THE Mammoth Hunters

Also by Jean M. Auel:

THE CLAN OF THE CAVE BEAR
THE VALLEY OF HORSES

EARTH'S CHILDREN™

THE Mammoth Hunters

JEAN M. AUEL

HODDER AND STOUGHTON
LONDON SYDNEY AUCKLAND TORONTO

DRUM
mammoth skull
Mezhirich (Ukraine)

MUSICAL INSTRUMENT
with distinctive tones,
mammoth shoulder blade,
Mezin (Ukraine)

HORSE SCULPTURE
mammoth ivory, Lourdes

N

0   MILES   400
0   KM   400

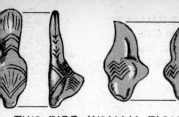

TWO BIRD-WOMAN FIGURES
mammoth ivory, Mezin

THER FIGURE
mammoth ivory,
stienki (Ukraine)

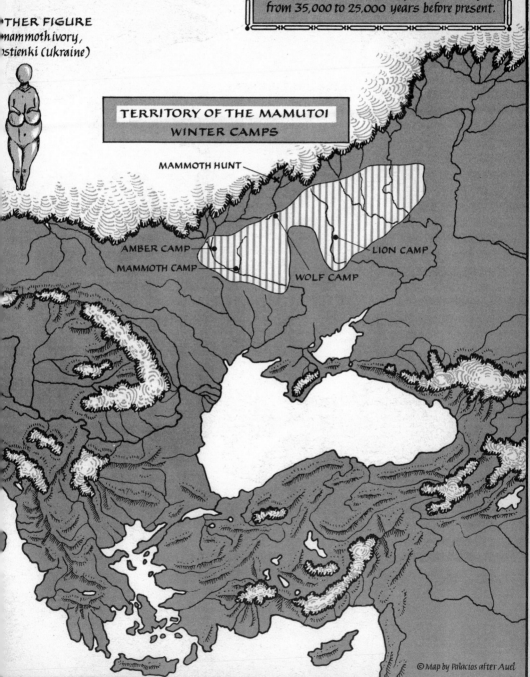

EARTH'S CHILDREN™

PREHISTORIC EUROPE
DURING THE ICE AGE
Extent of ice and change in coastlines during
10,000-year interstadial,
a warming trend during the Wurm glaciation
of the late Pleistocene Epoch extending
from 35,000 to 25,000 years before present.

TERRITORY OF THE MAMUTOI
WINTER CAMPS

MAMMOTH HUNT

AMBER CAMP

MAMMOTH CAMP

WOLF CAMP

LION CAMP

© Map by Palacios after Auel

British Library Cataloguing in Publication Data

Auel, Jean M.
  The mammoth hunters. – (Earth's children™)
  I. Title   II. Series
  813'.54[F]   PS3551.U36

  ISBN 0-340-34934-4

For MARSHALL,
    who has become a man to be proud of,
and for BEVERLY,
    who helped,
and for CHRISTOPHER, BRIAN and MELLISSA,
    with love.

ACKNOWLEDGMENTS

I could never have told this story without the books and materials of the specialists who have worked at the sites and have collected the artifacts of our prehistoric ancestors, and they have my deepest gratitude. To several people, I owe special thanks. I have enjoyed the discussions, the correspondence, and the papers, full of not only facts, but ideas and theories. I must make it clear, however, that those who provided me with information and offered help are in no way responsible for the viewpoints or ideas expressed in this story. This is a work of fiction, a story of my imagination. The characters, concepts, and cultural descriptions are my own.

Sincere thanks first to David Abrams, professor of anthropology and tour director extraordinaire, and to Diane Kelly, student of anthropology, and master of human relations, who planned, arranged, and accompanied us on the private research trip to sites and museums in France, Austria, Czechoslovakia, and the Soviet Union.

My thanks and great appreciation to Dr Jan Jelinek, Director, Anthropos Institute, Brno, Czechoslovakia, for taking the time to show me many of the actual artifacts from Eastern Europe that appear in his book, *The Pictorial Encyclopedia of the Evolution of Man* (The Hamlyn Publishing Group Ltd., London).

I am grateful to Dr Lee Porter of Washington State University, and to whatever fates put her, with her American accent, into our hotel in Kiev. She was there studying mammoth fossil bones, and meeting with the very person we had been desperately trying to see. She cut through all the red tape, and arranged the meeting.

I am indebted to Dr J. Lawrence Angel, Curator of Physical Anthropology at Smithsonian Institution, for many things: for some positive and encouraging words about my books; for giving me a "backstage" look and an explanation of some of the differences and similarities between Neanderthal and modern human bones, and particularly for suggesting people who could give me further information and assistance.

I deeply appreciate the special efforts of Dr Ninel Kornietz, Russian expert on the Ukrainian Upper Paleolithic, who was gracious and kind, even on short notice. With her we saw artifacts in two museums, and she presented me with the one book I had been searching for on the musical instruments made out of mammoth bones by Ice Age people, and a recording of their sounds. The book was in Russian, and I owe deep thanks to Dr Gloria y'Edynak, formerly an assistant of Dr Angel, who knows Russian, including the technical terminology of paleoanthropology, for arranging for a translator for this book, and especially for checking it over and filling in the correct technical words. Thanks are also due for her translation of the Ukrainian language articles comparing modern weaving patterns in the Ukraine with designs carved into Ice Age artifacts.

To Dorothy Yacek-Matulis I owe great appreciation for a good, readable, workable translation, in reasonable time and for reasonable cost, of the Russian mammoth music book. The material has proved invaluable.

Thanks are also in order to Dr. Richard Klein, author of *Ice-Age Hunters of the Ukraine* (University of Chicago Press), who kindly provided additional papers and information about the ancient people of the region.

I am particularly grateful to Alexander Marshack, Research Fellow of the Peabody Museum of Archaeology and Ethnology, Harvard University, and author of *The Roots of Civilization* (McGraw-Hill Book Co.), for copies of the results of his microscopic studies of Ukrainian Upper Paleolithic art and artifacts, which appeared in *Current Anthropology*, material from his as yet unpublished book on the Eastern European Ice Age people.

My sincerest appreciation to Dr Olga Soffer, Department of Anthropology, University of Wisconsin, and probably the leading expert in the United States today on the Ice Age populations of Russia, for the long, interesting, and useful conversation in the lobby of the Hilton, and her material, "Patterns of Intensification as Seen from the Upper Paleolithic Central Russian Plain," from *Prehistoric Hunter–Gatherers: the Emergence of Cultural Complexity*, T. Douglas Price and James A. Brown, editors (Academic Press).

Gratitude in great measure to Dr Paul C. Paquet, co-Editor, *Wolves of the World*, Noyes Publications, for interrupting his vacation to return my call, and for the long discussion on wolves and their possible domestication.

Thanks again to Jim Riggs, anthropologist and instructor of *Aboriginal Life Skills* classes. I continue to use the information I learned from him.

I am indebted to three people who read a fat manuscript on short notice and offered helpful comments from a reader's point of view: Karen Auel, who read a first draft and got caught up in it, and let me know I had a story; Doreen Gandy, poet and teacher, who squeezed the reading into the end of her school year without any loss of her usual insights; and Cathy Humble, who managed, again, to make astute observations.

Special thanks to Betty Prashker, my editor, whose perceptions I value, and whose commentary and suggestions were right on target.

Words are insufficient to thank Jean Naggar, friend, confidante, and literary agent beyond compare, who has continued to exceed my wildest expectations.

I am grateful to Judith Wilkes, my secretary and office assistant, whose intelligence I have come to depend upon, and who eases the pressure of my increased volume of correspondence, so I can write.

And to Ray Auel . . .

THE MAMMOTH HUNTERS

Lion Camp Earthlodge

ENTRY area – storage of fuel, implements, outer clothes

FIRST hearth – cooking hearth and space for gathering

SECOND   **– Lion Hearth**
          Talut – headman
          Nezzie
            Danug
            Latie
            Rugie
            Rydag

THIRD   **– Fox Hearth**
          Wymez
          Ranec

FOURTH   **– Mammoth Hearth** – space for ceremonies, gathering, projects, visitors
          Mamut – shaman
            Ayla
            Jondalar

FIFTH   **– Reindeer Hearth**
          Manuv
            Tronie
            Tornec
              Nuvie
              Hartal

SIXTH   **– Crane Hearth**
          Crozie
            Fralie
            Frebec
              Crisavec
              Tasher
            (Bectie)

SEVENTH – Aurochs Hearth
          Tulie – headwoman
          Barzec
            Deegie
            Druwez
            Brinan
            Tusie
            (Tarneg)

1

Trembling with fear, Ayla clung to the tall man beside her as she watched the strangers approach. Jondalar put his arm around her protectively, but she still shook.

He's so big! Ayla thought, gaping at the man in the lead, the one with hair and beard the colour of fire. She had never seen anyone so big. He even made Jondalar seem small, though the man who held her towered over most men. The red-haired man coming towards them was more than tall; he was huge, a bear of a man. His neck bulged, his chest could have filled out two ordinary men, his massive biceps matched most men's thighs.

Ayla glanced at Jondalar and saw no fear in his face, but his smile was guarded. They were strangers, and in his long travels he had learned to be wary of strangers.

"I don't recall seeing you before," the big man said without preamble. "What Camp are you from?" He did not speak Jondalar's language, Ayla noticed, but one of the others he had been teaching her.

"No Camp," Jondalar said. "We are not Mamutoi." He unclasped Ayla and took a step forward, holding out both hands, palms upwards showing he was hiding nothing, in the greeting of friendliness. "I am Jondalar of the Zelandonii."

The hands were not accepted. "Zelandonii? That's a strange . . . Wait, weren't there two foreign men staying with those river people that live to the west? It seems to me the name I heard was something like that."

"Yes, my brother and I lived with them," Jondalar conceded.

The man with the flaming beard looked thoughtful for a while, then, unexpectedly, he lunged for Jondalar and grabbed the tall blond man in a bone-crunching bear hug.

"Then we are related!" he boomed, a broad smile warming his face. "Tholie is the daughter of my cousin!"

Jondalar's smile returned, a little shaken. "Tholie! A Mamutoi woman named Tholie was my brother's cross-mate! She taught me your language."

"Of course! I told you. We are related." He grasped the hands that

Jondalar had extended in friendship, which he had rejected before. "I am Talut, headman of the Lion Camp."

Everyone was smiling, Ayla noticed. Talut beamed a grin at her, then eyed her appreciatively. "I see you are not travelling with a brother now," he said to Jondalar.

Jondalar put his arm around her again, and she noticed a fleeting look of pain wrinkle his brow before he spoke. "This is Ayla."

"It's an unusual name. Is she of the river people?"

Jondalar was taken aback by the abruptness of his questioning, then, remembering Tholie, he smiled inwardly. The short, stocky woman he knew bore little resemblance to the great hulk of a man standing there on the river bank, but they were chipped from the same flint. They both had the same direct approach, the same unselfconscious – almost ingenuous – candour. He didn't know what to say. Ayla was not going to be easy to explain.

"No, she has been living in a valley some days' journey from here."

Talut looked puzzled. "I have not heard of a woman with her name living nearby. Are you sure she is Mamutoi?"

"I'm sure she is not."

"Then who are her people? Only we who hunt mammoth live in this region."

"I have no people," Ayla said, lifting her chin with a touch of defiance.

Talut appraised her shrewdly. She had spoken the words in his language, but the quality of her voice and the way she made the sounds were . . . strange. Not unpleasant, but unusual. Jondalar spoke with the accent of a language foreign to him; the difference in the way she spoke went beyond accent. Talut's interest was piqued.

"Well, this is no place to talk," Talut said, finally. "Nezzie will give me the Mother's own wrath if I don't invite you to visit. Visitors always bring a little excitement, and we haven't had visitors for a while. The Lion Camp would welcome you, Jondalar of the Zelandonii, and Ayla of No People. Will you come?"

"What do you say, Ayla? Would you like to visit?" Jondalar asked, switching to Zelandonii so she could answer truthfully without fear of offending. "Isn't it time you met your own kind? Isn't that what Iza told you to do? Find your own people?" He didn't want to seem too eager, but after so long without anyone else to talk to, he was anxious to visit.

"I don't know," she said, frowning with indecision. "What will they think of me? He wanted to know who my people were. I don't have any people any more. What if they don't like me?"

"They will like you, Ayla, believe me. I know they will. Talut invited you, didn't he? It didn't matter to him that you have no people. Besides, you'll never know if they will accept you – or if you will like them – if you don't give them a chance. These are the kind of people you should have grown up with, you know. We don't have to stay long. We can leave any time."

"We can leave any time?"

"Of course."

Ayla looked down at the ground, trying to make up her mind. She wanted to go with them; she felt an attraction to these people, and a curiosity to know more about them, but she felt a tight knot of fear in her stomach. She glanced up and saw two shaggy steppe horses grazing on the rich grass of the plain near the river, and her fear intensified.

"What about Whinney! What will we do with her? What if they want to kill her? I can't let anyone hurt Whinney!"

Jondalar hadn't thought about Whinney. What would they think? he wondered. "I don't know what they will do, Ayla, but I don't think they would kill her if we tell them she is special and not meant for food." He remembered his surprise, and his initial feeling of awe over Ayla's relationship with the horse. It would be interesting to see their reaction. "I have an idea."

Talut did not understand what Ayla and Jondalar said to each other, but he knew the woman was reluctant, and the man was trying to coax her. He also noticed that she spoke with the same unusual accent, even in his language. His language, the headman realised, but not hers.

He was pondering the enigma of the woman with a certain relish – he enjoyed the new and unusual; the inexplicable challenged him. But then the mystery took on an entirely new dimension. Ayla whistled, loud and shrill. Suddenly, a hay-coloured mare and a colt of an unusually deep shade of brown galloped into their midst, directly to the woman, and stood quietly while she touched them! The big man suppressed a shudder of awe. This was beyond anything he had ever known.

Was she Mamut? he wondered, with growing apprehension. One with special powers? Many of Those Who Served the Mother claimed magic to call animals and direct the hunt, but he had never seen anyone with such control over animals that they would come at a signal. She had a unique talent. It was a little frightening – but think how much a Camp could benefit from such talent. Kills could be so easy!

Just as Talut was getting over the shock, the young woman gave him another. Holding on to the mare's stiff stand-up mane, she sprang up on the back of the horse and sat astride her. The big man's mouth gaped open in astonishment as the horse with Ayla on her back galloped along the edge of the river. With the colt following behind, they raced up the slope to the steppes beyond. The wonder in Talut's eyes was shared by the rest of the band, particularly a young girl of twelve years. She edged towards the headman and leaned against him as though for support.

"How did she do that, Talut?" the girl asked, in a small voice that held surprise and awe, and a tinge of yearning. "That little horse, he was so close, I could almost have touched him."

Talut's expression softened. "You'll have to ask her, Latie. Or, perhaps, Jondalar," he said, turning to the tall stranger.

"I'm not sure myself," he replied. "Ayla has a special way with animals. She raised Whinney from a foal."

"Whinney?"

"That's as close as I can say the name she has given the mare. When she says it, you'd think she was a horse. The colt is Racer. I named him – she asked me to. That's Zelandonii for someone who runs fast. It also means someone who tries hard to be best. The first time I saw Ayla, she was helping the mare deliver the colt."

"That must have been a sight! I wouldn't think a mare would let anyone get close to her at that time," one of the other men said.

The riding demonstration had the effect Jondalar had hoped for, and he thought the time was right to bring up Ayla's concern. "I think she'd like to come and visit your Camp, Talut, but she's afraid you may think the horses are just any horses to be hunted, and since they are not afraid of people, they would be too easy to kill."

"They would at that. You must have known what I was thinking, but who could help it?"

Talut watched Ayla riding back into view, looking like some strange animal, half-human and half-horse. He was glad he had not come upon them unknowing. It would have been . . . unnerving. He wondered for a moment what it would be like to ride on the back of a horse, and if it would make him appear so startling. And then, picturing himself sitting astride one of the rather short, though sturdy, steppe horses like Whinney, he laughed out loud.

"I could carry that horse easier than she could carry me!" he said.

Jondalar chuckled. It hadn't been hard to follow Talut's line of thought. Several people smiled, or chuckled, and Jondalar realised they must all have been thinking about riding a horse. It was not so strange. It had occurred to him when he first saw Ayla on Whinney's back.

Ayla had seen the shocked surprise on the faces of the small band of people and, if Jondalar had not been waiting for her, she would have kept on going right back to her valley. She'd had enough of disapproval during her younger years for actions that were not acceptable. And enough freedom since, while she was living alone, not to want to subject herself to criticism for following her own inclinations. She was ready to tell Jondalar he could visit these people if he wanted; she was going back.

But when she returned, and saw Talut still chuckling over his mental

16

picture of himself riding the horse, she reconsidered. Laughter had become precious to her. She had not been allowed to laugh when she lived with the Clan; it made them nervous and uncomfortable. Only with Durc, in secret, had she laughed out loud. It was Baby, and Whinney, who had taught her to enjoy the feeling of laughter, but Jondalar was the first person to openly share it with her.

She watched the man, laughing easily with Talut. He looked up and smiled, and the magic of his impossibly vivid blue eyes touched a deep place inside that resonated with a warm tingling glow, and she felt a great welling up of love for him. She couldn't go back to the valley, not without him. Just the thought of living without him brought a strangling constriction to her throat, and the burning ache of tears held back.

As she rode towards them, she noticed that, though Jondalar wasn't as big as the red-haired man in size, he was nearly as tall, and bigger than the other three men. No, one was a boy, she realised. And was that a girl with them? She found herself observing the group of people surreptitiously, not wanting to stare.

Her body movements signalled Whinney to a stop, then, swinging her leg over, she slid off. Both horses seemed nervous as Talut approached, and she stroked Whinney and put an arm around Racer's neck. She was as much in need of the familiar reassurance of their presence as they were of hers.

"Ayla, of No People," he said, not sure if it was a proper way to address her, though for this woman of uncanny talent, it well might be; "Jondalar says you fear harm will come to these horses if you visit with us. I say here, as long as Talut is headman of the Lion Camp, no harm will come to that mare or her young one. I would like you to visit, and bring the horses." His smile broadened with a chuckle. "No one will believe us otherwise!"

She was feeling more relaxed about it now, and she knew Jondalar wanted to visit. She had no real excuse to refuse, and she was drawn to the easy, friendly laughter of the huge red-haired man.

"Yes, I come," she said. Talut nodded, smiling, and wondered about her, her intriguing accent, her awesome way with horses. Who was Ayla of No People?

Ayla and Jondalar had camped beside the rushing river and had decided that morning, before they met the band from the Lion Camp, that it was time to turn back. The waterway was too large to cross without difficulty, and not worth the effort if they were going to turn around and retrace their route. The steppeland east of the valley where Ayla had lived alone for three years had been more accessible, and the young woman hadn't bothered to take the difficult roundabout way to the west out of the valley very often, and was largely unfamiliar with that area. Though they had started out towards the west, they had no particular destination in mind, and ended up travelling north, and then east instead, but much further than Ayla had ever travelled on her hunting forays.

Jondalar had convinced her to make the exploratory trip to get her used to travelling. He wanted to take her home with him, but his home was far to the west. She had been reluctant, and scared, to leave her secure valley to live with unknown people in an unknown place. Though he was eager to return after travelling for many years, he had reconciled himself to spending the winter with her in the valley. It would be a long trek back – likely to take a full year – and it would be better to start in late spring, anyway. By then, he was sure he could convince her to come with him. He didn't even want to consider any other alternative.

Ayla had found him, badly mauled and nearly dead, at the beginning of the warm season that was now seeing its last days, and she knew the tragedy he had suffered. They fell in love while she was nursing him back to health, though they were long in overcoming the barriers of their vastly different backgrounds. They were still learning each other's ways and moods.

Ayla and Jondalar finished breaking camp and much to the surprise – and interest – of the waiting people, packed their supplies and equipment on the horse, rather than in backframes or haversacks which they would have carried themselves. Though they had sometimes ridden double on the sturdy horse, Ayla thought Whinney and her colt would be less nervous if they saw her. The two of them walked behind the band of people, Jondalar leading Racer by a long rope attached to a halter, which he had devised. Whinney followed Ayla with no visible guidance.

They followed the course of the river for several miles through a broad valley that sloped down from the surrounding grassy plains. Chest-high standing hay, seed heads nodding ripe and heavy, billowed in golden waves on the near slopes matching the cold rhythm of frigid air that blew in fitful bursts from the massive glaciers to the north. On the open steppes, a few bent and gnarled pine and birch trees huddled along watercourses, their roots seeking the moisture given up to the desiccating winds. Near the river, reeds and sedges were still green, though a chill wind rattled through deciduous branches, bereft of leaves.

Latie hung back, glancing now and then at the horses and the woman, until they sighted several people around a bend in the river. Then she ran ahead, wanting to be the first to tell of the visitors. At her shouts, people turned and gawked.

Other people were coming out of what appeared to Ayla to be a large hole in the river bank, a cave of some sort, perhaps, but like none she had ever seen before. It seemed to have grown out of the slope facing the river, but it did not have the random shape of rock or earthen banks. Grass grew on the sod roof, but the opening was too even, too regular, and felt strangely unnatural. It was a perfectly symmetrical arch.

Suddenly, at a deep emotional level, it struck her. It was not a cave, and these people were not Clan! They did not look like Iza, who was the only mother she remembered, or like Creb or Brun, short and muscular, with large eyes shadowed by heavy brow ridges, a forehead that sloped back, and a chinless jaw that jutted forward. These people looked like her. They were like the ones she had been born to. Her mother, her real mother, must have looked like one of these women. These were the Others! This was their place! The realisation brought a rush of excitement and a tingle of fear.

Stunned silence greeted the strangers – and their even stranger horses – as they arrived at the permanent winter site of the Lion Camp. Then everyone seemed to talk at once.

"Talut! What have you brought this time?" "Where did you get those horses?" "What did you do to them?" Someone addressed Ayla: "How do you make them stay?" "What Camp are they from, Talut?"

The noisy, gregarious people crowded forward, eager to see and touch both the people and the horses. Ayla was overwhelmed, confused. She wasn't used to so many people. She wasn't used to people talking, particularly all of them talking at once. Whinney was side-stepping, flicking her ears, head high, neck arched, trying to protect her frightened colt and shy away from the people closing in.

Jondalar could see Ayla's confusion, and the nervousness of the horses, but he couldn't make Talut or the rest of the people understand. The mare was sweating, swishing her tail, dancing in circles. Suddenly, she could stand it no longer. She reared up, neighing in fear, and lashed out with hard hooves, driving the people back.

Whinney's distress focused Ayla's attention. She called her name with a sound like a comforting nicker, and signalled with gestures she had used to communicate before Jondalar had taught her to speak.

"Talut! No one must touch the horses unless Ayla allows it! Only she can control them. They are gentle, but the mare can be dangerous if she is provoked or feels her colt is threatened. Someone could get hurt," Jondalar said.

"Stay back! You heard him," Talut shouted with a booming voice that silenced everyone. When the people and horses settled down, Talut continued in a more normal tone. "The woman is Ayla. I promised her that no harm would come to the horses if they came to visit. I promised as headman of the Lion Camp. This is Jondalar of the Zelandonii, and a kinsman, brother of Tholie's cross-mate." Then, with a grin of self-satisfaction, he added, "Talut has brought some visitors!"

19

There were nods of agreement. The people stood around, staring with unfeigned curiosity, but far enough away to avoid the horse's kicking hooves. Even if the strangers had left that moment, they had brought enough interest and gossip to last for years to come. News that two foreign men were in the region, living with the river people to the southwest, had been talked about at Summer Meetings. The Mamutoi traded with the Sharamudoi, and since Tholie, who was a kinswoman, had chosen a river man, the Lion Camp had been even more interested. But they never expected one of the foreign men to walk into their Camp, particularly not with a woman who had some magic control over horses.

"Are you all right?" Jondalar asked Ayla.

"They frightened Whinney and Racer, too. Do people always talk at once like that? Women and men at the same time? It's confusing, and they are so loud, how do you know who is saying what? Maybe we should have gone back to the valley." She was hugging the mare's neck, leaning against her, drawing comfort as well as giving it.

Jondalar knew Ayla was almost as distressed as the horses. The noisy press of people had been a shock for her. Maybe they shouldn't stay too long. Perhaps it would be better to start with just two or three people at a time, until she became accustomed to her kind of people again, but he wondered what he'd do if she never really did. Well, they were here now. He could wait and see.

"Sometimes people are loud, and talk all at once, but mostly one person talks at a time. And I think they'll be careful around the horses now, Ayla," he said, as she started to unload the pack baskets tied on both sides of the animal by a harness she had made out of leather thongs.

While she was busy, Jondalar took Talut aside and quietly told him the horses, and Ayla, were a little nervous, and needed some time to get used to everyone. "It would be better if they could be left alone for a while."

Talut understood, and moved among the people of the Camp, talking to each one. They dispersed, turning to other tasks, preparing food, working on hides or tools, so they could watch without being so obvious about it. They were uneasy, too. Strangers were interesting, but a woman with such compelling magic might do something unexpected.

Only a few children stayed to watch with avid interest while the man and woman unpacked, but Ayla didn't mind them. She hadn't seen children for years, not since she'd left the Clan, and was as curious about them as they were about her. She took off the harness and Racer's halter, then patted and stroked Whinney, then Racer. After giving the colt a good scratching and an affectionate hug, she looked up to see Latie staring at the young animal with longing.

"You like touch horse?" Ayla asked.

"Could I?"

"Come. Give hand. I show." She took Latie's hand and held it to the shaggy winter coat of the half-grown horse. Racer turned his head to sniff and nuzzle the girl.

The girl's smile of gratitude was a gift. "He likes me!"

"He like scratch, too. Like this," Ayla said, showing the child the colt's special itchy places.

Racer was delighted with the attention, and showed it, and Latie was beside herself with joy. The colt had attracted her from the beginning. Ayla turned her back on the two to help Jondalar, and didn't notice another child approach. When she turned around, she gasped and felt the blood drain from her face.

"Is it all right if Rydag touches the horse?" Latie said. "He can't talk, but I know he wants to." Rydag always caused people to react with surprise. Latie was used to it.

"Jondalar!" Ayla cried in a hoarse whisper. "That child, he could be my son! He looks like Durc!"

He turned, and opened his eyes in stunned surprise. It was a child of mixed spirits.

Flatheads – the ones Ayla always referred to as Clan – were animals to most people, and children like this were thought of by many as "abominations", half-animal, half-human. He had been shocked when he first understood that Ayla had given birth to a mixed son. The mother of such a child was usually a pariah, cast out for fear she would draw the evil animal spirit again and cause other women to give birth to such abominations. Some people didn't even want to admit they existed, and to find one here living with people was more than unexpected. It was a shock. Where had the boy come from?

Ayla and the child were gazing at each other, oblivious to everything around them. He's thin for one who is half-Clan, Ayla thought. They are usually big-boned and muscular. Even Durc wasn't this thin. He's sickly, Ayla's trained medicine woman's eye told her. A problem since birth, with the strong muscle in the chest that pulsed and throbbed and made the blood move, she guessed. But those facts she stored without thinking; she was looking more closely at his face, and his head, for the similarities, and the differences, between this child and her son.

His large, brown, intelligent eyes were like Durc's, even to the look of ancient wisdom far beyond his years – she felt a pang of longing and a lump in her throat – but there was also pain and suffering, not all of it physical, which Durc had never known. She was filled with compassion. This child's brows were not as pronounced, she decided after careful study. Even at just three years old, when she left, the bony ridges above Durc's eyes had been well developed. Durc's eyes and protruding

21

brow ridges were all Clan, but his forehead was like this child's. Neither was pushed back and flattened like the Clan, but high and vaulted, like hers.

Her thoughts strayed. Durc would be six years now, she recalled, old enough to go with the men when they practised with their hunting weapons. But Brun will be teaching him to hunt, not Broud. She felt a flush of anger remembering Broud. She would never forget how the son of Brun's mate had nursed his hatred of her until he could take her baby away, out of spite, and force her out of the Clan. She closed her eyes as the pain of remembering tore through her like a knife. She didn't want to believe that she would never see her son again.

She opened her eyes to Rydag, and took a deep breath.

I wonder how old this boy is? He's small, but he must be close to Durc's age, she thought, comparing the two again. Rydag's skin was fair, and his hair was dark and curly, but lighter and softer than the bushy brown hair more common to the Clan. The biggest difference between this child and her son, Ayla noted, was his chin and neck. Her son had a long neck like hers – he had choked on his food sometimes, which the other Clan babies never did – and a receding but distinct chin. This boy had the Clan's short neck, and forward-thrusting jaw. Then she remembered Latie said he couldn't talk.

Suddenly, in a moment of understanding, she knew what this child's life must be like. It was one thing for a girl of five, who had lost her family in an earthquake and who had been found by a clan of people not capable of fully articulate speech, to learn the sign language they used to communicate. It was quite another to live with speaking people, and not be able to talk. She remembered her early frustration because she had been unable to communicate with the people who took her in, but even worse, how difficult it had been to make Jondalar understand her before she learned to speak again. What if she had not been able to learn?

She made a sign to the boy, a simple greeting gesture, one of the first she had learned so long ago. There was a moment of excitement in his eyes, then he shook his head and looked puzzled. He had never learned the Clan way of speaking with gestures, she realised, but must have retained some vestige of the Clan memories. He had recognised the signal for an instant, she was sure of it.

"Can Rydag touch the little horse?" Latie asked again.

"Yes," Ayla said, taking his hand. He is so slight, so frail, she thought, and then understood the rest. He could not run, like other children. He could not play normal rough-and-tumble games. He could only watch – and wish.

With a tenderness of feeling Jondalar had never seen on her face before, Ayla picked the boy up and put him on Whinney's back. Signalling the horse to follow, she walked them slowly around the Camp. There was a lull in conversation as everyone stopped to stare at Rydag sitting on the horse. Although they had been talking about it, except for Talut and the people who had met them by the river, no one had ever seen anyone ride a horse before. No one had ever thought of such a thing.

A large, motherly woman emerged from the strange dwelling, and seeing Rydag on the horse, which had kicked perilously close to her head, her first reaction was to rush to his aid. But as she neared, she became aware of the silent drama of the scene.

The child's face was filled with wonder and delight. How many times had he watched with wishful eyes, prevented by his weakness, or his difference, from doing what other children did? How many times had he wished he could do something to be admired or envied for? Now, for the first time, as he sat on the back of a horse, all the children of the Camp, and all the adults, were watching him with wishful eyes.

The woman from the dwelling saw and wondered. Had this stranger truly understood the boy so quickly? Accepted him so easily? She saw the way Ayla was looking at Rydag, and knew it was so.

Ayla saw the woman studying her, then smile at her. She smiled back and stopped beside her.

"You have made Rydag very happy," the woman said, holding out her arms to the youngster Ayla lifted off the horse.

"It is little," Ayla said.

The woman nodded. "My name is Nezzie," she said.

"I am named Ayla."

The two women looked at each other, considered each other carefully, not with hostility, but testing the ground for a future relationship.

Questions she wanted to ask about Rydag spun through Ayla's mind, but she hesitated, not sure if it was proper to ask. Was Nezzie the boy's mother? If so, how had she come to give birth to a child of mixed spirits? Ayla was puzzled again about a question that had bothered her since Durc was born. How did life begin? A woman only knew it was there when her body changed as the baby grew. How did it get inside a woman?

Creb and Iza had believed that a new life began when women swallowed the totem spirits of men. Jondalar thought the Great Earth Mother mixed the spirits of a man and a woman together and put them inside the woman when she became pregnant. But Ayla had formed her own opinion. When she noticed that her son had some of her characteristics, and some of the Clan's, she realised that no life started to grow inside her until after Broud forced his penetration into her.

She shuddered at the memory, but because it was so painful she could not forget it, and she had come to believe it was something about a man putting his organ inside the place where babies were born from that caused life to start inside a woman. Jondalar thought it was a strange idea when she told him, and tried to convince her it was the Mother who created life. She didn't quite believe him, now she wondered. Ayla had grown up with the Clan, she was one of them, for all that she looked different. Though she had hated it when he did it, Broud was only exercising his rights. But how could a man of the Clan have forced Nezzie?

Her thoughts were interrupted by the commotion of another small hunting band arriving. As one man approached, he pulled back his hood, and both Ayla and Jondalar gaped with surprise. The man was brown! The colour of his skin was a rich deep brown. He was nearly the colour of Racer, which was rare enough for a horse. Neither of them had ever seen a person with brown skin before.

His hair was black, tight wiry curls that formed a woolly cap like the fur of a black mouflon. His eyes were black, too, and they sparkled with delight as he smiled, showing gleaming white teeth and a pink tongue in contrast to his dark skin. He knew the stir he created when strangers first saw him, and rather enjoyed it.

He was a perfectly ordinary man in other respects, medium height, hardly more than an inch or so taller than Ayla, and medium build. But a compact vitality, an economy of movement, and an easy self-confidence created an impression of someone who knew what he wanted and wouldn't waste any time going after it. His eyes took on an added gleam when he saw Ayla.

Jondalar recognised the look as attraction. His brow furrowed into a frown, but neither the blonde woman nor the brown-skinned man noticed. She was captivated by the novelty of the man's unusual colouring, and stared with the unabashed wonder of a child. He was attracted as much by the aura of naïve innocence her response projected, as by her beauty.

Suddenly Ayla realised she had been staring, and blushed crimson as she looked down at the ground. From Jondalar she had learned that it was perfectly proper for men and women to look directly at each other, but to the people of the Clan it was not only discourteous, it was offensive to stare, particularly for a woman. It was her upbringing, the customs of the Clan, reinforced again and again by Creb and Iza so she would be more acceptable, that caused her such embarrassment.

But her obvious distress only fired the interest of the dark man. He was often the object of unusual attention by women. The initial surprise of his appearance seemed to arouse curiosity about what other differences he might have. He sometimes wondered if every woman at the Summer Meetings had to find out for herself that he was, indeed, a man like

24

every other man. Not that he objected, but Ayla's reaction was as intriguing to him as his colour was to her. He wasn't used to seeing a strikingly beautiful adult woman blushing as modestly as a girl.

"Ranec, have you met our visitors?" Talut called out, coming towards them.

"Not yet, but I'm waiting . . . eagerly."

At the tone in his voice Ayla looked up into deep black eyes full of desire – and subtle humour. They reached inside her and touched a spot only Jondalar had touched before. Her body responded with an unexpected tingle that brought a faint gasp to her lips, and widened her grey-blue eyes. The man leaned forward, preparing to take her hands, but before customary introductions could be made, the tall stranger stepped between them, and with a deep scowl on his face, thrust both hands forward.

"I am Jondalar of the Zelandonii," he said. "The woman I am travelling with is Ayla."

Something was bothering Jondalar, Ayla was sure, something about the dark man. She was used to reading meaning from posture and stance, and she had been watching Jondalar closely for cues upon which to base her own behaviour. But the body language of people who depended on words was so much less purposeful than that of the Clan, who used gestures to communicate, that she didn't trust her perceptions yet. These people seemed to be both easier and more difficult to read, as with this sudden shift in Jondalar's attitude. She knew he was angry, but she didn't know why.

The man took both of Jondalar's hands, and shook them firmly. "I am Ranec, my friend, the best, if only, carver of the Lion Camp of the Mamutoi," he said with a self-deprecating smile, then added, "When you travel with such a beautiful companion, you must expect her to attract attention."

Now it was Jondalar's turn to be embarrassed. Ranec's friendliness and candour made him feel like an oaf, and, with a familiar pain, brought to mind his brother. Thonolan had had the same friendly self-confidence, and had always made the first moves when they encountered people on their Journey. It upset Jondalar when he did something foolish – it always had – and he didn't like starting out a relationship with new people in the wrong way. He had displayed bad manners, at best.

But his instant anger had surprised him, and caught him off guard. The hot stab of jealousy was a new emotion to him, or at least one he hadn't experienced in so long it was unexpected. He would have been quick to deny it, but the tall and handsome man, with an unconscious charisma, and a sensitive skill in the furs, was more accustomed to women being jealous over his attentions.

25

Why should it bother him that some man looked at Ayla? Jondalar thought. Ranec was right, as beautiful as she was, he should expect it. And she had the right to make her own choice. Just because he was the first man of her kind she had met didn't mean he would be the only one she would ever find attractive. Ayla saw him smile at Ranec, but noticed that the tension across his shoulders had not eased.

"Ranec always speaks lightly of it, though he isn't in the habit of denying any of his other skills," Talut was saying as he led the way to the unusual cave which seemed to be made of earth growing out of the bank. "He and Wymez are alike in that way, if not many others. Wymez is as reluctant to admit to his skill as a maker of tools as the son of his hearth is to speak of his carving. Ranec is the best carver of all the Mamutoi."

"You have a skilled toolmaker? A flint knapper?" Jondalar asked with pleased expectation, his hot flash of jealousy gone with the thought of meeting another person knowledgeable in his craft.

"Yes, and he is the best, too. The Lion Camp is well known. We have the best carver, the best toolmaker, and the oldest Mamut," the headman declared.

"And a headman big enough to make everyone agree, whether they believe it or not," Ranec said, with a wry grin.

Talut grinned back, knowing Ranec's tendency to turn aside praise of his carving skill with a quip. It didn't stop Talut from bragging, however. He was proud of his Camp, and didn't hesitate to let everyone know.

Ayla watched the subtle interaction of the two men – the older one a massive giant with flaming red hair and pale blue eyes, the other dark and compact – and understood the deep bond of affection and loyalty they shared though they were as different as any two men could be. They were both Mammoth Hunters, both members of the Lion Camp of the Mamutoi.

They walked towards the archway Ayla had noticed earlier. It seemed to open into a hillock or perhaps a series of them, tucked into the slope that faced the large river. Ayla had seen people enter and leave. She knew it must be a cave or a dwelling of some kind, but one which seemed to be made entirely of dirt; hard-packed but with grass growing in patches out of it, particularly around the bottom and up the sides. It blended into the background so well that, except for the entrance, it was hard to distinguish the dwelling from its surroundings.

On closer inspection she noticed that the rounded top of the mound was the repository of several curious implements and objects. Then she saw a particular one just above the archway, and caught her breath.

It was the skull of a cave lion!

2

Ayla was hiding in a tiny cleft of a sheer rock wall watching a huge cave lion's claw reach in to get her. She screamed in pain and fear when it found her bare thigh and raked it with four parallel gashes. The Spirit of the Great Cave Lion himself had chosen her, and caused her to be marked to show he was her totem, Creb had explained, after a testing far beyond that which even a man had to endure, though she had been a girl of only five years. A sensation of quivering earth beneath her feet brought a rush of nausea.

She shook her head to dispel the vivid memory.

"What's wrong, Ayla?" Jondalar asked, noticing her distress.

"I saw that skull," she said, pointing to the decoration above the door, "and remembered when I was chosen, when the Cave Lion became my totem!"

"We are the Lion Camp," Talut announced, with pride, though he had said it before. He didn't understand them when they spoke Jondalar's language, but he saw the interest they were showing in the Camp's talisman.

"The cave lion holds strong meaning for Ayla," Jondalar explained. "She says the spirit of the great cat guides and protects her."

"Then you should be comfortable here," Talut said, beaming a smile at her, feeling pleased.

She noticed Nezzie carrying Rydag and thought again of her son. "I think so," she said.

Before they started in, the young woman stopped to examine the entrance arch, and smiled when she saw how its perfect symmetry had been achieved. It was simple, but she would not have thought of it. Two large mammoth tusks, from the same animal or at least animals of the same size, had been anchored firmly in the ground with the tips facing each other and joined together at the top of the arch in a sleeve made from a hollow short section of a mammoth leg bone.

A heavy curtain of mammoth hide covered the opening, which was high enough so that even Talut, moving the drape aside, could enter without ducking his head. The arch led to a roomy entrance area, with another symmetrical arch of mammoth tusks hung with leather directly across. They stepped down into a circular foyer whose thick walls curved up to a shallow domed ceiling.

As they walked through, Ayla noticed the side walls, which seemed to be a mosaic of mammoth bones, were lined with outer clothes hung on pegs and racks with storage containers and implements. Talut pulled back the inner drape, went on through and held it back for the guests.

Ayla stepped down again. Then stopped, and stared in amazement, overwhelmed by bewildering impressions of unknown objects, unfamiliar sights, and strong colours. Much of what she saw was incomprehensible to her and she grasped at that which she could make sense of.

The space they were in had a large fireplace near the centre. A massive haunch of meat was cooking over it, spitted on a long pole. Each end was resting in a groove cut in the knee joint of an upright leg bone of a mammoth calf, sunk into the ground. A fork from a large branching antler of a deer had been fashioned into a crank and a boy was turning it. He was one of the children who had stayed to watch her and Whinney. Ayla recognised him and smiled. He grinned back.

She was surprised by the spaciousness of the neat and comfortable earthlodge, as her eyes became accustomed to the dimmer light indoors. The fireplace was only the first of a row of hearths extending down the middle of the longhouse, a dwelling that was over eighty feet in length, and almost twenty feet wide.

Seven fires, Ayla counted to herself, pressing her fingers against her leg inconspicuously and thinking the counting words Jondalar had taught her.

It was warm inside, she realised. The fires warmed the interior of the semi-subterranean dwelling more than fires usually warmed the caves she was accustomed to. It was quite warm, in fact, and she noticed several people farther back who were very lightly clad.

But it wasn't any darker at the back. The ceiling was about the same height throughout, twelve feet or so, and had smoke holes above each fireplace that let in light as well. Mammoth bone rafters, hung with clothing, implements, and food, extended across, but the centre section of the ceiling was made of many reindeer antlers entwined together.

Suddenly Ayla became aware of a smell that made her mouth water. It's mammoth meat! she thought. She hadn't tasted rich, tender mammoth meat since she left the cave of the Clan. There were other delicious cooking odours, too. Some familiar, some not, but they combined to remind her that she was hungry.

As they were led along a well-trodden passageway that ran down the middle of the longhouse next to several hearths, she noticed wide benches with furs piled on them, extending out from the walls. Some people were sitting on them, relaxing or talking. She felt them looking at her as she walked past. She saw more of the mammoth tusk archways along the sides, and wondered where they led, but she hesitated to ask.

It is like a cave, she thought, a large comfortable cave. But the arching tusks and large, long mammoth bones used as posts, supports, and walls made her realise it was not a cave that someone had found. It was one they had built!

The first area, in which the roast was cooking, was larger than the rest, and so was the fourth, where Talut led them. Several bare sleeping benches along the walls, apparently unused, showed how they were constructed.

When they had excavated the lower floor, wide platforms of dirt were left just below ground level along both sides and braced with strategically placed mammoth bones. More mammoth bones were placed across the top of the platforms, filled in with matted grass between the spaces, to raise and support pallets of soft leather stuffed with mammoth wool and other downy materials. With several layers of furs added, the dirt platforms became warm and comfortable beds or couches.

Jondalar wondered if the hearth to which they were led was unoccupied. It seemed bare, but for all its empty spaces, it had a lived-in feeling. Coals glowed in the fireplace, furs and skins were piled up on some of the benches, and dried herbs hung from racks.

"Visitors usually stay at the Mammoth Hearth," Talut explained, "if Mamut doesn't object. I will ask."

"Of course they may stay, Talut."

The voice came from an empty bench. Jondalar spun around and stared as one of the piles of furs moved. Then two eyes gleamed out of a face marked, high on the right cheek, with tattooed chevrons that fell into the seams and stitched across the wrinkles of incredible age. What he had thought was the fur of a winter animal turned out to be a white beard. Two long thin shanks unwound from a cross-legged position and dropped over the edge of the raised platform to the floor.

"Don't look so surprised, man of the Zelandonii. The woman knew I was here," the old man said in a strong voice that carried little hint of his advanced years.

"Did you, Ayla?" Jondalar asked, but she didn't seem to hear him. Ayla and the old man were locked in the grip of each other's eyes, staring as though they would see into each other's soul. Then, the young woman dropped to the ground in front of the old Mamut, crossing her legs and bowing her head.

Jondalar was puzzled, and embarrassed. She was using the sign language which she had told him the people of the Clan used to communicate. That way of sitting was the posture of deference and respect a Clan woman assumed when she was asking permission to express herself.

The only other time he'd seen her in that pose was when she was trying to tell him something very important, something she could not communicate in any other way; when the words he had taught her were not enough to tell him how she felt. He wondered how something could be expressed more clearly in a language in which gestures and actions were used more than words, but he had been surprised to know those people communicated at all.

But he wished she hadn't done that here. His face reddened at seeing her use flathead signals in public like that, and he wanted to rush to tell her to get up, before someone else saw her. The posture made him feel uncomfortable anyway, as though she were offering to him the reverence and homage that was due to Doni, the Great Earth Mother. He had thought of it as something private between them, personal, not something to show someone else. It was one thing to do that with him, when they were alone, but he wanted her to make a good impression on these people. He wanted them to like her. He didn't want them to know her background.

The Mamut levelled a sharp look at him, then turned back to Ayla. He studied her for a moment, then leaned over and tapped her shoulder.

Ayla looked up and saw wise, gentle eyes in a face striated with fine creases and soft puckers. The tattoo under his right eye gave her a fleeting impression of a darkened eye socket and missing eye, and for a heartbeat she thought it was Creb. But the old holy man of the Clan, who, with Iza, had raised her and cared for her, was dead, and so was Iza. Then who was this man who had evoked such strong feelings in her? Why was she sitting at his feet like a woman of the Clan? *And how had he known the proper Clan response?*

"Get up, my dear. We will talk later," the Mamut said. "You need time to rest and eat. These are beds — sleeping places," he explained, indicating the benches, as though he knew she might need to be told. "There are extra furs and bedding over there."

Ayla rose gracefully to her feet. The observant old man saw years of practice in the movement, and added that bit of information to his growing knowledge of the woman. In their short meeting, he already knew more about Ayla and Jondalar than anyone else in the Camp. But then he had an advantage. He knew more about where Ayla came from than anyone else in the Camp.

The mammoth roast had been carried outside on a large pelvic bone platter along with various roots, vegetables and fruits so as to enjoy the meal in the late afternoon sun. Mammoth meat was just as rich and tender as Ayla remembered, but she'd had a difficult moment when the meal was served. She didn't know the protocol. On certain occasions, usually more formal ones, the women of the Clan ate separately from the men. Usually, though, they sat in family groups together, but even then, the men were served first.

Ayla didn't know that the Mamutoi honoured guests by offering them the first and choicest piece, or that custom dictated, in deference to the Mother, that a woman take the first bite. Ayla hung back when the food was brought out, keeping behind Jondalar, trying to watch the others unobtrusively. There was a moment of confused shuffling while everyone stood back waiting for her to start, and she kept trying to get behind them.

Some members of the Camp became aware of the action, and with mischievous grins began to make a game of it. But it didn't seem funny to Ayla. She knew she was doing something wrong, and watching Jondalar didn't help. He was trying to urge her forward, too.

Mamut came to her aid. He took her arm and led her to the large bone platter of thick-sliced mammoth roast. "You are expected to eat first, Ayla," he explained.

"But I am a woman!" she protested.

"That is why you are expected to eat first. It is our offering to the Mother, and it is better if a woman accepts it in Her place. Take the best piece, not for your sake, but to honour Mut," the old man explained.

She looked at him, first with surprise, and then with gratitude. She picked up a plate, a slightly curved piece of ivory flaked off a tusk, and with great seriousness carefully chose the best slice. Jondalar smiled at her, nodding approval, then others crowded forward to serve themselves. When she was through, Ayla put the plate on the ground where she had seen others put theirs.

"I wondered if you were showing us a new dance earlier," said a voice from close behind her.

Ayla turned to see the dark eyes of the man with brown skin. She didn't understand the word "dance", but his wide smile was friendly. She smiled back.

"Did anyone ever tell you how beautiful you are when you smile?" he said.

"Beautiful? Me?" She laughed and shook her head in disbelief.

Jondalar had said almost the same words to her once, but Ayla did not think of herself that way. Since long before she reached womanhood, she had been thinner and taller than the people who had raised her. She'd looked so different, with her bulging forehead and the funny bone beneath her mouth, that Jondalar said was a chin, she always thought of herself as big and ugly.

Ranec watched her, intrigued. She laughed with childlike abandon, as though she genuinely thought he'd said something funny. It was not the

31

response he had expected. A coy smile, perhaps, or a knowing, laughing invitation, but Ayla's grey-blue eyes held no guile, and there was nothing coy or self-conscious about the way she tossed her head back or pushed her long hair out of her way.

Rather, she moved with the natural fluid grace of an animal, a horse perhaps, or a lion. She had an aura about her, a quality that he couldn't quite define, but it had elements of complete candour and honesty, and yet some deep mystery. She seemed innocent, like a baby, open to everything, but she was every bit a woman, a tall, stunning, uncompromisingly beautiful woman.

He looked her over with interest and curiosity. Her hair, thick and long with a natural wave, was a lustrous deep gold, like a field of hay blowing in the wind; her eyes were large and wide-spaced and framed with lashes a shade darker than her hair. With a sculptor's knowing sense he examined the clean elegant structure of her face, the muscled grace of her body, and when his eyes reached her full breasts and inviting hips, they took on a look that disconcerted her.

She flushed and looked away. Though Jondalar had told her it was proper, she wasn't sure if she liked this looking straight at someone. It made her feel defenceless, vulnerable. Jondalar's back was turned to her when she looked in his direction, but his stance told her more than words. He was angry. Why was he angry? Had she done anything to make him angry?

"Talut! Ranec! Barzec! Look who's here!" a voice called out.

Everyone turned to look. Several people were coming over the rise at the top of the slope. Nezzie and Talut both started up the hill as a young man broke away and ran towards them. They met midway and embraced enthusiastically. Ranec rushed to meet one of those approaching, too, and though the greeting was more restrained, it was still with warm affection that he hugged an older man.

Ayla watched with a strangely empty feeling as the rest of the people of the Camp deserted the visitors in their eagerness to greet returning relatives and friends, all talking and laughing at the same time. She was Ayla of No People. She had no place to go, no home to return to, no clan to welcome her with hugs and kisses. Iza and Creb, who had loved her, were dead, and she was dead to the ones she loved.

Uba, Iza's daughter, had been as much a sister as anyone could be; they were related by love if not by blood. But Uba would shut her heart and her mind to her if she saw Ayla now; would refuse to believe her eyes; would not believe her eyes; would not see her. Broud had cursed her with death. She was, therefore, dead.

And would Durc even remember her? She'd had to leave him with Brun's clan. Even if she could have stolen him away, there would have

32

been just the two of them. If something had happened to her, he would have been left alone. It was best to leave him with the Clan. Uba loved him and would take care of him. Everyone loved him – except Broud. Brun would protect him, though, and would teach him to hunt. And he would grow up strong and brave, and be as good with a sling as she was, and be a fast runner, and . . .

Suddenly she noticed one member of the Camp who had not run up the slope. Rydag was standing by the earthlodge, one hand on a tusk, gazing round-eyed at the band of happy laughing people walking back down. She saw them, then, through his eyes, arms around each other, holding children, while other children were jumping up and down begging to be held. He was breathing too hard, she thought, feeling too much excitement.

She started towards him, and saw Jondalar moving in the same direction. "I was going to take him up there," he said. He had noticed the child, too, and they'd both had the same thought.

"Yes, do it," she said. "Whinney and Racer may get nervous again around all the new people. I'll go and stay with them."

Ayla watched Jondalar pick up the dark-haired child, put him on his shoulders, and stride up the slope towards the people of the Lion Camp. The young man, nearly Jondalar's match in height, whom Talut and Nezzie had welcomed so warmly, held out his arms to the youngster and greeting him with obvious delight, then lifted Rydag to his shoulders for the walk back down to the lodge. He is loved, she thought, and remembered that she, too, had been loved, in spite of her difference.

Jondalar saw her watching them and smiled at her. She felt such a warm rush of feeling for the caring, sensitive man, she was embarrassed to think she had been feeling so sorry for herself only moments be- fore. She wasn't alone any more. She had Jondalar. She loved the sound of his name, and her thoughts filled with him and her feeling for him.

Jondalar. The first one of the Others she had ever seen, that she could remember; the first with a face like hers; blue eyes like hers – only more so; his eyes were so blue it was hard to believe they were real.

Jondalar. The first man she'd ever met who was taller than she; the first one who ever laughed with her, and the first to cry tears of grief – for the brother he had lost.

Jondalar. The man who had been brought as a gift from her totem, she was sure, to the valley where she had settled after she left the Clan when she grew weary of searching for the Others like herself.

Jondalar. The man who had taught her to speak again, with words, not just the sign language of the Clan. Jondalar, whose sensitive hands could shape a tool, or scratch a young horse, or pick up a child and put

33

him on his back. Jondalar, who taught her the joys of her body – and his – and who loved her, and whom she loved more than she ever thought it was possible to love anyone.

She walked towards the river and around a bend, where Racer was tied to a stunted tree by a long rope. She wiped wet eyes with the back of her hand, overcome with the emotion that was still so new to her. She reached for her amulet, a small leather pouch attached to a thong around her neck. She felt the lumpy objects it contained, and made a thought to her totem.

"Spirit of the Cave Lion, Creb always said a powerful totem was hard to live with. He was right. Always the testing has been difficult, but always it has been worth it. This woman is grateful for the protection, and for the gifts of her powerful totem. The gifts inside, of things learned, and the gifts of those to care about like Whinney and Racer, and Baby, and most of all, for Jondalar."

Whinney came to her when she reached the colt and blew a soft greeting. She laid her head on the mare's neck. The woman felt tired, drained. She wasn't used to so many people, so much going on, and people who spoke a language were so *noisy*. She had a headache, her temples were pounding, and her neck and shoulders hurt. Whinney was leaning on her, and Racer, joining them, added pressure from his side, until she was feeling squeezed between them, but she didn't mind.

"Enough!" she said, finally, slapping the colt's flank. "You're getting too big, Racer, to get me in the middle like that. Look at you! Look how big you are. You're almost as big as your dam!" She scratched him, then rubbed and patted Whinney, noticing dried sweat. "It's hard for you, too, isn't it? I'll give you a good rub-down and brush you with a teasel later, but many people are coming now so you're probably going to get more attention. It won't be so bad once they get used to you."

Ayla didn't notice that she had slipped into the private language she had developed during her years alone with only animals for company. It was composed partly of Clan gestures, partly of verbalisations of some of the few words the Clan spoke, imitations of animals, and the nonsense words she and her son had begun to use. To anyone else, it was likely the hand signals would not have been noticed, and she would have seemed to be murmuring a most peculiar set of sounds: grunts and growls and repetitive syllables. It might not have been thought of as a language.

"Maybe Jondalar will brush Racer, too." Suddenly she stopped as a troubling thought occurred to her. She reached for her amulet again and tried to frame her thoughts. "Great Cave Lion, Jondalar is now your chosen, too, he bears the scars on his leg of your marking, just as I do."

She shifted her thoughts into the ancient silent language spoken only with hands; the proper language for addressing the spirit world.

"Spirit of the Great Cave Lion, that man who has been chosen has not a knowledge of totems. That man knows not of testing, knows not the trials of a powerful totem, or the gifts and the learning. Even this woman who knows has found them difficult. This woman would beg the Spirit of the Cave Lion . . . would beg for that man . . ."

Ayla stopped. She wasn't sure what she was asking for. She didn't want to ask the spirit not to test Jondalar – she did not want him to forfeit the benefits such trials would most assuredly bring – and not even to go easy on him. Since she had suffered great ordeals and gained unique skills and insights, she had come to believe benefits came in proportion to the severity of the test. She gathered her thoughts and continued.

"This woman would beg the Spirit of the Great Cave Lion to help that man who has been chosen to know the value of his powerful totem; to know that no matter how difficult it may seem, the testing is necessary." She finally finished and let her hands drop.

"Ayla?"

She turned around and saw Latie. "Yes."

"You seemed to be . . . busy. I didn't want to interrupt you."

"I am through."

"Talut would like you to come and bring the horses. He has already told everyone they should do nothing that you don't say. Not to frighten them or make them nervous . . . I think he made some people nervous."

"I will come," Ayla said, then she smiled. "You like ride horse back?" she asked.

Latie's face split into a wide grin. "Could I? Really?" When she smiled like that, she resembled Talut, Ayla thought.

"Maybe people not be nervous when see you on Whinney. Come. Here is rock. Help you get on."

As Ayla came back around the bend, followed by a full-grown mare with the girl on her back, and a frisky colt behind, all conversation stopped. Those who had seen it before, though still awed themselves, were enjoying the expressions of stunned disbelief on the faces of those who hadn't.

"See, Tulie. I told you!" Talut said to a dark-haired woman who resembled him in size, if not in colouring. She towered over Barzec, the man from the last hearth, who stood beside her with his arm around her waist. Near them were the two boys of that hearth, thirteen and eight years, and their sister of six, whom Ayla had recently met.

When they reached the earthlodge, Ayla lifted Latie down, then stroked and patted Whinney, whose nostrils were flaring as she picked up the scent of unfamiliar people again. The girl ran to a gangly, red-haired young man of, perhaps, fourteen years, nearly as tall as Talut and, except for age and a body not yet as filled out, almost identical.

"Come and meet Ayla," Latie said, pulling him towards the woman with the horses. He allowed himself to be pulled. Jondalar had strolled over to keep Racer settled down.

"This is my brother, Danug," Latie explained. "He's been gone a long time, but he's going to stay home now that he knows all about mining flint. Aren't you, Danug?"

"I don't know all about it, Latie," he said, a bit embarrassed.

Ayla smiled. "I greet you," she said, holding out her hands.

It made him even more embarrassed. He was the son of the Lion Hearth, he should have greeted the visitor first, but he was overwhelmed by the beautiful stranger who had such power over animals. He took her proffered hands and mumbled a greeting. Whinney chose that moment to snort and prance away, and he quickly let her hands go, feeling, for some reason, that the horse disapproved.

"Whinney would learn to know you faster if you patted her and let her get your scent," Jondalar said, sensing the young man's discomfort. It was a difficult age; no longer child but not quite man. "Have you been learning the craft of mining flint?" he asked conversationally, trying to put the boy at ease as he showed him how to stroke the horse.

"I am a worker of flint. Wymez has been teaching me since I was young," the young man said with pride. "He's the best, but he wanted me to learn some other techniques, and how to judge the raw stone." With the conversation turned to more familiar topics, Danug's natural enthusiasm surfaced.

Jondalar's eyes lit up with sincere interest. "I, too, am a worker of flint, and learned my craft from a man who is the best. When I was about your age, I lived with him near the flint mine he found. I'd like to meet your teacher sometime."

"Then let me introduce you, since I am the son of his hearth – and the first, though not the only, user of his tools."

Jondalar turned at the sound of Ranec's voice, and noticed the whole Camp was circled around. Standing beside the man with brown skin was the man he had greeted so warmly. Though they were the same height, Jondalar could see no further resemblance. The older man's hair was straight and light brown shot with grey, his eyes were an ordinary blue, and there was no similarity between his and Ranec's distinctly exotic features. The Mother must have chosen the spirit of another man for the child of his hearth, Jondalar thought, but why did She select one of such unusual colouring?

"Wymez of the Fox Hearth of the Lion Camp, Flint Master of the Mamutoi," Ranec said with exaggerated formality, "meet our visitors,

Jondalar of the Zelandonii, another of your ilk, it would seem." Jondalar felt an undercurrent of . . . he wasn't sure. Humour? Sarcasm? Something. "And, his beautiful companion, Ayla, a woman of No People, but great charm – and mystery." His smile drew Ayla's eyes, with the contrast between white teeth and dark skin, and his dark eyes sparkled with a knowing look.

"Greetings," Wymez said, as simple and direct as Ranec had been elaborate. "You work the stone?"

"Yes, I'm a flint knapper," Jondalar replied.

"I have some excellent stone with me. It's fresh from the source, hasn't dried out at all."

"I've got a hammerstone, and a good punch in my pack," Jondalar said, immediately interested. "Do you use a punch?"

Ranec gave Ayla a pained look as their conversation quickly turned to their mutual skill. "I could have told you this would happen," he said. "Do you know what the worst part of living at the hearth of a master toolmaker is? It's not always having stone chips in your furs, it's always having stone talk in your ears. And after Danug showed an interest . . . stone, stone, stone . . . that's all I heard." Ranec's warm smile belied his complaint, and everyone had obviously heard it before, since no one paid much attention, except Danug.

"I didn't know it bothered you so much," the young man said.

"It didn't," Wymez said the the youngster. "Can't you tell when Ranec is trying to impress a pretty woman?"

"Actually, I'm grateful to you, Danug. Until you came along, I think he was hoping to turn me into a flint worker," Ranec said to relieve Danug's concern.

"Not after I realised your only interest in my tools was to carve ivory with them, and that wasn't long after we got here," Wymez said, then he smiled and added, "And if you think chips of flint in your bed are bad, you ought to try ivory dust in your food."

The two dissimilar men were smiling at each other, and Ayla realised with relief that they were joking, teasing each other verbally, in a friendly way. She also noticed that for all their difference in colour and Ranec's exotic features, their smile was similar, and their bodies moved the same way.

Suddenly shouting could be heard coming from inside the longhouse. "Keep out of it, old woman! This is between Fralie and me." It was a man's voice, the man of the sixth hearth, next to the last one. Ayla recalled meeting him.

"I don't know why she chose you, Frebec! I should never have allowed it!" a woman screeched back at the man. Suddenly an older woman burst out through the archway, dragging a crying young woman with her. Two bewildered boys followed, one about seven, the other a toddler of two with a bare bottom and a thumb in his mouth.

"It's all your fault. She listens to you too much. Why don't you stop interfering?"

Everyone turned away – they had heard it all before, too many times. But Ayla stared in amazement. No woman of the Clan would have argued with any man like that.

"Frebec and Crozie are at it again, don't mind them," said Tronie. She was the woman from the fifth hearth – the Reindeer Hearth, Ayla recalled. It was the next after the Mammoth Hearth, where she and Jondalar were staying. The woman was holding a baby boy to her breast.

Ayla had met the young mother from the neighbouring hearth earlier and was drawn to her. Tornec, her mate, picked up the three-year-old who was clinging to her mother, still not accepting of the new baby who had usurped her place at her mother's breast. They were a warm and loving young couple, and Ayla was glad they were the ones who lived at the next hearth rather than the ones who squabbled. Manuv, who lived with them, had come to talk to her while they were eating, and told her that he had been the man of the hearth when Tornec was young, and was the son of a cousin of Mamut. He said he often spent time at the fourth hearth, which pleased her. She always did have a special fondness for older people.

She wasn't as comfortable with the neighbouring hearth on the other side, the third one. Ranec lived there – he had called it the Fox Hearth. She did not dislike him, but Jondalar acted so strangely around him. It was a smaller hearth, though, with only two men and took less space in the longhouse so she felt closer to Nezzie and Talut, at the second hearth, and to Rydag. She liked the other children of Talut's Lion Hearth, too, Latie and Rugie, Nezzie's younger daughter, close in age to Rydag. Now that she'd met Danug, she liked him, too.

Talut approached with the big woman. Barzec and the children were with them and Ayla assumed they were mated.

"Ayla, I would like you to meet my sister, Tulie of the Aurochs Hearth, headwoman of the Lion Camp."

"Greetings," the woman said, holding out both hands in the formal way. "In Mut's name, I welcome you." As sister to the headman, she was his equal, and conscious of her responsibilities.

"I greet you, Tulie," Ayla replied, trying not to stare.

The first time Jondalar was able to stand, it had been a shock to discover that he was taller than she was, but to see a woman who was taller was even more surprising. Ayla had always towered over everyone in the Clan. But the headwoman was more than tall, she was muscular and powerful-looking. The only one who exceeded her in size was her brother. She carried herself with the presence that only sheer height and mass can convey, and the undeniable self-assurance of a woman, mother, and leader completely confident and in control of her life.

Tulie wondered about the visitor's strange accent, but another problem concerned her more, and with the directness typical of her people, she did not hesitate to bring it up.

"I didn't know the Mammoth Hearth would be occupied when I invited Branag to return with us. He and Deegie will be joined this summer. He will only stay a few days, and I know she had hoped they could spend those days off by themselves a little, away from her brothers and sister. Since you are a guest, she would not ask, but Deegie would like to stay at the Mammoth Hearth with Branag, if you do not object."

"Is large hearth. Many beds. I do not object," Ayla said, feeling uncomfortable to be asked. It wasn't her home.

As they were talking, a young woman came out of the earthlodge, followed by a young man. Ayla looked twice. She was close to Ayla's age, stocky and a fraction taller! She had deep chestnut hair and a friendly face that many would have said was pretty, and it was evident that the young man with her thought she was quite attractive. But Ayla wasn't paying much attention to her physical appearance, she was staring with awe at the young woman's clothing.

She was dressed in leggings, and a tunic of leather of a colour that almost matched her hair – a long, profusely decorated, dark ochre red tunic that opened in front, belted to hold it closed. Red was a colour sacred to the Clan. Iza's pouch was the only object Ayla owned that had been dyed red. It held the special roots used to make the drink for the special ceremonies. She still had it, carefully tucked away in her medicine bag in which she carried various dried herbs used in the healing magic. A whole tunic made of red leather? It was hard to believe.

"It is so beautiful!" Ayla said, even before she could be properly introduced.

"Do you like it? It's for my Matrimonial, when we are joined. Branag's mother gave it to me, and I just had to put it on to show everyone."

"I not ever see anything like it!" Ayla said, her eyes open wide.

The young woman was delighted. "You're the one called Ayla, aren't you? My name is Deegie, and this is Branag. He has to go back in a few days," she said, looking disappointed, "but after next summer we'll be together. We're going to move in with my brother, Tarneg. He's living with his woman and her family now, but he wants to set up a new Camp and he's been after me to take a mate so he'll have a headwoman."

Ayla saw Tulie smiling and nodding at her daughter and remembered the request. "Hearth have much room, many empty beds, Deegie. You

39

stay at Mammoth Hearth with Branag? He is visitor, too . . . if Mamut not mind. Is hearth of Mamut."

"His first woman was the mother of my grandmother. I've slept at his hearth many times. Mamut won't mind, will you?" Deegie asked, seeing him.

"Of course you and Branag can stay, Deegie," the old man said, "but remember, you may not get much sleep." Deegie smiled with expectation as Mamut continued, "With visitors, Danug returning after being away for a whole year, your Matrimonial, and Wymez's success on his trading mission, I think there is reason to gather at the Mammoth Hearth tonight and tell the stories."

Everyone smiled. They expected the announcement, but that didn't diminish their anticipation. They knew that a gathering at the Mammoth Hearth meant recounting of experiences, storytelling, and perhaps other entertainment, and they looked forward to the evening with enjoyment. They were eager to hear news of other Camps, and to listen again to stories they knew. And they were as interested in seeing the reactions of the strangers to the lives and adventures of members of their own Camp as to hearing the stories they had to share.

Jondalar also knew what such a gathering meant, and it bothered him. Would Ayla tell much of her story? Would the Lion Camp be as welcoming afterwards? He thought about taking her aside to caution her, but he knew it would just make her angry and upset. In many ways she was like the Mamutoi, direct and honest in the expression of her feelings. It wouldn't do any good anyway. She didn't know how to lie. At best, she might refrain from speaking.

3

Ayla spent time in the afternoon rubbing down and currying Whinney with a soft piece of leather and the dried spiny head of a teasel. It was as relaxing for her as it was for the horse.

Jondalar worked companionably beside her using a teasel on Racer to soothe his itchy places while he smoothed the colt's shaggy winter coat, though the young animal wanted to play more than stand still. Racer's warm and soft inner layer had grown in much thicker, reminding the man how soon the cold would be upon them, which set him to thinking about where they would spend the winter. He still wasn't sure how Ayla felt about the Mamutoi, but at least the horses and the people of the Camp were getting used to each other.

Ayla noticed the easing of tensions, too, but she was worried about where the horses would spend the night when she was inside the earthlodge. They were used to sharing a cave with her. Jondalar kept assuring her they would be fine, horses were used to being outside. She finally decided to tether Racer near the entrance, knowing Whinney wouldn't wander far afield without her colt, and that the mare would wake her if any danger presented itself.

The wind turned cold as darkness fell, and there was a breath of snow in the air when Ayla and Jondalar went in, but the Mammoth Hearth in the middle of the semi-subterranean dwelling was snug and warm as people gathered. Many had stopped to pick at cold leftovers from the earlier meal which had been brought in: small white starchy groundnuts, wild carrots, blueberries, and slices of mammoth roast. They picked up the vegetables and fruit with fingers or a pair of sticks used as tongs, but Ayla noticed that each person, except for the youngest of children, had an eating knife for the meat. It intrigued her to watch someone take hold of a large slice with the teeth, then cut off a small bite with an upward flick of the knife – without losing a nose.

Small brown waterbags – the preserved waterproof bladders and stomachs of various animals – were passed around and people drank from them with great relish. Talut offered her a drink. It smelled fermented and somewhat unpleasant, and filled her mouth with a slightly sweet but strong burning taste. She declined a second offer. She didn't like it, though Jondalar seemed to enjoy it.

People were talking and laughing as they found places on platforms or on furs or mats on the floor. Ayla's head was turned, listening to a conversation, when the level of noise dropped off noticeably. She turned around and saw the old Mamut standing quietly behind the fireplace in which a small fire burned. When all conversation ceased, and he had everyone's attention, he picked up a small unlit torch and held it to the hot flames until it caught. In the expectant hush of held breaths he brought the flame to a small stone lamp that was in a niche in the wall behind him. The dried lichen wick sputtered in the mammoth fat, then flared up, revealing a small ivory carving of an ample, well-endowed woman behind the lamp.

Ayla felt a prickle of recognition, though she had never seen one like it before. That's what Jondalar calls a donii, she thought. He says it holds the Spirit of the Great Earth Mother. Or a part of it, maybe. It seems too small to hold all of it. But then how big is a spirit?

Her mind wandered back to another ceremony, the time when she was given the black stone which she carried in the amulet bag around her neck. The small lump of black manganese dioxide held a piece of the spirit of everyone in the entire Clan, not just her clan. The stone had been given to her when she was made a medicine woman, and she had given up a part of her own spirit in exchange, so that if she saved someone's life, that person incurred no obligation to give her something of like kind and value in return. It had already been done.

It still bothered her when she recalled that the spirits had not been returned after she was death-cursed. Creb had taken them back from Iza, after the old medicine woman died, so they would not go with her to the spirit world, but no one had taken them from Ayla. If she had a piece of the spirit of every member of the Clan, had Broud caused them to be cursed with death, too?

Am I dead? she wondered as she had wondered many times before. She didn't think so. She had learned that the power of the death curse was in the believing, and that when loved ones no longer acknowledged your existence, and you had no place to go, you might as well die. But why hadn't she died? What had kept her from giving up? And more important, what would happen to the Clan when she really did die? Might her death cause harm to those she loved? Perhaps to all the Clan? The small leather pouch felt heavy with the weight of the responsibility, as though the fate of the entire Clan hung around her neck.

Ayla was brought out of her musing by a rhythmic sound. With a hammer-shaped section of an antler, Mamut was beating on the skull of a mammoth, painted with geometric lines and symbols. Ayla thought she detected a quality beyond rhythm and she watched and listened carefully. The hollow cavity intensified the sound with rich vibrations, but it was more than the simple resonance of the instrument. When the old shaman played on the different areas marked on the bone drum, the pitch and tone changed with such complex and subtle variations, it seemed as though Mamut was drawing speech from the drum, making the old mammoth skull talk.

Low and deep in his chest, the old man began intoning a chant in closely modulated minor tones. As drum and voice interwove an intricate pattern of sound, other voices joined in from here and there around the room, fitting into the established mode, yet varying it independently. The drum rhythm was picked up by a similar sound across the room. Ayla looked over and saw Deegie playing another skull drum. Then Tornec began tapping with an antler hammer on another mammoth bone, a shoulder bone covered with evenly spaced lines and chevrons painted in red. The deep tonal resonances of the skull drums, and the higher-pitched tones of the scapula, filled the earthlodge with a beautiful haunting sound. Ayla's body pulsed with movement and she noticed others moving their bodies in time to the sound. Suddenly it stopped.

The silence was filled with expectancy, but it was left to fade away. No formal ceremony was planned, only an informal gathering of the Camp to spend a pleasant evening in one another's company, doing what people do best – talking.

Tulie began by announcing that agreement had been reached, and the nuptials of Deegie and Branag would be formalised the next summer. Words of approval and congratulations were spoken out, though everyone expected it. The young couple beamed their pleasure. Then Talut asked Wymez to tell them about his trading mission, and they learned that it involved exchanges of salt, amber, and flint. Several people asked questions or made comments, while Jondalar listened with interest, but Ayla did not comprehend and resolved to ask him later. Following that, Talut asked about Danug's progress, to the young man's discomfiture.

"He has talent, a deft touch. A few more years of experience, and he'll be very good. They were sorry to see him leave. He's learned well, it was worth the year away," Wymez reported. More words of approval were spoken out by the group. Then there was a lull filled with small private conversations before Talut turned to Jondalar, which caused rustlings of excitement.

"Tell us, man of the Zelandonii, how do you come to be sitting in the lodge of the Lion Camp of the Mamutoi?" he asked.

Jondalar took a swallow from one of the small brown waterbags of fermented drink, looked around at the people waiting expectantly, then smiled at Ayla. He's done this before! she thought, a little surprised, understanding that he was setting the pace and the tone to tell his story. She settled down to listen as well.

"It is a long story," he began. People were nodding. That's what they wanted to hear. "My people live a long way from here, far, far to the west, even beyond the source of the Great Mother River that empties into Beran Sea. We live near a river, too, as you do, but our river flows into the Great Waters of the west.

"The Zelandonii are a great people. Like you, we are Earth's Children; the one you call Mut, we call Doni, but She is still the Great Earth Mother. We hunt and trade, and sometimes make long Journeys. My brother and I decided to make such a Journey." For a moment, Jondalar closed his eyes and his forehead knotted with pain. "Thonolan . . . my brother . . . was full of laughter and loved adventure. He was a favourite of the Mother."

The pain was too real. Everyone knew it was not an affectation for the sake of the story. Even without his saying so, they guessed the cause. They also had a saying about the Mother taking the ones She favoured early. Jondalar hadn't planned to show his feelings like that. The grief caught him by surprise and left him somewhat embarrassed. But such loss is universally understood. His unintended demonstration drew their sympathy and caused them to feel for him a warmth that went beyond the normal curiosity and courtesy they usually extended to non-threatening strangers.

He took a deep breath and tried to pick up the thread of his tale. "The Journey was Thonolan's in the beginning. I planned to accompany him only a short way, only as far as the home of some relatives, but then I decided to go with him. We crossed over a small glacier, which is the source of Donau – the Great Mother River – and said we would follow her to the end. No one believed we would do it, I'm not sure if we did, but we kept going, crossing many tributaries and meeting many people.

"Once, during the first summer, we stopped to hunt, and while we were drying the meat, we found ourselves surrounded by men pointing spears at us . . ."

Jondalar had found his stride again, and held the camp enthralled as he recounted his adventures. He was a good storyteller, with a flair for drawing out the suspense. There were nods and murmurs of approval and words of encouragement, often shouts of excitement. Even when they listen, people who speak with words are not silent, Ayla thought.

She was as fascinated as the rest, but found herself for a moment watching the people who were listening to him. Adults held young children in their laps while the older children sat together watching the charismatic stranger with glistening eyes. Danug, in particular, seemed captured. He was leaning forward, in rapt attention.

"Thonolan went into the canyon, thinking he was safe with the lioness gone. Then we heard the roar of a lion . . ."

"What happened then?" Danug asked.

"Ayla will have to tell you the rest. I don't remember much after that."

All eyes turned towards her. Ayla was stunned. She didn't expect it; she had never spoken to a crowd of people before. Jondalar was smiling at her. He'd had the sudden thought that the best way to get her used to talking to people was to make her do it. It wouldn't be the last time she'd be expected to recount some experience, and with her control over the horses still fresh in everyone's mind, the story of the lion would be more believable. It was an exciting story, he knew, and one that would add to her mystery – and perhaps, if she satisfied them with this story, she wouldn't have to bring up her background.

"What happened, Ayla?" Danug said, still caught up in the tale. Rugie had been feeling shy and reticent around her big brother who had been gone for so long, but remembering former times when they sat around telling stories, she decided at that moment to climb into his lap. He welcomed her with an absentminded smile and hug, but looked at Ayla expectantly.

Ayla looked around at all the faces turned towards her, tried to speak, but her mouth was dry, though her palms were sweaty.

"Yes, what happened?" Latie repeated. She was sitting near Danug, with Rydag in her lap.

The boy's big brown eyes were filled with excitement. He opened his mouth to ask, too, but no one understood the sound he made – except Ayla. Not the word itself, but its intent. She had heard similar sounds before, had even learned to speak them. The people of the Clan were not mute, but they were limited in their ability to articulate. They had instead evolved a rich and comprehensive sign language to communicate, and used words only for emphasis. She knew the child was asking her to continue the story, and that to him the words had that meaning. Ayla smiled, and directed her words to him.

"I was with Whinney," Ayla began. Her way of saying the mare's name had always been an imitation of the soft nicker of a horse. The people in the lodge didn't realise she was saying the animal's name. Instead, they thought it was a wonderful embellishment to the story. They smiled, and spoke words of approval, encouraging her to continue in the same vein.

"She soon have small horse. Very big," Ayla said, holding her hands out in front of her stomach to indicate that the horse was very pregnant. There were smiles of understanding. "Every day we ride, Whinney need go out. Not far, not fast. Always go east, easy to go east. Too easy,

45

nothing new. One day, we go west, not east. See new place," Ayla continued, directing her words to Rydag.

Jondalar had been teaching her Mamutoi, as well as the other languages he knew, but she wasn't as fluent as she was in his language, the one she'd first learned to speak. Her manner of speaking was odd, different in a way that was hard to explain, and she struggled to find words, feeling shy about it. But when she thought of the boy who couldn't make himself understood at all, she had to try. Because he had asked.

"I hear lion." She wasn't sure why she did it. Perhaps it was the expectant look on Rydag's face, or the way he turned his head to hear, or an instinct for it, but she followed the word "lion" with a menacing growl, that sounded for all the world like a real lion. She heard little gasps of fear, then nervous chuckles, then smiling words of approval from the assembled group. Her ability to mimic the sounds of animals was uncanny. It added unexpected excitement to her story. Jondalar was nodding and smiling his approval, too.

"I hear man scream." She looked at Jondalar and her eyes filled with sorrow. "I stop, what to do? Whinney is big with baby." She made the little squealing sounds of a foal, and was rewarded with a beaming smile from Latie. "I worry for horse, but man scream. I hear lion again. I listen." She managed, somehow, to make a lion's roar sound playful. "It is Baby. I go in canyon then, I know horse not be hurt."

Ayla saw puzzled looks. The word she spoke was unfamiliar, although Rydag might have known it if his circumstances had been different. She had told Jondalar it was the Clan word for infant.

"Baby is lion," she said, trying to explain. "Baby is lion I know, Baby is . . . like son. I go in canyon, make lion go away. I find one man dead. Other man, Jondalar, hurt very bad. Whinney take back to valley."

"Ha!" a voice said derisively. Ayla looked up and saw that it was Frebec, the man who had been arguing with the old woman earlier. "Are you trying to tell me you told a lion to go away from a wounded man?"

"Not any lion. Baby," Ayla said.

"What is that . . . whatever you are saying?"

"Baby is Clan word. Mean child, infant. Name I give lion when he live with me. Baby is lion I know. Horse know, too. Not afraid." Ayla was upset, something was wrong, but she wasn't sure what.

"You lived with a lion? I don't believe that," he sneered.

"You don't believe it?" Jondalar said, sounding angry. The man was accusing Ayla of lying, and he knew only too well how true her story was. "Ayla does not lie," he said, standing up to untie the thong that was gathered around the waist of his leather trousers. He dropped down one side of them and exposed a groin and thigh disfigured with angry red scars. "That lion attacked me, and Ayla not only got me away from him, she is a Healer of great skill. I would have followed my brother to the next world without her. I will tell you something else. I saw her ride the back of that lion, just as she rides the horse. Will you call me a liar?"

"No guest of the Lion Camp is called a liar," Tulie said, glaring at Frebec, trying to calm a potentially ugly scene. "I think it is evident that you were badly mauled, and we have certainly seen the woman . . . Ayla . . . ride the horse. I see no reason to doubt you, or her."

There was a strained silence. Ayla was looking from one to the other, confused. The word "liar" was unfamiliar to her, and she did not understand why Frebec said he didn't believe her. Ayla had grown up among people who communicated with movement. More than hand signs, the Clan language included posture and expressions to shade meanings and give nuances. It was impossible to lie effectively with the entire body. At best, one could refrain from mentioning and even that was known, though allowed for the sake of privacy. Ayla didn't know how to lie.

But she did know something was wrong. She could read the anger and hostility that had sprung up as easily as if they'd shouted it. She also knew that they were trying to refrain from mentioning it. Talut saw Ayla look at the dark-skinned man, then look away. Seeing Ranec gave him an idea of a way to ease tensions and get back to storytelling.

"That was a good story, Jondalar," Talut boomed, giving Frebec a hard look. "Long Journeys are always exciting to hear about. Would you like to hear a story of another long Journey?"

"Yes, very much."

There were smiles all around as people relaxed. It was a favourite story of the group, and not often was there an opportunity to share it with people who hadn't heard it before.

"It's Ranec's story . . ." Talut began.

Ayla looked at Ranec expectantly. "I would know how man with brown skin comes to live at Lion Camp," she said.

Ranec smiled at her, but turned to the man of his hearth. "It's my story, but yours to tell, Wymez," he said.

Jondalar was seated again, not at all sure he liked the turn the conversation had taken – or perhaps Ayla's interest in Ranec – though it was better than the near-open hostility, and he was interested, too.

Wymez settled back, nodded to Ayla, then smiling at Jondalar, he began. "We have more in common than a feel for the stone, young man. I, too, made a long Journey in my youth. I travelled south towards the east first, past Beran Sea, all the way to the shores of a much larger sea farther south. This Southern Sea has many names, for many people live along its shores. I travelled around its eastern end then west along the south shore through lands of many forests, much warmer, and rainier, than here.

"I won't try to tell you all that happened to me. I will save that for another time. I will tell you Ranec's story. As I travelled west, I met many people and stayed with some of them, and learned new ways, but then I would get restless and travel again. I wanted to see how far west I could go.

"After several years I came to a place, not far from your Great Waters, I think, Jondalar, but across the narrow straits where the Southern Sea joins it. There, I met some people whose skin was so dark it seemed black, and there I met a woman. A woman I was drawn to. Perhaps at first it was her difference . . . her exotic clothes, her colour, her dark flashing eyes. Her smile compelled . . . and the way she danced, the way she moved . . . she was the most exciting woman I ever met."

Wymez talked in a direct, understated way, but the story was so enthralling it needed no dramatics. Yet, the demeanour of the stocky, quietly reserved man changed perceptibly when he mentioned the woman.

"When she agreed to join with me, I decided to stay there with her. I always had an interest in working stone, even as a youngster, and I learned their way of making spear points. They chip off both sides of the stone, you understand?" He directed the question to Jondalar.

"Yes, bifacially, like an axe."

"But these points were not so thick and crude. They had good technique. I showed them some things, too, and I was quite content to accept their ways, especially after the Mother blessed her with a child, a boy. She asked me for a name, as was their custom. I chose Ranec."

That explains it, Ayla thought. His mother was dark-skinned.

"What made you decide to come back?" Jondalar asked.

"A few years after Ranec was born, difficulties began. The dark-skinned people I was living with had moved there from farther south, and some people from neighbouring Camps didn't want to share hunting grounds. There were differences in customs. I almost convinced them to meet and talk about it. Then some young hotheads from both sides decided to fight about it instead. One death led to another for revenge, and then to attacks on home Camps.

"We set up good defences, but there were more of them. It went on for some time and they kept killing us off, one after another. After a while, the sight of a person with lighter skin began to cause fear and hatred. Though I was one of them, they started distrusting me, and even Ranec. His skin was lighter than the others, and his features had a different cast. I talked to Ranec's mother, and we decided to leave. It was a sad parting, leaving family and many friends, but it wasn't safe to stay. Some of the hotheads even tried to keep us from going, but with help, we stole away in the night.

"We travelled north, to the straits. I knew some people lived there who made small boats which they used to cross the open water. We were warned that it was the wrong season, and it was a difficult crossing during the best of conditions. But I felt we had to get away, and decided to chance it.

"It was the wrong decision," Wymez said in a tightly controlled voice. "The boat capsized. Only Ranec and I made it across, and one bundle of her belongings." He paused for a moment before he continued the story. "We were still far from home, and it took a long time, but we finally arrived here, during a Summer Meeting."

"How long were you gone?" Jondalar asked.

"Ten years," Wymez said, then smiled. "We created quite a stir. No one expected to see me again, much less with Ranec. Nezzie didn't even recognise me, but my little sister was only a girl when I left. She and Talut had just completed their Matrimonial and were setting up the Lion Camp with Tulie and both of her mates, and their children. They invited me to join them. Nezzie adopted Ranec, though he is still the son of my hearth, and took care of him as though he were her own, even after Danug was born."

When he stopped talking, it took a moment to realise he was through. Everyone wanted to hear more. Even though most of them had heard many of his adventures, he always seemed to have new stories or new twists to old stories.

"I think Nezzie would be everyone's mother, if she could," Tulie said, recalling the time of his return. "I had Deegie at the breast then, and Nezzie couldn't get enough of playing with her."

"She does more than mother me!" Talut said, with a playful grin as he patted her broad backside. He had gotten another waterbag of the powerful drink and was passing it on after taking a swallow.

"Talut! I'll do more than mother you, all right!" She was trying to sound angry, but stifling a smile.

"Is that a promise?" he countered.

"You know what I meant, Talut," Tulie said, brushing aside the rather obvious innuendos between her brother and his woman. "She couldn't even let Rydag go. He's so sickly, he'd have been better off."

Ayla's eye was drawn to the child. Tulie's comment had bothered him. Her words had not been intentionally unkind, but Ayla knew he didn't like being spoken of as though he wasn't there. There wasn't anything he could do about it, though. He couldn't tell her how he felt, and without thinking, she assumed that because he couldn't speak, he didn't feel.

Ayla wanted to ask about the child, too, but felt it might be presumptuous. Jondalar did it for her, though it was to satisfy his own curiosity.

"Nezzie, would you tell us about Rydag? I think Ayla would be particularly interested – and so would I."

Nezzie leaned over and took the child from Latie, and held him on her lap while she gathered her thoughts.

"We were out after megaceros, you know, the giant deer with the great antlers," she began, "and planned to build a surround to drive them into – that's the best way to hunt the big-antlered ones. When I first noticed the woman hiding near our hunting camp, I thought it was strange. You seldom see flathead women, and never alone."

Ayla was leaning close, listening intently.

"She didn't run away when she saw me looking at her, either, only when I tried to get closer. Then I saw she was pregnant. I thought she might be hungry, so I left some food out near the place she was hiding. In the morning it was gone, so I left more before we broke camp.

"I thought I saw her the next day a few times, but I wasn't sure. Then that night, when I was by the fire nursing Rugie, I saw her again. I got up and tried to get closer to her. She ran away again, but she moved like she was in pain, and I realised she was in labour. I didn't know what to do. I wanted to help, but she kept running away, and it was getting dark. I told Talut, and he got some people together to go after her."

"That was strange, too," Talut said, adding his part to Nezzie's story. "I thought we'd have to circle around and trap her, but when I yelled at her to stop, she just sat on the ground and waited. She didn't seem too frightened of me, and when I beckoned her to come, she got right up and followed behind me, like she knew what to do and understood I wouldn't hurt her."

"I don't know how she even walked," Nezzie continued. "She was in such pain. She was quick to understand that I wanted to help her, but I don't know how much help I was. I wasn't even sure she'd live to deliver her baby. She never cried out, though. Finally, near morning, her son was born. I was surprised to see he was one of mixed spirits. Even that young you could tell he was different.

"The woman was so weak I thought it might give her reason to live if I showed her that her son was alive, and she seemed eager to see him. But I guess she was too far gone, must have lost too much blood. It was as though she just gave up. She died before the sun came up.

"Everybody told me to leave him to die with his mother, but I was nursing Rugie anyway, and had a lot of milk. It wasn't that much trouble to put him to my breast, too." She hugged him protectively. "I know he's weak. Maybe I should have left him, but I couldn't love Rydag any more if he were my own. And I'm not sorry I kept him."

Rydag looked up at Nezzie with his big, glowing brown eyes, then put thin arms around her neck and laid his head on her breast. Nezzie rocked him as she held him.

"Some people say he's an animal because he can't talk, but I know he understands. And he's not an 'abomination' either," she added, with an angry look at Frebec. "Only the Mother knows why the spirits that made him were mixed."

Ayla was fighting to hold back tears. She didn't know how these people would react to tears; her watering eyes had always bothered people of the Clan. Watching the woman and the child, she was over-whelmed with memories. She ached to hold her son, and grieved anew for Iza, who had taken her in and mothered her, though she had been as different to the Clan as Rydag was to the Lion Camp. But more than anything, she wished there was some way she could explain to Nezzie how moved she was, how grateful she was for Rydag's sake . . . and her own. Inexplicably, Ayla felt it would somehow help repay Iza if she could find a way to do something for Nezzie.

"Nezzie, he knows," Ayla said softly. "He is not animal, not flathead. He is child of Clan, and child of Others."

"I know he is not an animal, Ayla," Nezzie said, "but what is Clan?"

"People, like mother of Rydag. You say flathead; they say Clan," Ayla explained.

"What do you mean, 'they say Clan'? They can't talk," Tulie inter-jected.

"Not say many words. But they talk. They talk with hands."

"How do you know?" Frebec asked. "What makes you so smart?"

Jondalar took a deep breath and held it, waiting for her answer.

"I lived with Clan before. I talked like Clan. Not with words until Jondalar came," Ayla said. "The Clan were my people."

There was a stunned silence as the meaning of her words became clear.

"You mean you lived with flatheads! You lived with those dirty animals!" Frebec exclaimed with disgust, jumping up and backing away. "No wonder she can't talk right. If she lived with them she's as bad as they are. Nothing but animals, all of them, including that mixed-up perversion of yours, Nezzie."

The Camp was in an uproar. Even if some might have agreed with him, Frebec had gone too far. He had overstepped the bounds of courtesy to visitors, and had even insulted the headman's mate. But it had long been an embarrassment to him that he belonged to the Camp that had taken in the "abomination of mixed spirits", and he was still chafing under the barbs of Fralie's mother in the most recent round of their long-standing battle. He wanted to take out his irritation on someone.

51

Talut roared to the defence of Nezzie and Ayla. Tulie was quick to defend the honour of the Camp. Crozie, smiling maliciously, was alternately haranguing Frebec and browbeating Fralie, and the others were voicing their opinions loudly. Ayla looked from one to another, wanting to put her hands over her ears to shut out the noise.

Suddenly Talut boomed a shout for silence. It was loud enough to startle everyone into quiet. Then Mamut's drum was heard. It had a settling, quieting effect.

"I think before anyone else says anything, we ought to hear what Ayla has to say," Talut said, as the drum stilled.

Tulie leaned forward attentively, more than willing to listen to find out about the mysterious woman. Ayla wasn't sure she wanted to say any more to these noisy, rude people, but she felt she had no choice. Then, lifting her chin a bit, she thought, if they wanted to hear it, she'd tell them, but she was leaving in the morning.

"I no . . . I do not remember young life," Ayla began, "only earthquake, and cave lion who make scars on my leg. Iza tell me she find me by river . . . what is word, Mamut? Not awake?"

"Unconscious."

"Iza find me by river, unconscious. I am close to age of Rydag, younger. Maybe five years. I am hurt on leg from cave lion claw. Iza is . . . medicine woman. She heal my leg. Creb . . . Creb is Mog–ur . . . like Mamut . . . holy man . . . knows spirit world. Creb teach me to speak Clan way. Iza and Creb . . . all Clan . . . they take care of me. I am not Clan, but they take care of me."

Ayla was straining to recall everything Jondalar had told her about their language. She hadn't liked Frebec's comment that she couldn't talk right, any more than the rest of what he said. She glanced at Jondalar. His forehead was furrowed. He wanted her to be careful of something. She wasn't entirely sure of the reason for his concern, but perhaps it was not necessary to mention everything.

"I grow up with Clan, but leave . . . to find Others, like me. I am . . ." She stopped to think of the right counting word. "Fourteen years then. Iza tell me Others live north. I look long time, not find anyone. Then I find valley and stay, to make ready for winter. Kill horse for meat, then see small horse, her baby. I have no people. Young horse is like baby, I take care of young horse. Later, find young lion, hurt. Take lion, too, but he grow up, leave, find mate. I live in valley three years, alone. Then Jondalar come."

Ayla stopped then. No one spoke. Her explanation, so simply told, with no embellishments, could only be true, yet it was difficult to believe. It posed more questions than it answered. Could she really have been taken in and raised by flatheads? Could they really talk, or at least communicate? Could they really be so humane, so human? And what about her? If she was raised by them, was she human?

In the silence that followed, Ayla watched Nezzie and the boy, and then remembered an incident early in her life with the Clan. Creb had been teaching her to communicate with hand signs, but there was one gesture she had learned herself. It was a signal shown often to babies, and always used by children to the women who take care of them, and she recalled how Iza had felt when she first made the signal to her.

Ayla leaned forward and said to Rydag, "I want show you word. Word you say with hands."

He sat up, his eyes showing his interest, and excitement. He had understood, as he always did, every word that was said, and the talk about hand signs had caused vague stirrings within him. With everyone watching, she made a gesture, a purposeful movement with her hands. He made an attempt to copy her, frowned with puzzlement. Then, suddenly comprehension came to him from some deeply buried place, and it showed on his face. He corrected himself as Ayla smiled and nodded her head. Then he turned to Nezzie and made the gesture again. She looked at Ayla.

"He say to you, 'mother'," Ayla explained.

"Mother?" Nezzie said, then closed her eyes, blinking back tears, as she held close the child she had cared for since his birth. "Talut! Did you see that? Rydag just called me 'mother'. I never thought I'd ever see the day Rydag would call me 'mother'."

4

The mood of the Camp was subdued. No one knew what to say, or what to think. Who were these strangers that had suddenly appeared in their midst? The man who claimed to come from some place far to the west was easier to believe than the woman who said she had lived for three years in a valley nearby, and even more amazing, with a pack of flatheads before that. The woman's story threatened a whole structure of comfortable beliefs, yet it was difficult to doubt her.

Nezzie had carried Rydag to his bed, with tears in her eyes, after he had signed his first silent word. Everyone else took it as a signal that the storytellings were over and moved to their own hearths. Ayla used the opportunity to slip away. Pulling her parka, a hooded outer fur tunic, over her head, she went outside.

Whinney recognised her leaving the lodge and nickered softly. Feeling her way in the dark, guided by the mare's snorting and blowing, Ayla found the horse.

"Is everything all right, Whinney? Are you comfortable? And Racer? Probably no more than I am," Ayla said, with thoughts as much as with the private language she used when she was with the horses. Whinney tossed her head, prancing delicately, then rested her head across the woman's shoulder as Ayla wrapped her arms around the shaggy neck and laid her forehead against the horse who had been her only companion for so long. Racer crowded in close and all three clung together for a moment of respite from all the unfamiliar experiences of the day.

After Ayla assured herself that the horses were fine, she walked down to the edge of the river. It felt good to be out of the lodge, away from people. She took a deep breath. The night air was cold and dry. Sparks of static crackled through her hair as she pushed back her fur-lined hood, stretched her neck and looked up.

The new moon, avoiding the great companion that held it tethered, had turned its shining eye out upon the distant depths whose whirling lights tantalised with promises of boundless freedom, but offered only cosmic emptiness. High thin clouds cloaked the fainter stars, but only veiled the more determined with shimmering halos, and made the sooty black sky feel close and soft.

Ayla was in a turmoil, conflicting emotions pulling at her. These were the Others she had looked for. The kind she had been born to. She would have grown up with people like them, comfortable, at home, if it hadn't been for the earthquake. Instead she had been raised by the Clan. She knew Clan customs, but the ways of her own people were strange. Yet if it hadn't been for the Clan, she wouldn't have grown up at all. She couldn't go back to them, but she didn't feel that she belonged here, either.

These people were so noisy, and disorderly. Iza would have said they had no manners. Like that Frebec man, speaking out of turn, without asking permission, and then everyone yelling and talking at once. She thought Talut was a leader, but even he had to shout to make himself heard. Brun would never have had to shout. The only time she ever heard him shout was to warn someone of impending danger. Everyone in the Clan kept the leader at a certain level of awareness; Brun had only to signal, and within heartbeats, he would have had everyone's attention.

She didn't like the way these people talked about the Clan, either, calling them flatheads and animals. Couldn't anyone see they were people, too? A little different, maybe, but people just the same. Nezzie knew it. In spite of what the rest said, she knew Rydag's mother was a woman, and the child to whom she gave birth only a baby. He's mixed, though, like my son, Ayla thought, and like Oda's little girl at the Clan Gathering. How could Rydag's mother have had a child of mixed spirits like that?

Spirits! Is it really spirits that make babies? Does a man's totem spirit overcome a woman's and make a baby grow inside her, the way the Clan thinks? Does the Great Mother choose and combine the spirits of a man and a woman and then put them inside a woman, the way Jondalar and these people believe?

Why am I the only one who thinks it's a man, not a spirit, that starts a baby growing inside a woman? A man, who does it with his organ . . . his manhood, Jondalar calls it. Why else would men and women come together like they do?

When Iza told me about the medicine, she said that it strengthened her totem and that's what kept her from having a baby for so many years. Maybe it did, but I didn't take it when I was living alone and no babies got started by themselves. It was only after Jondalar came that I even thought about looking for that golden thread plant and the antelope sage root again . . .

After Jondalar showed me it didn't have to hurt . . . after he showed me how wonderful it could be for a man and woman together . . .

I wonder what would happen if I stopped taking Iza's secret medicine? Would I have a baby? Would I have Jondalar's baby? If he put his manhood there, where babies come from?

The thought brought a flush of warmth to her face, and a tingling to her nipples. It's too late today, she thought, I already took the medicine this morning, but what if I just made an ordinary tea tomorrow? Could I start Jondalar's baby growing? We wouldn't have to wait, though. We could try tonight . . .

She smiled to herself. You just want him to touch you, and put his mouth on your mouth, and on . . . She shivered with anticipation, closing her eyes to let her body remember how he could make it feel.

"Ayla?" a voice barked.

She jumped at the sound. She hadn't heard Jondalar coming, and the tone he used wasn't in keeping with the way she was feeling. It dispelled the warmth. Something was bothering him. Something had been bothering him since they arrived; she wished she could discover what it was.

"Yes."

"What are you doing out here?" he snapped.

What had she been doing? "I am feeling the night, and breathing, and thinking about you," she answered, explaining as fully as she could.

It wasn't the answer Jondalar expected, though he wasn't sure what answer he did expect. He had been fighting down a hard knot of anger and anxiety that had made his stomach churn ever since the dark-skinned man appeared. Ayla seemed to find him so interesting, and Ranec was always looking at her. Jondalar had tried to swallow his anger and convince himself it was silly to think there was anything more to it. She needed other friends. Just because he was the first didn't mean he was the only man she would ever want to know.

Yet when Ayla asked Ranec about his background, Jondalar felt himself flush with hot rage and shudder with cold terror at the same time. Why did she want to know more about this fascinating stranger if she wasn't interested? The tall man resisted an urge to snatch her away, and was bothered because he had such a feeling. She had the right to choose her friends, and they were only friends. They had only talked and looked at each other.

When she went outside alone, Jondalar, seeing Ranec's dark eyes follow her, quickly put on his parka and went out after her. He saw her standing by the river, and for some reason he couldn't explain, felt sure she was thinking about Ranec. Her answer first caught him by surprise, then he relaxed, and smiled.

"I should have known, if I asked, I'd get a complete and honest answer. 'Breathing, and feeling the night' – you're wonderful, Ayla."

She smiled back. She wasn't sure what she had done, but something had made him smile, and put the happiness back in his voice. The warmth she had been feeling returned, and she moved towards him. Even in the dark of night, with barely enough starlight to show a face, Jondalar sensed her mood from the way she moved, and responded in kind. The next moment she was in his arms, with his mouth on hers, and all her doubts and worries fled from her mind. She would go anywhere, live with any people, learn any strange customs, so long as she had Jondalar.

After a moment she looked up at him. "Do you remember when I asked you what your signal was? How I should tell you when I wanted you to touch me, and wanted your manhood in me?"

"Yes, I remember," he said, smiling wryly.

"You said to kiss, or just ask. I am asking. Can you make your manhood ready?"

She was so serious, and so ingenuous, and so appealing. He bent his head to kiss her again, and held her so close she could almost see the blue of his eyes, and the love in them. "Ayla, my funny, beautiful woman," he said. "Do you know how much I love you?"

But as he held her, he felt a flush of guilt. If he loved her so much, why did he feel so embarrassed about the things she did? When that Frebec man backed away from her in disgust, he'd wanted to die of shame that he had brought her, that he could be associated with her. A moment later, he'd hated himself for it. He loved her. How could he be ashamed of the woman he loved?

That dark man, Ranec, wasn't ashamed. The way he looked at her, with his white gleaming teeth and his dark flashing eyes, laughing, coaxing, teasing; when Jondalar thought of it, he'd had to fight an impulse to strike out at him. Every time he thought of it, he had to fight the urge again. He loved her so much, he couldn't bear the thought that she might want someone else, maybe someone who wasn't embarrassed by her. He loved her more than he ever thought it was possible to love anyone. But how could he be ashamed of the woman he loved?

Jondalar kissed her again, harder, holding her so tight it hurt, then with an almost frenzied ardour, he kissed her throat and neck. "Do you know what it feels like to know, finally, that you can fall in love? Ayla, can't you feel how much I love you?"

He was so earnest, so fervent, she felt a pang of fear, not for herself, but for him. She loved him, more than she could ever find words for, but this love he felt for her was not quite the same. It wasn't so much stronger, as more demanding, more insistent. As though he feared he would lose that which he had finally won. Totems, especially strong totems, had a way of knowing, and testing, just such fears. She wanted to find a way to deflect his outpouring of powerful emotion.

"I can feel how ready you are," she said, with a little grin.

But he didn't respond with a lighter mood, as she had hoped. Instead he kissed her fiercely, crushing her until she thought her ribs would crack. Then he was fumbling inside her parka, under her tunic, reaching for her breasts, trying to untie the drawstring of her trousers.

She had never known him like this, needing, craving, imploring in his urgency. His way was usually more tender, more considerate of her needs. He knew her body better than she did, and he enjoyed his knowledge and skill. But this time his needs were stronger. Knowing the moment for what it was, she gave herself up to him, and lost herself in the powerful expression of his love. She was as ready for him as he was for her. She undid the drawstring and let her legged garment drop, then helped him with his.

Before she knew it, she was on the hard ground near the bank of the river. She caught a glimpse of faintly hazy stars before closing her eyes. He was on her, his mouth hard on hers, his tongue prodding, searching, as though he could find with it what he sought so eagerly with his warm and rigid member. She opened to him, her mouth and her thighs, then reached for him and guided him into her moist, inviting depths. She gasped as he entered, and heard an almost strangled moan, then felt his shaft sink in to fill her, as she strained to him.

Even in his frenzy, he marvelled at the wonder of her, at how suited they were, that her depths matched his size. He felt her warm folds embrace him fully, and almost, at that first instant, reached his peak. For a moment, he struggled to hold back, to exercise the control he was so accustomed to, then he let go. He plunged in, and again, and once more, and then with an inexpressible shudder, he felt a rising peak of wonder, and cried out her name.

"Ayla! Oh, my Ayla, my Ayla. I love you!"

"Jondalar, Jondalar, Jondalar . . ."

He finished a last few motions, then with a groan, buried his face in her neck and held her as he lay still, spent. She felt a stone jabbing her back, but she ignored it.

After a while he raised himself and looked down at her, his forehead furrowed with concern. "I'm sorry," he said.

"Why are you sorry?"

"It was too fast, and I didn't make you ready, didn't give you Pleasures, too."

"I was ready, Jondalar, I had Pleasure. Did I not ask you? I have Pleasure in your Pleasure. I have Pleasure in your love, in your strong feeling for me."

"But you did not feel the moment as I did."

"I did not need it. I had different feeling, different Pleasure. Is it always necessary?" she asked.

"No, I suppose not," he said, frowning. Then he kissed her and lingered over it. "And this night is not over yet. Come, get up. It's cold out here. Let's go find a warm bed. Deegie and Branag have already pulled their drapes closed. They will be separated until next summer and are eager."

Ayla smiled. "But not as eager as you were." She couldn't see it, but she thought he blushed. "I love you, Jondalar. Everything. All you do. Even your eager . . ." She shook her head. "No, that's not right, that's the wrong word."

The word you want is 'eagerness', I think."

"I love even your eagerness. Yes, that's right. At least I know your words better than Mamutoi." She paused. "Frebec said I didn't speak right. Jondalar, will I ever learn to speak right?"

"I don't speak Mamutoi quite right, either. It's not the language I grew up with. Frebec just likes to make trouble," Jondalar said, helping her up. "Why does every Cave, every Camp, every group have to have a troublemaker? Don't pay any attention to him, no one else does. You speak very well. I'm amazed at the way you pick up languages. You'll be speaking Mamutoi better than I do before long."

"I have to learn how to speak with words. I have nothing else now," she said softly. "I don't know anyone who speaks the language I grew up with, any more." She closed her eyes for a moment as a feeling of bleak emptiness came over her.

She shook it off and started to put her legged garments back on, and then stopped. "Wait," she said, taking them off again. "Long ago, when I first became a woman, Iza told me everything a woman of the Clan needed to know about men and women, even though she doubted that I'd ever find a mate and would need to know it. The Others may not believe the same way, even the signals between men and women are not the same, but the first night I sleep in a place of the Others, I think I should make a cleansing after our Pleasures."

"What do you mean?"

"I'm going to wash in the river."

"Ayla! It's cold. It's dark. It could be dangerous."

"I won't go far. Just here at the edge," she said, throwing down her parka, and pulling her inner tunic up over her head.

The water was cold. Jondalar watched from the bank, and got himself just wet enough to know how cold it was. Her feeling for the ceremony of the occasion made him think of the purifying rituals of First Rites, and he decided a little cleansing wouldn't hurt him either. She was shivering when she got out. He held her in his arms to warm her. The shaggy bison fur of his parka dried her, then he helped her get into her tunic and parka.

She felt alive, and tingly, and fresh as they walked back to the earthlodge. Most people were settling down for the night when they entered. Fires were banked low, and voices were softened. The first hearth was empty, though the mammoth roast was still in evidence. As they moved quietly along the passageway through the Lion Hearth, Nezzie got up and detained them.

"I just wanted to thank you, Ayla," she said, glancing at one of the beds along the wall. Ayla followed her eyes and saw three small forms sprawled out on one large bed. Latie and Rugie shared it with Rydag. Danug, sprawled out in sleep, took up another bed, and Talut, stretched to his full length propped up on an elbow waiting for Nezzie, smiled at her from a third. She nodded and smiled back, not sure what the proper response was.

They moved to the next hearth as Nezzie crawled in beside the red-haired giant, and tried to pass through silently, so as not to disturb anyone. Ayla felt someone watching her and looked towards the wall. Two shining eyes and a smile were observing them from the dark recess. She sensed Jondalar's shoulders stiffen and looked quickly away. She thought she heard a soft chuckle, then thought it must have been the snores coming from the bed along the opposite wall.

At the large fourth hearth, one of the beds was hung with a heavy leather drape, closing the space off from the passageway, though sounds and movement could be detected within. Ayla noticed that most of the other sleeping places in the longhouse had similar drapes tied up to mammoth bone rafters above or to posts alongside, though not all of them were closed. Mamut's bed on the side wall opposite theirs was open. He was in it, but she knew he wasn't asleep.

Jondalar lit a stick of wood on a hot coal in the fireplace, and shielding it with his hand, carried it to the wall near the head of their sleeping platform. There, in a niche, a thick, flattish stone in which a saucer-shaped depression had been pecked out, was half-filled with fat. He lit a wick of twisted cattail fuzz, lighting up a small Mother figure behind the stone lamp. Then he untied the thongs that held up the drape around their bed, and when it fell, motioned to her.

She slipped in and climbed up on the platform bed piled high with soft furs. Sitting in the middle, closed off by the drape and lit by the soft flickering light, she felt secluded, and secure. It was a private little place all their own. She was reminded of the small cave she had found when she was a girl, where she used to go when she wanted to be alone.

"They are so clever, Jondalar. I would not have thought of this."

Jondalar stretched out beside her, pleased by her delight. "You like the drape closed?"

"Oh, yes. It makes you feel alone, even if you know people are all around. Yes, I like it." Her smile was radiant.

He pulled her down to him, and kissed her lightly. "You are so beautiful when you smile, Ayla."

She looked at his face, suffused with love: at his compelling eyes, violet in the light of the fire instead of their usual vivid blue; at his long yellow hair disarrayed on the furs; at his strong chin and high forehead so different from the chinless jaw and receding forehead of the men of the Clan.

"Why do you cut off your beard?" she asked, touching the stubble on his jaw.

"I don't know. I'm used to it, I guess. In summer, it's cooler, not as itchy. I usually let it grow in winter. Helps keep the face warm when I'm outside. Don't you like it shaved?"

She frowned in puzzlement. "It is not for me to say. A beard is a man's, to cut or not as he pleases. I only asked because I had not ever seen a man who cut his beard before I met you. Why do you ask if I like it or not?"

"I ask, because I want to please you. If you like a beard, I'll let it grow."

"It does not matter. Your beard is not important. You are important. You give me please . . . No," she shook her head angrily. "You give me pleases . . . Pleasures . . . you please me," she corrected.

He grinned at her efforts, and the unintended double meaning of her word. "I would like to give you Pleasures." He pulled her to him again, and kissed her. She snuggled down beside him, on her side. He rolled over, then sat up and looked down at her. "Like the first time," he said. "There's even a donii to watch over us." He looked at the niche with the fire-lighted ivory carving of the motherly figure.

"It is the first time . . . in a place of the Others," she said, closing her eyes, feeling both anticipation and the solemnity of the moment.

He cupped her face in his hands and kissed both eyelids, then gazed for a long moment at the woman he thought more beautiful than any woman he'd ever known. There was a quality of the exotic about her. Her cheekbones were higher than Zelandonii women, her eyes more widely spaced. They were framed with thick lashes, darker than her heavy hair that was gold as autumn grass. Her jaw was firm, her chin slightly pointed.

She had a small straight scar in the hollow of her throat. He kissed it, and felt her shiver with pleasure. He moved back up and looked down at her again, then kissed the end of her fine, straight nose, and the corner of her full mouth, where it turned up in the hint of a smile.

He could feel her tension. Like a hummingbird, motionless but full of quivering excitement he couldn't see, only sense, she was keeping her eyes closed, making herself lie still and wait. He watched her, savouring the moment, then he kissed her mouth, opened his and sought entry with his tongue, and felt her receive it. No prodding this time, only gently seeking, and then accepting hers.

He sat up, saw her open her eyes and smile at him. He pulled off his tunic, and helped her off with hers. Easing her back down, he leaned over and took a firm nipple in his mouth, and suckled. She gasped as a shock of excitement coursed through her. She felt a warm wet tingling between her legs, and wondered why Jondalar's mouth on her nipple should make her feel sensation where he hadn't even touched.

He nuzzled and nibbled lightly, until she pushed towards him, then sucked in earnest. She moaned with pleasure. He reached for the other breast, caressed its full roundness and turgid tip. She was already breathing hard. He let go of her breast and began to kiss her neck and throat, found her ear and nibbled on a lobe, then blew in it, caressing her arms and her breasts with both hands. Shivers shook her.

He kissed her mouth, then ran his warm tongue slowly over her chin, down the middle of her throat, between her breasts, and down to her navel. His manhood had grown again, and pushed insistently against the restraints of the drawstring closure. He untied her drawstring first, and pulled the long pants off, then starting at her navel, continued in the direction he was going. He felt soft hair, and then his tongue found the top of her warm slit. He felt her jump when he reached a small, hard bump. When he stopped, she gave a small cry of dismay.

He untied his own drawstring then, and let his striving member free as he pulled off his trousers. Ayla sat up and took it in her hand, letting it slide back and forth over the full length, feeling the warmth, the smooth skin, the hard fullness. He was pleased that his size did not frighten her, as it had so many women when they first saw him, not even the first time. She bent down to him, and he felt her warm mouth enclose him. He felt pulling as she moved up and down, and he was glad he had already released his strongest urge or he might not have found the control now.

"Ayla, this time I want to Pleasure you," he said, pushing her away.

She looked at him with eyes dilated, dark and luminous, kissed him, and then nodded. He held her shoulders and pushed her back down on the furs, and kissed her mouth and throat again, giving her chills of Pleasure. He cupped both breasts in his hands, held them together, and went from one sensitive nipple to the other, and in between. Then his tongue found her navel again, and he circled it with an ever-increasing spiral, until he reached the soft hair of her mound.

He moved over between her thighs, spreading them, then spread her folds back with his hands and savoured a long slow taste. She shuddered, half sat up, cried out, and he felt himself surge anew. He loved to Pleasure her, to feel her response to his skill. It was like drawing a fine blade out of a piece of flint. It gave him a special feeling of joy to know he had been the first to give her Pleasure. She had only known force and pain before he had evoked in her the Gift of Pleasure which the Great Earth Mother had given to Her children.

He explored her tenderly, knowing where her pleasurable sensations lay, teasing them with his tongue, and with his skilled hands, reaching inside. She began to move against him, crying out and tossing her head, and he knew she was ready. He found the hard bump, began to work it, while her breath came fast, his own thrusting manhood eager for her. Then she cried out, he felt a wetness, as she reached for him.

"Jondalar . . . ahhh . . . Jondalar!"

She was beyond herself, beyond any knowing except him. She wanted him, wanted to feel his fullness inside her. He was on her, she was helping him, guiding him, then he was sliding in, and felt a surge that brought him to that inexpressible peak. It backed off, and he plunged in again, deep; she embraced him all.

He pulled out, and then pushed in again, and again, and again. He wanted to draw it out, make it last. He wanted it never to end, and yet he couldn't wait for it. With each powerful push, he felt closer. Sweat glistened on their bodies in the flickering light as they matched their timing, found their stride, and moved with the rhythm of life.

Breathing hard, they strained to meet at each stroke, reaching, pulsing, all will, all thought, all feeling concentrated. Then, almost unexpectedly, the intensity peaked. In a burst beyond them both, they reached the crest, and broke through with a spasm of joy. They held for a moment, as though trying to become one with each other, and then let go.

They lay unmoving, catching their breaths. The lamp sputtered, dimmed, flared up again, then went out. After a while Jondalar rolled over and lay beside her, feeling in a twilight state between sleeping and waking. But Ayla was still wide awake, her eyes open in the dark, listening, for the first time in years, to sounds of people.

The murmur of low voices, a man's and a woman's, came from the bed nearby, and a little beyond it, the shallow rasping breath of the sleeping shaman. She could hear a man snoring at the next hearth, and from the first hearth, the unmistakable rhythmic grunts and cries of Talut and Nezzie sharing Pleasures. From the other direction, a baby cried. Someone made comforting sounds until the crying stopped abruptly. Ayla smiled, no doubt a breast had been offered. Farther away voices of restrained anger rose in an outburst, then hushed, and still farther a hacking cough could be heard.

Nights had always been the worst time during her lonely years in the valley. During the day she could always find something to do to keep busy, but at night the stark emptiness of her cave had pressed heavily. In the beginning, hearing only the sound of her own breath, she even had trouble sleeping. With the Clan, there was always someone around at night – the worst punishment that could be inflicted was to be set apart, alone; avoidance, ostracism, the death curse.

She knew only too well that it was, indeed, a terrible punishment. She knew it even more at that moment. Lying in the dark, hearing the sounds of life around her, feeling the warmth of Jondalar beside her, for the first time since she met these people, whom she called Others, she felt at home.

"Jondalar?" she said softly.

"Hmmm."

"Are you sleeping?"

"Not yet," he mumbled.

"These are nice people. You were right, I did need to come and get to know them."

His brain cleared quickly. He had hoped, once she met her own kind of people and they were no longer so unknown, they would not seem so fearful to her. He had been gone many years, the Journey back to his home would be long and difficult, she had to want to come with him. But her valley had become home. It offered everything she needed to survive, and she had made a life for herself there, using the animals as a substitute for the people she lacked. Ayla did not want to leave; instead she had wanted Jondalar to stay.

"I knew you would, Ayla," he said warmly, persuasively, "if you just got to know them."

"Nezzie reminds me of Iza. How do you suppose Rydag's mother got pregnant with him?"

"Who knows why the Mother gave her a child of mixed spirits? The ways of the Mother are always mysterious."

Ayla was silent, for a while. "I don't think the Mother gave her mixed spirits. I think she knew a man of the Others."

Jondalar frowned. "I know you think men have something to do with starting life, but how could a flathead female know a man?"

"I don't know how, but women of the Clan don't travel alone and they stay away from the Others. The men don't want Others around the women. They think babies are started by a man's totem spirit, and they don't want the spirit of a man of the Others to get too close. And the women are afraid of them. There are always new stories at Clan Gatherings of people being bothered or hurt by the Others, particularly women.

"But Rydag's mother wasn't afraid of the Others. Nezzie said she followed them for two days, and she came with Talut when he signalled her. Any other Clan woman would have run away from him. She must have known one before, and one who treated her well, or at least did not hurt her, because she wasn't afraid of Talut. When she needed help, what gave her reason to think she might find it from the Others?"

"Maybe it was just because she saw Nezzie nursing," Jondalar suggested.

"Maybe. But that doesn't answer why she was alone. The only reason I can think of is that she was cursed and driven from her clan. Clan women are not often cursed. It is not their nature to bring it on themselves. Perhaps it had something to do with a man of the Others . . ."

Ayla paused for a moment, then added thoughtfully, "Rydag's mother must have wanted her baby very much. It took a lot of courage for her to approach the Others, even if she did know a man before. It was only when she saw the baby and thought he was deformed that she gave up. The Clan doesn't like mixed children, either."

"How can you be so sure she knew a man?"

"She came to the Others to have her baby, which means she had no clan to help her and she had some reason to think Nezzie and Talut would. Maybe she met him later, but I'm sure she knew a man who made Pleasures with her . . . or maybe just relieved his needs. She had a mixed child, Jondalar."

"Why do you think it's a man that causes life to start?"

"You can see it, Jondalar, if you think about it. Look at the boy that arrived today, Danug. He looks just like Talut. Only younger. I think Talut started him when he shared Pleasures with Nezzie."

"Does that mean she will have another child because they shared Pleasures tonight?" Jondalar asked. "Pleasures are shared often. They are a Gift of the Great Earth Mother and it honours Her when they are shared often. But women don't have children every time they share Her Gift. Ayla, if a man appreciates the Mother's Gifts, honours Her, then She may choose to take his spirit to mix with the woman he mates. If it is his spirit, the child may resemble him, as Danug resembles Talut, but it is the Mother who decides."

Ayla frowned in the dark. That was one question she hadn't resolved. "I don't know why a woman doesn't have a child every time. Maybe Pleasures must be shared several times before a baby can start, or perhaps only at certain times. Mabye it is only when a man's totem spirit is

65

especially powerful and so can defeat a woman's, or maybe the Mother does choose, but She chooses the man and makes his manhood more powerful. Can you say for sure how She chooses? Do you know how the spirits are mixed? Couldn't they be mixed inside the woman when they share Pleasures?"

"I've never heard of that," Jondalar said, "but I suppose it could be." Now he was frowning in the dark. He was silent for so long Ayla thought he had gone to sleep, but then he spoke. "Ayla, if what you think is true, we might be starting a baby inside you every time we share the Mother's Gift."

"I think so, yes," Ayla said, delighted with the idea.

"Then we must stop!" Jondalar said, sitting up suddenly.

"But why? I want to have a baby started by you, Jondalar." Ayla's dismay was evident.

Jondalar rolled over and held her. "And I want you to, but not now. It is a long Journey back to my home. It could take a year or more. It could be dangerous for you to travel so far if you are with child."

"Can't we just go back to my valley then?" she asked.

Jondalar was afraid if they returned to her valley so that she could have a child in safety, they would never leave.

"Ayla, I don't think that would be a good idea. You shouldn't be alone then. I wouldn't know how to help you, you need women around. A woman can die in childbirth," he said, his voice constricted with anguish. He had seen it happen not long before.

It was true, Ayla realised. She had come close to death giving birth to her son. Without Iza, she would not have lived. This wasn't the time to have a baby, not even one of Jondalar's.

"Yes, you are right," she said, feeling a crushing disappointment. "It can be difficult . . . I . . . I . . . would want women around," she agreed.

He was silent again for a long time. "Ayla," he said, his voice almost cracked with strain, "maybe . . . maybe we shouldn't share the same bed . . . if . . . but it *honours* the Mother to share Her Gift . . ." he blurted out.

How could she tell him truthfully that they didn't have to stop sharing Pleasures? Iza had warned her never to tell anyone, particularly a man, about the secret medicine. "I don't think you should worry about it," she said. "I don't know for sure if it is a man that causes children, and if the Great Mother chooses, She can choose any time, can't She?"

"Yes, and it has worried me. Yet if we avoid Her Gift, it might anger Her. She expects to be honoured."

"Jondalar, if She chooses, She chooses. If the time comes, we can make a decision then. I wouldn't want you to offend Her."

"Yes, you're right, Ayla," he said, somewhat relieved.

With a twinge of regret, Ayla decided she would keep taking the medicine that prevented conception, but she dreamed of having babies that night, some with long blond hair, and others who resembled Rydag and Durc. It was near morning when she had a dream that took on a different dimension, ominous and otherworldly.

In the dream she had two sons, brothers who no one would guess were brothers. One was tall and blond, like Jondalar, the other, older one, she knew was Durc though his face was in shadow. The two brothers approached each other from opposite directions in the middle of an empty, desolate, windblown prairie. She felt great anxiety; something terrible was about to happen, something she had to prevent. Then, with a shock of terror, she knew one of her sons would kill the other. As they drew closer, she tried to reach them, but a thick, viscous wall held her trapped. They were almost upon each other, arms raised as though to strike. She screamed.

"Ayla! Ayla! What's wrong?" Jondalar said, shaking her.

Suddenly Mamut was beside him. "Wake up, child. Wake up!" he said. "It is only a symbol, a message. Wake up, Ayla!"

"But one will die!" she cried, still filled with the emotions of the dream.

"It is not what you think, Ayla," Mamut said. "It may not mean one . . . brother will die. You must learn to search your dreams for their real meaning. You have the Talent; it is very strong, but you lack training."

Ayla's vision cleared and she saw two concerned faces looking at her, both tall men, one young and handsome, the other old and wise. Jondalar was holding up a stick of burning wood from the fireplace to help her wake up. She sat up and tried to smile.

"Are you all right now?" Mamut asked.

"Yes. Yes. I am sorry to wake you," Ayla said, lapsing into Zelandonii, forgetting the old man did not understand that language.

"We will talk later," he said, smiling gently, and returned to his bed.

Ayla noticed the drape to the other occupied bed fall shut as she and Jondalar settled back down on their sleeping platform, and felt a little embarrassed that she had created such a stir. She cuddled to Jondalar's side, resting her head in the hollow beneath his shoulder, grateful for his warmth and his presence. She was almost asleep when her eyes suddenly flew open again.

"Jondalar," she said in a whisper, "how did Mamut know I dreamed about my sons, about one brother killing the other?" But he was already sleeping.

5

Ayla woke with a start, then lay still and listened. She heard a loud wail, again. Someone seemed to be in great pain. Concerned, she pushed the drape aside and looked out. Crozie was standing in the passageway near the sixth hearth, with her arms outspread in an attitude of pleading despair calculated to draw sympathy.

"He would stab my breast! He would kill me! He would turn my own daughter against me!" Crozie shrieked as though she were dying, clutching her hands to her breast. Several people stopped to watch. "I give him my own flesh. Out of my own body . . ."

"Give! You didn't give me a thing!" Frebec yelled. "I paid your Bride Price for Fralie."

"It was trivial! I could have gotten much more for her," Crozie snapped, her lament no more sincere than her scream of pain had been. "She came to you with two children. Proof of the Mother's favour. You lowered her value with your pittance. And the value of her children. And look at her! Already blessed again. I gave her to you out of kindness, out of the goodness of my heart . . ."

"And because no one else would take Crozie, even with her twice-blessed daughter," a nearby voice added.

Ayla turned to see who had spoken. The young woman who had worn the beautiful red tunic the day before was smiling at her.

"If you had any plans to sleep late, you can forget them," Deegie said. "They're at it early today."

"No. I get up," Ayla said. She looked around. The bed was empty, and except for the two women, no one was around. "Jondalar up." She found her clothes and began to dress. "I wake up, think woman hurt."

"No one is hurt. At least not that anyone can see. But I feel sorry for Fralie," Deegie said. "It's hard being caught in the middle like that."

Ayla shook her head. "Why they shout?"

"I don't know why they fight all the time. I suppose they both want Fralie's favour. Crozie is getting old and doesn't want Frebec to undermine her influence, but Frebec is stubborn. He didn't have much before and doesn't want to lose his new position. Fralie did bring him a lot of status, even with her low Bride Price." The visitor was obviously interested and Deegie sat down on a platform bed while Ayla dressed, warming to her subject.

"I don't think she'd put him aside, though. I think she cares for him, for all that he can be so nasty sometimes. It wasn't so easy to find another man – one willing to take her mother. Everyone saw how it was the first time, no one else wanted to put up with Crozie. That old woman can scream all she wants about giving her daughter away. She's the one who brought down Fralie's value. I'd hate to be pulled both ways like that. But I'm lucky. Even if I were going to an established Camp instead of starting a new one with my brother, Tulie would be welcome."

"Your mother go with you?" Ayla said, puzzled. She understood a woman moving to her mate's clan, but taking her mother along was new to her.

"I wish she would, but I don't think she will. I think she'd rather stay here. I don't blame her. It's better to be headwoman of your own Camp than the mother of one at another. I will miss her, though."

Ayla listened, fascinated. She didn't understand half of what Deegie said, and wasn't sure if she believed she understood the other half.

"It is sad to leave mother, and people," Ayla said. "But you have mate soon?"

"Oh, yes. Next summer. At the Summer Meeting. Mother finally got everything settled. She set such a high Bride Price I was afraid they'd never meet it, but they agreed. It's so hard waiting, though. If only Branag didn't have to leave now. But they're expecting him. He promised he'd go back right away . . ."

The two young women walked towards the entrance of the longhouse together, companionably, Deegie chatting and Ayla avidly listening.

It was cooler in the entrance foyer, but it wasn't until she felt the blast of cold air when the drape at the front arch was pulled back that Ayla realised how much the temperature had dropped. The frigid wind whipped her hair back and tugged at the heavy mammoth hide entrance cover, billowing it out with a sudden gust. A light dusting of snow had fallen during the night. A sharp crosscurrent picked up the fine flakes, swirled them into pockets and hollows, then scooped out the wind-blasted crystals and flung them across the open space. Ayla's face stung with a peppering of tiny hard pellets of ice.

Yet it had been warm inside, much warmer than a cave. She had put on her fur parka only to come out; she wouldn't have needed extra clothing if she had stayed in. She heard Whinney neigh. The horse and the colt, still tied to his lead, were as far back as they could get from the people and their activities. Ayla started towards them, then turned back to smile at Deegie. The young woman smiled back, and went to find Branag.

The mare seemed relieved when Ayla neared, nickering and tossing her head in greeting. The woman removed Racer's bridle, then walked with them down towards the river and around the bend. Whinney and Racer relaxed once the Camp was out of sight, and after some mutual affection, settled down to graze on the brittle dry grass.

Before starting back up Ayla stopped beside a bush. She untied the waist thong of her legged garment, but still was not sure what to do so the leggings wouldn't get wet when she passed water. She'd had the same problem ever since she started wearing the clothes. She had made the outfit for herself during the summer, patterning it after the one she had made for Jondalar, which was copied from the clothing the lion had ripped. But she hadn't worn it until they started on their trip of exploration. Jondalar had been so pleased to see her wearing clothes like his, rather than the comfortable leather wrap usually worn by women of the Clan, she decided to leave it behind. But she hadn't discovered how to manage this basic necessity easily and she didn't want to ask him. He was a man. How would he know what a woman needed to do?

She removed the close-fitting trousers, which required that she also remove her footwear – high-topped moccasins that wrapped around the lower pant legs – then spread her legs and bent over in her usual manner. Balancing on one foot to put the lower garment back on, she noticed the smoothly rolling river and changed her mind. Instead, she pulled her parka and tunic up over her head, took off her amulet from around her neck, and walked down the bank towards the water. The cleansing ritual should be completed, and she always did enjoy a morning swim.

She had planned to swish out her mouth, and rinse off her face and hands in the river – she didn't know what means these people used to clean themselves, either. When it was necessary, if the woodpile was buried under ice and fuel was scarce, or if the wind was blowing hard through the cave, or if water was frozen so solid it was hard to break off enough even for drinking, she could do without washing, but she preferred to be clean. And in the back of her mind she was still thinking of the ritual, the completion of a purification ceremony after her first night in the cave – or the earthlodge – of the Others.

She looked out at the water. The current moved swiftly along the main channel, but ice in transparent sheets filmed puddles and the quieter backwaters of the river, and crusted white at the edge. A finger of the bank, sparsely covered with bleached and withered grass, stretched into the river forming a still pool between itself and the shore. A single birch tree, dwarfed to a shrub, grew on the spit of dirt.

Ayla walked towards the pool and stepped in, shattering the perfect pane of ice which glazed it. She gasped as the freezing water brought a hard shiver, and grabbed a skeletal limb of the small birch to steady herself, as she moved into the current. A sharp gust of freezing wind buffeted her bare skin, raising gooseflesh, and whipped her hair into her face. She clenched her chattering teeth and waded in deeper. When the water was nearly waist-high, she splashed icy water on her face, then with another quick indrawn breath of shock, stooped down and submerged up to her neck.

For all her gasps and shivers, she was used to cold water and, she thought, soon enough it would be impossible to bathe in the river at all. When she got out, she pushed the water off her body with her hands and dressed quickly. Tingling warmth replaced the numbing cold as she walked back up the slope from the river, making her feel renewed and invigorated, and she smiled as a tired sun momentarily bested the overcast sky.

As she approached the Camp she stopped at the edge of a trampled area near the longhouse and watched the several knots of people engaged in various occupations.

Jondalar was talking with Wymez and Danug, and she had no doubts as to the subject of the conversation of the three flint knappers. Not far from them four people were untying cords that had held a deer hide – now soft, flexible, nearly white leather – to a rectangular frame made of mammoth rib bones lashed together with thongs. Nearby, Deegie was vigorously poking and stretching a second hide, which was strung on a similar frame, with the smoothly blunted end of another rib bone. Ayla knew working the hide as it was drying was done to make the leather supple, but binding it to the mammoth bone frames was a new method of stretching leather. She was interested and noted the details of the process.

A series of small slits had been cut near the outside edge following the contour of the animal skin, then a cord was passed through each one, tied to the frame and pulled tight to stretch the hide taut. The frame was propped against the longhouse and could be turned around and worked from either side. Deegie was leaning with all her weight on the rib-bone staker, pushing the blunt end into the mounted hide until it seemed the long shaft would poke right through, but the strong flexible leather yielded without giving way.

A few others were busy with activities Ayla was not familiar with, but the rest of the people were putting the skeletal remains of mammoths into pits that had been dug in the ground. Bones and ivory were scattered all over. She looked up as someone called out and saw Talut and Tulie coming towards the Camp bearing on their shoulders a large curved ivory tusk still attached to the skull of a mammoth. Most of the bones did not come from animals they had killed. Occasional finds on the steppes provided some, but the majority came from the piles of bones that accumulated at sharp turns in rivers, where raging waters had deposited the remains of animals.

Then Ayla noticed another person watching the Camp not far from her. She smiled as she went to join Rydag, but was startled to see him smile back. People of the Clan did not smile. An expression showing bared teeth usually denoted hostility on a face with Clan features, or extreme nervousness and fear. His grin seemed, for a moment, out of place. But the boy had not grown up with the Clan and had learned a friendlier meaning for the expression.

"Good morning, Rydag," Ayla said, at the same time making the Clan greeting gesture with the slight variation that indicated a child was being addressed. Ayla noticed again the flicker of understanding at her hand signal. He remembers! she thought. He has the memories, I'm sure of it. He knows the signs, he would only have to be reminded. Not like me. I had to learn them.

She recalled Creb's and Iza's consternation when they discovered how difficult it was for her, compared with Clan youngsters, to remember anything. She had had to struggle to learn and memorise, while children of the Clan only had to be shown once. Some people had thought Ayla was rather stupid, but as she grew up she taught herself to memorise quickly so they wouldn't lose patience with her.

But Jondalar had been astonished at her skill. Compared to others like herself, her trained memory was a wonder, and it enhanced her ability to learn. He was amazed at how easily she learned new languages, for example, almost without effort it seemed. But gaining that skill had not been easy, and though she had learned to memorise quickly, she never did fully comprehend what Clan memories were. None of the Others could; it was a basic difference between them.

With brains even larger than those who came after, the Clan had not so much less intelligence as a different kind of intelligence. They learned from memories that were in some ways similar to instinct but more conscious, and stored in the backs of their large brains at birth was everything their forebears knew. They didn't need to learn the knowledge and skills necessary to live, they remembered them. As children, they needed only to be reminded of what they already knew to become accustomed to the process. As adults, they knew how to draw upon their stored memories.

They remembered easily, but anything new was grasped only with great effort. Once something new was learned – or a new concept understood or a new belief accepted – they never forgot it and they passed it on to their progeny, but they learned, and changed, slowly.

Iza had come to understand, if not comprehend, their difference when she was teaching Ayla the skills of a medicine woman. The strange girl child could not remember nearly as well as they, but she learned much more quickly.

Rydag said a word. Ayla did not understand him immediately. Then she recognised it. It was her name! Her name spoken in a way that had once been familiar, the way some people of the Clan had said it.

Like them, the child was not capable of a fully articulate speech; he could vocalise, but he could not make some of the important sounds that were necessary to reproduce the language of the people he lived with. They were the same sounds Ayla had difficulty with, from lack of practice. It was that limitation in the vocal apparatus of the Clan, and those that went before, that had led them to develop instead a rich and comprehensive language of hand signs and gestures to express the thoughts of their rich and comprehensive culture. Rydag understood the Others, the people he lived with; he understood the concept of language. He just couldn't make himself understood to them.

Then the youngster made the gesture he had made to Nezzie the night before; he called Ayla "mother". Ayla felt her heart beat faster. The last one who had made that sign to her was her son, and Rydag looked so much like Durc that for a moment she saw her son in him. She wanted to believe he was Durc, and she ached to pick him up and hold him in her arms, and say his name. She closed her eyes and repressed the urge to call out to him, shaking with the effort.

When she opened her eyes again, Rydag was watching her with a knowing, ancient, and yearning look, as though he understood her, and knew that she understood him. As much as she wished it, Rydag was not Durc. He was no more Durc than she was Deegie; he was himself. Under control again, she took a deep breath.

"Would you like more words? More hand signs, Rydag?" she asked.

He nodded, emphatically.

"You remember 'mother' from last night . . ."

He answered by making the sign again that had so moved Nezzie . . . and her.

"Do you know this?" Ayla asked, making the greeting gesture. She could see him struggling with knowledge he almost knew. "It is greeting. It means 'good morning', or 'hello'. This" – she demonstrated the gesture again with the variation she had used, "is when older person is speaking to younger."

He frowned, then made the gesture, then smiled at her with his startling grin. He made both signs, then thought again and made a third, and looked at her quizzically, not sure if he had really done anything.

73

"Yes, that is right, Rydag! I am woman, like mother, and that is way to greet mother. You do remember!"

Nezzie noticed Ayla and the boy together. He had caused her great distress a few times when he forgot himself and tried to do too much, so she was always aware of the child's location and activities. She was drawn towards the younger woman and the child, trying to observe and understand what they were doing. Ayla saw her, noted her expression of curiosity and concern, and called her over.

"I am showing Rydag language of Clan – mother's people," Ayla explained, "like word last night."

Rydag, with a big grin that showed his larger than usual teeth, made a deliberate gesture to Nezzie.

"What does that mean?" she asked, looking at Ayla.

"Rydag say, 'Good morning, mother,'" the young woman explained.

"Good morning, mother?" Nezzie made a motion that vaguely resembled the deliberate gesture Rydag had made. "That means, 'Good morning, mother'?"

"No. Sit here. I will show you. This" – Ayla made the sign – "means 'Good morning' and this way" – she made the variation – "means 'Good morning, mother'. He might make same sign to me. That would mean 'motherly woman'. You would make this way" – Ayla made another variation of the hand sign – "to say, 'Good morning, child'. And this" – Ayla continued with still another variation – "to say 'Good morning, my son'. You see?"

Ayla went through all the variations again as Nezzie watched carefully. The woman, feeling a bit self-conscious, tried again. Though the signal lacked finesse, it was clear to both Ayla and Rydag that the gesture she was trying to make meant "Good morning, my son."

The boy, who was standing at her shoulder, reached thin arms around her neck. Nezzie hugged him, blinking hard to hold back a flood that threatened, and even Rydag's eyes were wet, which surprised Ayla.

Of all the members of Brun's clan, only her eyes had teared with emotion, though their feelings were just as strong. Her son could vocalise the same as she could; he was capable of full speech – her heart still ached when she remembered how he had called out after her when she was forced to leave – but Durc could shed no tears to express his sorrow. Like his Clan mother, Rydag could not speak, but when his eyes filled with love, they glistened with tears.

"I have never been able to talk to him before – that I knew for sure he understood," Nezzie said.

"Would you like more signs?" Ayla asked, gently.

The woman nodded, still holding the boy, not trusting herself to speak at the moment for fear her control would break. Ayla went

74

through another set of signs and variations, with Nezzie and Rydag both concentrating, trying to grasp them. And then another. Nezzie's daughters, Latie and Rugie, and Tulie's youngest children, Brinan and his little sister Tusie, who were close to Rugie and Rydag in age, came to find out what was going on, then Fralie's seven-year-old son, Crisavec, joined them. Soon they were all caught up in what seemed to be a wonderful new game: talking with hands.

But unlike most games played by the children of the Camp, this was one in which Rydag excelled. Ayla couldn't teach him fast enough. She barely had to show him once, and before long he was adding the variations himself – the nuances and finer shades of meaning. She had a sense that it was all right there inside him, filled up and bursting to come out, needing only the smallest opening, and once released, there was no holding back.

It was all the more exciting because the children who were near his age were learning, too. For the first time in his life, Rydag could express himself fully, and he couldn't get enough of it. The youngsters he had grown up with easily accepted his ability to "speak" fluently in this new way. They had communicated with him before. They knew he was different, he had trouble talking, but they hadn't yet acquired the adult bias that assumed he was, therefore, lacking in intelligence. And Latie, as older sisters often do, had been translating his "gibberish" to the adult members of the Camp for years.

By the time they had all had enough of learning and went off to put the new game into serious play, Ayla noticed Rydag was correcting them and they turned to him for confirmation of the meaning of the hand signs and gestures. He had found a new place among his peers.

Still sitting beside Nezzie, Ayla watched them flashing silent signals to each other. She smiled, imagining what Iza would have thought of children of the Others speaking like the Clan, shouting and laughing at the same time. Somehow, Ayla thought, the old medicine woman would have understood.

"You must be right. That is his way to speak," Nezzie said. "I've never seen him so quick to learn anything. I didn't know flathe . . . What do you call them?"

"Clan. They say Clan. It means . . . family . . . the people . . . humans. The Clan of the Cave Bear, people who honour Great Cave Bear; you say Mamutoi, Mammoth Hunters who honour Mother," Ayla replied.

"Clan . . . I didn't know they could talk like that. I didn't know anyone could say so much with hands . . . I've never seen Rydag so happy." The woman hesitated, and Ayla sensed she was trying to find a way to say something more. She waited to give her a chance to gather

75

her thoughts. "I'm surprised you took to him so quickly," Nezzie continued. "Some people object because he's mixed, and most people are a little uncomfortable around him. But you seem to know him."

Ayla paused before she spoke, while she studied the older woman, not sure what to say. Then, making a decision, she said, "I knew someone like him once . . . my son. My son, Durc."

"Your son!" There was surprise in Nezzie's voice, but Ayla did not detect any sign of the revulsion that had been so apparent in Frebec's voice when he spoke of flatheads and Rydag the night before. "*You* had a mixed son? Where is he? What happened to him?"

Anguish darkened Ayla's face. She had kept thoughts of her son buried deep while she was alone in her valley, but seeing Rydag had awakened them. Nezzie's questions jolted painful memories and emotions to the surface, and caught her by surprise. Now she had to confront them.

Nezzie was as open and frank as the rest of her people, and her questions had come spontaneously, but she was not without sensitivity. "I'm sorry, Ayla. I should have thought . . ."

"Do not have concern, Nezzie," Ayla said, blinking to hold back tears. "I know questions come when I speak of son. It . . . pains . . . to think of Durc."

"You don't have to talk about him."

"Sometime must talk about Durc." Ayla paused, then plunged in. "Durc is with Clan. When she die, Iza . . . my mother, like you with Rydag . . . say I go north, find my people. Not Clan, the Others. Durc is baby then. I do not go. Later, Durc is three years, Broud make me go. I not know where Others live, I not know where I will go, I cannot take Durc. I give to Uba . . . sister. She love Durc, take care of him. Her son now."

Ayla stopped, but Nezzie didn't know what to say. She would have liked to ask more questions, but didn't want to press when it was obviously such an ordeal for the young woman to speak of a son, whom she loved but had to leave behind. Ayla continued of her own accord.

"Three years since I see Durc. He is . . . six years now. Like Rydag?"

Nezzie nodded. "It is not yet seven years since Rydag was born."

Ayla paused, seemed to be deep in thought. Then she continued. "Durc is like Rydag, but not. Durc is like Clan in eyes, like me in mouth." She made a wry smile. "Should be other way. Durc make words, Durc could speak, but Clan does not. Better if Rydag speak, but he cannot. Durc is strong." Ayla's eyes took on a faraway look. "He run fast. He is best runner, some day racer, like Jondalar say." Her eyes filled with sadness when she looked up at Nezzie. "Rydag weak. From birth. Weak in . . .?" She put her hand to her chest, she didn't know the word.

"He has trouble breathing sometimes," Nezzie said.

"Trouble is not breathing. Trouble is blood . . . no . . . not blood
. . . da-dump," she said, holding a fist to her chest. She was frustrated
at not knowing the word.

"The heart. That's what Mamut says. He has a weak heart. How did
you know that?"

"Iza was medicine woman, healer. Best medicine woman of Clan.
She teach me like daughter. I am medicine woman."

Jondalar had said Ayla was a Healer, Nezzie recalled. She was surprised
to learn that flatheads even thought about healing, but then she hadn't
known they could talk either. And she had been around Rydag enough
to know that even without full speech he was not the stupid animal that
so many people believed. Even if she wasn't a Mamut, there was no
reason Ayla couldn't know something about healing.

The two women looked up as a shadow fell across them. "Mamut
wants to know if you would come and talk to him, Ayla," Danug said.
Both of them had been so engrossed in conversation, neither one had
noticed the tall young man approaching. "Rydag is so excited with the
new hand game you showed him," he continued. "Latie says he wants
me to ask if you will teach me some of the signs, too."

"Yes. Yes. I teach you. I teach anyone."

"I want to learn more of your hand words, too," Nezzie said, as they
both got up.

"In morning?" Ayla asked.

"Yes, tomorrow morning. But you haven't had anything to eat yet.
Maybe tomorrow it would be better to have something to eat first,"
Nezzie said. "Come with me and I'll get you something, and for Mamut,
too."

"I am hungry," Ayla said.

"So am I," Danug added.

"When aren't you hungry? Between you and Talut, I think you could
eat a mammoth," Nezzie said, with pride in her eyes for her great
strapping son.

As the two women and Danug headed towards the earthlodge, the
others seemed to take it as a cue to stop for a meal and followed
them in. Outer clothes were removed in the entrance foyer and hung
on pegs. It was a casual, everyday, morning meal with some people
cooking at their own hearths and others gathering at the large first
hearth that held the primary fireplace and several small ones. Some
people ate cold leftover mammoth, others had meat or fish cooked
with roots or greens in a soup thickened with roughly ground wild
grains plucked from the grasses of the steppes. But whether they
cooked at their own place or not, most people eventually wandered

to the communal area to visit while they drank a hot tea before going outside again.

Ayla was sitting beside Mamut watching the activities with great interest. The level of noise of so many people talking and laughing together still surprised her, but she was becoming more accustomed to it. She was even more surprised at the ease with which the women moved among the men. There was no strict hierarchy, no order to the cooking or serving of food. They all seemed to serve themselves, except for the women and men who helped the youngest children.

Jondalar came over to them and lowered himself carefully to the grass mat beside Ayla while he balanced with both hands a watertight but handleless and somewhat flexible cup, woven out of bear grass in a chevron design of contrasting colours, filled with hot mint tea.

"You up early in morning," Ayla said.

"I didn't want to disturb you. You were sleeping so soundly."

"I wake when I think someone hurt, but Deegie tell me old woman . . . Crozie . . . always talk loud with Frebec."

"They were arguing so loud, I even heard them outside," Jondalar said. "Frebec may be a troublemaker, but I'm not so sure I blame him. That old woman squawks worse than a jay. How can anyone live with her?"

"I think someone hurt," Ayla said, thoughtfully.

Jondalar looked at her, puzzled. He didn't think she was repeating that she mistakenly thought someone was physically hurt.

"You are right, Ayla," Mamut said. "Old wounds that still pain."

"Deegie feels sorrow for Fralie." Ayla turned to Mamut, feeling comfortable about asking him questions, though she did not want to betray her ignorance generally. "What is Bride Price? Deegie said Tulie asked high Bride Price for her."

Mamut paused before answering, gathering his thoughts carefully because he wanted her to understand. Ayla watched the white-haired old man expectantly. "I could give you a simple answer, Ayla, but there is more to it than it seems. I have thought about it for many years. It is not easy to understand and explain yourself and your people, even when you are one of those whom others come to for answers." He closed his eyes in a frown of concentration. "You understand status, don't you?" he began.

"Yes," Ayla said. "In the Clan, leader has the most status, then chosen hunter, then other hunters. Mog-ur has high status, too, but is different. He is . . . man of spirit world."

"And the women?"

"Women have status of mate, but medicine woman has own status."

Ayla's comments surprised Jondalar. With all he had learned from her

78

about flatheads, he still had difficulty believing they could understand a concept as complex as comparative ranking.

"I thought so," Mamut said, quietly, then proceeded to explain. "We revere the Mother, the maker and nurturer of all life. People, animals, plants, water, trees, rocks, earth, She gave birth, She created all of it. When we call upon the spirit of the mammoth, or the spirit of the deer, or the bison, to ask permission to hunt them, we know it is the Mother's Spirit that gave them life; Her Spirit that causes another mammoth, or deer, or bison to be born to replace the ones She gives us for food."

"We say it is the Mother's Gift of Life," Jondalar said, intrigued. He was interested in discovering how the customs of the Mamutoi compared with the customs of the Zelandonii.

"Mut, the Mother, has chosen women to show us how She has taken the spirit of life into Herself to create and bring forth new life to replace those She has called back," the old holy man continued.

"Children learn about this as they grow up, from legends and stories and songs, but you are beyond that now, Ayla. We like to hear the stories even when we grow old, but you need to understand the current that moves them, and what lies beneath, so you can understand the reasons for many of our customs. With us, status depends upon one's mother, and Bride Price is the way we show value."

Ayla nodded, fascinated. Jondalar had tried to explain about the Mother, but Mamut made it seem so reasonable, so much easier to understand.

"When women and men decide to form a union, the man, and his Camp, give many gifts to the woman's mother and her Camp. The mother or the headwoman of the Camp sets the price – says how many gifts are required – for the daughter, or occasionally a woman may set her own price, but it depends on much more than her whim. No woman wants to be undervalued, but the price should not be so much that the man of her choice and his Camp can't afford or are unwilling to pay."

"Why payment for a woman?" Jondalar asked. "Doesn't that make her trade goods, like salt or flint or amber?"

"The value of a woman is much more. Bride Price is what a man pays for the privilege of living with a woman. A good Bride Price benefits everyone. It bestows a high status on the woman; tells everyone how highly she is thought of by the man who wants her, and by her own Camp. It honours his Camp, and lets them show they are successful and can afford to pay the price. It gives honour to the woman's Camp, shows them esteem and respect, and gives them something to compensate for losing her if she leaves, as some young women do, to join a new Camp or to live at the man's Camp. But most important, it helps them to pay a good Bride Price when one of their men wants a woman, so they can show their wealth.

"Children are born with their mother's status, so a high Bride Price benefits them. Though the Bride Price is paid in gifts, and some of the gifts are for the couple to start out their life together with, the real value is the status, the high regard, in which a woman is held by her own Camp and by all the other Camps, and the value she bestows on her mate, and her children."

Ayla was still puzzled, but Jondalar was nodding, beginning to understand. The specific and complex details were not the same, but the broad outlines of kinship relationships and values were not so different from those of his own people. "How is a woman's value known? To set a good Bride Price?" the Zelandonii man asked.

"Bride Price depends on many things. A man will always try to find a woman with the highest status he can afford because when he leaves his mother, he assumes the status of his mate, who is or will be a mother. A woman who has proven her motherhood has a higher value, so women with children are greatly desired. Men will often try to push the value of their prospective mate up because it is to their benefit; two men who are vying for a high-valued woman might combine their resources – if they can get along and she agrees – and push her Bride Price even higher.

"Sometimes one man will join with two women, especially sisters who don't want to be separated. Then he gets the status of the higher-ranked woman and is looked upon with favour, which gives a certain additional status. He is showing he is able to provide for two women and their future children. Twin girls are thought of as a special blessing, they are seldom separated."

"When my brother found a woman among the Sharamudoi, he had kinship ties with a woman named Tholie, who was Mamutoi. She once told me she was 'stolen', though she agreed to it," Jondalar said.

"We trade with the Sharamudoi, but our customs are not the same. Tholie was a woman of high status. Losing her to others meant giving up someone who was not only valuable herself – and they paid a good Bride Price – but who would have taken the value she received from her mother and given it to her mate and her children, value that eventually would have been exchanged among all the Mamutoi. There was no way to compensate for that. It was lost to us, as though her value was stolen from us. But Tholie was in love, and determined to join with the young Sharamudoi, so to get around it, we allowed her to be 'stolen'."

"Deegie say Fralie's mother made Bride Price low," Ayla said.

The old man shifted position. He could see where her question was leading, and it was not going to be easy to answer. Most people understood their customs intuitively and could not have explained as clearly as Mamut. Many in his position would have been reluctant to explain beliefs that would normally have been cloaked in ambiguous stories, fearing that such a forthright and detailed exposition of cultural values would strip them of their mystery and power. It even made him uncomfortable, but he had already drawn some conclusions and made some decisions about Ayla. He wanted her to grasp the concepts and understand their customs as quickly as possible.

"A mother can move to the hearth of any one of her children," he said. "If she does – and usually she won't until she gets old – most often it will be a daughter who still lives at the same Camp. Her mate usually moves with her, but he can go back to his mother's Camp, or live with a sister if he wants. A man often feels closer to his mate's children, the children of his hearth, because he lives with them and trains them, but his sister's children are his heirs, and he is their responsibility. Usually the elders are welcomed, but unfortunately, not always. Fralie is the only child Crozie has left, so where her daughter goes, she goes. Life has not been kind to Crozie, and she has not grown kindly with age. She grasps and clings and few men want to share a hearth with her. She had to keep lowering her daughter's Bride Price after Fralie's first man died, which rankles and adds to her bitterness."

Ayla nodded understanding, then frowned with concern. "Iza told me of old woman, live with Brun's clan before I am found. She came from other clan. Mate die, no children. She have no value, no status, but always have food, always place by fire. If Crozie not have Fralie, where she go?"

Mamut pondered the question a moment. He wanted to give Ayla a completely truthful answer. "Crozie would have a problem, Ayla. Usually someone who has no kin will be adopted by another hearth, but she is so disagreeable, there are not many who would take her. She could probably find enough to eat and a place to sleep at any Camp, but after a while they would make her leave, just as their Camp made them leave after Fralie's first man died."

The old shaman continued with a grimace. "Frebec isn't so agreeable, himself. His mother's status was very low, she had few accomplishments and little to offer except a taste for bouza, so he never had much to begin with. His Camp didn't want Crozie, and didn't care if he left. They refused to pay anything. That's why Fralie's Bride Price was so low. The only reason they are here is because of Nezzie. She convinced Talut to speak for them, so they were taken in. There are some here who are sorry."

Ayla nodded with understanding. It made the situation a little more clear. "Mamut, what . . ."

"Nuvie! Nuvie! O Mother! She's choking!" a woman suddenly screamed.

Several people were standing around while her three-year-old coughed and sputtered, and struggled to draw breath. Someone pounded the child on the back, but it didn't help. Others were standing around trying to offer advice, but they were at a loss as they watched the girl gasping to breathe, and turning blue.

6

Ayla pushed her way through the crowd and reached the child as she was losing consciousness. She picked the girl up, sat down and put her across her lap, then reached into her mouth with a finger to see if she could find the obstruction. When that proved unsuccessful, Ayla stood up, turned the child around and held her around the middle with one arm so that her head and arms hung down, and struck her sharply between the shoulder blades. Then, from behind, she put her arms around the limp toddler, and pulled in with a jerk.

Everyone was standing back, with held breaths, watching the woman who seemed to know what she was doing, in a life-and-death struggle to clear the blockage in the little girl's throat. The child had stopped breathing, though her heart was still beating. Ayla laid the child down and kneeled beside her. She saw a piece of clothing, the child's parka, and stuffed it under her neck to hold her head back and her mouth open. Then holding the small nose closed, the woman placed her mouth over the girl's, and pulled in her breath as hard as she could, creating a strong suction. She held the pressure until she was almost without breath herself.

Then suddenly, with a muffled pop, she felt an object fly into her mouth, and almost lodge in her own throat. Ayla lifted her mouth and spat out a piece of gristly bone with meat clinging to it. She took a deep gulp of air, flipped her hair back out of her way, and, covering the mouth of the still child with her mouth again, breathed her own life-giving breath into the quiet lungs. The small chest raised. She did it several more times.

Suddenly the child was coughing and sputtering again, and then she took a long, rasping breath of her own.

Ayla helped Nuvie to sit up as she started to breathe again, only then aware of Tronie sobbing her relief to see her daughter still alive.

Ayla pulled her parka on over her head, threw the hood back and looked down the row of hearths. At the last one, the Hearth of the Aurochs, she saw Deegie standing near the fireplace brushing her rich chestnut hair back and wrapping it into a bun while she talked to someone on a bed platform. Ayla and Deegie had become good friends in the past few days and usually went outside together in the morning. Poking an ivory hairpin – a long thin shaft carved from the tusk of a mammoth and polished smooth – into her hair, Deegie waved at Ayla and signalled, "Wait for me, I'll go with you."

Tronie was sitting on a bed at the hearth next to the Mammoth Hearth, nursing Hartal. She smiled at Ayla and motioned her over. Ayla walked into the area defined as the Reindeer Hearth, sat down beside her, then bent over to coo and tickle the baby. He let go for a moment, giggled and kicked his feet, then reached for his mother to suckle again.

"He knows you already, Ayla," Tronie said.

"Hartal is happy, healthy baby. Grows fast. Where is Nuvie?"

"Manuv took her outside earlier. He's such a help with her, I'm glad he came to live with us. Tornec has a sister he could have stayed with. The old and the young always seem to get along, but Manuv spends almost all his time with that little one, and he can't refuse her anything. Especially now, after we came so close to losing her." The young mother put the baby over her shoulder to pat his back, then turned to Ayla again. "I haven't really had a chance to talk to you alone. I want to tell you again. We are all so grateful . . . I was so afraid she was . . . I still have bad dreams. I didn't know what to do. I don't know what I would have done if you hadn't been there." She choked up as tears came to her eyes.

"Tronie, do not speak. I am medicine woman, is not necessary to thank. Is my . . . I don't know word. I have knowledge . . . is necessary . . . for me."

Ayla saw Deegie coming through the Hearth of the Crane and noticed that Fralie was watching her. There were deep shadows around her eyes, and she seemed more tired than she should be. Ayla had been observing her and thought she was far enough along in her pregnancy that she should not be suffering morning sickness any more, but Fralie was still vomiting regularly and not just in the morning. Ayla wished she could make a closer examination, but Frebec had created a big furor when she mentioned it. He claimed that because she stopped someone from choking didn't prove she knew anything about healing. He wasn't convinced, just because she said so, and he didn't want some strange woman giving Fralie bad advice. That gave Crozie something else to argue with him about. Finally, to stop their squabbling, Fralie declared she felt fine and didn't need to see Ayla.

Ayla smiled encouragingly at the besieged woman, then picking up an empty waterskin on the way, walked with Deegie towards the entrance. As they passed through the Mammoth Hearth, and stepped

84

into the Hearth of the Fox, Ranec looked up and watched them pass by. Ayla had the distinct feeling that he watched her all the way through the Lion Hearth and the cooking area until she reached the inner arch, and she had to restrain an urge to look back.

When they pushed back the outer drape, Ayla blinked her eyes at the unexpected brightness of an intense sun in a bold blue sky. It was one of those warm, gentle days of fall that came as a rare gift, to be held in memory against the season when vicious winds, raging storms, and biting cold would be the daily fare. Ayla smiled in appreciation and suddenly remembered, though she hadn't thought of it in years, that Uba had been born on a day like this, that first fall after Brun's clan found her.

The earthlodge and the levelled area in front of it were carved out of a west-facing slope, about midway down. The view was expansive from the entrance, and she stood for a moment, looking out. The racing river glinted and sparkled as it murmured a liquid undertone to the interplay of sunlight and water, and across, in a distant haze, Ayla saw a similar escarpment. The broad swift river, gouging a channel through the vast open steppes, was flanked by ramparts of eroded earth.

From the rounded shoulder of the plateau above to the wide floodplain below, the fine loess soil was sculpted by deep gullies; the handiwork of rain, melting snow, and the outflow of the great glaciers to the north during the spring runoff. A few green larch and pine stood straight and stiff in their isolation, scattered sparsely among the recumbent tangle of leafless shrubs on the lower ground. Downstream, along the river's edge, the spikes of cattails mingled with reeds and sedges. Her view upstream was blocked by the bend in the river, but Whinney and Racer grazed within sight on the dry standing hay that covered the balance of the stark, spare landscape.

A spattering of dirt landed at Ayla's feet. She looked up, startled, into Jondalar's vivid blue eyes. Talut was beside him with a big grin on his face. She was surprised to see several more people on top of the dwelling.

"Come up, Ayla. I'll give you a hand," Jondalar said.

"Not now. Later. I just come out. Why you up there?"

"We're putting the bowl boats over the smoke holes," Talut explained.

"What?"

"Come on. I'll explain," Deegie said. "I'm ready to overflow."

The two young women walked together towards a nearby gully. Steps had been roughly cut into the steep sides leading to several large, flat mammoth shoulder blades with holes cut in them braced over a deeper part of the dry gully. Ayla stepped out on one of the shoulder blades, untied the waist thong of her legged garment, lowered it, then bent down and squatted over the hole, beside Deegie, wondering again why she hadn't thought of the posture herself when she was having so much trouble with her clothes. It seemed so simple and obvious after she watched Deegie once. The contents of the night baskets were also thrown into the gully, as well as other refuse, all of which was washed away in the spring.

They climbed out and walked down to the river beside a broad gulch. A rivulet, whose source farther north was already frozen, trickled down the middle. When the season turned again, the trench would carry a raging torrent. The top sections of a few mammoth skulls were inverted and stacked near the bank along with some crude long-handled dippers, roughed out of leg bones.

The two women filled the mammoth skull basins with water dipped from the river, and from a pouch Ayla brought with her, she sprinkled withered petals – once the pale blue sprays of saponin-rich ceanothus flowers – into both their hands. Rubbing with wet hands created a foamy, slightly gritty washing substance which left a gentle perfume on clean hands and faces. Ayla snapped off a twig, and used the end on her teeth, a habit she had picked up from Jondalar.

"What is bowl boat?" Ayla asked as they walked back carrying the waterproof stomach of a bison, bulging with fresh water, between them.

"We use them to cross the river, when it's not too rough. You start with a frame of bone and wood shaped like a bowl that will hold two or maybe three people, and cover it with a hide, usually aurochs, hair side out and well oiled. Megaceros antlers, with some trimming, make good paddles . . . for pushing it through the water," Deegie explained.

"Why bowl boats on top of lodge?"

"That's where we always put them when we aren't using them, but in winter we cover the smoke holes with them so rain and snow won't come in. They were tying them down through the holes so they won't blow away. But you have to leave a space for the smoke to get out, and be able to move it over, and shake it loose from inside if snow piles up."

As they walked together, Ayla was thinking how happy she was to know Deegie. Uba had been a sister and she loved her, but Uba was younger, and Iza's true daughter; there had always been the difference. Ayla had never known anyone her own age who seemed to understand everything she said, and with whom she had so much in common. They put the heavy waterskin down and stopped to rest for a while.

"Ayla, show me how to say 'I love you' with signs, so I can tell Branag when I see him again," Deegie asked.

"Clan has no sign like that," Ayla said.

"Don't they love each other? You make them sound so human when you talk about them, I thought they would."

86

"Yes, they love each other, but they are quiet . . . no, that is not right word."

"I think 'subtle' is the word you want," Deegie said.

"Subtle . . . about showing feelings. A mother might say, 'You fill me with happiness' to child," Ayla replied, showing Deegie the proper sign, "but woman would not be so open . . . no, obvious?" She questioned her second choice of words and waited for Deegie's nod before continuing, "Obvious about feelings for man."

Deegie was intrigued. "What would she do? I had to let Branag know how I felt about him when I found out he'd been watching me at Summer Meetings, just as I'd been looking at him. If I couldn't have told him, I don't know what I would have done."

"A Clan woman does not say, she shows. Woman does things for man she loves, cooks food as he likes, makes favourite tea ready in morning when he wakes up. Makes clothes in special way – inner skin of fur wrap very soft, or warm foot-coverings with fur inside. Even better if woman can know what he wants before he asks. Shows she pays close attention to learn habits and moods, knows him, cares."

Deegie nodded. "That's a good way to tell someone you love him. It is nice to do special things for each other. But how does a woman know he loves her? What does a man do for a woman?"

"One time Goov put himself in danger to kill snow leopard that was frightening to Ovra because was prowling too close to cave. She know he did it for her even though he gave hide to Creb, and Iza made fur wrap for me," Ayla explained.

"That is subtle! I'm not sure if I would have understood." Deegie laughed. "How do you know he did it for her?"

"Ovra told me, later. I did not know then. I was young. Still learning. Hand signs not all of Clan language. Much more said in face, and eyes, and body. Way of walking, turning of head, tightening muscles of shoulders, if you know what means, says more than words. Took long time to learn language of Clan."

"I'm surprised, as fast as you've been learning Mamutoi! I can watch you. Every day you're better. I wish I had your gift for language."

"I am still not right. Many words I do not know, but I think of speaking words in Clan way of language. I listen to words and watch how face looks, feel how words sound and go together and see how body moves . . . and try to remember. When I show Rydag, and others, hand signs, I learn, too. I learn your language, more. I must learn, Deegie," Ayla added with a fervour that bespoke her earnestness.

"It isn't just a game for you, is it? Like the hand signs are for us. It's fun to think that we can go to the Summer Meeting and speak to each other without anyone else knowing it."

87

"I am happy everyone has fun and wants to know more. For Rydag. He has fun now, but is not a game for him."

"No, I don't suppose it is." They reached for the waterskin again, then Deegie stopped and looked at Ayla. "I couldn't understand why Nezzie wanted to keep him, at first. But then I got used to him, and grew to like him. Now he's just one of us, and I'd miss him if he wasn't here, but it never occurred to me before that he might want to talk. I didn't think he ever gave it a thought."

Jondalar stood at the entrance of the earthlodge watching the two young women deeply involved in conversation as they approached, pleased to see Ayla getting along so well. When he thought about it, it seemed rather amazing that of all the people they might have met up with, the one group they found had a child of mixed spirits in their midst and so was more willing than most would probably have been to accept her. He'd been right about one thing, though. Ayla didn't hesitate to tell anyone about her background.

Well, at least she hadn't told them about her son, he thought. It was one thing for a person like Nezzie to open her heart to an orphan, it was quite another to welcome a woman whose spirit had mingled with a flathead's, and who'd given birth to an abomination. There was always an underlying fear that it might happen again, and if she drew the wrong kind of spirits to her, they might spread to other women nearby.

Suddenly the tall handsome man flushed. Ayla doesn't think her son is an abomination, he thought, mortified. He had flinched with disgust when she first told him about her son, and she had been furious. He had never seen her so angry, but her son was her son, and she certainly felt no shame over him. She's right. Doni told me in a dream. Flatheads . . . the Clan . . . are children of the Mother, too. Look at Rydag. He's a lot brighter than I ever imagined one like him would be. He's a little different, but he's human, and very likeable.

Jondalar had spent some time with the youngster and discovered how intelligent and mature he was, even to a certain wry wit, particularly when his difference or his weakness was mentioned. He had seen the adoration in Rydag's eyes every time the boy looked at Ayla. She had told him that boys of Rydag's age were closer to manhood in the Clan, more like Danug, but it was also true that his weakness might have matured him beyond his years.

She's right. I know she's right about them. But if she just wouldn't talk about them. It would be so much easier. No one would even know if she didn't tell them . . .

She thinks of them as her people, Jondalar, he chided himself, feeling his face heat again, angry at his own thoughts. How would you feel if someone told you not to talk about the people who raised and took care

88

of you? If she's not ashamed of them, why should you be? It hasn't been so bad. Frebec's a troublemaker anyway. But she doesn't know how people can turn on you, and on anyone who's with you.

Maybe it's best that she doesn't know. Maybe it won't happen. She's already got most of this Camp talking like flatheads, including me.

After Jondalar had seen how eagerly nearly everyone wanted to learn the Clan way of communicating, he sat in on the impromptu lessons that seemed to spring up every time someone asked questions about it. He found himself caught up in the fun of the new game, flashing signals across a distance, making silent jokes, such as saying one thing and signing something else behind someone's back. He was surprised at the depth and the fullness of the silent speech.

"Jondalar, your face is red. What could you be thinking?" Deegie asked in a teasing tone when they reached the archway.

The question caught him off guard, reminded him of his shame, and he blushed deeper in his embarrassment. "I must have been too close to the fire," he mumbled, turning away.

Why does Jondalar say words that are not true? Ayla wondered, noticing that his forehead was furrowed in a frown and his rich blue eyes were deeply troubled before he averted them. He is not red from fire. He is red from feeling. Just when I think I am beginning to learn, he does something I don't understand. I watch him, I try to pay attention. Everything seems wonderful, then for no reason, suddenly he's angry. I can see that he's angry, but I can't see what makes him angry. It's like the games, saying one thing with words and another with signs. Like when he says nice words to Ranec, but his body says he's angry. Why does Ranec make him angry? And now, something bothers him, but he says fire makes him hot. What am I doing wrong? Why don't I understand him? Will I ever learn?

The three of them turned to go in and almost bumped into Talut coming out of the earthlodge.

"I was coming to look for you, Jondalar," the headman said. "I don't want to waste such a good day, and Wymez did some unplanned scouting on the way back. He says they passed a winter herd of bison. After we eat, we're going to hunt them. Would you like to join us?"

"Yes. I would!" Jondalar said with a big smile.

"I asked Mamut to feel the weather and Search for the herd. He says the signs are good, and the herd hasn't wandered far. He said something else, too, which I don't understand. He said, 'The way out is also the way in.' Can you make anything of that?"

"No, but that's not unusual. Those Who Serve the Mother often say things I don't understand." Jondalar smiled. "They speak with shadows on their tongues."

89

"Sometimes I wonder if they know what they mean," Talut said.

"If we are going to hunt, I'd like to show you something that could be helpful." Jondalar led them to their sleeping platform in the Mammoth Hearth. He picked up a handful of lightweight spears and an implement that was unfamiliar to Talut. "I worked this out in Ayla's valley, and we've been hunting with it ever since."

Ayla stood back, watching, feeling an awful tension building up inside. She wanted desperately to be included, but she was not sure how these people felt about women hunting. Hunting had been the cause of great anguish for her in the past. Women of the Clan were forbidden to hunt or even to touch hunting weapons, but she had taught herself to use a sling in spite of the taboo and the punishment had been severe when she was found out. After she had lived through it, she had even been allowed to hunt on a limited basis to appease her powerful totem who had protected her. But her hunting had been just one more reason for Broud to hate her and, ultimately, it contributed to her banishment.

Yet, hunting with her sling had increased her chances when she lived alone in the valley, and gave her the incentive and encouragement to expand on her ability. Ayla had survived because the skills she had learned as a woman of the Clan, and her own intelligence and courage, gave her the ability to take care of herself. But hunting had come to symbolise for her more than the security of depending on and being responsible for herself; it stood for the independence and freedom that were the natural results. She would not easily give it up.

"Ayla, why don't you get your spear-thrower, too?" Jondalar said, then turned back to Talut. "I've got more power, but Ayla is more accurate than I am, she can show you what this can do better than I can. In fact, if you want to see a demonstration of accuracy, you ought to see her with a sling. I think her skill with it gives her an advantage with these."

Ayla let out her breath – she didn't know she had been holding it – and went to get her spear-thrower and spears while Jondalar was talking to Talut. It was still hard to believe how easily this man of the Others had accepted her desire and ability to hunt, and how naturally he spoke in praise of her skill. He seemed to assume that Talut and the Lion Camp would accept her hunting, too. She glanced at Deegie, wondering how a woman would feel.

"You ought to let mother know if you are going to try a new weapon on the hunt, Talut. You know she'll want to see it, too," Deegie said. "I might as well get my spears and packboards out now. And a tent, we'll probably be gone overnight."

After breakfast, Talut motioned to Wymez and squatted down by an area of soft dirt near one of the smaller fireplaces in the cooking hearth, well lit by light coming in through the smoke hole. Stuck in the ground near the edge was an implement made from a leg bone of a deer. It was shaped like a knife or a tapered dagger, with a straight dull edge leading from the knee joint to a point. Holding it by the knob of the joint, Talut smoothed the dirt with the flat edge, then, shifting it, began to draw marks and lines on the level surface with the point. Several people gathered around.

"Wymez said he saw the bison not far from the three large outcrops to the northeast, near the tributary of the small river that empties upstream," the headman began, explaining as he drew a rough map of the region with the drawing knife.

Talut's map wasn't so much an approximate visual reproduction as a schematic drawing. It wasn't necessary to accurately depict the location. The people of the Lion Camp were familiar with their region and his drawing was no more than a mnemonic aid to remind them of a place they knew. It consisted of conventionalised marks and lines that represented landmarks or ideas that were understood.

His map did not show the route which the water took across the land; their perspective was not from such a bird's-eye view. He drew herringbone zigzag lines to indicate the river, and attached them to both sides of a straight line, to show a tributary. At the ground level of their open flat landscape, rivers were bodies of water, which sometimes joined.

They knew where the rivers came from and where they led, and that rivers could be followed to certain destinations, but so could other landmarks, and a rock outcrop was less likely to change. In a land that was so close to a glacier, yet subject to the seasonal changes of lower latitudes, ice and permafrost – ground that was permanently frozen – caused drastic alterations of the landscape. Except for the largest of them, the deluge of glacial runoff could change the course of a river from one season to the next as easily as the ice hill pingos of winter melted into the bogs of summer. The mammoth hunters conceived of their physical terrain as an interrelated whole in which rivers were only an element.

Neither did Talut conceive of drawing lines to scale to show the length of a river or trail in miles or paces. Such linear measures had little meaning. They understood distance not in terms of how far away a place was but how long it would take to get there, and that was better shown by a series of lines telling the number of days, or some other markings of number or time. Even then, a place might be more distant for some people than for others, or the same place might be farther away at one season than another because it took longer to travel to it. The distance travelled by the entire Camp was measured by the length of time it took the slowest. Talut's map was perfectly clear to the members of the Lion Camp, but Ayla watched with puzzled fascination.

"Wymez, tell me where they were," Talut said.

"On the south side of the tributary," Wymez replied, taking the bone drawing knife and adding some additional lines. "It's rocky, with steep outcrops, but the floodplain is wide."

"If they keep going upstream, there are not many outlets along that side," Tulie said.

"Mamut, what do you think?" Talut asked. "You said they haven't wandered far off."

The old shaman picked up the drawing knife, and paused for a moment with his eyes closed. "There is a stream that comes in, between the second and last outcrop," he said as he drew. "They will likely move that way, thinking it will lead out."

"I know the place!" Talut said. "If you follow it upstream, the floodplain narrows and then is hemmed in by steep rock. It's a good place to trap them. How many are there?"

Wymez took the drawing tool and drew several lines along the edge, hesitated, then added one more. "I saw that many, that I can say for certain," he said, stabbing the bone drawing knife in the dirt.

Tulie picked up the marking bone and added three more. "I saw those straggling behind, one seemed quite young, or perhaps it was weak."

Danug picked up the marker and added one more line. "It was a twin, I think. I saw another straggling. Did you see two, Deegie?"

"I don't recall."

"She only had eyes for Branag," Wymez said, with a gentle smile.

"That place is about half a day from here, isn't it?" Talut asked.

Wymez nodded. "Half a day, at a good pace."

"We should start out right away then." The headman paused thoughtfully. "It's been some time since I've been there. I'd like to know the lay of the land. I wonder . . ."

"Someone willing to run could get there faster and scout it, then meet us on the way back," Tulie said, guessing what her brother was thinking.

"That's a long run . . ." Talut said, and glanced at Danug. The tall, gangly youth was about to speak up, but Ayla spoke first.

"That is not long run for horse. Horse runs fast. I could go on Whinney . . . but I do not know place," she said.

Talut looked surprised at first, then smiled broadly. "I could give you a map! Like this one," he said, pointing at the drawing on the ground. He looked around and spied a cast-off flake of broken ivory near the bone fuel pile, then pulled out his sharp flint knife. "Look, you go north until you reach the big stream." He began incising zigzag lines to indicate water. "There is a smaller one you have to cross first. Don't let it confuse you."

Ayla frowned. "I do not understand map," she said. "I not see map before."

Talut looked disappointed, and dropped the ivory scrap back on the pile.

"Couldn't someone go with her?" Jondalar suggested. "The horse can take two. I've ridden double with her."

Talut was smiling again. "That's a good idea! Who wants to go?"

"I'll go! I know the way," a voice called out, followed quickly by a second. "I know the way. I just came from there." Latie and Danug had both spoken up, and several others looked ready to.

Talut looked from one to the other, then shrugged his shoulders, holding out both hands, and turned to Ayla. "The choice is yours."

Ayla looked at the youth, nearly as tall as Jondalar, with red hair the colour of Talut's, and the pale fuzz of a beginning beard. Then at the tall, thin girl, not quite a woman but getting close, with dark blonde hair a shade or two lighter than Nezzie's. There was earnest hope in both sets of eyes. She didn't know which one to choose. Danug was nearly a man. She thought she ought to take him, but something about Latie reminded Ayla of herself, and she remembered the look of longing she had seen on the girl's face the first time Latie saw the horses.

"I think Whinney go faster if not too much weight. Danug is man," Ayla said, giving him a big, warm smile. "I think Latie better this time."

Danug nodded, looking flustered, and backed off, trying to find a way to deal with the sudden flush of mixed emotions that had unexpectedly overwhelmed him. He was sorely disappointed that Latie was chosen, but Ayla's dazzling smile when she called him a man had caused the blood to rush to his face and his heart to beat faster – and an embarrassing tightening in his loins.

Latie rushed to change into the warm, lightweight reindeer skins she wore for travelling, packed her haversack, added the food and waterbag Nezzie prepared for her, and was outside and ready to go before Ayla was dressed. She watched while Jondalar helped Ayla fasten the side basket panniers on Whinney with the harness arrangement she had devised. Ayla put the travelling food Nezzie gave her, along with water, in one basket on top of her other things, and took Latie's haversack and put it in the other carrier. Then, holding on to Whinney's mane, Ayla made a quick leap and was astride her back. Jondalar helped the girl up. Sitting in front of Ayla, Latie looked down at the people of her Camp from the back of the dun yellow horse, her eyes brimming with happiness.

Danug approached them, a little shyly, and handed Latie the broken flake of ivory. "Here, I finished the map Talut started, to make the place easier to find," he said.

"Oh, Danug. Thank you!" Latie said, and grabbed him around the neck to give him a hug.

"Yes. Thank you, Danug," Ayla said, smiling her heart-pounding smile at him.

Danug's face turned almost as red as his hair. As the woman and the girl started up the slope on the back of the mare, he waved at them, his palm facing him in a "come-back" motion.

Jondalar, with one arm around the arched neck of the young horse, who was straining after them with his head raised and nose in the air, put his other arm around the young man's shoulder. "That was very nice of you. I know you wanted to go. I'm sure you'll be able to ride the horse another time." Danug just nodded. He wasn't exactly thinking of riding a horse at that moment.

Once they reached the steppes, Ayla signalled the horse with subtle pressures and body movements, and Whinney broke into a fast run, heading north. The ground blurred with motion beneath flying hooves, and Latie could hardly believe she was racing across the steppes on the back of a horse. She had smiled with elation when they started out, and it still lingered, though sometimes she closed her eyes and strained forward just to feel the wind in her face. She was exhilarated beyond description; she had never even dreamed anything could be so exciting.

The rest of the hunters followed behind them not long after they left. Everyone who was able and wanted to go went along. The Lion Hearth contributed three hunters. Latie was young and only recently allowed to join Talut and Danug. She was always eager to go, as her mother had been when she was younger, but Nezzie did not often accompany hunters any more. She stayed to take care of Rugie and Rydag, and help watch other young children. She had not gone on many hunts since she took in Rydag.

The Fox Hearth had only two men, and both Wymez and Ranec hunted, but none from the Mammoth Hearth did, except for the visitors, Ayla and Jondalar. Mamut was too old.

Though he would like to have gone, Manuv stayd behind so as not to slow them down. Tronie stayed, too, with Nuvie and Hartal. Except for an occasional drive, where even the children could help, she no longer went along on hunting trips either. Tornec was the only hunter from the Reindeer Hearth, just as Frebec was the only hunter from the Hearth of the Crane. Fralie and Crozie stayed at the Camp with Crisavec and Tasher.

Tulie had almost always found a way to join hunting parties, even when she had small children, and the Aurochs Hearth was well represented. Besides the headwoman, Barzec, Deegie, and Druwez all went. Brinan tried his best to convince his mother to let him go, but he was left with Nezzie, along with his sister Tusie, placated with a promise that soon he would be old enough.

The hunters hiked up the slope together, and Talut set a fast pace once they reached the level grassland.

"I think the day is too good to waste, too," Nezzie said, putting her cup down firmly and speaking to the group which gathered around the outdoor cooking hearth, after the hunters left. They were sipping tea and finishing up the last of breakfast. "The grains are ripe and dry, and I've been wanting to go up and collect a last good day's worth. If we head towards that stand of stone pines by the little creek, we can collect the ripe pine nuts from the cones, too, if there's time. Does anyone else want to go?"

"I'm not sure if Fralie should walk so far," Crozie said.

"Oh, mother," Fralie said. "A little walk will do me good, and once the weather turns bad, we'll all have to stay inside most of the time. That will come soon enough. I'd like to go, Nezzie."

"Well, I'd better go, then, to help you with the children," Crozie said as if she was making a great sacrifice, although the idea of an outing sounded good to her.

Tronie wasn't reluctant to admit it. "What a good idea, Nezzie! I'm sure I can put Hartal in the back carrier, so I can carry Nuvie when she gets tired. There's nothing I'd like better than spending a day outside."

"I'll carry Nuvie. You don't have to carry two," Manuv said. "But I think I'll get the pine nuts first, and leave the grain collecting to the rest of you."

"I think I'll join you, too, Nezzie," Mamut said. "Perhaps Rydag wouldn't mind keeping an old man company, and maybe teach me more of Ayla's signs, since he's so good at them."

"You very good at signs, Mamut," Rydag signalled. "You learn signs fast. Maybe you teach me."

"Maybe we can teach each other," Mamut signed back.

Nezzie smiled. The old man had never treated the child of mixed spirits any differently from the other children of the Camp, except to show extra consideration for his weakness, and he had often helped her with Rydag. There seemed to be a special closeness between them, and she suspected Mamut was coming along to keep the boy occupied while the rest were working. She knew he would also make sure no one exerted inadvertent pressure on Rydag to move faster than he should.

95

He could slow down if he saw the youngster straining too hard, and blame his advanced age. He had done so before.

When everyone was gathered outside the earthlodge, with collecting and burden baskets and leather tarps, waterbags and food for a midday meal, Mamut brought out a small figure of a mature woman carved out of ivory and stuck it in the ground in front of the entrance. He said some words understood by no one but him, and made evocative gestures. Everyone in the Camp would be gone, the lodge would be empty, and he was invoking the Spirit of Mut, the Great Mother, to guard and protect the dwelling in their absence.

No one would violate the prohibition against entering signified by the figure of the Mother at the door. Short of absolute need, no one would dare risk the consequences which everyone believed would result. Even if the need was dire – if someone was hurt, or caught in a blizzard and needed shelter – immediate actions would be taken to placate a possibly angry and vengeful protector. Compensation over and above the value of anything used would be paid by the person, or the family or Camp of the person, as promptly as possible. Donations and gifts would be given to members of the Mammoth Hearth to appease the Great Mother Spirit with entreaties and explanations, and promises of future good deeds or compensatory activities. Mamut's action was more effective than any lock.

When Mamut turned from the entrance, Nezzie hoisted a carrying basket to her back and adjusted the tumpline across her forehead, picked up Rydag and settled him on her ample hip to carry him up the slope, then, herding Rugie, Tusie, and Brinan ahead of her, started up to the steppes. The others followed suit, and soon the other half of the Camp was hiking across the open grasslands for a day of work harvesting the grains and seeds that had been sown and offered to them by the Great Mother Earth. The work and the contribution to their livelihood of the gatherers was counted no less valuable than the work of the hunters, but neither was only work. Companionship and sharing made the work fun.

Ayla and Latie splashed through one shallow creek, but Ayla slowed the horse before they came to the next somewhat larger watercourse.

"Is this stream we follow?" Ayla asked.

"I don't think so," Latie said, then consulted the marks on the piece of ivory. "No. See here, that's the little one we crossed. We cross this one, too. Turn and follow the next one upstream."

"Not look deep here. Is good place to cross?"

Latie looked up and down the stream. "There's a better place up a ways. We only have to take off boots and roll up leggings there."

They headed upstream, but when they reached the wide shallow crossing where water foamed around jutting rocks, Ayla didn't stop. She turned Whinney into the water and let the horse pick her way across. On the other side, the mare took off in a gallop, and Latie was smiling again.

"We didn't even get wet!" the girl exclaimed. "Only a few splashes."

When they reached the next stream and turned east, Ayla slowed the pace for a while to give Whinney a rest, but even the slower gait of the horse was so much faster than a human could walk, or consistently run, they covered ground quickly. The terrain changed as they continued, getting rougher and gradually gaining in elevation. When Ayla stopped and pointed to a stream coming in on the opposite side, forming a wide V with the one they had been following, Latie was surprised. She didn't expect to see the tributary so soon, but Ayla had noticed turbulence and was expecting it. Three large granite outcrops could be seen from where they stood, a jagged scarp face across the waterway, and two more on their side, upstream and offset at an angle.

They followed their branch of the stream and noticed that it angled off towards the outcrops, and when they approached the first, saw that the watercourse flowed between them. Some distance after they passed the outcrops which flanked the stream, Ayla noticed several dark shaggy bison grazing on still-green sedge and reeds near the water. She pointed, and whispered in Latie's ear.

"Don't talk loud. Look."

"There they are!" Latie said in a muffled squeal, trying to keep her excitement under control.

Ayla turned her head back and forth, then wet a finger and held it up, testing the wind direction. "Wind blows to us from bison. Good. Do not want to disturb until ready to hunt. Bison know horses. On Whinney, we get closer, but not too much."

Ayla guided the horse, carefully skirting the animals, to check farther upstream, and when she was satisfied, came back the same way. A big old cow lifted her head and eyed them, chewing her cud. The tip of her left horn was broken off. The woman slowed and let Whinney assume movement that was natural to her while her passengers held their breaths. The mare stopped and lowered her head to eat a few blades of grass. Horses did not usually graze if they were nervous, and the action seemed to reassure the bison. She went back to grazing as well. Ayla slipped around the small herd as fast as she could, then galloped Whinney downstream. When they reached previously noted landmarks, they turned south again. They stopped for water for Whinney and themselves after they crossed the next stream, and then continued south.

*   *   *

TMH-4

The hunting party was just beyond the first small creek when Jondalar noticed Racer pulling against his halter towards a cloud of dust moving in their direction. He tapped Talut and pointed. The headman looked ahead and saw Ayla and Latie galloping towards them on Whinney. The hunters did not have long to wait before the horse and riders pounded into their midst, and pranced to a stop. The smile on Latie's face was ecstatic, her eyes sparkled, and her cheeks were flushed with excitement as Talut helped her down. Then Ayla threw her leg over and slid off, as everyone crowded around.

"Couldn't you find it?" Talut asked, voicing the concern everyone felt. One other person mentioned it at almost the same time, but in a different tone.

"Couldn't even find it. I didn't think running ahead on a horse would do any good," Frebec sneered.

Latie responded to him with surprised anger. "What do you mean, we 'couldn't even find it'? We found the place. We even saw the bison!"

"Are you trying to say you have already been there and back?" he asked, shaking his head in disbelief.

"Where are the bison now?" Wymez asked the daughter of his sister, ignoring Frebec and blunting his snide remark.

Latie marched to the basket pannier on Whinney's left side and took out the piece of marked ivory. Then taking the flint knife from the sheath at her waist, she sat on the ground and began scratching some additional marks on the map.

"The south fork goes between two outcrops, here," she said. Wymez and Talut sat down beside her and nodded agreement, while Ayla and several others stood behind and around her. "The bison were on the other side of the outcrops, where the floodplain opens out and there is still some green feed near the water. I saw four little ones . . ." She cut four short parallel marks as she spoke.

"I think, five," Ayla corrected.

Latie looked up at Ayla, and nodded, then added one more short mark. "You were right, Danug, about the twins. And they're young ones. And seven cows . . ." She looked up at Ayla again for confirmation. The woman nodded agreement, and Latie added seven more parallel lines, slightly longer than the first ones. ". . . only four with young, I think." She pondered a moment. "There were more, farther off."

"Five young males," Ayla added. "And two, three others. Not sure. Maybe more we not see."

Latie made five slightly larger lines, somewhat apart from the first ones, then added three more lines, between the two sets, making them a bit smaller again. She cut a little Y tick in the last mark in the line to indicate she was done, that that was the full number of bison they had counted. Her counting marks had cut over some of the other marks that had been etched into the ivory earlier, but it didn't matter. They had already served their purpose.

Talut took the ivory flake from Latie and studied it. Then he looked at Ayla. "You didn't happen to notice which way they were heading, did you?"

"Upstream, I think. We go around herd, careful, not disturb. No tracks other side, grass not chewed," Ayla said.

Talut nodded and paused, obviously thinking. "You said you went around them. Did you go far upstream?"

"Yes."

"The way I remember it, the floodplain narrows until it disappears, and high rocks close in the stream, and there is no way out. Is that right?"

"Yes . . . but, maybe way out."

"A way out?"

"Before high rocks, side is steep, trees, thick brush with thorns, but near rocks is dry streambed. Like steep path. Is way out, I think," she said.

Talut frowned, looked at Wymez, and Tulie, then laughed out loud. "The way out is also the way in! That's what Mamut said!"

Wymez looked puzzled for only a moment, then he slowly grinned his understanding. Tulie looked at both of them. Then a dawning look of comprehension appeared on her face.

"Of course! We can go in that way, build a surround to trap them, then go around the other way and drive them into it," Tulie said, making it clear to everyone else as well. "Someone will have to watch and make sure they don't get wind of us and go back downstream while we're building it."

"That sounds like a good job for Danug and Latie," Talut said.

"I think Druwez can help them," Barzec added, "and if you think more help is needed, I'll go."

"Good!" Talut said. "Why don't you go with them, Barzec, and follow the river upstream? I know a faster way to get to the back end. We'll cut across from here. You keep them hemmed in, and as soon as we get the trap built, we'll come back around to help chase them into it."

7

The dry streambed was a swath of dried mud and rock cutting through a steep, wooded, brush-entangled hillside. It led to a level but narrow floodplain beside a rushing stream that gushed out between constraining rock in a series of rapids and low waterfalls. Once Ayla had gone down on foot, she went back for the horses. Both Whinney and Racer were accustomed to the steep path that had led to her cave in the valley, and made their way down with little trouble.

She removed the basket harness from Whinney so she could graze freely. But Jondalar worried about removing Racer's halter since neither he nor Ayla had much control over him without it, and he was getting old enough to be fractious when the mood struck him. Since it didn't keep him from grazing, she agreed to keep it on him, though she would have preferred to have given him complete freedom. It made her realise the difference between Racer and his dam. Whinney had always come and gone as she wished, but Ayla had spent all her time with the horse – she'd had no one else. Racer had Whinney, but less contact with her. Perhaps she, or Jondalar, ought to spend more time with him, and try to teach him, she thought.

The corral-like surround was already under construction by the time Ayla went to help. The fence was made of whatever materials they could find, boulders, bones, trees and branches, which were built up and intertwined together. The rich and varied animal life of the cold plains constantly renewed itself, and the old bones scattered across the landscape were often swept away by vagrant streams into jumbled piles. A quick search downstream had revealed a pile of bones a short distance away, and the hunters were hauling large leg bones and rib cages towards the focus of activity: an area near the bottom of the dry stream which they were fencing in. The fence needed to be sturdy enough to contain the herd of bison, but was not intended to be a permanent structure. It would only be used once, and in any case was not likely to last beyond spring when the rushing stream bloated into a raging torrent.

Ayla watched Talut swinging an enormous axe with a gigantic stone head, as though it were a toy. He had doffed his shirt and was sweating profusely as he chopped his way through a stand of straight young saplings, felling each tree with two or three blows. Tornec and Frebec, who were carrying them away, couldn't keep up with him. Tulie was supervising their placement. She had an axe nearly as large as her brother's, and handled it with as much ease, breaking a tree in half, or shattering a bone to make it fit. Few men could match the strength of the headwoman.

"Talut!" Deegie called. She was carrying the front end of a whole curved mammoth tusk that was over fifteen feet in length. Wymez and Ranec supported the middle and back. "We found some mammoth bones. Will you break this tusk?"

The huge red-haired giant grinned. "This old behemoth must have lived a good long life!" he said, straddling the tusk when they put it down.

Talut's enormous muscles bunched as he lifted the sledgehammer-sized axe, and the air resounded with the blows as splinters and flakes of ivory flew in all directions. Ayla was fascinated just watching the powerful man wield the massive tool with such skilful ease. But the feat was even more astounding to Jondalar, for a reason he never considered. Ayla was more accustomed to seeing men execute prodigious feats of muscular strength. Though she had exceeded them in height, the men of the Clan were massively muscled and extraordinarily robust. Even the women had a pronounced rugged strength, and the life Ayla had led as she grew up, expected to perform the tasks of a Clan woman, had caused her to develop unusually strong muscles for her thinner bones.

Talut put the axe down, hoisted the back half of the tusk to his shoulder and started towards the enclosure they were building. Ayla picked the huge axe up to move it, and knew she could not have handled it. Even Jondalar found it too heavy to use with skill. It was a tool uniquely suited to the big headman. The two of them lifted the other half-tusk to their shoulders and followed Talut.

Jondalar and Wymez stayed to help wedge the cumbersome pieces of ivory in with boulders; they would present a substantial barrier to any charging bison. Ayla went with Deegie and Ranec to get more bones. Jondalar turned to watch them go, and struggled to swallow his anger when he saw the dark man move beside Ayla and make a comment that caused her and Deegie to laugh. Talut and Wymez both noticed the red glowering face of their young and handsome visitor, and a significant looked passed between them, but neither commented.

The final element of the surround was a gate. A sturdy young tree, stripped of its branches, was positioned upright at one side of an opening in the fence. A hole was dug for the base, and a mound of stones was piled up around it for support. It was reinforced by tying it with thongs to the heavy mammoth tusks. The gate itself was constructed of leg bones, branches, and mammoth ribs lashed firmly to crosspieces of saplings chopped to size. Then with several people holding the gate in place, one end was attached in many places to the upright pole using a crossed-over lashing that allowed it to swing on its leather hinges. Boulders and heavy bones were piled near the other end, ready to be shoved in front of the gate after it was closed.

It was afternoon, the sun still high, when all was in readiness. With everyone working together, it had taken a surprisingly short time to build the trap. They gathered around Talut, and lunched on the dried travelling food they brought with them, while they made further plans.

"The difficult part will be to get them through the gate," Talut said. "If we get one in the others will probably follow. But if they get beyond the gate and start milling around in this small space at the end, they'll head for the water. That stream is rough here, and some may not make it, but that won't do us any good. We'll lose them. The best we could hope for would be to find a drowned carcass downstream."

"Then we'll have to block them," Tulie said. "Not let them get past the trap."

"How?" Deegie asked.

"We could build another fence," Frebec suggested.

"How you know bison will not turn into water, when they come to fence?" Ayla asked.

Frebec eyed her with a patronising expression, but Talut spoke before he did.

"That's a good question, Ayla. Besides, there's not much material left around here to build fences," Talut said.

Frebec gave her a dark look of anger. He felt as though she had made him appear stupid.

"Whatever we can erect to block the way would be helpful, but I think someone needs to be there to drive them in. It could be a dangerous stand," Talut continued.

"I'll stand. That's a good place to use this spear-thrower I've been telling you about," Jondalar said, showing the unusual implement. "It not only gives a spear more distance, it gives it more force than a hand-thrown spear. With a true aim, one spear can kill instantly, at close range."

"Is that true?" Talut said, looking with renewed interest at Jondalar. "We'll have to talk more about it later, but yes, if you want, you can take a stand. I think I will, too."

"And so will I," Ranec said.

Jondalar frowned at the smiling dark man. He wasn't sure he wanted to make a stand with the man so obviously interested in Ayla.

"I shall stand here, too," Tulie said. "But rather than try to build another fence, we should make separate piles for each of us to stand behind."

"Or to run behind," Ranec quipped. "What makes you think they won't end up chasing us?"

"Speaking of chasing, now that we've decided what to do once they get here, how are we going to get them here?" Talut said, glancing at the placement of the sun in the sky. "It's a long walk around to get behind them from here. We may not have enough day left."

Ayla had been listening with more than interest. She recalled the men of the Clan making hunting plans, and especially after she began hunting with her sling, often wished she could have been included. This time, she was one of the hunters. She noted that Talut had listened to her earlier comment, and recalled how readily they had accepted her offer to scout ahead. It encouraged her to make another suggestion.

"Whinney is good chaser," she said. "I chase herds many times on Whinney. Can go around bison, find Barzec and others, chase bison here soon. You wait, chase into trap."

Talut looked at Ayla, then at the hunters, and then back at Ayla. "Are you sure you can do that?"

"Yes."

"What about getting around them?" Tulie asked. "They have probably sensed we are here by now, and the only reason they aren't gone is that Barzec and the youngsters are keeping them penned in. Who knows how long they will be able to hold them? Won't you chase them back the wrong way if you go towards them from this direction?"

"I not think so. Horse not disturb bison much, but I go around if you want. Horse goes faster than you can walk," Ayla said.

"She's right! No one can deny that. Ayla could go around on the horse faster than we could walk it," Talut said, then he frowned in concentration. "I think we should let her do it her way, Tulie. Does it really matter if this hunt succeeds? It would help, particularly if this turns out to be a long, hard winter, and it would give us more variety, but we really do have enough stored. We wouldn't suffer if we lost this one."

"That's true, but we've gone to a lot of work."

"It wouldn't be the first time that we went to a lot of work and came up empty-handed." Talut paused again. "The worst thing that can happen is that we lose the herd, and if it works, we could be feasting on bison before it's dark, and be on our way back in the morning."

Tulie nodded. "All right, Talut. We'll try it your way."

"You mean Ayla's way. Go ahead, Ayla. See if you can bring those bison here."

Ayla smiled, and whistled for Whinney. The mare neighed and galloped towards her, followed by Racer. "Jondalar, keep Racer here," she said, and sprinted towards the horse.

"Don't forget your spear-thrower," he called.

She stopped to grab it and some spears from the holder on the side of her pack, then with a practised easy motion, she leaped on to the horse's back, and was off. For a while, Jondalar had his hands full with the young horse that didn't like being kept from joining his dam in an exciting run. It was just as well; it didn't give Jondalar time to notice the look on Ranec's face as he watched Ayla go.

The woman, bareback on the horse, rode hard along the floodplain beside the tumbling, boisterous stream, which wound along a sinuous corridor hemmed in by steep rolling hills on both sides. Naked brush screened by dry standing hay clung to the hillsides and crouched low on the windy crests, softening the craggy face of the land, but hidden beneath the windblown loess topsoil that filled in the cracks was a stony heart. Exposed projections of bedrock studding the slopes revealed the essential granite character of the region, dominated by lofty knolls which rose to the bare rock summits of the prominent outcrops.

Ayla slowed when she neared the area where she had seen the bison earlier in the day, but they were gone. They had sensed, or heard, the building activity and reversed their direction. She saw the animals just as she was moving into the shadow of one of the outcrops cast by the afternoon sun, and, just beyond the small herd, she saw Barzec standing near what appeared to be a small cairn.

Greener grass amid the bare slender trees near the water had coaxed the bison into the narrow valley, but once they moved past the twin outcrops that flanked the stream, there was no exit other than the way in. Barzec and the younger hunters had seen the bison strung out along the stream, still stopping to graze now and then, but steadily moving out. They had chased them back in, but that stopped them only temporarily, and caused them to bunch together and move with more determination when they tried to leave the valley the next time. Determination and frustration could lead to stampede.

The four had been sent to keep the animals from leaving, but they knew they'd never stop a stampede. They couldn't keep chasing them in. It took too much effort to keep it up and Barzec didn't want to start them stampeding in the other direction before the trap was ready, either. The pile of stones Barzec was standing near when Ayla first saw him was stacked around a sturdy branch. A piece of clothing was fastened to it and was flapping in the wind. Then she noticed several more stone piles supporting upright branches or bones, spaced at fairly close intervals between the outcrop and the water, and from each a sleeping fur or a piece of clothing or a tent covering had been hung. They had even used small trees and bushes, anything from which they could drape something that would move in the wind.

The bison were nervously eyeing the strange apparitions, not sure how threatening they were. They didn't want to go back the way they had come, but they didn't want to go forward, either. Sporadically a bison would move towards one of the things, then back off when it flapped. They were stalled, effectively being kept exactly where Barzec wanted them. Ayla was impressed with the clever idea.

She edged Whinney close to the outcrop, trying to work her way around the bison slowly, so as not to upset the delicate balance. She noticed the old cow with the broken horn edging forward. She didn't like being held in, and looked ready to make a break.

Barzec saw Ayla, looked behind him for the rest of the hunters, then looked back at her with a frown. After all their efforts, he didn't want her chasing the bison the wrong way. Latie moved up beside him, and they spoke quietly, but he still watched the woman and the horse with apprehension for the long moments it took her to reach them.

"Where are the others?" Barzec asked.

"They are waiting," Ayla said.

"What are they waiting for? We can't keep these bison here for ever!"

"They wait for us to chase bison."

"How can we chase them? There's not enough of us! They're getting ready to break out as it is. I'm not sure how much longer we can keep them here, much less chase them back in. We'd have to get them to stampede."

"Whinney will chase," Ayla said.

"The horse is going to chase them!"

"She chase before, but better if you chase, too."

Danug and Druwez, who had been spread out watching the herd and throwing stones at the occasional animal that dared the flapping sentinels, moved closer to hear. They were no less amazed than Barzec, but their lessened vigilance opened an opportunity and ended the conversation.

Out of the corner of her eye, Ayla saw a huge young bull bolt, followed by several more. In a moment, all would be lost as the pent-up herd broke free. She wheeled Whinney around, dropped her spear and spear-thrower, and went after him, grabbing the flapping tunic from the branch on her way.

She raced straight for the animal, leaning over, waving the tunic at him. The bison dodged, trying to go around. Whinney wheeled again as Ayla snapped the leather in the young bull's face. His next diverting move turned him back towards the narrow valley, and into the path of the animals that had followed his lead, with Whinney and Ayla, snapping the leather tunic, right behind him.

Another animal broke away, but Ayla managed to turn her around, too. Whinney seemed to know almost before the bison did which one would try next, but it was as much the woman's unconscious signals to the horse as the mare's intuitive sense that put her in the way of the shaggy animal. Ayla's training of Whinney had not been a conscious effort in the beginning. The first time she got on the horse's back had been sheer impulse, and no thought of controlling or directing entered her mind. It had happened gradually, as mutual understanding grew, and the control was exerted by tension of her legs and subtle shifts of her body. Though, eventually, she did begin to apply it purposefully, there was always an additional element of interaction between the woman and the horse, and they often moved as one, as though they shared one mind.

The instant Ayla moved, the others recognised the situation, and rushed to stop the herd. Ayla had chased herding animals with Whinney in the past, but she would not have been able to turn the bison around without help. The large hump-backed beasts were much harder to control than she imagined they would be. They'd been held back, and she had never tried to drive animals in a direction they didn't want to go. It was almost as though some instinctual sense warned them of the trap waiting for them.

Danug rushed to Ayla's aid, to help turn back the ones who first bolted, though she was concentrating so intensely on stopping the young bull that she hardly noticed him at first. Latie saw one of the twin calves break, and, pulling the branch out of the pile of stones, she dashed to block its path. She whacked it on the nose, and harried it back, while Barzec and Druwez descended upon a cow with stones and a flapping fur. Finally their determined efforts turned the incipient stampede around. The old cow with the broken horn and a few others managed to break out, but most of the bison pounded along the floodplain of the small river, heading upstream.

They breathed a little easier once the small herd was beyond the granite outcrops, but they would have to keep them going. Ayla stopped only long enough to slide off the horse, pick up her spear and spear-thrower, and leap back on.

Talut had just taken a drink from his waterbag when he thought he heard a faint rumbling, like low rolling thunder. He cocked his head downriver and listened a few moments, not expecting to hear anything so soon, not sure that he expected to hear them at all. He lay face down and put his ear to the ground.

"They're coming!" he shouted, jumping up.

All of them scrambled to find their spears, and rushed to the places they had decided to take. Frebec, Wymez, Tornec, and Deegie spread out along the steep slope at one side, ready to fall in behind and block the gate closed. Tulie was nearest the open gate on the opposite side, ready to slam it shut once the bison were inside the pen.

In the space between the corral-like enclosure and the tumultuous stream, Ranec was a few paces away from Tulie, and Jondalar a few more paces away, almost at the edge of the water. Talut chose a place somewhat forward of the visitor, and stood on the wet bank. Each person had a piece of leather or clothing to flap at the oncoming animals with hopes of turning them aside, but each also lifted a spear, juggled it slightly, then gripped it firmly around the shaft, and held it in readiness – except for Jondalar.

The narrow, flat, wooden implement he held in his right hand was about the length of his arm from elbow to fingertips, and grooved down the centre. It had a hook as a backstop at one end, and two leather loops on either side for his fingers at the front end. He held it horizontally, and fitted the feathered butt end of a light spear shaft, tipped with a long, tapered, wickedly sharp bone point, against the hook at the back of the spear-thrower. Holding the spear lightly in place with his first two fingers that were through the loops, he tucked his leather flap in his belt, and picked up a second spear with his left hand, ready to slap it in place for a second cast.

Then they waited. No one spoke, and in the still expectancy small sounds loomed large. Birds warbled and called. Wind rustled dry branches. Water cascading over rocks splashed and gurgled. Flies droned. The drumming of running hooves grew louder.

Then bawling and grunting and huffing could be heard above the approaching thunder, and human voices shouting. Eyes strained to see signs of the first bison at the bend downstream, but when it came, it wasn't just one. Suddenly, the entire herd was pounding around the turn, and the huge, shaggy, dark brown animals with long black deadly horns were stampeding straight for them.

Each person braced, waiting for the assault. In the lead was the big young bull who had almost bolted to safety before the long chase began. He saw the enclosure ahead and veered around, towards the water – and the hunters standing in his path.

Ayla, close on the heels of the small herd, had been holding her own spear-thrower loosely as they were chasing the animals, but as they neared the last turn, she shifted it into position, not knowing what to expect. She saw the bull veer . . . and head straight for Jondalar. Other bison were following.

Talut ran towards the animal, flapping his tunic at him, but the thick-maned bison had had his fill of flapping things, and would not be deterred. Without a second thought, Ayla leaned forward, and urged Whinney ahead at full speed. Dodging around and past other running bison, she closed on the big bull and hurled her spear, just as Jondalar was casting his. A third spear was thrown at the same time.

The mare clattered past the hunters, splashing Talut as her hooves hit the edge of the water. Ayla slowed and halted, then quickly turned back. By then, it was over. The big bison was on the ground. The ones behind him slowed, and those nearest the slope had no other place to go than into the surround. After the first went through the opening, the others followed with little prodding. Tulie followed the last straggler pushing the gate, and the moment it was closed, Tornec and Deegie rolled a boulder against it. Wymez and Frebec lashed it to well-secured uprights while Tulie shoved another boulder beside the first.

Ayla slid off Whinney, still a little shaken. Jondalar was kneeling beside the bull with Talut and Ranec.

"Jondalar's spear went in the side of the neck, and through the throat. I think it would have killed this bull by itself, but your spear could have done it, too, Ayla. I didn't even see you coming," Talut said, just a trifle awed by her feat. "Your spear went in deep, right through his ribs."

"But it was a dangerous thing to do, Ayla. You could have gotten hurt," Jondalar said. He sounded angry, but it was reaction from the fear he felt for her when he realised what she had done. Then he looked at Talut and pointed to a third spear. "Whose spear is this? It was well thrown, landed deep in the chest. It would have stopped him, too."

"That's Ranec's spear," Talut said.

Jondalar turned to the dark-skinned man, and each of them took the measure of the other. Differences they might have, and rivalries might put them at odds, but they were first human, men who shared a beautiful, but harsh, primeval world and knew that survival depended upon each other.

"I owe you my thanks," Jondalar said. "If my spear had missed, I would be thanking you for my life."

"Only if Ayla's had missed, too. That bison has been thrice killed. It didn't stand a chance going against you. It seems you are meant to live. You are fortunate, my friend, the Mother must favour you. Are you as lucky in everything?" Ranec said, then looked at Ayla with eyes full of admiration, and more.

Unlike Talut, Ranec had seen her coming. Careless of the danger of long sharp horns, her hair flying, her eyes full of terror and anger, controlling the horse as though it were an extension of herself, she was like an avenging spirit, or like every mother of every creature who had ever defended her own. It seemed not to matter that both horse and she could easily have been gored. It was almost as though she was a Spirit of the Mother, who could control the bison as easily as she controlled the horse. Ranec had never seen anything like her. She was everything he'd ever desired: beautiful, strong, fearless, caring, protective. She was all woman.

Jondalar saw how Ranec looked at her, and his gut wrenched. How could Ayla help but see it? How could she not respond? He feared he might lose Ayla to the exciting dark man, and he didn't know what to do about it. Clenching his teeth, his forehead knotted with anger and frustration, he turned away, trying to hide his feelings.

He'd seen men and women react as he was doing, and had felt pity for them, and a bit scornful. It was the behaviour of a child, an inexperienced child lacking knowledge and wisdom in the ways of the world. He thought he was beyond that. Ranec had acted to save his life, and he was a man. Could he blame him for being attracted to Ayla? Didn't she have the right to make her own choice? He hated himself for feeling the way he did, but he couldn't help it. Jondalar yanked his spear out of the bison and walked away.

The slaughter had already begun. From behind the safety of the fence the hunters threw spears at the lowing, bawling, confused animals milling around inside the surround-trap. Ayla climbed up and found a convenient place to hang on, and watched Ranec hurl a spear with force and precision. A huge cow staggered and fell to its knees. Druwez threw another at the same bison, and from another direction – she wasn't sure who threw it – came yet another. The hump-backed shaggy beast slumped down, and its massive low-slung head collapsed on its knees. Spear-throwers gave no advantage here, she realised. Their method was quite efficient with hand-thrown spears.

Suddenly a bull charged the fence, crashing into it with the force of tons. Wood splintered, lashings were torn loose, uprights were dislodged. Ayla could feel the fence shaking and jumped down, but it didn't stop. The bison's horns were caught! He was shaking the entire structure in his efforts to break loose. Ayla thought it would break apart.

Talut climbed the unsteady gate, and with one blow from his huge axe, cracked open the skull of the mighty beast. Blood spurted up in his face, and brains spilled out. The bison sagged and, his horns still caught, pulled the weakened gate and Talut down with him.

The big headman stepped nimbly off the falling structure as it reached the ground, then walked a few paces and delivered another skull-crushing blow to the last bison still standing. The gate had served its purpose.

"Now comes the work," Deegie said, gesturing towards the space surrounded by the makeshift fence. Fallen animals were scattered around like hummocks of dark brown wool. She walked to the first, pulled her razor-sharp flint knife from the sheath, and straddling the head, slit its throat. Blood spurted bright red from the jugular, then slowed and pooled dark crimson around the mouth and nose. It seeped slowly into the ground in a widening circle, staining the dun earth black.

"Talut!" Deegie called when she reached the next mound of shaggy fur. The long spear shaft sticking out of its side still shuddered. "Come put this one out of its pain, but try to save some of the brains this time. I want to use them." Talut quickly dispatched the suffering animal.

Then came the bloody job of cutting, skinning, and butchering. Ayla joined Deegie, and helped her roll a big cow over to bare its tender underside. Jondalar walked towards them, but Ranec was closer, and got there first. Jondalar watched, wondering if they would need help or if a fourth would just get in the way.

Starting at the anus, they slit the stomach to the throat, cutting the milk-filled udders away. Ayla grabbed one side and Ranec the other, to tear open the rib cage. They cracked it apart, then with Deegie almost climbing inside the still warm cavity, they pulled out the internal organs – stomach, intestines, heart, liver. It was done quickly, so the intestinal gases, which would soon start bloating the carcass, would not taint the meat. Next, they started on the hide.

It was obvious they needed no help. Jondalar saw Latie and Danug struggling with the rib cage of a smaller animal. He nudged Latie aside, and with both hands tore it open with one powerful angry rip. But butchering was hard work, and by the time they were ready to skin, the effort had taken the edge off his anger.

Ayla was not unfamiliar with the process; she had done it alone, many times. The hide was not cut off so much as it was stripped off. Once it was cut loose from around the legs, it separated rather easily from the muscle, and it was more efficient and cleaner to fist it loose from inside or to pull it off. Where a ligament was attached and it was easier to cut, they used a special skinning knife with a bone handle and a flint blade sharp on both edges but rounded and dull at the tip, so as not to pierce the skin. Ayla was so accustomed to using hand-held knives and tools she felt awkward using a hafted blade, though she could already tell she would have better control and leverage once she got used to it.

The tendons from legs and back were stripped out; sinew was put to a wide range of uses from sewing thread to snares. The hide would become leather or fur. The long shaggy hair was made into rope and cordage of various sizes, and netting for fishing, or trapping birds, or small animals in their season. All the brains were saved, also several of the hooves, to be boiled up with bones and scraps of hide for glue. The huge horns, which could span as much as six feet, were prized. The solid ends that extended for a third of their length could be used as levers, pegs, punches, wedges, daggers. The hollow portion with the solid distal end removed became conical tubes used to blow up fires, or funnels to fill skin bags with liquids or powders or seeds, and to empty them again. A central section, with some of the solid part left intact for a bottom, could serve as a drinking cup. Narrow transverse cuts could make buckles, bracelets, or retaining rings.

The noses and tongues of the bison were saved – choice delicacies along with livers – then the carcasses were cut into seven pieces: two hindquarters, two forequarters, the midsection halved, and the huge neck. The intestines, stomachs and bladders were washed and rolled in the hides. Later they would be blown up with air, to keep them from shrinking, and then used for cooking or storage containers for fats and liquids, or floats for fishing nets. Every part of the animal was used, but not every part of every animal was taken; only the choicest or most useful. Only so much as could be carried.

Jondalar had taken Racer partway up the steep path and, to the young horse's distress, tied him securely to a tree to keep him out of the way, and out of danger. Whinney found him as soon as the bison were penned and Ayla let her go. Jondalar went to get him after he finished helping Latie and Danug with the first bison, but Racer was skittish around all the dead animals. Whinney didn't like it either, but she was more accustomed to it. Ayla saw them coming, and noticed Barzec and Druwez walking downstream again, and it occurred to her that in the rush to get the bison turned and chased into the trap, their packs had been left behind. She went after them.

"Barzec, you go back for packs?" she asked.

He smiled at her. "Yes. And the spare clothes. We left in such a hurry . . . not that I'm sorry. If you hadn't turned them when you did, we would have lost them for sure. That was quite a trick you did with that horse. I wouldn't have believed it if I hadn't seen it, but I'm worried about leaving everything back there. All these dead bison are going to draw every meat-eating animal around. I saw wolf tracks while we were waiting, and they looked fresh. Wolves love to chew up leather when they find it. Wolverines will, too, and be nasty about it, but wolves will do it for fun."

"I can go for packs and clothes on horse," Ayla said.

"I didn't think of that! After we're through, there will be plenty to feed on, but I don't want to leave anything out that I don't want them to have."

"We hid the packs, remember?" Druwez said. "She'll never find them."

"That's true," Barzec said. "I guess we'll have to go ourselves."

"Druwez know where to find?" Ayla asked.

III

The boy looked at Ayla, and nodded.

Ayla smiled. "You want come on horse with me?"

The boy's face split in a wide grin. "Can I?"

She looked over at Jondalar, and caught his eye. Then beckoned him to come with the horses. He hurried over.

"I'm going to take Druwez and go get the packs and things they left behind when we started chasing," Ayla said, speaking Zelandonii. "I'll let Racer come, too. A good run might settle him down. Horses don't like dead things. It was hard for Whinney in the beginning, too. You were right about keeping the halter on him, but we ought to start thinking about teaching him to be like Whinney."

Jondalar smiled. "It's a good idea, but how do you do it?"

Ayla frowned. "I'm not sure. Whinney does things for me because she wants to, because we're good friends, but I don't know about Racer. He likes you, Jondalar. Maybe he would do things for you. I think we both need to try."

"I'm willing," he said. "Someday, I'd like to be able to ride on his back the way you ride on Whinney."

"I would like that, too, Jondalar," she said, remembering, with the warm feeling of love she'd felt even then, how she had once hoped that if the blond man of the Others grew to have feeling for Whinney's colt, it might encourage him to stay in her valley, with her. That was why she had asked him to name the foal.

Barzec had been waiting while the two strangers spoke in the language he didn't understand, getting a bit impatient. Finally he said, "Well, if you are going to get them, I'll go back and help with the bison."

"Wait a moment. I'll help Druwez up, and go with you," Jondalar said.

They both helped him up, and stood watching them go.

Shadows were already getting long by the time they returned, and both hurried to help. Later, as she was washing out long tubes of intestines at the edge of the small river, Ayla recalled skinning and butchering animals with the women of the Clan. Suddenly she realised this was the first time she had ever hunted as an accepted member of a hunting group.

Even when she was young, she had wanted to go with the men, though she knew women were forbidden to hunt. But the men were held in such high esteem for their prowess, and they made it seem so exciting, that she would daydream about herself as a hunter, especially when she wanted to escape from an unpleasant or difficult situation. That was the innocent beginning that led to situations far more difficult than she ever imagined. After she was allowed to hunt with a sling, though other hunting was still taboo, she had often quietly paid attention when the men were discussing hunting strategy. The men of the Clan did almost nothing but hunt – except discuss hunting, make hunting weapons, and engage in hunting rituals. The Clan women skinned and butchered the animals, prepared the hides for clothing and bedding, preserved and cooked the meat, in addition to making containers, cordage, mats and various household objects, and gathering vegetable products for food, medicine, and other uses.

Brun's clan had had almost the same number of people as the Lion Camp, but the hunters had seldom killed more than one or two animals at a time. Consequently, they had to hunt often. At this time of year, the Clan hunters were out almost every day to get as much as they could stored ahead for the coming winter. Since she arrived, this was the first time anyone of the Lion Camp had hunted and though she wondered, no one else seemed worried about it. Ayla paused to look at the men and women skinning and butchering a small herd. With two or three people working together on each animal, the work was accomplished far more quickly than Ayla had thought possible. It made her think about the differences between them and the Clan.

The Mamutoi women hunted; that meant, Ayla thought, there were more hunters. It was true that nine of the hunters were male and only four were female – women with children seldom hunted – but it made a difference. They could hunt more effectively with more hunters, just as they could process and butcher more efficiently with everyone working together. It made sense, but she felt there was more involved, some essential point she was missing, some fundamental way of thinking, too. They were not so rigid, so bound by rules of what was considered proper, and what had been done before. There was a blurring of roles, the behaviour of women and men was not so strictly defined. It seemed to depend more on personal inclination, and what worked best.

Jondalar had told her that among his people no one was forbidden to hunt and, though hunting was important and most people did hunt, at least when they were young, no one was required to hunt. Apparently the Mamutoi had similar customs. He had tried to explain that people might have other skills and abilities that were equally worthwhile, and used himself as an example. After he had learned to knap the flint, and had developed a reputation for quality workmanship, he could trade his tools and points for anything he needed. It wasn't necessary for him to hunt at all, unless he wanted to.

But Ayla still didn't quite understand. What kind of manhood ceremony did they have if it didn't matter whether a man hunted or not? Men of the Clan would have been lost if they hadn't believed it was essential for them to hunt. A boy didn't become a man until he made his first major kill. Then she thought about Creb. He had never hunted. He couldn't hunt, he was missing an eye, and an arm, and he was lame. He had been the greatest Mog-ur, the greatest holy man of the Clan, but he had never made his kill, never had a manhood ceremony. In his own heart, he wasn't a man. But she knew he was.

Though it was already dusk by the time they were through, none of the blood-spattered hunters hesitated to strip off clothes and head for the stream. The women washed somewhat upstream of the men, but they stayed in sight of each other. Rolled hides and split carcasses had been stacked together and several fires lit around them to keep four-legged predators and scavengers away. Driftwood, deadfall, and the green wood used in the construction of the fence were piled nearby. A joint was roasting on a spit over one of them, and several low tents were spaced around it.

The temperature dropped quickly as darkness engulfed them. Ayla was glad for the mismatched and ill-fitting garments that had been loaned to her by Tulie and Deegie while her outfit, which she had washed to remove the bloodstains, was drying by a fire along with several others. She spent some time with the horses, making sure they were comfortable and settling down. Whinney stayed just within the edge of light from the fire where the meat was roasting, but as far away as she could from the carcasses waiting to be transported back to the earthlodge, and from the pile of scraps beyond the pale guarded by fire, from which snarls and yaps could be heard occasionally.

After the hunters ate their fill of bison, browned and crisp outside and rare near the bone, they built up the fire and sat around it sipping hot herbal tea, and talking.

"You should have seen her turn that herd," Barzec was saying. "I don't know how much longer we could have held them. They were getting more and more nervous, and I was certain we'd lost them once that bull bolted."

"I think we have Ayla to thank for the success of this hunt," Talut said.

Ayla blushed at the unaccustomed praise, but shyness accounted for only part of it. The acceptance of her and appreciation of her skills and abilities implied by the praise made her glow with warmth. She had longed for such acceptance all her life.

"And think what a story it will make at a Summer Meeting!" Talut added.

The conversation paused. Talut picked up a dry branch, a piece of deadfall that had lain so long on the ground, the bark hung loosely around it like old and weathered skin. He cracked it in two across his knee and put both pieces in the fire. A geyser of sparks erupted, lighting the faces of the people sitting close together around the flames.

"Hunts are not always so lucky. Do you remember the time we almost got the white bison?" Tulie asked. "What a shame that it got away."

"That one must have been favoured. I was sure we had it. Have you ever seen a white bison?" Barzec asked Jondalar.

"I've heard of them, and I've seen a hide," Jondalar replied. "White animals are held sacred among the Zelandonii."

"The foxes and rabbits, too?" Deegie asked.

"Yes, but not as much. Even ptarmigan are, when they are white. We believe it means they have been touched by Doni, so the ones that are born white, and stay white all year, are more sacred," Jondalar explained.

"The white ones have special meaning for us, too. That's why the Hearth of the Crane has such high status . . . usually," Tulie said, glancing at Frebec with a touch of disdain. "The great northern crane is white, and birds are the special messengers of Mut. And white mammoths have special powers."

"I'll never forget the white mammoth hunt," Talut said. Expectant looks encouraged him to continue. "Everyone was excited when the scout reported seeing her. It's the highest honour of all for the Mother to give us a white she-mammoth, and since it was the first hunt of a Summer Meeting, it would mean good luck for everyone, if we could get her," he explained to the visitors.

"All the hunters who wanted to go on the hunt had to undergo ordeals of purification and fasting to make sure we were acceptable, and the Mammoth Hearth imposed taboos on us, even afterwards, but we all wanted to be chosen. I was young, not much older than Danug, but I was big like he is. Maybe that's why I was picked, and I was one who got a spear in her. Like the bison that went after you, Jondalar, no one knows whose spear killed her. I think the Mother didn't want any one person or one Camp to get too much honour. The white mammoth was everyone's. It was better that way. No envy or resentment."

"I've heard of a race of white bears that live far north," Frebec said, not wanting to be left out of the discussion. Perhaps no one person or Camp could take full credit for killing the white mammoth, but that didn't preclude all envy or resentment. Anyone chosen to go on it gained more status from that one hunt than Frebec was born with.

"I've heard of them, too," Danug said. "When I was staying at the flint mine, Sungaea visitors came to trade for flint. One woman was a storyteller, a good storyteller. She told about the World Mother, and the mushroom men who follow the sun at night, and many different animals.

She told us about the white bear. They live on the ice, she said, and eat only animals from the sea, but they are said to be mild-mannered, like the huge cave bear who eats no meat. Not like the brown bear. They are vicious." Danug didn't notice the irritated look Frebec gave him. He hadn't meant to interrupt, he was just pleased to join in with something to say.

"Men of Clan come back from hunt once and tell of white rhinoceros," Ayla said. Frebec was still irritated and scowled at her.

"Yes, the white are rare," Ranec said, "but the black are special, too." He was sitting back from the fire a bit and his face in shadow could hardly be seen, except for his white teeth and the roguish gleam in his eyes.

"You're rare, all right, and more than happy to let every woman at Summer Meeting, who wants to find out, know just how rare you are," Deegie remarked.

Ranec laughed. "Deegie, can I help it if the Mother's own are so curious? You wouldn't want me to disappoint anyone, would you? But I wasn't talking about me. I was thinking about black cats."

"Black cats?" Deegie asked.

"Wymez, I have a vague memory of a large black cat," he said, turning to the man with whom he shared a hearth. "Do you know anything about that?"

"It must have made a very strong impression on you. I didn't think you remembered," Wymez said. "You were hardly more than a baby, but your mother did scream. You had wandered away, and just when she saw you, she saw this big black cat, like a snow leopard, only black, leaping out of a tree. I think she thought it was going for you, but either her scream scared it off, or that wasn't its intention. It just kept on going, but she ran for you, and it was a long time before she let you out of her sight again."

"Were there many black ones like that where you were?" Talut asked.

"Not too many, but they were around. They stayed in forests and were night hunters, so they were hard to see."

"It would be as rare as the white ones here, wouldn't it? Bison are dark, and some mammoths, but they aren't really black. Black is special. How many black animals are there?" Ranec said.

"Today, when I go with Druwez, we see black wolf," Ayla said. "Not ever see black wolf before."

"Was it really black? Or just dark?" Ranec asked, very interested.

"Black. Lighter on belly, but black. Lone wolf, I think," Ayla added. "I do not see other tracks. In pack, would be . . . low status. Leave, maybe, find other lone wolf, make new pack."

"Low status? How do you know so much about wolves?" Frebec

116

asked. There was a hint of derision in his voice, as though he didn't want to believe her, but there was obvious interest, also.

"When I learn to hunt, I hunt only meat-eaters. Only with sling. I watch close, long time. I learn about wolves. Once I see white wolf in pack. Other wolves not like her. She leave. Other wolves not like wrong colour wolf."

"It was a black wolf," Druwez said, wanting to defend Ayla, especially after the exciting ride on the horse. "I saw it, too. I wasn't even sure at first, but it was a wolf, and it was black. And I think it was alone."

"Speaking of wolves, we should keep watch tonight. If there is a black wolf around, that's all the more reason," Talut said. "We can trade off, but someone ought to be awake and watching all night."

"We should get some rest," Tulie added, getting up. "We have a long hike tomorrow."

"I'll watch first," Jondalar said. "When I get tired, I can wake someone."

"You can wake me," Talut said. Jondalar nodded.

"I watch, too," Ayla said.

"Why don't you watch with Jondalar? It's a good idea to have a partner to watch with. You can keep each other awake."

8

"It was cold last night. This meat is starting to freeze," Deegie said, lashing a hindquarter to a packboard.

"That's good," Tulie said, "but there's more than we can carry. We will have to leave some."

"Can't we build a cairn over it with the rocks from the fence?" Latie asked.

"We can, and we probably should, Latie. It's a good idea," Tulie said, preparing a load for herself that was so huge Ayla wondered how even she, as strong as she was, could carry it. "But we may not get back for it until spring, if the weather turns. If it was closer to the lodge, it would be better. Animals don't come around as much, and we could watch it, but out here in the open if something like a cave lion, or even a determined wolverine, really wants the meat, it will find a way to break in."

"Can't we pour water over it to freeze it solid? That would keep animals out. It's hard to break into a frozen cairn even with picks and mattocks," Deegie said.

"It would keep animals out, yes, but how do you keep the sun out, Deegie?" Tornec asked. "You can't be sure it will stay cold. It's too early in the season."

Ayla was listening, and watching the pile of bison parts dwindle as everyone packed as much as they could carry. She wasn't used to surplus, to having so much that one could pick and choose and take only the best. There had always been plenty of food to eat when she lived with the Clan, and more than enough hides for clothing, bedding, and other uses, but little was wasted. She wasn't sure how much would be left, but so much had already been thrown into the heap of scraps, that it bothered her to think of leaving more, and it was obvious that no one else wanted to, either.

She noticed Danug pick up Tulie's axe and, wielding it as easily as the woman, chop a log in two and add it to the last fire left burning. She walked over to him.

"Danug," she said quietly. "Would help me?"

"Um . . . ah . . . yes," he stammered bashfully, feeling his face turn red. Her voice was so low and rich and her unusual accent was so exotic. She had caught him by surprise; he hadn't seen her coming, and standing close to the beautiful woman inexplicably flustered him.

"I need . . . two poles," Ayla said, holding up two fingers. "Young trees downstream. You cut for me?"

"Ah . . . sure. I'll cut down a couple of trees for you."

As they walked towards the bend in the small river, Danug felt more relaxed, but he kept glancing down at the blonde head of the woman who walked at his side and just a half-step ahead. She selected two straight young alders of approximately the same width, and after Danug chopped them down, she directed him to strip off the branches and cut the tips so that they were of equal length. By then most of the big strapping youth's bashfulness had eased.

"What are you going to do with these?" Danug asked.

"I will show you," she said, then with a loud, imperative whistle, she called Whinney. The mare galloped towards her. Ayla had outfitted her earlier in harness and panniers in preparation for leaving. Though Danug thought it looked odd to see a leather blanket across the horse's back, and a pair of baskets tied to her sides with thongs, he noticed it didn't seem to bother the animal or slow her down.

"How do you get her to do that?" Danug asked.

"Do what?"

"Come to you when you whistle."

Ayla frowned, thinking. "I am not sure, Danug. Until Baby come, I am alone in valley with Whinney. She is only friend I know. She grow up with me, and we learn . . . each other."

"Is it true that you can talk to her?"

"We learn, each other, Danug. Whinney not talk like you talk. I learn . . . her signs . . . her signals. She learn mine."

"You mean like Rydag's signs?"

"A little. Animals, people, all have signals, even you, Danug. You say words, signals say more. You speak when you not know you speak."

Danug frowned. He wasn't sure he liked the drift of the conversation. "I don't understand," he said, looking aside.

"Now we talk," Ayla continued. "Words not say, but signals say . . . you want ride horse. Is right?"

"Well . . . ah . . . yes, I'd like to."

"So . . . you ride horse."

"Do you mean it? Can I really have a ride on the horse? Like Latie and Druwez did?"

Ayla smiled. "Come here. Need big stone to help you get on first time."

Ayla stroked and patted Whinney, and talked to her in the unique language that had developed naturally between them: the combination of Clan signs and words, nonsense sounds she had invented with her son and imbued with meaning, and animal sounds which she mimicked perfectly. She told Whinney that Danug wanted a ride, and to make it exciting but not dangerous. The young man had learned some of the Clan signs that Ayla was teaching Rydag and the Camp, and was surprised that he could make out the meaning of a few that were part of her communication with the horse, but that only filled him with more awe. She *did* talk to the horse, but like Mamut when he was invoking spirits, she used a mystical, powerful, esoteric language.

Whether the horse understood explicitly or not, she did understand from Ayla's actions that something special was expected when the woman helped the tall young man on her back. To Whinney, he felt like the man she had come to know and trust. His long legs hung down low, and there was no sense of direction or control.

"Hold on to mane," Ayla instructed. "When you want to go, lean forward a little. When you want to slow or stop, sit up."

"You mean you're not going to ride with me?" Danug said, a touch of fear quaking his voice.

"Not need me," she said, then gave Whinney's flank a slap.

Whinney broke away with a sudden burst of speed. Danug jerked backwards, then clutching her mane to pull forward, wrapped his arms around her neck and hung on for dear life. But when Ayla rode, leaning forward was a signal to go faster. The sturdy horse of the cold plains surged ahead down the level floodplain, which had by now become quite familiar, leaping logs and brush and avoiding exposed, jagged rock and occasional trees.

At first, Danug was so petrified he could only keep his eyes squeezed shut and hang on. But after he realised he hadn't fallen off, though he could feel the mare's powerful muscles as he bounced with her stride, he opened his eyes a slit. His heart beat with excitement as he watched trees and brush and the ground below pass by in a blur of speed. Still holding on, he lifted his head up to look around.

He could hardly believe how far he had come. The large outcrops flanking the stream were just ahead! Vaguely, he heard a shrill whistle far behind him, and immediately noticed a difference in the horse's pace. Whinney burst beyond the guarding rocks then, slowing only slightly, turned around in a wide circle and headed back. Though still hanging on, Danug was less fearful now. He wanted to see where they were going, and assumed a somewhat more upright position, which Whinney interpreted as a signal to slow a little.

The grin on Danug's face as the horse approached made Ayla think of Talut, especially when he was pleased with himself. She could see the man in the boy. Whinney pranced to a stop, and Ayla led her to the rock so Danug could get down. He was so ecstatic he could hardly speak, but he could not stop smiling. He had never considered riding fast on the back of a horse – it was beyond his imagination – and the experience went beyond his wildest expectations. He would never forget it.

His grin made Ayla smile every time she glanced at him. She attached the poles to Whinney's harness and when they returned to the campsite, he was still grinning.

"What's wrong with you?" Latie asked. "Why are you smiling like that?"

"I rode the horse," Danug answered. Latie nodded and smiled.

Nearly everything that could be taken away from the hunting site had been lashed to packboards, or wrapped in skins ready to be swung hammock-like from stout poles carried across the shoulders of two people. There were still haunches and rolled hides left, but not as much as Ayla thought there might be. As with hunting and butchering, more could be taken back to the winter camp when everyone worked together.

Several people had noticed that Ayla was not preparing a load to carry back, and wondered where she had gone, but when Jondalar saw her return with Whinney dragging the poles, he knew what she had in mind. She rearranged the poles so that the thicker ends were crossed just above the basket panniers across the mare's withers and fastened to the harness, and the narrow ends angled out behind the horse and rested easily on the ground. Then between the two poles, she attached a makeshift platform made out of the tent covering, using branches for support. The people stopped to watch her, but it wasn't until she began transferring the balance of the bison parts to the travois that anyone guessed its purpose. She also filled up the panniers, and put the last of it on a packboard to carry herself. When she was through, much to everyone's surprise, there was nothing left in the stack.

Tulie looked at Ayla and the horse, with the travois and panniers, obviously impressed. "I never thought of using a horse to carry a load," she said. "In fact, it never occurred to me to use a horse for anything except food – until now."

Talut threw dirt on the fire, stirred it around to make sure it was out. Then he hoisted his heavy packboard to his back, drew his haversack over his left shoulder, picked up his spear and started out. The rest of the hunters followed him. Jondalar had wondered ever since he first met the Mamutoi why they made their packs to be worn over only one shoulder. As he adjusted his packboard to fit comfortably across his back, and pulled his haversack over his shoulder, he suddenly understood. It allowed them to carry fully loaded packboards on their backs. They must carry large quantities often, he thought.

Whinney walked behind Ayla, her head close to the woman's shoulder. Jondalar, leading Racer by the halter, walked beside her. Talut fell back and walked just in front of them, and they exchanged a few words while they hiked. As people trudged along under their heavy loads, Ayla noticed an occasional glance in the direction of her and the horse.

After a while, Talut began humming a rhythmic tune under his breath. Soon, he was vocalising sounds in time with their steps:

> *Hus-na, dus-na, teesh-na, keesh-na.*
> *Pec-na, sec-na, ha-na-nya.*
> *Hus-na, dus-na, teesh-na, keesh-na.*
> *Pec-na, sec-na, ha-na-nya!*

The rest of the group joined in, repeating the syllables and the tone. Then, with a mischievous grin, Talut, keeping the same tones and pace, looked at Deegie and changed to words.

> *What is pretty Deegie wishing?*
> *Branag, Branag, share my bed.*
> *Where is pretty Deegie going?*
> *Home to empty furs instead.*

Deegie blushed, but smiled, while everyone chuckled knowingly. When Talut repeated the first question, the rest of the group joined in on the answer, and after the second, they sang out the reply. Then they joined Talut in singing the refrain.

> *Hus-na, dus-na, teesh-na, keesh-na,*
> *Pec-na, sec-na, ha-na-nya!*

They repeated it several times, then Talut improvised another verse.

> *How does Wymez spend the winter?*
> *Making tools and wanting fun.*
> *How does Wymez spend the summer?*
> *Making up for having none!*

Everyone laughed, except Ranec. He roared. When the verse was repeated by the group, the usually undemonstrative Wymez turned red at the gentle jab. The toolmaker's habit of taking advantage of the Summer Meetings to compensate for his essentially celibate winter life was well known.

Jondalar was enjoying the teasing and joking as much as the others. It was just the kind of thing his people might do. But at first, Ayla didn't quite understand the situation, or the humour, especially when she noticed Deegie's embarrassment. Then she saw it was done with good-natured smiling and laughter, and the jibes were taken in good grace. She was beginning to understand verbal humour, and the laughter itself was contagious. She, too, smiled at the verse directed at Wymez.

Talut started the refrain of measured syllables again when everyone quieted down. Everyone joined him, anticipating now.

> Hus-na, dus-na, teesh-na, keesh-na,
> Pec-na, sec-na, ha-na-nya!

Talut looked at Ayla, then, with a smug grin, began:

> Who wants Ayla's warm affection?
> Two would like to share her furs.
> Who will be the rare selection?
> Black or white the choice is hers.

It pleased Ayla to be included in the joking, and though she wasn't sure if she completely understood the meaning of the verse, she flushed with warmth because it was about her. Thinking about the previous night's conversation, she thought the rare black and white must refer to Ranec and Jondalar. Ranec's delighted laughter confirmed her suspicion, but Jondalar's strained smile bothered her. He wasn't enjoying the joking now.

Barzec then picked up the refrain, and even Ayla's untrained ear detected a fine and distinctive quality in the timbre and tone of his voice. He, too, smiled at Ayla, signalling who would be the subject of his teasing verse.

> How will Ayla choose a colour?
> Black is rare but so is white.
> How will Ayla choose a lover?
> Two can warm her furs at night!

Barzec glanced at Tulie, while everyone repeated his verse, and she rewarded him with a look of tenderness and love. Jondalar, however, frowned, unable to maintain even the appearance that he was enjoying the direction the teasing had taken. He did not like the idea of sharing Ayla with anyone, particularly the charming carver.

Ranec picked up the refrain next, and the rest quickly joined in.

Hus-na, dus-na, teesh-na, keesh-na.
Pec-na, sec-na, ha-na-nya!

He did not look at anyone, at first, wanting to maintain some suspense. Then he flashed a big, toothy smile at Talut, the instigator of the teasing song, and everyone laughed in advance, waiting for Ranec to make a telling point on the one who had caused the others to squirm.

Who's big and tall and strong and wise?
Lion Camp's own red-haired brute.
Who wields a tool to match his size?
Every woman's friend, Talut!

The big headman roared at the innuendo, as the others shouted out the verse a second time, then he picked up the refrain again. As they hiked back to the Lion Camp, the rhythmic song set the pace, and the laughter eased the burden of carrying back the results of their hunting.

Nezzie came out of the longhouse and let the drape fall behind her. She gazed out across the river. The sun was low in the western sky, preparing to sink into a high bank of clouds near the horizon. She glanced up the slope, not sure why. She didn't really expect the hunters back yet; they had only left the day before and probably would be gone two nights, at least. Something made her look up again. Was that movement at the top of the path that led to the steppes?

"It's Talut!" she cried, seeing the familiar figure silhouetted against the sky. She ducked her head inside the earthlodge and shouted, "They're back! Talut and the rest, they're back!" Then she rushed up the slope to meet them.

Everyone came running out of the lodge to greet the returning hunters. They helped ease the heavy packboards off the backs of the people who had not only hunted, but carried the products of their efforts back. But the sight that caused the most surprise was the horse dragging behind her a load much larger than anyone could carry. People gathered around as Ayla unloaded even more from the basket panniers. The meat and the other parts of the bison were immediately brought into the lodge, passed from hand to hand, and put into storage.

Ayla made sure the horses were comfortable after everyone went in, removing Whinney's harness and Racer's halter. Even though they seemed not to be suffering any consequences from spending their nights outside alone, the woman still felt a pang of concern about leaving them each evening when she went inside the lodge. As long as the weather stayed reasonably nice, it wasn't bad. A little cold didn't bother her, but this was the season of unexpected changes. What if a bad storm blew up? Where would the horses go then?

She looked up with a worried frown. High wispy clouds in brilliant shades streamered overhead. The sun had set not long before, and left a panoply of strident colour trailing behind it. She watched until the ephemeral hues faded and the clear blue greyed.

When she went in, Ayla overheard a comment about her and the horse just before she pushed back the inner drape that led to the cooking hearth. People had been sitting around, relaxing, eating, and talking, but conversation stopped as she appeared. She felt uncomfortable entering the first hearth with everyone staring at her. Then Nezzie handed her a bone plate, and the talking started up again. Ayla began to serve herself, then stopped to look around. Where was the bison meat they had just brought back? There was no sign of it any place. She knew it must have been put away, but where?

Ayla pushed back the heavy outer mammoth hide and looked first for the horses. Assured that they were safe, she looked for Deegie and smiled as she approached. Deegie had promised to show her, with the fresh bison skins, how the Mamutoi tanned and processed hides. In particular, Ayla was interested in how they coloured leather red, like Deegie's tunic. Jondalar had said white was sacred to him; red was sacred to Ayla, because it was sacred to the Clan. A skin colouring paste of red ochre mixed with fat, preferably cave bear fat, was used in the naming ceremony; a piece of red ochre was the first object that went into an amulet bag, given at the time a person's totem was made known. From the beginning to the end of life, red ochre was used in many rituals, including the last, the burial. The small bag that contained the roots used to make the sacred drink was the only red thing Ayla had ever owned, and next to her amulet, it was her greatest treasure.

Nezzie came out of the lodge carrying a large piece of leather stained from use, and saw Ayla and Deegie together. "Oh, Deegie. I was looking for someone to help me," she said. "I thought I'd make a big stew for everyone. The bison hunt was so successful, Talut said he thought we should have a feast to celebrate. Will you set this up for cooking? I put hot coals in the pit by the big fireplace, and put the frame over it. There is a bag of dried mammoth dung out there to put in the coals. I'll send Danug and Latie for water."

"For one of your stews, I'll help any time, Nezzie."

"Can I help?" Ayla asked.

"And me," Jondalar said. He had just come up to talk to Ayla and overheard.

"You can help me carry some food out," Nezzie said as she turned to go back.

They followed her towards one of the mammoth tusk archways that were along the walls inside the earthlodge. She pulled back a rather stiff, heavy drape of mammoth hide, which had not been dehaired. The double layer of reddish fur, with its downy undercoat and long outer hair, faced the outside. A second drape hung behind it and when it was pulled back they felt a breath of cold air. Looking into the dimly lit area, they saw a large pit the size of a small room. It was about three feet deeper than the floor level with the bare earth of the slope high up the walls, and it was almost full of frozen slabs and chunks, and smaller carcasses of meat.

"Storage!" Jondalar said, holding back the heavy drapes while Nezzie let herself down. "We keep meat frozen for winter, too, but not as conveniently close. Our shelters are built underneath the cliff overhangs, or in the front of some caves. But it's hard to keep meat frozen there, so our meat is outside."

"Clan keeps meat frozen in cold season in cache, under pile of stones," Ayla said, understanding now what had happened to the bison meat they brought back.

Nezzie and Jondalar both looked surprised. They never thought about people of the Clan storing meat for winter, and were still amazed when Ayla mentioned activities that seemed so advanced, so human. But then Jondalar's comments about the place where he lived had surprised Ayla. She had assumed all of the Others lived in the same kind of dwelling, and didn't realise the earthlodges were constructions as unusual to him as they were to her.

"We don't have a lot of stones around here to make caches with," Talut said in his booming voice. They looked up at the red-bearded giant coming towards them. He relieved Jondalar of one of the drapes. "Deegie told me you decided to make a stew, Nezzie," he said with an appreciative grin. "I thought I'd come and help."

"That man can smell food before it's even cooking!" Nezzie chuckled, as she rummaged around in the pit below.

Jondalar was still interested in the storage rooms. "How does the meat stay frozen like this? It's warm inside the lodge," Jondalar asked.

"In winter, all the ground is frozen hard as a rock, but it melts enough to dig in summer. When we build a lodge, we dig down far enough to reach the ground that is always frozen, for storage rooms. They will keep food cold even in summer, though not always frozen. In fall, as soon as the weather turns cold outside, the ground starts to freeze up. Then meat will freeze in the pits and we start storing for winter. The hide of the mammoth keeps the warm inside and the cold outside,"

Talut explained. "Just like it does for the mammoth," he added with a grin.

"Here, Talut, take this," Nezzie said, holding out a hard, frosty, reddish-brown chunk with a thick layer of yellowish fat on one side.

"I will take," Ayla offered, reaching for the meat.

Talut reached for Nezzie's hands, and though she was by no means a small woman, the powerful man lifted her out as though she were a child. "You're cold. I'll have to warm you up," he said, then putting his arms around her waist, he picked her up and nuzzled her neck.

"Stop it, Talut. Put me down!" she scolded, though her face glowed with delight. "I have work to do, this is not the right time . . ."

"Tell me the right time, then I'll put you down."

"We have visitors," she remonstrated, but she put her arms around his neck, and whispered in his ear.

"That's a promise!" the huge man roared, setting her down lightly, and patting her ample backside, while the flustered woman straightened her clothes and tried to regain her dignity.

Jondalar grinned at Ayla, and put his arm around her waist.

Again, Ayla thought, they are making a game, saying one thing with words, and something else with their actions. But this time, she understood the humour and the underlying strong love shared by Talut and Nezzie. Suddenly she realised they showed love without being obvious, too, as the Clan did, by saying one thing that meant something else. With the new insight, an important concept fell into place that clarified and resolved many questions that had bothered her, and helped her to understand humour better.

"That Talut!" Nezzie said, trying to sound stern, but her pleased smile belied her tone. "If you've got nothing else to do, you can help get the roots, Talut." Then to the young woman, she added, "I'll show you where we keep them, Ayla. The Mother was bountiful this year, it was a good season and we dug up many."

They walked around a sleeping platform to another draped archway. "Roots and fruit are stored higher up," Talut said to the visitors, pulling back another drape and showing them baskets heaped with knobby, brown-skinned, starchy groundnuts; small, pale yellow wild carrots; the succulent lower stems of cattails and bulrushes; and other produce stored at ground level around the edge of a deeper pit. "They last longer if they are kept cold, but freezing makes them soft. We keep hides in the storage pits, too, until someone is ready to work them, and some bones to make tools and a little ivory for Ranec. He says freezing keeps it fresher and easier to work. Extra ivory, and bones for the fires, are stored in the entrance room and in the pits outside."

"That reminds me, I want a knee bone of a mammoth for the stew.

That always adds richness and flavour," Nezzie said as she was filling a large basket with various vegetables. "Now where did I put those dried onion flowers?"

"I always thought that rock walls were necessary to survive a winter, for protection from the worst of the winds and storms," Jondalar said, his voice full of admiration. "We build shelters inside caves, against the walls, but you don't have caves. You don't even have many trees for wood to build shelters. You've done it all with mammoths!"

"That's why the Mammoth Hearth is sacred. We hunt other animals, but our life depends on the mammoth," Talut said.

"When I stayed with Brecie and the Willow Camp south of here, I didn't see any structures like these."

"Do you know Brecie, too?" Talut interrupted.

"Brecie and some people from her Camp pulled my brother and me out of quicksand."

"She and my sister are old friends," Talut said, "and related, through Tulie's first man. We grew up together. They call their summering place Willow Camp, but their home is Elk Camp. Summer dwellings are lighter, not like this. Lion Camp is a wintering place. Willow Camp often goes to Beran Sea for fish and shellfish and for salt to trade. What were you doing there?"

"Thonolan and I were crossing the delta of the Great Mother River. She saved our lives . . ."

"You should tell that story later. Everyone will want to hear about Brecie," Talut said.

It occurred to Jondalar that most of his stories were also about Thonolan. Whether he wanted to or not, he was going to have to talk about his brother. It wouldn't be easy, but he would have to get used to it, if he was going to talk at all.

They walked through the area of the Mammoth Hearth, which, except for the central passageway, was defined by mammoth bone partitions and leather drapes, as were all the hearths. Talut noticed Jondalar's spear-thrower.

"That was quite a demonstration you both gave," the headman said. "That bison was stopped in its tracks."

"This will do much more than you saw," Jondalar said, stopping to pick up the implement. "With it, you can throw a spear both harder and farther."

"Is that true? Maybe you can give us another demonstration," Talut said.

"I would like to, but we should go up on the steppes, to get a better feel for the range. I think you'll be surprised," Jondalar said, then turned to Ayla. "Why don't you brings yours, too?"

Outside Talut saw his sister heading towards the river, and called out to the headwoman that they were going to look at Jondalar's new way of throwing spears. They started up the slope, and by the time they reached the open plains, most of the Camp had joined them.

"How far can you throw a spear, Talut?" Jondalar asked when they reached a likely place for a demonstration. "Can you show me?"

"Of course, but why?"

"Because I want to show you that I can throw one farther," Jondalar said.

General laughter followed his statement. "You'd better pick someone else to pit yourself against. I know you're a big man, and probably strong, but no one can throw a spear farther than Talut," Barzec advised. "Why don't you just show him, Talut? Give him a fair chance to see what he's up against. Then he can compete in his own range. I could give him a good contest, maybe even Danug could."

"No," Jondalar said, with a gleam in his eye. This was shaping up into a competition. "If Talut is your best, then only Talut will do. And I would wager that I can throw a spear farther . . . except I have nothing to wager. In fact, with this," Jondalar said, holding up the narrow, flat implement shaped out of wood, "I would wager that Ayla can throw a spear farther, faster, and with better accuracy than Talut."

There was a buzzing of amazement among the assembled Camp in response to Jondalar's claim. Tulie eyed Ayla and Jondalar. They were too relaxed, too confident. It should have been obvious to them that they were no match for her brother. She doubted that they'd even be a match for her. She was nearly as tall as the fair-haired man and possibly stronger, though his long reach might give him an edge. What did they know that she didn't? She stepped forward.

"I'll give you something to wager," she said. "If you win, I will give you the right to make a reasonable claim of me, and if it's within my power, I will grant it."

"And if I lose?"

"You will grant me the same."

"Tulie, are you sure you want to wager a future claim?" Barzec asked his mate, with a worried frown. Such undefined terms were high stakes, invariably requiring more than usual payment. Not so much because the winner made unusually high demands, although that happened, but because the loser needed to be certain the wager was satisfied and no further claim could be made. Who knew what this stranger might ask?

"Against a future claim? Yes," she replied. But she did not say that she believed she could not lose either way, because if he won, if it really did what he said, they would have access to a valuable new weapon. If he lost, she'd have a claim on him. "What do you say, Jondalar?"

TMH-5

Tulie was shrewd, but Jondalar was smiling. He'd wagered for future claims before; they always added flavour to the game, and interest for the spectators. He wanted to share the secret of his discovery. He wanted to see how it would be accepted, and how it would work in a communal hunt. That was the next logical step in testing his new hunting weapon. With a little experimentation and practice, anyone could do it. That was the beauty of it. But it took time to practise and learn the new technique, which would require eager enthusiasm. The wager would help to create that . . . and he'd have a future claim on Tulie. He had no doubt of that.

"Agreed!" Jondalar said.

Ayla was watching the interplay. She didn't quite understand this wagering, except that some competition was involved, but she knew more was going on beneath the surface.

"Let's get some targets up here to sight on, and some markers," Barzec said, taking charge of the competition. "Druwez, you and Danug get some long bones for posts."

He smiled, watching the two boys racing down the slope. Danug, so much like Talut, towered over the other boy, though he was only a year older, but at thirteen years Druwez was beginning to show a stocky, compact muscularity, similar to Barzec's build.

Barzec was convinced this youngster, and little Tusie, were the progeny of his spirit, just as Deegie and Tarneg were probably Darnev's. He wasn't sure about Brinan. Eight years since his birth, but it was still hard to tell. Mut may have chosen some other spirit, not one of the two men of the Aurochs Hearth. He resembled Tulie, and had her brother's red hair, but Brinan had his own look. Darnev had felt the same way. Barzec felt a lump in his throat, sharply aware for a moment of his co-mate's absence. It wasn't the same without Darnev, Barzec thought. After two years, he still grieved as much as Tulie.

By the time mammoth leg-bone posts – with red fox tails tied to them and baskets woven with brightly dyed grasses inverted on top – were raised to mark the throwing line, the day was beginning to take on a feeling of celebration. Starting at each post, shocks of long grass, still growing, were tied together with cord at intervals, creating a wide lane. The children were racing up and down the throwing course, stamping down the grass, and delineating the space even more. Others brought spears out, then someone got an idea to stuff an old sleeping pallet with grass and dry mammoth dung, which was then marked with figures in black charcoal to use as a movable target.

During the preparations, which seemed to grow more elaborate of their own accord, Ayla started to put together a morning meal for Jondalar, Mamut and herself. Soon it included all of the Lion Hearth so Nezzie could get the stew cooking. Talut volunteered his fermented drink for dinner, which made everyone feel it was a special occasion, since he usually brought out his bouza only for guests and celebrations. Then Ranec announced he would make his special dish, which surprised Ayla to learn that he cooked, and pleased everyone else. Tornec and Deegie said if they were going to have a festival, they might as well . . . do something. It was a word that Ayla did not understand, but which was greeted with even more enthusiasm than Ranec's speciality.

By the time the morning meal was over and cleaned up, the lodge was empty. Ayla was the last to leave. Letting the drape of the outer archway fall back behind her, she noticed it was midmorning. The horses had wandered a little closer, and Whinney tossed her head and snorted a greeting to the woman as she appeared. The spears had been left up on the steppes, but she had brought her sling back, and was holding it in her hand along with a pouch of round pebbles she had selected from a gravel bed near the bend in the river. She had no waist thong around her heavy parka to tuck the sling in, and no convenient fold in a wrap in which to carry the missiles. The tunic and parka she was wearing were loose-fitting.

The whole Camp was caught up in the competition; almost everyone was already up the slope, waiting in anticipation. She started up, too, then saw Rydag waiting patiently for someone to notice him and carry him up, but the ones who usually did – Talut, Danug, and Jondalar – were already on the steppes.

Ayla smiled at the child and went to pick him up, then got an idea. Turning around, she whistled for Whinney. The mare and the colt both galloped to her, and seemed so pleased to see her Ayla realised she hadn't spent much time with them recently. There were so many people who took up her time. She resolved to go out for a ride every morning, at least while the weather held. Then she picked up Rydag and put him on the mare's back to let Whinney carry him up the steep grade.

"Hold on to her mane so you don't fall backwards," she cautioned.

He nodded agreement, grabbed hold of the thick, dark hair standing up on the back of the neck of the hay-coloured horse, and heaved a great sigh of happiness.

The tension in the air was palpable when Ayla reached the spear-throwing course. It made her realise that, for all the festivities, the contest had become serious business. The wager had made it more than a demonstration. She left Rydag on Whinney's back so he would have a good view of the activities, and stood quietly beside both horses to keep them calm. They were more comfortable around these people now, but the mare sensed the tension, she knew, and Racer always sensed his dam's moods.

The people were milling around in anticipation, some throwing spears

131

of their own down the well-trampled course. No special time had been predetermined for the contest to begin, yet, as though someone had given a signal, everyone seemed to know the precise moment to clear the way and quiet down. Talut and Jondalar were standing between the two posts eyeing the course. Tulie was beside them. Though Jondalar had originally said he would wager that even Ayla could cast a spear farther than Talut, it seemed so farfetched the comment evidently had been ignored, and she watched with avid interest from the sidelines.

Talut's spears were bigger and longer than any of the others, as though his powerful muscles needed something with weight and mass to hurl, but, Ayla recalled, the spears of the men of the Clan had been even heavier and bulkier if not as long. Ayla noticed other differences as well. Unlike Clan spears, made for thrusting, these spears, along with hers and Jondalar's, were made for throwing through the air, and were all fletched, though the Lion Camp seemed to prefer three feathers attached to the butt end of the shafts, while Jondalar used two. The spears she had made for herself while living alone in her valley had sharpened, fire-hardened points, similar to ones she had seen in the Clan. Jondalar had shaped and sharpened bone into spear points and attached them to shafts. The Mammoth Hunters seemed to prefer flint-tipped spears.

Engrossed in her careful observation of the spears that various people were holding, she almost missed Talut's first hurl. He had stepped back a few paces, then, with a running start, let fly with a mighty cast. The spear whizzed past the bystanders and landed with a solid thunk, its point nearly buried in the ground and the shaft vibrating from the impact. The admiring Camp left no doubt what they thought of their headman's feat. Even Jondalar was surprised. He had suspected Talut's throw would be long, but the big man had far exceeded his expectations. No wonder the people had doubted his claim.

Jondalar paced the distance off to get a feel for the measure he would have to beat, then went back to the throwing line. Holding the spear-thrower horizontally, he laid the back end of the spear shaft in the groove that ran down the length of the device and fitted a hole carved out of the spear butt into the small protruding hook at the back end of the thrower. He put his first two fingers through the leather finger loops at the front end, which allowed him to hold the spear and the spear-thrower at a good balance point. He sighted down the field on Talut's upright spear, then pulled back and heaved.

As he hurled, the back end of the spear-thrower raised up, in effect, extending the length of his arm by another two feet, and adding the impetus of the extra leverage to the force of the throw. His spear whistled past the onlookers, and then to their surprise, past the upright spear of their headman, and well beyond it. It landed flat and slid a short way rather than lodging in the ground. With the device, Jondalar had doubled his own previous distance, and while he had by no means doubled Talut's cast, he had exceeded it by a good measure.

Suddenly, before the Camp could catch its breath, and mark the difference between the two casts, another spear came hurtling down the course. Startled, Tulie glanced back and saw Ayla at the throwing line, spear-thrower still in hand. She looked ahead in time to see the spear land. Though Ayla hadn't quite matched Jondalar's throw, the young woman had outdistanced Talut's mighty heave, and the look on Tulie's face was sheer disbelief.

9

"You have a future claim on me, Jondalar," Tulie stated. "I admit I might have given you an outside chance to beat Talut, but never would I have believed the woman could. I'd like to see that . . . aah . . . what do you call it?"

"A spear-thrower. I don't know what else to call it. I got the idea from Ayla, when I was watching her with her sling one day. I kept thinking, if only I could throw a spear as far, and as fast, and as well as she can throw a stone with a sling. Then I started thinking about how to do it," Jondalar said.

"You've talked about her skill before. Is she really that good?" Tulie asked.

Jondalar smiled. "Ayla, why don't you get your sling and show Tulie?"

Ayla's brow creased. She wasn't used to public demonstrations. She had perfected her skill in secret, and after she was grudgingly allowed to hunt, she always went out alone. It had made both the Clan and her uncomfortable for them to see her use a hunting weapon. Jondalar was the first one who ever hunted with her, and the first to see her display her self-taught expertise. She watched the smiling man for a moment. He was relaxed, confident. She could detect no cues warning her to refuse.

She nodded her head and went to get her sling and the bag of stones from Rydag, to whom she had given them when she decided to throw the spear. The boy was smiling at her from Whinney's back, feeling a part of the excitement, delighted at the stir she had caused.

She looked around for targets. She noticed the upright mammoth rib bones and sighted on them first. The resonant, almost musical, sound of stones hitting bone left no doubt that she had hit the posts, but that was too easy. She looked around trying to find something else to hit. She was used to searching out birds and small animals to hunt, not objects to throw stones at.

Jondalar knew she could do much more than hit posts, and recalling one afternoon during the summer just past, his smile turned into a grin as he looked around, then kicked loose some clods of dirt. "Ayla," he called.

She turned and looking down the throwing lane, saw him standing with legs apart, his hands on his hips, and a clod of dirt balanced on each shoulder. She frowned. He had done something similar once before with two rocks, and she didn't like to see him put himself in jeopardy. Stones from a sling could be fatal. But, when she thought about it, she had to admit that it was more dangerous in appearance than in actuality. Two unmoving objects should be an easy target for her. She hadn't missed a shot like that in years. Why should she miss it now, just because a man happened to be supporting the objects – the man she loved?

She closed her eyes, took a deep breath, then nodded again. Picking out two stones from the pouch on the ground at her feet, she brought together the two ends of the leather strap and fitted one of the stones into the worn pocket in the middle, holding the other stone in readiness. Then she looked up.

A nervous stillness hovered over and filled the empty spaces around the onlookers. No one spoke. No one even breathed, it seemed. All was quiet, except for the screaming tension in the air.

Ayla concentrated on the man with the clumps of dirt on his shoulders. When she started to move, the entire Camp strained forward. With the lithe grace and subtle movement of a trained hunter who has learned to signal her intention as little as possible, the young woman wound up and let fly the first missile.

Even before the first stone had reached its mark, she was readying the second. The hard clump of dirt on Jondalar's right shoulder exploded with the impact of the harder stone. Then, before anyone was even aware she had cast it, the second stone followed the first, pulverising the lump of grey-brown loess soil on his left shoulder in a cloud of dust. It happened so fast some of the watchers felt as though they'd missed it, or that it was a trick of some kind.

It was a trick, a trick of skill few could have duplicated. No one had taught Ayla to use a sling. She had learned by secretly watching the men of Brun's clan, and by trial and error, and practice. She had developed the rapid-fire double-stone throw technique as a means of self-defence after she'd missed her first shot once, and barely escaped an attacking lynx. She didn't know that most people would have said it was impossible; there had been no one to tell her.

Though she didn't realise it, it was doubtful if she would ever meet anyone who could match her skill, and it didn't matter to her in the least. Pitting herself against another to see who was best was of no interest to her. Her only competition was with herself; her only desire was to better her own skill. She knew her capabilities, and when she thought of a new technique, such as the double stone throw or hunting from horseback, she tried several approaches and when she found one that seemed to work, she practised until she could do it.

In every human activity, a few people, through concentration and practice, and deep desire, can become so skilled that they excel all others. Ayla was such an expert with her sling.

There was a moment of silence as people released held breaths, then murmurs of surprise, then Ranec began slapping his thighs with his hands. Soon the entire Camp was applauding in the same way. Ayla wasn't sure what it meant, and glanced at Jondalar. He was beaming with delight, and she began to sense the applause was a sign of approval.

Tulie was applauding, too, though in a somewhat more restrained manner than some of the others, not wanting to seem too impressed, though Jondalar felt sure she was.

"If you think that was something, watch this!" he said, reaching down for two more hard lumps of dirt. He saw that Ayla was watching him, and was ready with two more stones. He threw both chunks into the air at one time. Ayla discharged one and then the other in a burst of dust and falling dirt. He threw up two more, and she blasted them before they hit the ground.

Talut's eyes were gleaming with excitement. "She is good!" he said.

"You throw two up," Jondalar said to him. Then he caught Ayla's eye and picked up two more hunks of dirt himself and held them up to show her. She reached into the pouch and came up holding four stones, two in each hand. It would take exceptional coordination just to load and throw four stones with a sling before four clods thrown up in the air fell back to earth, but to do it with enough accuracy to hit them would be a challenge that would certainly test her skill. Jondalar overheard Barzec and Manuv making a wager between themselves; Manuv was betting on Ayla. After saving little Nuvie's life, he was sure she could do anything.

Jondalar hurled the clods up, one after the other, with his strong right hand as Talut heaved two more dry clumps of dirt as high as he could into the air.

The first two, one of Jondalar's and one of Talut's, were hit in quick succession. Dirt rained down from the collision, but it took extra time to transfer the additional stones from one hand to the other. Jondalar's other clump was falling, and Talut's was slowing as it neared the top of its arc, before Ayla could ready the sling again. She sighted on the lowest target, gaining speed as it was falling, and flung a stone out of the sling. She watched it hit, waiting longer than she should have before reaching again for the loose end of the sling. She would have to hurry.

With a smooth motion, Ayla put the last stone into the sling, and then, faster than anyone could believe, whipped it out again, shattering the last lump of dirt just before it hit the ground.

The Camp burst into shouts of approval and congratulations, and thigh-slapping applause.

"That was quite a demonstration, Ayla," Tulie said, her voice warm with praise. "I don't think I've ever seen anything like it."

"I thank you," Ayla answered, flushed with pleasure from the head-woman's response, as well as her achievement. More people crowded around her, full of compliments. She smiled shyly, then looked for Jondalar, feeling a little uncomfortable with all the attention. He was talking to Wymez and Talut, who had Rugie on his shoulders and Latie at his side. He saw her looking at him, and smiled, but kept on talking.

"Ayla, how did you ever learn to handle a sling like that?" Deegie asked.

"And where? Who taught you?" Crozie asked.

"I would like to learn to do that," Danug added, shyly. The tall young man was standing behind the others looking at Ayla with adoring eyes. The first time he saw her, Ayla had awakened youthful stirrings in Danug. He thought she was the most beautiful woman he'd ever seen, and that Jondalar, whom he admired, was very lucky. But after his ride on the horse, and now her demonstration of skill, his budding interest had suddenly blossomed into a full-blown crush.

Ayla gave him a tentative smile.

"Perhaps you'll give us some instruction, when you and Jondalar show us your spear-throwers," Tulie suggested.

"Yes. I wouldn't mind knowing how to use a sling like that, but that spear-thrower really looks interesting, if it's reasonably accurate," Tornec added.

Ayla backed up. The questions and the crowding were making her nervous. "Spear-thrower is accurate . . . if hand is accurate," she said, remembering how diligently she and Jondalar had practised with the implement. Nothing was accurate by itself.

"That's always the way. The hand, and the eye, make the artist, Ayla," Ranec said, reaching for her hand and looking into her eyes. "Do you know how beautiful, how graceful you were? You are an artist with a sling."

The dark eyes that looked into hers held her, compelled her to see the strong attraction, and pulled from the woman in her a response as ancient as life itself. But her heart beat with a warning as well; this was not the right man. This was not the man she loved. The feeling Ranec drew from her was undeniable, but of a different nature.

She forced her eyes away, looked frantically around for Jondalar . . .

and found him. He was staring at them, and his vivid blue eyes were filled with fire and ice, and pain.

Ayla pulled her hand away from Ranec and backed off. It was too much. All the questions and crowding, and uncontrollable emotions overpowering her. Her stomach tightened into a knot, her chest pounded, her throat ached; she had to get away. She saw Whinney with Rydag still on her back, and without thinking, swooped up the pouch of stones with the hand that still held her sling as she raced towards the horse.

She vaulted on to the mare's back and wrapped a protective arm around the boy as she leaned forward. With the signals of pressure and movement, and the subtle, inexplicable communication between horse and woman, Whinney sensed her need to flee and, leaping to a start, raced across the open plains in a fast gallop. Racer followed behind, keeping up with his dam with no trouble.

The people of the Lion Camp were stunned. Most of them had no idea why Ayla had run for her horse, and only a few had seen her ride hard. The woman, long blonde hair flying in the wind behind her, clinging to the back of the galloping mare, was a startling and awesome sight, and more than one would have gladly traded places with Rydag. Nezzie felt a twinge of worry for him, then, feeling that Ayla wouldn't let him come to harm, she relaxed.

The boy didn't know why he had been granted this rare treat, but his eyes glistened with delight. Though the excitement caused his heart to pound a bit, with Ayla's arm around him, he felt no fear, only a breathless wonder to be racing into the wind.

Flight from the scene of her distress and the familiar feel and sound of the horse relieved Ayla's tension. As she relaxed, she noticed Rydag's heart beating against her arm with its peculiar indistinct rumbling sound, and felt a moment's concern. She wondered if she was wise to have taken him with her, then realised the heartbeat, though abnormal, was not unduly stressed.

She slowed the horse, and making a wide circle, headed back. As they neared the throwing course, they passed near a pair of ptarmigan, their mottled summer plumage not yet fully changed to winter white, concealed in the high grass. The horses flushed them out. Out of habit, as they took to the air, Ayla readied her sling, then looked down and saw that Rydag had two stones in his hand from the pouch he held in front of him. She took them, and guiding Whinney with her thighs, she knocked one of the low-flying fat fowl down from the sky, and then the other.

She halted Whinney, and holding Rydag, slid off the mare's back with the boy in her arms. She put him down and retrieved the birds, wrung their necks, and with a few stringy stalks of standing hay, she tied together their feathered feet. Though they could fly fast and far when they chose, ptarmigan did not fly south. Instead, with a heavy winter growth of white feathers, that camouflaged and warmed their bodies and made snowshoes of their feet, they endured the bitter season, feeding on seeds and twigs, and when a blizzard struck, scratched out small caves in the snow to wait it out.

Ayla put Rydag on Whinney's back again. "Will you hold the ptarmigan?" she signed.

"You will let me?" he signalled back, his sheer joy showing in more than his hand signs. He had never run fast just for the pleasure of running fast; for the first time he felt what it was like. He had never hunted or really understood the complex feelings that came from the exercise of intelligence and skill in the pursuit of sustenance for himself and his people. This was as close as he had ever come, it was as close as he ever could.

Ayla smiled, draped the birds across the horse's withers in front of Rydag, then turned and started walking towards the throwing course. Whinney followed. Ayla wasn't in a hurry to get back, she was still upset, remembering Jondalar's angry look. Why does he get so angry? One moment he was smiling at her, so pleased . . . when everyone was crowding in on her. But when Ranec . . . She flushed, remembering the dark eyes, the smooth voice. Others! she thought, shaking her head as if to clear her mind. I don't understand these Others!

The wind blowing from her back whipped tendrils of her long hair in her face. Annoyed, she brushed them out of her way with her hand. She had thought several times about braiding her hair again, the way she had worn it when she lived alone in the valley, but Jondalar liked her hair worn loose, so she left it down. It was a nuisance sometimes. Then, with a touch of irritation, she noticed that she still held her sling in her hand because she had no place to put it, no convenient thong to tuck it in. She wasn't even able to wear her medicine bag with these clothes that she wore because Jondalar liked them; she had always tied it to the thong that held her wrap closed.

She lifted her hand to push her hair out of her eyes again, and then noticed her sling. She stopped, and pulling her hair back out of her eyes, she wrapped the supple leather sling around her head. Tucking the loose end under, she smiled, pleased with herself. It seemed to work. Her hair still hung loose down her back, but the sling kept her hair out of her eyes, and her head seemed to be a good place to carry her sling.

Most people assumed Ayla's flying leap on the horse, and the fast ride ending with the quick dispatch of the ptarmigan, were part of her sling demonstration. She refrained from correcting them, but she avoided looking at Jondalar and Ranec.

Jondalar knew she was upset when she turned and ran, and was sure the fault was his. He was sorry, mentally chided himself, but was having trouble coping with his unfamiliar mixed emotions, and didn't know how to tell her. Ranec hadn't realised the depth of Ayla's distress. He knew he was provoking some feeling from her, and suspected that may have contributed to her disconcerted rush towards the horse, but he thought her actions were naïve and charming. He was finding himself even more attracted to her and wondered just how strong her feeling was for the big blond man.

Children were racing up and down the throwing course again when she returned. Nezzie came for Rydag, and took the birds as well. Ayla let the horses go. They moved off and began to graze. Ayla stayed to watch when a friendly disagreement led several people to an informal spear-throwing contest, which then led them to an activity beyond her realm of experience. They played a game. She understood competitions, contests that tested necessary skills – who could run the fastest or throw a spear the farthest – but not an activity whose object seemed to be simply enjoyment, with the testing or improving of essential skills incidental.

Several hoops were brought up from the lodge. They were about the size that would fit over a thigh, and had been made of strips of wet rawhide, braided and allowed to dry stiff, then wrapped tightly with bear grass. Sharpened feathered shafts – light spears, but not tipped with bone or flint points – were also part of the equipment.

The hoops were rolled on the ground, and the shafts thrown at them. When someone stopped a hoop by throwing a shaft through the hole and embedding it in the ground, shouts and thigh-slapping applause signalled approval. The game, which also involved the counting words and this thing called wagering, had aroused great excitement, and Ayla was fascinated. Both men and women played, but took turns rolling the hoops and throwing the shafts, as though they were opposing each other.

Finally, some conclusion was reached. Several people headed back to the lodge. Deegie, flushed with excitement, was among them. Ayla joined her.

"This day seems to be turning into a festival," Deegie said. "Contests, games, and it looks like we are going to have a real feast. Nezzie's stew, Talut's bouza, Ranec's dish. What are you going to do with the ptarmigan?"

"I have a special way I like to cook. You think I should make?"

"Why not? It would add to the feast to have another special dish."

Before they reached the lodge, preparations for the feast were evident in the delicious cooking smells that reached out with tantalising promise. Nezzie's stew was largely responsible. It was quietly bubbling in the large cooking hide, tended at the moment by Latie and Brinan, though everyone seemed to be involved in some way with food preparations. Ayla had been interested in the stew cooking arrangement, and had watched Nezzie and Deegie set it up.

In a large pothole that had been dug near a fireplace, hot coals were placed on top of ashes, accumulated from previous use, that lined the bottom. A layer of powdered, dried mammoth dung was poured on the coals, and on top of that was placed a large, thick piece of mammoth hide supported by a frame, and filled with water. The coals smouldering under the dung began to heat the water, but by the time the dung caught fire, enough of the fuel had been burned away that the hide no longer rested on it, but was supported by the frame. The liquid slowly seeping through the hide, though it had reached boiling, kept the leather from catching fire. When the fuel under the cooking hide was burned away, the stew was kept boiling by the addition of river stones that had been heated red hot in the fireplace, a chore some children were tending to.

Ayla plucked the two ptarmigan and gutted them, using a small flint knife. It had no handle, but the back had been dulled by retouching to prevent cutting the user, and a notch had been chipped away from behind the point. It was held with the thumb and index finger on either side, and the forefinger on the notch, making it easy to control. It was not a knife for heavy work, only for cutting meat or leather, and Ayla had only learned to use it since she arrived, but found it very convenient.

She had always cooked her ptarmigan in a pit lined with stones in which a fire was lit and allowed to go out before the birds were put in and covered over. But large stones were not easy to find in this region, so she decided to adapt the stewpot heating pit to her use. It was the wrong season for the greens she liked to use – coltsfoot, nettles, pigweed – and for ptarmigan eggs, or she would have stuffed the cavity with them, but some of the herbs in her medicine bag, used lightly, were good for seasoning as well as healing, and the hay she wrapped the birds in added a subtle flavour of its own. It might not have been exactly Creb's favourite dish when she was through, but the ptarmigan should taste good, she thought.

When she finished cleaning the birds, she went inside, and saw Nezzie at the first hearth starting a fire in the large fireplace.

"I would like to cook ptarmigan in hole, like you cook stew in hole. Can I have coals?" Ayla asked.

"Of course. Is there anything else you need?"

"I have dried herbs. I like fresh greens in birds. Wrong season."

"You could look in the storage room. There are some other vegetables you might think of using, and we do have some salt," Nezzie volunteered.

Salt, Ayla thought. She hadn't cooked with salt since she left the Clan. "Yes, would like salt. Maybe vegetable. Will look. Where I find hot coals?"

"I'll give you some, as soon as I get this going."

Ayla watched Nezzie make the fire, idly at first, not paying much attention, but then she found herself intrigued. She knew, but had not really thought about it before, that they did not have many trees. They burned bone for fuel, and bone did not burn very easily. Nezzie had produced a small ember from another fireplace, and with it set fire to some fluff from the seed pods of fireweed collected for tinder. She added some dried dung, which made a hotter and stronger flame, and then small shavings and chips of bone. They did not catch hold well.

Nezzie blew at the fire to keep it going while she moved a small handle the young woman had not noticed before. Ayla heard a slight whistling sound of wind, noticed a few ashes blowing around, and saw the flame burn brighter. With the hotter flame, the bone chips began to singe around the edges, then burst into flame. And Ayla suddenly realised the source of something that had been nagging at her, something she had barely noticed but that had bothered her ever since she arrived at the Lion Camp. The smell of smoke was wrong.

She had burned some dried dung occasionally and was familiar with the strong sharp odour of its smoke, but her primary fuel had been of plant origin; she was used to the smell of wood smoke. The fuel used by the Lion Camp was of animal origin. The smell of burning bone had a different character, a quality reminiscent of a roast left too long on the fire. In combination with the dried dung, which they also used in large quantities, a distinctive pungent odour permeated the entire encampment. It wasn't unpleasant, but unfamiliar, which created in her a slight uneasiness. Now that she had identified the cause, a certain undefined tension was relieved.

Ayla smiled as she watched Nezzie add more bone, and adjust the handle, which made it burn hotter.

"How you do that?" she asked. "Make fire so hot?"

"Fire needs to breathe, too, and wind is the fire's breath. The Mother taught us that when She made women keepers of the hearth. You can see it when you give your breath to fire; when you blow on it, the fire gets hotter. We dig a trench from underneath the fireplace to the outside to bring the wind in. The trench is lined with the intestines of an animal that are blown full with air before they are dried, then covered over with bone before the dirt is put back. The trench for this hearth goes out that way, under those grass mats. See?"

Ayla looked where Nezzie pointed, and nodded.

"It comes in here," the woman continued, showing her a hollow bison horn protruding out of an opening in the side of the firepit, which was lower than the level of the floor. "But you don't always want the same amount of wind. It depends how hard it is blowing outside and how much fire you want. You block the wind, or open it up here," Nezzie said, showing her the handle that was attached to a damper made of thin scapular bone.

In concept, it seemed simple enough, but it was an ingenious idea, a true technical achievement, and essential to survival. Without it the Mammoth Hunters could not have lived on the subarctic steppes, except in a few isolated locations, for all the abundance of game. At most, they would have been seasonal visitors. In a land nearly devoid of trees, and with the harsh winters only known when glaciers advance upon the land, the forced-air fireplace enabled them to burn bone, the only fuel available in quantities large enough to allow year-around occupation.

After Nezzie got the fire started, Ayla looked through the storage rooms to see if there was anything that appealed to her to stuff the ptarmigan with. She was tempted by some dried embryos from the eggs of birds, but they would probably have to be soaked, and she wasn't sure how long that would take. She thought about using wild carrots or the peas from milk vetch pods, but changed her mind.

Then she caught sight of the woven container that still held the gruel of grains and vegetables she had stone-boiled that morning. It had been put aside to lunch on as anyone wished, and had thickened and settled. She tasted it. Without salt, people preferred distinctive, spicy flavours, and she had flavoured the gruel with sage and mint, and added bitter roots, onions, and wild carrots to the mixed rye and barley grains.

With some salt, she thought, and the sunflower seeds she had seen in a storage room, and the dried currants . . . and perhaps coltsfoot and rose hips from her medicine bag, it might make an interesting filling for the ptarmigan. Ayla prepared and stuffed the birds, wrapped them in fresh-cut hay, and buried them in a pit with some bone coals and covered them with ashes. Then she went to see what other people were doing.

A lot of activity was going on near the entrance to the lodge and most of the Camp had congregated there. As she drew near, she saw that large piles of grain-bearing stalks had been collected. Some people were threshing, trampling, beating and flailing bunches of the stalks to free the grain from the straw and hulls. Others were removing the chaff that was left by tossing the grain into the air from wide, flat winnowing trays made of willow withes, to let the lighter husks blow away. Ranec was putting the grain in a mortar made from a hollowed-out mammoth foot bone extended by a section of leg bone. He picked up a mammoth tusk, severed crosswise, which served as the pestle, and began pounding the grains.

Soon Barzec took off his outer fur parka and standing opposite him, picked up the heavy tusk every other stroke, so that the work alternated back and forth between them. Tornec began clapping his hands together matching the rhythm, and Manuv picked it up with a repetitive, chanting refrain.

"I-yah, wo-wo, Ranec pounding grains go yah!

"I-yah, wo-wo, Ranec pounding grains go neh!"

Then Deegie came in on the alternating stroke harmonising with a contrasting phrase.

"Neh neh neh neh, Barzec makes it easy yah!

"Neh neh neh neh, Barzec makes it easy nah!"

Soon others were chanting or slapping their thighs, and male voices sang with Manuv while the female voices joined Deegie. Ayla felt the strong rhythm, and hummed along under her breath, not entirely sure about joining in, but enjoying it.

After a time, Wymez, who had taken off his parka, moved close beside Ranec and relieved him without missing a beat. Manuv was just as quick to change the refrain, and on the following beat sang a new line.

"Nah nah we-ye, Wymez takes the grinder yoh!"

When Barzec seemed to tire, Druwez took it from him and Deegie changed her phrase, and then Frebec took a turn.

They stopped then to check the results and poured the ground grain into a sieve basket of plaited cattail leaves, and shook it through. Then more grain was put into the bone mortar, but this time Tulie and Deegie took up the mammoth tusk pestle, and Manuv made up a refrain for both, but sang the female part in a falsetto voice that made everyone laugh. Nezzie took over from Tulie, and on impulse, Ayla stepped up beside Deegie, which brought smiles and nods.

Deegie banged the tusk down and let go. Nezzie reached out and lifted as Ayla moved into Deegie's place. Ayla heard a "yah!" as the pestle slammed down again, and grabbed the thick, slightly curved, ivory shaft. It was heavier than she expected, but she lifted it and heard Manuv sing.

"A-yah wa-wa, Ayla here is welcome nah!"

She almost dropped the mammoth tusk. She hadn't expected the spontaneous gesture of friendship, and on the next beat when the whole Lion Camp sang it out, both men and women, she was so moved she had to blink back tears. It was more than just a simple message of warmth and friendship to her; it was acceptance. She had found the Others, and they had made her welcome.

Tronie replaced Nezzie, and after a while Fralie made a move towards them, but Ayla shook her head, and the pregnant woman stepped back, readily acquiescing. Ayla was glad she did, but it confirmed her suspicion that Fralie was not feeling well. They continued to pound the grain, until Nezzie stopped them to pour it into the sieve and refill the mortar again.

This time Jondalar stepped up to take a turn at the tedious and difficult task of grinding the wild grain by hand, made easier by cooperative effort and fun. But he frowned when Ranec came forward, too. Suddenly the tension between the dark-skinned man and the blond visitor charged the friendly atmosphere with a subtle undercurrent of enmity.

When the two men, alternating the heavy tusk between them, began to pick up the pace, everyone felt it. As they continued to speed up, the chanting songs faded out, but some people began stamping their feet, and the clapping became louder and sharper. Imperceptibly, Jondalar and Ranec increased the force along with the pace, and instead of a cooperative work effort, it became a contest of strength and will. The pestle was slammed down so hard by one man it bounced back up for the other to grab and slam back down again.

Sweat beaded up on their foreheads, ran down their faces and into their eyes. It soaked their tunics as they kept pushing each other, faster, and harder, smashing the large heavy pestle into the mortar, one then the other, back and forth. It seemed to go on forever, but they wouldn't quit. They were breathing hard, showing signs of strain and fatigue, but refused to give in. Neither man was willing to yield to the other; it seemed each would rather die first.

Ayla was beside herself. They were pushing too hard. She looked at Talut with panic in her eyes. Talut nodded to Danug and they both moved towards the stubborn men who seemed determined to kill themselves.

"It's time to give someone else a turn!" Talut thundered, as he shoved Jondalar out of the way and grabbed the pestle. Danug snatched it away from Ranec on the rebound.

Both men were so dazed with exhaustion they hardly seemed to know the contest was over as they staggered away, gasping for breath. Ayla wanted to rush to their aid, but indecision held her back. She knew that somehow she was the cause of their struggle, and no matter which one she went to first, the other would lose face. The people of the Camp were worried, too, but reluctant to offer help. They were afraid that if they expressed their concern, it would acknowledge that the competition

145

between the two men was more than a game, and lend credence to a rivalry that no one was ready to take so seriously.

As Jondalar and Ranec began to recover, attention shifted back to Talut and Danug, who were still pounding the grain – and making a competition of it. A friendly competition, but not any less intense. Talut was grinning at the young copy of himself as he smashed the ivory pestle into the foot bone. Danug, unsmiling, slammed it back with grim determination.

"Good for you, Danug!" Tornec shouted.

"He doesn't stand a chance," Barzec countered.

"Danug's younger," Deegie said. "Talut will give out first."

"He doesn't have Talut's stamina," Frebec disagreed.

"He doesn't have Talut's strength yet, but Danug has the stamina," Ranec said. He had finally caught his breath enough to contribute to the commentary. Though still suffering from the exertion, he saw their contest as a way to make his competition with Jondalar seem less than the dead serious effort it had been.

"Come on, Danug!" Druwez shouted.

"You can do it!" Latie added, caught up in the enthusiasm, though she wasn't sure if she meant it for Danug or Talut.

Suddenly, with a hard bang from Danug, the foot bone cracked.

"That's just enough!" Nezzie scolded. "You don't have to pound so hard you break the mortar. Now we need a new one, and I think you should make it, Talut."

"I think you are right!" Talut said, beaming with delight. "That was a good match, Danug. You have grown strong while you were away. Did you see that boy, Nezzie?"

"Look at this!" Nezzie said, removing the contents of the mortar. "This grain has been beaten to powder! I just wanted it cracked. I was going to parch it and store it. You can't parch this to keep it."

"What kind of grain is it? I'll ask Wymez, but I think my mother's people made something from grain pounded to dust," Ranec said. "I'll take some of it, if no one else wants it."

"It's mostly wheat, but some rye and oats are mixed in. Tulie already has enough for little loaves of ground grain everyone likes, they just have to be cooked. Talut wanted some grain to mix with the cattail root starch for his bouza. But you can have it all, if you want it. You worked for it."

"Talut worked for it, too. If he wants some he can have it," Ranec said.

"Use what you want, Ranec. I'll take what's left," Talut said. "The cattail root starch I have soaking is starting to ferment. I don't know what would happen if I put this in it, but it might be interesting to try it and see."

Ayla watched both Jondalar and Ranec to assure herself that they were all right. When she saw Jondalar pull off his sweaty tunic, slosh water over himself, and go into the lodge, she knew he had suffered no ill effects. Then she felt a little foolish for worrying about him so much. He was a strong, vigorous man, after all, certainly a little exertion wouldn't hurt him, or Ranec. But she avoided both of them. She was confused by their actions, and her feelings, and she wanted some time to think.

Tronie came out of the arched doorway of the lodge, looking harried. She was holding Hartal on one hip and a shallow bone dish piled with baskets and implements on the other. Ayla hurried towards her.

"I help? Hold Hartal?" she asked.

"Oh, would you?" the young mother asked, handing the baby over to Ayla. "Everyone has been cooking and making special food today, and I wanted to make something for the feast, too, but I kept getting distracted. And then Hartal woke up. I fed him, but he's not in any mood to go back to sleep yet."

Tronie found a place to spread out near the big outside fireplace. Holding the baby, Ayla watched Tronie pour shelled sunflower seeds into the shallow bone dish from one of the baskets. With a piece of knucklebone – Ayla thought it came from a woolly rhinoceros – Tronie mashed the seeds to a paste. After a few more batches of seeds had been mashed, she filled another basket with water. She picked up two straight bone sticks, which had been carved and shaped for the purpose, and with one hand, she deftly plucked hot cooking stones from the fire. With a hiss and a cloud of steam, she plunked the stones in the water, pulled out cooled ones and added more hot until it came to a boil. Then she added the sunflower nut paste. Ayla was intrigued.

The cooking released the oil from the seeds, and with a large ladle, Tronie skimmed it and poured it into another container, this time made of birchbark. When she had skimmed off as much as she could, she added cracked wild grain of some indistinguishable variety and small black pigweed seeds to the boiling water, flavouring it with herbs, and added more cooking stones to keep it boiling. The birchbark containers were set off to the side to cool until the sunflower seed butter congealed. She gave Ayla a taste from the tip of the ladle, and she decided it was delicious.

"It's especially good on Tulie's loaf cakes," Tronie said. "That's why I wanted to make it. While I had boiling water, I thought I might as well make something for breakfast tomorrow. No one feels much like cooking the morning after a big festival, but children, at least, like to eat. Thanks so much for helping with Hartal."

"No give thanks. Is my pleasure. I not hold baby in long time," Ayla said, and realised it was true. She found herself looking at Hartal closely, comparing him in her mind with the babies of the Clan. Hartal had no brow ridges, but they weren't fully developed in Clan babies, either. His forehead was straighter and his head rounder, but they were not really so very different at this young age, she thought, except that Hartal laughed and giggled and cooed, and Clan babies did not make as many sounds.

The baby started to fuss a bit, when his mother went to wash off the implements. Ayla bounced him on her knee, then changed his position until she was looking at him. She talked to him and watched his interested response. That satisfied him for a while, but not for long. When he got ready to cry again, Ayla whistled at him. The sound surprised him and he stopped crying to listen. She whistled again, this time making a bird song.

Ayla had spent many long afternoons when she was alone in her valley practising bird whistles and calls. She had become so adept at mimicking birdsong that certain varieties came to her whistle, but those birds were not unique to the valley.

As she whistled to entertain the baby, a few birds landed nearby, and began pecking at some of the grain and seeds that had fallen from Tronie's baskets. Ayla noticed them, whistled again, and held out a finger. After some initial wariness, one brave finch hopped on her finger. Carefully, with whistles that calmed and intrigued the little creature, Ayla picked it up and brought the bird close for the baby to see. A delighted giggle and a reaching chubby fist scared it off.

Then, to her surprise, Ayla heard applause. The sound of thigh slapping caused her to look up and see the faces of most of the people of the Lion Camp smiling at her.

"How do you do it, Ayla? I know some people can imitate a bird, or an animal, but you do it so well it fools them," Tronie said. "I've never met anyone with so much control over animals."

Ayla blushed, as though she had been caught in the act of doing something . . . not right, caught in the act of being different. For all the smiles and approval, she felt uncomfortable. She didn't know how to answer Tronie's question. She didn't know how to explain that when you are entirely alone, you have all the time in the world to practise whistling like a bird. When there is no one in the world you can turn to, a horse or even a lion may give you companionship. When you don't know if there is anyone in the world like you, you seek contact with something living however you can.

10

There was a lull in the activities of the Lion Camp in the early afternoon. Though their largest meal of the day was usually around noon, most people skipped the midday meal, or picked at leftovers from the morning, in anticipation of a feast that promised to be delicious for all that it was unplanned. People were relaxing; some were napping, others checked on food now and then, a few were talking quietly, but there was a feeling of excitement in the air and everyone was looking forward to a special evening.

Inside the earthlodge, Ayla and Tronie were listening to Deegie, who was telling them the details of her visit to Branag's Camp, and the arrangements for their joining. Ayla listened with interest at first, but when the two young Mamutoi women began speaking about this relative or that friend, none of whom she knew, she got up, with a comment about checking the ptarmigan, and went out. Deegie's talk of Branag and her coming Matrimonial made Ayla think of her relationship with Jondalar. He had said he loved her, but he had never proposed a joining to her, or spoke of Matrimonials, and she wondered about it.

She went to the pit where her birds were cooking, checked to make sure she could feel heat, then noticed Jondalar and Wymez and Danug off to the side, where they usually worked, away from the paths people normally used. She knew what they were talking about, and even if she hadn't, she could have guessed. The area was littered with broken hunks and sharp chips of flint, and several large nodules of the workable stone were lying on the ground near the three toolmakers. She often wondered how they could spend so much time talking about flint. Certainly they must have said everything there was to say by now.

While she was not an expert, until Jondalar came, Ayla had made her own stone tools, which adequately served her needs. When she was young, she had often watched Droog, the Clan toolmaker, and learned by copying his techniques. But Ayla had known the first time she watched Jondalar that his skill far surpassed hers, and while there was a similarity in feeling towards the craft, and perhaps even in relative ability, Jondalar's methods and the tools he produced far outstripped the

Clan's. She was curious about the methods Wymez used, and had meant to ask if she could watch sometime. She decided this was a good time.

Jondalar was aware of her the moment she came out of the lodge, but he tried not to show it. He was sure she had been avoiding him ever since her sling demonstration on the steppes, and he didn't want to force his attentions on her if she didn't want him around. When she started in their direction, he felt a great knot of anxiety in his stomach, afraid she would change her mind, or that she only seemed to be coming towards them.

"If not disturb, I like to watch toolmaking," Ayla said.

"Of course. Sit down," Wymez said, smiling a welcome.

Jondalar visibly relaxed; his furrowed brow smoothed and the tightness of his jaws eased. Danug tried to say something when she sat down next to him, but her presence rendered him speechless. Jondalar recognised the look of adoration in his eyes, and stifled an indulgent smile. He had developed a real fondness for the youngster, and he knew calf-eyed young love was no threat to him. He could afford to feel a bit like a patronising older brother.

"Is your technique commonly used, Jondalar?" Wymez asked, obviously continuing a discussion that Ayla had interrupted.

"More or less. Most people detach blades from a prepared core to make into other tools – chisels, knives, scrapers, or points for smaller spears."

"What about bigger spears? Do you hunt mammoth?"

"Some," Jondalar said. "We don't specialise in it the way you do. Points for bigger spears are made out of bone – I like to use the foreleg of deer. A chisel is used to rough it out by cutting grooves in the general outline and going over them until it breaks free. Then it is shaved to the right shape with a scraper made on the side of a blade. They can be brought to a strong, sharp point with wet sandstone."

Ayla, who had helped him make the bone spear points they used, was impressed by their effectiveness. They were long and deadly, and pierced deep when the spears were thrown with force, particularly with the spear-thrower. Much lighter weight than the ones she had used, which were patterned after the heavy spear of the Clan, Jondalar's spears were all meant for throwing, not thrusting.

"A bone point punctures deep," Wymez said. "If you hit a vital spot, it's a quick kill, but there's not much blood. It's harder to get to a vital spot on a mammoth or rhinoceros. The fur is deep, skin is thick, if you get between ribs, there is still a lot of fat and muscle to go through. The eye is a good target, but it's small, and always moving. A mammoth can be killed with a spear in the throat, but that's dangerous. You have to get too close. A flint spear point has sharp edges. It cuts through tough skin easier, and it draws blood, and that weakens an animal. If you can make them bleed, the gut or the bladder is the best place to aim. It's not quite as quick, but a lot safer."

Ayla was fascinated. Toolmaking was interesting enough, but she had never hunted mammoth.

"You are right," Jondalar said, "but how do you make a big spear point straight? No matter what technique you use to detach a blade, it's always curved. That's the nature of the stone. You can't throw a spear with a curved point, you'd lose accuracy, you'd lose penetration, and probably half your force. That's why flint points are small. By the time you pressure-flake off enough of the underside to shape a straight point, there isn't much left."

Wymez was smiling, nodding his head in agreement. "That's true, Jondalar, but let me show you something." The older man got a heavy hide-wrapped bundle from behind him and opened it up. He picked up a huge axe head, a gigantolith the size of a sledgehammer, made from a whole nodule of flint. It had a rounded butt, and had been shaped to a rather thick cutting end that came to a point. "You've made something like this, I'm sure."

Jondalar smiled. "Yes, I've made axes, but nothing as big as that. That must be for Talut."

"Yes, I was going to haft this to a long bone for Talut . . . or maybe Danug," Wymez said, smiling at the young man. "These are used to break mammoth bones or to sever tusks. It takes a powerful man to wield one. Talut handles it like a stick. I think Danug can do the same by now."

"He can. He cut poles for me," Ayla said, looking at Danug with appreciation, which brought on a flush and a shy smile. She, too, had made and used hand axes, but not of that size.

"How do you make an axe?" Wymez continued.

"I usually start by breaking off a thick flake with a hammerstone, and retouching on both sides to give it an edge and a point."

"Ranec's mother's people, the Aterians, make a spear point with a bifacial retouch."

"Bifacial? Knapped on both sides like an axe? To get it reasonably straight, you'd have to start with a big slab of a flake, not a fine, thin blade. Wouldn't that be too clumsy for a spear point?"

"It was somewhat thick and heavy, but a definite improvement over an axe. And very effective for the animals they hunted. It's true, though. To pierce a mammoth or a rhino, you need a flint point that is long and straight, and strong, and thin. How would you do it?" Wymez asked.

"Bifacially. It's the only way. On a flake that thick, I'd use flat pressure retouch to remove fine slivers from both sides," Jondalar said,

151

thoughtfully, trying to imagine how he would make such a weapon, "but that would take tremendous control."

"Exactly. The problem is control, and the quality of the stone."

"Yes. It would have to be fresh. Dalanar, the man who taught me, lives near an exposed cliff of chalk that bears flint at ground level. Maybe some of his stone would work. But even then, it would be hard. We've made some fine axes, but I don't know how you'd make a decent spear point that way."

Wymez reached for another package wrapped in fine soft leather. He opened it carefully and exposed several flint points.

Jondalar's eyes opened in surprise. He looked up at Wymez, then at Danug who was smiling with pride for his mentor, then he picked up one of the points. He turned it over in his hands tenderly, almost caressing the beautifully worked stone.

The flint had a slippery feel, a smooth, not-quite-oily quality, and a sheen that glistened from the many facets in the sunlight. The object had the shape of a willow leaf, with near perfect symmetry in all dimensions, and it extended the full length of his hand from the base of his palm to his fingertips. Starting at one end in a point, it spread out to the breadth of four fingers in the middle, then back to a point at the other end. Turning it on edge, Jondalar saw that it did indeed lack the characteristic bowed shape of the blade tools. It was perfectly straight, with a cross-section about the thickness of his small finger.

He felt the edge professionally. Very sharp, just slightly denticulated by the scars of the many tiny flakes that had been removed. He ran his fingertips lightly over the surface and felt the small ridges left behind by the many similar tiny flakes that had been detached to give the flint point such a fine, precise shape.

"This is too beautiful to use for a weapon," Jondalar said. "This is a work of art."

"That one is not used for a weapon," Wymez said, pleased by the praise of a fellow craftsman. "I made it as a model to show the technique."

Ayla was craning her neck to look at the exquisitely crafted tools nestled in the soft leather on the ground, not daring to touch. She had never seen such beautifully made points. They were of variable sizes and types. Besides the leaf-shaped ones, there were asymmetrical shouldered points that tapered sharply back on one side to a projecting shank, which would be inserted in a handle so it could be used as a knife, and more symmetrical stemmed points with a centred tang that might be spear points or knives of another kind.

"Would you like to examine them closer?" Wymez asked.

Her eyes gleaming with wonder, she picked each one up, handling them as though they were precious jewels. They very nearly were.

"Flint is . . . smooth . . . alive," Ayla said. "Not see flint like this before."

Wymez smiled. "You have discovered the secret, Ayla," he said. "That is what makes these points possible."

"Do you have flint like this nearby?" Jondalar asked, incredulous. "I've never seen any quite like it, either."

"No, I'm afraid not. Oh, we can get good-quality flint. A large Camp to the north lives near a good flint mine. That's where Danug has been. But this stone has been specially treated . . . by fire."

"By fire!" Jondalar exclaimed.

"Yes. By fire. Heating changes the stone. Heating is what makes it feel so smooth . . ." Wymez looked at Ayla. ". . . so alive. And heating is what gives the stone its special qualities." While he was talking, he picked up a nodule of flint that showed definite signs of having been in a fire. It was sooty and charred, and the chalky outer cortex was a much deeper colour when he cracked it open with a blow from a hammerstone. "It was an accident the first time. A piece of flint fell in a fireplace. It was a big, hot fire – you know how hot a fire it takes to burn bone?"

Ayla nodded her head knowingly. Jondalar shrugged, he hadn't paid much attention, but since Ayla seemed to know, he was willing to accept it.

"I was going to roll the flint out, but Nezzie decided, since it was there, it would make a good support for a dish to catch drippings from a roast she was cooking. It turned out that the drippings caught fire, and ruined a good ivory platter. I replaced it for her, since it turned out to be such a stroke of good fortune. But I almost discarded the stone at first. It was all burnt like this, and I avoided using it until I was low on material. The first time I cracked it open, I thought it was ruined. Look at it, you can see why," Wymez said, giving them each a piece.

"The flint is darker, and it does have that slick feel," Jondalar said.

"It happened that I was experimenting with Aterian spear points trying to improve on their technique. Since I was just trying out new ideas, I thought it didn't matter if the stone was less than perfect. But as soon as I started working with it, I noticed the difference. It happened shortly after I returned, Ranec was still a boy. I've been perfecting it ever since."

"What kind of difference do you mean?" Jondalar asked.

"You try it, Jondalar, you'll see."

Jondalar picked up his hammerstone, an oval stone, dented and chipped from use, that fitted comfortably in his hand, and began knocking off the balance of the chalky cortex in preparation for working it.

"When flint is heated very hot before it is worked," Wymez continued while Jondalar worked, "control over the material is much greater. Very

153

small chips, much finer, thinner, and longer, can be removed by applying pressure. You can make the stone take almost any shape you want."

Wymez wrapped his left hand with a small rag of leather to protect it from the sharp edges, then positioned another piece of flint, recently flaked from one of the burned hunks, in his left hand, to demonstrate. With his right hand, he picked up a short, tapered bone retoucher. He placed the pointed end of the bone against the edge of the flint and pushed with a strong forward and downward motion, and detached a small, long, flat sliver of stone. He held it up. Jondalar took it from him, then experimented on his own, quite obviously surprised and pleased with the results.

"I've got to show this to Dalanar! This is unbelievable! He's improved on some of the processes – he has natural feel for working with the stone, like you, Wymez. But you can almost shave this stone. This is caused by heating?"

Wymez nodded. "I wouldn't say you can shave it. It's still stone, not quite as easy to shape as bone, but if you know how to work stone, heating makes it easier."

"I wonder what would happen with indirect percussion . . . have you tried using a piece of bone or antler with a point to direct the force of a blow from a hammerstone? You can get blades that are much longer and thinner that way."

Ayla thought that Jondalar had a natural feel for working with the stone, too. But more than that, she sensed in his enthusiasm and spontaneous desire to share this marvellous discovery with Dalanar, an aching desire to go home.

In her valley, when she had been hesitant about facing the unknown Others, she had thought Jondalar only wished to leave so he could be with other people. She had never quite understood before just how powerful was his desire to return to his home. It came as a revelation, an insight; she knew that he could never be truly happy any other place.

Though she desperately missed her son and the people she loved, Ayla hadn't felt homesickness in Jondalar's sense, as a yearning to go back to a familiar place, where people were known, and customs were comfortable. She had known when she left the Clan she could never return. To them, she was dead. If they saw her, they would think she was a malicious spirit. And now, she knew she would not go back to live with them even if she could. Though she had been with the Lion Camp only a short time, she already felt more comfortable and at home than she had in all the years she lived with the Clan. Iza had been right. She was not Clan. She was born to the Others.

Lost in thought, Ayla had missed some further discussion. Hearing Jondalar mention her name brought her back.

". . . I think Ayla's technique must be close to theirs. That's where she learned. I have seen some of their tools, but I had never seen them made before she showed me. They are not without skill, but it's a long step from preshaping a core to an intermediary punch, and that makes the difference between a heavy flake tool and a fine, light blade tool."

Wymez smiled and nodded. "Now, if we could only find a way to make a blade straight. No matter how you do it, the edge of a knife is never quite as sharp after it's been retouched."

"I've thought about that problem," Danug said, making a contribution to the discussion. "How about cutting a groove in bone or antler, and gluing in bladelets? Small enough to be almost straight?"

Jondalar thought about it for a moment. "How would you make them?"

"Couldn't you start with a small core?" Danug suggested, a little tentatively."

"That might work, Danug, but a small core could be hard to work with," Wymez said. "I've thought about starting with a bigger blade and breaking it into smaller ones . . ."

They were still talking about flint, Ayla realised. They never seemed to tire of it. The material and its potential never ceased to fascinate them. The more they learned, the more it stimulated their interest. She could appreciate flint and toolmaking, and she thought the points Wymez had shown them were finer than any she had ever seen, as much for their beauty as for their use. But she had never heard the subject discussed in such exhaustive detail. Then, she remembered her fascination with medical lore and healing magic. The times she had spent with Iza, and Uba, when the medicine woman was teaching them, were among her happiest memories.

Ayla noticed Nezzie coming out of the lodge, and got up to see if she could help. Though the three men smiled and made comments as she left, she didn't think they would even notice that she had gone.

That wasn't entirely true. Though none of the men made comments out loud, there was a break in their conversation as they watched her leave.

She's a beautiful young woman, Wymez thought. Intelligent, and knowledgeable, and interested in many things. She'd bring a high Bride Price, if she were Mamutoi. Think what status she'd bring to a mate, and pass on to her children.

Danug's thoughts ran along much the same lines, though they were not as clearly formed in his mind. Vague ideas about Bride Price and Matrimonials and even co-mating occurred to him, but he didn't think he would stand a chance. Mostly, he just wanted to be around her.

Jondalar wanted her even more. If he could have thought of a reasonable excuse, he would have gotten up and followed her. Yet he feared to clutch too tight. He remembered his feelings when women tried too hard to make him love them. Instead it made him want to avoid them, and feel pity. He did not want Ayla's pity. He wanted her love.

A choking gorge of bile rose in his throat when he saw the dark-skinned man come out of the earthlodge, and smile at her. He tried to swallow it down, to control the anger and frustration he felt. He had never known such jealousy, and he hated himself for it. He was sure Ayla would hate him, or worse, pity him, if she knew how he felt. He reached for a large nodule of flint, and with his hammerstone, he smashed it open. The piece was flawed, shot through with the white crumbly chalk of its outer cortex, but Jondalar kept hitting the stone, breaking it into smaller and smaller pieces.

Ranec saw Ayla coming from the direction of the flint-knapping area. The growing excitement and attraction he felt every time he saw her could not be denied. He had been drawn from the beginning to the perfection of form she presented to his aesthetic sense, not just as a beautiful woman to look at, but in the subtle, unstudied grace of her movements. His eye for such detail was sharp, and he could not detect the slightest posturing or affectation. She carried herself with a self-possession, an unafraid confidence, that seemed so completely natural he felt she must have been born with it, and it generated a quality he could only think of as presence.

He flashed a warm smile. It wasn't a smile that could easily be ignored, and Ayla returned it with matching warmth.

"Have your ears been filled with flint-talk?" Ranec said, making the last two words into one, and thereby giving the phrase a slightly derogatory meaning. Ayla detected the nuance, but wasn't entirely sure of its meaning, though she thought it was meant to be humorous, a joke.

"Yes. They talk flint. Making blades. Making tools. Points. Wymez make beautiful points."

"Ah, he brought out his treasures, did he? You are right, they are beautiful. I'm not always sure if he knows it, but Wymez is more than a craftsman. He is an artist."

A frown creased Ayla's forehead. She remembered he had used that word to describe her when she used her sling, and she wasn't sure if she understood the word the way he used it.

"Are you artist?" she asked.

He made a wry grimace. Her question had touched at the heart of an issue about which he had strong feelings.

His people believed that the Mother had first created a spirit world, and the spirits of all things in it were perfect. The spirits then produced living copies of themselves, to populate the ordinary world. The spirit was the model, the pattern from which all things were derived, but no copy could be as perfect as the original; not even the spirits themselves could make perfect copies, that was why each was different.

People were unique, they were closer to the Mother than other spirits. The Mother gave birth to a copy of Herself and called her Spirit Woman, then caused a Spirit Man to be born of her womb, just as each man was born of woman. Then the Great Mother caused the spirit of the perfect woman to mingle with the spirit of the perfect man, and so give birth to many different spirit children. But She Herself chose which man's spirit would mingle with a woman's before She breathed Her life force into the woman's mouth to cause pregnancy. And to a few of Her children, women and men, the Mother gave special gifts.

Ranec referred to himself as a carver, a maker of objects carved in the likeness of living or spiritual things. Carvings were useful objects. They personified living spirits, made them visual, realisable, and they were essential tools for certain rites, necessary for the ceremonies conducted by the Mamutoi. Those who could create such objects were held in great esteem; they were gifted artists, whom the Mother had chosen.

Many people thought that all carvers, indeed, all people who could create or decorate objects to make them something more than simply utilitarian, were artists, but in Ranec's opinion, not all artists were equally gifted, or perhaps they didn't give equal care to their work. The animals and figures they made were crude. He felt such representations were an insult to the spirits, and to the Mother who created them.

In Ranec's eye the finest and most perfect example of anything was beautiful, and anything beautiful was the finest and most perfect example of spirit; it was the essence of it. That was his religion. Beyond that, at the core of his aesthetic soul, he felt that beauty had an intrinsic value of its own, and he believed there was a potential for beauty in everything. While some activities or objects could be simply functional, he felt that anyone who came close to achieving perfection in any activity was an artist, and the results contained the essence of beauty. But the art was as much in the activity as in the results. Works of art were not just the finished product, but the thought, the action, the process that created them.

Ranec sought out beauty, almost as a holy quest, with his own skilled hands but more with his innately sensitive eye. He felt a need to surround himself with it, and he was beginning to view Ayla, herself, as a work of art, as the finest, most perfect expression of woman he could imagine. It was not just her appearance that made her beautiful. Beauty was not a static picture; it was essence, it was spirit, it was that which animated. It was best expressed in movement, behaviour, accomplishment. A beautiful woman was a complete and dynamic woman. Though he did not say it in so many words, Ayla was coming to represent for him a perfect incarnation of the original Spirit Woman. She was the essence of woman, the essence of beauty.

The dark man with the laughing eyes and the ironic wit, which he had learned to use to mask his deep longings, strove to create perfection and beauty in his own work. For his efforts, he was acclaimed by his people as the finest carver, an artist of true distinction, but, as with many perfectionists, he was never quite satisfied with his own creations. He would not refer to himself as an artist.

"I am a carver," he said to Ayla. Then, because he saw her puzzlement, he added, "Some people will call any carver an artist." He hesitated a moment, wondering how she would judge his work, then said, "Would you like to see some of my carvings?"

"Yes," she said.

The simple directness of her reply stopped him for a moment, then he threw his head back and laughed out loud. Of course, what else would she say? His eyes crinkling with delight, he beckoned her into the lodge.

Jondalar watched them go through the arched entrance together and felt a heaviness descend upon him. He closed his eyes and dropped his head to his chest in dejection.

The tall and handsome man had never suffered for lack of female attention, but since he lacked understanding of the quality that made him so attractive, he had no faith in it. He was a maker of tools, more comfortable with the physical than the metaphysical, better at applying his considerable intelligence to understanding the technical aspects of pressure and percussion on homogeneous crystalline silica – flint. He perceived the world in physical terms.

He expressed himself physically as well; he was better with his hands than with words. Not that he was inarticulate, just not especially gifted with words. He had learned to tell a story well enough, but he wasn't quick with glib answers and humorous retorts. He was a serious and private man, who didn't like to talk about himself, though he was a sensitive listener, which attracted confessions and confidences from others. At home, he had been renowned as a fine craftsman, but the same hands that could so carefully shape hard stone into fine tools were also skilled in the ways of a woman's body. It was another expression of his physical nature, and, though not as openly, he had been equally renowned for it. Women pursued him, and jokes were made of his "other" craft.

It was a skill he had learned as he had learned to shape flint. He knew where to touch, was receptive and responsive to subtle signals, and he derived pleasure from giving Pleasure. His hands, his eyes, his entire body, spoke more eloquently than any words he ever uttered. If Ranec had been a woman, he would have called him an artist.

Jondalar had developed genuine affection and warmth for some women, and enjoyed them all physically, but he did not love, until he met Ayla, and he did not feel confident that she truly loved him. How could she? She had no basis for comparison. He was the only man she knew until they came here. He recognised the carver as a man of distinction and considerable charm, and saw the signs of his growing attraction to Ayla. He knew that if any man could, Ranec was capable of winning Ayla's love. Jondalar had travelled half the world before he found a woman he could love. Now that he had finally found her, would he lose her so soon?

But did he deserve to lose her? Could be bring her back with him knowing how his people felt about women like her? For all his jealousy, he was beginning to wonder if he was the right person for her. He told himself that he wanted to be fair to her, but in his innermost heart he wondered if he could bear the stigma of loving the wrong woman, again.

Danug saw Jondalar's anguish and looked at Wymez with troubled eyes. Wymez only nodded knowingly. He, too, had once loved a woman of exotic beauty, but Ranec was the son of his hearth, and overdue in finding a woman to settle down and raise a family with.

Ranec led Ayla to the Hearth of the Fox. Though she had passed through it several times every day, she had studiously avoided curious looks at the private quarters; it was one custom from her life with the Clan that applied to the Lion Camp. In the open-house plan of the earthlodge, privacy was not so much a matter of closed doors as of consideration, respect, and tolerance for each other.

"Sit down," he said, motioning her to a bed platform strewn with soft, luxurious furs. She looked around, now that it was acceptable to satisfy her curiosity. Though they shared a hearth, the two men who lived on opposite sides of the central passageway had living spaces that were uniquely individual.

Across the fireplace, the toolmaker's area had a look of indifferent simplicity. There was a bed platform with a stuffed pad and furs, and a leather drape haphazardly tied above that looked as though it hadn't been untied in years. Some clothing hung from pegs, and more was piled on a section of the bed platform extending along the wall beyond the partition at the head of the bed.

The working area took up most of the room, defined by chunks, broken pieces, and chips of flint surrounding a mammoth foot bone used as both a seat and an anvil. Various stone and bone hammers and retouchers were in evidence on the extension of the bed platform at the foot. The only decorative objects were an ivory figurine of the Mother in a niche on the wall, and hanging next to it, an intricately decorated girdle from which a dried and withered grass skirt hung. Ayla knew without asking that it had belonged to Ranec's mother.

In contrast, the carver's side was tastefully sumptuous. Ranec was a collector, but a very selective one. Everything was chosen with care, and displayed to show its best qualities and to complement the whole with a textural richness. The furs on the bed invited touching, and gratified the touch with exceptional softness. The drapes on both sides, hanging in careful folds, were velvety buckskin of a deep tan shade, and smelled faintly, but pleasantly, of the pine smoke that gave them their colour. The floor was covered with mats of some aromatic grass exquisitely woven with colourful designs.

On an extension of the bed platform were baskets of various sizes and shapes; the larger ones held clothing arranged to show the decorative beadwork or feather and fur designs. In some of the baskets and hanging from pegs were carved ivory armbands and bracelets, and necklaces of animal teeth, freshwater mollusc shells, seashells, cylindrical lime tubes, natural and coloured ivory beads and pendants, and prominent among them, amber. A large flake of mammoth tusk, incised with unusual geometric designs, was on the wall. Even hunting weapons and outer clothing that hung from pegs added to the overall effect.

The more she looked, the more she saw, but the objects that seemed to reach for and hold her attention were a beautifully made ivory Mother figure in a niche, and the carvings near his work area.

Ranec watched her, noting where her eyes stayed, and knowing what she was seeing. When her eyes settled on him, he smiled. He sat down at his workbench, the lower leg bone of a mammoth sunk into the floor so that the flat, slightly concave knee joint reached just about chest high when he sat on a mat on the floor. On the curved horizontal work surface, amid a variety of burins, chisel-like flint tools which he used for carving, was an unfinished carving of a bird.

"This is the piece I'm working on," he said, watching her expression as he held it out to her.

She carefully cradled the ivory sculpture in her hands, looked at it, then turned it over and examined it closer. Then looking puzzled, she turned it one way, and then the other again. "Is bird when I look this way," she said to Ranec, "but now"—she held it up the other way—"is woman!"

"Wonderful! You saw it right away. It's something I've been trying to work out. I wanted to show the transformation of the Mother, Her spiritual form. I want to show Her when She takes on Her bird form to fly from here to the spirit world, but still as the Mother, as woman. To incorporate both forms at once!"

Ranec's dark eyes flashed, he was so excited he almost couldn't speak fast enough. Ayla smiled at his enthusiasm. It was a side of him she hadn't seen before. He usually seemed much more detached, even when he laughed. For a moment, Ranec reminded her of Jondalar when he was developing the idea for the spear-thrower. She frowned at the thought. Those summer days in the valley seemed so long ago. Now Jondalar almost never smiled, or if he did, he was angry the next moment. She had a sudden feeling that Jondalar would not like her to be there, talking to Ranec, hearing his pleasure and excitement, and that made her unhappy, and a little angry.

TMH-6

11

"Ayla, there you are," Deegie said, passing through the Fox Hearth. "We're going to start the music. Come along. You, too, Ranec."

Deegie had collected most of the Lion Camp on her way through. Ayla noticed that she carried the mammoth skull and Tornec the scapula which was painted with red ordered lines and geometric shapes, and that Deegie had used the unfamiliar word again. Ayla and Ranec followed them outside.

Wispy clouds raced across a darkening sky to the north, and the wind picked up, parting the fur on hoods and parkas, but none of the people gathering in a circle seemed to notice. The outdoor fireplace, which had been constructed with mounds of soil and a few rocks to take advantage of the prevailing north wind, burned hotter as more bone and some wood was added, but the fire was an invisible presence overpowered by the coruscating glow descending in the west.

Some large bones that seemed to have been randomly left lying around took on a planned purpose as Deegie and Tornec joined Mamut and seated themselves on them. Deegie placed the marked skull down so that it was held off the ground, supported front and back by other large bones. Tornec held the painted scapula in an upright position, and tapped it in various places with the hammer-shaped implement made of antler, adjusting the position slightly.

Ayla was astounded at the sounds they produced, different from the sounds she had heard inside. There was a sense of drum rhythms, but this sound had distinct tones, like nothing she had heard before, yet it had a hauntingly familiar quality. In variability, the tones reminded her of voice sounds, like the sounds she sometimes hummed quietly to herself, yet more distinct. Was that music?

Suddenly a voice sang out. Ayla turned and saw Barzec, his head thrown back, making a loud ululating cry that pierced the air. He dropped to a low vibrato that evoked a lump of feeling in Ayla's throat, and ended with a sharp, high-pitched burst of air, that somehow managed to leave a question hanging. In response, the three musicians began a rapid beating on the mammoth bones, which repeated the sound Barzec had made, matching it in tone and feeling in a way that Ayla couldn't explain.

Soon others joined in singing, not with words, but with tones and voice sounds, accompanied by the mammoth bone instruments. After a time, the music changed and gradually took on a different quality. It became slower, more deliberate, and the tones created a feeling of sadness. Fralie began to sing in a high, sweet voice, this time with words. She told a story of a woman who lost her mate, and whose child had died. It touched Ayla deeply, made her think of Durc, and brought tears to her eyes. When she looked up, she saw she was not alone, but she was most moved when she noticed Crozie, impassively staring ahead, her old face expressionless, but with rivulets of tears streaming down her cheeks.

As Fralie repeated the last phrases of the song, Tronie joined in, then Latie. On the next repetition, the phrase was varied, and Nezzie and Tulie, whose voice was a rich, deep contralto, sang with them. The phrase varied once more, more voices were added, and the music changed character again. It became a story of the Mother, and a legend of the people, the spirit world and their beginnings. When the women came to the place where Spirit Man was born, the men joined in, and the music alternated between the women's and the men's voices, and a friendly spirit of competition entered in.

The music became faster, more rhythmic. In a burst of exuberance, Talut pulled off his outer fur and landed in the centre of the group with feet moving, fingers snapping. Amid laughter, shouts of approval, feet stomping and thigh slapping, Talut was encouraged in an athletic dance of kicking feet and high leaps in time to the music. Not to be outdone, Barzec joined him. As they were both tiring, Ranec entered the circle. His fast-stepping dance, displaying more intricate movements, brought on more shouts and applause. Before he stopped, he called for Wymez, who hung back at first, but then encouraged by the people, began a dance whose movements had a distinctly different character to them.

Ayla was laughing and shouting with the rest, enjoying the music, singing, and dancing, but mostly the enthusiasm and fun, which filled her with good feelings. Druwez jumped in with a nimble display of acrobatics, then Brinan tried to copy him. His dance lacked the polish of his older brother's, but he was applauded for his efforts, which encouraged Crisavec to join him. Then Tusie decided she wanted to dance. Barzec, with a doting smile, took both her hands in his and danced with her. Talut, taking a cue from Barzec, found Nezzie and brought her into the circle. Jondalar tried to coax Ayla to join, but she held back, then noticing Latie looking with glistening eyes at the dancers, nudged him to see her.

"Will you show me the steps, Latie?" he asked.

She gave the tall man a grateful smile, Talut's smile, Ayla noted again, and took both his hands as they moved towards the others. She was slender and tall for her twelve years, and moved gracefully. Comparing her with the other women with an outsider's vision, Ayla thought she would be a very attractive woman one day.

More women joined the dance, and as the music changed character again, nearly everyone was moving in time to it. People began singing, and Ayla felt herself drawn forward to join hands and form a circle. With Jondalar on one side and Talut on the other, she moved forward and back and round and round, dancing and singing, as the music pushed them faster and faster.

Finally, with a last shout, the music ended. People were laughing, talking, catching their breath, the musicians as well as the dancers.

"Nezzie! Isn't that food ready yet? I've been smelling it all day, and I'm starving!" Talut shouted.

"Look at him," Nezzie said, nodding towards her great hulk of a man. "Doesn't he look like he's starving?" People chuckled. "Yes, the food is ready. We've just been waiting until everyone was ready to eat."

"Well, I'm ready," Talut replied.

While some people went to get their dishes, the ones who had cooked brought out the food. Each person's dishes were individual possessions. Plates were often flat pelvic or shoulder bones from bison or deer, cups and bowls might be tightly woven, waterproof small baskets or sometimes the cup-shaped frontal bones of deer with the antlers removed. Clamshells and other bivalves, traded for, along with salt, from people who visited or lived near the sea, were used for smaller dishes, scoops, and the smallest ones for spoons.

Mammoth pelvic bones were trays and platters. Food was served with large ladles carved from bone or ivory or antler or horn, and with straight pieces casually manipulated like tongs. Smaller straight tongs were used for eating along with the flint eating knives. Salt, rare and special so far inland, was served separately from a rare and beautiful mollusc shell.

Nezzie's stew was as rich and delicious as the aroma had proclaimed it would be, complemented by Tulie's small loaf cakes of ground grain which had been dropped in the boiling stew to cook. Though two birds did not go far in feeding the hungry Camp, everyone sampled Ayla's ptarmigan. Cooked in the ground oven, it was so tender it fell apart. Her combination of seasonings, though unusual to the palates of the Mamutoi, was well received by the Lion Camp. They ate it all. Ayla decided she liked the grain stuffing.

Ranec brought out his dish near the end of the meal, surprising everyone because it was not his usual speciality. Instead he passed around crisp little cakes. Ayla sampled one, then reached for another.

"How you make this?" she asked. "Is so good."

"Unless we can get a contest going every time, I don't think they will be too easy to make again. I used the powdered grain, mixed it with rendered mammoth fat, then added blueberries and talked Nezzie out of a little of her honey, and cooked it on hot rocks. Wymez said my mother's people used boar's fat to cook with, but he wasn't sure how. Since I don't remember even seeing a boar, I thought I'd settle for mammoth fat."

"Taste is same, almost," Ayla said, "but nothing taste like this. Disappears in mouth." Then she looked speculatively at the man with brown skin and black eyes and tight curly hair, who was, in spite of his exotic appearance, as much a Mamutoi of the Lion Camp as anyone. "Why you cook?"

He laughed. "Why not? There are only two of us at the Hearth of the Fox, and I enjoy it, though I'm glad enough to eat from Nezzie's fire most of the time. Why do you ask?"

"Men of the Clan not cook."

"A lot of men don't, if they don't have to."

"No, men of the Clan not able to cook. Not know how. Not have memories for cooking." Ayla wasn't sure if she was making herself clear, but Talut came then pouring drinks of his fermented brew, and she noticed Jondalar eyeing her trying not to look upset. She held out a bone cup and watched Talut fill it with bouza. She hadn't liked it very much the first time she tasted it, but everyone else seemed to enjoy it so much she thought she'd try it again.

After Talut had poured for everyone, he picked up his plate and went back for a third helping of stew.

"Talut! Are you going back for more?" Nezzie said, in the not-quite-scolding tone that Ayla was coming to recognise as Nezzie's way of saying she was pleased with the big headman.

"But you've outdone yourself. This is the best stew I've ever eaten."

"Exaggerating again. You're saying that so I won't call you a glutton."

"Now, Nezzie," Talut said, putting his dish down. Everyone was smiling, giving each other knowing looks. "When I say you're the best, I mean you're the best." He picked her up and nuzzled her neck.

"Talut! You big bear. Put me down."

He did as he was bid, but fondled her breast and nibbled an earlobe. "I think you're right. Who needs more stew? I think I'll finish off dinner with you. Didn't I get a promise earlier?" he replied, with feigned innocence.

"Talut! You're as bad as a bull in heat!"

"First I'm a wolverine, then I'm a bear, now I'm an aurochs." He bellowed a laugh. "But you're the lioness. Come to my hearth," he said, making motions as if he was going to pick her up and carry her off to the lodge.

Suddenly she gave in and laughed. "Oh, Talut. How dull life would be without you!"

Talut grinned, and the love and understanding in their eyes when they looked at each other spread its warmth. Ayla felt the glow, and deep in her soul she sensed that their closeness had come from learning to accept each other as they were, over a lifetime of shared experiences.

But their contentment brought disquieting thoughts to her. Would she ever know such acceptance? Would she ever understand anyone so well? She sat mulling her thoughts, staring out across the river, and shared a quiet moment with the others as the broad empty landscape staged an awesome display.

The clouds to the north had expanded their territory by the time the Lion Camp finished the feast, and presented their reflecting surfaces to a rapidly retreating sun. In a flagrant blaze of glory, they proclaimed their triumph across the far horizon, flaunting their victory in blaring banners of orange and scarlet – careless of the dark ally, the other side of day. The lofty show of flying colours, flamboyant in its brazen splendour, was a short-lived celebration. The inexorable march of night sapped the volatile brilliance, and subdued the fiery tones to sanguine shades of carmine and carnelian. Flaming pink faded to smoky lavender, was overcome by ash purple, and finally surrendered to sooty black.

The wind increased with the coming night, and the warmth and shelter of the earthlodge beckoned. In the fading light, individual dishes were scoured by each person with sand and rinsed with water. The balance of Nezzie's stew was poured into a bowl and the large cooking hide was scoured the same way, then hung over the frame to dry. Inside, outer clothing was pulled off and hung on pegs, and fireplaces were stoked and fed.

Tronie's baby, Hartal, fed and contented, went to sleep quickly, but three-year-old Nuvie, struggling to keep her eyes open, wanted to join the others who were beginning to congregate at the Mammoth Hearth. Ayla picked her up and held her when she toddled over, then carried her back to Tronie, sound asleep, before the young mother even left her hearth.

At the Hearth of the Crane, though he had eaten from his mother's dish, Ayla noticed that Fralie's two-year-old son, Tasher, wanted to nurse, then fussed and whined, which convinced Ayla that his mother's milk was gone. He had just fallen asleep when an argument erupted between Crozie and Frebec and woke him. Fralie, too tired to spend energy on anger, picked him up and held him, but seven-year-old Crisavec had a scowl on his face.

He left with Brinan and Tusie when they came through. They found Rugie and Rydag, and all five children, who were near the same age, immediately began talking with words and hand signs, and giggling. They crowded on to a vacant bed platform together next to the one shared by Ayla and Jondalar.

Druwez and Danug were huddled together near the Fox Hearth. Latie was standing nearby, but either they didn't see her or weren't talking to her. Ayla watched her turn her back on the boys finally and, with her head down, shuffle slowly towards the younger children. The girl was not yet a young woman, Ayla guessed, but not far from it. It was a time when girls wanted other girls to talk to, but there were no girls her age at the Lion Camp, and the boys were ignoring her.

"Latie, you sit with me?" she asked. Latie brightened and sat beside Ayla.

The rest of the Aurochs Hearth came through the longhouse along the passageway. Tulie and Barzec joined Talut, who was conferring with Mamut. Deegie sat on the other side of Latie, and smiled at her.

"Where's Druwez?" she asked. "I always knew if I wanted to find him, I just had to find you."

"Oh, he's talking to Danug," Latie said. "They're always together now. I was so glad when my brother came back, I thought all three of us would have so much to talk about. But they just want to talk to each other."

Deegie and Ayla caught each other's eye, and a knowing glance passed between them. The time had come when the friendships made as children needed to be looked at in a new light, and rearranged into the patterns of adult relationships when they would know each other as women and men, but it could be a confusing, lonely time. Ayla had been excluded and alienated, one way or another, for most of her life. She understood what it meant to be lonely, even when surrounded by people who loved her. Later, in her valley, she had found a way to ease a more desperate loneliness, and she recalled the yearning and excitement in the girl's eyes whenever she looked at the horses.

Ayla looked at Deegie, then at Latie to include her in the conversation. "This is so busy day. Many days so busy. I need help, could help me, Latie?" Ayla asked.

"Help you? Of course. What do you want me to do?"

"Before, every day I brush horses, go for ride. Now, I not have so much time, but horses need. Could help me? I show you."

Latie's eyes grew big and round. "You want me to help you take care of the horses?" she asked in a surprised whisper. "Oh, Ayla, could I?"

"Yes. As long as I am stay here, would be so much help," Ayla replied.

Everyone had crowded into the Mammoth Hearth. Talut and Tulie and several others were talking about the bison hunt with Mamut. The old man had made the Search, and they were discussing whether he should Search again. Since the hunt had been so successful, they wondered if another would be possible soon. He agreed to try.

The big headman passed around more of the bouza, the fermented drink he had made from the starch of cattail roots, while Mamut was preparing himself for the Search, and filled Ayla's cup. She drank most of the fermented brew he had given her outside, but felt a little guilty for throwing some away. This time, she smelled it, swished it around a few times, then took a deep breath and swallowed it down. Talut smiled and filled her cup again. She returned an insipid smile, and drank it, too. He filled her cup once more when he passed by and found it empty. She didn't want it, but it was too late to refuse. She closed her eyes and gulped the strong liquid. She was getting more used to the taste, but she still couldn't understand why everyone seemed to like it so much.

While she was waiting, a dizziness came over her, her ears buzzed, and her perceptions grew foggy. She didn't notice when Tornec began a rhythmic tonal beating on the mammoth shoulder bone; it seemed instead to have happened inside her. She shook her head and tried to pay attention. She concentrated on Mamut and watched him swallow something, and had a vague feeling that it wasn't safe. She wanted to stop him, but stayed where she was. He was Mamut, he must know what he was doing.

The tall, thin, old man with the white beard and the long white hair sat cross-legged behind another skull drum. He picked up an antler hammer and after a pause to listen, played along with Tornec, then began a chanting song. The chanting was picked up by others, and soon most of the people were deeply involved in a mesmerising sequence that consisted of repetitive phrases sung in a pulsating beat with little change in tone, alternating with arhythmic drumming that had more tonal variation than the voices. Another drum player had joined them, but Ayla only noticed that Deegie was not beside her any more.

The pounding of the drums matched the pounding in Ayla's head. Then she thought she heard more than just the chanting and the beating drums. The changing tones, the various cadences, the alterations of pitch and volume in the drumming, began to suggest voices, speaking voices, saying something she could almost, but not quite, understand. She tried to concentrate, strained to listen, but her mind wasn't clear and the harder she tried, the further from comprehension the voices of the drums seemed to be. Finally she let go, gave in to the whirling dizziness that seemed to engulf her.

Then she heard the drums, and suddenly she was swept away.

She was travelling, fast, across the bleak and frozen plains. In the empty landscape stretched out below her, all but the most distinctive features were shrouded in a veil of windblown snow. Slowly, she became aware she was not alone. A fellow traveller viewed the same scene, and in some inexplicable way, exercised a degree of control over their speed and direction.

Then, faintly, like a distant aural beacon, a point of reference, she heard voices chanting and drums talking. In a moment of clarity, she heard a word, spoken in an eerie staccato throbbing that approximated, if it did not exactly reproduce, the pitch, tone, and resonance of a human voice.

"Zzzlloooow." Then again, "Zzllooow heeerrrr."

She felt their speed slow, and looking down, saw a few bison huddled in the lee of a high river bank. The huge animals stood in stoic resignation in the driving blizzard, snow clinging to their shaggy coats, their heads lowered as though weighted down by the massive black horns that extended out. Only the steam blowing from the nostrils of their distinctively blunted faces gave a hint that they were living creatures and not features of the land.

Ayla felt herself drawn closer, close enough to count them and to notice individual animals. A young one moved a few steps to crowd against her mother; an old cow, whose left horn was broken off at the tip, shook her head and snorted; a bull pawed the ground, pushing snow aside, then nibbled on the exposed clump of withered grass. In the distance a howl could be heard; the wind, perhaps.

The view expanded again as they pulled back, and she caught a glimpse of silent four-legged shapes moving with stealth and purpose. The river flowed between twin outcrops below the huddled bison. Upstream, the floodplain where the bison had sought shelter narrowed between high banks and the river rushed through a steep gorge of jagged rock, then gushed out in rapids and small waterfalls. The only outlet was a steep rocky defile, a runoff for spring floods, that led back up to the steppes.

"Hhooomme."

The long vowel of the word resonated in Ayla's ear with intensified vibrations, and then she was moving again, streaking over the plains.

"Ayla! Are you all right?" Jondalar said.

Ayla felt a spastic jump wrench her body, then opened her eyes to see a pair of startling blue ones looking at her with a worried frown.

"Uh . . . Yes. I think so."

"What happened? Latie said you fell back on the bed, then got stiff and then started jerking. After that you went to sleep, and no one could wake you."

"I don't know . . ."

"You came with me, of course, Ayla." They both turned at Mamut's voice.

"I go with you? Where?" Ayla asked.

The old man gave her a searching look. She's frightened, he thought. No wonder, she didn't expect it. It's fearful enough the first time when you're prepared for it. But I didn't think to prepare her. I didn't suspect her natural ability would be so great. She didn't even take the somuti. Her gift is too powerful. She must be trained, for her own protection, but how much can I tell her now? I don't want her to think of her Talent as a burden she must bear all her life. I want her to know it is a gift, even though it carries a heavy responsibility . . . but She doesn't usually bestow Her Gifts on those who cannot accept them. The Mother must have a special purpose for this young woman.

"Where do you think we went, Ayla?" the old shaman asked.

"Not sure. Outside . . . I was in blizzard, and I see bison . . . with broken horn . . . by river."

"You saw clearly. I was surprised when I felt you with me. But I should have realised it might happen, I knew you had potential. You have a gift, Ayla, but you need training, guidance."

"A gift?" Ayla asked, sitting up. She felt a chill, and for an instant, a shock of fear. She didn't want any gifts. She only wanted a mate and children, like Deegie, or any other woman. "What kind of gift, Mamut?"

Jondalar saw her face pale. She looks so scared, and so vulnerable, he thought, putting his arm around her. He wanted only to hold her, to protect her from harm, to love her. Ayla leaned into his warmth and felt her apprehension lessen. Mamut noted the subtle interactions and added them to his considerations about this young woman of mystery who had suddenly appeared in their midst. Why, he wondered, in their midst?

He didn't believe it was chance that led Ayla to the Lion Camp. Accident or coincidence did not figure largely in his conception of the world. The Mamut was convinced that everything had a purpose, a directing guidance, a reason for being, whether or not he understood what it was, and he was sure the Mother had a reason for directing Ayla to them. He had made some astute guesses about her, and now that he knew more about her background, he wondered if part of the reason she was sent to them was because of him. He knew it was likely that he, more than anyone, would understand her.

170

"I'm not sure what kind of gift, Ayla. A gift from the Mother can take many forms. It seems you have a gift for Healing. Probably your way with animals is a gift as well."

Ayla smiled. If the healing magic she learned from Iza was a gift, she didn't mind that. And if Whinney and Racer and Baby were gifts from the Mother, she was grateful. She already believed the Spirit of the Great Cave Lion had sent them to her. Maybe the Mother had something to do with it, too.

"And from what I learned today, I would say you have a Gift for Searching. The Mother has been lavish with Her Gifts to you," Mamut said.

Jondalar's forehead furrowed with concern. Too much attention from Doni was not necessarily desirable. He had been told often enough how well-favoured he was; it hadn't brought him much happiness. Suddenly he remembered the words of the old white-haired Healer who had Served the Mother for the people of the Sharamudoi. The Shamud had told him once that the Mother favoured him so much no woman could refuse him, not even the Mother Herself could refuse him – that was his gift – but he warned him to be wary. Gifts from the Mother were not an unmixed blessing, they put one in Her debt. Did that mean Ayla was in Her debt?

Ayla wasn't sure if she liked the last gift very much. "I not know Mother, or gifts. I think Cave Lion, my totem, send Whinney."

Mamut looked surprised. "The Cave Lion is your totem?"

Ayla noticed his expression, and recalled how difficult it had been for the Clan to believe that a female could have a powerful male totem protecting her. "Yes. Mog-ur told me. Cave Lion choose me, and make mark. I show you," Ayla explained. She untied the waist thong of the legged garment, and lowered the flap enough to expose her left thigh, and the four parallel scars made by a sharp claw, evidence of her encounter with a cave lion.

The marks were old, long healed, Mamut noted. She must have been quite young. How had a young girl escaped from a cave lion? "How did you get that mark?" he asked.

"I not remember . . . but have dream."

Mamut was interested. "A dream?" he encouraged.

"Comes back, sometimes. I am in dark place, small place. Light comes in small opening. Then," she closed her eyes and swallowed, "something block light. I am frightened. Then big lion claw come in, sharp nails. I scream, wake up."

"I have had a dream about cave lions recently," Mamut said. "That's why I was so interested in your dream. I dreamed of a pride of cave lions, sunning themselves out on the steppes on a hot summer day.

There are two cubs. One of them, a she-cub, tries to play with the male, a big one with a reddish mane. She reaches up with a paw, and bats his face, gently, more like she just wants to touch him. The big male shoves her aside, and then holds her down with a huge forearm, and washes her with his long raspy tongue."

Both Ayla and Jondalar listened, entranced.

"Then, suddenly," Mamut continued, "there is a disturbance. A herd of reindeer is running straight at them. At first I thought they were attacking – dreams often have deeper meaning than they seem – but these deer are in a panic, and when they see the lions, they scatter. In the process, the she-cub's brother gets trampled. When it's over, the lioness tries to get the little male to get up, but she can't revive him, so finally she leaves with just the little she-cub and the rest of the pride."

Ayla was sitting in a state of shock.

"What's wrong, Ayla?" Mamut asked.

"Baby! Baby was brother. I chase reindeer, hunting. Later, I find little cub, hurt. Bring to cave. Heal him. Raise him like baby."

"The cave lion you raised had been trampled by reindeer?" It was Mamut's turn to feel shock. This could not be merely coincidence or similarity of environment. This had powerful significance. He had felt the cave lion dream should be interpreted for its symbolic values, but there was more meaning here than he had realised. This went beyond Searching, beyond his previous experience. He would have to think deeply about it, and he felt he needed to know more. "Ayla, if you wouldn't mind answering . . ."

They were interrupted by loud arguing.

"You don't care about Fralie! You didn't even pay a decent Bride Price!" Crozie screeched.

"And you don't care about anything but your status! I'm tired of hearing about her low Bride Price. I paid what you asked when no one else would."

"What do you mean, no one else would? You begged me for her. You said you'd take care of her and her children. You said you'd welcome me to your hearth . . ."

"Haven't I? Haven't I done that?" Frebec shouted.

"You call this making me welcome? When have you shown your respect? When have you honoured me as a mother?"

"When have you shown me respect? Whatever I say, you argue about."

"If you ever said something intelligent, no one would need to argue. Fralie deserves more. Look at her, full of the Mother's blessing . . ."

"Mother, Frebec, please, stop fighting," Fralie interjected. "I just want to rest . . ."

She looked drawn and pale, and she worried Ayla. As the argument raged, the medicine woman in her could see how it distressed the pregnant woman. She got up and was drawn to the Hearth of the Crane.

"Can't you see Fralie upset?" Ayla said when both the old woman and the man stopped just long enough for her to speak. "She need help. You not help. You make sick. Not good, this fighting, for pregnant woman. Make lose baby."

Both Crozie and Frebec looked at her with surprise, but Crozie was quicker to recover.

"See, didn't I tell you? You don't care about Fralie. You don't even want her to talk to this woman who knows something about it. If she loses the baby, it will be your fault!"

"What does she know about it!" Frebec sneered. "Raised by a bunch of dirty animals, what can she know about medicine? Then she brings animals here. She's nothing but an animal herself. You're right, I'm not going to let Fralie near this abomination. Who knows what evil spirits she has brought into this lodge? If Fralie loses the baby it will be her fault! Her and her Mother-damned flatheads!"

Ayla staggered back as though she had been dealt a physical blow. The force of the vituperative attack took her breath away, and rendered the rest of the Camp speechless. In the stunned silence, she gasped a strangled, sobbing cry, turned and ran out through the lodge. Jondalar grabbed her parka, and his, and ran after her.

Ayla pushed through the heavy drape of the outer archway into the teeth of screaming wind. The ominous storm that had been threatening all day brought no rain or snow, but howled with fierce intensity beyond the thick walls of the earthlodge. With no barrier to check their savage blast, the difference in atmospheric pressures caused by the great walls of glacial ice to the north created winds of hurricane force across the vast open steppes.

She whistled for Whinney, and heard an answering neigh close by. Coming out of the dark on the lee side of the longhouse, the mare and her colt appeared.

"Ayla! You weren't thinking of going for a ride in this wind storm, I hope," Jondalar said, coming out of the lodge. "Here, I brought your parka. It's cold out here. You must be freezing already."

"Oh, Jondalar. I can't stay here," she cried.

"Put your parka on, Ayla," he insisted, helping to pull it over her head. Then he took her in his arms. He had expected a scene such as the one Frebec had just made, much earlier. He knew it was bound to happen when she talked so openly about her background. "You can't leave now. Not in this. Where would you go?"

"I don't know. I don't care," she sobbed. "Away from here."

173

"What about Whinney? And Racer? This is no weather for them to be out in."

Ayla clung to Jondalar without answering, but on another level of consciousness, she had noticed that the horses had sought shelter close to the earthlodge. It bothered her that she had no cave to offer them for protection from bad weather, as they were used to. And Jondalar was right. She couldn't possibly leave on a night like this.

"I don't want to stay here, Jondalar. As soon as it clears up, I want to go back to the valley."

"If you want, Ayla. We'll go back. After it clears. But now, let's go back inside."

12

"Look how much ice is clinging to their coats," Ayla said, trying to brush away with her hand the icicles hanging in matted clumps to Whinney's long shaggy hair. The mare snorted, raising a steaming cloud of warm vapour in the cold morning air, which was quickly dissipated by the sharp wind. The storm had let up, but the clouds overhead still looked ominous.

"But horses are always outside in winter. They don't usually live in caves, Ayla," Jondalar said, trying to sound reasonable.

"And many horses die in winter, even though they stay in sheltered places when the weather is bad. Whinney and Racer have always had a warm and dry place when they wanted one. They don't live with a herd, they aren't used to being out all the time. This is not a good place for them . . . and it's not a good place for me. You said we could leave any time. I want to go back to the valley."

"Ayla, haven't we been made welcome here? Haven't most people been kind and generous?"

"Yes, we were welcomed. The Mamutoi try to be generous to their guests, but we are only visitors here, and it's time to leave."

Jondalar's forehead wrinkled with concern as he looked down and scuffed his foot. He wanted to say something, but didn't quite know how. "Ayla . . . ah . . . I told you something like this might happen if you . . . if you talked about the . . . ah . . . people you lived with. Most people don't think about . . . them the way you do." He looked up. "If you just hadn't said anything . . ."

"I would have died if it hadn't been for the Clan, Jondalar! Are you saying I should be ashamed of the people who took care of me? Do you think Iza was less human than Nezzie?" Ayla stormed.

"No, no, I didn't mean that, Ayla. I'm not saying you should be ashamed, I'm just saying . . . I mean . . . you don't have to talk about them to people who don't understand."

"I'm not sure you understand. Who do you think I should talk about when people ask who I am? Who my people are? Where I come from? I am not Clan any more – Broud cursed me, to them I am dead – but I wish I could be! At least they finally accepted me as a medicine woman. They wouldn't keep me from helping a woman who needs help. Do you know how terrible it is to see her suffer and not be allowed to help? I am a medicine woman, Jondalar!" she said with a cry of frustrated helplessness, and angrily turned back to the horse.

Latie stepped out of the entrance to the earthlodge, and seeing Ayla with the horses, approached eagerly. "What can I do to help?" she asked, smiling broadly.

Ayla recalled her request for help the evening before, and tried to compose herself. "Not think I need help now. Not stay, go back to valley soon," she said, speaking in the girl's language.

Latie was crushed. "Oh . . . well . . . I guess I'd be in the way, then," she said, starting back to the archway.

Ayla saw her disappointment. "But horses need coat brushed. Full of ice. Maybe could help today?"

"Oh, yes," the girl said, smiling again. "What can I do?"

"See, there, on ground near lodge, dry stalks?"

"You mean this teasel?" Latie asked, picking up a stiff stem with a rounded spiny dried top.

"Yes, I get from river bank. Top make good brush. Break off, like this. Wrap hand with small piece leather. Make easier to hold," Ayla explained. Then she led her to Racer and showed the girl how to hold the teasel to curry the shaggy winter coat of the young horse. Jondalar stayed nearby to keep him calm until he became accustomed to the unfamiliar girl when Ayla went back to breaking up and brushing away the ice clinging to Whinney.

Latie's presence temporarily ended their talk about leaving, and Jondalar was grateful for it. He felt he had said more than he should have, and said it badly, and now was at a loss for words. He didn't want Ayla to go under these circumstances. She might never want to leave the valley again if she went back now. As much as he loved her, he didn't know if he could stand to spend the rest of his life with no other people. He didn't think she should, either. She has been getting along so well, he thought. She wouldn't have any trouble fitting in anywhere, even with the Zelandonii. If only she wouldn't talk about . . . but she's right. What is she supposed to say when someone asks who her people are? He knew that if he took her home with him, everyone would ask.

"Do you always brush the ice out of their coats, Ayla?" Latie asked.

"No, not always. At valley, horses come in cave when bad weather. Here, no place for horses," Ayla said. "I leave soon. Go back to valley, when weather clear."

Inside the lodge, Nezzie had walked through the cooking hearth and the entrance foyer on her way out, but as she approached the outer archway, she heard them talking outside, and stopped to listen. She had been afraid Ayla might want to leave after the trouble the night before, and that would mean no more sign language lesssons for Rydag and the Camp. The woman had already noticed the difference in the way people treated him, now that they could talk to him. Except Frebec, of course. I'm sorry I asked Talut to invite them to join us . . . except where would Fralie be now if I hadn't? She's not well; this pregnancy is hard on her.

"Why do you have to leave, Ayla?" Latie asked. "We could make a shelter for them here."

"She's right. It wouldn't be hard to set up a tent, or lean-to, or something near the entrance to protect them from the worst winds and snows," Jondalar added.

"I think Frebec not like to have *animal* so close," Ayla said.

"Frebec is only one person, Ayla," Jondalar said.

"But Frebec is Mamutoi. I am not."

No one refuted her statement, but Latie blushed with shame for her Camp.

Inside, Nezzie hurried back to the Lion Hearth. Talut, just waking up, flung back the furs, swung his huge legs over the edge of the bed platform and sat up. He scratched his beard, stretched his arms in a wide reach and opened his mouth in a terrific yawn, and then made a grimace of pain and held his head in his hands for a moment. He looked up and saw Nezzie, and smiled sheepishly.

"I drank too much bouza last night," he announced. Getting up, he reached for his tunic and pulled it on.

"Talut, Ayla is planning to leave as soon as the weather clears," Nezzie said.

The big man scowled. "I was afraid she might. It's too bad. I was hoping they would winter with us."

"Can't we do anything? Why should Frebec's bad temper drive them away when everyone else wants them to stay?"

"I don't know what we can do. Have you talked to her, Nezzie?"

"No. I heard her talking outside. She told Latie there was no place here to shelter the horses, they were used to coming in her cave when the weather was bad. Latie said we could make a shelter, and Jondalar suggested a tent or something near the entrance. Then Ayla said she didn't think Frebec would like to have an animal so close, and I know she didn't mean the horses."

Talut headed for the entrance and Nezzie walked along. "We probably could make something for the horses," he said, "but if she wants to go, we can't force her to stay. She's not even Mamutoi, and Jondalar is Zel . . . Zella . . . whatever it is."

Nezzie stopped him. "Couldn't we make her a Mamutoi? She says she has no people. We could adopt her, then you and Tulie could make the ceremony to bring her into the Lion Camp."

Talut paused, considering. "I'm not sure, Nezzie. You don't make just anyone Mamutoi. Everyone would have to agree, and we'd need some good reasons to explain it to the Council at the Summer Meeting. Besides, you said she's leaving," Talut said, then pushed the drape aside and hurried to the gully.

Nezzie stood just outside the archway watching Talut's back, then shifted her gaze to the tall blonde woman who was combing the thick coat of the hay-coloured horse. Pausing to study her carefully, Nezzie wondered who she really was. If Ayla had lost her family on the peninsula to the south, they could have been Mamutoi. Several Camps summered near Beran Sea, and the peninsula wasn't much farther, but somehow the older woman doubted it. Mamutoi knew that was flathead territory and stayed away as a rule, and there was something about her that didn't quite look Mamutoi. Perhaps her family had been Sharamudoi, those river people to the west that Jondalar stayed with, or maybe Sungaea, the people who lived northeast, but she didn't know if they travelled as far south as the sea. Maybe her people had been strangers travelling from some other place. It was hard to say, but one thing was certain. Ayla was not a flathead . . . and yet they took her in.

Barzec and Tornec came out of the lodge followed by Danug and Druwez. They motioned morning greetings to Nezzie in the way Ayla had shown them; it was becoming customary with the Lion Camp, and Nezzie encouraged it. Rydag came out next, motioned his greeting and smiled at her. She motioned and smiled back, but when she hugged him, her smile faded. Rydag didn't look well. He was puffy and pale and seemed more tired than usual. Perhaps he was getting sick.

"Jondalar! There you are," Barzec said. "I've made one of those throwers. We were going to try it out up on the steppes. I told Tornec a little exercise would help him get over his headache from drinking too much last night. Care to come along?"

Jondalar glanced at Ayla. It wasn't likely they were going to get anything resolved this morning, and Racer seemed to be quite content to have Latie giving him attention.

"All right. I'll get mine," Jondalar said.

While they waited, Ayla noticed that both Danug and Druwez seemed to be avoiding Latie's efforts to get their attention, though the gangly red-haired young man smiled shyly at her. Latie watched after her brother and her cousin with unhappy eyes when they left with the men.

"They could have asked me to go along," she mumbled under her breath, then turned determinedly back to brushing Racer.

"You want learn spear-thrower, Latie?" Ayla asked, remembering

178

early days when she watched after departing hunters wishing she could go along.

"They could have asked me. I always beat Druwez at Hoops and Darts, but they wouldn't even look at me," Latie said.

"I will show, if you want, Latie. After horses brushed," Ayla said.

Latie looked up at Ayla. She remembered the woman's surprising demonstrations with the spear-thrower and sling, and had noticed Danug smiling at her. Then a thought occurred to her. Ayla didn't try to call attention to herself, she just went ahead and did what she wanted to do, but she was so good at what she did, people had to pay attention to her.

"I would like you to show me, Ayla," she said. Then, after a pause, she asked, "How did you get so good? I mean with the spear-thrower and the sling?"

Ayla thought, then said, "I want to very much, and I practise . . . very much."

Talut came walking up from the direction of the river, his hair and beard wet, his eyes half closed.

"Oooh, my head," he said with an exaggerated moan.

"Talut, why did you get your head wet? In this weather, you'll get sick," Nezzie said.

"I am sick. I dunked my head in cold water to try to get rid of this headache. Oooh."

"No one forced you to drink so much. Go inside and dry off."

Ayla looked at him with concern, a little surprised that Nezzie seemed to feel so little sympathy for him. She'd had a headache and felt a little ill when she woke up, too. Was it caused by the drink? The bouza that everyone liked so well?

Whinney lifted her head and nickered, then bumped her. The ice on the horses' coats did not hurt them, though a big build-up could be heavy, but they enjoyed the brushing and the attention, and the mare had noticed that Ayla had paused, lost in thought.

"Whinney, stop that. You just want more attention, don't you?" she said, using the form of communication she usually did with the horse.

Though she'd heard it before, Latie was still a little startled by the perfect imitation of Whinney's nicker that Ayla made, and noticed the sign language now that she was more accustomed to it, though she wasn't sure she understood the gestures.

"You can talk to horses!" the girl said.

"Whinney is friend," Ayla said, saying the horse's name the way Jondalar did because the people of the Camp seemed more comfortable hearing a word rather than a whinny. "For long time, only friend." She patted the mare, then looked over the coat of the young horse and patted him. "I think enough brush. Now we get spear-thrower and go practise."

They went into the earthlodge, passing by Talut, who was looking miserable, on their way to the fourth hearth. Ayla picked up her spear-thrower and a handful of spears, and on her way out, noticed the leftover yarrow tea she had made for her morning headache. The dried flower umbel and brittle feathery leaves of the plant still clung to a stalk that had been growing near the teasel. Spicy and aromatic when fresh, the yarrow which had grown near the river was sapped of its potency by rain and sun, but it reminded her of some she had prepared and dried earlier. She had an upset stomach along with her headache, so she decided to use it as well as the willow bark.

Perhaps it would help Talut, she thought, though from the sound of his complaints she wondered if the preparation of ergot she made for particularly bad headaches might be better. That was very powerful medicine, though.

"Take this, Talut. For headache," she said on the way out. He smiled weakly, and took the cup and drank it down, not really expecting much, but glad for the sympathy which no one else seemed disposed to offer.

The blonde woman and girl walked up the slope together, heading for the trampled track where the contests had been held. When they reached the level ground of the steppes, they saw that the four men who had gone up earlier were practising at one end; they headed for the opposite end. Whinney and Racer trailed along behind. Latie smiled at the dark brown horse when he nickered at her and tossed his head. Then he settled down to graze beside his dam, while Ayla showed Latie how to cast a spear.

"Hold like this," Ayla began, holding the narrow wooden implement that was about two feet long in a horizontal position. She put the first and second fingers of her right hand into the leather loops.

"Then put spear on," she continued, resting the shaft of a spear, perhaps six feet long, in a groove cut down the length of the implement. She fitted the hook, carved as a backstop, into the butt end of the spear, being careful not to crush the feathers. Then, holding the spear steady, she pulled back and hurled it. The long free end of the spear-thrower rose up, adding length and leverage, and the spear flew with speed and force. She gave the implement to Latie.

"Like this?" the girl said, holding the spear-thrower the way Ayla had explained. "The spear rests in this groove, and I put my fingers through the loops to hold it, and put the end against this back part."

"Good. Now throw."

Latie lobbed the spear a good distance. "It's not so hard," she said, pleased with herself.

"No. Is not hard to throw spear," Ayla agreed. "Is hard to make spear go where you want."

"You mean to be accurate. Like making the dart go in the hoop."

Ayla smiled. "Yes. Need practice, to make dart go in hoop . . . go in the hoop." She had noticed Frebec coming up to see what the men were doing, and it suddenly made her conscious of her speech. She still wasn't speaking right. She needed to practise, too, she thought. But why should it matter? She wasn't staying.

Latie practised while Ayla coached, and they both become so involved they didn't notice that the men had drifted in their direction and had stopped their practice to watch.

"That's good, Latie!" Jondalar called out after she had hit her mark. "You may turn out to be better than anyone! I think these boys got tired of practising and wanted to come and watch you instead."

Danug and Druwez looked uncomfortable. There was some truth in Jondalar's teasing, but Latie's smile was radiant. "I will be better than anyone. I'm going to practise until I am," she said.

They decided they'd had enough practising for one day, and tramped back down to the earthlodge. As they approached the tusk archway, Talut came bursting out.

"Ayla! There you are. What was in that drink you gave me?" he asked, advancing on her.

She took a step back. "Yarrow, with some alfalfa, and a little raspberry leaf, and . . ."

"Nezzie! Do you hear that? Find out how she makes it. It made my headache go away! I feel like a new man!" He looked around. "Nezzie?"

"She went down to the river with Rydag," Tulie said. "He seemed tired this morning, and Nezzie didn't think he should go so far. But he said he wanted to go with her . . . or maybe, he wanted to be with her . . . I'm not sure of the sign. I said I'd go down and help her carry him, or the water, back. I'm just on my way."

Tulie's remarks caught Ayla's attention for more than one reason. She felt some concern about the child, but more than that, she detected a distinct change in Tulie's attitude towards him. He was Rydag now, not just "the boy", and she spoke about what he had said. He had become a person to her.

"Well . . ." Talut hesitated, surprised for a moment that Nezzie wasn't in his immediate vicinity, then, reproaching himself for expecting her to be, he chuckled. "Will you tell me how to make it, Ayla?"

"Yes," she said. "I will."

He looked delighted. "If I'm going to make the bouza, then I ought to know a remedy for the morning after."

Ayla smiled. For all his size, there was something so endearing about the huge red-haired headman. She had no doubt he could be formidable if brought to anger. He was as agile and quick as he was strong, and he certainly did not lack for intelligence, but there was a gentle quality to him. He resisted anger. Though he was not averse to making a joke at someone else's expense, he laughed as often at his own foibles. He dealt with the human problems of the people with genuine concern and his compassion extended beyond his own Camp.

Suddenly a high-pitched keening pulled everyone's attention towards the river. Her first glance sent Ayla running down the slope; several people followed behind. Nezzie was kneeling over a small figure, wailing in anguish. Tulie was standing beside her looking distraught and helpless. When Ayla arrived, she saw that Rydag was unconscious.

"Nezzie?" Ayla said, asking with her expression what had happened.

"We were walking up the slope," Nezzie explained. "He started having trouble breathing. I decided I'd better carry him, but as I was putting down the waterbag, I heard him cry out in pain. When I looked up, he was lying there like that."

Ayla bent down and examined Rydag carefully, putting her hand, and then her ear, to his chest, feeling his neck near the jaw. She looked at Nezzie with troubled eyes, then turned to the headwoman.

"Tulie, carry Rydag to lodge, to Mammoth Hearth. Hurry!" she commanded.

Ayla ran back up ahead and dashed through the archways. She rushed to the platform at the foot of her bed, and pawed through her belongings until she found an unusual pouch that had been made from a whole otter skin. She dumped its contents on the bed and searched through the pile of packets and small pouches it had contained, looking at the shape of the container, the colour and type of cord that held it closed, and the number and spacing of knots in it.

Her mind raced. It's his heart, I know the trouble is his heart. It didn't sound right. What should I do? I don't know as much about the heart. No one in Brun's clan had heart problems. I must remember what Iza explained to me. And that other medicine woman at the Clan Gathering, she had two people in her clan with heart problems. First think, Iza always said, what exactly is wrong. He's pale and swollen up. He's having trouble breathing, and he's in pain. His pulse is weak. His heart must work harder, make stronger pushes. What is best to use? Datura, maybe? I don't think so. What about hellebore? Belladonna? Henbane? Foxglove? Foxglove . . . leaves of foxglove. It's so strong. It could kill him. But he will die without something strong enough to make his heart work again. Then, how much to use? Should I boil it or steep it? Oh, I wish I could remember the way Iza did. Where is my foxglove? Don't I have any?

"Ayla, what's wrong?" She looked up to see Mamut beside her.

"It's Rydag . . . his heart. They bring him. I look for . . . plant. Tall stem . . . flowers hang down . . . purple, red spots inside. Big leaves, feel like fur, underside. Make heart . . . push. You know?" Ayla felt stifled by her lack of vocabulary, but she had been more clear than she realised.

"Of course, purpurea, foxglove is another name. That's very strong . . ." Mamut watched Ayla close her eyes and take a deep breath.

"Yes, but necessary. Must think, how much . . . Here is bag! Iza say, always keep with."

Just then Tulie came in carrying the small boy. Ayla grabbed a fur off her bed, put it on the ground near the fire, and directed the woman to lay him down on it. Nezzie was right behind her, and everyone else crowded around.

"Nezzie, take off the parka. Open clothes. Talut, too much people here. Make room," Ayla directed, not even realising she was issuing commands. She opened the small leather pouch she held and sniffed the contents, and looked up at the old shaman, concerned. Then with a glance at the unconscious child, her face hardened with determination. "Mamut, need hot fire. Latie, get cooking stones, bowl of water, cup to drink."

While Nezzie loosened his clothing, Ayla bunched up more furs to put behind him and raise his head. Talut was making the people of the Camp stand back to give Rydag air, and Ayla working room. Latie was anxiously feeding the fire Mamut had made, trying to make the stones heat faster.

Ayla checked Rydag's pulse; it was hard to find. She laid her ear to his chest. His breathing was shallow and raspy. He needed help. She moved back his head, to open his air passage, then clamped her mouth over his to breathe her air into his lungs, as she had done with Nuvie.

Mamut observed her for a while. She seemed too young to have much healing skill, and certainly there had been an indecisive moment, but that had passed. Now she was calm, focusing on the child, issuing orders with quiet assurance.

He nodded to himself, then sat behind the mammoth skull drum and began a measured cadence accompanied by a low chant, which, strangely, had the effect of easing some of the strain Ayla was feeling. The healing chant was quickly picked up by the rest of the Camp; it relieved their tensions to feel they were contributing in a beneficial way. Tornec and Deegie joined in with their instruments, then Ranec appeared with rings made out of ivory that rattled. The music of drums and chanting and rattle was not loud or overpowering, but instead gently pulsing and soothing.

Finally the water boiled and Ayla measured out a quantity of dried foxglove leaves into her palm and sprinkled it on the water simmering

183

in the bowl. She waited then, letting them steep and trying to stay calm, until finally the colour and her intuitive sense told her it was right. She poured some of the liquid from the cooking bowl into a cup. Then she cradled Rydag's head in her lap, and closed her eyes for a moment. This was not medicine to be used lightly. The wrong dosage would kill him, and the strength in the leaves of each plant was variable.

She opened her eyes to see two vivid blue eyes, full of love and concern, looking back at her, and gave Jondalar a fleeting smile of gratitude. She brought the cup to her mouth and dipped her tongue into it, testing the strength of the preparation. Then she put the bitter brew to the child's lips.

He choked on the first sip, but that roused him slightly. He tried to smile his recognition of Ayla, but made a grimace of pain instead. She made him drink more, slowly, while she carefully watched his reactions: changes in skin temperature and colour, the movement of his eyes, the depth of his breathing. The people of the Lion Camp watched, too, anxiously. They hadn't realised how much the child had come to mean to them until his life was threatened. He had grown up with them, he was one of them, and recently they had begun to realise he was not so different from them.

Ayla wasn't sure when the rhythms and chanting stopped, but the quiet sound of Rydag taking a deep breath sounded like a roar of victory in the absolute silence of the tension-filled lodge.

Ayla noticed a slight flush as he took a second deep breath, and felt her apprehension ease a bit. The rhythms started again with a changed tempo, a child cried, voices murmured. She put down the cup, checked the pulse in his neck, felt his chest. He was breathing easier, and with less pain. She looked up and saw Nezzie smiling at her through eyes filled with tears. She was not alone.

Ayla held the boy until she was sure he was resting comfortably, and then held him just because she wanted to. If she half closed her eyes, she could almost forget the people of the Camp. She could almost imagine this boy, who looked so much like her son, was indeed the child to whom she had given birth. The tears that wet her cheeks were as much for herself, for the son she longed to see, as they were for the child in her arms.

Rydag fell asleep, finally. The ordeal had taken much out of him, and Ayla as well. Talut picked him up and carried him to his bed, then Jondalar helped her up. He stood with his arms around her, while she leaned against him, feeling drained and grateful for his support.

There were tears of relief in the eyes of most of the assembled Camp, but appropriate words were hard to find. They didn't know what to say to the young woman who had saved the child. They gave her smiles, nods of approval, warm touches, a few murmured comments, hardly more than sounds. More than enough for Ayla. At that moment, she would have been uncomfortable with too many words of gratitude or praise.

After Nezzie made sure Rydag was comfortably settled, she went to talk to Ayla. "I thought he was gone. I can't believe he's only sleeping," she said. "That medicine was good."

Ayla nodded. "Yes, but strong. But he should take every day, some, not too much. Should take with other medicine. I will mix for him. You make like tea, but boil little first. I will show. Give him small cup in morning, another before sleep. He will pass water at night more, until swelling down."

"Will that medicine make him well, Ayla?" Nezzie asked, hope in her voice.

Ayla reached to touch her hand, and looked directly at her. "No, Nezzie. No medicine can make him well," she replied in a firm voice that was tinged with sorrow.

Nezzie bowed her head in acquiescence. She'd known all along, but Ayla's medicine had effected such a miraculous recovery, she couldn't help but hope.

"Medicine will help. Make Rydag feel better. Not pain so much," Ayla continued. "But I not have much. Leave most medicine in valley. I not think we go for long. Mamut knows foxglove, may have some."

Mamut spoke up. "My Gift is for Searching, Ayla. I have little Gift for Healing, but the Mamut of the Wolf Camp is a good Healer. We can send someone to ask if she has some, after the weather clears. It will take a few days, though."

Ayla hoped she had enough of the heart stimulant made from the digitalis foxglove leaves to last until someone could go to get some, but wished even more that she had the rest of her own preparation with her. She wasn't sure of someone else's methods. She was always very careful to dry the large, fuzzy leaves slowly, in a cool, dark place out of the sun, to retain as much of the active principle as possible. In fact, she wished she had all her carefully prepared herbal medicines, but they were still stored in her small cave in the valley.

Just as Iza had done, Ayla always carried her otter skin medicine bag which contained certain roots and barks, leaves, flowers, fruits, and seeds. But that was little more than first aid to her. She had an entire pharmacopoeia in her cave, even though she'd lived alone and had no real use for it there. It was training and habit that caused her to collect medicinal plants as they appeared with the passing seasons. It was almost as automatic as walking. She knew of many other uses for the plant life in her environment, from fibres for cordage to food, but it was the medicinal properties that interested her most. She could hardly pass a plant she knew to have healing properties without gathering it, and she knew hundreds.

She was so familiar with the vegetation that unknown plants always intrigued her. She looked for similarities to known plants, and understood categories within larger categories. She could identify related types and families, but knew well that similar appearance did not necessarily mean similar reactions, and cautiously experimented on herself, tasting and testing with knowledge and experience.

She was also careful with dosages and methods of preparation. Ayla knew that an infusion, prepared by pouring boiling water over various leaves, flowers, or berries and letting it steep, extracted aromatic and volatile principles and essences. Boiling, which produced a decoction, withdrew the extractive, resinous, and bitter principles and was more effective on hard materials like barks, roots, and seeds. She knew how to withdraw the essential oils, gums, and resins of a herb, how to make poultices, plasters, tonics, syrups, ointments or salves using fats or thickening agents. She knew how to mix ingredients, and how to strengthen or dilute as needed.

The same process of comparison that was applied to plants revealed the similarities between animals. Ayla's knowledge of the human body and its functions was the result of a long history of drawing conclusions from trial and error, and an extensive understanding of animal anatomy derived from butchering the animals that were hunted. Their relationship to humans could be seen when accidents or injuries were sustained.

Ayla was a botanist, pharmacist, and doctor; her magic consisted of the esoteric lore passed down and improved upon by generation after generation for hundreds, thousands, perhaps millions of years of gatherers and hunters whose very existence depended on an intimate knowledge of the land on which they lived and its products.

Out of that timeless resource of unrecorded history, passed on to her through the training she had received from Iza, and aided by an inherent analytical talent and intuitive perception, Ayla could diagnose and treat most ailments and injuries. With a razor-sharp flint blade she even did minor surgical operations occasionally, but Ayla's medicine depended more on the complex active principles of healing plants. She was skilled, and her remedies were effective, but she could not perform major surgery to correct a congenital defect of the heart.

As Ayla watched the sleeping boy who looked so much like her son, she felt a deep relief and gratitude knowing that Durc had been sound and healthy when he was born – but that did not assuage the pain of having to tell Nezzie that no medicine could make Rydag well.

Later in the afternoon, Ayla sorted through her packets and pouches of herbs to prepare the mixture she had promised Nezzie she would make. Mamut silently watched her again. There could be little doubt now of her healing skills by anyone, including Frebec, though he still might not want to admit it, or Tulie, who had not been as vocal, but who, the old man knew, had been very sceptical. Ayla appeared to be an ordinary young woman, quite attractive even to his old eyes, but he was convinced there was much more to her than anyone knew; he doubted if she even knew the full extent of her potential.

What a difficult – and fascinating – life she has led, he mused. She looks so young, but she is already much older in experience than most people will ever be. How long did she live with them? How had she become so skilled in their medicine? he wondered. He knew that such knowledge was not usually taught to one not born to it, and she had been an outsider, more than most people could ever understand. Then there was her unexpected talent for Searching. What other talents might lie untapped? What knowledge not yet used? What secrets unrevealed?

Her strength comes out in a crisis; he remembered how Ayla had given orders to Tulie, and Talut. Even me, he thought with a smile, and no one objected. Leadership comes to her naturally. What adversity has tested her to give her such presence so young? The Mother has plans for her, I'm sure of it, but what about the young man, Jondalar? He is certainly well-favoured, but his gifts are not extraordinary. What is Her purpose for him?

She was putting the balance of her packages of herbs away when Mamut suddenly looked more closely at her otter skin medicine bag. It was familiar. He could close his eyes and almost see one so similar that it brought back a flood of memories.

"Ayla, may I see that?" he asked, wanting to see it more closely.

"This? My medicine bag?" she queried.

"I've always wondered how they were made."

Ayla handed him the unusual pouch, noticing the arthritic bumps in his long, thin, old hands.

The ancient shaman examined it carefully. It showed signs of wear; she'd had it for some time. It had been made, not by sewing or attaching pieces together, but from the skin of a single animal. Rather than slitting the otter's belly, which was the usual way to skin an animal, only the throat had been cut, leaving the head attached by a strip at the back. The bones and insides were drawn out through the neck and the brain case was drained, leaving it somewhat flattened. The entire skin was then cured and small holes had been cut at intervals around the neck with a stone awl for a cord to be threaded through as a drawstring. The result was a pouch of sleek, waterproof otter fur with the feet and tail still intact, and the head used as a cover flap.

187

Mamut gave it back to her. "Did you make that?"

"No. Iza make. She was medicine woman of Brun's clan, my . . . mother. She teach me since little girl, where plants grow, how to make medicine, how to use. She was sick, not go to Clan Gathering. Brun need medicine woman. Uba too young, I am only one."

Mamut nodding with understanding, then he looked at her sharply. "What was the name you said just now?"

"My mother? Iza?"

"No, the other one."

Ayla thought for a moment. "Uba?"

"Who is Uba?"

"Uba is . . . sister. Not true sister, but like sister to me. She is daughter of Iza. Now she is medicine woman . . . and mother of . . ."

"Is that a common name?" Mamut interrupted in a voice that carried an edge of excitement.

"No . . . I do not think . . . Creb name Uba. Mother of Iza's mother had same name. Creb and Iza had same mother."

"Creb! Tell me, Ayla, this Creb, did he have a bad arm and walk with a limp?"

"Yes," Ayla replied, puzzled. How could Mamut know?

"And was there another brother? Younger, but strong and healthy?"

Ayla frowned in the face of Mamut's eager questions. "Yes. Brun. He was leader."

"Great Mother! I can't believe it! Now I understand."

"I do not understand," Ayla said.

"Ayla, come, sit down. I want to tell you a story."

He led her to a place by the hearth near his bed. He perched on the edge of the platform, while she sat on a mat on the floor and looked up expectantly.

"Once, many, many years ago, when I was a very young man, I had a strange adventure that changed my life," Mamut began. Ayla felt a sudden, eerie tingling just under her skin and had a feeling that she almost knew what he was going to say.

"Manuv and I are from the same Camp. The man his mother chose for a mate was my cousin. We grew up together, and as youngsters do, we talked about making a Journey together, but the summer we were going to go, he got sick. Very sick. I was anxious to start, we'd been planning the trip for years and I kept hoping he'd get better, but the sickness lingered. Finally, near the end of the summer I decided to Journey alone. Everyone advised against it, but I was restless.

"We had planned to skirt Beran Sea and then follow the eastern shore of the big Southern Sea, much the way Wymez did. But it was so late

188

in the season, I decided to take a short cut across the peninsula and the eastern connection to the mountains."

Ayla nodded. Brun's clan had used that route to the Clan Gathering.

"I didn't tell anyone my plan. It was flathead country, and I knew I'd get a lot of objections. I thought if I was careful I could avoid any contact, but I didn't count on the accident. I'm still not sure how it happened. I was walking along a high bank of a river, almost a cliff, and the next thing I knew I slipped and fell down it. I must have been unconscious for a while. It was late afternoon when I came to. My head hurt and was none too clear, but worse was my arm. The bone was dislocated and broken, and I was in great pain.

"I stumbled along the river for a while, not sure where I was going. I'd lost my pack and didn't even think to look for it. I don't know how long I walked, but it was almost dark when I finally noticed a fire. I didn't consider that I was on the peninsula. When I saw some people near it, I headed for it.

"I can imagine their surprise when I stumbled into their midst, but by then I was so delirious I didn't know where I was. My surprise came later. I woke up in unfamiliar surroundings, with no idea how I had got there. When I discovered a poultice on my head and my arm in a sling, I remembered falling, and thought how lucky I was to have been found by a Camp with a good Healer, then the woman appeared. Perhaps you can imagine, Ayla, how shocked I was to discover I was in the Camp of a clan."

Ayla was feeling shocked herself. "You! You are man with broken arm? You know Creb and Brun?" Ayla said in stunned disbelief. A rush of feeling overwhelmed her and tears squeezed out of the corners of her eyes. It was like a message from her past.

"You have heard of me?"

"Iza told me, before she is born, her mother's mother heal man with broken arm. Man of the Others. Creb tell me, too. He said Brun let me stay with Clan because he learn from that man – from you, Mamut – Others are men, too." Ayla stopped, stared at the white hair, the wrinkled old face, of the venerable old man. "Iza walk in spirit world now. She was not born when you come . . . and Creb . . . he was boy, not yet chosen by Ursus. Creb was old man when he die . . . how can you still live?"

"I have wondered myself why the Mother chose to grant me so many seasons. I think She has just given me an answer."

13

"Talut? Talut, are you asleep?" Nezzie whispered in the big headman's ear as she shook him.

"Huh? Wha's wrong?" he said, coming abruptly awake.

"Shhh. Don't wake everybody. Talut, we can't let Ayla go now. Who will take care of Rydag the next time? I think we should adopt her, make her part of our family, make her Mamutoi."

He looked up and saw her eyes glistening a reflection of the red coals of the banked fire. "I know you care for the boy, Nezzie. I do, too. But is your love for him a reason to make a stranger one of us? What would I say to the Councils?"

"It's not just Rydag. She is a Healer. A good Healer. Do the Mamutoi have so many Healers that we can afford to let such a good one go? Look what has happened in just a few days. She saved Nuvie from choking to death . . . I know Tulie said that could just have been a technique she learned, but your sister can't say that about Rydag. Ayla knew what she was doing. That was Healing medicine. She's right about Fralie, too. Even I can see this pregnancy is hard on her, and all that fighting and arguing isn't helping. And what about your headache?"

Talut grinned. "That was more than Healing magic, that was amazing!"

"Shhhh! You'll wake the whole lodge up. Ayla is more than a Healer. Mamut says she's an untrained Searcher, too. And look at her way with animals, I wouldn't doubt if she isn't a Caller besides. Think what a benefit that would be to a Camp if it turns out that she can not only Search out animals to hunt, but Call them to her?"

"You don't know that, Nezzie. You're just guessing."

"Well, I don't have to guess about her skill with those weapons. You know she'd bring a good Bride Price if she were Mamutoi, Talut. With everything she has to offer, tell me what you think she'd be worth as the daughter of your hearth?"

"Hmmm. If she were Mamutoi, and the daughter of the Lion Hearth . . . But she may not want to become Mamutoi, Nezzie. What about the young man, Jondalar? It's obvious that there is strong feeling between them."

Nezzie had been thinking about it for some time, and she was ready. "Ask him, too."

"Both of them!" Talut exploded, sitting up.

"Hush! Keep your voice down!"

"But he has people. He says he's Zel . . . Zel . . . whatever it is."

"Zelandonii," Nezzie whispered. "But his people live a long way from here. Why should he want to make such a long trip back if he can find a home with us? You could ask him, anyway, Talut. That weapon he invented ought to be reason enough to satisfy the Councils. And Wymez says he is an expert toolmaker. If my brother gives him a recommendation, you know the Councils won't refuse."

"That's true . . . but, Nezzie," Talut said, lying down again, "how do you know they will want to stay?"

"I don't know, but you can ask, can't you?"

It was midmorning when Talut stepped out of the longhouse, and noticed Ayla and Jondalar leading the horses away from the Camp. There was no snow, but early morning hoarfrost still lingered in patches of crystal white, and their heads were wreathed in steam with each breath. Static crinkled in the dry freezing air. The woman and man were dressed for the cold in fur parkas with hoods pulled tight around their faces, and fur leggings which were tucked into footwear that was wrapped around the lower edge of the trousers and tied.

"Jondalar! Ayla! Are you leaving?" he called, hurrying to catch up with them.

Ayla nodded an affirmative reply, which made Talut lose his smile, but Jondalar explained, "We're just going to give the horses some exercise. We'll be back after noon."

He neglected to mention that they were also looking for some privacy, a place to be alone for a while to discuss, without interruption, whether to go back to Ayla's valley. Or rather, in Jondalar's mind, to talk Ayla out of wanting to go.

"Good. I'd like to arrange for some practice sessions with those spear-throwers, when the weather clears. I'd like to see how they work and what I could do with one," Talut said.

"I think you might be surprised," Jondalar replied, smiling, "at how well they work."

"Not by themselves. I'm sure they work well for either of you, but it takes some skill, and there may not be much time for practice before spring." Talut paused, considering.

Ayla waited, her hand on the mare's withers, just below her short, stiff mane. A heavy fur mitten dangled by a cord out of the sleeve of her parka. The cord was drawn up through the sleeve, through a loop at the back of the neck, down the other sleeve, and attached to the other mitten. With the cord attached to them, if the dexterity of a bare hand was needed, the mittens could be pulled off quickly, without fear of losing them. In a land of such deep cold and strong winds, a lost mitten could mean a lost hand, or a lost life. The young horse was snorting and prancing with excitement, and bumped against Jondalar impatiently. They seemed anxious to be on their way, and were waiting for him to finish only out of courtesy, Talut knew. He decided to plunge ahead anyway.

"Nezzie was talking to me last night, and this morning I spoke to some others. It would be helpful to have someone around to show us how to use those hunting weapons."

"Your hospitality has been more than generous. You know I would be happy to show anyone how to use the spear-thrower. It is small enough thanks for all you have done," Jondalar said.

Talut nodded, then went on, "Wymez tells me you are a fine flint knapper, Jondalar. The Mamutoi can always use someone who can produce good quality tools. And Ayla has many skills that would benefit any Camp. She is not only proficient with the spear-thrower and that sling of hers – you were right," he turned from Jondalar to Ayla – "she is a Healer. We would like you to stay."

"I was hoping we might winter with you, Talut, and I appreciate your offer, but I'm not sure how Ayla feels about it," Jondalar replied, smiling, feeling that Talut's offer couldn't have come at a better time. How could she leave now? Certainly Talut's offer meant more than Frebec's nastiness.

Talut continued, addressing his remarks to the young woman. "Ayla, you have no people now, and Jondalar lives far away, perhaps farther than he cares to travel if he can find a home here. We would like you both to stay, not only through the winter, but always. I invite you to become one of us, and I speak for more than myself. Tulie and Barzec would be willing to adopt Jondalar to the Aurochs Hearth, and Nezzie and I want you to become a daughter of the Lion Hearth. Since Tulie is headwoman, and I am headman, that would give you a high standing among the Mamutoi."

"You mean, you want to adopt us? You want us to become Mamutoi?" Jondalar blurted, a little stunned, and flushed with surprise.

"You want me? You want adopt me?" Ayla asked. She had been listening to the conversation, frowning with concentration, not entirely sure she believed what she was hearing. "You want make Ayla of No People, Ayla of the Mamutoi?"

The big man smiled. "Yes."

Jondalar was at a loss for words. Hospitality to guests might be a matter of custom, and of pride, but no people made a custom of asking strangers to join their tribe, their family, without serious consideration.

"I . . . uh . . . don't know . . . what to say," he said. "I am very honoured. It is a great compliment to be asked."

"I know you need some time to think about it. Both of you," Talut said. "I would be surprised if you didn't. We haven't mentioned it to everyone, and the whole Camp must agree, but that shouldn't be a problem with all you bring, and Tulie and I both speaking for you. I wanted to ask you first. If you agree, I will call a meeting."

They silently watched the big headman walk back to the earthlodge. They had planned to find a place to talk, each hoping to resolve problems that they felt had begun to arise between them. Talut's unexpected invitation had added an entirely new dimension to their thoughts, to the decisions they needed to make, indeed, to their lives. Without saying a word, Ayla mounted Whinney and Jondalar got on behind her. With Racer following along, they started out up the slope and across the open countryside, each lost in thought.

Ayla was moved beyond words by Talut's offer. When she lived with the Clan, she had often felt alienated, but it was nothing to the aching emptiness, the desperate loneliness she had known without them. From the time she left the Clan until Jondalar came, hardly more than a season before, she had been alone. She'd had no one, no sense of belonging, no home, no family, no people, and she knew she would never see her clan again. Because of the earthquake that left her orphaned, before she was found by the Clan, the earthquake on the day she was expelled gave her separation a profound sense of finality.

Underlying her feeling was a deep elemental fear, a combination of the primordial terror of heaving earth and the convulsive grief of a small girl who had lost everything, even her memory of those to whom she had belonged. There was nothing Ayla feared more than wrenching earth movements. They always seemed to signal changes in her life as abrupt and violent as the changes they wrought on the land. It was almost as though the earth itself was telling her what to expect . . . or shuddering in sympathy.

But after the first time she lost everything, the Clan had become her people. Now, if she chose, she could have people again. She could become Mamutoi, she would not be alone.

But what about Jondalar? How could she choose a people different from his? Would he want to stay and become Mamutoi? Ayla doubted it. She was sure he wanted to return to his own home. But he had been afraid all of the Others would behave towards her as Frebec did. He

193

didn't want her to speak of the Clan. What if she went with him and they would not accept her? Maybe his people were all like Frebec. She would *not* refrain from mentioning them, as though Iza, and Creb, and Brun, and her son, were people she should be ashamed of. She would not be ashamed of the people she loved!

Did she want to go to his home and risk being treated like an animal? Or did she want to stay here where she was wanted, and accepted? The Lion Camp had even taken in a mixed child, a boy like her son . . . Suddenly a thought struck her. If they had taken in one, might they take another? One who was not weak or sickly? One who could learn to talk? Mamutoi territory extended all the way to Beran Sea. Didn't Talut say someone had a Willow Camp there? The peninsula where the Clan lived was not far beyond. If she became one of the Mamutoi, maybe, someday, she could . . . But what about Jondalar? What if he left? Ayla felt a deep ache in the pit of her stomach at the thought. Could she bear to live without Jondalar? she wondered, as she wrestled with mixed feelings.

Jondalar struggled with conflicting desires, too. He hardly considered the offer made to him, except that he wanted to find a reason to refuse that would not offend Talut and the Mamutoi. He was Jondalar of the Zelandonii, and he knew his brother had been right. He could never be anything else. He wanted to go home, but it was a nagging ache rather than a great urgency. It was impossible to think in any other terms. His home was so far away, it would take a year just to travel the distance.

His mental turmoil was about Ayla. Though he'd never lacked for willing partners, most of whom would have been more than willing to form a more lasting tie, he'd never found a woman he wanted as much as Ayla. None of the women among his own people, and none of the women he met on his travels, had been able to cause in him that state he had seen in others, but had not felt himself, until he met her. He loved her more than he thought was possible. She was everything he'd ever wanted in a woman, and more. He could not bear the thought of living without her.

But he also knew what it was like to bring disgrace upon himself. And the very qualities that attracted him – her combination of innocence and wisdom, of honesty and mystery, of self-confidence and vulnerability – were the result of the same circumstances that would cause him to feel the pain of disgrace and exile again.

Ayla had been raised by the Clan, people who were different in unexplainable ways. To most people he knew, the ones Ayla referred to as Clan were not human. They were animals, but not like the other animals created by the Mother for their needs. Though not admitted, the similarities between them were recognised, but the Clan's obvious human characteristics did not cause close feelings of brotherhood. Rather, they were seen as a threat and their differences were emphasised. To people like Jondalar, the Clan was viewed as an unspeakably bestial species not even included in the Great Earth Mother's pantheon of creations, as though they had been spawned of some great unfathomable evil.

But there was more recognition of their mutual humanity in deed than in word. Jondalar's kind had moved into the Clan's territory not so many generations before, often taking over good living sites near bountiful foraging and hunting areas, and forcing the Clan into other regions. But just as wolf packs divide up a territory among themselves, and defend it from each other, not other creatures, prey or predatory, the acceptance of the boundaries of each other's territories was a tacit agreement that they were the same species.

Jondalar had come to realise, about the time he realised his feeling for Ayla, that all life was a creation of the Great Earth Mother, including flatheads. But though he loved her, he was convinced that among his people Ayla would be an outcast. It was more than her association with the Clan that made her a pariah. She would be viewed as an unspeakable abomination, who was condemned by the Mother, because she had given birth to a child of mixed spirits, half-animal and half-human.

The taboo was common. All the people Jondalar had met on his travels held the belief, though some more strongly than others. Some people did not even admit to the existence of such misbegotten offspring, others thought of the situation as an unpleasant joke. That was why he had been so shocked to find Rydag at the Lion Camp. He was sure it could not have been easy for Nezzie, and in truth, she had borne the brunt of harsh criticism and prejudice. Only someone serenely confident and sure of her position would have dared to face down her detractors, and her genuine compassion and humanity had eventually prevailed. But even Nezzie had not mentioned the son Ayla had told her about, when she was trying to persuade the others to take her in.

Ayla didn't know the pain Jondalar felt when Frebec had ridiculed her, though he had expected more of it. His pain was more than just empathy for her, however. The whole angry confrontation reminded him of another time that his emotions had led him astray, and it exposed a deep and buried pain of his own. But even worse was his own unexpected reaction. That caused his anguish now. Jondalar still flushed with guilt because, for a moment, he had been embarrassed to be associated with her when Frebec hurled his invective. How could he love a woman and be ashamed of her?

Ever since that terrible time when he was young, Jondalar had fought to keep himself under control, but he seemed unable to contain the conflicts that tormented him now. He wanted to take Ayla home with him. He wanted her to meet Dalanar and the people of his Cave, and his mother, Marthona, and his older brother and young sister, and his cousins, and Zelandoni. He wanted them to welcome her, to establish his own hearth with her, a place where she could have children that might be of his spirit. There was no one else on earth he wanted, yet he cringed at the thought of the contempt that might be heaped on him for bringing home such a woman, and he was reluctant to expose her to it.

Especially if it didn't have to be. If only she wouldn't speak about the Clan, no one would know. Yet, what could she say when someone asked who her people were? Where she came from? The people who raised her were the only ones she knew, unless . . . she accepted Talut's offer. Then, she could be Ayla of the Mamutoi, just as though she had been born to them. Her peculiar way of saying some words would just be an accent. Who knows? he thought. Maybe she is Mamutoi. Her parents could have been. She doesn't know who they were.

But if she becomes Mamutoi, she might decide to stay. What if she does? Would I be able to stay? Could I learn to accept these people as my own? Thonolan did it. Did he love Jetamio more than I love Ayla? But the Sharamudoi were her people. She was born and raised there. The Mamutoi are not Ayla's people any more than they are mine. If she could be happy here, she could be happy with the Zelandonii. But if she becomes one of them, she might not want to come home with me. She wouldn't have any trouble finding someone here . . . I'm sure Ranec wouldn't mind at all.

Ayla felt him clutch her possessively, and wondered what had brought it on. She noticed a line of brush ahead, thought it was probably a small river, and urged Whinney towards it. The horses smelled the water and needed little prodding. When they reached the stream, Ayla and Jondalar dismounted and looked for a comfortable place to sit.

The watercourse had a thickening at the edges which they knew was only the beginning. The white border that had been built up, layer upon layer, out of the dark waters still swirling down the centre, would grow as the season waxed, and close in until the turbulent flow was stilled, held in suspension until the cycle turned. Then the waters would burst forth once again in a gush of freedom.

Ayla opened a small parfleche, a carrying case made of stiff rawhide, in which she had packed food for them, some dried meat that she thought was aurochs, and a small basket of dried blueberries and little tart plums. She brought out a brassy grey nodule of iron pyrite and a piece of flint to start a small fire to boil water for tea. Jondalar marvelled again at the ease with which the fire was started with the firestone. It was magic, a miracle. He had never seen anything like it before he met Ayla.

Nodules of iron pyrite – firestones – had littered the rocky beach in her valley. Her discovery that a hot spark, long-lived enough to start a fire, could be drawn from the iron pyrite by striking it with flint, had been an accident, but one she was ready to take advantage of. Her fire had gone out. She knew how to make fire by the laborious process most people used, twirling a stick against a base, or platform, of wood until the friction caused heat enough to make a smouldering ember. So she understood how to apply the principle when she picked up a chunk of iron pyrite, by mistake, instead of her flint-shaping hammerstone, and struck that first spark.

Jondalar had learned the technique from Ayla. Working with flint, he had often caused small sparks, but he thought of it as the living spirit of the stone released as part of the process. It didn't occur to him to attempt to make a fire with the sparks. But then he was not alone in a valley living on the bare edge of survival, he was usually around people who nearly always had a fire going. The sparks he made with just flint were not usually long-lived enough to make fire, anyway. It was Ayla's adventitious combination of flint and iron pyrite that created the spark which could be made into fire. He understood immediately the value of the process and the firestones, however, and the benefits to be gained by being able to make fire so quickly and easily.

While they ate, they laughed at the antics of Racer enticing his mother into a game of "come get me", and then at both horses rolling on their backs, their legs kicking up in the air, on a sandy bank protected from the wind and warmed by the sun. They carefully avoided any mention of the thoughts that were on their minds, but the laughter relaxed them both, and the seclusion and privacy reminded them of their days of closeness in the valley. By the time they were sipping hot tea, they were ready to venture into more difficult topics.

"Latie would enjoy watching those two horses play like that, I think," Jondalar said.

"Yes. She does like the horses, doesn't she?"

"She likes you, too, Ayla. She's become quite an admirer." Jondalar hesitated, then continued, "Many people like you and admire you here. You don't really want to go back to the valley and live alone, do you?"

Ayla looked down at the cup in her hands, swirled the last of the tea around with the dregs of the leaves, and took a shallow sip. "It is a relief to be alone, by ourselves, again. I didn't realise how good it could feel to get away from all the people, and there are some of my things in the cave at the valley that I wish I had. But, you are right. Now that I've met the Others, I don't want to live alone all the time. I like Latie, and Deegie, and Talut and Nezzie, everyone . . . except Frebec."

Jondalar sighed with relief. The first and biggest hurdle had been easy. "Frebec is only one. You can't let one person spoil everything. Talut . . . and Tulie . . . would not have invited us to stay with them if they didn't like you, and didn't feel that you had something valuable to offer."

"You have something valuable to offer, Jondalar. Do you want to stay and become a Mamutoi?"

"They have been kind to us, much kinder than simple hospitality requires. I could stay, certainly through the winter, and even longer, and I'd be happy to give them anything I could. But they don't need my flint-knapping. Wymez is far better than I am, and Danug will soon be as good. And I've already shown them the spear-thrower. They have seen how it's made. With practice, they could use it. They just have to want it. And I am Jondalar of the Zelandonii . . ."

He stopped and his eyes took on an unfocused look as though he were seeing across a great distance. Then he looked back the way they had come and his forehead knotted in a frown as he tried to think of some explanation. "I must return . . . someday . . . if only to tell my mother of my brother's death . . . and to give Zelandoni a chance to find his spirit and guide it to the next world. I could not become Jondalar of the Mamutoi knowing that, I cannot forget my obligation."

Ayla looked at him closely. She knew he didn't want to stay. It wasn't because of obligations, though he might feel them. He wanted to go home.

"What about you?" Jondalar said, trying to keep his tone and expression neutral. "Do you want to stay and become Ayla of the Mamutoi?"

She closed her eyes, searching for a way to express herself, feeling that she didn't know enough words, or the right words, or that words were just not enough. "Since Broud cursed me, I have had no people, Jondalar. It has made me feel empty. I like the Mamutoi and respect them. I feel at home with them. The Lion Camp is . . . like Brun's clan . . . most are good people. I don't know who my people were before the Clan, I don't think I will ever know, but sometimes at night I think . . . I wish they were Mamutoi."

She looked hard at the man, at his straight yellow hair against the dark fur of his hood, at his handsome face that she thought of as beautiful though he'd told her that wasn't the right word for a man, at his strong, sensitive body and large expressive hands, at his blue eyes that seemed so earnest, and so troubled. "But, before the Mamutoi, you came. You took the emptiness away and filled me with love. I want to be with you, Jondalar."

The anxiety left his eyes, replaced now by the relaxed and easy warmth she had grown used to in the valley, and then by the magnetic, compelling desire that made her body respond with a will of its own. Without any conscious volition, she was drawn to him, felt his mouth find hers and his arms surround her.

"Ayla, my Ayla, I love you so," he cried in a harsh strangulated sob that was filled with anguish and relief. He held her tight against his chest, and yet gently, as they sat on the ground, as though he never wanted to let go, but was afraid she would break. He released his hold just enough to tilt her face up to his, and kissed her forehead, and her eyes, and the tip of her nose, then her mouth, and felt his desire mount. It was cold, they had no place of shelter or warmth, but he wanted her.

He untied the drawstring of her hood, and found her throat and neck, while his hands reached beneath her parka and her tunic, and found her warm skin and full breasts, with their hard, erect nipples. A low moan escaped her lips as he fondled them, squeezing and pulling firmly. He untied the drawstring of her trousers and reached in to find her furry mound. She pressed up to him when he found her warm moist slit, and felt a tightening, a tingling.

Then she felt under his parka and tunic for his drawstring, untied it, then reached for his hard, throbbing member and rubbed her hands along its shaft. He breathed a loud sigh of pleasure when she bent down and took him into her mouth. She felt the smoothness of his skin with her tongue, and drew him in as far as she could, then pushed him out and drew him in again, still rubbing his warm, curved shaft with her hands.

She heard him moan, start to cry out, and then take a deep breath and gently push her away. "Wait, Ayla, I want you," he said.

"I'd have to take off my leggings and my foot-coverings for that," she said.

"No, you don't, it's too cold out. Turn around, remember?"

"Like Whinney and her stallion," Ayla whispered.

She turned around, went down on her knees. For an instant, the position reminded her not of Whinney and her eager stallion, but of Broud, of being thrown down and forced. But Jondalar's loving touch was not the same. She lowered her waistband, baring her warm, firm backside, and an opening that beckoned to him like a flower to bees with its soft petals and deep pink throat. The invitation was almost too much. He felt a surge of pressure that ached to break loose. After a moment to hold back, he crouched up close to keep her warm while he caressed her smooth fullness, and explored her inviting pocket and ridges and folds of warm wetness and Pleasure with his gentle, knowing touch, until her cries and a new font of warmth told him to hold back no more.

Then he spread her twin mounds apart and guided his full and ready manhood into the deep and willing entrance of her womanhood with an agonising Pleasure that tore a cry from both of them. He withdrew, almost fully, and entered again, pulling her to him, and revelled in her deep embrace. Again he withdrew and entered, and again, and again, until finally in a great burst, the glorious release came.

After a few final strokes that drew out the final measure, and still deep within her warmth, he wrapped his arms around her and rolled them both over on their sides. He held her close, covering her with his body and his parka for a moment while they rested.

Finally they pulled apart and Jondalar sat up. The wind was picking up, and Jondalar glanced at massing clouds with apprehension.

"I should clean myself a little," Ayla said, getting up. "These are new leggings from Deegie."

"When we get back, you can leave them outside to freeze, and then brush it off."

"The stream still has water . . ."

"It's icy, Ayla!"

"I know. I'll be quick."

Testing her way on the ice, she squatted near the water, and rinsed herself with her hand. As she stepped back on the bank, Jondalar came up behind her, and dried her with the fur of his parka.

"I don't want that to freeze," he said, with a big grin as he patted her with the fur, and then caressed her.

"I think you'll keep it warm enough," she said with a smile, tying her drawstring and straightening her parka.

This was the Jondalar she loved. The man who could make her feel warm and quivery inside with a look of his eyes, or a touch of his hands; the man who knew her body better than she did, and could draw out feelings she didn't know were there; the man who had made her forget the pain of Broud's first forcible entry, and taught her what Pleasures were and should be. The Jondalar she loved was playful, and caring, and loving. That was how he had been in the valley, and now when they were alone. Why was he so different around the Lion Camp?

"You are getting very quick with words, woman. I'm going to have trouble keeping up with you, in my own language!" He put his arms around her waist, and looked down at her, his eyes full of love and pride. "You are good with language, Ayla. I can't believe how fast you learn. How do you do it?"

"I have to. This is my world now. I have no people. I am dead to the Clan, I can't go back."

"You could have people. You could be Ayla of the Mamutoi. If you want to be. Do you?"

"I want to be with you."

"You can still be with me. Just because someone adopts you doesn't mean you can't leave . . . someday. We could stay here . . . for a while. And if something happened to me – it could, you know – it might not be so bad to have people. People who want you."

"You mean you wouldn't mind?"

"Mind? No, I wouldn't mind, if that's what you want."

Ayla thought she detected a little hesitation, but he did seem sincere. "Jondalar, I am only Ayla. I have no people. If I am adopted, I would have someone. I would be Ayla of the Mamutoi." She stepped back, away from him. "I need to think about it."

She turned around and walked towards the pack she had been carrying. If I'm going to leave with Jondalar soon, I shouldn't agree, she thought. It wouldn't be fair. But he said he'd be willing to stay. For a while. Maybe, after he lives with the Mamutoi, he'll change his mind and want to make this his home. She wondered if she was trying to find an excuse.

She reached inside her parka for her amulet, and sent out a thought to her totem. Cave Lion, I wish there was some way I could know what is right. I love Jondalar, but I want to belong to people of my own, too. Talut and Nezzie want to adopt me, they want to make me a daughter of the Lion . . . the *Lion* Hearth. And the *Lion* Camp! Oh, Great Cave Lion, have you been guiding me all along, and I just wasn't paying attention?

She spun around. Jondalar was still standing where she left him, silently watching her.

"I've decided. I will do it! I will be Ayla of the Lion Camp of the Mamutoi!"

She noticed a fleeting frown cross his face before he smiled. "Good, Ayla. I'm glad for you."

"Oh, Jondalar. Will it be right? Will everything turn out all right?"

"No one can answer that. Who could know?" he said, coming towards her, one eye on the darkening sky. "I hope it will . . . for both of us." They clung to each other for a moment. "I think we should be getting back."

Ayla reached for the parfleche to pack it, but something caught her eye. She went down on one knee, and picked up a deep golden stone. Brushing it off, she looked at it closer. Completely encapsulated within the smooth stone, that had begun to feel warm to the touch, was a complete winged insect.

"Jondalar! Look at this. Have you ever seen anything like it?"

He took it from her, looked it over closely, then looked at her with a bit of awe. "This is amber. My mother has one like it. She places great value on it. This one may be even better." He noticed Ayla staring at him. She looked stunned. He didn't think he'd said anything all that startling. "What is it, Ayla?"

"A sign. It's a sign from my totem, Jondalar. The Spirit of the Great Cave Lion is telling me I made the right decision. He wants me to become Ayla of the Mamutoi!"

The force of the wind intensified as Ayla and Jondalar rode back, and though it was just past noon, the light of the sun was dimmed by clouds of dry loess soil billowing up from the frozen ground. Soon they could hardly see their way through the windblown dust. Flashes of lightning crackled around them in the dry, freezing air, and thunder growled and boomed. Racer reared up in fright as a bolt flashed and a clap of thunder cracked nearby. Whinney nickered anxiously. They dismounted to calm the nervous young horse, and continued on foot leading them both.

By the time they reached the Camp, winds of gale force were driving a dust storm that blackened the sky, and blasted their skin. As they came close to the earthlodge, a figure emerged out of the wind-driven gloom holding on to something which flapped and strained as though it were alive.

"There you are. I was getting worried," Talut shouted above the howling and thunder.

"What are you doing? Can we help?" Jondalar asked.

"We made a lean-to for Ayla's horses when it looked like a storm was brewing. I didn't know it would be a dry storm. The wind blew it apart. I think you'd better bring them in. They can stay in the entrance room," Talut said.

"Is it like this often?" Jondalar said, grabbing an end of the large hide that was supposed to have been a windbreak.

"No. Some years we don't have dry storms at all. It will settle down once we get a good snow," Talut said, ". . . then we'll just have blizzards!" he finished with a laugh. He ducked into the earthlodge, then held back the heavy mammoth hide drape so Ayla and Jondalar could lead the horses inside.

The horses were nervous about entering the strange place full of so many unfamiliar smells, but they liked the noisy windstorm even less, and they trusted Ayla. The relief was immediate once they were out of the wind, and they settled down quickly. Ayla was grateful to Talut for his concern for them, though a little surprised. As she went through the second archway, Ayla noticed how cold she was. The stinging grains of dust had distracted her, but the sub-freezing temperature and strong wind had chilled her to the bone.

*   *   *

The wind still raged outside the longhouse, rattling the covers over the smoke holes and bellying out the heavy drapes. Sudden draughts sent dust flying and caused the fire in the cooking hearth to flare up. People were gathered in casual groups around the area of the first hearth, finishing up the evening meal, sipping herb tea, talking, waiting for Talut to begin.

Finally he got up and strode towards the Lion Hearth. When he returned he was carrying an ivory staff, taller than he was, thicker at the bottom, tapering at the top. It was decorated with a small, spoked wheel-like object, which had been fastened to the staff about a third of the way down from the top. White crane feathers were attached to the top half, fanning out in a semicircle, while between the spokes of the bottom half enigmatic pouches, carved ivory, and pieces of fur dangled from thongs. On closer look, Ayla saw that the staff was made from a single, long, mammoth tusk which, by some unknown method, had been made straight. How, she wondered, did someone take the curve out of a mammoth tusk?

Everyone quieted and turned their attention to the headman. He looked at Tulie, she nodded. Then he banged the butt end of the Staff on the ground four times.

"I have a serious matter to present to the Lion Camp," Talut began. "Something that is the concern of everyone, therefore I talk with the Speaking Staff so all will listen carefully and no one may interrupt. Anyone who wishes to speak on this matter may request the Speaking Staff."

There was a rustle of excitement as people sat up and took notice.

"Ayla and Jondalar came to the Lion Camp not long ago. When I numbered the days they have been here, I was surprised that it has been such a short time. They already feel like old friends, like they belong. I think most of you feel the same. Because of such warm feelings of friendship for our relative, Jondalar, and his friend, Ayla, I had hoped they would extend their visit and planned to ask them to stay through the winter. But in the short time they have been here, they have shown more than friendship. Both of them have brought valuable skills and knowledge, and offered them to us without reservation, just as though they were one of us.

"Wymez recommends Jondalar as a skilled worker of flint. He has shared his knowledge freely with both Danug and Wymez. More than that, he has brought with him a new hunting weapon, a spear-thrower that extends both the range and power of a spear."

There were nods and comments of approval, and Ayla noticed again that the Mamutoi seldom sat quietly, but spoke out with comments in active participation.

"Ayla brings many unusual talents," Talut continued. "She is skilled and accurate with the spear-thrower, and with her own weapon, the sling. Mamut says she is a Searcher, though untrained, and Nezzie thinks she may be a Caller as well. Perhaps not, but it is true that she can make horses obey her, and they allow her to ride on their backs. She has even taught us a way of speaking without words, which has helped us to understand Rydag in a new way. But perhaps most important, she is a Healer. She has already saved the lives of two children . . . and she has a wonderful remedy for headaches!"

The last comment brought a wave of laughter.

"Both of them bring so much, I do not want the Lion Camp or the Mamutoi to lose them. I have asked them to stay with us, not just for the winter, but always. In the name of Mut, Mother of All," Talut pounded the ground with his staff once, firmly, "I ask that they join us, and that you accept them as Mamutoi."

Talut nodded to Ayla and Jondalar. They stood up and approached him with the formality of a prearranged ceremony. Tulie, who had been waiting off to the side, moved up to stand beside her brother.

"I ask for the Speaking Staff," she said.

Talut passed it to her.

"As headwoman of the Lion Camp, I state my agreement with Talut's comments. Jondalar and Ayla would be valuable additions to the Lion Camp, and to the Mamutoi." She faced the tall blond man. "Jondalar," she said, stamping the Speaking Staff three times. "Tulie and Barzec have asked you to be a son of the Aurochs Hearth. We have spoken for you. How do you speak, Jondalar?"

He approached her, and took the Staff she offered and stamped it three times. "I am Jondalar of the Ninth Cave of the Zelandonii, son of Marthona, former leader of the Ninth Cave, born to the hearth of Dalanar, leader of the Lanzadonii," he began. Since it was a formal occasion he decided to use his more formal address and name his primary ties, which brought smiles and nods of approval. All the foreign names gave the ceremony an exotic and important flavour. "I am greatly honoured by your invitation, but I must be fair and tell you I have strong obligations. Someday I must return to the Zelandonii. I must tell my mother of my brother's death, and I must tell Zelandoni, our Mamut, so a Search for his spirit can be made to guide him to the world of the spirits. I value our kinship, I am so warmed by your friendship, I do not want to leave. I wish to stay with you, my friends and relatives, for as long as I can." Jondalar passed the Speaking Staff back to Tulie.

"We are saddened that you cannot join our hearth, Jondalar, but we understand your obligations. You have our respect. Since we are related, through your brother who was a cross-mate of Tholie, you are welcome to remain as long as you wish," Tulie said, then passed the Staff back to Talut.

"Ayla," Talut said, stamping the Staff three times on the ground, "Nezzie and I want to adopt you as a daughter of the Lion Hearth. We have spoken for you. How do you speak?"

Ayla took the Staff and banged it on the ground three times. "I am Ayla. I have no people. I am honoured and pleased to be asked to become one of you. I would feel proud to be Ayla of the Mamutoi," she said, in a carefully rehearsed speech.

Talut took the Staff back and stamped it four times. "If there are no objections, I will close this special meeting . . ."

"I request the Speaking Staff," a voice from the audience called out. Everyone looked surprised to see Frebec approaching.

He took the Staff from the headman, struck the ground three times. "I do not agree. I do not want Ayla," he said.

14

The people of the Lion Camp were stunned into silence. Then there was a hubbub of shocked surprise. The headman had sponsored Ayla, with the headwoman in full accord. Though everyone knew Frebec's feelings about Ayla, no one else seemed to share them. What's more, Frebec and the Crane Hearth hardly seemed in a position to object. They had been accepted by the Lion Camp only recently themselves, after several other Camps had turned them down, only because Nezzie and Talut had argued on their behalf. The Crane Hearth once had a high status, and there had been people in other Camps who had been willing to sponsor them, but there had always been dissenters, and there could be no dissenters. Everyone had to agree. After all the headman's support, it seemed ungrateful for Frebec to oppose him, and no one had expected it, least of all Talut.

The commotion quickly died down when Talut took the Speaking Staff from Frebec, held it up and shook it, invoking its power. "Frebec has the Staff. Let him speak," Talut said, handing the ivory shaft back.

Frebec hit the ground three times and continued, "I do not want Ayla because I don't think she has offered enough to make her a Mamutoi." There was an undercurrent of objection to his statement, especially after Talut's words of praise, but not enough to interrupt the speaker. "Do we ask any stranger who stops for a visit to become Mamutoi?"

Even with the constraint of the Speaking Staff, it was difficult for the Camp to keep from speaking out. "What do you mean she has nothing to offer? What about her hunting skill?" Deegie called out, full of righteous anger. Her mother, the headwoman, had not accepted Ayla on first appearances. Only after careful consideration had she agreed to go along with Talut. How could this Frebec object?

"So what if she hunts? Is everyone who hunts made one of us?" Frebec said. "That's not a good reason. She won't be hunting much longer anyway, not after she has children."

"Having children is more important! That will give her more status," Deegie flared.

"Don't you think I know that? We don't even know if she can have children, and if she doesn't have children, she won't be of much value at all. But we weren't talking about children, we were talking about hunting. Just because she hunts is not a good enough reason to make her a Mamutoi," Frebec argued.

"What about the spear-thrower? You can't deny it is a weapon of value, and she is good at it and already showing others how to use it," Tornec said.

"She did not bring it. Jondalar did, and he is not joining us."

Danug spoke out. "She might be a Searcher, or a Caller. She can make horses obey her, she even rides on one."

"Horses are food. The Mother meant for us to hunt them, not live with them. I'm not even sure it's right to ride them. And no one knows for sure what she might be. She might be a Searcher, she might be a Caller. She might be the Mother on earth, but she might not. Since when is 'might be' a reason to make someone one of us?" No one had been able to counter his objections. Frebec was beginning to enjoy himself, and all the attention he was getting.

Mamut looked at Frebec with some surprise. Though the shaman completely disagreed with him, he had to concede that Frebec's arguments were clever. It was too bad they were so misdirected.

"Ayla has taught Rydag to talk, when no one thought he could," Nezzie shouted, joining in the debate.

"Talk!" he sneered. "You can call a lot of hand waving 'talking' if you want to, but I don't. I can't think of anything more useless than making stupid gestures at a flathead. That's not a reason to accept her. If anything, it's a reason not to."

"And in spite of the obvious, I suppose you still don't believe she is a Healer?" Ranec commented. "You realise, I hope, that if you drive Ayla out, you may be the one who is sorry if there is no one here to help Fralie when she delivers."

Ranec had always been an anomaly to Frebec. In spite of his high status and renown as a carver, Frebec didn't know what to make of the brown-skinned man, and was not comfortable around him. Frebec always had the feeling Ranec was being disdainful or making fun of him when he used that subtle ironic tone. He didn't like it, and besides, there was probably something unnatural about such dark skin.

"You're right, Ranec," Frebec said in a loud voice. "I don't think she's a Healer. How could anyone growing up with those animals learn to be a Healer? And Fralie has already had babies. Why should this time be any different? Unless having that animal woman here brings her bad luck. That flathead boy already brings down the status of this Camp. Can't you see? She'll only bring it down more. Why would anyone want a woman raised by animals? And what would people think if anyone came here and found horses inside a lodge? No, I don't want an animal woman who lived with flatheads to be one of the Lion Camp."

There was a great commotion over his comments about the Lion Camp, but Tulie raised her voice above the tumult. "By whose measure do you say the status of this Camp has been brought down? Rydag does not take my status from me, I am still a leading voice on the Council of Sisters. Talut has lost no standing either."

"People are always saying 'that Camp with the flathead boy'. It makes me ashamed to say I am a member," Frebec shouted back.

Tulie stood her tallest beside the rather slightly built man. "You are welcome to leave at any time," she said in her coldest voice.

"Now look what you've done," Crozie cried. "Fralie expecting a child, and you're going to force her out, in this cold, with no place to go. Why did I ever agree to your joining? Why did I ever believe someone who paid such a low Bride Price would be good enough for her? My poor daughter, my poor Fralie . . ."

The old woman's wails were drowned out by the general noise level of angry voices and arguments aimed at Frebec. Ayla turned her back and walked towards the Mammoth Hearth. She noticed Rydag watching the meeting with big sad eyes from the Lion Hearth, and went to him instead. She sat down beside him, felt his chest and looked at him carefully to make sure he was all right. Then, without trying to make any conversation, because she didn't know what to say, she picked him up. She held him on her lap, rocking back and forth, humming a tuneless monotone under her breath. She had once rocked her son that way, and later, alone in her cave in her valley, she had often rocked herself to sleep the same way.

"Does no one respect the Speaking Staff?" Talut roared, overpowering the rest of the furor. His eyes blazed. He was angry. Ayla had never seen him so angry, but she admired his self-control when he next spoke. "Crozie, we would not turn Fralie out into the cold, and you insult me and the Lion Camp by suggesting that we would."

The old woman looked at the headman with mouth agape. She hadn't really thought they would turn Fralie out. She had merely been haranguing Frebec, and didn't think about it being taken as an insult. She had the decency to blush with shame, which surprised some people, but she did understand the finer points of accepted behaviour. Fralie's status, after all, had first come from her. Crozie was highly esteemed in her own right, or had been until she lost so much, and made herself and everyone around her so miserable. She could still claim the distinction if not the substance.

"Frebec, you may feel embarrassment to be a member of the Lion Camp," Talut said, "but if this Camp has lost any status, it is because this was the only Camp that would take you in. As Tulie said, no one is forcing you to stay. You are free to leave any time, but we will not put you out, not with a sick woman who will be giving birth this winter. Perhaps you have not been around pregnant women very much before, but whether you realise it or not, Fralie's illness is more than pregnancy. Even I know that much.

"But that is not the reason this meeting was called. No matter how you feel about it, or how we feel about it, you are a member of the Lion Camp. I have stated my wish to adopt Ayla to my hearth, to make her Mamutoi. But everyone must agree, and you have objected . . ."

By this time, Frebec was squirming. It was one thing to make himself feel important by objecting and thwarting everyone else, but Talut had just reminded him of the humiliation and desperation he had felt when he was trying so hard to find a Camp to establish a new hearth, with his treasured new woman, who was more desirable and had brought him more status than he ever had in his life.

Mamut was observing him closely. Frebec had never been particularly outstanding. He had little status, since his mother had little to bestow on him, no accomplishments to his credit, and few obvious qualities or talents of any real merit. He wasn't hated, but neither was he well liked. He seemed to be a rather mediocre man of average abilities. But he showed skill in arguing. Though false, his arguments had logic. He might have more intelligence than he had been given credit for, and apparently he had high aspirations. Joining with Fralie was a great achievement, for a man like him. He would bear closer watching.

Even to make an offer for a woman like her showed a certain daring. Bride Price was the basis of economic value among the Mamutoi; brides were the standard of currency. A man's standing in his society came from the woman who gave birth to him and the woman or women he could attract – by status, or hunting prowess, or skill, or talent, or charm – to live with him. Finding a woman of high status willing to become his woman was like finding great riches, and Frebec was not going to let her go.

But why had she accepted him? Mamut wondered. Certainly there were other men who had made offers; Frebec had added to her difficulties. He had so little to offer, and Crozie was so disagreeable, that Fralie's Camp had turned them out, and Frebec's Camp had refused them. Then one after another of the other Camps had turned him down, even with a pregnant, high-status woman. And each time, out of her own feelings of panic, Crozie made it worse, berating him and blaming him, and making them even less desirable.

Frebec had been grateful when the Lion Camp had said yes, but they had been one of the last he'd tried. It wasn't that they didn't have a high station, but they were looked upon as having an unusual assortment of members. Talut had the ability to see the unusual as special rather than odd. He'd known status all his life, he was looking for something more, and he found it in the unusual. He came to relish that quality and fostered it in his Camp. Talut, himself, was the biggest man anyone had ever seen, not only among the Mamutoi, but the neighbouring peoples as well. His sister, Tulie, was the biggest and strongest woman. Mamut was the oldest man. Wymez was the best flint knapper, Ranec not only the darkest man, but the best carver. And Rydag was the only flathead child. Talut wanted Ayla, who was most unusual with her horses, and her skills, and her gifts, and he wouldn't mind Jondalar, who had come from the farthest away.

Frebec didn't want to be unusual, especially since he could only see himself viewed as the least of something. He was still seeking standing among the ordinary, and he had begun by making a virtue of the most common. He was Mamutoi, therefore he was better than everyone who was not, better than anyone different. Ranec, with his dark skin – and his biting, satiric wit – wasn't really Mamutoi. He hadn't even been born among them, but Frebec was, and he was certainly better than those animals, those flatheads. That boy Nezzie loved so much had no status at all since he was born to a flathead woman.

And that Ayla, who came with her horses and her tall stranger, had already caught the disdainful eye of dark Ranec, whom all the women wanted in spite of his difference, or because of it. She hadn't even looked at Frebec, as though she knew he wasn't worth her attention. It didn't matter that she was skilled, or gifted, or beautiful, he was certainly better than she; she wasn't a Mamutoi and he was. What's more, she had lived with those flatheads. Now Talut wanted to make her a Mamutoi.

Frebec knew he was the cause of the unpleasant scene that had erupted. He had proved he was important enough to keep her out, but he had made the big headman angrier than he'd ever seen him, and it was a little frightening to see the huge bear of a man so angry. Talut could pick him up and break him in two. At the very least, Talut could make him leave. Then how long would he keep his high-status woman?

Yet, for all his controlled anger, Talut was treating Frebec with more respect than he was accustomed to receiving. His comments had not been ignored or cast aside.

"Whether your objections are reasonable does not matter," Talut continued, coldly. "I believe she has many unusual talents that could bring benefit to us. You have disputed that and say she has nothing of value to offer. I don't know what could possibly be offered that someone could not dispute, if they wished . . ."

"Talut," Jondalar said, "excuse my interruption while you hold the

Speaking Staff, but I think I know something that could not be disputed."

"You do?"

"Yes, I think so. May I speak with you alone?"

"Tulie, will you hold the Staff?" Talut said, then walked towards the Lion Hearth with Jondalar. A murmur of curiosity followed them.

Jondalar went to Ayla and spoke with her. She nodded and laying Rydag down, got up and hurried to the Mammoth Hearth.

"Talut, are you willing to put out all the fires?" Jondalar said.

Talut frowned. "All the fires? It's cold out, and windy. It could get cold inside quickly."

"I know, but believe me, it will be worth it. For Ayla to demonstrate this to the best effect, it needs to be dark. It won't be cold for long."

Ayla came back with some stones in her hands. Talut looked from her, to Jondalar, and back to her again. Then he nodded his head in agreement. A fire could always be started again, even if it took some effort. They went back to the cooking hearth, and Talut spoke to Tulie, privately. There was some discussion and Mamut was drawn in, then Tulie spoke to Barzec. Barzec signalled Druwez and Danug, and all three put on parkas, picked up large, tightly woven baskets and went outside.

The murmur of conversation was full of excitement. Something special was going on and the Camp was full of anticipation, almost the way it was before a special ceremony. They hadn't expected secret consultations and a mysterious demonstration.

Barzec and the boys were back quickly with baskets full of loose dirt. Then starting at the far end, at the Hearth of the Aurochs, they stirred the banked coals or small sustaining fires in each of the firepits and poured the dirt over them to smother the flames. The people of the Camp became nervous when they realised what was going on.

As the longhouse darkened with each fire that was put out, everyone stopped talking and the lodge grew still. The wind beyond the walls howled louder, and the draughts felt colder and brought with them a deeper and more ominous chill. Fire was appreciated and understood, if somewhat taken for granted, but they knew their life depended on it when they saw their fires go out.

Finally only the fire in the large cooking hearth remained. Ayla had her fire-starting materials ready beside the fireplace, and then, with a nod from Talut, Barzec, sensing the dramatic moment, dumped the dirt on the fire as the people gasped.

In an instant the lodge was filled with darkness. It wasn't just an absence of light, but a fullness of dark. A smothering, uncompromising, deep black occupied every empty space. There were no stars, no glowing orb, no nacreous, shimmering clouds. A hand brought in front of the eyes could not be seen. There was no dimension, no shadow, no silhouette of black on black. The sense of sight had lost all value.

A child cried and was hushed by his mother. Then breathing was noticed, and shuffling, and a cough. Someone spoke in a quiet voice and was answered by one with a deeper tone. The smell of burned bone was strong, but mingled in was a multitude of other odours, scents, and aromas: processed leathers, food that was cooked and food that was stored, grass mats, dried herbs, and the smell of people, of feet and bodies and warm breaths.

The Camp waited in the dark, wondering. Not exactly frightened, but a little apprehensive. A long time seemed to pass and they began to get restless. What was taking so long?

The timing had been left up to Mamut. It was second nature to the old shaman to create dramatic effects, almost instinct to know just the right moment. Ayla felt a tap on her shoulder. It was the signal she was waiting for. She had a piece of iron pyrite in one hand, flint in the other, and on the ground in front of her was a small pile of fireweed fluff. In the pitch-black darkness of the lodge, she closed her eyes and took a deep breath, then struck the iron pyrite with the flint.

A large spark glowed, and in the perfect dark, the tiny light illuminated just the young woman kneeling on the ground for a long moment, bringing forth a startled gasp and sounds of awe from the Camp. Then it went out. Ayla struck again, this time closer to the tinder she had prepared. The spark fell on the quickly flammable material. Ayla bent close to blow, and in a moment, it burst into flame, and she heard *ahhs* and *ohhs* and exclamations of wonder.

She fed small shavings of woody brush from a nearby pile, and when they caught, slightly larger sticks and kindling. Then she sat back and watched while Nezzie cleaned the dirt and ashes out of the cooking hearth and transferred the flame to it. Regulating the damper of the flue that brought wind from outside, she started the bone burning. The attention of the people of the Camp had been riveted on the process, but after the fire was going, they realised how short a time it had taken. It was magic! What had she done to create fire so fast?

Talut shook the Speaking Staff, and struck the ground three times with the thick end. "Now does anyone have any more objections to Ayla becoming a Mamutoi, and a member of the Lion Camp?" he asked.

"Will she show us how to do that magic?" Frebec said.

"She will not only show us, she has promised to give one of her firestones to each hearth in this Camp," Talut replied.

"I have no more objections," Frebec said.

Ayla and Jondalar sorted through their travelling packs to gather together all the iron pyrite nodules they had with them and selected six of the best. She had relit the fires of each hearth the night before, showing them the process, but she was tired and it was too late to look through their packs for firestones before they went to bed.

The six stones, greyish yellow with a metallic sheen, made a small, insignificant pile on the bed platform, yet one like them had made the difference between her acceptance and her rejection. Seeing them, no one would ever guess what magic lay hidden in the soul of those rocks.

Ayla picked them up and, holding them in her hands, looked at Jondalar.

"If everyone else wanted me, why would they let one person keep me out?" she asked.

"I'm not sure," he said, "but everyone in a group like this has to live with everyone else. It can cause a lot of bad feeling if one person really doesn't like another person, especially when the weather keeps everyone inside for a long time. People end up taking sides, arguments can lead to fights, and someone may get hurt, or worse. That leads to anger, and then someone wants revenge. Sometimes the only way to avert more tragedy is to break up the group . . . or to pay a high penalty and send the troublemaker away . . ."

His forehead knotted in pain as he closed his eyes for a moment, and Ayla wondered what caused his grief.

"But Frebec and Crozie fight all the time, and people don't like that," she said.

"The rest of the Camp knew about that before they agreed, or at least they had some idea. Everyone had a chance to say no, so no one can blame anyone else. Once you've agreed to something, you tend to feel it's up to you to work it out, and you know it's only for the winter. Changes are easier to make in summer."

Ayla nodded. She still wasn't entirely certain that he wanted her to become one of these people, but showing the firestone had been his idea, and it worked. They both walked to the Lion Hearth to deliver the stones. Talut and Tulie were deep in conversation. Nezzie and Mamut were occasionally drawn in, but they listened more than talked.

"Here are firestones I promised," Ayla said when they acknowledged her approach. "You can give them today."

"Oh, no," Tulie said. "Not today. Save them for the ceremony. We were just talking about that. They will be part of the gifts. We have to decide on a value for them so we can plan what else will be necessary to give. They should have a very high value, not only for themselves, but for trading, and for the status they will give you."

"What gifts?" Ayla said.

"It is customary, when someone is adopted," Mamut explained, "for gifts to be exchanged. The person who is adopted receives gifts from everyone, and in the name of the hearth that is adopting, gifts are distributed to the rest of the hearths in the Camp. They can be small, just a token exchange, or they can be quite valuable. It depends on the circumstances."

"I think the firestones are valuable enough to be a sufficient gift for each hearth," Talut said.

"Talut, I would agree with you if Ayla was Mamutoi already and her value was established," Tulie said, "but in this case, we are trying to set her Bride Price. The entire Camp will benefit if we can justify a high value for her. Since Jondalar has declined to be adopted, at least for now . . ." Tulie's smile, to show she bore him no animosity, was almost flirtatious, but not in the least coy. It simply expressed her conviction that she was attractive and desirable. ". . . I will be happy to contribute some gifts for distribution."

"What kind of gifts?" Ayla asked.

"Oh, just gifts . . . they can be many things," Tulie said. "Furs are nice, and clothes . . . tunics, leggings, boots, or the leather to make them. Deegie makes beautifully dyed leather. Amber and seashells, and ivory beads, for necklaces and decorating clothes. Long teeth of wolves and other meat eaters are quite valuable. So are ivory carvings. Flint, salt . . . food is good to give, especially if it can be stored. Anything well-made, baskets, mats, belts, knives. I think it's important to give as much as possible, so when everyone shows the gifts at the Meeting, it will appear that you have an abundance, to show your status. It doesn't really matter if most of it is donated to Talut and Nezzie for you."

"You and Talut and Nezzie do not have to give for me. I have things to give," Ayla said.

"Yes, of course, you have the firestones. And they are the most valuable, but they don't look very impressive. Later people will realise their worth, but first impressions make a difference."

"Tulie is right," Nezzie said. "Most young women spend years making and accumulating gifts to give away at their Matrimonials, or if they are adopted."

"Are so many people adopted by the Mamutoi?" Jondalar asked.

"Not outsiders," Nezzie said, "but Mamutoi often adopt other Mamutoi. Every Camp needs a sister and brother to be headwoman and headman, but not every man is lucky enough to have a sister like Tulie. If something happens to one or the other, or if a young man or a young woman wants to start a new Camp, a sister or a brother may be adopted. But, don't worry. I have many things that you can give, Ayla, and even Latie has offered some of her things for you to give."

"But I have things to give, Nezzie. I have things in cave at valley," Ayla said. "I spent years making many things."

"It's not necessary for you to go back . . ." Tulie said, privately thinking that whatever she might have would be very primitive with her flathead background. How could she tell the young woman that her gifts probably would not be suitable? It could be awkward.

"I want to go back," Ayla insisted. "Other things I need. My healing plants. Food stored. And food for horses." She turned to Jondalar. "I want to go back."

"I suppose we could. If we hurried and didn't stop along the way, I think we could make it . . . if the weather clears."

"Usually, after the first cold snap like this, we get some nice weather," Talut said. "It's unpredictable, though. It can turn any time."

"Well, if we get some decent weather maybe we'll take a chance and go back to the valley," Jondalar said, and was rewarded by one of Ayla's beautiful smiles.

There were some things he wanted, too. Those firestones had made quite an impression, and the rocky beach at the bend of the river in Ayla's valley had been full of them. Someday, he hoped, he would return and share with his people everything he had learned and discovered: the firestones, the spear-thrower, and for Dalanar, Wymez's trick of heating flint. Someday . . .

"Hurry back," Nezzie called out, holding her hand up with the palm facing her, and waving goodbye.

Ayla and Jondalar waved back. They were mounted double on Whinney, with Racer on a rope behind, and looked down on the people of the Lion Camp who had gathered to see them off. As excited as she felt about returning to the valley that had been her home for three years, Ayla felt a pang of sorrow at leaving behind people who already seemed like family.

Rydag, standing on one side of Nezzie, and Rugie on the other, clung to her as they waved. Ayla couldn't help noticing how little resemblance there was between them. One was a small image of Nezzie, the other half-Clan, yet they had been raised as brother and sister. With a sudden insight, Ayla recalled that Oga had nursed Durc, along with her own son, Grev, as milk brothers. Grev was fully Clan and Durc only half; the difference between them had been as great.

Ayla signalled Whinney with pressure of legs and shift in position, so second nature she hardly thought of it as guiding the mare. They turned and started up the slope.

The journey back was not the leisurely trip they had made on their way out. They travelled steadily, making no exploratory side trips or hunting forays, no early stops to relax or enjoy Pleasures. Expecting to return, they had noted landmarks as they were travelling from the valley, certain outcrops, highlands, and rock formations, valleys and watercourses, but the changing season had altered the landscape.

In part, the vegetation had changed its aspect. The protected valleys where they had stopped had taken on a seasonal variation that caused an uneasy sense of unfamiliarity. The arctic birch and willow had lost all their leaves, and their scrawny limbs shivering in the wind seemed shrivelled and lifeless. Conifers – white spruce, larch, stone pine – hale and proud in their green-needled vigour, were prominent instead, and even the isolated dwarfs on the steppes, contorted by winds, gained substance by comparison. But more confusing were the changes in surface features wrought, in that frigid periglacial land, by perma-frost.

Permafrost – permanently frozen ground – any part of the earth's crust, from the surface to deep bedrock, that remains frozen year-around, was brought on, in that land far south of polar regions so long ago, by continent-spanning sheets of ice, a mile or two – or more – high. A complex interaction of climate, surface, and underground conditions created and maintained the frozen ground. Sunshine had an effect, and standing water, vegetation, soil density, wind, snow.

Average yearly temperatures only a few degrees less than those that would later maintain temperate conditions, were enough to cause the massive glaciers to encroach upon the land, and the permafrost farther south. The winters were long and cold, and occasional storms brought heavy snows and intense blizzards, but the snowfall over the season was relatively light, and many days were clear. The summers were short, with a few days so hot they belied the nearness of any glacial mass of ice, but generally it was cloudy and cool, with little rain.

Though some portion of the ground was always frozen, permafrost was not a permanent, unchanging state; it was as inconstant and fickle as the seasons. In the depths of winter when it was frozen solid all the way through, the land seemed passive, hard, and ungiving, but it was not what it seemed. When the season turned, the surface softened, only a few inches where thick ground cover or dense soils or too much shade resisted the gentle warmth of summer, but the active layer thawed down several feet on sunny slopes of well-drained gravels with little vegetation.

The yielding layer was an illusion, though. Beneath the surface the iron-hard grip of winter still ruled. Impenetrable ice held sway, and with the thaw and forces of gravity, saturated soils, and their burden of rocks and trees, crept and slid and flowed across the water-lubricated table of ground still frozen below. Slumps occurred and cave-ins as the surface warmed, and where the summer melt could find no outlet, bogs and swamps and thaw-lakes appeared.

When the cycle turned once more, the active layer above the frozen ground turned hard again, but its cold and icy countenance disguised a restless heart. The extreme stresses and pressures caused heaving, thrusting, and buckling. The frozen ground split and cracked and then filled with ice, which, to relieve stress, was expelled as ice wedges. Pressures filled holes with mud, and caused fine silt to rise in silt boils and frost blisters. As the freezing water expanded, mounds and hills of muddy ice – pingos – rose up out of swampy lowlands reaching heights of up to two hundred feet and diameters of several hundred.

As Ayla and Jondalar retraced their steps, they discovered that the relief of the landscape had changed, making landmarks misleading. Certain small streams they thought they remembered had disappeared. They had iced over closer to their source, and become dry downstream. Hills of ice had appeared where none had been before, risen out of summer bogs and swampy lowlands where dense, fine-textured substrates caused poor drainage. Stands of trees grew on talik – islands of unfrozen layers surrounded by permafrost – which sometimes gave a misleading impression of a small valley, where they could not recall having seen one.

Jondalar was not familiar with the general terrain and more than once deferred to Ayla's better memory. When she was unsure, Ayla followed Whinney's lead. Whinney had brought her home more than once before, and seemed to know where she was going. Sometimes riding double on the mare, other times trading off, or walking to give the horse a rest, they pushed on until they were forced to stop for the night. Then they made a simple camp with a small fire, their hide tent and sleeping furs. They cooked cracked, parched wild grain into a hot mush, and Ayla brewed a hot herbal beverage.

In the morning, they drank a hot tea for warmth while they packed up, then on the way they ate ground dried meat and dried berries that were mixed with fat and shaped into small cakes. Except for a hare they accidentally flushed, which Ayla brought down with her sling, they didn't hunt. But they did supplement the travelling food Nezzie had given them with the oily rich and nutritious pignon seeds from the cones of stone pines, gathered at stopping places along the way, and thrown on the fire to open with a pop.

As the terrain around them gradually changed, becoming rocky and more rugged with ravines and steep-walled canyons, Ayla felt a growing sense of excitement. The territory had a familar feel, like the landscape south and west of her valley. When she saw an escarpment with a particular pattern of colouration in the strata, her heart leaped.

"Jondalar! Look! See that!" she cried, pointing. "We're almost there!"

Even Whinney seemed excited, and without being urged, increased her pace. Ayla watched for another landmark, a stone outcrop with a distinctive shape which reminded her of a lioness crouching. When she found it, they turned north until they came to the edge of a steep slope strewn with gravel and loose rocks. They stopped and looked over the edge. At the bottom, a small river, flowing east, glinted in the sun as it splashed over rocks. They dismounted and carefully picked their way down. The horses started across, then paused to drink. Ayla found the stepping-stones jutting out of the water, with only one wide space to jump, that she had always used. She took a drink, too, when they reached the other side.

"The water is sweeter here. Look how clear it is!" she exclaimed. "It's not muddy at all. You can see the bottom. And look, Jondalar, the horses are here!"

Jondalar smiled affectionately at her exuberance, feeling a similar, if milder, sense of homecoming at the sight of the familiar long valley. The harsh winds and frost of the steppes brushed the protected pocket with a lighter touch, and even stripped of summer leaves, a richer, fuller growth was apparent. The steep slope, which they had just descended, rose precipitously to a sheer rock wall as it advanced down the valley on the left. A wide fringe of brush and trees bordered the opposite bank of the stream running along its base, then thinned out to a meadow of golden hay billowing in waves in the afternoon sun. The level field of waist-high grass sloped gradually up to the steppes on the right, but it narrowed and the incline steepened towards the far end of the valley until it became the other wall of a narrow gorge.

Halfway down, a small herd of steppe horses had stopped grazing and was looking their way. One of them neighed. Whinney tossed her head and answered. The herd watched them approach until they were quite close. Then, as the strange scent of humans continued to advance, they wheeled as one, and with pounding hooves and flying tails, galloped up the gentle slope to the open steppes above. The two humans on the back of one horse stopped to watch them go. So did the young horse attached by a rope.

Racer, with head high and ears pitched forward, followed them as far as his lead would allow, then stood with neck outstretched and nostrils wide, watching after them. Whinney nickered to him as they started down the valley again, and he came back and followed behind.

As they hurried upstream towards the narrow end of the valley, they could see the small river swirling in a sharp turn around a jutting wall and a rocky beach on the right. On the other side of it was a large pile of rocks, driftwood, and bones, antlers, horns, and tusks of every variety. Some were skeletons from the steppes, others were the remains of animals caught in flash floods, carried downstream, and thrown against the wall.

Ayla could hardly wait. She slid off Whinney's back and raced up a steep narrow path alongside the bone pile to the top of the wall, which formed a ledge in front of a hole in the face of the rock cliff. She almost ran inside, but checked herself at the last minute. This was the place where she had lived alone, and she had survived because never for a moment did she forget to be alert to possible danger. Caves were used not only by people. Edging up along the outside wall, she unwound her sling from her head and stooped to pick up some chunks of rock.

Carefully, she looked inside. She saw only darkness, but her nose detected a faint smell of wood burned long ago, and a somewhat fresher musky scent of wolverine. But that, too, was old. She stepped inside the opening and let her eyes adjust to the dim light, and then looked around.

She felt the pressure of tears filling her eyes, and struggled to hold them back to no avail. There it was, her cave. She was home. Everything was so familiar, yet the place where she had lived for so long seemed deserted and forlorn. The light streaming in from the hole above the entrance showed her that her nose had been right, and closer inspection brought a gasp of dismay. The cave was in a shambles. Some animal, perhaps more than one, had indeed broken in, and had left the evidence scattered around. She wasn't sure how much damage had been done.

Jondalar appeared at the entrance then. He came in, followed by Whinney and Racer. The cave had been home to the mare, too, and the only home Racer knew until they met the Lion Camp.

"It looks as if we've had a visitor," he said when he became aware of the devastation. "This place is a mess!"

Ayla heaved a big sigh and wiped a tear away. "I'd better get a fire going and torches lit so we can see how much has been ruined. But first I'd better unpack Whinney so she can rest and graze."

"Do you think we should just let them run free like that? Racer looked like he was ready to follow those horses. Maybe we should tie them up." Jondalar had a worried frown.

"Whinney has always run free," Ayla said, feeling a little shocked. "I can't tie her up. She's my friend. She stays with me because she wants to. She went to live with a herd once, when she wanted a stallion. I missed her so much, I don't know what I would have done if I hadn't had Baby. But she came back. She will stay, and, as long as she does, so will Racer, at least until he grows up. Baby left me, Racer might, too, just like children leave their mothers' hearths when they grow up.

But horses are different from lions. I think if he becomes a friend, like Whinney, he might stay."

Jondalar nodded. "All right, you know them better than I do." Ayla was, after all, the expert. The only expert when it came to horses. "Why don't I make the fire while you unpack, then?"

As he went to the places where Ayla had always kept the fire-starting materials and wood, not realising how familiar her cave had become to him in the short summer he had lived there with her, Jondalar wondered how he could make Racer a good friend. He still didn't understand completely how Ayla communicated with Whinney so that she went where the woman wanted her to when they were riding, and stayed nearby though she had the freedom to leave. Maybe he'd never learn, but he would like to try. Still, until he learned, it wouldn't hurt to keep Racer on a rope, at least when they travelled where there might be other horses.

A check of the cave and its contents told its story. A wolverine or a hyena, Ayla couldn't tell which since both had been in the cave at different times and their tracks were intermixed, had broken into one of the caches of dried meat. It was cleaned out. One basket of grain they had picked for Whinney and Racer, which had been left fairly exposed, had been chewed into in several places. A variety of small rodents judging by the tracks – voles, pikas, ground squirrels, jerboas, and giant hamsters – had made off with the bonanza and hardly a seed was left. They found one nest stuffed with the plunder beneath a pile of hay nearby. But most of the baskets of grains and roots and dried fruits, which had either been set into holes dug into the dirt floor of the cave, or protected by rocks piled on them, suffered far less damage.

Ayla was glad they had decided to put the soft leather hides and furs she had made over the years in a sturdy basket and stash it in a cairn. The large pile of rocks had proved too much for the marauding beasts, but the leather left over from the clothes Ayla had made for Jondalar and herself before they left, which had not been put away, was chewed to shreds. Another cairn which held, among other things, a rawhide container filled with carefully rendered fat stored in small sausagelike sections of deer intestines, had been the object of repeated assaults. One corner of the parfleche had been torn out by teeth and claws, one sausage broken into, but the cairn had stood.

In addition to getting into the stored food, the animals had prowled through other storage areas, knocked over stacks of handcrafted and smoothed wooden bowls and cups, dragged around baskets and mats twined and woven in subtle patterns and designs, defecated in several places, and in general created havoc with whatever they could find. But the actual damage was much less than it first appeared, and they had

220

essentially ignored her large pharmacopoeia of dried and preserved herbal medicines.

By evening, Ayla was feeling much better. They had cleaned and restored order to the cave, determined that the loss was not too great, cooked and eaten a meal, and even explored the valley to see what changes had taken place. With a fire in the hearth, sleeping furs spread out over clean hay in the shallow trench which Ayla used as a bed, and Whinney and Racer comfortably settled in their place on the other side of the entrance, Ayla finally felt at home.

"It's hard to believe I'm back," Ayla said, sitting on a mat in front of the fire beside Jondalar. "I feel as though I've been gone a lifetime, but it hasn't been long at all."

"No, it hasn't been long."

"I've learned so much, maybe that's why it seems long. It was good that you convinced me to go with you, Jondalar, and I'm glad we met Talut and the Mamutoi. Do you know how afraid I was to meet the Others?"

"I knew you were worried about it, but I was sure once you got to know some people, you'd like them."

"It wasn't just meeting people. It was meeting the *Others*. To the Clan, that's what they were, and though I'd been told all my life I was born to the Others, I still thought of myself as Clan. Even when I was cursed and knew I couldn't go back, I was afraid of the Others. After Whinney came to live with me, it was worse. I didn't know what to do. I was afraid they wouldn't let me keep her, or would kill her for food. And I was afraid they wouldn't allow me to hunt. I didn't want to live with people who wouldn't let me hunt if I wanted to, or who might make me do something I didn't want to do," Ayla said.

Suddenly the recollection of her fears and anxieties filled her with discomfort and nervous energy. She got up and walked to the mouth of the cave, then pushed aside the heavy windbreak, and walked out on to the top of the jutting wall that formed a broad front porch to the cave. It was cold out and clear. The stars, hard and bright, glittered out of a deep black sky with an edge as sharp as the wind. She hugged herself, and rubbed her arms as she walked towards the end of the ledge.

She started to shiver, and felt a fur being wrapped around her shoulders, and turned to face Jondalar. He enfolded her in his arms and she snuggled up close to his warmth.

He bent to kiss her, then said, "It's cold out here. Come back inside."

Ayla let him lead her in, but stopped just past the heavy hide that she had used for a windbreak since her first winter.

"This was my tent . . . no, this was Creb's tent," she corrected herself. "He never used it, though. It was the tent I used when I was one of the women chosen to go along with the men when they hunted, to butcher the meat and help carry it back. But it didn't belong to me. It belonged to Creb. I took it along with me when I left because I thought Creb wouldn't have minded. I couldn't ask him. He was dead, but he wouldn't have seen me if he'd been alive. I had just been cursed." Tears had begun to stream down her face, though she didn't seem to notice. "I was dead. But Durc saw me. He was too young to know he wasn't supposed to see me. Oh, Jondalar, I didn't want to leave him." She was sobbing now. "But I couldn't take him with me. I didn't know what might happen to me."

He wasn't sure what to say, or what to do, so he just held her and let her cry.

"I want to see him again. Every time I see Rydag, I think of Durc. I wish he was here with me now. I wish we both were being adopted by the Mamutoi."

"Ayla, it's late. You're tired. Come to bed," Jondalar said, leading her to the sleeping furs, but he was feeling uneasy. Such thinking was unrealistic, and he didn't want to encourage her.

She turned obediently and let him guide her. Silently, he helped her out of her clothes, then sat her down and pushed her gently back, and covered her with the furs. He added wood and banked the coals in the fireplace to last longer, then quickly undressed, and crawled into bed beside her. He put his arm around her and kissed her, gently, barely touching her lips with his.

The effect was tantalising, and he felt her tingling response. With the same light, almost tickling touch, he began kissing her face; her cheeks, her closed eyes, and then her soft full lips again. He reached up and tilted her jaw back, and caressed her throat and her neck the same way. Ayla made herself lie still, and instead of feeling tickled, shivers of exquisite fire followed his lambent touch, and dispelled her sorrowful mood.

His fingertips traced the curve of her shoulder and brushed the length of her arm. Then, slowly, with a whisper of touch, he drew his hand back up the inside of her arm. She shook with a tingling spasm that sensitised every nerve with quickened expectation. As he followed the outline of her body down her side, his skilful hand glanced over her soft nipple. It rose up firm and ready as an intense shock of pleasure shot through her.

Jondalar couldn't resist, and bent over to take it in his mouth. She pressed up to him as he suckled and pulled and nibbled, feeling a warm wetness between her thighs as the acute sensations sent corresponding twinges deep inside. He smelled the woman-scent of her skin, and felt a drawing fullness in his loins as he sensed her readiness. He never seemed able to get enough of her, and she was always ready for him.

Not once, that he could remember, had she ever turned him away. No matter what the circumstances, indoors or out, in warm furs or on cold ground, however he wanted her, she was there for him, not just acquiescing, but an active, willing partner. Only during her moon time was she a little subdued, as though she felt shy about it, and respecting her wishes, he held back.

As he reached to caress her thigh and she opened to him, he felt so strong an urge that he could have taken her that instant, but he wanted it to last. They were in a warm dry place, alone, for probably the last time all winter. Not that he hesitated in the longhouse of the Mamutoi, but being alone together lent a special quality of freedom and intensity to their Pleasures. His hand encountered her moistness, then her small, erect centre of pleasure, and he heard her breath explode in gasps and cries as he rubbed and fondled it. He reached lower, and entered with two fingers and explored her depths and textures as she arched her back and moaned. Oh, how he wanted her, he thought, but not yet.

He let go of her nipple, and found her mouth, slightly open. He kissed her firmly, loving the slow sensuous touch of her tongue that found his as he reached hers. He pulled back for a moment, to exercise some control before he gave in entirely to his overpowering drive and this beautiful, willing woman he loved. He looked at her face until she opened her eyes.

In daylight, her eyes were grey-blue, the colour of fine flint, but now they were dark and so full of longing and love his throat hurt with the feeling that arose from the depths of his being. He touched her cheek with the back of his forefinger, outlined her jaw, and ran it over her lips. He couldn't get enough of looking at her, of touching her, as though he wanted to etch her face into his memory. She looked up at him, at eyes so vividly blue they looked violet in firelight, and were so compelling with his love and desire, she wanted to melt into them. If she wanted to, she couldn't have refused him, and she didn't want to.

He kissed her, then moved his warm tongue down her throat and to the depression between her breasts. With both hands, he cupped their full roundness, then reached for a nipple and suckled. She kneaded and massaged his shoulders and arms, moaning softly as waves of tingling sensation coursed through her body.

He worked his way down with his tongue and his mouth, wetted the depression of her navel with his tongue, then felt the texture of soft hair. She arched a little in invitation, and with a moist and sensitive tongue he found the top of her slit, and then the small centre of pleasure. She cried out as he reached it.

Then she sat up, curled around until she found his rigid manhood, and took it into her mouth as far as she could. He gave way a little, and she tasted a spurt of warmth, while her hands reached for his soft pouches.

He felt the pressure building, the drawing from his loins, and the throbbing pulsations in his full member as he tasted of her womanness, and rediscovered her folds and ridges and her deep lovely well. He almost couldn't get enough. He wanted to touch every part of her, taste every part of her, wanted more and more of her, and felt her warmth and a pulling sensation, and both her hands moving up and down his long and full shaft. He ached to enter her.

With supreme effort, he pulled away, turned around and found the source of her womanhood again, explored her with his knowing hands. Then bent down to her node, nuzzling until her breath came in spasms and cries. She felt the surging, building of inexpressible and exquisite tension. She called for him, reached for him, and then he rose up between her thighs, and with a trembling of expectation and control, finally entered her, and exulted in her warm welcome.

He'd held back so long it took a moment to let go. He drove in again, deep, revelling in the wonder of her who could accept all his full size. With joyous abandon, he pushed in again, and out, and in, faster, surging to higher peaks, while she rose up to meet him, matching him stroke for stroke. Then with cries that rose in pitch, he felt it coming, it surged within her, and they burst forth in that final overwhelming rush of energy and pleasure, and release.

They were both too drained, too sensually spent, to move. He was sprawled on top of her, but she always loved that part, the weight of his body on her. She smelled the faint odour of herself on him, which always reminded her how loved she had just been, and why she felt so deliciously drowsy. She still felt the sheer unexpected wonder of the Pleasures. She hadn't known her body could feel such delight and joy. She had only known the degradation of being mounted out of hatred and contempt. Until Jondalar, she didn't know there was any other way.

He pulled himself up, finally, kissing a breast and nuzzling her navel as he backed off and got up. Then she got up, and headed towards the back, dropping some cooking stones in the fire.

"Will you pour some water in that cooking basket, Jondalar? I think the large waterbag is full," she said, on her way to the far corner of the cave, which she used when it was too cold to go outside to relieve herself.

When she returned, she picked the hot stones out of the fire the way she had learned from the Mamutoi, and dropped them into the water that was in a watertight basket. They hissed and steamed as their heat warmed the water. She fished them out and put them back in the fire, and added others that were hot.

When the water was simmering, she scooped out a few cupfuls, put them in a wooden basin, and from her supply of herbals, added a few dried ceanothus lilac-like flowers. A fragrant, spicy perfume filled the air, and when she dipped in a soft scrap of leather, the solution of plant saponin foamed slightly, but it would need no rinsing and leave only a pleasant scent. He watched her standing by the fire while she wiped her face and washed her body, drinking in her beauty as she moved, and wishing he could begin again.

She gave Jondalar a piece of absorbent rabbit skin and passed the basin to him. While he cleansed himself – it was a custom she developed after Jondalar arrived, which he adopted – she looked over her herbs again, pleased to have her entire supply available. She selected individual combinations for a tea for each. For herself, she started with her usual golden thread and antelope root, wondering for a moment if she should stop taking it and see if a baby would start growing inside her. In spite of his explanations, she still believed it was a man, not spirits, that started the life growing. But whatever the cause, Iza's magic seemed to work, and her woman's curse, or rather moon time, as Jondalar called it, still came regularly. It would be nice to have a baby that came from Pleasures with Jondalar, she thought, but maybe it was best to wait. If he decides to become a Mamutoi, too, then perhaps.

She looked at thistle next for her tea, a strengthener of the heart and breath, and good for mother's milk, but she chose damiana instead, which helped keep women's cycles in balance. Then she selected red clover and rose hips for general good health and taste. For Jondalar she picked ginseng, for male balance, energy, and endurance, added yellow dock, a tonic and purifier, then liquorice root, because she had noticed him frowning, which was usually a sign that he was worried or stressed about something, and to sweeten it. She put in a pinch of camomile for nerves as well.

She straightened and rearranged the furs, and gave Jondalar his cup, the wooden one she had made that he liked so well. Then, a little chilly, they both went back to bed, finished their tea and snuggled together.

"You smell nice, like flowers," he said, breathing in her ear, and nibbling her earlobe.

"So do you."

He kissed her, gently, then lingered, with more feeling. "The tea was good. What was in it?" he asked, kissing her neck.

"Just camomile and some things to make you feel good, and give you strength and endurance. I don't know your names for all of them."

225

He kissed her then, with more heat, and she responded with warmth. He propped himself up on one elbow, and looked down at her.

"Ayla, do you have any idea how amazing you are?"

She smiled and shook her head.

"Any time, every time I want you, you are ready for me. You have never put me off or turned me away, even though the more I have you, the more I seem to want you."

"Is that amazing? That I should want you as often as you want me? You know my body better than I do, Jondalar. You have made me feel Pleasures I didn't know were there. Why should I not want you whenever you want me?"

"But for most women, there are some times when they are not in the mood, or it's just not convenient. When it's freezing cold out on the steppes, or on the damp bank of a river when the warm bed is a few steps away. But you never say no. You never say wait."

She closed her eyes, and when she opened them, she had a slight frown. "Jondalar, that's how I was raised. A woman of the Clan never says no. When a man gives her the signal, wherever she is, or whatever she is doing, she stops and answers his need. Any man, even if she hates him, as I hated Broud. Jondalar, you give me nothing but joy, nothing but pleasure. I love it when you want me, any time, any place. If you want me, there is no time I am not ready for you. I always want you. I love you."

He clutched her suddenly, and held her so tightly she could hardly breathe. "Ayla, Ayla," he cried in a hoarse whisper, his head buried in her neck, "I thought I'd never fall in love. Everyone was finding a woman to mate, setting up a hearth and a family. I was just getting older. Even Thonolan found a woman on the Journey. That's why we stayed with the Sharamudoi. I knew many women. I liked many women, but there was always something missing. I thought it was me. I thought the Mother wouldn't let me fall in love. I thought it was my punishment."

"Punishment? For what?" Ayla asked.

"For . . . for something that happened a long time ago."

She didn't press. That was also part of her upbringing.

15

A voice called to him, his mother's voice, but distant, wavering across a fitful wind. Jondalar was home, but home was strange; familiar, yet unfamiliar. He reached beside him. The place was empty! In a panic, he bolted up, fully awake.

Looking around, Jondalar recognised Ayla's cave. The windbreak across the entrance had come loose at one end and was flapping in the wind. Chill gusts of air were blowing into the small cave, but the sun was streaming in through the entrance and the hole above it. He quickly drew on trousers and tunic, and then noticed the steaming cup of tea near the fireplace and beside it, a fresh twig stripped of its bark.

He smiled. How did she do it? he thought. How did she always manage to have hot tea ready and waiting for him when he woke up? At least here, at her cave, she did. At the Lion Camp, there was always something going on, and meals were usually shared with others. He as often took his morning drink at the Lion Hearth or the cooking hearth as the Mammoth Hearth, and then, someone else usually joined them. He didn't notice, there, whether she always had a hot drink waiting for him when he woke up, but when he thought about it, he knew she did. It was never her way to make an issue of it. It was just always there, like so many other things she did for him without him ever having to ask.

He picked up the cup and sipped. There was mint in it – she knew he liked mint in the morning – camomile, too, and something else he couldn't quite discern. The tea had a reddish tinge, rose hips perhaps?

How easy it is to fall into old habits, he thought. He had always made a game out of trying to guess what was in her morning tea. He picked up the twig and chewed on an end as he went outside, and used the chewed end to scrub his teeth. He swished his mouth out with a drink of tea, as he walked to the far end of the ledge to pass his water. He tossed the twig and spat out the tea, then stood at the edge, musing, watching his steaming stream arc down.

The wind was not strong, and the morning sun reflecting off the light-coloured rock gave an impression of warmth. He walked across the uneven surface to the jutting tip and looked down at the small river below. Ice was building up along its edges, but it still ran swiftly around the sharp bend, which shifted its generally southward direction to the east for a few miles before turning back to its southerly course. On his left, the peaceful valley stretched out alongside the river, and he noticed Whinney and Racer grazing nearby. The view upstream, on his right, was entirely different. Beyond the bone pile, at the foot of the wall, and the rocky beach, high stone walls closed in and the river flowed at the bottom of a deep gorge. He remembered swimming upstream once, as far as he could go, to the foot of a tumultuous waterfall.

He saw Ayla come into view as she ascended the steep path, and smiled. "Where have you been?"

A few more steps up and his question was answered, without her saying a word. She was carrying two fat, almost white, ptarmigan by their feathered feet. "I was standing right where you are and saw them in the meadow," she said, holding them out. "I thought fresh meat might be nice for a change. I started a fire in my cooking pit down on the beach. I'll pluck them and start them cooking after we finish breakfast. Oh, here's another firestone I found."

"Are there many on the beach?" he asked.

"Maybe not as many as before. I had to look for this."

"I think I'll go down and look for some later."

Ayla went in to finish preparing breakfast. The meal included grains cooked with red huckleberries that she had found still clinging to bushes that were bare of leaves. The birds had not left many, and she had to pick diligently to gather a few handfuls, but she was pleased to find them.

"That's what it was!" Jondalar said, as he was finishing another cup of tea. "You put red huckleberries in the tea! Mint, camomile, and red huckleberries."

She smiled agreement, and he felt pleased with himself for solving the little puzzle.

After the morning meal, they both went down to the beach, and while Ayla prepared the birds for roasting in the stone oven, Jondalar began searching for the small nodules of iron pyrite that were scattered on the beach. He was still searching when she went back up to the cave. He also found some good-sized chunks of flint, and set them aside. By midmorning, he had accumulated a pile of the firestones, and was bored with staring at the stony beach. He walked around the jutting wall, and seeing the mare and the young horse some distance down the valley, he started towards them.

As he got closer, he noticed that they were both looking in the direction of the steppes. Several horses were at the top of the slope looking back at them. Racer took a few steps towards the wild herd, his neck arched and his nose quivering. Jondalar reacted without thinking.

"Go on! Get away from here!" he shouted, racing towards them, waving his arms.

Startled, the horses jumped back, neighing and snorting, and raced off. The last, a hay-coloured stallion, charged towards the man, then reared as if in warning, before galloping after the rest.

Jondalar turned back and walked to Whinney and Racer. Both were nervous. They, too, had been startled, and they had sensed the herd's panic. He patted Whinney and put his arm around Racer's neck.

"It's all right, boy," he said to the young horse, "I didn't mean to scare you. I just didn't want them enticing you away before we had a chance to become good friends." He scratched and stroked the animal with affection. "Imagine what it would be like to ride a stallion like that yellow one," he mused aloud. "He would be difficult to ride, but then he wouldn't let me scratch him like this, either, would he? What would I have to do for you to let me ride your back and go where I want to go? When should I begin? Should I try to ride you now, or should I wait? You're not full grown yet, but you will be soon. I'd better ask Ayla. She must know. Whinney always seems to understand her. I wonder, do you understand me at all, Racer?"

When Jondalar finally started back to the cave, Racer followed him, bumping him playfully and nuzzling his hand, which greatly pleased the man. The young horse did seem to want to be friends. Racer trailed him all the way back, and up the path into the cave.

"Ayla, do you have anything I can give Racer? Like some grain or something?" he asked as soon as he went in.

Ayla was sitting near the bed with an assortment of piles and mounds of objects arrayed around her. "Why don't you give him some of those little apples in that bowl over there? I looked over some, and those have bruises," she said.

Jondalar scooped out a handful of the small round tart fruits, and fed them to Racer one at a time. After a few more pats, the man walked over to Ayla. He was followed by the friendly horse.

"Jondalar, push Racer out of there! He might step on something!"

He turned around and bumped into the young animal. "That's enough, now, Racer," the man said, walking back with him to the other side of the cave opening, where the young stallion and his dam customarily stayed. But when Jondalar went to leave, he was followed again. He took Racer back to his place again, but had no more luck getting him to stay. "Now that he's so friendly, how do I get him to stop?"

Ayla had been watching the antics, smiling. "You might try pouring a little water in his bowl, or putting some grain in his feeding tray."

Jondalar did both, and when the horse was finally distracted enough, walked back to Ayla, carefully watching behind him to make sure the young horse was no longer there. "What are you doing?" he asked.

"I'm trying to decide what to take with me and what to leave behind," she explained. "What do you think I should give Tulie at the adoption ceremony? It has to be something especially nice."

Jondalar looked over the piles and stacks of things Ayla had made to occupy herself during the empty nights and long cold winters she had spent alone in the cave. Even when she lived with the Clan, she had become recognised for her skill and the quality of her work, and during her years in the valley, she'd had little else to do. She gave extra time and careful attention to each project, to make it last. The results showed.

He picked up a bowl from a stack of them. It was deceptively simple. It was almost perfectly circular and had been made from a single piece of wood. The quality of the finish was so smooth, it almost felt alive. She had told him how she made them. The process was essentially the same as any he knew of; the difference was the care and attention to detail. First, she gouged out the rough shape with a stone adze, then carved it closer with a hand-held flint knife. With a rounded stone and sand, she smoothed both inside and out until hardly a ripple could be felt, and gave it a final finish with scouring horsetail fern.

Her baskets, whether open weave or watertight, had the same quality of simplicity and expert craftsmanship. There was no use of dyes or colours, but textural interest had been created by changing the style of weave, and by using natural colour variations of the fibres. Mats for the ground had the same characteristic. Coils of ropes and twines of sinew and bark, no matter what size, were even and uniform, as were the long thongs, cut in a spiral from a single hide.

The hides she made into leather were soft and supple, but more than anything, he was impressed with her furs. It was one thing to make buckskin pliable by scraping off the grain with the fur on the outside, as well as scraping the inside, but with the fur left on, hides were usually stiffer. Ayla's were not only luxurious on the fur side, but velvety soft and yielding on the inside.

"What are you giving Nezzie?" he asked.

"Food, like those apples, and containers to hold it."

"That's a good idea. What were you thinking of giving Tulie?"

"She is very proud of Deegie's leather, so I don't think I should give her that, and I don't want to give her food like Nezzie. Nothing too practical. She's headwoman. It should be something special to wear, like amber or seashells, but I don't have anything special like that," Ayla said.

"Yes, you do."

"I thought about giving her the amber I found, but that's a sign from my totem. I can't give that away."

"I don't mean the amber. She probably has plenty of amber. Give her fur. It was the first thing she mentioned."

"But she must have many furs, too."

"No furs are as beautiful and special as yours, Ayla. Only once in my life before have I ever seen anything like them. I'm sure she never has. The one I saw was made by a flathe – by a Clan woman."

By evening, Ayla had made some hard decisions, and the accumulation of years of work was settling into two piles. The larger one was to be left behind, along with the cave and the valley. The smaller one was all she would take with her . . . and her memories. It was a wrenching, sometimes agonising process that left her feeling drained. Her mood was communicated to Jondalar, who found himself thinking more of his home and his past and his life than he had for many years. His mind kept straying to painful memories he thought he'd forgotten, and wished he could. He wondered why he kept remembering now.

The evening meal was quiet. They made sporadic comments, and often lapsed into silence, each occupied with private thoughts.

"The birds are delicious, as usual," Jondalar remarked.

"Creb liked them that way."

She had mentioned that before. It was still hard to believe, sometimes, that she had learned so much from the flatheads she lived with. When he thought of it, though, why wouldn't they know how to cook as well as anyone?

"My mother is a good cook. She would probably like them, too."

Jondalar has been thinking a lot about his mother lately, Ayla thought. He said he woke up this morning dreaming about her.

"When I was growing up, she had special foods she liked to make . . . when she wasn't busy with the matters of the Cave."

"Matters of the Cave?"

"She was the leader of the Ninth Cave."

"You told me that, but I didn't understand. You mean she was like Tulie? A headwoman?"

"Yes, something like that. But there was no Talut, and the Ninth Cave is much bigger than the Lion Camp. Many more people." He stopped and closed his eyes in concentration. "Maybe as many as four people for every one."

Ayla tried to think about how many that would be, then decided she would work it out later with marks on the ground, but she wondered how so many people could live together all the time. It seemed to be almost enough for a Clan Gathering.

"In the Clan, no women were leaders," she said.

"Marthona became leader after Joconnan. Zelandoni told me she was so much a part of his leadership that after he died, everyone just turned to her. My brother, Joharran, was born to his hearth. He's leader now, but Marthona is still an adviser . . . or she was when I left."

Ayla frowned. He had spoken of them before, but she hadn't quite understood all his relationships. "Your mother was the mate of . . . how did you say it? Joconnan?"

"Yes."

"But you always talk of Dalanar."

"I was born to his hearth."

"So your mother was the mate of Dalanar, too."

"Yes. She was already a leader when they mated. They were very close, people still tell stories about Marthona and Dalanar, and sing sad songs about their love. Zelandoni told me they cared too much. Dalanar didn't want to share her with the Cave. He grew to hate the time she spent on leadership duties, but she felt a responsibility. Finally they severed the knot and he left. Later, Marthona made a new hearth with Willomar, and then gave birth to Thonolan and Folara. Dalanar travelled to the northeast, discovered a flint mine and met Jerika, and founded the First Cave of the Lanzadonii there."

He was silent for a while. Jondalar seemed to feel a need to talk about his family, so Ayla listened even though he was repeating some things he'd said before. She got up, poured the last of the tea into their cups, added wood to the fire, then sat on the furs on the end of the bed and watched its flickering light move shadows across Jondalar's pensive face. "What does it mean, Lanzadonii?" she asked.

Jondalar smiled. "It just means . . . people . . . children of Doni . . . children of the Great Earth Mother who live in the northeast, to be exact."

"You lived there, didn't you? With Dalanar?"

He closed his eyes. His jaw worked as he ground his teeth and his forehead knotted with pain. Ayla had seen that expression before, and wondered. He had spoken about that period in his life during the summer, but it upset him and she knew he held back. She felt a tension in the air, a great pressure building up centred on Jondalar, like a swelling of the earth getting ready to burst forth from great depths.

"Yes, I lived there," he said, "for three years." He jumped up suddenly, knocking over his tea, and strode to the back wall of the cave. "O, Mother! It was terrible!" He put his arm up to the wall and leaned his head against it, in the dark, trying to keep himself under control. Finally, he walked back, looked down at the wet spot where the liquid had seeped into the hard-packed dirt floor, and hunkered down on one knee to right the cup. He turned it over in his hands and stared at the fire.

"Was it so bad living with Dalanar?" Ayla finally asked.

"Living with Dalanar? No." He looked surprised at what she had said. "That isn't what was so bad. He was glad to see me. He welcomed me to his hearth, taught me my craft right along with Joplaya, treated me like an adult . . . and he never said a word about it."

"A word about what?"

Jondalar took a deep breath. "The reason I was sent there," he said, and looked down at the cup in his hand.

As the silence deepened, the breathing of the horses filled the cave, and the loud reports of the fire burning and crackling rebounded off the stone walls. Jondalar put the cup down and stood up.

"I always was big for my age, and older than my years," he began, striding the length of the cleared space around the fire, and then back again. "I matured young. I was no more than eleven years when the donii first came to me in a dream . . . and she had the face of Zolena."

There was her name again. The woman who had meant so much to him. He'd talked about her, but only briefly and with obvious distress. Ayla hadn't understood what caused him such anguish.

"All the young men wanted her for their donii-woman, they all wanted her to teach them. They were supposed to want her, or someone like her" – he whirled and faced Ayla – "but they weren't supposed to love her! Do you know what it means to fall in love with your donii-woman?"

Ayla shook her head.

"She is supposed to show you, teach you, help you understand the Mother's great Gift, to make you ready when it is your turn to bring a girl to womanhood. All women are supposed to be donii-women at least once, when they are older, just as all men are supposed to share a young woman's First Rites, at least once. It is a sacred duty in honour of Doni." He looked down. "But a donii-woman represents the Great Mother, you don't fall in love and want her for your mate." He looked up at her again. "Can you understand that? It's forbidden. It's like falling in love with your mother, like wanting to mate your own sister. Forgive me, Ayla. It's almost like wanting to mate a flathead woman!"

He turned and in a few long paces was at the entrance. He pushed the windbreak aside, then his shoulders slumped and he changed his mind and walked back. He sat down beside her, and looked off into the distance.

"I was twelve, and Zolena was my donii-woman, and I loved her. And she loved me. At first it was just that she seemed to know exactly how to please me, but then it was more. I could talk to her, about

233

anything; we liked to be with each other. She taught me about women, what pleased them, and I learned well because I loved her and wanted to please her. I loved pleasing her. We didn't mean to fall in love, we didn't even tell each other, at first. Then we tried to keep it a secret. But I wanted her for my mate. I wanted to live with her. I wanted her children to be the children of my hearth."

He blinked and Ayla saw a glistening wetness at the corners of his eyes as he stared at the fire.

"Zolena kept saying I was too young, I'd get over it. Most men are at least fifteen before they seriously start looking for a woman to be a mate. I didn't feel too young. But it didn't matter what I wanted. I couldn't have her. She was my donii-woman, my counsellor and teacher, and she wasn't supposed to let me fall in love with her. They blamed her more than me, but that made it worse. She wouldn't have been blamed at all if I hadn't been so stupid!" Jondalar said, spitting it out.

"Other men wanted her, too. Always. Whether she wanted them or not. One was always bothering her – Ladroman. She had been his donii-woman a few years before. I suppose I can't blame him for wanting her, but she wasn't interested in him any more. He started following us, watching us. Then one time he found us together. He threatened her, said if she didn't go with him, he'd tell everyone about us.

"She tried to laugh him off, told him to go ahead; there was nothing to tell, she was just my donii-woman. I should have done the same, but when he mocked us with words we had said in private, I got angry. No . . . I did not just get angry. I lost my temper, and went out of control. I hit him."

Jondalar pounded his fist on the ground beside him, then again, and again. "I couldn't stop hitting him. Zolena tried to make me stop. Finally, she had to get someone else to pull me away. It's good that she did. I think I would have killed him."

Jondalar got up and began striding back and forth again. "Then it all came out. Every sordid detail. Ladroman told everything, in public . . . in front of everyone. I was embarrassed to find out how long he'd been watching us, and how much he had heard. Zolena and I were both questioned," he blushed just remembering, "and both denounced, but I hated it when she was held responsible. What made it worse was that I am my mother's son. She was the leader of the Ninth Cave, and I disgraced her. The whole Cave was in an uproar."

"What did she do?" Ayla asked.

"She did what she had to do. Ladroman was badly hurt. He lost several teeth. That makes it hard to chew, and women don't like a man without teeth. Mother had to pay a large penalty for me as restitution, and when Ladroman's mother insisted, she agreed to send me away."

He stopped and closed his eyes, his forehead knotting with the pain of remembering. "I cried that night." The admission was obviously difficult for him to make. "I didn't know where I would go. I didn't know mother had sent a runner to Dalanar to ask him to take me."

He took a breath and continued. "Zolena left before I did. She had always been drawn to the Zelandonii, and she went to join Those Who Serve the Mother. I thought about Serving, too, maybe as a carver – I thought I had a little talent for carving then. But word came from Dalanar, and the next thing I knew, Willomar was taking me to the Lanzadonii. I didn't really know Dalanar. He left when I was young, and I only saw him at Summer Meetings. I didn't know what to expect, but Marthona did the right thing."

Jondalar stopped talking, and hunkered down near the fire again. Then picked up a broken branch, dry and brittle, and added it to the flames. "Before I left, people avoided me, reviled me," he continued. "Some people took their children away when I was around so they wouldn't be exposed to my foul influence, as though looking at me might corrupt them. I know I deserved it, what we did was terrible, but I wanted to die."

Ayla waited, silently watching him. She didn't understand entirely the customs he spoke of, but she hurt for him with an empathy born of her own pain. She, too, had broken taboos and paid the harsh consequences, but she had learned from them.. Perhaps because she was so different to begin with, she had learned to question whether what she had done was really so bad. She had come to understand that it wasn't wrong for her to hunt, with sling or spear or anything she wanted, just because the Clan believed it was wrong for women to hunt, and she didn't hate herself because she had stood up to Broud against all tradition.

"Jondalar," she said, aching for him as he hung his head in defeat and recrimination, "you did a terrible thing – " he nodded agreement " – when you beat that man so hard. But what did you and Zolena do that was so wrong?" Ayla asked.

He looked at her, surprised at her question. He had expected scorn, derision, the kind of contempt he felt for himself. "You don't understand. Zolena was my donii-woman. We dishonoured the Mother. Offended Her. It was shameful."

"What was shameful? I still don't know what you did that was so wrong?"

"Ayla, when a woman assumes that aspect of the Mother, to teach a young man, she takes on an important responsibility. She is preparing him for manhood, to be the woman-maker. Doni has made it a man's responsibility to open a woman, to make her ready to accept the mingled spirits from the Great Earth Mother so the woman can become a mother.

It is a sacred duty. It is not a common, everyday relationship that anyone can have at any time, not something to be taken lightly," Jondalar explained.

"Did you take it lightly?"

"No. Of course not!"

"Then what did you do wrong?"

"I profaned a sacred rite. I fell in love . . ."

"You fell in love. And Zolena fell in love. Why should that be wrong? Don't those feelings make you feel warm and good? You didn't plan to do it. It just happened. Isn't it natural to fall in love with a woman?"

"But not that woman," Jondalar protested. "You don't understand."

"You are right. I don't understand. Broud forced me. He was cruel and hateful, and that's what gave him pleasure. Then you taught me what Pleasures should be, not painful, but warm and good. Loving you makes me feel warm and good, too. I thought love always made you feel that way, but now you tell me it can be wrong to love someone, and it can cause great pain."

Jondalar picked up another piece of wood and put it on the fire. How could he make her understand? You could love your mother, too, but you don't want to mate her, and you don't want your donii-woman to have the children of your hearth. He didn't know what to say, but the silence was strained.

"Why did you leave Dalanar and go back?" Ayla asked, after a while.

"My mother sent for me . . . no, it was more than that. I wanted to return. As good as Dalanar was to me, as much as I liked Jerika, and my cousin, Joplaya, it was never quite home. I didn't know if I could ever return. I was very worried about going back, but I wanted to go. I vowed never to lose my temper, never to lose control again."

"Were you glad you went home?"

"It wasn't the same, but after the first few days, it was better than I thought it would be. Ladroman's family had left the Ninth Cave, and without him there to remind everyone, people forgot about it. I don't know what I would have done if he'd still been there. It was bad enough at Summer Meetings. Every time I saw him I'd remember the disgrace. There was a lot of talk when Zolena first returned, a little later. I was afraid to see her again, but I wanted to. I couldn't help it, Ayla, even after all that, I think I still loved her." His look pleaded for understanding.

He stood again and started pacing. "But she had changed a lot. She'd already moved up in the ranks of the Zelandonii. She was very much One Who Serves the Mother. I didn't want to believe it at first. I wanted to see how much she had changed, to see if she had any feelings left for me. I wanted to be alone with her, and planned how to do it. I waited until the next festival to Honour the Mother. She must have guessed.

236

She tried to avoid me, but then changed her mind. Some people were scandalised the next day, even though it was entirely proper to share Pleasures with her at a festival." He snorted with derision. "They needn't have bothered. She said she still cared about me, wanted the best for me, but it wasn't the same. She really didn't want me any more.

"The truth of it is," he said, with bitter irony, "I think she does care about me. We're good friends now, but Zolena knew what she wanted . . . and she got it. She is not Zolena now. Before I started my Journey, she became Zelandoni, First among Those Who Serve the Mother. I left with Thonolan soon afterwards. I think that's why I went."

He walked to the entrance again, and stood there looking out over the top of the repaired windbreak. Ayla got up and joined him. She closed her eyes, feeling the wind on her face, and listened to Whinney's even breathing, and Racer's more nervous huffing. Jondalar took a deep breath, then went back and sat down on a mat by the fire, but he made no move to go to sleep. Ayla followed him, took down the large waterbag and poured some water into a cooking basket, then put stones in the fire to heat. He didn't seem ready for bed yet. He wasn't through.

"The best part of going back home was Thonolan," he said, picking up the thread again. "He'd grown up while I was gone, and after I got back, we became good friends and started doing all kinds of things together . . ."

Jondalar stopped, and his face filled with grief. Ayla remembered how hard his brother's death had been on him. He slumped down beside her, his shoulders sagging, drained and exhausted, and she realised what an ordeal it had been for him to talk about his past. She wasn't sure what had brought it on, but she knew something had been building up in him.

"Ayla, on our way back, do you think we can find . . . the place where Thonolan was . . . killed?" he said, turning to her, his eyes brimming, and his voice breaking.

"I'm not sure, but we can try." She added more stones to the water and picked out soothing herbs.

Suddenly she remembered, with all the worry and fear she'd felt then, his first night in her cave, when she wasn't sure he would live. He'd called for his brother then, and though she hadn't understood his words, she understood he was asking for the man who was dead. When she finally made him understand, he spent his great racking grief in her arms.

"That first night, do you know how long it had been since I cried?" he asked, startling her, almost as though he knew what she had been thinking, but then he'd been talking about Thonolan. "Not since then, not since my mother told me I would have to leave. Ayla, why did he have to die?" he said, with a pleading, strained voice. "Thonolan was younger than I was! He shouldn't have died so young. I couldn't bear knowing he was gone. Once I started, I couldn't seem to stop. I don't know what I would have done if you hadn't been there, Ayla. I never told you that before. I think I was ashamed because . . . because I lost control again."

"There is no shame in grieving, Jondalar . . . or in loving."

He looked away from her. "You think not?" His voice held an edge of self-contempt. "Even when you use it for yourself, and hurt someone else?"

Ayla frowned in puzzlement.

He turned and faced the fire again. "The summer after I was back, I was selected at the Summer Meeting for First Rites. I was worried; most men are. You worry about hurting a woman, and I'm not a small man. There are always witnesses, to verify that a girl has been opened, but also to make sure that she's not really hurt. You worry that maybe you won't be able to prove your manhood and they'll have to get another man at the last moment, and you'll be shamed. Many things can happen. I have to thank Zelandoni." His laugh was caustic. "She did exactly what a donii-woman is supposed to. She counselled me . . . and it helped.

"But, I thought of Zolena that night, not the aspiring Zelandoni. Then I saw this scared girl and I realised she was a lot more worried than I was. She really got frightened when she saw me full; many women do, the first time. But I remembered what Zolena had taught me, how to make her ready, how to limit and control myself, how to please her. It turned out to be wonderful, to see her go from a nervous, scared girl to an open, willing woman. She was so grateful, and so loving . . . I felt that I loved her, that night."

He closed his eyes in that frown of pain Ayla had seen so much recently. Then he jumped up again and paced. "I never learn! I knew the next day I didn't really love her, but she loved me! She was not supposed to fall in love with me any more than I was supposed to fall in love with my donii-woman. I was supposed to make her a woman, teach her about Pleasures, not make her love me. I tried not to hurt her feelings, but I could see her disappointment when I finally made her understand."

He was striding back from the cave opening, and stopped in front of her and almost shouted at her. "Ayla, it is a sacred act, to make a girl a woman, a duty, a responsibility, and I had profaned it again!" He started walking. "That wasn't the last time. I told myself I would never do that again, but it happened the same way the next time. I told myself I would not accept the role again, I didn't deserve it. But the next time they selected me, I couldn't say no. I wanted it. They chose me often, and I began to look forward to it, to the feelings of love and warmth on that night, even though I hated myself the next day for using those young women and the Mother's sacred rite for myself."

He stopped, and clung to one of the posts of her herb drying rack, and looked down at her. "But after a couple of years, I realised something was wrong, and I knew the Mother was punishing me. The men my age were finding women, settling down, showing off the children of their hearths. But I couldn't find a woman to love that way. I knew many women, I enjoyed them for their company and their Pleasures, but I only felt love when I wasn't supposed to, at First Rites . . . and only on that night." He hung his head.

He looked up, startled, when he heard a gentle laugh. "Oh, Jondalar. But you fell in love. You love me, don't you? Don't you understand? You weren't being punished. You were waiting for me. I told you my totem led you to me, maybe the Mother did, too, but you had to come a long way. You had to wait. If you had fallen in love before, you would never have come. You would never have found me."

Could that be true? he wondered. He wanted to believe it. For the first time in years he felt the load that had weighed down his spirit lighten, and a look of hope crossed his face. "What about Zolena, my donii-woman?"

"I don't think it was wrong to love her, but even if it went against your customs, you were punished, Jondalar. You were sent away. That's over now. You don't have to keep reminding yourself, punishing yourself."

"But the young women, at First Rites, who . . ."

Ayla's expression turned hard. "Jondalar, do you know how terrible it is to be forced the first time? Do you know what it is to hate and have to endure what is not a Pleasure, but painful and ugly? Maybe you weren't supposed to fall in love with those women, but it must have been a wonderful feeling for them to be treated gently, to feel the Pleasures that you know so well how to give, and to feel loved that first time. If you gave them even a little of what you give me, then you gave them a beautiful memory to carry with them all their lives. Oh, Jondalar, you didn't hurt them. You did exactly the right thing. Why do you think you were chosen so often?"

The burden of shame and self-contempt he had carried, buried deep inside for so long, began to slip. He began to think that maybe there was a reason for his life, that the painful experiences of his childhood had some purpose. In the catharsis of confession, he saw that perhaps his actions had not been as contemptible as he thought, that perhaps he was worthwhile – and he wanted to feel worthwhile.

But the emotional baggage he had dragged around with him for so long was hard to unload. Yes, he'd finally found a woman to love, and it was true that she was everything he'd ever wanted – but what if he brought her home and she told someone that she was raised by flatheads? Or worse, that she had a mixed son? An abomination? Would he be reviled, again, along with her, for bringing such a woman? He flushed at the thought.

Was it fair to her? What if they turned her away, heaped insults on her? And what if he didn't stand by her? What if he let them do it? He shuddered. No, he thought. He wouldn't let them do such a thing to her. He loved her. But what if he did?

Why was Ayla the one he had found to love? Her explanation seemed too simple. His belief that the Great Mother was punishing him for his sacrilege could not be laid to rest so easily. Perhaps Ayla was right, maybe Doni had led him to her, but wasn't it a punishment that this beautiful woman he loved would be no more acceptable to his people than the first woman he had loved? Wasn't it ironic that this woman he had finally found was a pariah who had given birth to an abomination?

But the Mamutoi held similar beliefs and they weren't turning her away. The Lion Camp was adopting her, even knowing she had been raised by flatheads. They had even welcomed a mixed child. Maybe he shouldn't try to take her home with him. She might be happier staying. Maybe he should stay, too, let Tulie adopt him and become Mamutoi. His forehead furrowed. But he wasn't Mamutoi. He was Zelandonii. The Mamutoi were good people, and their ways were similar, but they weren't his people. What could he offer Ayla here? He had no affiliations, no family, no kin among these people. What could he offer her if he took her home?

He was torn in so many directions, he suddenly felt exhausted. Ayla saw his face go slack, his shoulders slump.

"It's late, Jondalar. Drink a little of this, and let's go to bed," she said, handing him a cup.

He nodded, drank the warm beverage, slipped out of his clothes and crawled into the furs. Ayla lay beside him, watching him until the furrows on his forehead eased and smoothed out, and his breath was deep and regular, but sleep for her was slower in coming. Jondalar's distress troubled her. She was glad he had told her more about himself, and his younger life. She had long believed something deep within himself caused him great anguish, and perhaps talking about it had relieved some of his discomfort, but something still bothered him. He had not told her everything, and she felt a deep uneasiness about it.

240

She lay awake, trying not to disturb him, wishing she could sleep. How many nights had she spent alone in this cave, unable to sleep? Then she remembered the cloak. Slipping quietly out of bed, she rummaged through her pack and pulled out a soft, old piece of leather, and held it to her cheek. It was one of the few things she had taken with her from the rubble of the Clan's cave before she left. She had used it to help carry Durc when he was an infant, and to support him on her hip when he was a toddler. She didn't know why she had taken it. It had not been a necessity, yet more than once, when she was alone, she had rocked herself to sleep with it. But not since Jondalar came.

She crumpled the soft old hide into a ball, stuffed it to her stomach, and wrapped herself around it. Then, she closed her eyes and went to sleep.

"It's too much, even with the travois and carrying baskets on Whinney. I need two horses to carry all this!" Ayla said, looking over the pile of bundles and neatly tied objects she wanted to take with her. "I'll have to leave more behind, but I've been through everything so many times, I don't know what else to leave." She glanced around trying to find something that would give her an idea for a solution to her dilemma.

The cave seemed deserted. Everything useful that they weren't taking with them had been put back in the storage holes and cairns, just in case they might want to come back for it someday, though neither one believed they ever would. All that was left in view was a pile of discards. Even Ayla's herb drying rack was bare.

"You've got two horses. Too bad you can't use both of them," Jondalar said, seeing the two horses in their place near the entrance, munching on hay.

Ayla studied the horses, speculatively. Jondalar's comment had started her thinking. "I still think of him as Whinney's colt, but Racer is almost as big as she is. Maybe he could carry a small load."

Jondalar was immediately interested. "I've been wondering when he would be big enough to do some of the things Whinney does, and how you would teach him to do them. When did you first ride Whinney? And what made you think about it in the first place?"

Ayla smiled. "I was just running with her one day, wishing I could run as fast, and suddenly the idea came to me. She was a little frightened at first and started running, but she knew me. When she got tired, she stopped, and didn't seem to mind. It was wonderful! It was running like the wind!"

Jondalar watched her as she recalled her first ride, her eyes glistening and breathing hard with remembered excitement. He had felt the same way the first time Ayla had let him ride on Whinney, and he shared her excitement. He was moved by a sudden desire for her. It never ceased to amaze him how he could be so easily and unexpectedly provoked to want her. But her mind was on Racer.

"I wonder how long it would take to get him used to carrying something? I was riding Whinney before I started having her carry a load, so it didn't take her long. But if he started first with a small load, it might make it easier to get him to carry a rider later. Let's see if I can find something to practise with."

She rummaged through the discard pile pulling out skins, some baskets, extra rocks she had used to sand bowls and knap flint tools with, and the sticks she had marked to keep track of the days she had lived in the valley.

She paused for a moment, holding one stick, and put each finger of one hand over the first marks, the way Creb had shown her so long ago. She swallowed hard, thinking about Creb. Jondalar had used the marks on the sticks to confirm how long she had been there, and to help her put into his counting words the number of years of her life. She was seventeen years, then, in the beginning of summer; in late winter or spring she would add another year. He had said he was twenty years and one, and laughingly called himself an old man. He had begun his Journey three years before, the same time she had left the Clan.

She gathered everything up and headed outside, whistling for Whinney and Racer to follow. In the field, they both spent some time stroking and scratching the young stallion. Then Ayla picked up a leather hide. She let him smell it and chew on it, and rubbed him down with it. Then she draped it across his back, and let it hang. He grabbed an end with his teeth and pulled it off, then brought it to her to play some more. She put it across his back again. The next time, Jondalar put it on his back while Ayla set out a coiled long thong and busied herself with making something. They draped the hide on Racer and let him pull it off a few more times. Whinney nickered, watching with interest, and got some attention, too.

The next time Ayla put the hide across Racer's back, she dropped a long strip of leather with it, reached under him to grab the loose end, and tied the hide on with it. This time when Racer went to pull it off with his teeth, it didn't come immediately. At first, he didn't like it, and tried to buck it off, but then he found a flapping end and started tugging with his teeth until he pulled it out from under the thong. He began working the loose thong around until he found the knot, and worked at it with his teeth until he untied it. He picked the hide up with his teeth and dropped it at Ayla's feet, then went back for the thong. Both Ayla and Jondalar laughed, as Racer pranced away with his head held high, looking proud of himself.

The young horse allowed Jondalar to tie the hide on him again, and walked around with it on his back before he made a game of tugging and pulling and working it off. By then, he seemed to be losing interest. Ayla tied the hide on him again, and he let it stay while she petted and talked to him. Then she reached for the training device she had constructed, two baskets tied together so that they would hang down on both sides, with stones to add weight, and sticks jutting up like the front ends of travois poles.

She draped it across Racer's back. He flattened his ears, and turned his head back to look. He was unaccustomed to a weight on his back, but he'd been leaned across and handled so much of his life, he was used to feeling some pressure and weight. It wasn't a totally unfamiliar experience, but most important, he trusted the woman, and so did his dam. She left the basket carrier in place while she patted and scratched and talked to him, and then she took it off along with the thong and the hide. He sniffed it again, then ignored it.

"We may have to stay an extra day or so to get him used to it, and I will still go through everything one more time, but I think it will work," Ayla said, beaming with pleasure as they walked back to the cave. "Maybe not dragging a load on poles, like Whinney does, but I think Racer could carry some things on his back."

"I just hope the weather holds a few more days," Jondalar said.

"If we don't try to ride at all, we can put a bundle of hay where we sit, Jondalar. I tied it up tight," Ayla said, calling down to the man making one last search for firestones on the rocky beach below. The horses were on the beach, too. Whinney, outfitted with packed travois and carrying baskets plus a hide-covered lumpy load on her rump, was waiting patiently. Racer was more skittish about the baskets hanging down his sides and the small load tied to his back. He was still unaccustomed to carrying any load, but the steppe horse was the original breed, a stocky, sturdy horse, used to living in the wild and exceptionally strong.

"I thought you were bringing grain for them, why do you want hay? There's more grass out there than all the horses can eat."

"But when it snows heavily or, worse, when the ice crusts on top, it's hard for them to get at it, and too much grain can make them bloat. It's good to have a few days' supply of hay on hand. Horses can die of starvation in winter."

"You wouldn't let those horses starve if you had to break through the ice and cut the grass yourself, Ayla," Jondalar said with a laugh, "but I don't care if we ride or walk." His smile faded as he looked up at the clear blue sky. "It's going to take longer to get back than it did getting here, as loaded as the horses are, either way."

Holding three more pieces of the innocuous-looking stones in his hand, Jondalar started up the steep path to the cave. When he reached the entrance, he found Ayla standing there looking in with tears in her eyes. He deposited the pyrites in a pouch near his travelling pack and then went to stand beside her.

"This was my home," she said, overcome by loss as the finality of the move struck her. "This was my own place. My totem led me here, gave me a sign." She reached for the small leather bag she wore around her neck. "I was lonely, but I did what I wanted to do here, and what I had to do. Now the Spirit of the Cave Lion wants me to leave." She looked up at the tall man beside her. "Do you think we'll ever come back?"

"No," he said. There was a hollow ring to his voice. He was looking in the small cave, but he was seeing another place and another time. "Even if you go back to the same place, it's not the same."

"Then why do you want to go back, now, Jondalar? Why not stay here, become a Mamutoi?" she asked.

"I can't stay. It's hard to explain. I know it won't be the same, but the Zelandonii are my people. I want to show them the firestones. I want to show them how to hunt with the spear-thrower. I want them to see what can be done with flint that has been heated. All these things are important and worthwhile and can bring many benefits. I want to bring them to my people." He looked down at the ground and lowered his voice. "I want them to look at me and think that I am worthwhile."

She looked into his expressive, troubled eyes, and wished she could remove the pain she saw there. "Is it so important what they think? Isn't it more important that you know you are?" she said.

Then she remembered that the Cave Lion was his totem, too, chosen by the Spirit of the powerful animal just as she had been. She knew it was not easy living with a powerful totem, the tests were difficult, but the gifts, and the knowledge that came inside, were always worth it. Creb had told her that the Great Cave Lion never chose someone who wasn't worthy.

Rather than the smaller, one-shouldered Mamutoi haversack, they settled into heavy travelling packs, similar to the type Jondalar once used, designed to be worn on the back, with straps over the shoulders. They made sure the hoods of their parkas were free to slip on or off. Ayla had added tumplines, which could be worn across the forehead for added support, if they chose, though she usually dispensed with the tumpline in favour of wearing her sling wrapped around her head. Their food, fire-making materials, tent, and sleeping furs were packed inside.

Jondalar also carried two good-sized nodules of flint carefully selected from several he had found on the beach, and a pouch full of firestones.

In a separate holder attached to the side, they both carried spears and spear-throwers. Ayla carried several good throwing stones in a pouch, and under her parka, attached to a thong she had tied around her tunic, was her otter skin medicine bag.

The hay, which Ayla had bound into a round bale, was tied on the mare. She gave both horses a critical appraisal, checking their legs, their stance, their carriage to make sure they were not overloaded. With a last look up the steep path, they started out down the long valley, Whinney following Ayla, Jondalar leading Racer by a rope. They crossed over the small river near the stepping-stones. Ayla considered removing some of Whinney's load to make it easier for her to get up the gravelled slope, but the sturdy mare made it with little trouble.

Once up on the western steppes, Ayla went a different way from the one they had arrived by. She took a wrong turn, then backtracked, until she found the one she was looking for. Finally, they arrived at a blind canyon strewn with huge, sharp-angled boulders, which had been sheared from crystalline granite walls by the cutting edge of frost and heat and time. Watching Whinney for signs of nervousness – the canyon had once been home to cave lions – they started in, drawn to the slope of loose gravel at the far end.

When Ayla had found them, Thonolan was already dead and Jondalar gravely injured. Except for a request to the Spirit of her Cave Lion to guide the man to the next world, she'd had no time for burial rites, but she couldn't leave the body exposed to predation. She had dragged him to the end, and using her heavy spear, fashioned after the kind used by the men of the Clan, she levered aside a rock which held back an accumulation of loose stone. She had grieved as the gravel covered the lifeless, bloody form of a man she never knew, and now, never would; a man like herself, a man of the Others.

Jondalar stood at the foot of the slope wishing there was something he could do to acknowledge this burial place of his brother. Perhaps Doni had already found him, since She called him back to Her so soon, but he knew Zelandoni would try to find this resting place of Thonolan's spirit and guide him if she could. But how could he tell her where this place was? He couldn't even have found it himself.

"Jondalar?" Ayla said. He looked at her and noticed she had a small leather pouch in her hand. "You have told me his spirit should return to Doni. I don't know the ways of the Great Earth Mother, I only know of the spirit world of the Clan totems. I asked my Cave Lion to guide him there. Maybe it is the same place, or maybe your Great Mother knows of that place, but the Cave Lion is a powerful totem and your brother is not without protection."

"Thank you, Ayla. I know you did the best you could."

"Maybe you don't understand, just as I don't understand Doni, but the Cave Lion is your totem, too, now. He chose you, as he chose me, and marked you, as he marked me."

"You told me that before. I'm not sure what it means."

"He had to choose you, when he chose you for me. Only a man with a Cave Lion totem is strong enough for a woman with a Cave Lion totem, but there is something you must know. Creb always told me, it is not easy living with a powerful totem. His Spirit will test you, to know you are worthy. It will be very hard, but you will gain more than you know." She held up the small pouch. "I made an amulet for you. You don't have to wear it around your neck, as I do, but you should keep it with you. I put a piece of red ochre in it, so it can hold a piece of your spirit and a piece of your totem's, but I think your amulet should hold one more thing."

Jondalar was frowning. He didn't want to offend her, but he wasn't sure if he wanted this Clan totem amulet.

"I think you should take a piece of stone from your brother's grave. A piece of his spirit will stay with it, and you can carry it back with yours to your people."

The knots of consternation on his forehead deepened then suddenly cleared. Of course! That might help Zelandoni find this place in a spirit trance. Maybe there was more to Clan totems than he realised. After all, didn't Doni create the spirits of all the animals?

"Ayla, how do you know exactly what to do? How could you learn so much, where you grew up? Yes, I'll keep this and put a stone from Thonolan's grave in it," he said.

He looked at the loose, sharp-edged gravel sloping against the wall in a tenuous equilibrium, created by the same forces that had split the stone slabs and blocks from the steep canyon sides. Suddenly a stone, giving way to the cosmic force of gravity, rolled down amid a spattering of other rocks and landed at Jondalar's feet. He picked it up. At first glance, it appeared to be the same as all the other innocuous little pieces of broken granite and sedimentary rock. But when he turned it over, he was surprised to see a shining opalescence where the stone had broken. Fiery red lights gleamed from the heart of the milky white stone, and shimmering streaks of blues and greens danced and sparkled in the sun as he turned it this way and that.

"Ayla, look at this," he said, showing her the small piece of opal. "You'd never guess it from the back of this. You'd think it was just an ordinary stone, but look here, where it broke off. The colours seem to come from deep inside, and they're so bright. It almost seems alive."

"Maybe it is, or maybe it is a piece of the spirit of your brother," she replied.

246

16

A cold eddy of air curled beneath the edge of the low tent; an exposed arm was quickly brought under a fur. A stiff breeze whistled through the flap across the opening; a frown of worry creased a sleeping brow. A gust caught the flap with a sharp crack and snapped it back and forth, opening the way for bellowing draughts, which brought both Ayla and Jondalar fully awake in an instant. Jondalar tied the loose end down, but the wind, increasing steadily through the night, made sleep fitful and uneasy as it gasped and groaned, heaved and howled around the small hide shelter.

In the morning, they struggled to fold the tent hide between them in the blustery wind and packed quickly, not bothering to make a fire. Instead they drank cold water from the icy stream nearby and ate travelling food. The wind abated around midmorning, but there was a tension in the atmosphere which made them doubt that the worst was over.

When the wind picked up again around noon, Ayla noticed a fresh, almost metallic scent to the air, more like an absence of smell than an actual odour. She sniffed, turning her head, testing, evaluating.

"There's snow on this wind." Ayla shouted to be heard above the roar. "I can smell it."

"What did you say?" Jondalar said, but the wind whipped his words away and Ayla understood his meaning more from the shapes his mouth took as he spoke than from hearing him. She stopped to let him come abreast.

"I can smell snow on the way. We've got to find a place to shelter before it comes," Ayla said, searching the broad, flat expanse with troubled eyes. "But where can we find shelter out here?"

Jondalar was equally worried as he scanned the empty steppes. Then he recalled the nearly frozen stream they had camped near the night before. They hadn't crossed over, it would still be on their left no matter how much it meandered. He strained to see through blowing dust, but nothing was clear. He turned left anyway.

"Let's try to find that little river," he said. "There may be trees or high banks along it that will give us some protection." Ayla nodded, following his lead. Whinney did not object either.

The subtle quality to the air that the woman had detected, and thought of as the smell of snow, had been an accurate warning. Before long, a light powdery sifting whirled and blew in an erratic pattern, defining and giving shape to the wind. It soon gave way to larger flakes that made it more difficult to see.

But when Jondalar thought he saw the outline of vague shapes looming ahead, and stopped to try to make them out, Whinney pushed on and they all followed her lead. Low-bent trees and a screen of brush marked the edge of a watercourse. The man and woman could have crouched behind it, but the mare kept going downstream until they reached a turn where the water had cut deep into a bank of hard-packed soil. There, next to the low bluff, out of the full force of the wind, Whinney urged the young horse, and stood on the outside to protect him.

Ayla and Jondalar quickly removed the horses' loads and set up their small tent almost under the mare's feet, then crawled inside to wait out the storm.

Even in the lee of the bank, out of the direct force of the wind, the storm threatened their simple shelter. The roaring gale blew from all directions at once, and seemed determined to find a way inside. It succeeded often. Draughts and gusts stole under the edges or in through cracks where the skin across the opening overlapped or the smoke-hole cover was fastened, often bringing a dusting of snow. The woman and the man crawled under their furs to keep warm, and talked. Incidents of their childhood, stories, legends, people they'd known, customs, ideas, dreams, hopes; they never seemed to run out of things to talk about. As night came on, they shared Pleasures, and then slept. Sometime in the middle of the night, the wind stopped its assault on their tent.

Ayla awoke and lay with her eyes open, looking around the dim interior, fighting down a growing panic. She didn't feel well, she had a headache, and the muffled stillness felt heavy in the stale air of the tent. Something was wrong, but she didn't know what. She sensed a familiarity about the situation, or a memory, as though she'd been there before, but not quite. It was more like a danger she ought to recognise, but what? Suddenly she couldn't bear it and sat up, pushing the warm covers off the man lying beside her.

"Jondalar! Jondalar!" She shook him, but she didn't need to. He was awake the moment she bolted up.

"Ayla! What is it?"

"I don't know. Something is wrong!"

"I don't see anything wrong," he said. He didn't, but something was obviously bothering Ayla. He wasn't used to seeing her so close to panic. She was usually so calm, so completely in control even when she was in imminent danger. No four-legged predator could bring such abject terror to her eyes. "Why do you think something is wrong?"

"I had a dream. I was in a dark place, darker than night, and I was suffocating, Jondalar. I couldn't breathe!"

A familiar look of concern spread across his face as he looked around the tent once more. It just wasn't like Ayla to be so frightened; perhaps something was wrong. It was dark in the tent, but not completely dark. A faint light filtered through. Nothing seemed out of place, the wind hadn't torn anything or snapped any cords. In fact, it wasn't even blowing. There was no movement at all. It was absolutely still . . .

Jondalar threw back the furs, scrambled to the entrance. He unfastened the tent flap, exposing a wall of soft white, which collapsed into the tent, but showed only more of the same beyond.

"We're buried, Jondalar! We're buried in snow!" Ayla's eyes were wide with terror and her voice cracked with the strain of trying to keep it under control.

Jondalar reached for her and held her. "It's all right, Ayla. It's all right," he murmured, not at all sure that it was.

"It's so dark and I can't breathe!"

Her voice sounded so strange, so remote, as though it came from afar, and she had become limp in his arms. He laid her down on her furs, and noticed her eyes were closed, but she still kept crying out in that eerie, distant voice that it was dark, and she couldn't breathe. Jondalar was at a loss, frightened for her, and of her, a little. Something strange was going on, something more than their snowy entombment, as frightening as that was.

He noticed his pack near the opening, partly covered with snow, and stared at it for a moment. Suddenly he crawled over to it. Brushing off the snow, he felt for the side holder and found a spear. Rising to his knees, he unfastened the smoke-hole cover that was near the middle. With the butt end of the spear he poked up through the snow. A pile plopped down on their sleeping furs, and then sunlight and a gust of fresh air swept through the small tent.

The change in Ayla was immediate. She visibly relaxed and soon opened her eyes. "What did you do?" she asked.

"I poked a spear through the smoke hole and broke through the snow. We'll have to dig our way out, but the snow may not be as deep as it seems." He looked at her closely with concern. "What happened to you, Ayla? You had me worried. You kept saying you couldn't breathe. I think you fainted."

"I don't know. Maybe it was the lack of fresh air."

"It didn't seem that bad. I wasn't having much trouble breathing. And you were really afraid. I don't think I've ever seen you so scared."

Ayla was uncomfortable under his questioning. She did feel strange, a little light-headed still, and seemed to recall unpleasant dreams, but she couldn't explain it.

"I remember once that snow covered up the opening of the small cave I stayed in when I had to leave Brun's clan. I woke up in the dark and the air was bad. That must have been it."

"I suppose that could make you afraid if it happened again," Jondalar said, but somehow he didn't quite believe it, and neither did Ayla.

The big red-bearded man was still outside working, though the twilight was fast fading into dark. He was the first to see the strange procession round the crest at the top of the slope and start down. First came the woman, plodding wearily through the deep snow, followed by a horse whose head was hanging with exhaustion, with a load on her back and dragging the travois behind her. The young horse, also carrying a load, was led by a rope held by the man following the mare. His way was easier going since the snow had already been trampled down by those in the lead, though Jondalar and Ayla had traded places on the way to give each other a rest.

"Nezzie! They're back!" Talut shouted as he started up to meet them, and tramped the snow down for Ayla for the last few steps of the way. He led them, not to the familiar arched entrance at the front end, but to the middle of the longhouse. To their surprise a new addition to the structure had been built in their absence. It was similar to the entrance foyer, but larger. From it, a new entrance opened directly to the Hearth of the Mammoth.

"This is for the horses, Ayla," Talut announced once they were inside, with a huge, self-satisfied grin at her expression of stunned disbelief. "I knew after that last windstorm that a lean-to would never be enough. If you, and your horses, are going to live with us, we needed to make something more substantial. I think we should call it the Hearth of the Horses!"

Tears filled Ayla's eyes. She was tired to the bone, grateful to have finally made their way back, and she was overwhelmed. No one had ever gone to so much trouble because they wanted her. As long as she lived with the Clan, she had never felt fully accepted, never quite belonged. She was sure they would never have allowed her to keep horses, much less build a place for them.

"Oh, Talut," she said, a catch in her voice, then she reached up and put her arms around his neck and pressed her cold cheek to his. Ayla had always seemed so reserved to him, her spontaneous expression of affection was a delightful surprise. Talut hugged her and patted her back, smiling with obvious pleasure and feeling very smug.

Most of the Lion Camp crowded around them in the new annexe, welcoming the woman and man as though they were both full-fledged members of the group.

"We were getting worried about you," Deegie said, "especially after it snowed."

"We'd have been back sooner if Ayla hadn't wanted to bring so much with her," Jondalar said. "The last couple of days, I wasn't sure we would make it back."

Ayla had already begun to unload the horses, for the last time, and as Jondalar went to help her, the mysterious bundles aroused great curiosity.

"Did you bring anything for me?" Rugie finally asked, speaking the question that everyone was wondering.

Ayla smiled at the little girl. "Yes, I brought something for you. I brought something for everyone," she answered, making them all wonder what gift she had brought for each.

"Who is that for?" Tusie asked, when Ayla began cutting the ties on the largest bundle.

Ayla glanced up at Deegie, and they both smiled, trying not to let Deegie's little sister notice their somewhat patronising amusement in hearing Tulie's tone and inflections in the voice of her youngest daughter.

"I even brought something for the horses," Ayla said to the little girl as she cut the last cords and the bale of hay burst open. "This is for Whinney and Racer."

After she spread it out for them, she started to untie the load on the travois. "I should bring the rest of this inside."

"You don't have to do it now," Nezzie said. "You haven't even taken off your outer clothes. Come in and have something hot to drink, and some food. Everything will be fine here for now."

"Nezzie is right," Tulie added. She was just as curious as the rest of the Camp, but Ayla's packages could wait. "You both need to rest and have something to eat. You look exhausted."

Jondalar smiled gratefully at the headwoman as he followed Ayla into the lodge.

In the morning, Ayla had many helping hands to carry in her bundles, but Mamut had quietly suggested that she keep her gifts covered until the ceremony that evening. Ayla smiled her agreement, quickly understanding the element of mystery and anticipation he implied, but her evasive replies to Tulie's hints to show her what she had brought annoyed the headwoman, though she didn't want to show it.

Once the packages and bundles were piled on one of the empty bed platforms and the drapes closed, Ayla crawled into the private, enclosed space, lit three stone lamps and spaced them for good lighting, and there examined and arranged the gifts she had brought. She made some minor changes to the choices she had made previously, adding or exchanging a few items, but when she snuffed out the lamps and emerged, letting the drapes fall closed behind her, she was satisfied.

She went out through the new opening, a space formerly occupied by a section of an unused platform bed. The floor of the new annexe was higher than the floor of the earthlodge, and three wide, four-inch-high steps had been cut for easier access. She paused to look around the addition. The horses were gone. Whinney was accustomed to nosing aside a hide windbreak, and Ayla only had to show her once. Racer picked up the trick from his dam. Obeying an impulsive urge to check on them – like a mother with children, a part of her mind was always conscious of the horses – the young woman walked through the enclosed space to the mammoth tusk archway, pulled back the heavy hide drape, and looked out.

The world had lost all form and definition; solid colour without shadow or shape spilled across the landscape in two hues: blue, rich, vibrant, startling blue sky unbroken by a single wisp of cloud; and white, blinding white snow reflecting a fulgent late morning sun. Ayla squinted against the glare of white; the only evidence of the storm that had raged for days. Slowly, as her eyes adjusted to the light, and a previous sense of depth and distance informed her perception, details filled in. The water, still rippling down the middle of the river, sparkled more brightly than the soft, white snow-covered banks, which blended into jagged white shards of ice, blunted by snow, at the edges of the watercourse. Nearby, mysterious white mounds took on the shapes of mammoth bones and piles of dirt.

She stepped outside a few paces to see around the bend of the river where the horses liked to graze, just out of sight. It was warm in the sun and the top of the snow glistened with a hint of melt. The horses would have to paw the deep, soft, cold layer aside to find the dried grass it covered. As Ayla prepared to whistle, Whinney, stepping into view, raised her head, and saw her. She whinnied a greeting as Racer came out from behind her. Ayla nickered back.

As the woman turned to go, she noticed Talut watching her with a peculiar, almost awed expression.

"How did the mare know you had come out?" he asked.

"I think she did not know, but horse have good nose, smell far. Good ears, hear far. Anything moves, she sees."

The big man nodded. She made it sound so simple, so logical, but still . . . He smiled, then, glad they were back. He was looking forward to Ayla's adoption. She had so much to offer, she would be a welcome, and valuable, Mamutoi woman.

They both went back into the new annexe, and as they entered, Jondalar came in from the lodge.

"I notice your gifts are all ready," he said with a big grin as he strode towards them. He enjoyed the anticipation her mysterious packages had caused, and being in on the surprise. He had overheard Tulie voicing concern about the quality of her gifts, but he had no doubts. They would be unusual to the Mamutoi, but fine workmanship was fine workmanship, and he felt sure hers would be recognised.

"Everyone is wondering what you have brought, Ayla," Talut said. He loved the anticipation and excitement as much, or more, than anyone.

"I do not know if my gifts enough," Ayla said.

"Of course they will be enough. Don't worry about it. Whatever you brought will be enough. Just the firestones would be enough. Even without firestones, just *you* would be enough," Talut said, then added with a smile, "Giving us a reason to have a big celebration could be enough!"

"But, you say gifts exchanged, Talut. In Clan, for exchange, must give same kind, same worth. What can be enough to give, for you, for everyone, who make this place for horses?" Ayla said, glancing around at the annexe. "Is like cave, but you make it. I do not know how people can make a cave like this."

"I've wondered that myself," Jondalar said. "I must admit, I've never seen anything like it and I've seen a lot of shelters: summer shelters, shelters built inside a cave or under an overhanging ledge, but your lodge is as solid as rock itself."

Talut laughed. "It has to be, to live here, especially in winter. As hard as the wind blows, anything less would get blown away." His smile faded, and a soft look of something akin to love suffused his face. "Mamutoi land is rich land, rich in game, in fish, in foods that grow. It is a beautiful, a strong land. I wouldn't want to live any other place . . ." The smile returned. "But strong shelters are needed to live here, and we don't have many caves."

"How do you make a cave, Talut? How do you make a place like this?" Ayla asked, remembering how Brun had searched for just the right cave for his clan, and how homeless she had felt until she found a valley that had a livable cave.

"If you want to know, I will tell you. It is not a big secret!" Talut said, grinning with pleasure. He was delighted with their obvious admiration. "The rest of the lodge is made the same way, more or less, but for this addition, we started by pacing off a distance from the wall outside the Mammoth Hearth. When we reached the centre of an area

253

that we thought would be large enough, a stick was put in the ground – that's where we would put a fireplace, if we decide we need a fire in here. Then we measured off a rope that same distance, fastened one end to the stick, and with the other end, marked a circle to show where the wall would go." Talut acted out his explanation, striding through the paces and tying an imaginary rope to a nonexistent stick.

"Next, we cut through the sod, lifted it out carefully, to save it, and then dug down about the length of my foot." To further clarify his remarks, Talut held up an unbelievably long, but surprisingly narrow and shapely foot encased in a snug-fitting soft shoe. "Then we marked off the width of the bench – the platform that can be beds or storage – and some extra for the wall. From the inside edge of the bench, we dug down deeper, about the depth of two or three of my feet, to excavate the middle for the floor. The dirt was piled up evenly all around the outside in a bank that helps support the wall."

"That's a lot of digging," Jondalar said, eyeing the enclosure. "I'd say the distance from one wall to the one opposite is, maybe, thirty of your feet, Talut."

The headman's eyes opened in surprise. "You're right! I measured it off exactly. How did you know?"

Jondalar shrugged. "Just a guess."

It was more than a guess, it was another manifestation of his instinctive understanding of the physical world. He could accurately judge distance with his eye alone, and he measured space with the dimensions of his own body. He knew the length of his stride and the width of his hand, the reach of his arm and the span of his grasp; he could estimate a fraction against the thickness of his thumb, or the height of a tree by pacing its shadow in the sun. It was not something he learned, it was a gift he was born with and developed with use. It never occurred to him to question it.

Ayla thought it was a lot of digging, too. She had dug her share of pit-traps and understood the work involved, and she was curious. "How do you dig so much, Talut?"

"How does anyone dig? We use mattocks to break up the loam, shovels to scoop it out, except for the hard-packed sod on top. We cut that out with the sharpened edge of a flat bone."

Her puzzled look made it plain she didn't understand. Perhaps she didn't know the words for the tools in his language, he thought, and stepping outside the door, returned with some implements. They all had long handles. One had a piece of mammoth rib bone attached to it, which had been ground to a sharp edge at one end. It resembled a hoe with a long curved blade. Ayla examined it carefully.

"Is like digging stick, I think," she said, looking to Talut for confirmation.

He smiled. "Yes, it's a mattock. We use pointed digging sticks, too, sometimes. They are easier to make in a hurry, but this is easier to use." Then he showed her a shovel made from the wide palmation of a giant antler of a megaceros, split lengthwise through the spongy centre, then shaped and sharpened. Antlers of young animals were used; the antlers of mature giant deer could reach eleven feet in length, and were too big. The handle was attached by means of strong cord strung through three pairs of holes bored down the centre. It was used, spongy side down, not to dig, but for scooping up and throwing out the fine loess soil loosened by the mattock, or, if they chose, for snow. He also had a second shovel, more scoop-shaped, made from an outer section of ivory flaked from a mammoth tusk.

"These are shovels," Talut said, telling her the name. Ayla nodded. She had used flat pieces of bone and antler in much the same way, but her shovels had had no handles.

"I'm just glad the weather stayed nice for a while after you left," the headman continued. "As it is, we didn't dig down as far as we usually would. The ground is already hard underneath. Next year, we can dig down deeper and make some storage pits, too, maybe even a sweatbath, when we get back from the Summer Meeting."

"Weren't you going to hunt again, when the weather got nice?" Jondalar said.

"The bison hunt was very successful, and Mamut isn't having much luck Searching. All he seems to find are the few bison we missed, and it isn't worthwhile to go after them. We decided to make the addition instead, to make a place for the horses, since Ayla and her horse were such a help."

"Mattock and shovel make easier, Talut, but is work . . . a lot of digging," Ayla said, surprised and a little overcome.

"We had a lot of people to work at it, Ayla. Nearly everyone thought it was a good idea and wanted to help . . . to make you welcome."

The young woman felt a sudden rush of emotion and closed her eyes to control tears of gratitude that threatened. Jondalar and Talut saw her, and turned aside out of consideration.

Jondalar examined the walls, still intrigued with the construction. "It looks like you dug it out between the platforms, too," he commented.

"Yes, for the main supports," Talut said, pointing to the six enormous mammoth tusks, wedged in at the base with smaller bones – parts of spines and phalanges – with their tips pointing towards the centre. They were spaced at regular intervals around the wall on both sides of the two pairs of mammoth tusks, which were used for the arched doorways. The strong, long, curved tusks were the primary structural members of the lodge.

As Talut of the Mammoth Hunters continued describing the construction of the semi-subterranean earthlodge, Ayla and Jondalar became even more impressed. It was far more complex than either had imagined. Midway between the centre and the tusk wall supports were six wooden posts – tapering trees, stripped of bark and crotched on top. Around the outside of the annexe, braced against the bottom of the bank, mammoth skulls stood upright in the ground, supported by shoulder blades, hip bones, spinal bones, and several strategically placed long bones, legs and ribs. The upper part of the wall, consisting mainly of shoulder blades, hip bones, and smaller tusks of mammoth, merged into the roof, which was supported by wooden beams stretched across and between the outer circle of tusks and the inner circle of posts. The mosaic of bones, all deliberately chosen and some trimmed to shape, were wedged in and lashed to the sturdy tusks, creating a curved wall that fitted together like interlocking pieces of a puzzle.

Some wood was available from river valleys, but for building purposes mammoth bones were in greater supply. But the mammoths they hunted contributed only a small portion of the bones they used. The great majority of their building materials were selected from the prodigious pile of bones at the bend in the river. Some bones even came from scavenger-stripped carcasses found on the nearby steppes, but the open grasslands were more important for providing materials of another variety.

Each year the migratory herds of reindeer dropped their antlers to make way for the next year's rack, and each year they were gathered up. To complete the dwelling, the antlers of the reindeer were bound to one another to make a strong framework of interlaced supports for a domed roof, leaving a hole in the centre for smoke to escape. Then, willow boughs from the river valley were tied together into a thick mat, which was laid across and bound securely over and around the antlers, and tapered down the bone wall, to create a sturdy base over the roof and the wall. Next, an even thicker thatch of grass, overlapped to shed water, was fastened to the willows all the way to the ground. On top of the grass thatch was a layer of dense sod. Part of the sod came from the ground that had been excavated for the addition, and part from land nearby.

The walls of the entire structure were two or three feet thick, but one final layer of material remained to complete the annexe.

They were standing outside admiring the new structure when Talut finished his detailed explanation of earthlodge construction. "I was hoping the weather would clear," he said, making an expansive gesture towards the clear blue sky. "We need to finish it. Without finishing, I'm not sure how long this will last."

"How long will a lodge last?" Jondalar asked.

"As long as I live, sometimes more. But earthlodges are winter homes. We usually leave in summer, for the Summer Meeting and the big mammoth hunt, and other trips. Summer is for travelling, to gather plants or seeds, to hunt or fish, to trade or visit. We leave most of our things here when we go, because we come back every year. The Lion Camp is our home."

"If you expect this part to be home to Ayla's horses for very long, then we better finish it while we have the chance," Nezzie interjected. She and Deegie set down the large, heavy skin of water they had hauled up from the partially frozen river.

Ranec arrived then, carrying digging tools and dragging a large basket full of compact wet soil. "I've never heard of anyone making a lodge, or even part of one, this late in the season," he said.

Barzec was right behind him. "It will be an interesting test," he said, setting down a second basket of slick mud, which they had dug from a particular place of the river bank. Danug and Druwez appeared then, each carrying additional baskets of the wet mud.

"Tronie has a fire started," Tulie said, picking up the heavy skin of water brought up by Nezzie and Deegie, by herself. "Tornec and some others are piling up snow to melt, once we get this water heating."

"I like to help," Ayla said, wondering how much help she would be. Everyone seemed to know exactly what to do, but she didn't have any idea what was going on, much less what she could do to help.

"Yes, can we help?" Jondalar added.

"Of course, it's for the horses," Deegie commented, "but let me get you something old of mine to wear, Ayla. It's a messy job. Does Talut or Danug have something for Jondalar?"

"I'll find something for him," Nezzie said.

"If you are still so eager after we are through, you can come and help put up the new lodge Tarneg and I will be making to start our Camp . . . after I join with Branag," Deegie added, smiling.

"Has anyone started fires in the sweatbaths?" Talut asked. "Everyone will want to clean up after this, especially if we're going to have a celebration tonight."

"Wymez and Frebec started them early this morning. They are getting more water now," Nezzie said. "Crozie and Manuv have gone off with Latie and the young ones to get fresh pine boughs to make the baths smell nice. Fralie wanted to go, too, but I didn't like the idea of her climbing up and down hills, so I asked her if she would watch Rydag. She's watching Hartal, too. Mamut is busy doing something for the ceremony tonight, too. I have a feeling he's planning some kind of a surprise."

257

"Oh . . . Mamut asked me, when I was coming out, to tell you that the signs are good for a hunt in a few days, Talut. He wants to know if you want him to Search," Barzec said.

"The signs *are* good for a hunt," the big headman said. "Look at this snow! Soft underneath, melting on top. If we get a good freeze, it will have a crust of ice, and animals always get stuck when the snow is in that condition. Yes, I think it would be a good idea."

Everyone had been walking towards the fireplace, where a large hide, filled with the icy water from the river, had been propped over a frame directly over the flames. The river water was only to start the process of melting the snow that was dumped in. As it melted, baskets of water were dipped out and poured into another large, stained, and dirty hide that lined a depression in the ground. The special soil, taken from a bank near the river, was added and mixed with the water to form a thick slurry of gummy, slick clay.

Several people climbed on top of the new sod-covered annexe with waterproof baskets of the fine, smooth, runny mud, and, with scoops, began pouring it down the sides. Ayla and Jondalar watched, and soon joined them. Others at the bottom spread it around to make sure that the entire surface had a thick coat.

The tough sticky clay, washed and sorted into fine particles by the river, would absorb no water. It was impervious to water. Rain, sleet, melting snow, nothing could penetrate. Even when wet, it was waterproof. As it dried, and with long use, the surface became quite hard, and was often used as a handy place to store objects and implements. When the weather was pleasant, it was a place to lounge, to visit, to expound in loud discussion, or to sit quietly and meditate. Children climbed up when visitors came, to watch without being in the way, and everyone used the perch when an audience was needed or there was something to see.

More clay was mixed and Ayla carried a heavy basket up, slopping it over the edge, and spilling it on herself. It didn't matter. She was already covered with mud, just as everyone else was. Deegie was right. It was a messy job. As they finished the sides, they moved away from the edge and began coating the top, but as the surface of the dome became covered with wet slippery mud, footing became treacherous.

Ayla poured out the last of the mud from her basket, and watched it oozing slowly down. She turned to go, not watching carefully where she was stepping. Before she knew it, her feet slipped out from under her. She fell with a plop into the fresh, soft clay she had just poured, and went slipping and sliding over the rounded edge of the roof and down the side of the horse annexe, letting out an involuntary scream.

The next instant she found herself caught by strong arms just as she reached the ground, and startled, looked at the mud-spattered, laughing face of Ranec.

"That's one way to spread it down the side," he said, steadying her, while she regained her composure. Then, still holding her, he added, "If you want to do it again, I'll wait here for you."

She felt warmth where he touched the cool skin of her arm, and she was entirely aware of his body pressing against her. His dark eyes, glistening and deep, were filled with a yearning that stirred an unbidden response from the core of her womanness. She trembled slightly, and felt her face flush before she looked down, and then moved away from his touch.

Ayla glanced at Jondalar, confirming what she expected to see. He was angry. His fists were clenched and his temples throbbed. She looked away quickly. She understood his anger a little more now, realising it was an expression of his fear – fear of loss, fear of rejection – but she felt a touch of irritation at his reaction, nonetheless. She couldn't help it that she slipped, and she was grateful that Ranec happened to be there to catch her. She flushed again, recalling her response to his lingering touch. She couldn't help that either.

"Come on, Ayla," Deegie said. "Talut says it's enough and the sweatbaths are hot. Let's go clean this mud off and get ready for the celebration. It's for you."

The two young women walked into the earthlodge through the new annexe. As they reached the Mammoth Hearth, Ayla suddenly turned to the other young woman. "Deegie, what is sweatbath?"

"Haven't you ever taken a sweatbath?"

"No." Ayla shook her head.

"Oh, you'll love it! You might as well take those muddy clothes off at the Aurochs Hearth. The women usually use the back sweatbath. The men like this one." As she spoke, Deegie indicated an archway just beyond Manuv's bed as they passed through the Reindeer Hearth and into the Crane Hearth.

"Is not for storage?"

"Did you think all the side rooms were for storage? I suppose you wouldn't know, would you? You feel so much a part of us already, it's hard to remember that you really haven't been here that long." She stopped then, and turned to look at Ayla. "I'm glad you will be one of us, I think you were meant to be."

Ayla smiled shyly. "I am glad, too, and I am glad you are here, Deegie. Is nice to know woman . . . young . . . like me."

Deegie smiled back. "I know. I just wish you had come sooner. I am going to be leaving after the summer. I almost hate to go. I want to be headwoman of my own Camp, like my mother, but I'm going to miss her, and you, and everyone."

259

"How far away you go?"

"I don't know. We haven't decided yet," Deegie said.

"Why go far? Why not build new lodge nearby?" Ayla asked.

"I don't know. Most people don't but I guess I could. I didn't think of that," Deegie said, with a look of quizzical surprise. Then, as they reached the last hearth in the earthlodge, she added, "Take off those dirty things and just leave them in a pile there."

Both Deegie and Ayla peeled off their muddy garments. Ayla could feel the warmth radiating from behind a drape of red leather suspended from a rather low mammoth tusk archway in the farthest back wall of the structure. Deegie ducked down and went in first. Ayla followed, but stopped a moment before entering with the drape held aside, trying to see in.

"Hurry in and close it! You're letting the heat out!" a voice called from the steamy, dimly lit, somewhat smoky interior.

She quickly scuttled in, letting the drape fall in place behind her, but, rather than cold, she felt the heat assault her. Deegie led her down a rough stairway made of mammoth bones placed up against the dirt wall of a pit that was about three feet deep. Ayla stood at the bottom on a floor that was covered with a soft, deep-piled fur of some kind waiting for her eyes to adjust, then looked around. The space that had been excavated was about six feet wide and ten feet long. It consisted of two circular sections joined together, each with a low domed ceiling – from where she stood, only three or four inches above her head.

Hot bone coals scattered across the floor of the larger section glowed brightly. The two young women walked through the smaller section to join the others, and Ayla saw that the walls were covered with skins, and the floor of the larger space was covered with mammoth bones spaced carefully apart. It gave them a place to walk above the bits of burning coals. Later, when they poured water on the floor to make steam, or to wash, it would drain into the dirt below the bones, which would keep feet above the mud.

More coals were piled up in the fireplace at the centre. They furnished both heat and the only source of light, except for a faint outline of daylight around the covered smoke hole. Naked women sat around the fireplace on makeshift benches made of flat bones stretched across other mammoth bone supports. Containers of water were lined up along one wall. Large, sturdy, tightly woven baskets held cold water, while steam issued from the stomachs of large animals supported by frames of antlers. Someone picked a red-hot stone out of the fireplace with two flat bones and dropped it into one of the water-filled stomachs. A cloud of pine-scented steam rose and enveloped the room.

"Here, you can sit between Tulie and me," Nezzie said, moving her ample body over one way, making room. Tulie moved the other way. She was a big woman, too, but most of her size was sheer muscular mass, though her full female shape left no doubt about her gender.

"I want to wash some of the mud off first," Deegie said. "Probably Ayla will, too. Did you see her slide down the side?"

"No. Did you hurt yourself, Ayla?" Fralie asked, looking concerned, and slightly uncomfortable with her advancing pregnancy.

Deegie laughed before Ayla could answer. "Ranec caught her, and didn't look at all unhappy about it, either." There were smiles and nods.

Deegie picked up a mammoth skull basin, dipped both hot and cold water into it, accidentally picking up a twig of pine from the hot water, and from a dark mound of some soft substance, pulled off a handful for Ayla and one for herself.

"What is this?" Ayla asked, feeling the luxuriously soft and silky texture of the material.

"Mammoth wool," Deegie said. "The undercoat they grow in winter. They shed it in big bunches every spring, right through the long outer hair. It gets caught on bushes and trees. Sometimes you can pick it up off the ground. Dip it in the water and use it to wash off the mud."

"Hair muddy, too," Ayla said, "should wash."

"We'll wash up good later, after we sweat awhile."

They rinsed off to billows of steam, then Ayla sat down between Deegie and Nezzie. Deegie leaned back and closed her eyes, sighing contentedly, but Ayla, wondering why they were all sitting together sweating, observed everyone in the room. Latie, sitting on the other side of Tulie, smiled at her. She smiled back.

There was a movement at the entrance. Ayla felt a cool breeze and realised how hot she was. Everyone looked to see who was coming. Rugie and Tusie clambered down, followed by Tronie holding Nuvie.

"I had to nurse Hartal," Tronie announced. "Tornec wanted to take him for a sweatbath, and I didn't want him fussing."

Were men not allowed here, not even male babies? Ayla wondered.

"Are all the men in the sweatbath, Tronie? Maybe I should get Rydag," Nezzie said.

"Danug took him in. I think the men decided they wanted all the males this time," Tronie said. "Even the children."

"Frebec took Tasher and Crisavec," Tusie mentioned.

"It's about time he started taking more interest in those boys," Crozie grumbled. "Isn't that the only reason you joined with him, Fralie?"

"No, mother. That's not the only reason."

Ayla was surprised. She'd never heard Fralie disagree with her mother before, even mildly. No one else seemed to notice. Maybe in here, with only the women, Fralie didn't have to worry about seeming to take sides. Crozie was sitting back with her eyes closed; it was amazing how much her daughter resembled her. In fact, she resembled her too much. Except for a stomach big with pregnancy, Fralie was so thin she looked almost as old as her mother, Ayla noticed. Her ankles were swollen. That was not a good sign. She wished she could examine her, then realised she might be able to, in here.

"Fralie, ankles swell much?" Ayla asked, somewhat hesitantly. Everyone sat up, waiting for Fralie's reply, as though they all suddenly realised what had just occurred to Ayla. Even Crozie watched her daughter without saying a word.

Fralie looked down at her feet, seeming to examine her swollen ankles, considering. Then she looked up. "Yes. They've been swollen lately," she said.

Nezzie breathed an audible sigh of relief, which everyone else felt.

"Still sick in morning?" Ayla asked, leaning forward.

"I wasn't sick this long with the first two."

"Fralie, will let me . . . look at you?"

Fralie looked around at the women. No one said a word. Nezzie smiled, and nodded at her, silently urging her to agree.

"All right," Fralie said.

Ayla quickly got up, looked at her eyes, smelled her breath, felt her forehead. It was too dark to see much, and it was too hot in the sweatbath to judge fever. "Will lie down?" Ayla asked.

Everyone moved out of the way to make a place for Fralie to stretch out. Ayla felt, and listened, and examined with thoroughness and obvious knowledge, while everyone else watched with curiosity.

"Sick more than morning, I think," Ayla said, when she was through. "I fix something, help make food not come up. Help feel better. Help swelling. Will take?"

"I don't know," Fralie said. "Frebec watches everything I eat. I think he's worried about me, but he won't admit to it. He'll ask where it came from."

Crozie was sitting, tight-lipped, obviously biting back words she wanted to say, fearing if she said them, Fralie might take Frebec's side and refuse Ayla's help. Nezzie and Tulie exchanged glances. It wasn't like Crozie to exercise so much self-restraint.

Ayla nodded. "I think I know way," she said.

"I don't know about the rest of you, but I'm ready to clean up and go out," Deegie said. "How would a quick plunge in the snow feel right now, Ayla?"

"I think good. I am hot."

17

Jondalar opened the drape that hung closed in front of the bed platform he shared with Ayla, and smiled. She was sitting cross-legged in the middle, naked, her skin pink and glowing, brushing her wet hair.

"I feel so good," she said, smiling back. "Deegie said I would love it. Did you like the sweatbath?"

He climbed in beside her, letting the drape fall. His skin was pink and glowing, too, but he had finished dressing and had just combed his hair and tied it in a club at the back of his neck. The sweatbath had felt so refreshing, he had even considered shaving, but just trimmed his beard instead.

"I always enjoy them," he said. Then he couldn't resist. He took her in his arms, kissed her, and began caressing her warm body. She responded willingly, giving herself up to his embrace, and he heard a soft moan when he bent to take a nipple in his mouth.

"Great Mother, woman, you are tempting," he said as he pulled back. "But what will people say when they start arriving at the Mammoth Hearth for your adoption, and find us sharing Pleasures instead of being dressed and ready?"

"We could tell them to come back later," she answered with a smile.

Jondalar laughed out loud. "I believe you would, wouldn't you?"

"Well, you gave me your signal, didn't you?" she said with a mischievous grin.

"My signal?"

"Remember, after you showed me what Pleasures were, I asked you what your signal was? The signal a man gives a woman when he wants her? You said I'd always know, then you kissed me and touched me like that. Well, you just gave me your signal, and when a man gives her the signal, a woman of the Clan never refuses."

"Is it really true she never refuses?" he asked, still not quite able to believe it.

"That's what she is taught, Jondalar. That's how a proper woman of the Clan behaves," she answered, with a perfectly matter-of-fact seriousness.

"Hmmm, you mean the choice is mine? If I said let's stay here and share Pleasures, you'd make everyone wait?" He was trying to be serious, but his eyes twinkled with delight at what he considered their private joke.

"Only if you give me the signal," she replied, in the same vein.

He took her in his arms and kissed her again, and feeling her warm skin and warmer response, he was almost tempted to find out if she was joking or if she really meant it, but, reluctantly, he let her go.

"It's not what I'd rather do, but I think I'd better let you get dressed. People will be here before long. What are you going to wear?"

"I don't really have anything, except some Clan wraps, and the outfit I've been wearing, and an extra pair of leggings. I wish I did. Deegie showed me what she's going to wear. It's so beautiful – I've never seen anything like it. She gave me one of her brushes, after I started to brush my hair with teasel," Ayla said, showing Jondalar the stiff mammoth-hair brush, tightly wrapped around one end with rawhide to form the handle, giving it the shape of a wide, tapering paint brush. "She gave me some strings of beads and shells, too. I think I'll wear them in my hair, like she does."

"I'd better let you finish getting ready," Jondalar said, opening the drape to leave. He leaned over to kiss her again, then got up. After the leather drape closed, he stood looking at it for a moment, and a frown creased his brow. He wished he could have stayed with her and not had to worry about other people. When they were in her valley they could do what they wanted whenever they wanted to. And she wouldn't be getting ready to be adopted by people who lived so far from his home. What if she wanted to stay here? He had a sinking feeling that after this night, nothing would ever be the same.

As he turned to go, Mamut caught his eye, and beckoned him. The tall young man walked towards the tall old shaman.

"If you are not busy, I could use your help," Mamut said.

"I'd be glad to help. What can I do?" Jondalar asked.

From the back of a storage platform, Mamut showed him four long poles. On close inspection, Jondalar realised they were not wood, but solid ivory; curved mammoth tusks, that had been shaped and straightened. Then the old man gave him a large, hafted, stone maul. Jondalar stopped to examine the heavy hammerlike tool since he had not seen one quite like it before. It was completely covered with hide. He could feel that a circular groove had been nicked around the large stone, and a flexible willow withe wrapped around the groove, then bound to a bone handle. The entire maul had then been wrapped with wet, unprocessed hide, which had only been scraped clean. The rawhide shrunk tight as it dried, encasing both stone maul and handle in hard, tough leather, thus holding them firmly together.

The shaman led him towards the firepit, and lifting up a grass mat, Mamut showed him a hole, about six inches across, that was filled with small stones and pieces of bone. They removed them, then Jondalar brought one of the ivory poles and dropped the end in the hole. While Mamut held it straight, Jondalar wedged the stones and bones around the pole, tamping them down firmly with a stone maul. When the post was firmly embedded, they put another post in, and then another, in an arc around, but somewhat away from, the fireplace.

Then the old man brought out a package and carefully, with reverence, unwrapped it and withdrew a neatly rolled sheet of thin membranous material of a parchmentlike quality. When it was opened, Jondalar saw that several animal figures – a mammoth, birds, and a cave lion among them – and strange geometric designs had been painted on it. They fastened it around the upright ivory poles creating a translucent painted screen set back from the hearth. Jondalar retreated a few steps to absorb the overall effect, then he looked closer, curious. Intestines, after they were cut open, cleaned, and dried, were usually translucent, but this screen was made of something else. He thought he knew what the material was, but he wasn't sure.

"That isn't made of intestines, is it? They would have had to be sewn together, and that is all one piece." The Mamut nodded agreement. "Then it has to be the membrane layer from the inner side of the hide of a very big animal, somehow removed in one piece."

The old man smiled. "A mammoth," he said. "A white female mammoth."

Jondalar's eyes opened wide, and he looked again at the screen with awe.

"Each Camp received a part of the white mammoth, since she gave up her spirit during the first hunt of a Summer Meeting. Most Camps wanted something white. I asked for this; we call it the shadow skin. It has less substance than any of the white pieces, and it cannot be displayed for all to see its obvious power, but I believe that which is subtle can be more powerful. This is more than a small piece, this encircled the inner spirit of the whole."

Brinan and Crisavec suddenly burst into the space in the middle of the Mammoth Hearth, running down the passageway from the Aurochs and Crane hearths, chasing each other. They tumbled together in a heap, wrestling, and almost ran into the delicate screen, but stopped when Brinan noticed the thin shank of a long leg barring their way. They looked up, directly at the drawing of the mammoth, and both gasped. Then they looked at Mamut. To Jondalar, the shaman's face showed no expression, but when the seven- and eight-year-old boys turned their gaze on the old shaman, they quickly got up, and carefully sidestepping the screen, walked towards the first hearth as though they had been severely scolded.

"They looked contrite, almost scared, but you didn't say a word and they've never been frightened of you before," Jondalar said.

"They saw the screen. Sometimes, when you look upon the essence of a powerful spirit, you see your own heart."

Jondalar smiled and nodded, but he wasn't sure he understood what the old shaman meant. He's talking like a zelandoni, the young man thought, talking with a shadow on his tongue, like those of his calling so often did. Still, he wasn't sure if he wanted to see his own heart.

As the boys walked through the Hearth of the Fox, they nodded at the carver, who smiled back. Ranec's smile grew bigger when he turned his attention back to the Mammoth Hearth, which he had been observing for some time. Ayla had just appeared, and was standing in front of the drape tugging on her tunic to straighten it. Though it didn't show under his dark skin, his face flushed at the sight of her. He felt his heart pound and a tension in his loins.

The more he saw her, the more exquisite she was. The long rays of the sun, streaming in through the smoke hole, directed its shimmering light on her on purpose, or so it seemed to him. He wanted to remember that moment, to fill his eyes with the sight of her. He thought of her in ardent hyperbole. Her rich, luxuriant hair falling in soft waves around her face was like a golden cloud playing with sunbeams; her unself-conscious movements embodied ultimate grace. No one knew the anxiety he had suffered while she was gone, or the happiness he felt that she was becoming one of them. He frowned when Jondalar saw her, walked towards her and put an arm around her possessively, then stood between them, blocking his view.

They walked together towards him on their way to the first hearth. She stopped to look at the screen, with obvious awe and admiration. Jondalar fell in behind her as they came to the passageway through the Fox Hearth. Ranec saw Ayla flush with warm feeling when she saw him, before she looked down. The tall man's face flushed red when he saw Ranec, too, but the look in his eye made it clear that there was no pleasure in his emotion. Each man tried to stare the other down as they passed by – Jondalar's hard anger and jealousy apparent, Ranec trying very hard to seem self-confident and cynical. Ranec's eyes automatically went next to the steady stare of the man behind Jondalar, the man who was the essence of spirituality to the Camp, and for some reason he felt a little abashed.

They approached the first hearth, and went out through the entrance foyer. Ayla began to understand why she had not noticed hectic preparations for a feast. Nezzie was supervising the removal of wilted leaves and steaming grass from a roasting hole in the ground, and the smells that arose from the cooking pit made everyone's mouth water. Preparations had begun before they went to get clay from the river, and the food had been cooking all the while they worked. Now, it only needed to be served to the Camp of hungry people.

A certain variety of round, hard starchy roots that took well to long cooking came out first, followed by baskets of a mixture of bone marrow, blue bearberries, and a variety of cracked and ground seeds—pigweed, a mixture of grains, and oily pignon seeds from the stone pine. The result, after hours of steaming, had a heavy, puddinglike consistency that retained the shape of the basket after it was removed, and while not sweet, though the berries gave it a light fruit flavour, was deliciously rich. A full haunch of mammoth meat was brought out next, self-basted by the steam and the thick edge of fat, and falling apart with tenderness.

The sun was setting and a sharp wind hurried everyone back inside the lodge, carrying the food with them. This time, when Ayla was asked to select first, she wasn't as shy. This feast was in her honour, and though being the centre of attention was still not easy for her, she was happy for the reason.

Deegie came to sit with her, and Ayla caught herself staring. Deegie's thick reddish-brown hair was pulled back from her face and wrapped into a coil that was piled high on her head. A string of round ivory beads, each one carved and pierced by hand, had been coiled in with her hair and stood out as contrasting highlights. She wore a long, loose dress of pliable leather – Ayla thought of it as a long tunic – that draped in soft folds from the belted waist, dyed deep brown with a rather shiny, burnished finish. It was sleeveless, but wide at the shoulders, giving the appearance of short sleeves. A fringe of long, reddish-brown mammoth hair fell from her shoulders in back and from a V-shaped yoke in front, and hung to just below her waist.

The neckline was outlined by a triple row of ivory beads, and around her neck she wore a necklace of conical seashells, spaced by cylindrical lime tubes and pieces of amber. Around her right upper arm was an ivory armband incised with an alternating chevron pattern. The pattern was repeated in colours of ochre reds, yellows, and browns in the belt, which was woven of animal hair, some of it dyed. Attached to the belt by a loop was an ivory-handled flint knife in a rawhide sheath, and suspended from another loop, the lower section of a hollow black aurochs horn, a drinking cup that was a talisman of the Aurochs Hearth.

The skirt had been cut on the diagonal, starting at the sides above the knee, to a point both in front and back. Three rows of ivory beads, a strip of rabbit fur, and a second strip of fur that had been pieced together from the striped backs of several ground squirrels accented the diagonal hemline, and hanging from it was another fringe of the long outer guard hairs of the woolly mammoth, reaching to her lower calf. She was not wearing leggings, and her legs showed through the fringe, as well as dark brown high boots, moccasin-like at the feet, burnished to a waterproof shine.

Ayla found herself wondering how they made leather shine. All of her hides and pelts had the soft natural texture of buckskin. But mostly she just stared at Deegie in awe, and thought she was the most beautiful woman she had ever seen.

"Deegie, that is beautiful . . . tunic?"

"You could call it a long tunic. It's really a summer dress. I made it for the Meeting last year, when Branag first declared for me. I changed my mind about the outfit I was going to wear. I knew we'd be inside, and with all the celebrating, it will get warm."

Jondalar came to join them, and it was obvious that he thought Deegie was quite attractive, too. When he smiled at her, the charisma that made him irresistibly appealing not only communicated his feeling but somehow intensified it, and provoked the invariable response. Deegie smiled warmly and invitingly at the tall handsome man with the intense blue eyes.

Talut approached them with a huge platter of food in his hand. Ayla gaped, staring. He wore a fantastic hat that stood so high on his head it brushed the ceiling. It was constructed of leather dyed in various colours, several different kinds of fur, including a long, bushy squirrel tail hanging down his back, and the front ends of two relatively small mammoth tusks jutting straight up from both sides of his head, and joined together at the tips like the entrance archways. His tunic, which fell to his knees, was a deep maroon – at least the parts of it she could see were maroon. The front of it was so richly decorated with a complex pattern of ivory beads, animal teeth, and various shells, it was difficult to see the leather.

In addition, around his neck was a heavy necklace of cave lion claws and a canine tooth, interspersed with amber, and suspended from it down his chest was an ivory plaque incised with enigmatic marks. A wide black leather belt, worn low, circled his waist and fastened in front with ties that hung down in tassels. Hanging from it by loops was a dagger, made by sharpening the tip of a mammoth tusk, and cross-hatching the grip for better purchase, a rawhide sheath with an ivory-handled flint knife, and a round, wheel-shaped object with spokelike divisions from which were suspended, by thongs, a pouch, some canine teeth, and most prominent, the brushy tip of a cave lion tail. A fringe of long mammoth hair that nearly swept the ground, revealed when he moved that his leggings were as ornamented as his tunic.

His shiny black footwear was particularly interesting, not for its decoration, because it had none, but for its lack of any visible seam. It appeared to be a single piece of soft leather shaped exactly like his foot. It was one more of several puzzles Ayla wanted to find answers to, later.

"Jondalar! I see you've found the two most beautiful women here!" Talut said.

"You're right," Jondalar said, smiling.

"I wouldn't hesitate to wager that these two could hold their own in any company," Talut continued. "You've travelled, what would you say?"

"I wouldn't argue with that. I've seen many women, but nowhere have I seen any more beautiful than right here," Jondalar said, looking directly at Ayla. Then he smiled at Deegie.

Deegie laughed. She enjoyed the byplay, but there was no doubt where Jondalar's heart lay. And Talut always paid her extravagant compliments; she was his acknowledged offspring and heir, the daughter of his sister, who was the daughter of his mother. He loved the children of his hearth and provided for them, but they were Nezzie's, and the heirs of Wymez, her brother. She had adopted Ranec, as well, since his mother was dead, which made him both the child of Wymez's hearth and his legitimate offspring and heir, but that was an exception.

All the people of the Camp had welcomed the opportunity to show off their finery, and Ayla kept trying to avoid staring at one or another. Their tunics were of various lengths, with and without sleeves, and in a variety of colours, with individual decorations. The men's tended to be shorter, more heavily decorated, and they usually wore headwear of some kind. Women generally favoured the V-shaped hemline, though Tulie's was more like a belted shirt worn over leggings. It was covered, in intricate and artistic designs, with beads, shells, teeth, carved ivory and, particularly, heavy pieces of amber. Though she didn't wear a hat, her hair was so elaborately arranged and decorated, she might as well have been wearing one.

But of all, Crozie's tunic was the most unusual. Instead of coming to a point in front, it was diagonally cut all the way across the front, with a rounded point on her right side, and a rounded cutout on her left. Most stunning, though, was its colour. It was white, not off-white or ivory, but true white, and fringed and decorated with, among other things, the white feathers of the large northern crane.

Even the children were dressed for a ceremony. When Ayla saw Latie standing at the edge of the group that was milling around her and Deegie, she asked Latie to come and show her outfit, in effect inviting her to join them. Latie commented on the way Ayla was wearing the beads and shells Deegie had given her, and thought she'd try them that way.

Ayla smiled. She hadn't been able to think of a way to wear them, and finally just twisted them together and wrapped them around her head, across her forehead, the way she carried her sling. Latie was quickly included in the general banter, and smiled shyly when Wymez told her she looked nice – an extravagant compliment from the laconic man. Once Latie joined them, Rydag was quick to follow. Ayla held him on her lap. His tunic was modelled after Talut's, but much less ornamented. He couldn't have begun to carry the weight – Talut's ceremonial outfit weighed several times what Rydag did. Few people could have worn his headdress alone.

But Ranec was slow to make an appearance. Several times Ayla noticed his absence and looked for him, but when she did see him, it caught her by surprise. Everyone had enjoyed showing Ayla their dress-up clothing just to see her reaction; she was so delighted and impressed and made no pretence about it. Ranec had been observing her and wanted to create an especially memorable effect, so he returned to the Fox Hearth to change. He had been watching from the Lion Hearth, and slipped up beside her while she was involved in conversation. When she turned her head, suddenly he was there, and by her amazed look, he knew he had achieved his desired effect.

The cut and style of his tunic were unusual; its tapered body and wide flaring sleeves gave it a distinctly different look and betrayed its foreign origin. It was not a Mamutoi tunic. It was one he had traded for – and paid dearly – but he knew he had to have it from the first moment he saw it. One of the northern Camps had made a trading expedition a few years before to a western people that were distantly related to the Mamutoi, and the leader had been given the shirt as a token of mutual ties and future friendly relations. He was not inclined to give it up, but Ranec had been so persistent, and finally offered him so much for it, he couldn't refuse.

Most of the garments worn by the people of the Lion Camp had been dyed shades of browns, deep reds, and dark yellows, and heavily decorated with light-coloured ivory beads, teeth, seashells and amber, enhanced with fur and feathers. Ranec's tunic was a creamy ivory, nearly as light, but richer than true white, and he knew it made a stunning contrast to his dark skin, but even more stunning was the decoration. Both front and back of the shirt had been used as a background for a picture created with porcupine quills and fine cords which had been dyed strong, bright, primary colours.

On the front of the shirt was an abstract portrayal of a seated woman, made out of an arrangement of concentric circles in shades of true reds, oranges, blues, blacks, and browns; one set of circles represented her belly, two more were her breasts. Arcs of circles within circles indicated hips, shoulders and arms. The head was a design based on a triangle, with a pointed chin and a flat top, with enigmatic lines instead of features on the face. In the middle of the breast and stomach circles, obviously meant to represent navel and nipples, were bright red garnets, and a line of coloured stones – green and pink tourmalines, red garnets, aquamarines – had been fastened along the flat top of the head. The back of the shirt showed the same woman from the back view, with concentric circles or portions of them representing buttocks and shoulders. The same series of colours was repeated several times around the flared ends of the sleeves.

Ayla just stared, unable to speak. Even Jondalar was amazed. He had travelled far, had met many different people with many different ways of dressing, both for everyday and for ceremonial purposes. He had seen quill embroidery, and understood and admired the process of dyeing it and sewing it on, but he had never seen quite so impressive or colourful a garment before in his life.

"Ayla," Nezzie said, taking her dish from her, "Mamut wants to see you for a moment."

As she got up, everyone began to clear away food, scrape plates, and prepare for the ceremony. During the long winter ahead, a number of feasts and ceremonies would be held to add interest and variety to a relatively inactive period – the Celebration of Brothers and Sisters, the Feast of the Long Night, the Laughing Contest, several festivals and celebrations in honour of the Mother – but Ayla's adoption was an unexpected occasion, and therefore all the more welcome.

While people began moving towards the Mammoth Hearth, Ayla prepared the materials for fire-making, as Mamut had requested. Then she waited, suddenly feeling nervous and excited. The general ceremony had been explained to her, so she would know what to expect, and what would be expected of her, but she hadn't grown up with the Mamutoi. Accepted attitudes and patterns of behaviour were not second nature to her, and though Mamut had seemed to understand and tried to calm her fears, she worried that she might do something inappropriate.

She was sitting on a mat near the firepit watching people. Out of the corner of her eye, she saw Mamut drink something in one gulp. She noticed Jondalar sitting on their bed platform alone. He seemed worried, and didn't look very happy, and she found herself wondering if she was doing the right thing to become a Mamutoi. She closed her eyes and sent a silent thought to her totem. If the Spirit of the Cave Lion had not wanted it, would he have given her a sign?

She knew the ceremony was about to begin when Talut and Tulie came and stood on either side of her, and Mamut poured cold ashes on the last small fire left burning in the lodge. Even though it had happened before, and the Camp knew what to expect, waiting in the dark for fire was an unnerving experience. Ayla felt the hand on her shoulder, and struck the spark, to a chorus of relieved sighs.

When the fire was well established, she stood up. Both Talut and Tulie stepped forward, one on either side, each holding a long ivory shaft. Mamut stood behind Ayla.

"In the name of Mut, the Great Earth Mother, we are here to welcome Ayla into the lodge of the Lion Camp of the Mamutoi," Tulie began. "But we do more than welcome this woman into the Lion Camp. She came here as a stranger; we wish to make her one of us, to make her Ayla of the Mamutoi."

Talut continued. "We are hunters of the great woolly mammoth, given to us by the Mother to use. The mammoth is food, is clothing, is shelter. If we honour Mut, She will cause the Spirit of the Mammoth to renew herself and return each season. If ever we dishonour the Mother, or fail to appreciate the Gift of the Spirit of the Mammoth, the mammoth will leave and never return again. So we have been told.

"The Lion Camp is like the great cave lion; each of us walks fearlessly and with pride. Ayla, too, walks fearlessly and with pride. I, Talut, of the Lion Hearth, headman of the Lion Camp, offer Ayla a place among the Mamutoi in the Lion Camp."

"It is a great honour she is offered. What makes her worthy?" a voice called out from the assembled group. Ayla recognised it as Frebec's, and was glad she had been told that it would be part of the ceremony.

"By the fire you see, Ayla has proven her value. She has discovered a great mystery, a stone from which fire can be drawn, and she has offered this magic freely, to each hearth," Tulie responded.

"Ayla is a woman of many Gifts, many Talents," Talut added to the response. "By the saving of life, she has proven her value as a skilled Healer. By the bringing of food, she has proven her value as a skilled hunter with a sling, and with a new weapon brought with her when she came, a spear-thrower. By the horses beyond that arch, she has proven her value as a Controller of animals. She would bring esteem to any hearth, and value to the Lion Camp. She is worthy of the Mamutoi."

"Who speaks for this woman? Who will be responsible for her? Who will offer her the kinship of Hearth?" Tulie called out, loudly and clearly, looking at her brother. But before Talut could answer, another voice spoke out.

"The Mamut speaks for Ayla! The Mamut will be responsible! Ayla is a daughter of the Mammoth Hearth!" the old shaman said, his voice deeper, stronger, and more commanding than Ayla ever would have thought possible.

Surprised gasps and murmured conversations could be heard from the darkened area. Everyone thought she was going to be adopted into the Lion Hearth. This was unexpected . . . or was it? Ayla never said she was a shaman, or that she wanted to be; she didn't behave like a person familiar with the unknown and unknowable; she was not trained to control special powers. Yet, she was a Healer. She did have extraordinary control over horses, and maybe other animals. She might be a Searcher, perhaps even a Caller. Still, the Mammoth Hearth represented the spiritual essence of those Earth's children who called themselves the mammoth hunters. Ayla couldn't even express herself completely in their language yet. How could someone who did not know their ways, and who had no knowledge of Mut, interpret the needs and wishes of the Mother for them?

"Talut was going to adopt her, Mamut," Tulie said. "Why should she go to the Mammoth Hearth? She has not dedicated herself to Mut, and is not trained to Serve the Mother."

"I didn't say she was trained, or that she ever will be, Tulie, though she is more gifted than you can imagine and I think training would be very wise, for her sake. I did not say she *will* be a daughter of the Mammoth Hearth. I said she *is* a daughter of the Mammoth Hearth. She was born to it, dedicated by the Mother Herself. Whether or not she decides to be trained is a choice only she can make, but it doesn't matter in the least. Ayla does not have to dedicate herself, it is out of her hands. Trained or not, her life will Serve the Mother. I speak for her not to accept her into training, unless she wants it. I wish to adopt her as the daughter of my hearth."

As Ayla listened to the old man, she felt a sudden chill. She didn't think she liked the idea that her destiny was ordained, out of her hands, chosen for her at birth. What did he mean that she was dedicated by the Mother, that her life would Serve the Mother? Was she chosen by the Mother, too? Creb had told her, when he was explaining about totems, that there was a reason why the Spirit of the Great Cave Lion had chosen her. He said she would have need of powerful protection. What did it mean to be chosen by the Mother? Was that why she needed protection? Or did it mean if she became Mamutoi the Cave Lion would no longer be her totem? No longer protect her? It was a disquieting thought. She didn't want to lose her totem. She shook herself, trying to dispel her sense of foreboding.

If Jondalar had been feeling uneasy about her adoption, this sudden turn of events made him even more uncomfortable. He heard the whispered comments of the people around him and wondered if it was true that she was meant to become one of them. She might even have been Mamutoi, before she was lost, if Mamut said she was born to the Mammoth Hearth.

Ranec was overjoyed. He had wanted Ayla to become one of them, but if she was adopted to the Lion Hearth, she would be his sister. He had no wish to be her brother. He wanted to join with her, and brother and sister could not join. Since both would be adopted, and obviously did not have the same mother, he was prepared to find another hearth that would adopt him so he could pursue his suit, much as he would hate to give up his ties with Nezzie and Talut. But if she was adopted into the Mammoth Hearth, he didn't have to. He was particularly pleased that she would be adopted as the daughter of Mamut, and not as One dedicated to Serve, although even that would not have deterred him.

Nezzie was a little disappointed; she already felt as though Ayla were a daughter. But most important to Nezzie was that Ayla stay with them, and if Mamut wanted her, it would just make her all that more acceptable to the Council at the Summer Meeting. Talut glanced at her, and when she nodded, he conceded to Mamut. Tulie had no objection, either. The four of them quickly conferred, and Ayla agreed. For some reason she couldn't quite define, it pleased her to be the daughter of Mamut.

As the darkened lodge quieted again, Mamut held his hand up, palm backward, facing him. "Will the woman, Ayla, step forward?"

Ayla's stomach churned and her knees felt weak as she approached the old man.

"Do you wish to be one with the Mamutoi?" he asked.

"Yes," she whispered, her voice cracking.

"Will you honour Mut, the Great Mother, revere all her Spirits, and especially, never offend the Spirit of the Mammoth; will you strive to be worthy of the Mamutoi, to bring honour to the Lion Camp, and always respect Mamut and the meaning of the Mammoth Hearth?"

"Yes." She could hardly say more. She wasn't sure what she was supposed to do to accomplish all of it, but she would certainly try.

"Does this Camp accept this woman?" Mamut said to the assembly.

"We accept her," they replied in unison.

"Are there any here that reject her?"

There was a long pause, and Ayla wasn't at all sure that Frebec wouldn't speak out in objection, but none replied.

"Talut, headman of the Lion Camp, will you inscribe the mark?" Mamut intoned.

As Ayla saw Talut withdraw his knife from the sheath, her heart beat fast. This was unexpected. She didn't know what he was going to do with the knife, but whatever it was, she was sure she wouldn't like it. The big headman took Ayla's arm, pushed up her sleeve, and poised the flint knife, then quickly cut a straight mark on her upper arm, drawing blood. Ayla felt the pain, but she didn't flinch. With the blood still wet on the knife, Talut incised a straight mark on the piece of ivory hanging as a plaque around his neck, held by Mamut, making a red-stained gouge. Then Mamut said some words Ayla did not understand. She didn't realise no one else understood them either.

"Ayla is now counted among the people of the Lion Camp, numbered among the Mammoth Hunters," Talut said. "This woman is and will forever be Ayla of the Mamutoi."

Mamut picked up a small bowl and poured stinging liquid on the cut on her arm – she realised it was an antiseptic cleansing solution – then he turned her around to face the group. "Welcome Ayla of the Mamutoi, member of the Lion Camp, daughter of the Mammoth Hearth." He paused for a moment, then added, "Chosen of the Spirit of the Great Cave Lion."

The group repeated the words, and Ayla realised it was the second time in her life that she had been taken in, accepted, and made a member of a people whose ways she hardly knew. She closed her eyes, hearing the words echo in her mind. Then it struck her. Mamut had included her totem! Even though she was not Ayla of the Clan any more, she had not lost her totem! She was still under the protection of the Cave Lion. But even more, she was not Ayla of No People; she was Ayla of the Mamutoi!

18

"You may always claim the sanctuary of the Mammoth Hearth, Ayla, wherever you are. Please accept this token, daughter of my Hearth," Mamut said as he removed a circlet of ivory carved with zigzag lines from his arm and tied the pierced ends together on Ayla's arm, just below her cut. Then he gave her a warm embrace.

Ayla had tears in her eyes when she went to the bed platform where her gifts were laid out but she wiped them away before she picked up a wooden bowl. It was round, strong, but of uniformly fine thinness. The bowl boasted neither painted nor carved design, only a subtle pattern of the wood grain, but that was symmetrically balanced.

"Please accept gift of medicine bowl from daughter of Hearth, Mamut," Ayla said. "And if you allow, daughter of Hearth will fill bowl every day with medicine for aching joints, of fingers and arms and knees."

"Ah, I would welcome some relief from my arthritis this winter," he said with a smile, taking the bowl and passing it to Talut, who looked it over, nodded, and passed it to Tulie.

Tulie examined it critically, at first judging it to be simplistic because it lacked the additional design, either carved or painted, that she was accustomed to. But as she looked more closely, running her fingertips over the remarkably smooth finish, noting the perfect shape and symmetry, she had to concede that it was certainly a finely crafted piece of work, perhaps the finest piece of workmanship of its kind she had ever seen. As the bowl was passed around, it aroused the interest and curiosity about the other gifts Ayla had brought even more as each person wondered if every gift would be as beautifully unusual.

Talut came forward next and gave Ayla a big hug, then presented her with an ivory-handled flint knife in a red-dyed rawhide sheath which was carved with an intricate design, similar to the knife Deegie wore on her belt. Ayla took the knife out of the sheath, and immediately guessed that the blade had probably been made by Wymez, and suspected that Ranec had carved and shaped the handle.

Ayla brought out a heavy pile of dark fur for Talut. He grinned wide when he shook out the mantle made from an entire bison hide, and flung it over his shoulders. The thick mane and shoulder fur made the big man seem even bigger than he was, and he enjoyed the effect. Then he noticed the way it clung to his shoulders and hung down in pliant folds, and examined the soft and supple inside of the warm cloak more closely.

"Nezzie! Look at this," he said. "Have you ever seen softer hide on a bison pelt? And this is warm. I don't think I want this made into anything, not even a parka! I'm going to wear it just as it is."

Ayla smiled at his delight, pleased that her gift was so well liked. Jondalar was standing back, looking over several heads that were crowding in closer, enjoying Talut's reaction, too. He'd anticipated it, but was glad to see his expectations borne out.

Nezzie gave Ayla a warm hug, and then a necklace of matched and graduated spiral shells, each one separated by carefully sawed small sections of the hard hollow leg bones of arctic fox, and suspended as a pendant in front, a large canine tooth of a cave lion. Ayla held it on while Tronie tied it at the back, then she looked down and admired it, holding up the cave lion tooth, and wondering how they had managed to pierce the hole through the root.

Ayla pushed the drape in front of the platform aside and brought out a very large covered basket, and set it down at Nezzie's feet. It seemed quite plain. None of the grasses out of which it was made had been dyed, and no coloured patterns of geometric designs or stylised figures of birds or animals graced the sides or cover. But on close inspection, the woman noticed the subtle design, and saw how expertly it was made. It was watertight enough to be a cooking basket, she knew.

Nezzie lifted the cover to examine it, and the whole camp voiced their surprise. The basket, divided into sections by flexible birch bark, was full of food. There were small hard apples, sweet and spicy wild carrots, peeled gnarled roots of starchy groundnuts, pitted dried cherries, dried but still green day-lily buds, round green milk vetch dried in the pod, dried mushrooms, dried stalks of green onions, and some unidentifiable dried leaves and slices. Nezzie smiled warmly at her as she examined the selection. It was a perfect gift.

Tulie approached next. Her embrace of welcome was not lacking in warmth, but more formal, and her presentation of her gift to Ayla, while not exactly done with a flourish, demonstrated a proper sense of ceremony. The gift was a small container, exquisitely decorated. It had been carved out of wood into the shape of a small box with rounded corners. Designs of fish were both carved and painted on it, and pieces of shell glued on it as well. The overall design gave the impression of water alive with fish and underwater plants. When Ayla lifted the lid, she discovered the purpose of so precious a box. It was filled with salt.

She had some idea of the value of salt. When she grew up with the Clan, who lived near Beran Sea, she had taken salt for granted. It was fairly easy to obtain, and some of the fish were even cured with it, but inland, when she lived in her valley, she had had no salt, and it had taken some time to get used to it. The Lion Camp was farther away from the sea than her valley. The salt, as well as the seashells, had to be transported over a long distance, yet Tulie had given her this whole box of it. It was a rare and costly gift.

Ayla felt properly awed as she brought out her gift for the headwoman, and she hoped that Jondalar had been right in his suggestion of what would be appropriate. The fur she had selected was the pelt of a snow leopard, one that had attempted to snatch a kill away from her the winter she and Baby were learning to hunt together. She had just planned to scare it off, but the adolescent cave lion had other ideas. Ayla had stunned the mature, though smaller, cat with a stone from her sling when it looked like a fight would ensue, and then finished it off with another.

The gift was obviously unexpected, and Tulie's eyes showed her pleasure, but it wasn't until she succumbed to the temptation to throw the luxurious, thick, winter fur around her shoulders that she noticed its unique quality, the same quality Talut had remarked upon. It felt unbelievably soft on the inner side. Furs were usually stiffer than hides. By its nature, fur could only be worked on one side with the scrapers used to stretch and soften. While it made a longer-lasting, sturdier material than Ayla's, which were only dressed with fat, the Mamutoi method of preserving skins was not as soft and pliable. Tulie was more impressed than she had expected to be, and decided she would find out what Ayla's method was.

Wymez approached with an object wrapped in a soft skin. She opened it, and caught her breath. It was a magnificent spear point, like the ones she had so admired. It sparkled in the firelight like a faceted gem, and was more valuable. Her gift to him was a sturdy grass floor mat for him to sit on when he worked. Most of Ayla's basket and mat weaving had no coloured designs, but the last winter in her cave she had begun to experiment with different grasses that had natural colour variations. The result, in combination with her usual weaving patterns, was a mat with a subtle but distinctive starburst pattern. She had been quite pleased when she made it, and when she was selecting gifts, its pointed rays extended out from the centre reminded her of Wymez's beautiful points, and the woven texture was suggestive of the small ridges of fine slivers he flaked off. She wondered if he would notice.

After he examined it, he gave her one of his rare smiles. "This is beautiful. It reminds me of the work done by Ranec's mother. She understood weaving with grasses better than anyone I ever knew. I suppose I should save it, hang it on the wall, but I will use it instead. I will sit on this when I work. It will help me keep my purpose in mind." His welcoming hug had none of the reticence of his verbal manner. She realised that beneath his quiet exterior Wymez was a man of friendly warmth and perceptive feeling.

There was no special sequence or order to the gift-giving, and the next person Ayla noticed, standing near the platform waiting to get her attention, was Rydag. She sat down near him, and returned his fierce hug. Then he opened his hand and held out a long round tube, the hollow leg bone of a bird, with holes cut in it. She took it from the boy, and turned it around in her hands, not sure of its purpose. He took it back, held it to his mouth, and blew. The whistle emitted a loud, piercing sound. Ayla tried it and smiled. Then she gave him a warm, waterproof, wolverine hood made in the style of the Clan, but she felt a wrenching pain when he put it on. He reminded her too much of Durc.

"I gave him a whistle like that to call me if he needs me. Sometimes he doesn't have breath enough to yell, but enough to blow a whistle," Nezzie explained, "but he made that one himself."

Deegie surprised her with the outfit she had planned to wear that evening. But when she saw the look in Ayla's eyes at the sight of it, Deegie decided to give it to her. Ayla was beyond words, and just stared at it until her eyes filled with tears. "I have never had anything to wear that was so beautiful."

She gave Deegie her gift then, a stack of baskets, and several beautifully finished wooden bowls of various sizes, which could be used as drinking cups for soups, or even to cook in, for her to use at her hearth after she joined with Branag. In a region where wood was relatively rare, and bone and ivory more commonly used for utensils, the bowls were a special gift. They were both delighted, and hugged with the warmth of sisters.

To show that he did not begrudge her a decent gift, Frebec gave her a pair of knee-high fur boots, decorated and quilled near the top, and she was glad she had selected some of her best summer reindeer pelts for him. The hair of the reindeer was hollow, a minute air-filled tube, and naturally insulating. The summer hide was both the warmest and the lightest weight, the most practical and comfortable to wear during cold weather hunting of any animal's fur, and therefore the most valuable. From the pieces she gave him, a complete outfit of tunic and trousers could be made that would be so warm, only a single additional outer garment would be needed even during the coldest weather, freeing him from bulky weight. He noticed the softness of her finished skins as the others had, but he did not remark on it and his hug of welcome was stiff.

Fralie gave her fur mittens to match the boots, and Ayla gave the pregnant woman a beautiful wooden cooking bowl, filled with a pouch of dried leaves. "I hope you like this tea, Fralie," she said, giving her a direct stare, as though to emphasise her words. "Is good to drink cup in morning when first wake up, and maybe another at night, before sleep. If you like, I will give more when this gone."

Fralie nodded agreement as they embraced. Frebec looked at them suspiciously, but Ayla was only giving a gift, and he could hardly complain about Fralie's gift from the newest member of the Lion Camp, could he? Ayla was not entirely happy with the circumstances. She would have preferred to treat Fralie directly and openly, but the subterfuge was better than not helping her at all, and Fralie refused to be put into a situation where it might seem that she was making a choice between her mother and her mate.

Crozie came forward next and nodded approvingly at Ayla. Then she gave her a small leather bag, sewn together around the sides and gathered at the top. The pouch was dyed red, beautifully decorated with small ivory beads, and embroidered in white with downward pointing triangles. Small white crane feathers were arrayed around the circular bottom edge. Ayla admired it, but when she made no move to do so, Deegie told her to open it. Inside were cords and threads made of mammoth wool, sinew, animal fur, and plant fibres, all carefully wound into circles or around small phalanges of bone. The sewing sack also contained sharp blades and awls for cutting and piercing. Ayla was delighted. She wanted to learn the Mamutoi ways of making and decorating clothes.

From her platform she took a small wooden bowl with a close-fitting lid and gave it to the old woman. When Crozie opened it, she looked at Ayla with a puzzled expression. It was filled with pure white marbleised softened tallow – tasteless, colourless, odourless animal fat that had been rendered in simmering water. She smelled it, and smiled, but was still puzzled.

"I make rose water, from petals . . . mix with . . . other things," Ayla started to explain.

"That's what makes it smell nice, I suppose, but what is it for?" Crozie asked.

"Is for hands, for face, elbows, feet. Feels good. Make smooth," Ayla said, taking a small dab and rubbing it on the back of the woman's dry, chapped, wrinkled old hand. After it was rubbed in, Crozie touched her hand, then closed her eyes, and slowly felt the smoother skin. When the old harridan opened her eyes, Alya thought they glistened more, though no tears were in evidence, but when the woman gave her a hard hug of welcome, Ayla felt her shaking underneath.

Each gift exchanged made everyone anticipate the next one more, and Ayla was enjoying the giving as much as the receiving. Her gifts were as unusual to them as theirs were to her, and it was as much fun to see her gifts well received as it was to feel overwhelmed by the gifts presented to her. She had never felt so special, had never been made to feel so welcome, so wanted. If she let herself think about it, tears of joy threatened.

Ranec was hanging back, waiting until all the other gifts were exchanged. He wanted to be last so his gift would not be confused with all the others. Among all the special and unique gifts she had received, he wanted his to be most memorable. Ayla was putting her things away on the platform that was just as full as when she began, when she saw the gift she had chosen for Ranec. She had to think for a moment before she realised she hadn't exchanged gifts with him yet. With it in her hands, she turned around to look for him, only to find herself looking into the teeth of his teasing smile.

"Did you forget one for me?" he said. He was standing so close she could see large black pupils and, for the first time, converging faint streaks of light within the dark brown of his eyes – his deep, liquid, compelling dark eyes. She felt a warmth emanating from him that disconcerted her.

"No, ah . . . did not forget . . . Here," she said, remembering the gift was in her hands and holding it up. He glanced down and his eyes showed his pleasure at the thick, lush, winter-white pelts of arctic foxes she held out to him. The moment of hesitation gave her the chance to compose herself, and when he looked back at her, her eyes held a teasing smile. "I think you forget."

He grinned, as much because she was so quick to catch on and play along with his joking as because it gave him an appropriate opening to present his gift.

"No. I did not forget. Here," he said, and brought out the object he had been hiding behind his back. She looked at the piece of carved ivory cradled in his hands, and almost didn't believe what she saw. And even when he relieved her of the white furs she held in her hands, she didn't reach for it. She was almost afraid to touch it. She looked up at him with sheer wonder.

"Ranec," she breathed, reaching, then hesitating. He had to urge it on her, and then she held it as though it might break. "This is Whinney! Is like you take Whinney and make small," she exclaimed, turning the exquisite, carved ivory horse, no more than three inches in length, over in her hands. A touch of colour had been applied to the sculpture: yellow ochre on the coat, and ground black charcoal on the legs, the stiff mane and along the spine to the tail to match Whinney's colouring. "Look, little ears, just right. And hooves, and tail. Even markings like her coat. Oh, Ranec, how you do it?"

Ranec couldn't have been happier as he gave her a warm embrace of welcome. Her reaction was exactly what he had been hoping for, even dreaming of, and the look of love in his eyes when he watched her was so obvious, it brought tears to Nezzie's eyes. She glanced at Jondalar and knew he saw it, too. Anguish was etched on his face. She shook her head knowingly.

After all the gifts were exchanged, Ayla went with Deegie to the Aurochs Hearth to change into the new outfit. Ever since Ranec had acquired the foreign shirt, Deegie had been trying to match the colour. She had finally come close, and from the cream-coloured leather she had made a short-sleeved V-necked tunic with a V-shaped hemline, with leggings to match, belted with finger-woven ties of bright colours similar to the colours of the designs on the shirt. The summer spent outside left Ayla's skin deeply tanned, and her blonde hair lightened, almost the colour of the leather. The outfit suited her as though it had been made especially for her.

With Deegie's help, Ayla put back Mamut's ivory armband, then added Talut's red-sheathed knife, and the necklace from Nezzie, but when the young Mamutoi woman suggested that she remove the worn, dirt-stained, lumpy leather pouch from around her neck, Ayla adamantly refused.

"Is my amulet, Deegie. Holds Spirit of Cave Lion, of Clan, of me. Little pieces, like Ranec's carving is little Whinney. Creb told me, if I lose amulet, totem cannot find me. I will die," Ayla tried to explain.

Deegie thought for a moment, looking at Ayla. The whole effect was spoiled by the grubby little leather bag. Even the thong around her neck was frayed, but that gave her an idea.

"Ayla, what do you do when it wears out? That thong looks like it will break soon," Deegie asked.

"I make new bag, new thong."

"Then, it's not the bag that is so important, but what's inside it, right?"

"Yes . . ."

Deegie looked around and suddenly spotted the sewing sack Crozie had given Ayla. She picked it up, emptied the contents carefully on to a platform, and held it out to her. "Is there any reason you can't use this? We can fasten it to a string of beads – one from your hair will be fine – and you can wear it around your neck."

Ayla took the beautiful, decorated bag from Deegie, looked at it, then wrapped her hand around the familiar old leather pouch and felt the sense of comfort the Clan amulet gave her. But she wasn't Clan any more. She hadn't lost her totem. The Spirit of the Cave Lion still protected her, and the signs she had been given were still important, but she was Mamutoi now.

When Ayla went back to the Mammoth Hearth, she was every inch a Mamutoi woman, a beautiful, well-dressed Mamutoi woman of high status and obvious value, and every eye had approving looks for the newest member of the Lion Camp. But two sets of eyes showed more than approval. Love and longing gleamed from dark laughing eyes full of eager hope no less than from the miserably unhappy eyes of an impossibly vivid shade of blue.

Manuv, with Nuvie on his lap, smiled warmly at Ayla as she passed by on her way to put her other clothes away, and she beamed back, so full of joy and happiness she didn't think she could contain it all. She was Ayla of the Mamutoi, and she was going to do everything she could to be completely one of them. Then she saw Jondalar talking to Danug, only from the back, but felt her elation collapse. Perhaps it was his stance, or the way he held his shoulders, but something at a subliminal level made her pause. Jondalar was not happy. But what could she do about it now?

She hurried to get the firestones. Mamut had told her to wait until later before giving them away. Appropriate ceremony would invest the stones with proper significance, and enhance their value. She picked up the small, yellow-grey metallic-coloured nodules of iron pyrite and brought them with her to the hearth. On her way, she passed behind Tulie, who was talking to Nezzie and Wymez, and overheard her speaking.

". . . but I had no idea she had so much wealth. Just look at the furs alone. The bison hide, and the white fox pelts, and this snow leopard – you don't see many of these around . . ."

Ayla smiled as her feeling of joy returned. Her gifts had been acceptable, and appreciated.

The old man of mystery had not been idle. While she was changing, Mamut was changing, too. His face was painted with zigzag lines that accented and enhanced his tattoo, and he wore as a cape the hide of a cave lion, the same cave lion whose tail Talut sported. Mamut's necklace was made of short hollowed-out sections of the tusk of a small mammoth interspersed with canine teeth of several different animals, including one of a cave lion that matched hers.

"Talut is planning a hunt, so I will Search," the shaman told her. "Join me, if you can – and want to. In any case, be prepared."

Ayla nodded, but her stomach churned.

Tulie came towards the hearth and smiled at her. "I didn't know Deegie was going to give that to you," she said. "I'm not sure if I would have approved earlier; she worked hard on it, but I must admit, it becomes you, Ayla."

Ayla just smiled, not sure how to respond.

"That's why I gave it to her, mother," Deegie said, approaching with her skull instrument. "I was trying to work out the process of getting finished leather to come out so light. I can always make another outfit."

"I'm ready," Tornec announced as he arrived with his mammoth bone instrument.

"Good. You can start as soon as Ayla starts handing out the stones," Mamut said. "Where's Talut?"

"He's been pouring his brew," Tornec said, smiling, "and he's being very generous. He said he wants this to be a suitable celebration."

"And it will be, too!" the big headman said. "Here, Ayla, I brought you a cup. After all, you are the reason for this occasion!"

Ayla tasted the drink, still finding the fermented flavour not entirely to her taste, but all the rest of the Mamutoi seemed to enjoy it. She decided she would learn to enjoy it, too. She wanted to be one of them, to do what they did, to like what they liked. She drank it down. Talut filled her cup again.

"Talut will tell you when to start giving out the stones, Ayla. Strike each one and get a spark just before you give it," Mamut instructed. She nodded, looked at the cup in her hand, then drank the contents, shaking her head at the potent beverage, and put the cup down to pick up the stones.

"Ayla is now counted among the Lion Camp," Talut said, as soon as everyone settled down, "but she has one more gift. For each hearth, a stone to make fire. Nezzie is the keeper of the Lion Hearth. Ayla will give the firestone to her to keep."

As Ayla walked towards Nezzie, she struck the iron pyrite with flint, drawing a bright spark, then she gave her the stone.

"Who is the keeper of the Fox Hearth?" Talut continued as Deegie and Tornec began beating on the bone instruments.

"I am. Ranec is the keeper of the Fox Hearth."

Ayla brought him a stone, and struck it. But when she gave it to him, he whispered, in a low, warm voice, "The fox furs are softer and more beautiful than any I have ever seen. I will keep them on my bed and think of you every night when I feel their softness against my bare skin." He touched her face, only lightly, with the back of his hand, but she felt it as a physical shock.

She backed away, confused, as Talut asked for the keeper of the Reindeer Hearth, and had to strike the stone twice to get a spark for

Tronie. Fralie took the stone for the Crane Hearth, and by the time Tulie took hers, and she gave one to Mamut, for the Mammoth Hearth, Ayla was feeling dizzy, and more than willing to sit down near the fire where Mamut indicated.

The drums began to have their effect. The sound was soothing and compelling at the same time. The lodge was darkened – a small fire diffused through the screen was the only light. She could hear breathing, close by, and looked to see where it was coming from. Crouched, near the fire, was a man – or was it a lion? The breathing became a low growl, almost, but not quite – to her perceptive ear – like the warning growl of a cave lion. The vocalised drumming picked up the sound, giving it resonance and depth.

Suddenly, with a savage snarl, the lion figure leaped, and the silhouette of a lion moved across the screen. But it almost jerked to a stop in a startled response to Ayla's unintentional reaction. She challenged the shadow lion with a growl so realistic and so menacing, it brought a gasp from most of the people watching. The silhouette recovered its lion stance and answered with the soothing growl of a lion backing down. Ayla voiced an angry snarl of victory, then began a series of *"hnk, hnk, hnk"* grunts that faded as though the lion was walking away.

Mamut smiled to himself. Her lion is so perfect it would fool a lion, he thought, pleased that she had spontaneously joined him. Ayla didn't know why she did, herself, except that after her first impromptu challenge, it was fun to talk like a lion with Mamut. She hadn't done anything like it since Baby left her valley. The drums had picked up and enhanced the scene, but now were following the silhouette moving sinuously across the screen. She was close enough to see that it was Mamut creating the action, but even she became caught up in the effect. She wondered, though, how the normally stiff and arthritic old man could move with such ease. Then she remembered seeing him gulp something down earlier, and suspected it might have been a strong painkiller. He would probably suffer for this the next day.

Suddenly Mamut leaped out from behind the screen and squatted by his mammoth skull drum. He beat on it rapidly for a short time, then stopped suddenly. He picked up a cup Ayla hadn't noticed before, drank from it, then approaching her, offered it. Without even thinking about it, she took a small sip, and then another, though the taste was strong, musky, and unpleasant. Encouraged by the talking drums, she soon began to feel the effects.

The leaping flames behind the screen gave the animals painted on it a feeling of movement. She was entranced by them, concentrated her entire attention on them, and heard only in the distance the voices of the Camp beginning to chant. A baby cried, but it seemed to come from some other world as she was drawn along by the strange flickering motion of the animals on the screen. They seemed almost alive, as the drum music filled her with pounding hooves, bawling calves, trumpeting mammoths.

Then, it was dark no longer. Instead, a hazy sun overlooked a snowy plain. A small herd of musk-oxen were huddled together, a blizzard swirling around them. As she swooped low, she sensed she was not alone. Mamut was with her. The scene shifted. The storm was over, but wind-driven whirling snow-devils wailed across the steppes like ghostly apparitions. She and Mamut moved away from the desolate emptiness. Then, she noticed a few bison standing stoically on the lee side of a narrow valley, trying to stay out of the wind. She was racing ahead, darting along the river valley that cut deep ravines. They followed a tributary that narrowed into a steep-walled canyon ahead, and she saw the familiar side path up to the dry bed of a seasonal stream.

And then she was in a dark place looking down at a small fire and people huddled around a screen. She heard a slow chant, a continuous repetition of sound. When she flickered her eyelids and saw blurred faces, she saw Nezzie and Talut and Jondalar looking down at her with worried expressions.

"Are you all right?" Jondalar asked, speaking Zelandonii.

"Yes, yes. I'm all right, Jondalar. What happened? Where was I?"

"You'll have to tell me."

"How do you feel?" Nezzie asked. "Mamut always likes this tea, afterwards."

"I am fine," she said, sitting up and taking the cup. She did feel fine. A little tired, and a little dizzy, but not bad.

"I don't think it was as frightening for you this time, Ayla," Mamut said, coming towards her.

Ayla smiled. "No, I am not frightened, but what we do?"

"We Searched. I thought you were a Searcher. That's why you are a daughter of the Mammoth Hearth," he said. "You have other natural talents, Ayla, but you need training." He saw her frown. "Don't worry about it now. There is time to think about it later."

Talut poured out more of his brew for Ayla and several others while Mamut told them about the Search, where they went, what they found. She gulped it down – it didn't seem so bad that way – then tried to listen, but it seemed to go to her head quickly. Her mind wandered and she noticed that Deegie and Tornec were still playing their instruments, but with tones so rhythmic and appealing it made her want to move with them. It reminded her of the Women's Dance of the Clan, and she found it hard to concentrate on Mamut.

She felt someone watching her, and glanced around. Near the Fox

Hearth she saw Ranec staring at her. He smiled and she smiled back. Suddenly Talut was filling her cup again. Ranec came forward and offered his cup for filling; Talut complied, then turned back to the discussion.

"You're not interested in this, are you? Let's go over there, where Deegie and Tornec are playing," Ranec said, in a low voice, leaning close to her ear.

"I think not. They talk about hunt." Ayla turned back to the serious discussion, but she had missed so much of it she didn't know where they were, and they didn't seem to notice if she was listening or not.

"You won't miss anything. They'll tell us all about it later. Listen to that," he said, pausing to let her hear the pulsing musical sounds coming from the other side of the hearth. "Wouldn't you rather see how Tornec does that? He's really very good."

Ayla leaned towards the sound, pulled by the rhythmic beat. She glanced at the group making plans, then looked at Ranec and broke into a full beaming smile. "Yes, I rather see Tornec!" she said, feeling pleased with herself.

As they got up, Ranec, standing close, stopped her. "You must stop smiling, Ayla," he said, his tone serious and stern.

"Why?" she asked with deep concern, her smile gone, wondering what she had done wrong.

"Because you are so lovely when you smile, you take my breath away," Ranec said, and he meant every word, but then he continued, "and how will I walk with you if I'm gasping for breath?"

Ayla's smile returned at his compliment, then the idea of him gasping for breath because she smiled made her giggle. It was a joke, of course, she thought, though she wasn't entirely sure he was joking. They walked towards the new entrance to the Mammoth Hearth.

Jondalar observed them as they approached. He had been enjoying the rhythms and music while he was waiting for her, but he did not enjoy seeing Ayla walking towards the music makers with Ranec. He felt jealousy rise in his throat, and had a wild urge to strike out at the man who dared to advance on the woman he loved. But Ranec, for all that he looked different, was Mamutoi, and belonged to the Lion Camp. Jondalar was only a guest. They would stand up for their own, and he was alone. He tried to exert control and reason. Ranec and Ayla were only walking together. How could he object to that?

He had had mixed feeling about her adoption from the beginning. He wanted her to belong to some group of people, because she wanted it, and, he admitted, so she would be more acceptable to his people. He had seen how happy she was when they were exchanging gifts, and he was pleased for her, but felt distant from it, and more worried than ever that she might not want to leave. He wondered if he should have allowed himself to be adopted after all.

He had felt a part of Ayla's adoption in the beginning. But he felt like an outsider now, even to Ayla. She was one of them, now. This was her night, her celebration, hers and the Lion Camp's. He had given her no gift, and had not received one in exchange. He hadn't even thought of it, though now he wished he had. But he had no gifts to give, to her or anyone. He had arrived here with nothing, and he had not spent years making and accumulating things. He had learned many things in his travels and had accumulated knowledge, but he'd had no opportunity to benefit from his acquisitions, yet. All he had brought with him was Ayla.

With a dark scowl, Jondalar watched her smiling and laughing with Ranec, feeling like an unwanted intruder.

19

When the discussion broke up, Talut doled out more of his fermented beverage, made from the starch of cattail roots and various other ingredients, which he was constantly experimenting with. The festivities centred on Deegie and Tornec became more lively. They played music, people sang, sometimes together and other times individually. Some people danced, not the energetic kind of dance Ayla had seen earlier, outside, but a subtle form of body movement made standing in one place in time to the rhythm, often with a singing accompaniment.

Ayla noticed Jondalar often, hanging back somewhat, and started towards him several times, but something always interrupted. There were so many people, and all of them seemed to be vying for her attention. She was not entirely in control of herself from Talut's drink, and her concentration was easily distracted.

She took a turn on Deegie's musical skull drum, with enthusiastic encouragement, and remembered some of the Clan rhythms. They were complex, distinctive and, to the Lion Camp, unusual and intriguing. If Mamut had any doubts left about Ayla's origins, the memories triggered by her playing eliminated them completely.

Then Ranec stood up to dance and sing a humorous song full of innuendo and double meanings about the Pleasures of Gifts, directed at Ayla. It brought broad grins and knowing glances, and was obvious enough to make Ayla blush. Deegie showed her how to dance and sing the satirical response, but at the end, where a hint of acceptance or rejection was supposed to finish it, Ayla stopped. She could do neither. She didn't quite understand the subtleties of the game, and while it wasn't her intention to encourage him, she didn't want him to think she didn't like him, either. Ranec smiled. Disguised as humour, the song was often used as a face-saving means of discovering if interest was mutual. Not even a flat rejection would have stopped him; he considered anything less, promising.

Ayla was giddy with the drink and the laughter, and the attention. Everyone wanted to include her, everyone wanted to talk to her, to listen to her, to put an arm around her and feel close. She couldn't

TMH–10

remember ever having so much fun, or feeling so warm and friendly, or so wanted. And every time she turned around, she saw an enraptured, gleaming smile and flashing dark eyes concentrated on her.

As the evening wore on, the group began to diminish. Children dropped off to sleep and were carried to their beds. Fralie had gone to bed early, at Ayla's suggestion, and the rest of Crane Hearth followed soon after. Tronie, complaining of a headache – she hadn't been feeling well that evening – went to her hearth to nurse Hartal, and fell asleep. Jondalar slipped away then, too. He stretched out on the sleeping platform, waiting for Ayla, and watching her.

Wymez was uncommonly voluble, after a few cups of Talut's bouza, and told stories and made teasing remarks first to Ayla, then to Deegie, then to all the women. Tulie began to find him suddenly interesting, after all this time, and teased and joked back. She ended up inviting him to spend the night at the Aurochs Hearth with her and Barzec. She hadn't shared her bed with a second man since Darnev died.

Wymez decided it might be a good idea to leave the hearth to Ranec, and perhaps not so unwise to let it be known that a woman could choose two men. He was not blind to the situation that was developing, though he doubted that any agreement could be reached between Ranec and Jondalar. But the big woman did seem particularly attractive this evening, and she was a highly valued headwoman who had a great deal of status to bestow. Who could tell what changes he might want to make if Ranec decided to change the composition of the Fox Hearth?

Not long after the three of them headed towards the back of the lodge, Talut teased Nezzie to the Lion Hearth. Deegie and Tornec got involved in experimenting with their instruments, to the exclusion of everyone else, and Ayla thought she heard some of her rhythms. Then she realised she and Ranec were talking alone, and it made her self-conscious.

"I think everyone go to bed," she said, her voice a little slurred. She was feeling the effects of the bouza, and weaved back and forth where she stood. Most of the lamps were gone, and the fire had burned low.

"Perhaps we should," he said, smiling. Ayla felt the unspoken invitation gleaming in his eyes, and was drawn to it, but she didn't know how to deal with it.

"Yes. I am tired," she said, starting towards her bed platform. Ranec took her hand and held her back.

"Ayla, don't go." His smile was gone, and his tone was insistent. She turned back, and the next instant, his arms were around her, and his mouth was hard on hers. She opened hers slightly, and his response was immediate. He kissed her all over, her mouth, her neck, her throat. His hands reached for her breasts, then caressed her hips, and her thighs, and cupped her mound, as though he couldn't get enough of her and wanted her all at once. Unexpected shocks of excitement coursed through her. He pressed her to him, and she felt a hard hot lump against her, and a sudden warmth of her own between her legs.

"Ayla, I want you. Come to my bed," he said with commanding urgency. With unexpected complaisance, she followed him.

All evening, Jondalar had watched the woman he loved laughing and joking and dancing with her new people, and the longer he watched, the more of an outsider he felt. But it was the attentive dark-skinned carver, in particular, that galled him. He wanted to vent his wrath, step in and take Ayla away, but this was her home now, this was the night of her adoption. What right did he have to interfere in their celebration? He could only put on a face of acceptance, if not pleasure, but he felt miserable, and went to the bed platform wishing for the oblivion of sleep that would not come.

From the dark enclosed space, Jondalar watched Ranec embrace Ayla and lead her away towards his bed, and felt a shock of disbelief. How could she be going with another man when he was waiting for her? No woman had ever chosen someone else when he wanted her, and this was the woman he loved! He wanted to jump up, grab her away, and smash his fist into that smiling mouth.

Then he imagined broken teeth and blood, and remembered the agony of shame and exile. These were not even his people. They would surely turn him out, and in the freezing cold night of the periglacial steppes there was no place to go. And how could he go anyplace without his Ayla?

But she had made the choice. She had chosen Ranec, and it was her right to choose anyone she wanted. Just because Jondalar was waiting didn't mean she had to go to him, and she hadn't. She chose a man of her own people, a Mamutoi man who sang and danced and flirted with her, and with whom she had laughed and had fun. Could he blame her? How many times had he chosen someone with whom he had laughed and had fun?

But how could she do it? This was the woman he loved! How could she choose someone else when he loved her? Jondalar anguished and despaired, but what could he do? Nothing but swallow his bitter gorge of jealousy, and watch the woman he loved follow another man to his bed.

Ayla wasn't thinking clearly, her mind was muddled from Talut's brew, and there was no question that she was attracted to Ranec, but those weren't the reasons she went with him. She would have gone no matter what. Ayla was brought up by the Clan. She was taught to comply, without question, with any man who commanded her, who gave her the signal that he desired to copulate with her.

If any man of the Clan gave the signal to any woman, she was expected to render the service, just as she would bring him food or water. Though it was deemed a courtesy to request a woman's services of her mate, or the man she was usually associated with, first, it was not required, and would have been given as a matter of course. A man's mate was his to command, but not exclusively. The bond between a woman and a man was mutually beneficial, companionate and often, after a time, affectionate, but to show jealousy, or any strong emotion, was unthinkable. It didn't make a man's mate any less his because she rendered a small service to someone else; and he didn't love the children of his mate any less. He assumed a certain responsibility for them, in terms of care and training, but his hunting provided for his clan, and all food, gathered and hunted, was shared.

Ranec had given Ayla what she had come to interpret as the "signal" of the Others, a command to satisfy his sexual needs. Like any properly raised woman of the Clan, it didn't even occur to her to refuse. She looked towards her bed platform once, but did not see the blue eyes full of shock and pain. It would have surprised her if she had.

Ranec's ardour had not cooled by the time they walked to the Fox Hearth, but he was more controlled once Ayla was within its boundaries, though he could hardly believe it. They sat down on his bed platform. She noticed the white furs she had given him. She started to untie her belt, but Ranec stopped her.

"I want to undress you, Ayla. I've dreamed of this, and I want it to be just right," Ranec said.

She shrugged, agreeably. She had already noticed that Ranec was different from Jondalar in certain ways, and it made her curious. It wasn't a matter of judging which man was better, just noting differences.

Ranec looked at her for a while. "You are so beautiful," he said, finally, as he leaned over to kiss her. His mouth was soft, though it could be hard when he kissed her hard. She noticed his dark hand outlined by the white fur, and rubbed his arm gently. His skin felt the same as any other skin.

He started by taking off the beads and shells she had in her hair, then he ran his hands through it, and brought it to his face to feel and smell. "Beautiful, so beautiful," he murmured. He unfastened her necklace, and then her new amulet bag, and put them carefully beside her beads on the storage bench near the head of the bed. Then he untied her belt, stood up, and pulled her up beside him. Suddenly, he was kissing her face and her throat again, and feeling her body underneath her tunic, as though he couldn't wait. Ayla felt his excitement. His fingertips brushing her nipple sent a current of feeling through her. She leaned towards him, giving herself up to him.

He stopped then, and taking a deep breath, lifted the tunic up over her head, and folded it neatly beside her other things. Then he just looked at her, as though he was trying to memorise her. He turned her one way, and then another, filling his eyes as though they, too, needed satisfaction.

"Perfect, just perfect. Look at them, full, yet shapely, just right," he said, running a fingertip lightly along the profile of her breast. She closed her eyes and shivered from the tender touch. Suddenly a warm mouth was sucking on a nipple, and she felt a shock deep inside. "Perfect, so perfect," he whispered, changing to the other breast. He pressed his face between them, then with both hands held them together and suckled both nipples at once, making little grunting noises of pleasure. She arched her neck back and pressed towards him, feeling twin surges of sensation, then reached for his head, and noticing his hair, so full and tightly curled, let her hands enjoy the new experience.

They were still standing when he backed away and looked at her, a smile on his face, while he untied the waist cord and lowered her leggings. He couldn't resist feeling the texture of her curly blonde hair, and cupping her mound to touch her warm moistness, then he sat her down. He quickly removed his own shirt, and put it beside hers, then he kneeled in front of her and removed one moccasin-type indoor shoe.

"Are you ticklish?" he asked.

"Little, on bottom."

"How does this feel?" He rubbed her foot, gently but firmly, applying pressure on the instep.

"Feel good." Then he kissed her instep. "Feel good," she said again with a smile.

He smiled back, then took off her other shoe, and rubbed her foot. He pulled the leggings off, and put them and the shoes with her other things. Taking her hands, he pulled her up again so she stood naked in the last light of the dying coals from the Mammoth Hearth. He turned her again, from front to back, looking at her. "O Mother! So beautiful, so perfect. Just like I knew you would be," he crooned, more to himself than to her.

"Ranec, I am not beautiful," she chided.

"You should see yourself, Ayla. Then you would not say that."

"It is nice you say, nice you think, but I am not beautiful," Ayla insisted.

"You are lovelier than anyone I've ever seen."

She only nodded. He could think so, if he wanted. She couldn't stop him.

After filling his eyes, he began to touch, first lightly, all over, outlining her with his fingertips from different angles. Then in finer detail, he traced the muscle structure under her skin. Suddenly he stopped and peeled the rest of his clothes off, leaving them where they fell, and took her in his arms, wanting to feel her body with his. She felt him as well, his warm compact muscular body, his hard upright throbbing manhood. She inhaled his pleasant masculine smell. He kissed her mouth, then her face and her neck, nipping her shoulders with gentle bites, that made her quiver, and murmuring under his breath, "So, so perfect. Ayla, I want you in every way. I want to see you and touch you and hold you. O Mother, so beautiful."

His hands were on her breasts again, his mouth on her nipples, sucking, then nipping lightly, then sucking both, making his little pleasure noises. He suckled one breast, trying to take as much in his mouth as he could, then the other. He got down on his knees in front of her, nuzzled her navel, and wrapped his arms around her legs and smooth round twin mounds, caressing them, then the split between. He nuzzled her hair, and lightly, teasingly, found her slit with a wet tongue. She moaned, and he felt her quivering response.

He stood up then, and eased her down to his bed, to the utterly soft, luxurious, caressing furs. He crawled in beside her, kissed her with soft biting lips, not teeth, suckled and nibbled her breasts, and with his hand, fondled and rubbed the folds and crevices of her womanhood. She moaned and cried out as he seemed to touch every place at once.

He took her hand and put it on his firm, fully engorged organ. She sat up, curled around and rubbed her cheek against it, to his delight. In the dim light, she could see the outline of her light hand against his darkness. He felt smooth. His man smell was different, though, similar but different, and his hair was wiry and tight. He moaned with sweet ecstasy when he felt a warm wetness enclose his maleness, and a drawing, pulling sensation. This was more than he'd ever imagined, more than he'd even dared dream. He thought he'd never contain himself when she began to use techniques she had so recently learned, quickly circling her tongue, drawing him in and releasing, adding firm strokes to the upright shaft. "O, Ayla, Ayla. You are She! I knew you were. So beautiful, so perfect, so knowing. You honour me."

Suddenly, Ranec sat up. "I want you, and I can't wait. Please, now," he said, in a throaty, strained whisper.

She rolled over and opened to him. He mounted and entered, voicing a long, shuddering cry. Then he pulled back and drove in again, and again, and again, his voice rising in pitch with each stroke. Ayla arched to meet him, trying to match his pace. "Ayla, I am ready. Here it is," he cried, straining, then suddenly, he moaned a great sigh of relief, pushed in and out a few more times, and relaxed on top of her. It took a bit longer for Ayla to relax.

After a while, Ranec pulled himself up, disengaged himself, and rolled over on his side and, propping himself up on an arm, looked down at Ayla. "I'm afraid I wasn't as perfect as you are," he said.

She frowned. "I do not understand this perfect, Ranec. What is perfect?"

"It was too fast. You are so wonderful, so perfect in what you do, I was ready too soon. I couldn't wait, and I think it wasn't as perfect for you," he said.

"Ranec, this is Gift of Pleasure, right?"

"Yes, that is one name for it."

"You think it was not Pleasure for me? I had Pleasures. Many Pleasures."

"Many, but not the perfect Pleasure. If you can wait, I think with a little time, I will be ready again."

"Is not necessary."

"Maybe not necessary, Ayla, but I want to," he said, bending down to kiss her. "I almost could now," he added caressing her breast, her stomach, and reaching for her mound. She jumped at his touch, and still quivered. "I'm sorry, you were almost ready. If I could only have held off a little longer."

She didn't answer. He was kissing her breast, rubbing the small knob within her slit, and in an instant, she was ready again. She was moving her hips, pushing against him, crying out. Suddenly, with a surge and a cry, the release came, and he felt a warmth of wetness. She relaxed then.

She smiled at him. "I think now perfect Pleasures," she said.

"Not quite, but next time, maybe. I hope there will be many next times, Ayla," he replied, lying on his side beside her, his hand resting on her stomach. She frowned, feeling confused. She wondered if she was misunderstanding something.

· In the dim light, he could see his dark hand on her light skin, and smiled. He always did like the contrast his deep colouring made against the lightness of the women he Pleasured. It left an impression no other man could make, and women noticed. They always remarked, and never forgot him. He was glad the Mother had chosen to give him such dark colour. It made him distinctive, unusual, unforgettable. He liked the feel of her stomach under his hand, too, but even more he liked knowing she was there beside him in his bed. He had hoped for it, wished it, dreamed it, and even now, with her there, it seemed impossible.

After a while he moved his hand up to her breast, fondled a nipple, and felt it harden. Ayla had begun to doze, tired and a little headachy, and when he nuzzled her neck, and then put his mouth on hers, she realised he wanted her, had given her a signal again. She felt a moment's annoyance and for an instant felt an urge to refuse. It surprised her, almost shocked her, and brought her fully awake. He was kissing her neck, stroking her shoulder and arm, then feeling the fullness and roundness of her breast. By the time he took a nipple in his mouth, she was no longer annoyed. Pleasurable sensations coursed through her depths reaching her place of perfect Pleasure. He changed to her other breast, fondling both and suckling each in turn, making his little pleasure noises in the back of his throat.

"Ayla, beautiful Ayla," Ranec murmured. Then he sat up and looked down at her on his bed. "O, Mother! I can't believe you're here. So lovely. This time it will be perfect, Ayla. This time I know it will be perfect."

Jondalar lay rigid on the bed, jaw clamped shut, desperately wanting to use his clenched fists on the carver, but forcing himself not to move. She had looked directly at him, then turned and went with Ranec. Every time he closed his eyes he saw her face, looking directly at him, then turning away.

It's her choice! It's her choice, he kept telling himself. She said she loved him, but how could she even know? Of course, she might have cared about him, even loved him, when they were alone in her valley; she didn't know anyone else then. He was the first man she ever met. But now that she had met other men, why couldn't she love someone else? He tried to convince himself that it was only fair for her to meet others and choose for herself, but he could not get it out of his mind that, on that night, she had chosen someone else.

Ever since he'd returned from his stay with Dalanar, the tall, muscular, almost beautifully handsome man had had his choice of women. A look of invitation from his unbelievable eyes, and any woman he ever wanted was his. In fact, they did everything they could to encourage him. They followed him, hungered after him, wished he would invite them. And he did, but no woman could match his memory of his first love, or overcome his burden of guilt over it. Now, the one woman in the world he had finally found, the one woman he loved, was in another man's bed.

The mere thought that she had chosen someone else brought pain, but when he heard the unmistakable sounds of her sharing Pleasures with Ranec, he muffled a moan, pounded the bed, and doubled up in agony. It was like a hot coal was boiling in his belly. His chest felt tight, his throat burned, he breathed in muffled gasps as though choking on smoky steam. Pressure forced hot tears out at the corners of his eyes though he squeezed them shut as tightly as he could.

Finally it ended, and when he was sure, he relaxed a little. But then it started again, and he couldn't stand it. He jumped up, stood irresolute for a moment, then raced out the entrance to the new annexe. Whinney's ears perked up and turned towards him as he ran past and through the exterior arch to the outside.

The wind buffeted him against the earthlodge. The sudden cold took his breath away and startled him into awareness of his surroundings. He looked out across the frozen river, and watched clouds streaming across the moon, trailing ragged edges. He took a few steps away from the shelter. Knives of wind tore through his tunic, and it seemed, through his skin and muscle to the marrow of his bone.

He went back inside, shivering, plodded past the horses and into the Mammoth Hearth again. He tensed up, listening, and heard nothing at first. Then came the sounds of breathing and moaning and grunting. He looked at his bed platform, then turned back towards the annexe, not knowing which way to go. He couldn't stand it inside; he couldn't stay alive outside. Finally he couldn't bear it. He had to go out. Grabbing his travelling sleeping furs, he went back through the archway to the horses' annexe.

Whinney snorted and tossed her head, and Racer, who was lying down, lifted his head off the ground and nickered a soft greeting. Jondalar headed towards the animals, spread his furs out on the ground beside Racer, and got in them. It was cold in the annexe, but not nearly as cold as outside. There was no wind, some heat filtered through, and the horses generated more. And their breathing covered up the sounds of other heavy breathing. Even so, he lay awake most of the night, his mind recalling sounds, replaying scenes, real and imagined, over and over again.

Ayla woke as the first slivers of daylight stole through cracks around the cover of the smoke hole. She reached across the bed for Jondalar, and was disconcerted to find Ranec. With the memory of the night before came the knowledge that she was going to have a bad headache; the effects of Talut's bouza. She slipped out of bed, picked up the clothes Ranec had arranged so neatly, and hurried to her own bed. Jondalar was not there, either. She looked around the Mammoth Hearth at the other beds. Deegie and Tornec were sleeping in one, and she wondered if they had shared Pleasures. Then she recalled that Wymez had been invited to the Aurochs Hearth and Tronie wasn't feeling well. Perhaps Deegie and Tornec had just found it more convenient to sleep there. It didn't matter, but she wondered where Jondalar was.

She remembered that she hadn't seen him after it grew late the night before. Someone said he had gone to bed, but where was he now? She noticed Deegie and Tornec again. He must be sleeping at a different hearth, too, she thought. She was tempted to check, but no one else seemed to be up and about, and she didn't want to wake anyone. Feeling uneasy, she crawled into her empty bed, pulled the furs around her, and after a while, slept again.

When she awoke the next time, the smoke-hole cover had been moved aside and bright daylight beamed in. She started to get up, then, feeling an enormous throbbing pain in her head, dropped back down and closed her eyes. Either I am very sick, or this is from Talut's bouza, she thought. Why do people like to drink it if it makes them so sick? Then she thought about the celebration. She didn't have a clear memory of it all, but she did recall playing rhythms, dancing and singing, though she didn't really know how. She had laughed a lot, even at herself when she found she had little voice for singing, not minding at all that she was the centre of attention. That wasn't like her. Normally she preferred to stay in the background and watch, and do her learning and practising in private. Was it the bouza that changed her normal inclination and caused her to be less careful? More forward? Is that why people drank it?

She opened her eyes again, and then got up very carefully, holding her head. She relieved herself in the indoor night basket – a tightly woven basket about half full of the dry pulverised dung of grazing animals from the steppes, which absorbed liquid and fecal matter. She washed herself with cold water. Then she stirred up the fire and added hot cooking stones. She dressed in the clothing she had made before she came, thinking of it now as a rather plain everyday outfit, though when she made it, it had seemed very exotic and complex.

Still moving carefully, she took several packets from her medicine bag and mixed up willow bark, yarrow, wood betony, and camomile in various proportions. She poured cold water into the cooking basket she used for morning tea, added hot rocks until it boiled, then the tea. Then hunkered in front of the fire with her eyes closed while she waited for the tea to steep. Suddenly, she jumped up, feeling her head throb but ignoring it, and reached for her medicine bag again.

I almost forgot, she thought, taking out her packets of Iza's secret contraceptive herbs. Whether it helped her totem fight off the spirit of a man's totem, as Iza thought, or somehow resisted the essence of a man's organ, as she suspected, Ayla did not want to take the chance of starting a baby now. Everything was too unsettled. She had wanted a baby started by Jondalar, but while she was waiting for the tea, she began to wonder how a baby, who was a mixture of her and Ranec, would look. Like him? Like me? Or a little of both? Probably both, like

Durc . . . and Rydag. They were mixtures. A dark son from Ranec would look different, too, except, she thought with a trace of bitterness, no one would call him an abomination, or think he was an animal. He would be able to talk and laugh and cry, just like everyone else.

Knowing how Talut had appreciated her headache remedy the last time he drank his brew, Ayla made enough for several people. After she drank hers, she went out to look for Jondalar. The new annexe leading out directly from the Mammoth Hearth was proving to be quite a convenience, and for some reason she was glad she didn't have to go through the Fox Hearth. The horses were outside, but as she walked through, she noticed Jondalar's travelling sleeping fur rolled up next to the wall and wondered, in passing, how it got there.

As she pushed aside the drape and stepped through the second arch, she saw Talut, Wymez, and Mamut talking with Jondalar, whose back was to her.

"How is head, Talut?" she asked as she approached.

"Are you offering me some of your magic morning-after medicine?"

"I have headache, and make tea. There is more, inside," she said, then turned to Jondalar with a full happy smile now that she had found him.

For an instant her smile brought a like response, but just for an instant. Then his face clouded into a dark frown and his eyes filled with a look she had never seen there before. Her smile left her.

"You want tea, too, Jondalar?" she asked, confused and distraught.

"Why do you think I need it? I didn't drink too much last night, but I don't suppose you noticed," he replied in a voice so cold and distant she hardly recognised it.

"Where you go? I look for you early, but not in bed."

"Neither were you," he said. "I hardly think it mattered to you where I was." He turned and walked away from her. She looked at the other three men. She saw embarrassment on Talut's face. Wymez looked uncomfortable, but not entirely unhappy. Mamut had a look she couldn't decipher.

"Ah . . . I think I'll go to get some of that tea you offered," Talut said, quickly ducking into the lodge.

"Perhaps I'll try a cup, too," Wymez said, and followed him.

What did I do wrong? Ayla thought, and the uneasiness she had been feeling grew into a hard knot of distress in the pit of her stomach.

Mamut studied her, then said, "I think you should come and talk to me, Ayla. Later, when we can have a moment alone. Your tea may bring several visitors to the hearth now. Why don't you get something to eat?"

"I am not hungry," Ayla said, her stomach churning. She did not want to start out with her new people doing something wrong, and she wondered why Jondalar was so angry.

Mamut smiled reassuringly. "You should try to eat something. There is mammoth meat left over from your feast, and I think Nezzie saved one of those steamed loaves for you."

Ayla nodded. As she walked towards the main entrance of the long-house, upset and worried, she looked for the horses with the part of her mind that was always concerned for them. When she saw them she noticed Jondalar was with them, and felt a small sense of relief. She had often drawn comfort from the animals when she was troubled, and while not a completely formed thought, she hoped that turning to them would eventually make Jondalar feel better.

She passed through the foyer and into the cooking hearth. Nezzie was sitting with Rydag and Rugie, eating. She smiled when she saw Ayla and got up. For all that she was amply proportioned, Nezzie was active and graceful in her movements and, Ayla suspected, probably quite strong.

"Get yourself some meat. I'll get the loaf I put aside for you. It's the last one," Nezzie said. "And get a cup of hot tea, if you want. It's fireweed and mint."

Ayla broke off pieces of the firm, moist loaf for Rydag and Rugie when she sat down with them and Nezzie, but only picked at her own food.

"Is something wrong, Ayla?" the woman asked. She knew there was, and had some idea of the cause.

Ayla looked at her with troubled eyes. "Nezzie, I know Clan ways, not Mamutoi ways. Want to learn, want to be good Mamutoi woman, but not know when I do wrong. I think last night I do something wrong."

"What makes you think so?"

"When I go out, Jondalar angry. I think Talut not happy. Wymez, too. They leave, quick. Tell me what I did wrong, Nezzie."

"You didn't do anything wrong, Ayla, unless being loved by two men is wrong. Some men feel possessive when they have strong feelings for a woman. They don't want her to be with other men. Jondalar feels he has a claim on you and is angry because you shared Ranec's bed. But it is not just Jondalar. I think Ranec feels the same way, and would be just as possessive if he could. I raised him since he was a boy, and I have never seen him so taken with a woman. I think Jondalar is trying not to show how he feels, but he can't help it, and if he showed his anger, it probably embarrassed Talut and Wymez. That might be why they left in a hurry.

"Sometimes we yell a lot, or tease each other. We take pride in

300

hospitality and like to be friendly, but the Mamutoi do not show their deepest feelings too much. It can cause trouble, and we try to avoid disputes and discourage fighting. The Council of Sisters even frowns on the raids the young men like to make on other people, like the Sungaea, and are trying to ban them. The Sisters say it just invites raids in return, and people have been killed. They say it's better to trade than raid. The Council of Brothers is more lenient. Most of them did a bit of raiding in their youth, and say it's just a way to use young muscles and make a little excitement for themselves.''

Ayla was no longer listening. Rather than clarifying anything, Nezzie's explanation only made her more confused. Was Jondalar angry because she had responded to another man's signal? Was that a reason to get angry? No man of the Clan would indulge in such an emotional response. Broud was the only man who had ever shown the least interest in her, and then only because he knew she hated it. But many people wondered why he was bothering with such an ugly woman and he would have welcomed interest by another man. When she thought about it, she realised that Jondalar had been bothered by Ranec's interest from the beginning.

Mamut came in from the entrance foyer walking with discernible difficulty.

"Nezzie, I promised to fill Mamut's medicine bowl with help for arthritis," Ayla said.

She got up to help him, but he waved her away. "You go ahead. I'll be there. It will just take me a little longer."

She rushed through the Lion Hearth and the Fox Hearth, relieved to find it empty, and added fuel to the fire at the Mammoth Hearth. As she sorted through her medications, she recalled the many times she had applied poultices and plasters, and made painkilling drinks to ease Creb's aching joints. It was one aspect of her medicine she knew very well.

She waited until Mamut was resting comfortably, sipping a warm tea after she had drawn off and soaked away most of his ancient aches, before she asked any questions. It was soothing for her as well as the old shaman to apply her knowledge, skill, and intelligence in the practice of her craft, and it relieved some of the stress she had been feeling. Yet when she picked up a cup of tea and sat opposite Mamut, she didn't quite know where to begin.

"Mamut, did you stay long with Clan?" she finally asked.

"Yes, it takes a while for a bad break to heal, and by then, I wanted to know more, so I stayed until they left for the Clan Gathering."

"You learn Clan ways?"

"Some of them."

"You know about signal?"

"Yes, Ayla, I know about the signal a man gives a woman." He paused, seeming to consider, then continued, "I will tell you something I have never told anyone else. There was a young woman who helped to take care of me while my arm was mending, and after I was included in a hunting ceremony and hunted with them, she was given to me. I know what the signal is, and what it means. I used the signal, though at first I was not comfortable about it. She was a flathead woman, and not very appealing to me, particularly since I'd heard so many stories about them while I was growing up. But I was young and healthy, and I was expected to behave like a man of the Clan.

"The longer I stayed, the more appealing she became – you have no idea how appealing it can be to have someone waiting on your every need or desire. It wasn't until later that I discovered she had a mate. She was a second woman, her first mate had died so one of the other hunters took her in, a little reluctantly since she came from a different clan and had no children. When I left, I did not want to leave her behind, but I felt she would be happier with a clan than with me and my people. And I wasn't sure how I would be welcomed if I returned with a flathead woman. I have often wondered what happened to her."

Ayla closed her eyes as memories flooded over her. It seemed uncanny to be learning bits and pieces about her clan from this man whom she had met such a short time ago. She fitted his story together with her own knowledge of the history of Brun's clan.

"She not ever have children, always second woman, but always someone take in. She die in earthquake, before they find me."

He nodded. He, too, was glad to have an important bit of his past filled in.

"Mamut, Nezzie say Jondalar angry because I share Ranec's bed. Is true?"

"I think that's true."

"But Ranec give me signal! How can Jondalar be angry if Ranec give me signal?"

"Where did Ranec learn the Clan signal?" Mamut asked, surprised.

"Not Clan signal. Signal of the Others. When Jondalar find my valley, and teach me First Rites and Gift of Pleasure from Great Earth Mother Doni, I ask, what his signal is? He put mouth on mine, make kiss. Put hand on me, make . . . feel Pleasure. He say that is how I will know when he want me; he tell me his signal. Ranec give me signal last night. Then he say, 'I want you. Come to my bed.' Ranec give me signal. He make command."

Mamut looked up at the ceiling, and said, "O, Mother!" Then he looked back at her. "Ayla, you don't understand. Ranec certainly did give you a signal that he wanted you, but it wasn't a command."

Ayla looked at him with intense puzzlement. "I not understand."

"No one can command you, Ayla. Your body belongs to you, it's your choice. You decide what you want to do and who you want to do it with. You can go to any man's bed you choose, so long as he is willing – and I don't see much problem there – but you don't have to share Pleasures with any man you don't want to, ever."

She stopped to think about his words. "What if Ranec commands again? He said, wants me again, many times."

"I don't doubt that he wants, but he cannot command you. No one can command you, Ayla. Not against your will."

"Not even man I mate? Not ever?"

"I don't think you'd remain mated for very long under those circumstances, but no, not even your mate can command you. Your mate does not own you. Only you can decide."

"Mamut, when Ranec gave me signal, I not have to go?"

"That's right." He looked at her frown. "Are you sorry you went to his bed?"

"Sorry?" She shook her head. "No. Not sorry. Ranec is . . . good. Is not rough . . . like Broud. Ranec . . . care for me . . . make good Pleasures. No. Not sorry about Ranec. Sorry about Jondalar. Sorry Jondalar angry. Ranec make good Pleasures, but Ranec is . . . not Jondalar."

20

Ayla turned her head to the side as she leaned into the screaming wind, trying to shield her face from the raw blast of gale-driven snow. Each careful step forward was violently opposed by a force made visible only by the swirling mass of frozen white grit hurled against her. As the angry blizzard raged, she faced the lash of stinging pellets and squinted her eyes open, then turned away and took another few steps. Buffeted by the fierce storm, she looked again. The smooth rounded shape ahead beckoned, and she was relieved finally to touch the solid ivory arch.

"Ayla, you shouldn't have gone out in that blizzard!" Deegie said. "You can lose your way a few steps beyond the entrance."

"But it has been blowing like that for many, many days, and Whinney and Racer go out. I want to know where they go."

"Did you find out?"

"Yes. They like to feed at place around bend. Wind does not blow so hard, and snow does not cover dry grass too high. Blows drift on other side. I have some grain, but have not grass left. Horses know where is grass, even when blizzard blows. I will give water here, when they come back," Ayla said, stamping her feet, and shaking the snow off the parka she had just pulled off. She hung it up on a peg near the entrance to the Mammoth Hearth, on her way in.

"Can you believe it? She went outside. In this weather!" Deegie announced to the several people who were congregated at the fourth hearth.

"But why?" Tornec asked.

"Horses need to eat, and I . . . ." Ayla started to reply.

"I thought you were gone a long time," Ranec said. "When I asked Mamut, he said he had last seen you go into the horse hearth, but when I looked you weren't there."

"Everyone started looking for you, Ayla," Tronie said.

"Then Jondalar noticed your parka was gone, and the horses, too. He thought you might have gone out with them," Deegie said, "so we decided we'd better look for you outside. When I looked out to see how the weather was, I saw you coming."

"Ayla, you should let someone know if you are going out when the weather is bad," Mamut chided, gently.

"Don't you know you make people worry when you go out in a blizzard like this?" Jondalar said, his tone more angry.

Ayla tried to answer, but everyone was talking at once. She looked at all the faces watching her, and flushed. "I am sorry. I did not mean to make worry. I live alone long time, have no people to worry. I go out and come in when I want. I am not used to people, to have someone worry," she said, looking at Jondalar, then at the others. Mamut saw Ayla's brow knit in a frown as the tall blond man turned away.

Jondalar felt himself flush as he walked away from the people who had been worried about Ayla. She was right, she had lived alone and taken care of herself just fine. What right did he have to question her actions, or take her to task for not telling anyone she was going out? But he had been fearful from the moment he discovered she was missing and had probably gone outside into the blizzard. He had seen bad weather – winters where he grew up were exceptionally cold and bleak – but he had never seen weather so severe. This storm had raged without let-up for half the season, it seemed.

No one had been more fearful for her safety than Jondalar, but he didn't want to show his deep concern. He'd been having difficulty talking to her since the night of her adoption. At first, he was so hurt that she had chosen someone else, he had withdrawn, and was ambivalent about his own feelings. He was wildly jealous, yet he doubted his love for her because he had been ashamed that he brought her.

Ayla had not shared Ranec's furs again, but every night Jondalar was afraid she might. It made him tense and nervous, and he found himself staying away from the Mammoth Hearth until after she was in bed. When he did finally join her on their sleeping platform, he turned his back and resisted touching her, afraid he might lose control, afraid he might break down and beg her to love him.

But Ayla didn't know why he was avoiding her. When she tried to talk to him, he answered in monosyllables, or pretended to be asleep; when she put an arm around him, he was stiff and unresponsive. It seemed to her that he didn't like her any more, especially after he brought separate furs to sleep in, so he wouldn't feel the searing touch of her body next to his. Even during the day, he stayed away from her. Wymez, Danug, and he had set up a flint-working area in the cooking hearth and Jondalar spent most of his waking hours there – he couldn't stand working with Wymez at the Fox Hearth, across the passageway from the bed Ayla had shared with Ranec.

After a while, when her friendly advances had been rebuffed too often, she became confused and hesitant and drew back from him. Only then did he finally begin to realise that the growing distance between them was his own doing, but he didn't know how to resolve it. As experienced and knowledgeable as he was about women, he had no experience with being in love. He found himself reluctant to tell her how he felt about her. He remembered young women following him around, declaring their strong feelings for him, when he didn't feel strongly about them. It had made him uncomfortable, made him want to get away. He didn't want Ayla to feel that way about him, so he held back.

Ranec knew they were not sharing Pleasures. He was excruciatingly conscious of Ayla every moment, though he tried not to make it obvious. He knew when she went to bed and when she woke, what she ate and with whom she spoke, and he spent as much time as he could at the Hearth of the Mammoth. Among those who gathered there, Ranec's wit, sometimes directed at one member or another of the Lion Camp, was often the cause of raucous laughter. He was scrupulously careful, however, never to denigrate Jondalar, whether Ayla was nearby or not. The visitor was aware of Ranec's way with words, but such cleverness had never been Jondalar's strong point. Ranec's compact muscularity and insouciant self-confidence had the effect of making the tall, dramatically handsome man feel like a big oaf.

As the winter progressed, Jondalar and Ayla's unresolved misunderstanding kept getting worse. Jondalar was becoming afraid that he would lose her entirely to the dark, exotic, and engaging man. He kept trying to convince himself that he should be fair, and let her make the choice, that he didn't have any right to make demands on her. But he stayed away because he didn't want to present her with a choice which would give her the opportunity to reject him.

The Mamutoi did not seem disturbed by the harsh weather. They had plenty of food stored, and busied themselves with their usual winter diversions, snug and secure inside their semi-subterranean longhouse. The older members of the Camp tended to gather around the cooking hearth, sipping hot tea, telling stories, reminiscing, gossiping, and playing games of chance with pieces of carved ivory or bone, when they were not busy on some project. The younger people congregated around the Mammoth Hearth, laughing and joking, singing songs and practising musical instruments, though there was a great deal of intermixing among everyone, and the children were welcome everywhere. This was the time of leisure; the time to make and mend tools and weapons, utensils and jewellery; the time to weave baskets and mats, to carve ivory, bone and antler, to make thongs, ropes, cords, and nets, and the time to make and decorate clothing.

Ayla was interested in how the Mamutoi processed their leather and, especially, how they coloured it. She was also intrigued with the coloured embroidery, quill and beadwork. Decorated and sewn clothing was new and unusual to her.

"You said you would show me how to make leather red after I make skin ready. I think bison skin I am working on is ready," Ayla said.

"All right, I'll show you," Deegie said. "Let's see how it looks."

Ayla went to the storage platform near the head of her bed and unfolded a complete hide, and spread it out. It was incredibly soft to the touch, pliable, and nearly white. Deegie examined it critically. She had watched Ayla's process without comment, but with great interest.

First Ayla had cut off the heavy mane with a sharp knife close to the skin, then she beamed it; draped it over a large smooth mammoth leg bone and scraped it using the slightly dulled edge of a flint flake. She scraped the inside to remove clinging bits of fat and blood vessels, and the outside, against the lay of the hair, taking off the outer layer of skin, which included the grain of the leather, as well. Deegie would have rolled it up and left it near the fire for a few days, allowing it to begin to decay, to loosen the hair. When she was ready, the hair would come out leaving behind the outer layer of skin, which would become the grain of the leather. To make the softer buckskin, as Ayla had done, she would have tied it to a frame to scrape off the hair and the grain.

Ayla's next step incorporated a suggestion from Deegie. After soaking and washing, Ayla had planned to rub fat into the hide to soften it, as she was accustomed to doing. But Deegie showed Ayla how to make a thin gruel of the putrefying brains of the animal to soak the hide in instead. Ayla was both surprised and pleased at the results. She could feel the change in the hide, the softening and elasticity which the brain tissue imparted, even while she was rubbing it in. But it was after thoroughly wringing out the hide that the work began. It had to be pulled and stretched constantly while it was drying, and the quality of the finished leather depended upon how well the hide was worked at this stage.

"You do have a good hand for leather, Ayla. Bison hide is heavy, and this is so soft. It feels wonderful. Have you decided what you want to make out of it?"

"No." Ayla shook her head. "But I want to make leather red. What do you think? Footwear?"

"It's heavy enough for it, but soft enough for a tunic. Let's go ahead and colour it. You can think about what to make with it later," Deegie said, and as they walked towards the last hearth together, she asked,

"What would you do with that hide now? If you were not going to colour it?"

"I would put over very smoky fire, so leather will not get stiff again, if it gets wet, from rain, or even from swimming," Ayla said.

Deegie nodded. "That's what I would do, too. But what we are going to do to the hide will make the rain slide off."

They passed by Crozie when they walked through the Crane Hearth, which reminded Ayla of something she had been meaning to ask about. "Deegie, do you know how to make leather white, too? Like tunic Crozie wear? I like red, but after that, I would like to learn white. I think I know someone who would like white."

"White is hard to do, hard to get leather really snowy white. I think Crozie could show you better than I could. You would need chalk . . . Wymez might have some. Flint is found in chalk, and usually the pieces he gets from the mine up north have a covering of chalk on the outside," Deegie said.

The young women walked back to the Mammoth Hearth with some small mortars and pestles, and several lumps of red ochre colouring material in various shades. Deegie set some fat to melting over the fire, then arrayed the coloured bits of material around Ayla. There were bits of charcoal for black, manganese for a blue-black, and a bright sulphurous yellow, in addition to ochres of many colours: browns, reds, maroons, yellows. The mortars were the natural bowl shapes of certain bones, such as the frontal bone of a deer, or pecked out of granite or basalt, just as the stone lamps were. Pestles were shaped out of hard ivory or bone, except one, which was an elongated natural stone.

"What shade of red do you want, Ayla? Deep red, blood red, earth red, yellow red; that's sort of a sun colour."

Ayla didn't know she would have so many choices. "I don't know . . . red red," she replied.

Deegie studied the colours. "I think if we take this one," she said, picking up a piece that was a rather bright earth red, "and add a little yellow to it, to bring out the red more, it might be a colour you would like."

She put the small lump of red ochre in the stone mortar and showed Ayla how to grind it very fine, then had her grind up the yellow colour in a separate bowl. In a third bowl, Deegie mixed the two colours until she was satisfied with the shade. Then she added the hot fat, which changed the colour, and brightened it to a shade that made Ayla smile.

"Yes. That is red. That is nice red," she said.

Next Deegie picked up a long deer rib, which had been split lengthwise so that the porous inner bone was exposed at the convex end. Using the rib burnisher with the spongy side down, she picked up a dab of the cooled red fat, and rubbed the mixture into the prepared bison skin, pressing hard as she held the hide in her hand. As she worked the mineral colouring into the pores of the material, the leather acquired a smooth sheen. On leather with grain, the burnishing tool and colouring agents would have given it a hard shiny finish.

After watching a while, Ayla picked up another rib bone and copied Deegie's technique. Deegie watched her, offered a few corrections. When a corner of the hide was finished, she stopped Ayla for a moment.

"Look," she said, sprinkling a few drops of water on the hide as she held up the corner. "It runs off, see?" The water beaded up and ran down, leaving no mark on the impervious finish.

"Have you decided what you are going to do with your red piece of leather, yet?" Nezzie asked.

"No," Ayla said. She had unfolded the full bison hide to show Rydag and to admire it herself again. It was hers, because she had dressed and treated the hide, and she had never owned so much of anything that was red, and the leather had turned out to be remarkably red. "Red was sacred to Clan. I would give to Creb . . . if I could."

"It is the brightest red I think I have ever seen. You would certainly see someone coming for a long way wearing that."

"It is soft, too," Rydag signed. He often came to the Mammoth Hearth to visit with her, and she welcomed him.

"Deegie showed me how to make soft with brain, first," Ayla said, smiling at her friend. "I use fat before. Hard to do, and stains, sometimes. Better using brain of bison." She paused with a thoughtful expression, then asked, "Will work for every animal, Deegie?" Then, when Deegie nodded, "How much brain should use? How much for reindeer? How much for rabbit?"

"Mut, the Great Mother, in Her infinite wisdom," Ranec replied instead, with the hint of a grin, "always gives just enough brains to each animal to preserve its hide."

Rydag's soft guttural chuckle puzzled Ayla for a moment, then she smiled. "Some have enough brains, do not get caught?"

Ranec laughed, and Ayla joined him, pleased with herself for understanding the joke hidden in the meaning. She was becoming much more comfortable with the language.

Jondalar, just walking into the Mammoth Hearth and seeing Ayla and Ranec laughing together, felt his stomach churn into a knot. Mamut saw him close his eyes as though in pain. He glanced at Nezzie and shook his head.

Danug, who had been following behind the visiting flint worker, watched him stop, clutch a post and drop his head. The feelings of Jondalar and Ranec for Ayla, and the problem that was developing because of them was apparent to all, though most people did not acknowledge it. They didn't want to interfere, hoping to give the three of them room to work it out for themselves. Danug wished he could do something to help, but he was at a loss. Ranec was a brother, since Nezzie had adopted him, but he liked Jondalar and felt empathy for his anguish. He, too, had strong, if undefined, feelings for the beautiful new member of the Lion Camp. Beyond the inexplicable flushes and physical sensations when he was near her, he felt an affinity with her. She seemed to be as confused about how to handle the situation as he often felt about the new changes and complications in his life.

Jondalar took a deep breath and straightened up, then continued into the area. Ayla's eyes followed him as he walked over to Mamut and handed him something. She watched them exchange a few words, then Jondalar left, quickly, without saying a word to her. She had lost the thread of the conversation going on around her, and when Jondalar left, she hurried to Mamut, not hearing the question Ranec had asked her, or seeing the fleeting look of disappointment on his face. He made a joke, which she also did not hear, to cover his dismay. But Nezzie, who was sensitive to the subtle nuances of his deeper feelings, noticed the hurt in his eyes, and then saw him set his jaw and square his shoulders with resolution.

She wanted to advise him, to give him the benefit of her experience and the wisdom of her years, but she held her tongue. They must work out their own destinies, she thought.

Since the Mamutoi lived in close quarters for extended periods of time, they had to learn to tolerate each other. There was no real privacy in the earthlodge, except the privacy of each person's thoughts, and they were very careful not to intrude into another's private thoughts. They shied away from asking personal questions, or pressing uninvited offers of assistance and advice, or intervening in private squabbles unless they were asked, or the squabbles got out of hand and became a problem for everyone. Instead, if they saw a troubling situation developing, they quietly made themselves available and waited with patience and forbearance until a friend was wanted to discuss worries, fears, and frustrations. They were not judgmental or highly critical, and they imposed few restrictions on personal behaviour if it did not hurt or seriously disturb others. A solution to a problem was one that worked, and satisfied everyone involved. They were gentle with each other's souls.

"Mamut . . ." Ayla began, then realised she didn't know exactly what she wanted to say. "Ah . . . I think now is good time to make medicine for arthritis."

"I would not object," the old man said, smiling. "I have not had as comfortable a winter in many years. If for no other reason, I am glad you are here, Ayla. Let me put away this knife I won from Jondalar, and I will put myself in your hands."

"You win knife from Jondalar?"

"Crozie and I were wagering with the knucklebones. He was watching and looked interested, so I invited him to play. He said he would like to, but he had nothing to wager. I told him as long as he had his skill, he always had something, and said I'd bet against a special knife that I wanted to be made in a certain way. He lost. He should know better than to wager against One Who Serves." Mamut chuckled. "Here's the knife."

Ayla nodded. His answer satisfied her curiosity, but she wished someone could tell her why Jondalar didn't want to talk to her. The group of people who had been admiring Ayla's red leather hide broke up and left the Mammoth Hearth, except for Rydag, who joined Ayla and Mamut. There was something comforting about watching her treat the old shaman. He settled himself on a corner of the bed platform.

"I will make hot poultice for you first," she said, and began to mix ingredients in a wooden bowl.

Mamut and Rydag watched her measuring, mixing, heating water. "What do you use in the poultice?" Mamut asked.

"I do not know your words for plants."

"Describe them to me. Maybe I can tell you. I know a few plants and some remedies; I've had to learn some."

"One plant, grows higher than knee," Ayla explained, thinking about the plant carefully. "Has big leaves, not bright green, like dust on them. Leaves grow together with stem first, then get big, then come to point at end. Under leaf, soft, like fur. Leaves good for many things, and roots, too, especially broken bones."

"Comfrey! That must be comfrey. What else is in the poultice?" This is interesting, he thought.

"Other plant, smaller, does not reach knee. Leaves like small spear point Wymez makes, dark shiny green, stay green in winter. Stem comes up from leaves, has little flowers, light colour, small red spots inside. Good for swellings, rash, too," Ayla said.

Mamut was shaking his head. "Leaves stay green in winter, spotted flowers. I don't think I know that one. Why not just call it spotted wintergreen."

Ayla nodded. "Do you want to know other plants?" she asked.

"Yes, go ahead and describe another."

"Big plant, bigger than Talut, almost tree. Grows on low ground, near rivers. Dark purple berries stay on plant even in winter. Young leaves good to eat, big old ones too strong, can make sick. Dried root in poultice is good for swelling, red swelling, too, and for pain. I put dried berries in tea I make for your arthritis. Do you know name?"

"No, I don't think so, but as long as you know the plant, I'm satisfied," Mamut said. "Your remedies for my arthritis have helped, you are good with medicine for elders."

"Creb was old. He was lame and had pain from arthritis. I learn from Iza how to help. Then I help others in Clan." Ayla paused and looked up from her mixing. "I think Crozie suffer pains of age, too. I want to help. You think she object, Mamut?"

"She doesn't like to admit to the failings of age. She was a proud beauty in her younger years, but I think you are right. You could ask her, especially if you can think of a way that wouldn't bruise her pride. That's all she has left now."

Ayla nodded. When the preparation was ready, Mamut removed his clothing. "When you are resting, with poultice," she said, "I have root powder of other plant I want to put on hot coals for you to smell. Will make you sweat, and is good for pain. Then, before you sleep tonight, I have new wash for joints. Apple juice and hot root . . . ."

"You mean horseradish? The root Nezzie uses, with food."

"I think, yes, with apple juice and Talut's bouza. Will make skin warm, and inside skin warm, too."

Mamut laughed. "How did you ever get Talut to let you put his bouza outside on the skin, and not inside?"

Ayla smiled. "He likes 'magic morning-after medicine.' I say I will always make for him," she said while she applied a thick, gummy, hot healing plaster to the old man's aching joints. He lay back comfortably, and closed his eyes.

"This arm look good," Ayla commented, working on the arm that had been broken. "I think was bad break."

"It was a bad break," Mamut said, opening his eyes again. He glanced at Rydag, who was quietly taking everything in. Mamut had not spoken of his experience to anyone but Ayla. He paused, then nodded sharply with decision. "It's time you knew, Rydag. When I was a young man on a Journey, I fell down a cliff and broke my arm. I was dazed, and finally wandered into a Camp of flatheads, people of the Clan. I lived with them for a while."

"That is why you quick to learn signs!" Rydag smiled. "I thought you very smart."

"I am very smart, young man," Mamut said, grinning back, "but I also remembered some of them, once Ayla reminded me."

Rydag's smile widened. Except for Nezzie, and the rest of his Lion Hearth family, he loved these two people more than anyone in the world, and he had never been so happy since Ayla came. For the first time in his life, he could talk, he could make people understand him, he could even make someone smile. He watched Ayla working on Mamut, and even he could recognise her thoroughness and knowledge. When Mamut looked in his direction, he signalled, "Ayla is good Healer."

"The medicine women of the Clan are very skilled – she learned from them. No one could have done a better job on my arm. The skin was scraped, with dirt ground in, and it was torn open with the broken bone poking through. It looked like a piece of meat. The woman, Uba, cleaned it and set it right, and it did not even swell up with pus and fever. I had full use when it healed, and only in these later years have I felt a little ache now and then. Ayla learned from the granddaughter of the woman who fixed my arm. I was told she was considered the best," Mamut announced, watching Rydag's reaction. The boy looked at both of them quizzically, wondering how they could know the same people.

"Yes. And Iza was best, like her mother and her grandmother," Ayla said, finishing up. She hadn't been paying attention to the silent communication between the boy and the old man. "She knew all her mother knew, had mother's memories, and grandmother's memories."

Ayla moved some stones from the fireplace closer to Mamut's bed, scooped up a few live coals with two sticks and put them on the stones, then sprinkled powdered honeybloom root on the coals. She went to get covers for Mamut to keep the heat in, but while she was tucking them around him, he got up on one elbow and looked at her thoughtfully.

"The people of the Clan are different in a way that most people don't realise. It's not that they don't talk, or that the way they talk is different. It's that the way they think is a little different. If Uba, the woman who took care of me, was the grandmother of your Iza, and she learned from her mother's and grandmother's memories, how did you learn, Ayla? You don't have Clan memories." Mamut noticed an embarrassed flush, and a quick little gasp of surprise before Ayla looked down. "Or do you?"

Ayla looked up at him again, then down. "No. I do not have Clan memories," she said.

"But . . . ?"

Ayla looked back at him. "What do you mean, 'but'?" she said. Her expression was wary, almost frightened. She looked down again.

"You do not have Clan memories, but . . . you have something, don't you? Something of the Clan?"

Ayla kept her head bowed. How could he know? She had never told anyone, not even Jondalar. She hardly even admitted it to herself, but she had never been quite the same afterwards. There were those times, that came on her . . .

"Does it have something to do with your skill as a medicine woman?" Mamut asked.

She looked up and shook her head. "No," she said, her eyes pleading for him to believe her. "Iza teach me, I was very young, I think I was not yet age of Rugie when she begin. Iza knew I did not have memories, but she make me remember, make me tell her again and again until I do not forget. She is very patient. Some people tell her, is foolish to teach me, I cannot remember . . . I am too stupid. She tell them no, I am just different. I do not want to be different. I make myself remember. I say to myself, over and over, even when Iza is not teaching me. I learn to remember, my way. Then I make myself learn fast so they won't think I am so stupid."

Rydag's eyes were opened big and round. More than anyone, he understood exactly how she had felt, but he didn't know anyone had ever felt the same way, especially someone like Ayla.

Mamut looked at her with amazement. "So you memorised Iza's Clan 'memories'. That's quite an accomplishment. They go back generation after generation, don't they?"

Rydag was listening closely now, sensing something very important to him.

"Yes," Ayla said, "but I do not learn all her memories. Iza could not teach me all she knew. She told me she did not even know how much she knew, but she teach me how to learn. How to test, how to try carefully. Then, when I am older, she said I was her daughter, medicine woman of her line. I ask, how can I claim her line? I am not her true daughter. I am not even Clan, I do not have memories. Then she tell me I have something else, as good as memories, maybe better. Iza thought I was born to line of medicine women of the Others, best line, like her line was best. That is why I am medicine woman of her line. She said someday I would be best."

"Do you know what she meant? Do you know what you have?" Mamut asked.

"Yes, I think so. When someone not well, I see what is wrong. I see look of eyes, colour of face, smell of breath. I think about it, sometimes know just looking, other times, know what to ask. Then make medicine to help. Not always same medicine. Sometimes new medicine, like bouza in arthritis wash."

"Your Iza may have been right. The best Healers have that gift," the Mamut said, then a thought occurred to him, and he continued, "I have noticed one difference between you and the Healers I know, Ayla. You

314

use plant remedies and other treatments to heal, Mamutoi Healers call upon the assistance of the spirits as well."

"I do not know world of spirits. In Clan only Mog-urs know. When Iza want help of spirits, she ask Creb."

The Mamut stared hard into the eyes of the young woman. "Ayla, would you like to have the help of the spirit world?"

"Yes, but I have no Mog-ur to ask."

"You don't have to ask anyone. You can be your own Mog-ur."

"Me? A Mog-ur? But I am a woman. A woman of the Clan cannot be a Mog-ur," Ayla said, stunned at the suggestion.

"But you are not a woman of the Clan. You are Ayla of the Mamutoi. You are a daughter of the Mammoth Hearth. The best Mamutoi Healers know the ways of the spirits. You are a good Healer, Ayla, but how can you be the best if you cannot ask the help of the spirit world?"

Ayla felt a great knot of anxiety tighten in her stomach. She was a medicine woman, a good medicine woman, and Iza said someday she would be the best. Now Mamut said she could not be the best without the help of the spirits, and he must be right. Iza always asked Creb to help, didn't she?

"But I do not know world of spirits, Mamut," Ayla said, feeling desperate, almost panicky.

Mamut leaned close to her, sensing the moment was right, and drawing from some inner source a power to compel. "Yes, you do," he said, his tone commanding, "don't you, Ayla?"

Her eyes flew open in fear. "I do not want to know spirit world!" she cried.

"You only fear that world because you don't understand it. I can help you to understand it. I can help you to use it. You were born to the Hearth of the Mammoth, born to the mysteries of the Mother, no matter where you were born or where you go. You cannot help yourself, you are drawn to it, and it seeks you. You cannot escape it, but with training and understanding, you can control it. You can make the mysteries work for you. Ayla, you cannot fight your destiny, and it is your destiny to Serve the Mother."

"I am medicine woman! That is my destiny."

"Yes, that is your destiny, to be a medicine woman, but that is Serving the Mother, and someday, you may be called to serve in another way. You need to be prepared. Ayla, you want to be the best medicine woman, don't you? Even you know that some sickness cannot be healed by medicines and treatments alone. How do you cure someone who no longer wants to live? What medicine gives someone the will to recover from a serious accident? When someone dies, what treatment do you give the ones left behind?"

Ayla bowed her head. If someone had known what to do for her when Iza died, she might not have lost her milk and had to give her son to the other women with babies to nurse. Would she know what to do if that happened to someone she was taking care of? Would knowledge of the spirit world help her to know what to do?

Rydag was watching the tense scene, knowing he had been forgotten for the moment. He was afraid to move, afraid it would distract them from something very important, though he wasn't sure what it was.

"Ayla, what is it you fear? What happened to make you turn away? Tell me about it," Mamut said, his voice persuasively warm.

Ayla got up suddenly. She picked up the warm furs and tucked them around the old shaman. "Must cover, keep warm for poultice to work," she said, obviously distracted and upset. Mamut lay back, allowed her to complete her treatment of him without objection, realising she needed time. She began to pace, nervous and agitated, her eyes unfocused, staring into space or at some internal scene. She spun around and faced him.

"I did not mean to!" she said.

"What didn't you mean to do?" Mamut said.

"Go into cave . . . see Mog-urs."

"When did you go into the cave, Ayla?" Mamut knew the restrictions against women participating in Clan rituals. She must have done something she wasn't supposed to, broken some taboo, he thought.

"At Clan Gathering."

"You went to a Clan Gathering? They hold a Gathering once every seven years, isn't that right?"

Ayla nodded.

"How long ago was this Gathering?"

She had to stop, think about it, and the concentration cleared her mind a bit. "Durc was just born then, in spring. Next summer, will be seven years! Next summer, is Clan Gathering. Clan will go to Gathering, bring Ura back. Ura and Durc will mate. My son will be man soon!"

"Is that true, Ayla? He will be only seven years when he mates? Your son will be a man so young?" Mamut asked.

"No, not so young. Maybe three, four more years. He is . . . like Druwez. Not yet man. But mother of Ura ask me for Durc, for Ura. She is child of mixed spirits, too. Ura will live with Brun and Ebra. When Durc and Ura old enough, will mate."

Rydag stared at Ayla in disbelief. He didn't entirely understand all the implications, but one thing seemed certain. She had a son, mixed like him, who lived with the Clan!

"What happened at the Clan Gathering seven years ago, Ayla?" Mamut asked, not wanting to let it drop when he had seemed so close to getting an agreement from Ayla to begin training, although she had brought up some intriguing points he would like to ask her about. He was convinced that it was not only important, it was essential, for her own sake.

Ayla closed her eyes with a pained expression. "Iza is too sick to go. She tell Brun I am medicine woman, Brun make ceremony. She tell me how to chew root to make drink for Mog-urs. Tell only, cannot show me. Is too . . . sacred to make for practice. Mog-urs at Clan Gathering not want me, I am not Clan. But no one else knows, only Iza's line. Finally say yes. Iza tell me not swallow juice when I chew, spit into bowl, but I cannot. I swallow some. Later, I am confused, go into cave, follow fires, find Mog-urs. They not see me, but Creb knows."

She became agitated again, paced back and forth. "It is dark, like deep hole and I am falling." She hunched her shoulders, rubbed her arms, as though she was cold. "Then Creb come, like you, Mamut, but more. He . . . he . . . take me with him."

She was silent then, pacing. Finally she stopped and spoke again. "Later, Creb is very angry and unhappy. And I am . . . different. I never say, but sometimes I think I go back there, and I am . . . frightened."

Mamut waited, to see if she was finished. He had some idea what she had gone through. He had been allowed at a Clan ceremony. They used certain plants in unique ways, and he had experienced something unfathomable. It changed him in ways he couldn't explain. He had tried, but he had never been able to duplicate the experience, even after he became Mamut. He was about to say something when Ayla spoke again.

"Sometimes I want to throw root away, but Iza tell me is sacred."

It took a moment for the meaning of Ayla's words to register, but the shock of recognition nearly brought him to his feet.

"Are you saying you have that root with you?" he asked, finding it difficult to control his excitement.

"When I leave, take medicine bag. Root is in medicine bag, in special red pouch."

"But is it still good? You say it's been more than three years since you left. Wouldn't it lose potency in that time?"

"No, is prepared special way. After root is dried, keeps long time. Many years."

"Ayla," the Mamut began, trying to phrase his words just right, "it could be very fortunate that you have it still. You know, the best way to overcome a fear is to face it. Would you be willing to prepare that root again? Just for you and me?"

Ayla shivered at the thought. "I do not know, Mamut. I do not want to. I am frightened."

"I don't mean right away," he said. "Not until you have had some

317

training and are prepared for it. And it should be a special ceremony, with deep meaning and significance. Perhaps the Spring Festival, the beginning of new life." He saw her shake again. "It's up to you, but you do not have to decide now. All I ask is that you allow me to begin training and preparation. When spring comes, if you don't feel ready, you can say no."

"What is training?" Ayla asked.

"First, I would want you to learn certain songs and chants, and how to use the mammoth skull. Then there is the meaning of certain symbols and signs."

Rydag watched her close her eyes and frown. He hoped she would agree. He had just learned more about his mother's people than he ever knew, but he wanted to learn more. If Mamut and Ayla planned a ceremony with Clan rituals, he was sure he would.

When Ayla opened them, her eyes looked troubled, but she swallowed hard, and then nodded. "Yes, Mamut. I try to face fear of spirit world, if you will help me."

As Mamut lay back down, he didn't notice Ayla clutch the small decorated bag she wore around her neck.

21

"Hu! Hu! Hu! That's three!" Crozie cried out, chuckling shrewdly as she counted the discs that had been caught with the marked side up in the shallow woven bowl.

"Your turn again," Nezzie said. They were sitting on the floor beside the circular pit of dry loess soil, which Talut had used to map out a hunting plan. "You still have seven to go. I'll bet two more." She made two more lines on the smoothed surface of the drawing pit.

Crozie picked up the wicker bowl and shook the seven small ivory discs together. The discs, which bellied out slightly so that they rocked when they were on a flat surface, were plain on one side; the other side was carved with lines and coloured. Keeping the wide shallow basket near the floor, Crozie flipped the discs into the air. Moving it smartly across the red-bordered mat that outlined the boundaries of the playing area, she caught the discs in the basket. This time four of the discs had their marked side up and only three were plain.

"Look at that! Four! Only three to go. I'll wager five more."

Ayla, sitting on a mat nearby, sipped tea from her wooden cup and watched the old woman shake the discs together in the bowl again. Crozie threw them up and caught them once more. This time five discs had the side with marks carved into them showing.

"I win! Do you want to try again, Nezzie?"

"Well, maybe one more game," Nezzie said, reaching for the wicker bowl and shaking it. She tossed the discs in the air, and caught them in the flat basket.

"There's the black eye!" Crozie cried, pointing to a disc that had turned up a side which was coloured black. "You lose! That makes twelve you owe me. Do you want to play another game?"

"No, you're too lucky today," Nezzie said, getting up.

"How about you, Ayla?" Crozie said. "Do you want to play a game?"

"I am not good at that game," Ayla said. "I do not catch all the pieces sometimes."

She had watched the gaming many times as the bitter cold of the long season deepened, but had played little, and then only for practice. She knew Crozie was a serious player who did not play for practice, and had little patience with inept or indecisive players.

"Well, how about Knucklebones? You don't need any skill to play that."

"I would play, but I do not know what to bet," Ayla said.

"Nezzie and I play for marks and settle it out later."

"Now or later, I do not know what to bet."

"Certainly you have something you can wager," Crozie said, somewhat impatient to get on with the game. "Something of value."

"And you wager something of same value?"

The old woman nodded brusquely. "Of course."

Ayla frowned with concentration. "Maybe . . . furs, or leather, or something to make. Wait! I think I know something. Jondalar played with Mamut and bet skill. He made special knife when he lost. Is skill good to bet, Crozie?"

"Why not?" she said. "I'll mark it, here," Crozie said, smoothing the dirt with the flat side of the drawing knife. The woman picked up two objects from the ground beside her and held them out, one in each hand. "We'll count three marks to a game. If you guess right, you get a mark. If you guess wrong, I get a mark. The first one to get three, wins the game."

Ayla looked at the two metacarpal bones of a musk-ox which she held, one painted with red and black lines, the other plain. "I should pick the plain one, that is right?" she asked.

"That is right," Crozie said, a crafty gleam in her eye. "Are you ready?" She rubbed both palms together with the knucklebones inside, but she looked over at Jondalar sitting with Danug in the flint-working area. "Is he really as good as they say?" she said, cocking her head in his direction.

Ayla glanced towards the man, blond head bent close to the red-haired boy's. When she looked back around, Crozie had both hands behind her back.

"Yes. Jondalar is good," she said.

Had Crozie purposely tried to direct her attention elsewhere, to distract her? she wondered. She looked at the woman carefully, noticing the slight tilt of her shoulders, the way she held her head, the expression on her face.

Crozie brought her hands in front of her again and held them out, each closed into a fist around a bone. Ayla studied the wrinkled face, which had become blank and unexpressive, and the white-knuckled arthritic old hands. Was one hand pulled in just a trifle closer to her chest? Ayla picked the other.

"You lose!" Crozie gloated, as she opened the hand to show the bone marked with red and black. She drew a short line in the drawing pit. "Are you ready to try again?"

"Yes," Ayla said.

This time Crozie began humming to herself as she rubbed the bones together between her palms. She closed her eyes, then looked up at the ceiling and stared, as though she saw something interesting near the smoke hole. Ayla was tempted to look up to see what was so fascinating, and started to follow Crozie's gaze. Then remembering the cunning trick that had been used to divert her attention before, she quickly looked back, in time to see the crafty old woman glance between her palms as she snatched her hands behind her back. A knowing smile of grudging respect flitted across the old face. The movement of her shoulders and arm muscles gave the impression of movement between the hidden hands. Did Crozie think Ayla had glimpsed one of the bones, and was she exchanging the pieces? Or did Crozie just want her to think so?

There was more to this game than guessing, Ayla thought, and it was more interesting to play than to watch. Crozie showed her bony-knuckled fists again. Ayla looked at her carefully, not making it obvious. It wasn't polite to stare, for one thing, and on a more subtle level, she didn't want Crozie to know what she was looking for. It was hard to tell, the woman was an old hand at the game, but it did seem that the other shoulder was a shade higher, and wasn't the other hand pulled in slightly this time? Ayla chose the hand she thought Crozie wanted her to pick, the wrong one.

"Ha! You lost again!" Crozie said, elated, then quickly added, "Are you ready?"

Before Ayla could nod in agreement, Crozie had her hands behind her back, and out for her to guess, but she was leaning forward this time. Ayla resisted, smiling. The old woman was always changing something, trying to keep from giving any consistent signal. Ayla chose the hand she thought was right, and was rewarded with a mark in the drawing pit. The next time, Crozie changed her position again, lowering her hands, and Ayla guessed wrong.

"That's three! I win. But you can't really test your luck with only one game. Do you want to play another?" Crozie said.

"Yes. Would like to play again," Ayla said.

Crozie smiled, but when Ayla guessed correctly the next two times, her expression was much less agreeable. She frowned as she rubbed the musk-ox knucklebones together a third time.

"Look over there! What's that?" Crozie said, pointing with her chin, in a blatant attempt to distract the young woman.

Ayla looked, and when she looked back, the old woman was smiling

321

again. The young woman took her time selecting the hand which held the winning bone, though she had decided quickly. She didn't want Crozie to feel too upset, but she had learned to interpret the unconscious body signals the woman made when playing the game, and she knew in which hand the plain bone was as clearly as if Crozie had told her.

It would not have pleased Crozie to know she was giving herself away so easily, but Ayla had an unusual advantage. She was so accustomed to observing and interpreting subtle details of posture and expression, it was almost instinctive. They were an essential part of the language of the Clan that communicated nuances and shades of meaning. She had noticed that body movements and postures also expressed meaning among these people who communicated primarily with verbal sounds, but that it was not purposeful.

Ayla had been so busy trying to learn the spoken language of her new people, she hadn't made any real effort to understand their unconscious unspoken language. Now that she was comfortably, if not precisely, fluent, she could expand her communication to include language skills that were not normally considered a part of speaking. The game she played with Crozie made her realise how much she could learn about her own kind of people by applying the knowledge and insight she had learned from the Clan. And if the Clan could not lie because body language was impossible to hide, the ones she had known as the Others could keep secrets from her even less. They didn't even know they were "talking". She wasn't fully able to interpret the body signals of the Others, yet . . . but she was learning.

Ayla chose the hand that held the plain musk-ox knucklebone, and with a jab of irritation, Crozie marked a third line for Ayla. "The luck is yours, now," she said. "Since I won a game, and you won a game, we might as well call it even and forget the bets."

"No," Ayla said. "We bet skill. You win my skill. My skill is medicine. I will give you. I want your skill."

"What skill?" Crozie said. "My skill at gaming? That's what I do best these days, and you already beat me. What do you want me for?"

"No, not gaming. I want to make white leather," Ayla said.

Crozie gaped in surprise. "White leather?"

"White leather, like tunic you wear at adoption."

"I haven't made white leather in years," Crozie said.

"But you can make?" Ayla asked.

"Yes." Crozie's eyes softened with a distant look. "I learned as a girl, from my mother. At one time it was sacred to the Hearth of the Crane, or so the legends say. No one else could wear it . . ." The old woman's

322

eyes hardened. "But that was before the Crane Hearth fell into such low esteem that even Bride Price is a pittance." She looked hard at the young woman. "What is white leather to you?"

"It is beautiful," Ayla said, which brought an involuntary softening to Crozie's eyes again. "And white is sacred to someone," she finished, looking down at her hands. "I want to make special tunic the way someone likes. Special white tunic."

Ayla didn't notice Crozie glance towards Jondalar, who happened at that moment to be staring at them. He looked aside quickly, seemingly embarrassed. The old woman shook her head at the young one, whose head was still bowed.

"And what do I get for it?" Crozie said.

"You will teach me?" Ayla said, looking up and smiling. She noticed a gleam of avarice in the old eyes, but something else, too. Something more distant, and softer. "I will make medicine for arthritis," she said, "like Mamut."

"Who says I need it?" Crozie snapped. "I'm not nearly as old as he is."

"No, you are not so old, Crozie, but you have pain. You do not say you have pain, you make other complaint, but I know, because I am medicine woman. Medicine cannot cure aching bones and joints, nothing can make it go away, but can make you feel better. Hot poultice will make easier to move and bend, and I will make medicine for pain, some for morning, some for other times," Ayla said. Then sensing the woman needed some way to save face, she added, "I need to make medicine for you, to pay my bet. It is my skill."

"Well, I guess I should let you pay your bet," Crozie said, "but I want one more thing."

"What? I will do, if I can."

"I want more of that soft white tallow that makes dry old skin feel smooth . . . and young," she said, quietly. Then she straightened up and snapped, "My skin always did get chapped in winter."

Ayla smiled. "I will do. Now, you tell me what is best hide for white leather, and I will ask Nezzie what is in cold rooms."

"Deerskin. Reindeer is good, though it is best to use it as a fur, for warmth. Any deer will do, red deer, elk, megaceros. Before you get the hide, though, you will need something else."

"What is that?"

"You will need to save your water."

"My water?"

"The water you pass. Not only yours, anyone's, though your own is best. Start collecting it now, even before you thaw out a deerskin. It must be left out where it's warm for a while," Crozie said.

"I usually pass water behind the curtain, in the basket with mammoth dung and ashes in it. It is thrown out."

"Don't go in the basket. Save it, in a mammoth skull basin, or a tight basket. Something that won't leak."

"Why is that water needed?"

Crozie paused and appraised the young woman before she answered. "I'm not getting any younger," she said, finally, "and I have no one, except Fralie . . . any more. Usually a woman passes her skills on to her children and grandchildren but Fralie has no time, and not much interest in working leather – she likes stitching and beadwork – and she has no daughters. Her sons . . . well, they're young. Who knows? But my mother gave me the knowledge, and I should pass it on . . . to someone. It's hard work, treating hides, but I've seen your leatherwork. Even the furs and skins you brought show skill, care, and that is necessary to make white leather. I haven't even thought of making it for many years, and no one else has shown much interest, but you asked. So I will tell you."

The woman bent forward and clutched Ayla's hand. "The secret of white leather is in the water you pass. That may seem strange to you, but it is true. After it is left in a warm place for a while, it changes. Then, if you soak hides in it, all the bits of fat that might be left come out, and any grease stains. The hair will come out more quickly, it won't rot easily, and it stays soft even without smoking, so it won't be tan or brown. In fact, it whitens the hide, still not true white, but close. Afterwards, when it is washed and wrung out several times, and worked dry, it is ready for the white colour."

If someone had asked her, Crozie could not have explained that urea, which was the major component of urine, would decompose, become ammoniacal, in a warm environment. She only knew that if urine was allowed to go stale, it became something else. Something that would both dissolve grease and act as a bleach, and in the same process, help to preserve the leather from bacterial decay. She didn't have to know why, or call it ammonia, she only had to know that it worked.

"Chalk . . . do we have any chalk?" Crozie asked.

"Wymez does. He said the flint he just brought back came from a chalk cliff, and he still has several stones coated with it," Ayla said.

"Why did you ask Wymez about chalk? How did you know I would agree to show you?" Crozie asked suspiciously.

"I did not. I have been wanting to make a white tunic for a long time. If you did not show me, I would try myself, but I did not know about saving the water, and I would not have thought of it. I am happy you will show me to do it right," Ayla said.

"Hmmf," was Crozie's only comment, convinced, but not wanting

324

to admit it. "Be sure you make that soft white tallow." Then she added, "And, make some for the leather, too. I think it would be good to mix with the chalk."

Ayla held the drape aside and looked out. The late-afternoon wind moaned and keened a dreary dirge, a fitting accompaniment to the drab, bleak landscape and the grey, overcast sky. She longed for some relief from the confining bitter cold, but the oppressive season seemed as though it would never come to an end. Whinney snorted and she turned around to see Mamut coming into the horse hearth. She smiled at him.

Ayla had felt a deep respect for the old shaman from the beginning, but since he had begun training her, her respect had grown into love. Partly, she perceived a strong similarity between the tall, thin, incredibly old shaman, and the short, crippled, one-eyed magician of the Clan, not in appearance but in nature. It was almost as though she had found Creb again, or at least his counterpart. Both exhibited a deep reverence and understanding for the world of the spirits, though the spirits they revered had different names; both could command awesome powers, though each was physically frail; and both were wise in the ways of people. But perhaps the strongest reason for her love was that, like Creb, Mamut had welcomed her, helped her to understand, and taken her in as a daughter of his hearth.

"I was looking for you, Ayla. I thought you might be here, with your horses," Mamut said.

"I was looking outside, wishing it was spring," Ayla said.

"This is the time most people start wishing for a change, for something new to do or see. They are getting bored, sleeping more. I think that's why we have more feasts and celebrations in the last part of winter. The Laughing Contest will be coming soon. Most people enjoy that one."

"What is the Laughing Contest?"

"Just what it sounds like. Everyone tries to make everyone else laugh. Some people wear funny clothes, or wear their clothes backwards, make funny faces at each other, act funny, make jokes about each other, play tricks on each other. And if anyone gets angry about it, they get laughed at all the more. Almost everyone looks forward to it, but no celebration is as eagerly anticipated as the Spring Festival. In fact, that's why I was looking for you," Mamut said. "There are still many things you should learn before then."

"Why is the Spring Festival so special?" Ayla wasn't sure she was anticipating it.

"For many reasons, I suppose. It is both our most solemn and our happiest celebration. It marks the end of the long deep cold, and the beginning of warmth. It is said that if you watch the cycle of seasons one year, you will understand life. Most people count three seasons. Spring is the season of birth. In the gush of Her birth waters, the spring floods, the Great Earth Mother brings forth new life again. Summer, the warm season, is the time of growth and increase. Winter is the 'little death'. In Spring, life is renewed again, reborn. Three seasons are enough for most purposes, but the Mammoth Hearth counts five. The Mother's sacred number is five."

In spite of her initial reservations, Ayla found herself fascinated by the training Mamut had insisted upon. She was learning so much: new ideas, new thoughts, even new ways of thinking. It was exciting to discover and think about so many new things, to be included instead of excluded. Knowledge of spirits, knowledge of numbers, even knowledge of hunting, had been kept from her when she had lived with the Clan; it was reserved for the men. Only Mog-urs and their acolytes studied them in depth, and no woman could become a Mog-ur. Women were not even admitted to discussions about such concepts as spirits or numbers. Hunting had been taboo for her, too, but they didn't bar women from listening; they had just assumed no woman could learn.

"I would like to go over the songs and chants we have been practising, and I want to begin showing you something special. Symbols. I think you will find them interesting. Some are about medicine."

"Medicine symbols?" Ayla asked. Of course she was interested. They walked into the Mammoth Hearth together.

"Are you going to do anything with the white leather?" Mamut asked, putting mats by the fire near his bed. "Or are you going to save it, like the red?"

"I don't know about the red yet, but I want to make a special tunic with the white. I am learning to sew, but I feel very clumsy. It turned out so perfect, I don't want to spoil the white until I get better. Deegie is showing me, and Fralie, sometimes, when Frebec doesn't make it difficult for her."

Ayla slivered some bone and added it to the flames while Mamut brought out a rather thin oval section of ivory with a large curved surface. The oval outline had been etched into a mammoth tusk with a stone chisel, then repeated until it was a deep groove. A sharp blow accurately placed at one end detached the flake of ivory. Mamut picked out a piece of bone charcoal from the fire as Ayla got a mammoth skull and a hammer-shaped drumstick made of antler and sat down beside him.

"Before we practise with the drum, I want to show you certain symbols that we use to help us memorise things, like songs, stories, proverbs, places, times, names, anything that someone wants to remember," Mamut began. "You have been teaching us hand signals and signs, and I know you've noticed that we use certain gestures, too, though not as many as the Clan. We wave goodbye and beckon to someone if we want him to come, and it is understood. We use other hand symbols, particularly when we are describing something, or telling a story, or when One Who Serves is conducting a ceremony. Here is one that will be easy. It is similar to a Clan symbol."

Mamut made a circular motion with his hand, palm facing outwards. "That means 'all', everyone, everything," he explained, then picked up the charcoal. "Now, I can make the same motion with this piece of charcoal on the ivory, see?" he said, drawing a circle. "Now that symbol means 'all' and any time you see it, even if it is drawn by another Mamut, you will know it means 'all'."

The old shaman enjoyed teaching Ayla. She was bright and quick to learn, but even more, her pleasure at learning was so transparent. Her face showed her feelings as he explained, her curiosity and interest, and her sheer wonder when she comprehended.

"I never would have thought of that! Can anyone learn this knowledge?" she asked.

"Some knowledge is sacred, and only those pledged to the Mammoth Hearth may be told, but most things can be learned by anyone who shows an interest. It often turns out that those who show great interest eventually dedicate themselves to the Mammoth Hearth. The sacred knowledge is often hidden behind a second meaning, or even a third meaning. Most people know this – " he drew another circle on the ivory – "means 'all', but it has another meaning. There are many symbols for the Great Mother, this is one of them. It means Mut, the Creator of All Life. Many other lines and shapes have meaning," he continued. "This means 'water'," he said, drawing a zigzag line.

"That was on the map, when we hunted the bison," she said. "I think it meant river."

"Yes, it can mean river. How it is drawn, or where it is drawn, or what it is drawn with can change the meaning. If it is like this," he said, making another zigzag with some additional lines, "it means the water is not drinkable. And like the circle, it has a second meaning. It is the symbol for feelings, passions, for love, and sometimes for hate. It can also be a reminder for a saying we have: the river runs silent when the water is deep."

Ayla frowned, sensing some meaning for her in the saying.

"Most Healers give the symbols meanings to help them remember, like reminders for sayings, except the sayings are about medicine or healing, and are not usually understood by anyone else," Mamut said. "I don't know many of them, but when we go to the Summer Meeting, you will meet other Healers. They can tell you more."

Ayla was interested. She remembered meeting other medicine women at the Clan Gathering, and how much she had learned from them. They had shared their treatments and remedies, even taught her new rhythms, but best of all was having other people to share experiences with. "I would like to learn more," she said. "I know only Clan medicine."

"I think you have more knowledge than you know, Ayla, certainly more than many of the Healers there will believe, at first. Some could learn from you, but I hope you understand that it may take some time before you are completely accepted." The old man watched her frown again, and wished there was some way he could ease her initial introduction. He could think of several reasons why it would not be easy for her to meet other Mamutoi, especially in large numbers. But no need to worry about that yet, he thought, and shifted the subject. "There is something about Clan medicine I'd like to ask you. Is it all just the 'memories'? Or do you have ways to help you remember?"

"How plants look, in seed, and shoot, and ripe; where they grow; what they are good for; how to mix, prepare and use them; that is from memory. Other kinds of treatments are remembered, too. I think about a new way to use something, but that is because I know how to use it," she said.

"Don't you use any symbols or reminders?"

Ayla thought for a moment, then, smiling, got up and brought back her medicine bag. She dumped out the contents in front of her, an assortment of small pouches and packets carefully tied with cords and small thongs. She picked up two of them.

"This one has mint," she said, showing Mamut one, "and this one has rose-hips."

"How do you know? You haven't opened them, or smelled them."

"I know because mint has a cord made from the stringy bark of a certain bush, and there are two knots on one end of the cord. The cord on the packet of rose-hips is from the long hair of a horse tail, and it has three knots in a row, close together," Ayla said. "I can smell difference, too – if I don't have a cold, but some very strong medicine has little smell. It is mixed with strong-smelling leaves of plant with little medicine, so wrong medicine will not be used. Different cord, different knots, different smell, sometimes different packet. They are reminders, right?"

"Clever . . . very clever," Mamut said. "Yes, they are reminders. But you have to remember the cords and the knots for each one, don't you? Still, it's a good way to make sure you are using the proper medicine."

Ayla's eyes were open, but she lay still and didn't move. It was dark except for the dim nightlight of banked fires. Jondalar was just climbing into bed, trying to make as little disturbance as possible as he moved around her. She had thought of moving to the inside once, but decided against it. She didn't want to make it easy for him to slip quietly in and out of bed. He rolled up in his separate furs and lay on his side, facing the wall, unmoving. She knew he did not go to sleep quickly, and she ached to reach over and touch him, but she'd been rebuffed before and didn't want to chance it again. It had hurt when he said he was tired or pretended to be asleep, or did not respond to her.

Jondalar waited until the sound of her breathing indicated that she had finally fallen off to sleep. Then he quietly rolled over, got up on an elbow and filled his eyes with the sight of her. Her tousled hair was strewn across the furs, and one arm was flung outside the covers, baring a breast. A warmth emanated from her and a faint woman-scent. He could feel himself shaking with wanting to touch her, but he felt certain she wouldn't want him bothering her when she was sleeping. After his confused and angry reaction to her night with Ranec, he feared she didn't want him any more. Lately, every time they accidentally brushed together, she flinched back. Several times he'd considered moving to a different bed, even a different hearth, but as difficult as it was to sleep beside her, it would be far worse to sleep away from her.

A wispy tendril of hair lay across her face and moved with each breath she took. He reached over and gently moved it aside, then carefully lowered himself back down to the bed, and allowed himself to relax. He closed his eyes and fell asleep to the sound of her breathing.

Ayla awoke with the feeling that someone was looking at her. The fires were built up and daylight was coming in through the partially uncovered fireplace hole. She turned her head to see Ranec's dark intense eyes quietly watching her from the Fox Hearth. She smiled sleepily at him, and was rewarded with a big, delighted smile. She was sure the place beside her would be empty, but she reached across the piled-up furs just to make sure. Then she pushed back her covers and sat up. She knew Ranec would wait until she was up and dressed before coming into the Mammoth Hearth to visit.

It had made her uncomfortable when she first became aware that he watched her all the time. In a way, it was flattering and she knew there was no malice in his attention, but within the Clan, it was considered discourteous to stare across the boundary stones into another family's living area. There had been no more real privacy in the cave of the Clan than there was in the earthlodge of the Mamutoi, but Ranec's attention felt like a mild intrusion upon her privacy – such as it was – and accentuated an undercurrent of tension she felt. Someone was always around. It had been no different when she lived with the Clan, but these were people whose ways she had not grown up with. The differences were often subtle, but in the close proximity of the earthlodge, they were heightened, or she was more sensitive to them. Occasionally, she wished she could get away. After three years of loneliness in the valley, she never imagined the time would come when she would wish to be alone, but there were times when she longed for the solitude, and the freedom, of loneliness.

Ayla hurried through her usual morning routine, eating only a few bites from the food left over from the night before. The open smoke holes usually meant it was clear outside, and she decided to go out with the horses. When she pushed aside the drape that led to the annexe, she saw Jondalar and Danug with the horses, and paused to reconsider.

Tending to the needs of the horses, either inside the annexe, or when the weather allowed, outside, gave her some respite from people when she wanted a moment to herself, but Jondalar also seemed to like to spend time with them. When she saw him with them, she often stayed away because he left them to her whenever she joined them, with mumbled comments about not wanting to interfere in her time with her horses. She wanted to allow him time with the animals. Not only did they provide a connection between her and Jondalar, their mutual care of the horses required communication, however reserved. His desire to be with them and sensitivity towards them made her think that he might need their companionship even more than she did.

Ayla went on into the Horse Hearth. Perhaps with Danug there, Jondalar wouldn't be so quick to leave. As she approached them, he was already backing away, but she rushed to say something that would keep him engaged in conversation.

"Have you thought, yet, about how you are going to teach Racer, Jondalar?" Ayla asked. She smiled a greeting at Danug.

"Teach him what?" Jondalar asked, a little disconcerted by her question.

"Teach him to let you ride him."

He had been thinking about it. In fact, he had just been making a comment to Danug, in what he hoped was a casual way. He didn't want to betray his increasingly strong desire to ride the animal. Particularly when he felt thwarted by his inability to deal with Ayla's apparent attraction to Ranec, he imagined himself galloping across the steppes on the back of the brown stallion, as free as the wind, but he wasn't sure if he still should be. Perhaps she would want Ranec to ride Whinney's colt, now.

"I have thought about it, but I didn't know if . . . how to begin," Jondalar said.

"I think you should keep doing what we started in the valley. Get him used to things on his back. Get him used to carrying loads. I'm not sure how to teach him to go where you want him to go. He will follow on a rope, but I don't know how he can follow a rope when you are on his back," Ayla said, talking fast, making suggestions on the spur of the moment, trying to keep him involved.

Danug watched her, then Jondalar, wishing he could say or do something that would suddenly make everything right, not only between them, but for everyone. An awkward moment of silence settled uneasily around them when Ayla stopped speaking. Danug rushed to fill the gap.

"Maybe he could hold the rope from behind, while he's sitting on the horse's back, instead of holding Racer's mane," the young man said.

Suddenly, as though someone had struck a piece of flint with iron pyrite in the dark lodge, Jondalar could visualise exactly what Danug had said. Instead of backing away, looking as though he was ready to sprint off at the first opportunity, Jondalar closed his eyes and wrinkled his forehead in concentration. "You know, that might work, Danug!" he said. Caught up in his excitement about an idea that might be a solution to a problem he had been worrying about, he forgot for a moment his uncertainty about his future. "Perhaps I could fasten something to his halter and hold it from behind. A strong cord . . . or a thin leather strap . . . two of them, maybe."

"I have some narrow thongs," Ayla said, noticing that he seemed less strained. She was pleased about his continuing interest in training the young stallion, and curious how it might work. "I will get them for you. They are inside."

Jondalar followed her through the inner arch into the Mammoth Hearth. Then stopped suddenly as she went to the storage platform to get the thong. Ranec was talking to Deegie and Tronie, and turned to flash his winning smile at Ayla. Jondalar felt his stomach churn, closed his eyes and gritted his teeth. He started edging back towards the opening. Ayla turned to give him a narrow roll of flexible leather.

"This is lashing, it is strong," she said, giving it to him. "I made it last winter." She looked up into the troubled blue eyes that revealed the pain, the confusion, and the indecision that tormented him. "Before you came to my valley, Jondalar. Before the Spirit of the Great Cave Lion chose you, and led you there."

He took the roll and hurried out. He couldn't stay. Whenever the carver came to the Mammoth Hearth, he had to leave. He couldn't be nearby when the dark man and Ayla were together, which was more often recently. He had watched from a distance when the younger people gathered in the larger space of the ceremonial area to spread out their work, share ideas and skills. He heard them practise music and sing, listened to their jokes and laughter. And every time he heard Ayla's laughter coupled with Ranec's, he winced.

Jondalar put the roll of lashing down near the young animal's halter, took his parka from the peg in the annexe, and went outside, smiling bleakly at Danug on his way. He slipped it over his head, pulled the hood tight around his face, and stuffed his hands in the mittens dangling from the sleeves, then walked up to the steppes.

The strong wind blowing a grey rack across the sky was no more than normal for the season, and the sun shining intermittently between the high broken clouds seemed to have little effect on the temperature that remained well below freezing. The snow cover was scant, and the dry air crackled and stole moisture from his lungs in clouds of steam with each breath. He would not be out long, but the cold calmed him with its insistent demand to put survival ahead of every other consideration. He didn't know why he reacted so strongly to Ranec. Part of it, without doubt, was his fear of losing Ayla to him, and part was visualising them together in his imagination, but there was also a nagging guilt about his own hesitation in accepting her fully and without reservation. Part of him believed Ranec deserved her more than he did. But one thing at least seemed certain. Ayla wanted him and not Ranec to try to learn to ride Racer.

Danug watched Jondalar start up the slope, then let the drape fall back, and walked slowly back inside. Racer neighed and tossed his head as the young man walked past and Danug looked at the horse and smiled. Nearly everyone seemed to enjoy the animals now, patting and talking to them, though not with Ayla's familiarity. It seemed so natural to have horses in an annexe of the lodge. How easy it was to forget the wonder and the amazement he had felt the first time he had seen them. He passed through the second archway, and saw Ayla standing beside her bed platform. He paused, then joined her.

"He's taking a walk on the steppes," he said to Ayla. "It's not a good idea to go out alone when it's cold and windy, but it's not as bad out as it can be sometimes."

"Are you trying to tell me he will be all right, Danug?" Ayla smiled at him, and he felt foolish for a moment. Of course Jondalar would be all right. He had travelled far, he could take care of himself. "Thank you," she said, "for your help, and for wanting to help," reaching over and touching his hand. Her hand was cool, but her touch warm, and he felt it with that special intensity she aroused in him, but on a deeper level, he felt that she had offered something more, her friendship.

"Maybe I'll go out and check some snares I set," he said.

"Try it this way, Ayla," Deegie said.

Deftly, she poked a hole near the edge of the leather with a small bone, a hard, tough bone from the leg of an arctic fox which had a natural sharp point, that had been made even sharper with sandstone. Then she laid a fine piece of sinew thread over the hole, and with the point of the sewing awl, pushed it through the hole. She grabbed it with her fingers from the back side of the leather and pulled the sinew through. At a corresponding place on another piece of leather which she was sewing to the first piece, she made another hole and repeated the process.

Ayla took the practice pieces of leather back. Using a square of tough mammoth skin as a thimble, she pushed the sharp arctic fox bone through the leather, making a small perforation. Then she tried to lay the thin sinew over the hole and push it through, but she couldn't seem to master the technique, and again felt thoroughly frustrated.

"I don't think I'll ever learn this, Deegie!" she wailed.

"You just have to practise, Ayla. I've been doing this since I was a girl. Of course it's easy for me, but you'll get it, if you keep trying. It's the same idea as cutting a little slit with a flint point and pulling leather lashing through to make working clothes, and you can do that just fine."

"But it is much harder to do with fine sinew and tiny holes. I can't get the sinew to go through. I feel so clumsy! I don't know how Tronie can sew on beads and quills like she does," Ayla said, looking at Fralie, who was rolling a long thin cylinder of ivory in the groove of a block of sandstone. "I was hoping she would show me, so I could decorate the white tunic after I made it, but I don't know if I'll even be able to make it the way I want."

"You will, Ayla. I don't think there is anything you can't do if you really want to," Tronie said.

"Except sing!" Deegie said.

Everyone laughed, including Ayla. Though her speaking voice was low-pitched and pleasant, singing was not one of her gifts. She could maintain a limited range of tones sufficient for the lulling monotony of a chant, and she did have an ear for music. She knew when she was off and she could whistle a melody, but any facility of voice was beyond her. The virtuosity of someone like Barzec was sheer wonder. She could listen to him all day, if he would consent to sing so long. Fralie, too, had a fine, clear, high, sweet voice, which Ayla loved to hear. In fact, most members of the Lion Camp could sing, but not Ayla.

Jokes were made about her singing and her voice, which included comments about her accent, though it was more speech mannerism than accent. She laughed as much as anyone. She couldn't sing and she knew it, and if they joked about her voice, many people had also, individually, praised her speech. They took it as a compliment that she had become so fluent in their language, so fast, and the joking about her singing made her feel that she belonged.

Everyone had some trait or characteristic that the others poked fun at:

Talut's size, Ranec's colour, Tulie's strength. Only Frebec took offence, so they joked about that behind his back, in sign language. The Lion Camp had also become fluent, without even thinking about it, in a modified version of the language of the Clan. As a result, Ayla wasn't the only one feeling the warmth of acceptance. Rydag, too, was included in the fun.

Ayla glanced towards him. He was sitting on a mat with Hartal on his lap, keeping the active baby occupied with a pile of bones, mostly deer vertebrae, so he wouldn't go crawling after his mother and scatter the beads she was helping Fralie make. Rydag was good with the babies. He had the patience to play with them and entertain them as long as they wished.

He smiled at her. "You not only one cannot sing, Ayla," he signed.

She smiled back. No, she thought, she was not the only one who could not sing. Rydag could not sing. Or talk. Or run and play. Or even live out a full life. In spite of her medicine, she didn't know how long he would live. He could die that day, or he could survive several years. She could only love him each day that he lived, and hope she could love him the next.

"Hartal cannot sing, either!" he signalled, and laughed with his odd guttural laugh.

Ayla chuckled, shaking her head with bemused delight. He had known what she was thinking, and made a joke about it that was clever, and funny.

Nezzie stood near the fireplace and watched them. Maybe you do not sing, Rydag, but you can talk now, she thought. He was stringing several vertebrae on a heavy cord through the spinal cord hole, and rattling them together for the baby. Without the hand-signal words, and the increased awareness they had brought of Rydag's intelligence and understanding, he would never have been allowed the responsibility of tending Hartal so his mother could work, not even right beside her. What a difference Ayla had brought to Rydag's life. This winter, no one questioned his essential humanity, except Frebec, and Nezzie was sure that was more out of stubbornness than belief.

Ayla continued to struggle with the awl and sinew. If she could only get the fine threads of sinew to go into the hole and out the other side. She tried to do it the way Deegie had shown her, but it was a knack that came from years of experience, and she was a long way from that. She dropped the practice pieces in her lap in frustration, and began watching the others making ivory beads.

A sharp blow to a mammoth tusk at the proper angle caused a fairly thin curved section to flake off. Grooves were cut in the large flake with chisel-like burins by etching a line and retracing it several times until the long pieces broke off. They were shaved and whittled into rough cylinders with scrapers and knives that peeled off long curled slivers, then they were rubbed smooth with sandstone kept wet to be more abrasive. Sharp flint blades, given a sawtooth edge and hafted to a long handle, were used to saw the ivory cylinders into small sections, and then the edges of them were smoothed.

The final step was to make a hole in the centre, to string them on a cord, or to sew them to a garment. It was done with a special tool. Flint, carefully shaped into a long thin point by a skilled toolmaker, was inserted into the end of a long narrow rod, perfectly straight and smooth. The point of the hand drill was centred on a small, thick disc of ivory and then, similar to the process of making fire, the rod was rotated back and forth between the palms while exerting downward pressure, until a hole was bored through.

Ayla watched Tronie twirl the rod between her palms, concentrating on making the hole just right. It occurred to her that they were going to a lot of work to make something that had no apparent use. Beads were no help in the securing or preparing of food, and they did not make the clothing to which they were attached more useful. But she began to understand why the beads had such value. The Lion Camp could never have afforded such an investment of time and effort without the security of warmth and comfort, and the assurance of adequate food. Only a cooperative, well-organised group could plan and store enough necessities ahead to assure the leisure to make beads. Therefore, the more beads they wore, the more it showed that the Lion Camp was a flourishing, desirable place to live, and the more respect and status they could command from the other Camps.

She picked up the leather in her lap and the bone awl, and made the last hole she had made a little bigger, then she tried to poke the sinew through the hole with the awl. She got it through, and pulled it from the back, but it didn't have the neat look of Deegie's tight stitches. She glanced up again, discouraged, and watched Rydag thread a backbone segment on a rope through the natural hole of its spinal cord. He picked up another vertebra and poked the rather stiff rope through its hole.

Ayla took a deep breath, and picked up her work again. It wasn't so hard forcing the point through the leather, she thought. She almost pushed the whole bone through the hole. If only she could attach the thread to it, she thought, it would be easy . . .

She stopped and examined the small bone carefully. Then she looked at Rydag tying the ends of the rope together and shaking the backbone rattle for Hartal. She watched Tronie spinning the hand drill between her palms, then turned to look at Fralie smoothing an ivory cylinder in the groove in a small block of sandstone. Then she closed her eyes, recalling Jondalar making spear points out of bone in her valley the previous summer . . .

She looked at the bone-sewing awl again. "Deegie!" she cried.

"What?" the young woman answered, startled.

"I think I know a way to do it!"

"Do what?"

"Get the sinew to go through the hole. Why not put a hole through the back end of a bone with a sharp point and then put the thread through the hole? Like Rydag put that rope through those backbones. Then, you can push it all the way through the leather and the thread will follow it. What do you think? Would it work?" Ayla asked.

Deegie closed her eyes for a moment, then took the awl from Ayla and looked it over. "It would have to be a very small hole."

"The holes Tronie is making in those beads are small. Would it have to be much smaller?"

"This bone is very hard, and tough. It would not be easy to make a hole in it, and I don't see a good place for a hole."

"Couldn't we make something out of mammoth tusk, or some other kind of bone? Jondalar makes long, narrow spear points out of bone, and smooths and sharpens them with sandstone, like Fralie is doing. Couldn't we make something like a tiny spear point, and then drill a hole in the other end?" Ayla asked, tense with excitement.

Deegie considered again. "We'd have to get Wymez or someone to make a smaller drill, but . . . it might work. Ayla, I think it might work!"

Nearly everyone seemed to be milling around the Mammoth Hearth. They were gathered together in groups of three or four, chatting, but expectancy was in the air. Word had somehow been passed that Ayla was going to try out the new thread-puller. Several people had worked on developing it, but since it had been her idea originally, Ayla was going to be the first to use it. Wymez and Jondalar had worked together to devise a way to make a flint borer small enough to make the hole. Ranec had selected the ivory, and using his carving tools, had shaped several very small, long, pointed cylinders. Ayla had smoothed and sharpened them to her satisfaction, but Tronie had actually bored the hole.

Ayla could sense the excitement. When she got out the practice leather and the sinew, everyone gathered around, all pretence that they were only casually visiting forgotten. The hard, dry deer tendon, brown as old leather and as big around as a finger, resembled a stick of wood. It was pounded until it became a bundle of white collagen fibres that separated easily into filaments of sinew, which could be coarse strings or thin, fine thread depending upon what was wanted. She felt the moment needed drama and took time examining the sinew, then finally pulled a thin filament away. She wet it with her mouth to soften it, and bind it together, then holding the thread-puller in her left hand, she examined the small hole critically. This could be difficult, getting the thread through the hole. The sinew was starting to dry, and harden slightly, which made it easier. Ayla carefully poked the sinew thread into the tiny hole, and breathed a small sigh of relief when she pulled it through, and held up the ivory sewing point with thread dangling from the end.

Next she picked up the piece of worn leather she was using for practice, and near an edge, she jabbed in the point, making a perforation. But this time she pushed it through, and smiled when she saw it pulling the thread after itself. She held it up to show, to exclamations of wonder. Then she picked up another piece of leather that she wanted to attach, and repeated the process, though she had to use the square of mammoth hide as a thimble to force the point through the thicker, tougher hide. She pulled the two pieces together, and then made a second stitch, and held the two pieces up to show.

"It works!" Ayla said, with a big smile of victory.

She gave the leather and needle to Deegie, who made a few stitches. "It does work. Here, mother, you try it," she said, handing the leather and the thread-puller to the headwoman.

Tulie also took a few stitches and nodded approvingly, then gave it to Nezzie, who tried it out, then let Tronie take a turn. Tronie gave it to Ranec, who tried pushing the point through both pieces at once, and discovered that thick leather was hard to penetrate.

"I think if you made a small cutting point out of flint," he said as he passed it to Wymez, "it would make it easier to poke this through heavy leather. What do you think?"

Wymez tried it and nodded agreement. "Yes, but this thread-puller is very clever."

Every person in the Camp tried the new implement, and agreed. It did make sewing much easier to have something that pulled, rather than pushed, the thread through.

Talut held the small sewing tool up and examined it from all angles, nodding his head with admiration. A long slender shaft, point at one end, hole at the other, it was an invention whose worth was recognised instantly. He wondered why no one had thought of it sooner. It was simple, so obvious once it was seen, but so effective.

22

Two sets of hooves pounded in unison across the hard ground. Ayla crouched low over the mare's withers, squinting into a wind burning cold on her face. She rode lightly, the controlling interplay of tension in her knees and hips in perfect accord with the powerful, striving muscles of the galloping horse. She noticed a change in the rhythm of the other hoofbeats, and glanced at Racer. He had pulled ahead, but, showing unmistakable signs of tiring, he was falling back. She brought Whinney to a gradual stop, and the young stallion halted, as well. Enveloped in clouds of steam from their hard breathing, the horses hung their heads. Both animals were tired, but it had been a good run.

Sitting upright and bouncing easily in rhythm with the horse's gait, Ayla headed back towards the river at a comfortable pace, enjoying the opportunity to be outside. It was cold, but beautiful, with the glare of an incandescent sun made brighter by sparkling ice and the white of a recent blizzard.

As soon as Ayla had stepped outside the earthlodge that morning, she decided to take the horses for a long run. The air itself enticed her out. It seemed lighter, as though an oppressive burden had been lifted. She thought the cold was not as intense, though nothing was visibly changed. The ice was just as frozen, the tiny pellets of wind-driven snow just as hard.

Ayla had no absolute means of knowing that the temperature had risen and the wind blew with less force, but she had detected subtle differences. Though it might have been interpreted as intuition, a feeling, it was in reality an acute sensitivity. To people who lived in climates of extreme cold, conditions even a little less severe were noticeable, and often greeted with exuberant good feelings. It wasn't yet spring, but the relentless grip of the deep grinding cold had eased, and the slight but noticeable warming brought with it the promise that life would stir again.

She smiled when the young stallion pranced ahead, his neck arched proudly and his tail held out. She still thought of Racer as the baby she had helped deliver, but he wasn't a baby any more. Though still not filled out completely, he was bigger than his dam, and he was a racer. He loved to run, and he was fast, but there was a difference in the running patterns of the two horses. Racer was invariably faster than his dam in a short run, easily outdistancing her at the start, but Whinney had more endurance. She could run hard longer and if they went on for any distance, she inevitably caught up and surged ahead of him.

Ayla dismounted, but stopped momentarily before pushing aside the drape and entering the earthlodge. She'd often used the horses as an excuse to get away, and on that morning she had been particularly relieved that the weather felt right for a long run. As happy as she was to have found people again, and to be accepted as one of them and included in their activities, she needed to be alone, occasionally. It was especially true when uncertainties and unresolved misunderstandings heightened tensions.

Fralie had been spending much of her time at the Mammoth Hearth with the young people, to Frebec's growing annoyance. Ayla had been hearing arguments from the Crane Hearth, or rather, harangues by Frebec complaining of Fralie's absence. She knew he didn't like Fralie to associate too closely with her, and was sure the pregnant woman would stay away more to keep the peace. It bothered Ayla, particularly since Fralie had just confided that she had been passing blood. She had warned the woman that she could lose the baby if she didn't rest, and promised her some medicine, but now it would be more difficult to treat her with Frebec hovering disapprovingly.

Added to that was her growing confusion about Jondalar and Ranec. Jondalar had been distant, but recently, he seemed more like himself. A few days before, Mamut had asked him to come and talk to him about a particular tool he had in mind, but the shaman had been busy all day, and only found time to discuss his project in the evening, when the young people usually gathered at the Mammoth Hearth. Though they sat quietly off to the side, the laughter and usual banter were easily overheard.

Ranec was more attentive than ever, and had been pressing Ayla lately, in the guise of teasing and joking, to come to his bed again. She still found it difficult to refuse him outright; acquiescence to a man's wishes had been too thoroughly ingrained in her to overcome easily. She laughed at his jokes – she was understanding humour more all the time, even the serious intent it sometimes masked – but skilfully evaded his implied invitation, to a chorus of laughter at Ranec's expense. He laughed as well, enjoying her wit, and she felt attracted to his easy friendliness. He was comfortable to be with.

Mamut noticed that Jondalar smiled, too, and nodded his head approvingly. The flint knapper had avoided the gathering of young people, only watching the friendly joking from a distance, and the laughter had only increased his jealousy. He didn't know that it was often sparked by Ayla's refusals of Ranec's offers, though Mamut did.

The next day, Jondalar smiled at her, for the first time in too long, Ayla thought, but she felt her breath catch in her throat and her heart speed up. During the next few days, he began coming back to the hearth earlier, not always waiting until she was asleep. Though she was reluctant to push herself on him still, and he seemed hesitant to approach her, she was beginning to hope that he was getting over whatever had been bothering him. Yet she was afraid to hope.

Ayla took a deep breath, then pulled back the heavy drape, and held it aside for the horses. After shaking out her parka and hanging it on a peg, she went inside. For a change, the Mammoth Hearth was nearly empty. Only Jondalar was there, talking to Mamut. She was pleased, but surprised to see him, and it made her realise how little she had seen of him lately. She smiled and hurried towards them, but Jondalar's scowl pulled down the corners of her mouth. He did not seem very happy to see her.

"You've been gone all morning, alone!" he blurted. "Don't you know it's dangerous to go out alone? You worry people. Soon someone would have had to go looking for you." He didn't say he had been the one who was worried, or that he was the one who was considering going out to look for her.

Ayla backed off at his vehemence. "I was not alone. I was with Whinney and Racer. I took them for a run. They needed it."

"Well, you shouldn't have gone out like that when it's so cold. It is dangerous to go out alone," he said, rather lamely, glancing at Mamut, hoping for support.

"I said I was not alone. I was with Whinney and Racer, and it is nice out, sunny, not as cold." She was flustered by his anger, not realising that it masked a fear for her safety that was almost unbearable. "I have been out alone in winter before, Jondalar. Who do you think went out with me when I lived in the valley?"

She's right, he thought. She knows how to take care of herself. I shouldn't keep trying to tell her when and where she can go. Mamut did not seem overly concerned when he had asked where Ayla was, and she is the daughter of his hearth. He should have paid more attention to the old shaman, Jondalar thought, feeling foolish, as though he had made a scene over nothing.

"Uh . . . well . . . maybe I should go look at the horses," he mumbled, backing away and hurrying towards the annexe.

Ayla watched him go, wondering if he thought she wasn't looking after them. She was confused and upset. It seemed impossible to understand him at all.

Mamut was watching her closely. Her hurt and distress were plain to see. Why was it that the people who were involved found it so hard to understand their own problems? He was inclined to confront them and force them to see what seemed obvious to everyone else, but he resisted. He had already done as much as he felt he should. He had sensed from the beginning an undercurrent of tension in the Zelandonii man, and was convinced that the problem was not as obvious as it seemed. It was best to let them work it out for themselves. They would all learn more from the experience if left to find their own solutions. But he could encourage Ayla to talk to him about it or, at least, help her to discover her choices, and know her own wishes and potential.

"Did you say it is not as cold out, Ayla?" Mamut asked.

It took a moment for the question to find its way through the maze of other pressing thoughts that worried her. "What? Oh . . . yes. I think so. It doesn't really feel warmer, it just doesn't seem as cold."

"I was wondering when She would break the back of winter," Mamut said. "I thought it should be getting close."

"Break the back? I do not understand."

"It's just a saying, Ayla. Sit down, I'll tell you a winter story about the Great Bountiful Earth Mother who created all that lives," the old man said, smiling. Ayla sat beside him on a mat near the fire.

"In a great struggle, the Earth Mother took a life force from Chaos, which is a cold and unmoving emptiness, like death, and from it She created life and warmth, but She must always fight for the life She created. When the cold season is coming on, we know the struggle has begun between the bountiful Earth Mother who wants to bring forth warm life, and cold death of Chaos, but first She must care for Her children."

Ayla was warming to the story, now, and smiled encouragingly. "What does She do to care for Her children?"

"Some She puts to sleep, some She dresses warmly to resist the cold, some She bids gather food and hide. As it gets colder and colder, death seems to be winning, the Mother is pushed back farther and farther. In the depths of the cold season, when the Mother is locked in the battle of life and death, nothing moves, nothing changes, everything seems to be dead. For us, without a warm place to live and the food that is stored, death would win in winter; sometimes, if the battle goes on longer than usual, it does. No one goes out much, then. People make things, or tell stories, or talk, but they don't move around much and they sleep more. That's why winter is called the little death.

"Finally, when the cold has pushed Her down as far as She will go, She resists. She pushes and pushes until She breaks the back of winter.

341

It means spring will return but it is not spring, yet. She has had a long fight, and She must rest before She can bring forth life again. But you know She has won. You can smell it, you can feel it in the air."

"I did! I did feel it, Mamut! That's why I had to take the horses for a run. The Mother broke the back of winter!" Ayla exclaimed. The story seemed to explain exactly how she felt.

"I think it's time for a celebration, don't you?"

"Oh, yes. I think so!"

"Perhaps you would be willing to help me arrange it?" He waited only long enough for Ayla to nod. "Not everyone feels Her victory, yet, but they will soon. We can both watch for the signs, and then decide when the time is right."

"What signs?"

"As life begins to stir again, each person feels it in a different way. Some get happy and want to go outside, but it's still too cold to go out very much, so they get edgy, or irritated. They want to acknowledge the life stirrings within them, but there are many big storms yet to come. Winter knows all is lost and gets angriest at this time of year, and people feel it and get angry, too. I'm glad you have alerted me. Between now and spring, people will be more restless. I think you will notice it, Ayla. That's when a celebration is best. It gives people a reason to express happiness instead of anger."

I knew she would notice, Mamut thought, when he saw her frown. I have barely begun to feel the difference, and she has recognised it already. I knew she was gifted, but her abilities still astound me, and I'm sure I have not yet discovered her full range. I may never know; her potential could be far greater than mine. What did she say about that root, and the ceremony with the Mog-urs? I'd like to get her prepared . . . the hunting ceremony with the Clan! It changed me, the effects were profound. It lives with me still. She, too, had an experience . . . could that have changed her? Enhanced her natural tendencies? I wonder . . . the Spring Festival, is it too soon to bring up the root again? Maybe I should wait until after she works with me on the Back Breaking Celebration . . . or the next one . . . there will be many between now and Spring . . .

Deegie walked down the passageway towards the Mammoth Hearth carrying heavy outer wear.

"I was hoping I would find you, Ayla. I want to check those snares I set to see if I caught any white foxes to trim Branag's parka. Do you want to come with me?"

Ayla, just waking up, looked up at the partially uncovered smoke hole. "It does look nice out. Let me get dressed."

She pulled back the covers, sat up, stretched and yawned, then went to the curtained-off area near the horse annexe. On her way, she passed by a platform bed on which a half-dozen children were sleeping, sprawled on top of each other in a heap, like a litter of wolf pups. She saw Rydag's large brown eyes open, and smiled at him. He closed them again, and snuggled down between the youngest, Nuvie, almost four years, and Rugie, who was approaching eight. Crisavec, Brinan, and Tusie were also in the pile, and lately, she had seen Fralie's youngest, Tasher, who was not yet three, beginning to take notice of the other youngsters. Latie, verging on womanhood, Ayla noticed, played with them less and less.

The children were benevolently spoiled. They could eat and sleep, where and when they wanted. They seldom observed the territorial customs of their elders; the entire lodge was theirs. They could demand the attention of adult members of the Camp, and often found it was welcomed as an interesting diversion; no one was in any particular hurry or had any place to go. Wherever their interests led the children, an older member of the group was ready to assist or explain. If they wanted to sew skins together, they were given the tools, and scraps of leather, and strings of sinew. If they wanted to make stone tools, they were given pieces of flint, and stone or bone hammers.

They wrestled and tumbled, and invented games, which were often versions of adult activities. They made their own small hearths, and learned to use fire. They pretended to hunt, spearing pieces of meat from the cold storage chambers, and cooked it. When playing "hearths" extended to mimicking the copulating activities of their elders, the adults smiled indulgently. No part of normal living was singled out as something to be hidden or repressed; all of it was necessary instruction to becoming an adult. The only taboo was violence, particularly extreme or unnecessary violence.

Living so closely together, they had learned that nothing could destroy a Camp, or a people, like violence, particularly when they were confined to the earthlodge during the long, cold winters. Whether by accident or design, every custom, manner, convention, or practice, even if not overtly directed at it, was aimed at keeping violence to a minimum. Sanctioned conduct allowed a wide range of individual differences in activities that did not, as a rule, lead to violence, or that might be acceptable outlets for draining off strong emotions. Personal skills were fostered. Tolerance was encouraged; jealousy or envy, while understood, discouraged. Competitions, including arguments, were actively used as alternatives, but were ritualised, strictly controlled, and kept within defined boundaries. The children quickly learned the basic rules. Yelling was acceptable; hitting was not.

As Ayla checked the large waterbag, she smiled again at the sleeping children, who had been up until late the night before. She enjoyed having children around again. "I should get snow before we leave. We are low on water, and it hasn't snowed for a while. Clean snow nearby is getting hard to find."

"Let's not take the time," Deegie said. "We have water at our hearth, and so has Nezzie. We can get more when we come back." She was putting on her warm winter outdoor clothes while Ayla was dressing. "I have a waterbag, and some food to take with us, so if you're not hungry, we can just go."

"I can wait for the food, but I need to make some hot tea," Ayla said. Deegie's eagerness to leave was infecting her. They were still just beginning to stir around outside the lodge, and spending some time alone just with Deegie seemed like fun.

"I think Nezzie has some hot tea, and I don't think she'd mind if we had a cup."

"She makes mint in the morning, I will just get something to add to it . . . something I like to drink in the morning. I think I will get my sling, too."

Nezzie insisted that the two young women eat some hot cooked grains as well, and gave them slices of meat from her roast of the night before to take along. Talut wanted to know which way they planned to go, and the general location of Deegie's snares. When they stepped outside the main entrance, the day had begun; the sun had risen above a bank of clouds on the horizon, and begun its journey across a clear sky. Ayla noticed the horses were already out. She didn't blame them.

Deegie showed Ayla the quick twist of the foot that turned the leather loop, attached to the elongated circular frame woven across with sturdy willow withes, into a convenient snowshoe hitch. With a little practice, Ayla was soon striding across the top of the snow alongside Deegie.

Jondalar watched them leaving from the entrance to the annexe. With a frown, he looked at the sky and considered following them, then changed his mind. He saw a few clouds, but nothing to portend danger. Why was he always so worried about Ayla whenever she left the earthlodge? It was ridiculous for him to follow her around. She wasn't going out alone, Deegie was with her, and the two young women were perfectly able to take care of themselves . . . even if it did snow . . . or worse. They'd notice him following after a while, and then he'd just be in the way when they wanted to be off by themselves. He let the drape fall, and turned back inside, but he couldn't shake his feeling that Ayla might be in danger.

★   ★   ★

"Oh, look, Ayla!" Deegie cried, on her knees examining the frozen solid white-furred carcass dangling from a noose pulled tight around its neck. "I set other traps. Let's hurry and check them."

Ayla wanted to stay and examine the snare, but she followed after Deegie. "What are you going to do with it?" she asked when she caught up.

"It depends on how many I get. I wanted to make a fringe on a fur parka for Branag, but I'm making him a tunic, too, a red one – not as bright as your red. It will have long sleeves, and take two hides, and I'm trying to match the colour of the second skin to the first. I think I'd like to decorate it with the fur and teeth of a winter fox. What do you think?"

"I think it will be beautiful." They schussed through the snow for a while, then Ayla said, "What do you think would be best for a white tunic?"

"It depends. Do you want other colours or do you want to keep it all white?"

"I think I want it to be white, but I'm not sure."

"White fox fur would be nice."

"I thought about that, but . . . I don't think it would be quite right," Ayla said. It wasn't so much the colour that was bothering her. She remembered that she had selected white fox furs to give to Ranec at her adoption ceremony, and didn't want any reminders about that time.

The second snare had been sprung, but it was empty. The sinew noose had been bitten through, and there were wolf tracks. The third had also caught a fox, and it had apparently frozen hard in the snare, but it had been gnawed at, most of it was eaten, in fact, and the fur was useless. Again Ayla pointed out wolf tracks.

"I seem to be trapping foxes for wolves," Deegie said.

"It looks like only one, Deegie," Ayla said.

Deegie was beginning to fear she would not get another good fur, even if one had been caught in her fourth snare. They hurried to the place where she had set it.

"It should be over there, near those bushes," she said as they approached a small wooded copse, "but I don't see . . ."

"There it is, Deegie!" Ayla shouted, hurrying ahead. "It looks good, too. And look at that tail!"

"Perfect!" Deegie sighed with relief. "I wanted at least two." She untangled the frozen fox from the noose, tied it together with the first fox, and slung them over the branch of a tree. She was feeling more relaxed now that she had trapped her two foxes. "I'm hungry. Why don't we stop and have something to eat here?"

"I do feel hungry, now that you say it."

They were in a sparsely wooded glen, more brush than trees, formed by a creek that had cut through thick deposits of loess soil. A sense of bleak and weary exhaustion pervaded the small vale in the waning days of the long harsh winter. It was a drab place of blacks and whites and dreary greys. The snow cover, broken by the woody underbrush, was old and compacted, disturbed by many tracks, and seemed used and grimy. Broken branches exposing raw wood showed the ravages of wind, snow and hungry animals. Willow and alder clung close to the earth, bent by the weight of climate and season to prostrate shrubs. A few scrawny birch trees stood tall and thin, scraping bare branches noisily together in the wind, as though clamouring for the fulfilling touch of green. Even the conifers had lost their colour. The twisted pines, bark scabbed with patches of grey lichen, were faded, and the tall larches were dark and sagged heavily from their burden of snow.

Dominating one shallow slope was a mound of snow armed with long canes spiked with sharp thorns; the dry woody stems of runners which had been sent out the previous summer to claim new territory. Ayla noted it in her mind, not as an impenetrable thicket of thorny briars, but as a place to look for berries and healing leaves in their proper season. She saw beyond the bleak, tired scene to the hope it held, and after the long confinement, even a winter-weary landscape looked promising, especially with the sun shining.

The two young women piled snow together to make seats on what would be the bank of a little stream if it were summer. Deegie opened her haversack and took out the food she had packed, and even more important, the water. She opened a birchbark packet and gave Ayla a compact cake of travelling food – the nutritious mixture of dried fruits and meat and energy-giving essential fat, shaped into a round patty.

"Mother made some of her steamed loaves with pine nuts last night, and gave me one," Deegie said, opening another packet and breaking off a piece for Ayla. They had become a favourite of hers.

"I will have to ask Tulie how to make these," Ayla said, taking a bite before she unwrapped the slices of Nezzie's roast, and put some down beside each of them. "I think we are having a feast out here. All we need are some fresh spring greens."

"That would make it perfect. I can hardly wait for spring. Once we have the Back Breaking Celebration, it seems to get harder and harder to wait," Deegie replied.

Ayla was enjoying the companionable outing with just herself and Deegie, and was even beginning to feel warm in the shallow depression, protected from winds. She untied the thong at her throat and pushed back her hood, then straightened her sling around her head. She closed her eyes and tipped her face up to the sun. She saw the circular after-image of the dazzling orb against the red background of her lowered eyelids, and felt the welcoming warmth. After she opened her eyes again, she seemed to see with greater clarity.

"Do people always wrestle at Back Breaking Celebrations?" Ayla asked. "I have never seen anyone wrestle without moving his feet before."

"Yes, it's to honour . . ."

"Look, Deegie! It is Spring!" Ayla interrupted, jumping up and rushing towards a willow shrub nearby. When the other woman joined her, she pointed to the hint of swelling buds along a slender twig, and one, coming into season too early to survive, that had burst forth in bright spring green. Both women smiled at each other in wonder, full of the discovery, as though they had invented Spring themselves.

The sinew snare loop still dangled not far from the willow. Ayla held it up. "I think this is a very good way to hunt. You do not have to look for animals. You make a trap and come back later to get them, but how do you make it, and how do you know that you will catch a fox?"

"It's not hard to make. You know how sinew gets hard if you wet it and let it dry, just like leather that is not treated?"

Ayla nodded.

"You make a little loop at the end," Deegie continued, showing her the loop. "Then you take the other end and put it through to make another loop, just big enough for a fox's head to go through. Then you wet it, and let it dry with the loop open so it will stay open. Then you have to go where the foxes are, usually where you've seen them or caught them before. My mother showed me this place. Usually there are foxes here every year, you can tell if there are tracks. They often follow the same paths when they are near their dens. To set the snare, you find a fox trail, and where it goes through bushes or near trees, you set the loop right across the trail, at about the height of their heads, and fasten it, like this, here and here," Deegie demonstrated as she explained. Ayla watched, her forehead furrowed in concentration.

"When the fox runs along the trail, the head goes through the loop, and as he runs, it tightens the noose around his neck. The more the fox struggles, the tighter the noose gets. It doesn't take long. Then the only problem is finding the fox before something else does. Danug was telling me about the way the people to the north have started setting snares. He says they bend down a young sapling and tie it to the noose so that it comes loose as soon as the animal is caught, and jerks it up when the tree springs back. That keeps the fox off the ground until you get back."

"I think that's a good idea," Ayla said, walking back towards their seats. She looked up, then suddenly, to Deegie's surprise, she whipped her sling off her head and was scanning the ground. "Where is a stone?" she whispered. "There!"

With a movement so swift Deegie could hardly follow, Ayla picked up the stone, set it in her sling, whipped it around and let fly. Deegie heard the stone land, but only when she got back to the seats did she see the object of Ayla's missile. It was a white ermine, a small weasel about fourteen inches long overall, but five of the inches was a white furry tail with a black tip. In summer the elongated, soft-furred animal would have a rich brown coat with a white underbelly, but in winter, the sinuous little stoat turned pure silky white, except for its black nose, sharp little eyes, and the very tip of its tail.

"It was stealing our roast meat!" Ayla said.

"I didn't even see it next to that snow. You've got good eyes," Deegie said. "And you're so quick with that sling, I don't know why you need to worry about snares, Ayla."

"A sling is good for hunting when you see what you want to hunt, but a snare can hunt for you when you are not even there. Both are useful to know," Ayla replied, taking the question seriously.

They sat down to finish their meal. Ayla's hand kept returning to rub the soft thick fur of the little weasel as they talked. "Ermines have the nicest fur," she said.

"Most of those long weasels do," Deegie said. "Minks, sables, even wolverines have good fur. Not so soft, but the best for hoods, if you don't want frost clinging around your face. But it's hard to snare them, and you can't really hunt them with a spear. They're quick and vicious. Your sling seemed to work, though I still don't know how you did it."

"I learned to use the sling hunting those kind of animals. I only hunted meat-eaters in the beginning and learned their ways first."

"Why?" Deegie asked.

"I was not supposed to hunt at all, so I did not hunt any animals that were food, only those that stole food from us." She snorted a wry chuckle of realisation. "I thought that would make it all right."

"Why didn't they want you to hunt?"

"Women of the Clan are forbidden to hunt . . . but they finally allowed me to use a sling." Ayla paused for an instant, remembering. "Do you know, I killed a wolverine long before I killed a rabbit?" She smiled at the irony.

Deegie shook her head in amazement. What a strange childhood Ayla must have had, she thought.

They got up to leave, and as Deegie went to get her foxes, Ayla picked up the soft, white little ermine. She rubbed her hand along the body all the way to the tip of the tail.

"That is what I want!" Ayla said, suddenly. "Ermine!"

"But that's what you have," Deegie said.

"No. I mean for the white tunic. I want to trim it with white ermine fur, and the tails. I like those tails with the little black tips."

"Where are you going to get enough ermine to decorate a tunic?" Deegie asked. "Spring is coming, they will be changing colour again soon."

"I do not need very many, and where there is one, there are usually more nearby. I will hunt them. Now," Ayla said. "I need to find some good stones." She started pushing snow out of the way, looking for stones near the bank of the frozen creek.

"Now?" Deegie said.

Ayla stopped and looked up. She had almost forgotten Deegie's presence in her excitement. She could make tracking and stalking more difficult. "You do not have to wait for me, Deegie. Go back. I will find my way."

"Go back? I wouldn't miss this for anything."

"You can be very quiet?"

Deegie smiled. "I have hunted before, Ayla."

Ayla blushed, feeling she had said the wrong thing. "I did not mean . . ."

"I know you didn't," Deegie said, then smiled. "I think I could learn some things from someone who killed a wolverine before she killed a rabbit. Wolverines are more vicious, mean, fearless, and spiteful than any animal alive, including hyenas. I've seen them drive leopards away from their own kills, they'll even stand up to a cave lion. I'll try to stay out of your way. If you think I'm scaring the ermine off, tell me, and I'll wait for you here. But don't ask me to go back."

Ayla smiled with relief, thinking how wonderful it was to have a friend who understood her so quickly. "Ermine are as bad as wolverines. They are just smaller, Deegie."

"Is there anything I can do to help?"

"We still have roast meat left. It might be useful, but first we must find tracks . . . after I get a good supply of stones."

When Ayla had accumulated a pile of satisfactory missiles, and put them in a pouch, which was attached to her belt, she picked up her haversack, and slung it over her left shoulder. Then she stopped and studied the landscape, looking for the best place to begin. Deegie stood beside her and just a step behind, waiting for her to take the lead. Almost as though she was thinking out loud, Ayla began speaking to her in a quiet voice.

"Weasels do not make dens. They use whatever they find, even a rabbit's burrow – after they kill the rabbits. Sometimes I think they would not need a den, if they did not have young. They are always moving: hunting, running, climbing, standing up and looking, and they are always killing, day and night, even after they have just eaten, though they might leave it. They eat everything, squirrels, rabbits, birds, eggs, insects, even dead and rotten meat, but most meat they kill and eat fresh. They make stinky musk when they are cornered, not to squirt like a skunk, but smells as bad, and they make sound like this . . ." Ayla uttered a cry that was half strangled scream and half grunt. "In the season of their Pleasures, they whistle."

Deegie was utterly astonished. She had just learned more about weasels and ermine than she had learned in her entire life. She didn't even know they made a sound at all.

"They are good mothers, have many babies, two hands . . ." Ayla stopped to think of the name of the counting word. "Ten, more sometimes. Other times, only few. Young stay with mother until almost grown." She stopped again to eye the landscape critically. "This time of year, litter might still be with mother. We look for track . . . I think near canebrake." She started towards the mound of snow that covered, more or less, the tangled mass of stems and runners that had been growing from the same place for many years.

Deegie followed her, wondering how she could have learned so much, when Ayla wasn't much older than she was. Deegie had noticed that Ayla's speech had lapsed just slightly – it was the only sign of her excitement – but it made her realise how well Ayla did speak now. She seldom spoke fast, but her Mamutoi was close to perfect, except for the way she said certain sounds. Deegie thought she might never lose that speech mannerism, and rather hoped she wouldn't. It made her distinctive . . . and more human.

"Look for small tracks with five toes, sometimes only four show, they make the smallest tracks of any meat-eater, and the back paws go in the same tracks that front-feet paws were in."

Deegie hung back, not wanting to trample delicate spoor, watching. Ayla slowly and carefully scanned each area of the space around her with every step she took, the snow-covered ground and each fallen log, each twig on each bush, the slender boles of bare birches and the weighted boughs of dark-needled pines. Suddenly her eyes stopped their constant vigilance, stilled by a sight that caught her breath. She lowered her foot slowly while reaching into the haversack for a large piece of rare roast bison, and laid it on the ground in front of her. Then she backed off carefully, and reached into the pouch of stones.

Deegie looked beyond Ayla without moving, trying to see what she saw. Finally she noticed movement, and then focused on several small white shapes sinuously moving towards them. They raced with surprising speed though they were climbing over deadfall, up and down trees, through brush, in and around small pockets and cracks, and devouring everything they found in their path. Deegie had never taken the time to notice the small voracious carnivores before, and she watched in rapt fascination. They stood up occasionally, shiny black eyes alert, ears cocked for every sound, but drawn unerringly by scent to their hapless prey.

Squirming through nests of voles and mice, under tree roots for hibernating newts and frogs, and darting after small birds too chilled and hungry to flee, the ravaging horde of eight or ten small white weasels closed in. Heads weaving back and forth, black little beads of eyes eager, they pounced with deadly accuracy at the brain, the nape of the neck, the jugular vein. Striking without compunction, they were the most efficient, bloodthirsty killers of the animal world, and Deegie was suddenly very glad they were small. There seemed no reason for such wanton destruction but a lust to kill – except the need to keep a continuously active body fuelled in the way they were intended and ordained by nature to do.

The ermines were drawn to the slab of rare meat, and without hesitation began to make short work of it. Suddenly there was confusion, hard-flung stones landed among the feeding weasels, striking some down, and the unmistakable scent of weasel musk choked the air. Deegie had been so absorbed in watching the animals she had missed Ayla's carefully controlled preparations and swift casts.

Then, out of nowhere, a large black animal bounded among the white weasels, and Ayla was stunned to hear a menacing growl. The wolf went after the slab of bison, but was held off by two bold and fearless ermine. Backing off only a bit, the black carnivore spied an ermine recently made harmless and grabbed for it instead.

But Ayla was not about to let the black wolf steal her ermine; she had put in too much effort to get them. They were her kills and she wanted them for the white tunic. As the wolf was trotting away with the small white weasel in its mouth, Ayla went after it. Wolves were also meat-eaters. She had studied them just as closely as weasels when she was teaching herself to use a sling. She understood them, too. She picked up a fallen branch as she ran after the animal. A single wolf usually gave way in the face of a determined charge, and might drop the ermine.

If it had been a pack, or even just two wolves, she would not have tried such a reckless assault, but when the black wolf paused to re-position the ermine in its mouth, Ayla went after it with the branch, hauling back to give it a solid blow. She didn't think of the branch as much of a weapon, but she planned only to scare the wolf off, and startle it into dropping the small furry animal it held. But Ayla was the one who was startled. The wolf dropped the ermine at its feet, and with a mean and ugly snarl, sprang straight for her.

Her instant reaction was to throw the branch across her as a defence, to hold off the attacking wolf, and her quick surge of energy said run. But in the wooded copse, the cold and brittle branch broke as she pulled it around and hit a tree. She was left holding a rotten stump, but the broken end flew into the wolf's face. It was enough to hold it off. The wolf had been bluffing, too, and wasn't very eager to attack. Stopping to pick up the dead ermine, the wolf climbed out of the wooded glen.

Ayla was frightened, but angry, and in shock, too. She couldn't just let that ermine go like that. She chased after the wolf once more.

"Let it go!" Deegie shouted. "You've got enough! Let the wolf have it."

But Ayla didn't hear; she wasn't paying attention. The wolf was heading for open ground and she was close behind. Reaching for another stone, and finding only two left, Ayla ran after the wolf. Though she expected that the large carnivore would soon outdistance her, she had to give it one more try. She loaded a stone in her sling and hurled it after the fleeing canine. The second stone that followed soon afterwards finished what the first had begun. Both found their mark.

She felt a sense of satisfaction when the wolf dropped. That was one animal that would not be stealing anything from her again. As she ran to get the ermine, she decided she might as well take the wolf pelt, too, but when Deegie found her, Ayla was sitting beside the dead black wolf, and the white ermine, and hadn't moved. The expression on her face gave Deegie cause for concern.

"What's wrong, Ayla?"

"I should have let her have it. I should have known she had a reason for going after that roast meat, even though the ermines wanted it. Wolves know how vicious weasels are, and usually a lone wolf will back down without attacking in an unfamiliar place. I should have let her have that ermine."

"I don't understand. You got your ermine back, and a black wolf pelt besides. What do you mean you should have let her have it?"

"Look," Ayla said, pointing to the black wolf's underbelly. "She's nursing. She's got pups."

"Isn't it early for wolves to whelp?" Deegie asked.

"Yes. She's out of season. And she's a loner. That is why she was having so much trouble finding enough to eat. And why she came for the roast meat, and wanted the ermine so much. Look at her ribs. The pups have been taking a lot out of her. She's hardly more than bones and fur. If she lived with a pack, they'd be helping her feed those pups, but if she lived with a pack she would not have had pups. Only the female leader of a pack has pups, usually, and this wolf is the wrong colour. Wolves get used to certain colours and marks. She's like that white wolf I used to watch when I was learning about them. They didn't like her either. She was always trying to make up to the female leader and the male leader, but they didn't want her around. After the pack got so big, she left. Maybe she got tired of no one liking her."

Ayla looked down at the black wolf. "Like this one did. Maybe that's why she wanted to have pups, because she was lonely. But she shouldn't have had them so early. I think this is the same black wolf I saw when we hunted bison, Deegie. She must have left her pack to look for a lone male to start her own pack, new packs get started that way. But it's always hard on the loners. Wolves like to hunt together, and they take care of each other. The male leader always helps the female leader with her pups. You should see them sometimes, they like to play with the babies. But where is her male? Did she ever find one? Did he die?"

Deegie was surprised to see that Ayla was fighting tears, over a dead wolf. "They all die some time, Ayla. We all go back to the Mother."

"I know, Deegie, but first she was different, and then she was alone. She should have had something while she lived, a mate, a pack to belong to, at least some babies."

Deegie thought she was beginning to understand why Ayla was feeling so strongly about a scrawny old black wolf. She was putting herself in the wolf's place. "She did have pups, Ayla."

"And now they are going to die, too. They don't have a pack. Not even a male leader. Without a mother, they will die." Suddenly Ayla jumped up. "I'm not going to let them die!"

"What do you mean? Where are you going?"

"I'm going to find them. I'm going to track the black wolf back to her den."

"That could be dangerous. Maybe there are other wolves around. How can you be sure?"

"I'm sure, Deegie. I just have to look at her."

"Well, if I can't change your mind, I only have one thing to say, Ayla."

"What?"

"If you expect me to tramp all over the place chasing after wolf tracks with you, you can carry your own ermines," Deegie said, dumping out five white weasel carcasses from her haversack. "I've got enough to carry with my foxes!" Deegie was grinning with delight.

"Oh, Deegie," Ayla said, smiling back with warmth and affection. "You brought them!" The two young women hugged each other out of their fullness of love and friendship.

"One thing is certain, Ayla. Nothing is ever dull around you!" Deegie helped load Ayla's haversack with the ermine. "What are you going to do about the wolf? If we don't take her, something else will, and a black wolf pelt is not too common."

"I'd like to take her, but I want to find her pups, first."

"All right, I'll carry her," Deegie said, hoisting the limp carcass over her shoulder. "If we have time later, I'll skin it out." She started to ask one more question, then changed her mind. She'd find out soon enough exactly what Ayla planned to do if she found any wolf pups left alive.

They had to go back to the vale to pick up the correct sets of tracks. The wolf had done a good job of covering her trail, knowing how precarious was the life she was leaving untended. Several times, Deegie was sure they'd lost it and she was a good tracker herself, but Ayla was motivated to persist until she found it again. By the time they had found the place that Ayla was sure was the den, the sun was showing late afternoon.

"I have to be honest, Ayla. I don't see any signs of life."

"That's the way it should be if they are alone. If there were signs of life, it would just invite trouble."

"You might be right, but if there are pups in there, how are you going to get them to come out?"

"I guess there is only one way. I'll have to go in after them."

"You can't do that, Ayla! It's one thing to watch wolves from a distance, but you can't go into their dens. What if there are more than pups? There could be another adult wolf around."

"Have you seen any other adult tracks besides the black's?"

"No, but I still don't like the idea of you going into a wolf's den."

"I haven't come this far to go away without finding out if there are any wolf pups around. I have to go in, Deegie."

Ayla put down her haversack and headed for the small dark hole in the ground. It was dug out of an old lair, abandoned long before because it was not the most favourable location, but it was the best the black wolf could find after her mate, an old lone wolf drawn to her too-early heat, died in a fight. Ayla got down on her belly, and started to wriggle in.

"Ayla, wait!" Deegie called. "Here, take my knife."

Ayla nodded, put the knife in her teeth, and started into the dark hole. It sloped downward at first, and the passage was narrow. Suddenly she found herself stuck and had to back out.

"We better go, Ayla. It's getting late, and if you can't get in, you can't get in."

"No," she said, pulling her parka off over her head. "I'll get in."

She shivered with the cold until she was inside the den, but it was a tight fit through the first tunnel section, where it sloped down. Near the bottom, where it levelled out, there was more room, but the den seemed deserted. With her own body still blocking the light, it took a while for her eyes to become accustomed to the darkness, but it wasn't until she started to back out that she thought she heard a sound.

"Wolf, little wolf, are you here?" she called, then remembering the many times she had watched and listened to wolves, she voiced a pleading whine. Then she listened. A tiny soft whimper came from the deepest, dark recess of the den, and Ayla felt like shouting for joy.

She wormed her way closer to the sound, and whined again. The whimper was closer, and then she saw two shining eyes, but when she reached for the pup, the wolf backed up and hissed a little snarl, and she felt sharp needle teeth bite her hand.

"Ow! You've got some fight in you," Ayla said, and then smiled, "some life in you, yet. Come on now, little wolf. It's going to be all right. Come on." She reached for the wolf pup again, making her pleading whine, and felt a fuzzy ball of fur. Getting a good hold, she pulled the pup, spitting and fighting all the way, towards her. Then she backed up out of the den.

"Look what I found, Deegie!" Ayla said, grinning triumphantly as she held up a little grey fuzzy wolf puppy.

23

Jondalar was outside the lodge, pacing back and forth between the main entrance and the horse annexe. Even in the warm parka he wore, an old one of Talut's, he was feeling the drop in temperature as the sun closed with the horizon. Several times he had climbed the slope in the direction Ayla and Deegie had taken and was considering climbing it again.

He had been trying to quell his anxiety ever since the two young women left that morning, and when he first began his worried pacing early in the afternoon, others in the earthlodge smiled condescendingly, but he was no longer alone in his concern. Tulie had hiked up the slope a few times herself, and Talut was talking about getting a group together to go look for them with torches. Even Whinney and Racer seemed nervous.

As the brilliant fire in the west slid behind a bank of clouds hanging near the edge of the earth, it emerged as a sharply defined bright red circle of light; an otherworldly circle without depth or dimension, too perfect, too symmetrical to belong to the natural environment. But the glowing red orb lent colour to clouds and a tinge of health to the pale partial face of the other unearthly companion, which was low in the eastern sky.

Just as Jondalar was about to climb up the slope again, two figures appeared at the top, silhouetted against a vivid lavender background that shaded into deep indigo. A single star glinted overhead. He breathed a great sigh and slumped against the arched tusks, feeling light-headed with the sudden release of tension. They were safe. Ayla was safe.

But why were they gone so long? They should know better than to make everyone worry so much. What could have kept them out so long? Maybe they were in trouble. He should have followed them.

"They're here! They're here!" Latie was shouting.

People ran out of the earthlodge half clothed; those that were out and dressed raced up to meet them.

"What took you so long? It's almost dark. Where were you?" Jondalar demanded as soon as Ayla reached the lodge.

She looked at him in astonishment.

"Let's get them inside first," Tulie said. Deegie knew her mother was not pleased, but they had been out all day, they were tired, and it was getting colder fast. Recriminations could come later, after Tulie made sure they were all right. They were hustled in, straight through the foyer and into the cooking hearth.

Deegie, grateful to unload, lifted off the carcass of the black wolf, which had stiffened to the shape of her shoulder. When she dropped it on a mat, there were exclamations of surprise, and Jondalar blanched. There had been trouble.

"That's a wolf!" Druwez said, eyeing his sister with awe. "Where did you get that wolf?"

"Wait until you see what Ayla has," Deegie said, taking the white foxes out of her haversack.

Ayla was dumping frozen ermine out of her carrier with one hand, holding the other carefully against her midriff on top of her warm, hooded, fur tunic.

"Those are very nice ermine," Druwez said, not nearly as impressed with the small white weasels as he was with the black wolf, but not wanting to offend.

Ayla smiled at the boy, then she untied the thong she had belted around her parka, and reaching under, withdrew a small grey ball of fur. Everyone looked to see what she had. Suddenly it moved.

The wolf puppy had slept comfortably against Ayla's warm body underneath her outer garment, but the light, and the noise, and the unfamiliar smells were frightening. The pup whimpered and tried to snuggle against the woman whose smell and warmth had become familiar. She put the small fuzzy creature down on the soil of the drawing pit. The puppy stood up, wobbled a few steps, then promptly squatted and made a puddle that was quickly absorbed by the soft dry dirt.

"It's a wolf!" Danug said.

"A baby wolf!" Latie added, her eyes filled with delight.

Ayla noticed Rydag hunkering close to look at the small animal. He reached out a hand, and the puppy sniffed it, and then licked it. Rydag's smile was pure joy.

"Where you get little wolf, Ayla?" the boy signed.

"Is long story," she signalled back, "will tell later." She quickly pulled off her parka. Nezzie took it and handed her a cup of hot tea. She smiled gratefully and took a sip.

"It doesn't matter where she got it. What is she going to do with it?" Frebec demanded. Ayla knew he understood the silent language, though he claimed he didn't. He had obviously understood Rydag. She turned and faced him.

"I am going to take care of it, Frebec," Ayla said, her eyes blazing with defiance. "I killed its mother" – she motioned towards the black wolf – "and I'm going to take care of this baby."

"That's not a baby. That's a wolf! An animal that can hurt people," he said. Ayla seldom took such a strong stand with him or anyone, and he had discovered she would often give in on small issues to avoid conflict if he was nasty enough. He didn't expect the direct confrontation, and he didn't like it, especially when he could sense it was not likely to go his way.

Manuv looked at the wolf puppy, and then at Frebec, and his face split into a wide grin. "Are you afraid that animal is going to hurt you, Frebec?"

The raucous laughter made Frebec flush with anger. "I didn't mean that. I mean wolves can hurt people. First it's horses, now it's wolves. What next? I am not an animal, and I don't want to live with animals," he said. Then he stomped away, not ready to test whether the rest of the Lion Camp would rather have him or Ayla and her animals if he forced them to make a choice.

"Do you have meat left from that bison roast, Nezzie?"

"You must be starving. I'll fix you a plate of dinner."

"Not for me. For the wolf puppy," Ayla said.

Nezzie brought Ayla a slab of roast meat, wondering how such a small wolf was going to eat it. But Ayla remembered a lesson she had learned long ago: babies can eat whatever their mothers eat, but it must be softer and easier to chew and swallow. She had once brought an injured young cave lion cub to her valley and fed him meat and broth instead of milk. Wolves were meat-eaters, too. She recalled that when she was watching wolves to learn about them, older wolves often chewed up food and swallowed it to bring it back to the den, then regurgitated it for the puppies. But she didn't have to chew it up, she had hands and a sharp knife, she could cut it up.

After mincing the meat to a pulp, Ayla put it in a bowl and added warm water, to bring the temperature closer to mother's milk. The puppy had been sniffing around the edges of the drawing pit, but seemed afraid to venture beyond its boundaries. Ayla sat down on the mat, held out her hand and softly called to the wolf. She had taken the baby from a cold and lonely place and brought it warmth and comfort, and her scent was already associated with security. The fuzzy fur ball waddled towards her outstretched hand.

She picked it up first to examine it. Close scrutiny revealed the little wolf was a male, and very young, probably no more than one full cycle of moon phases had passed since he was born. She wondered if he'd had siblings, and if he did, when they died. He was not injured in any way that she could tell, and he did not seem to be malnourished, though the black wolf had certainly been scrawny. When Ayla thought about the terrible odds the black had fought to keep this one pup alive, it reminded her of an ordeal she had once faced and it strengthened her resolve. If she could, she was going to keep the mother wolf's son alive, whatever it took, and not Frebec or anyone else was going to stop her.

Holding the pup in her lap, Ayla dipped her finger in the bowl of finely minced meat and held it under the baby wolf's nose. He was hungry. He nosed it, licked it, and then licked her finger clean. She scooped up another fingerful, and he eagerly licked that off, too. She held him on her lap, and continued to feed him, feeling his little belly round out. When she felt he had enough, she held a little water under his nose, but he only sampled. Then she got up and carried him to the Mammoth Hearth.

"I think you'll find some old baskets on that bench over there," Mamut said, following behind her.

She smiled at him. He knew exactly what she had in mind. She rummaged around and found a large woven cooking container, falling apart at one end, and put it on the platform near the head of her bed. But when she put the wolf in it, he whimpered to get out. She picked him up and looked around again, not sure what would work. She was tempted to take him into her bed, but she'd been through that with growing baby horses and lions. It was too hard getting them to change their habits later, and besides, Jondalar might not want to share his bed with a wolf.

"He's not happy in the basket. He probably wants his mother or other puppies to sleep with," Ayla said.

"Give him something of yours, Ayla," Mamut said. "Something soft, comfortable, familiar. You're his mother now."

She nodded and looked over her small assortment of clothes. She didn't have much. Her beautiful outfit from Deegie, the one she had made in the valley before she came, and some used odds and ends given to her by other people for changes. She'd had plenty of spare wraps when she lived with the Clan, and even in the valley . . .

She noticed the backframe she had brought from the valley put aside in a far corner of the storage platform. She looked through it and pulled out Durc's cloak, but after holding it for a moment, she folded it and put it back. She couldn't bear to give it up. Then she found her old Clan wrap, a large old hide of soft leather. She had worn one like it, wrapped around her and tied with a long thong, for as long as she could remember, until the day she first left her valley with Jondalar. It seemed so long ago now. She lined the basket with the Clan wrap, and put the wolf puppy in it. He sniffed around, then quickly snuggled in and was soon sound asleep.

Suddenly she realised how tired she was, and hungry, and her clothes were still damp from the snow. She took off wet boots, and the lining made of felted mammoth wool, and changed into one of her dry outfits and the soft indoor footwear Talut had shown her how to make. She had been intrigued by the pair he had worn at her adoption ceremony, and prevailed upon him to show her how they were made.

They were based on a natural characteristic of elk or deer: the hind leg bends so sharply at the gambrel joint, it conforms to the natural shape of a human foot. The skin was cut above and below the joint and taken off in one piece. After curing, the lower end was then sewn with sinew to the desired size, and the upper part wrapped and laced above the ankle with cords or thongs. The result was a seamless, warm, and comfortable leather stocking-shoe.

After she changed, Ayla went into the annexe to check on the horses, and reassure them, but she noticed a hesitation and a resistance from the mare when she went to pet her.

"You smell the wolf, don't you, Whinney? You will have to get used to it. Both of you. The wolf is going to be here with us, for a while." She held out her hands and let both horses sniff them. Racer backed off, snorted and tossed his head, and sniffed again. Whinney put her muzzle into the woman's hands, but her ears flattened back and she bobbed indecisively. "You got used to Baby, Whinney, you can get used to . . . Wolf. I'll bring him out here tomorrow, when he wakes up. When you see how little he is, you will know he can't hurt you."

When Ayla went back in, she saw Jondalar by the bed looking at the wolf puppy. His expression was unreadable, but she thought she saw curiosity and something like tenderness in his eyes. He looked up and saw her, and his forehead furrowed in a familiar way.

"Ayla, why did you stay out so long?" he said. "Everyone was getting ready to search for you."

"We didn't plan to, but once I saw that the black wolf I killed was nursing, I had to see if I could find her pups," Ayla said.

"What difference did it make? Wolves die all the time, Ayla!" He had started out talking to her in a reasonable tone, but his fear for her safety was putting an edge on his voice. "It was stupid to go tracking after a wolf like that. If you had found a wolf pack, they could have killed you." Jondalar had been beside himself with worry, but with relief came uncertainty, and a touch of frustrated anger.

"It made a difference to me, Jondalar," she flared, jumping to the defence of the wolf. "And I am not stupid. I hunted meat-eaters before I hunted anything else. I know wolves. If there had been a pack, I would not have backtracked to her den. The pack would have taken care of her pups."

"Even if she was a lone wolf, why did you spend all day chasing after a wolf puppy?" Jondalar's voice had got louder. He was releasing his own tensions as well as trying to convince her not to take such chances again.

"That puppy was all that mother wolf ever had. I could not let him starve because I killed his mother. If someone hadn't cared about me when I was young, I would not be alive. I have to care, too, even for a wolf puppy." Ayla's voice had risen, too.

"It's not the same. A wolf is an animal. You should have better sense, Ayla, than to threaten your own life for the sake of a wolf puppy," Jondalar shouted. He couldn't seem to make her understand. "This is not the kind of weather to be out in all day."

"I have good sense, Jondalar," Ayla said with anger flashing in her eyes. "I was the one who was out. Don't you think I know what the weather was like? Don't you think I know when my life is in danger? I took care of myself before you came, and faced far worse dangers. I even took care of you. I don't need you to tell me I am stupid and don't have sense."

People who were gathering at the Mammoth Hearth were reacting to the quarrel, smiling nervously and trying to make less of it. Jondalar glanced around and noticed several people smiling and talking among themselves, but the one who stood out was the dark man with the flashing eyes. Was there a hint of condescension in his broad smile?

"You're right, Ayla. You don't need me, do you? For anything," Jondalar spat, then seeing Talut approaching, he asked, "Would you mind if I moved to the cooking hearth, Talut? I'll try to stay out of everyone's way."

"No, of course I don't mind, but . . ."

"Good. Thank you," he said, and grabbed his bedding and belongings from the bed platform he shared with Ayla.

Ayla was stricken, beside herself to think he might really want to sleep away from her. She was almost ready to beg him not to leave, but her pride held her tongue. He had shared her bed, but they hadn't shared Pleasures in so long she was sure he had stopped loving her. If he didn't love her any more, she would not try to force him to stay, though the thought of it wrenched her stomach into a knot of fear and grief.

"You'd better take your share of food, too," she said, as he stuffed things into a back carrier. Then, trying to find a way to make the separation not quite so complete, she added, "Though I don't know who will cook for you there. It is not a real hearth."

"Who do you think cooked for me when I was on my Journey? A

donii? I don't need a woman to take care of me. I'll cook for myself!"
He stomped away, his arms full of furs, through the Fox Hearth and the
Lion Hearth, and threw his bedding down near the tool-working area.
Ayla watched him go, not wanting to believe it.

The lodge was buzzing with talk about their separation. Deegie hurried
down the passageway after hearing the news, finding it hard to believe.
She and her mother had gone to the Aurochs Hearth while Ayla was
feeding the wolf and spoken together quietly for some time. Deegie,
who had also changed into dry clothes, looked both chastened and
resolute. Yes, they should not have stayed out so long, for their own
safety as well as for the concern they caused others, but no, under the
circumstances, she would not have done anything differently. Tulie
would like to have spoken to Ayla as well, but felt it would be inappropriate, especially after hearing Deegie's story. Ayla had told Deegie to go
back before they started their senseless wolf attacking, and they were
both grown young women who should be perfectly able to take care of
themselves by now, but Tulie had never been so worried about Deegie
in her life.

Nezzie nudged Tronie, and they both filled plates with warmed food
and brought it to the Mammoth Hearth for Ayla and Deegie. Maybe
things would straighten out after they had something to eat and had a
chance to tell their story.

Everyone had held off asking about the wolf pup until the necessities
of warmth and food for the young women, and the little wolf, had been
attended to. Though she had been hungry, Ayla found it hard now to
put food in her mouth. She kept looking in the direction Jondalar had
gone. Everyone else seemed to find their way to the Mammoth Hearth,
anticipating the story of an exciting and unusual adventure, which could
be told and retold. Whether she was in the mood or not, they all wanted
to know the story of how she arrived back at the lodge with a baby
wolf.

Deegie began by relating the strange circumstances of the white foxes
in the snares. She was quite certain now it was the black wolf, weakened
and hungry, and unable to hunt deer or horse or bison alone, that had
been driven to taking the foxes from the traps for food. Ayla suggested
that the black might have followed Deegie's trail from trap to trap when
she set them. Then Deegie told of Ayla wanting white fur to make
something for someone, but not white fox fur this time, and tracking
the ermine.

Jondalar arrived after the storytelling began, and was trying to remain
quietly unnoticed sitting near the far wall. He was already sorry and
berating himself for leaving so hastily, but he felt the blood drain from
his face when he heard Deegie's remark. If Ayla was making something

362

with white fur for someone, and did not want winter fox, it must be because she had already given that someone white winter fox. And he knew to whom she had given white fox furs at her adoption ceremony. Jondalar closed his eyes and clenched his fists in his lap. He didn't even want to think it, but he couldn't keep the thoughts from his mind. Ayla must be making something for the dark man who looked so stunning in white fur; for Ranec.

Ranec wondered, too, who the someone was. He suspected it was Jondalar, but he hoped it might be someone else, maybe even him. It gave him an idea, though. Whether she was making something for him or not, he could still make something for her. He recalled her excitement and delight over the carved horse he had given her, and grew warm at the thought of carving something else for her; something that would delight her and excite her again, especially now that the big blond man had moved away. Jondalar's presence had always acted as a restraining influence, but if he was willingly abdicating his primary position, leaving her bed and her hearth, then Ranec felt free to pursue her more actively.

The little wolf whimpered in his sleep, and Ayla, sitting on the edge of her bed platform, reached over and stroked him to calm him. The only time in his young life that he had felt as warm and secure as he did now was when he had been nestled beside his mother, and she had left him alone many times in the cold dark den. But Ayla's hand had taken him out of that cheerless and frighteningly alone place, and brought him warmth and food and a feeling of safety. He settled down under her reassuring touch without even waking.

Ayla let Deegie continue the story, only adding comments and explanations. She didn't feel much like talking, and it was interesting that the other young woman's story was not the same one she would have told. It wasn't less true, but seen from a different viewpoint, and Ayla was a little surprised at some of her companion's impressions. She hadn't seen the situation as quite so dangerous. Deegie had been much more frightened of the wolf; she didn't seem to really understand them.

Wolves were among the gentlest of meat-eaters, and very predictable, if you paid attention to their signals – weasels were far more bloodthirsty and bears more unpredictable. It was rare for wolves to attack humans. But Deegie didn't see them that way. She described the wolf as viciously attacking Ayla, and she had been afraid. It had been dangerous, but even if Ayla hadn't fended it off, the attack was defensive. She might have been hurt, but she probably would not have been killed, and the wolf had backed down as soon as she could grab the dead ermine and get away. When Deegie described Ayla diving head first into the wolf's den, the Camp looked at her in awe. She was either very brave or very foolhardy, but Ayla didn't think she was either. She knew there were no other adult wolves around, there were no other tracks. The black had been a lone wolf, probably far from her home territory, and the black was dead.

Deegie's vivid recounting of Ayla's exploits did more than cause awe in one of the listeners. Jondalar had been growing more and more agitated. In his mind he embellished the story even more, envisioned Ayla not only in great danger, but attacked by wolves, hurt and bleeding, and perhaps worse. He couldn't bear the thought, and his earlier anxiety returned in redoubled force. Other people had similar feelings.

"You should not have put yourself in such danger, Ayla," the head-woman said.

"Mother!" Deegie said. The woman had indicated earlier that she would not bring up her concerns.

People who were still caught up in the adventure scowled at her for interrupting a dramatic story, told with skill. That it was true, made it more exciting, and though it would be told and retold, it would never again have the fresh impact of the first hearing. The mood was being spoiled – after all, she was back home and safe now.

Ayla looked at Tulie, then glanced at Jondalar. She had known the moment he came back to the Mammoth Hearth. He had been angry, and so, it seemed, was Tulie. "I was not in such danger," she said.

"You do not think it is dangerous to go into a wolves' den?" Tulie asked.

"No. There was no danger. It was the den of a lone wolf, and she was dead. I only went in to look for her babies."

"That may be, but was it necessary to stay out so late tracking the wolf? It was almost dark before you returned," Tulie said.

Jondalar had said the same thing. "But I knew the black had young, she was nursing. Without a mother, they would die," Ayla explained, although she had said it before and thought it was understood.

"So you endanger your own life" – and Deegie's, she thought, though she did not say it – "for the life of a wolf? After the black one attacked you, it was foolhardy to continue to chase it just to get back the ermine it took. You should have let it go."

"I disagree, Tulie," Talut interjected. Everyone turned towards the headman. "There was a starving wolf in the vicinity, one that had already trailed Deegie when she set her traps. Who's to say it wouldn't have trailed her back here? The weather is getting warmer, children are playing outside more. If that wolf got desperate enough, it might have attacked one of the children, and we would not have expected it. Now we know the wolf is dead. It's better that way."

People were nodding their heads in agreement, but Tulie was not to be put off so easily. "Perhaps it was better that the wolf was killed, but you can't say it was necessary to stay out so long looking for the wolf's young. And now that she's found the wolf pup, what are we going to do with it?"

"I think Ayla did the right thing in going after the wolf and killing it, but it is a shame that a nursing mother had to be killed. All mothers deserve the right to raise their young, even mother wolves. But more than that, it was not an entirely useless effort for Ayla and Deegie to track back to the wolf den, Tulie. They did more than find a wolf pup. Since they found only one set of tracks, now we know there are no other starving wolves nearby. And if in the name of the Mother, Ayla took pity on the wolf mother's young, I don't see any harm in that. It's such a tiny little pup."

"Now it's a tiny little pup, but it won't stay little. What do we do with a full-grown wolf around the lodge? How do you know it won't attack the children, then?" Frebec asked. "There will soon be a small baby at our hearth."

"Considering her way with animals, I think Ayla would know how to keep that wolf from hurting anyone. But more than that, I will say now, as headman of the Lion Camp, if there is even a hint that that wolf might hurt someone –" Talut stared pointedly at Ayla – "I will kill him. Do you agree to that, Ayla?"

All eyes turned to her. She flushed and stammered at first, and then spoke what she felt. "I cannot say for certain that this pup will not hurt someone when he is grown. I cannot even say if he will stay. I raised a horse from a baby. She left to find her stallion and joined a herd for a while, but she came back. I also raised a cave lion until he was full-grown. Whinney was like a mother's helper to Baby when he was little and they became friends. Even though cave lions hunt horses, and could easily have harmed me, he did not threaten either of us. He was always just my Baby.

"When Baby left to find a mate, he did not come back, not to stay, but he visited, and sometimes we met him on the steppes. He never threatened Whinney or Racer, or me, even after he found a mate and started his own pride. Baby attacked two men who went into his den, and killed one, but when I told him to go away and leave Jondalar and his brother alone, he went. A cave lion and a wolf are both meat-eaters. I have lived with a cave lion, and I have watched wolves. I do not think a wolf that grows up with the people of a Camp will ever hurt them, but I will say here, that if there is any hint of danger to any child, or any person" – she swallowed a few times – "I, Ayla of the Mamutoi, will kill him myself."

Ayla decided to introduce the wolf pup to Whinney and Racer the following morning so they could get accustomed to his scent and avoid unnecessary nervousness. After feeding him, she picked up the little canine and took him out to the horse annexe to meet the equine pair. Unknown to her, several people had seen her go.

Before she approached the horses with the young wolf, however, she picked up a dried chunk of horse dung, crushed it and rubbed him with the fibrous dust. Ayla hoped the steppes horse would be willing to befriend another baby hunting animal as she had the cave lion, but she recalled that Whinney had been more accepting of Baby after he had rolled in her dung.

When she held out the handful of fuzzy fur to Whinney, the mare shied away at first, but her natural curiosity won out. She advanced cautiously, and smelled the comforting, familiar scent of horse along with the more disturbing wolf odour. Racer was equally curious, and less cautious. While he had an instinctive wariness of wolves, he had never lived with a wild herd and had never been the object of pursuit by a pack of proficient hunters. He stepped up to the warm and living, interesting, though vaguely threatening, furry thing which Ayla held cupped in both hands, and stretched forward for a closer inspection.

After the two horses had sniffed sufficiently to familiarise themselves with the puppy, Ayla put him down on the ground in front of the two large grazers, and heard a gasp. She glanced towards the Mammoth Hearth entrance and noticed Latie holding open the drape. Talut, Jondalar, and several others crowded close behind her. They didn't want to disturb her, but they, too, were curious, and couldn't resist the urge to see the first meeting of the baby wolf and the horses. Small though he was, the wolf was a predator, and horses were wolves' natural prey. But hooves and teeth could be formidable weapons. Horses had been known to wound or kill full-grown attacking wolves and could easily make short work of so small a predator.

The horses knew they were in no danger from the young hunter, and quickly overcame their initial wariness. More than one person smiled to see the wobbly little wolf, not much bigger than a hoof, looking up the massive legs of the strange giants. Whinney lowered her head and nosed forward, pulled back, then poked her long mobile nose towards the wolf again. Racer approached the interesting baby from the other side. The wolf puppy huddled down and cringed when he saw the huge heads approaching him. But from the point of view of the small puppy, the world was populated by giants. The humans, even the woman who fed and comforted him, were gigantic, too.

He detected no threat in the warm breath blowing from the flaring nostrils. To the wolf's sensitive nose, the scent of these horses was familiar. It permeated Ayla's clothing and belongings, and even the woman herself. The baby wolf decided that these four-legged giants were part of his pack, too, and with his normal puppyish eagerness to please, reached up to touch his tiny black nose to the soft warm nose of the mare.

"They're touching noses!" Ayla heard Latie say in a loud whisper.

When the wolf started to lick the muzzle of the mare, which was the usual way puppies approached members of their pack, Whinney lifted her head quickly. But she was too intrigued to stay away for long from the startling little animal, and was soon accepting the caressing warm licks of the tiny predator.

After a few moments of mutual getting acquainted, Ayla picked up the young wolf to carry him back in. It had been an auspicious beginning, but she decided not to overdo it. Later, she would take him out for a ride.

Ayla had seen a look of amused tenderness on Jondalar's face when the animals met. It was an expression that once had been so familiar to her, it filled her with an unaccountable surge of happiness. Perhaps he would be willing to move back to the Mammoth Hearth, now that he had time to think about it. But when she went inside and smiled at him – her big beautiful smile – he averted his face and lowered his eyes, then quickly followed Talut back to the cooking hearth. Ayla bowed her head as her joy evaporated, leaving an aching heaviness in its place, convinced he didn't care about her any more.

Nothing was further from the truth. He was sorry he had acted so hastily, ashamed that he had displayed such immature behaviour, and certain that he was no longer welcome after his abrupt departure. He did not think her smile was really intended for him. He believed that it was a result of the successful meeting of the animals, but the sight of it filled him with such an agony of love and yearning, he couldn't bear to be near her.

Ranec saw Ayla's eyes follow after the back of the big man. He wondered how long their separation would last, and what effect it would have. Though he was almost afraid to hope, he could not help but think that Jondalar's absence might increase his chances with Ayla. He had some notion that he was in part a cause of the separation, but he felt the problem between them went deeper. Ranec had made his interest in Ayla obvious, and neither of them had indicated that it was wholly misplaced. Jondalar had not confronted him with a definitive statement of his intention to join with Ayla in an exclusive union; he had just acted with suppressed anger and withdrawn. And while Ayla had not exactly encouraged him, she had not turned him away either.

It was true, Ayla did welcome Ranec's company. She wasn't sure what was causing Jondalar to be so aloof, but she felt certain it was something that she was doing wrong. Ranec's attentive presence made her feel that her behaviour could not be entirely inappropriate.

Latie was standing beside Ayla, her eyes bright with interest in the wolf puppy she held. Ranec joined them.

"That was a sight I'll never forget, Ayla," Ranec said. "That tiny thing touching noses with that huge horse. He's a brave little wolf."

She looked up and smiled, as pleased at Ranec's praise as she would have been if the animal were her own child. "Wolf was frightened at first. They are much bigger than he is. I'm glad they made friends so fast."

"Is that what you are going to call him? Wolf?" Latie asked.

"I haven't really thought about it. It does seem a fitting name, though."

"I can't think of one more fitting," Ranec conceded.

"What do you think, Wolf?" Ayla asked, holding the baby wolf up and looking at him. The puppy squirmed towards her eagerly, and licked her face. They all smiled.

"I think he likes it," Latie said.

"You do know animals, Ayla," Ranec said, then with a questioning look, he added, "There is something I'd like to ask you, though. How did you know the horses wouldn't hurt him? Wolf packs hunt horses, and I've seen horses kill wolves. They are mortal enemies."

Ayla paused and considered. "I'm not sure. I just knew. Maybe because of Baby. Cave lions kill horses, too, but you should have seen Whinney with him when he was little. She was so protective, like a mother, or at least an aunt. Whinney knew a baby wolf couldn't hurt her, and Racer seemed to know it, too. I think if you start when they are babies, many animals can be friends, and friends of people, too."

"Is that why Whinney and Racer are your friends?" Latie asked.

"Yes, I think so. We've had time to get used to each other. That's what Wolf needs."

"Do you think he might get used to me?" Latie asked, with such yearning, Ayla smiled with recognition of the feeling.

"Here," she said, holding the puppy out to the girl. "Hold him."

Latie cuddled the warm and wriggling animal in her arms, then bent

368

her cheek to feel the soft fuzzy fur. Wolf licked her face, too, including her in his pack.

"I think he likes me," Latie said. "He just kissed me!"

Ayla smiled at the delighted reaction. She knew such friendliness was natural to wolf puppies; the humans seemed to find it as irresistible as adult wolves did. Only when they grew older did wolves become shy, defensive, and suspicious of strangers.

The young woman observed the pup with curiosity as Latie held him. Wolf's coat was still the unshaded dark grey colour of the very young. Only later would the hair develop the dark and light bars of the typical agouti colouration of an adult wolf – if it would at all. His mother had been solid black, even darker than the pup, and Ayla wondered what colour Wolf would turn out to be.

They all turned their head at Crozie's screech.

"Your promises mean nothing. You promised me respect! You promised I would always be welcome, no matter what!"

"I know what I promised. You don't have to remind me," Frebec shouted.

The squabble was not unexpected. The long winter had provided time to make and mend, to carve and to weave, to tell stories, sing songs, play games and musical instruments; to indulge in all the pastimes and diversions ever invented. But as the long season drew to a close, it was also the time when close confinement caused tempers to flare. The undercurrent of conflict between Frebec and Crozie had caused such strained relations that most people felt an outbreak was imminent.

"Now you say you want me to leave. I am a mother with no place to go, and you want me to leave. Is that keeping your promise?"

The verbal battle was carried along the passageway and soon arrived in full force at the Mammoth Hearth. The wolf puppy, frightened by the noise and commotion, squirmed out of Latie's arms, and was gone before she could see where he went.

"I keep my promises," Frebec said. "You didn't hear me right. What I meant was . . ." He had made promises to her, but he didn't know then what it would be like to live with the old harridan. If only he could just have Fralie and not have to put up with her mother, he thought, looking around trying to think of some way to get out of the corner Crozie had put him in.

"What I meant was . . ." He noticed Ayla and looked directly at her. "We need more room. The Crane Hearth isn't big enough for us. And what are we going to do when the baby comes? There seems to be plenty of room in this hearth, even for animals!"

369

"It's not for the animals, the Mammoth Hearth was this size before Ayla came," Ranec said, coming to Ayla's defence. "Everyone in the Camp congregates here, it has to be larger. Even then it gets crowded. You can't have a hearth this big."

"Did I ask for one this big? I only said ours wasn't big enough. Why should the Lion Camp make room for animals but not for people?"

More people were coming to see what was going on. "You can't take room from the Mammoth Hearth," Deegie said, making room for the old shaman to come forward. "Tell him, Mamut."

"No one made room for the wolf. He sleeps in a basket near her head," Mamut began in a reasonable tone. "You imply Ayla has this entire hearth, but she has little space to call her own. People gather here whether there is a ceremony or not, particularly the children. There is always someone around, including Fralie and her children sometimes."

"I have told Fralie I don't like her to spend so much time here, but she says she needs more room to spread out her work. Fralie would not have to come here to work if we had more room at our hearth."

Fralie blushed, and went back to the Crane Hearth. She had told Frebec that, but it wasn't entirely true. She also liked to spend time at the Mammoth Hearth for the company, and because Ayla's advice had helped with her difficult pregnancy. Now Fralie felt she would have to stay away.

"Anyway, I wasn't talking about the wolf," Frebec continued, "though no one asked me if I wanted to share the lodge with that animal. Just because one person wants to bring animals here, I don't know why I should have to live with them. I'm not an animal, and I didn't grow up with them, but around here animals are worth more than people. This whole Camp will build a separate room for horses, while we are squeezed into the smallest hearth in the lodge!"

An uproar ensued with everybody shouting at once, trying to make themselves heard.

"What do you mean, 'the smallest hearth in the lodge'?" Tornec stormed. "We have no more room than you, maybe less, and just as many people!"

"That's true," Tronie said. Manuv was vigorously nodding his head in agreement.

"No one has much room," Ranec said.

"He's right!" Tronie agreed again, with more vehemence. "I think even the Lion Hearth is smaller than yours, Frebec, and they have more people than you, and bigger ones, too. They are really cramped. Maybe they should have some of the space from the cooking hearth. If any hearth deserves it, they do."

"But the Lion Hearth is not asking for more room," Nezzie tried to say.

Ayla looked from one person to the next, unable to understand how the entire Camp had suddenly become embroiled in a vociferous argument, but feeling that somehow it was all her fault.

In the midst of it all, a loud bellow suddenly roared out that overpowered all the commotion and stopped everyone. Talut stood in the middle of the hearth with commanding assurance. His feet were spread apart and in his right hand was the enigmatically decorated, long, straight ivory shaft. Tulie joined him, lending her presence and authority. Ayla felt daunted by the powerful pair.

"I have brought the Speaking Staff," Talut said, holding up the shaft and shaking it to make his point. "We will discuss this problem peaceably and settle it equitably."

"In the name of the Mother, let no one dishonour the Speaking Staff," Tulie added. "Who will speak first?"

"I think Frebec should speak first," Ranec said. "He's the one with the problem."

Ayla had been edging towards the periphery, trying to get away from the noisy, shouting people. She noticed that Frebec seemed uncomfortable and nervous with all the unfriendly attention focused on him. Ranec's comment had carried the strong implication that the imbroglio was entirely his fault. Ayla, standing somewhat hidden behind Danug, studied Frebec closely for perhaps the first time.

He was of average height, perhaps a bit less. Now that she noticed it, she thought she was probably slightly taller than he, but she was somewhat taller than Barzec, too, and probably matched Wymez in height. She was so used to being taller than everyone, she hadn't paid attention before. Frebec had light brown hair, thinning somewhat, eyes of a medium shade of blue, and straight, even features with no disfigurements. He was an ordinary-looking man and she could find nothing to account for his belligerent, offensive behaviour. There were times when Ayla was growing up that she wished she had looked as much like the rest of the Clan as Frebec looked like his people.

As Frebec stepped forward and took the Speaking Staff from Talut, Ayla noticed Crozie out of the corner of her eye, with a gloating smirk on her face. Certainly the old woman was at least partially to blame for Frebec's actions, but was that all? There had to be more to it. Ayla looked for Fralie, but didn't see her among the people gathered in the Mammoth Hearth. Then she noticed the pregnant woman watching from the edge of the Crane Hearth.

371

Frebec cleared his throat a few times, then shifting his hold on the ivory shaft and grasping firmly, he began. "Yes, I do have a problem." He looked around nervously, then scowling, he stood up straighter. "I mean, we have a problem, the Crane Hearth. There is not enough space. We have no room to work, it is the smallest hearth in the lodge . . ."

"It is not the smallest. Theirs is bigger than ours!" Tronie spoke out, unable to restrain herself.

Tulie fixed her with a stern eye. "You will have a chance to speak, Tronie, when Frebec is through."

Tronie blushed and mumbled apologies. Her embarrassment seemed to give Frebec encouragement. His stance became more aggressive.

"We don't have enough room now, Fralie doesn't have enough room to work, and . . . and Crozie needs more space. And soon there will be another person. I think we should have more room." Frebec gave the Staff back to Talut and stepped back.

"Tronie, you may speak now," Talut said.

"I don't think . . . I was just . . . well, maybe I will," she said, stepping forward to take the staff. "We don't have any more room than the Crane Hearth, and we have just as many people." Then she added, trying to enlist Talut's assistance, "I think even the Lion Hearth is smaller . . ."

"That is not important, Tronie," Talut said. "The Lion Hearth isn't asking for space and we are not close enough to the Crane Hearth to be affected by Frebec's desire for more room. You, at the Reindeer Hearth, do have a right to speak up since changes in the Crane Hearth are more likely to cause changes in your space. Is there anything else you want to say?"

"No, I don't think so," Tronie said, shaking her head, as she handed him the staff.

"Anyone else?"

Jondalar wished he could say something that would help, but he was an outsider and felt it wasn't his place to intrude. He wanted to be by Ayla's side, and was even more sorry now that he had moved his sleeping place. He was almost glad when Ranec stepped up and took the ivory shaft. Somebody needed to speak for her.

"It's not terribly important, but Frebec is exaggerating. I can't say whether or not they need more space, but the Crane Hearth is not the smallest hearth in the lodge. The Fox Hearth has that honour. But we are only two, and we are content."

There were murmurs, and Frebec glared at the carver. There had never been much understanding between the two men. Ranec had always felt they had little in common, and tended to ignore him. Frebec took it as disdain, and there was some truth to the feeling. Particularly since he had begun making disparaging remarks to Ayla, Ranec found little of worth in Frebec.

Talut, attempting to forestall another general argument, raised his voice and addressed Frebec. "How do you think the space in the lodge ought to be changed to give you more room?" He gave the long ivory pole to the man.

"I never said I wanted to take any space from the Reindeer Hearth, but it seems to me that if some people have space for animals, they have more room than they need. A whole annexe was added to the lodge for the horses, but no one seems to care that we will soon be adding another person. Maybe things could be . . . moved over." Frebec finished lamely. He was not happy to see Mamut reach for the Speaking Staff.

"Are you suggesting that in order to make more room at the Crane Hearth, the Reindeer Hearth should move into the Mammoth Hearth? That would be a great inconvenience for them. As for Fralie coming here to work, you are not suggesting that she confine herself to the Crane Hearth, are you? It would be unhealthy, and deprive her of the companionship she finds here. This is where she is supposed to bring her projects. This hearth is meant to accommodate work that takes more room than there is in anyone's personal hearth. The Mammoth Hearth belongs to everyone and it is almost too small for gatherings now."

When Mamut turned the Speaking Staff back to Talut, Frebec looked chastened, but he bristled defensively when Ranec took it again.

"As for the horse annexe, we will all benefit from that space, especially after storage cellars are dug. Even now, it has become a convenient entrance for many people. I notice you keep your outer clothes in there, and use it more often than the front way, Frebec," Ranec said. "Besides, babies are small. They don't take much space. I don't think you need more room."

"How would you know?" Crozie interjected. "You've never had one born to your hearth. Babies do take room, a lot more than you think."

Only after she said it did Crozie realise that for the first time, she had sided with Frebec. She frowned, then decided maybe he was right. Maybe they did need more room. It was true that the Mammoth Hearth was a gathering place, but it did seem to accord Ayla greater status because she lived at such a large hearth. Though everyone had considered it theirs when Mamut had lived there alone, now, except for ceremonial gatherings, everyone treated it as though it were Ayla's. A larger space for the Crane Hearth might increase the status of its members.

Everyone seemed to take Crozie's interruption as a signal for general comment, and with a knowing look passing between them, Talut and

Tulie allowed the outburst to run its course. Sometimes people needed to speak their minds. During the interruption, Tulie caught Barzec's eye and after things quieted down, he stepped forward and requested the Staff. Tulie nodded agreement, as though she knew what he was going to say although they had not spoken to each other.

"Crozie is right," he said, nodding towards her. She stood up straighter, accepting the acknowledgment, and her opinion of Barzec rose. "Babies do take room, much more room than one would think from their size. Perhaps it is time for some changes, but I don't think the Mammoth Hearth should give up space. The needs of the Crane Hearth are growing, but the needs of the Aurochs Hearth are less. Tarneg has gone to live at the Camp of his woman, and soon he will be starting a new Camp with Deegie. Then she will be gone, too. Therefore, the Hearth of the Aurochs, understanding the needs of a growing family, will give up some space to the Hearth of the Crane."

"Is that satisfactory to you, Frebec?" Talut asked.

"Yes," Frebec replied, hardly knowing how to respond to this unexpected turn of events.

"Then I will leave it to you to work out together how much space will be given by the Aurochs Hearth, but I think it is only fair that no changes be made until after Fralie has her baby. Do you agree?"

Frebec nodded, still overwhelmed. At his former Camp, he wouldn't have dreamed of asking for more space; if he had, he would have been laughed at. He didn't have the prerogative, the status, to make such requests. When the argument with Crozie began, space wasn't on his mind at all. He had just been groping for some way to respond to her stinging, though true, accusations. Now, he was convincing himself that lack of space had been the reason all along for the argument, and for once, she had taken his side. He felt the thrill of success. He had won a battle. Two battles: one with the Camp, one with Crozie. As the people dispersed, he saw Barzec talking with Tulie, and it occurred to him that he owed them thanks.

"I appreciate your understanding," Frebec said to the headwoman and the man of the Aurochs Hearth.

Barzec made the customary disclaimers, but they would not have been pleased if Frebec had failed to acknowledge the accommodation made to him. They knew full well the value of their concession went far beyond a few feet of space. It announced that the Crane Hearth had the status to merit such a grant from the hearth of the headwoman, though it was the status of Crozie and Fralie that they had in mind when Tulie and Barzec had previously discussed a shift in boundary between themselves. They had already anticipated the changing needs of the two families. Barzec had even considered bringing up the issue earlier, but

374

Tulie suggested they wait for a more appropriate moment, perhaps as a gift for the baby.

They both knew this was the moment. It had taken no more than looks and nods to signal each other. And since Frebec had just won a nominal victory, the Crane Hearth was bound to be conciliatory about adjusting the boundary. Barzec had just been remarking with pride how wise Tulie was when Frebec approached to make his thanks. As Frebec walked back to the Crane Hearth, he savoured the incident, tallying up the points he felt he had won, just as though it had been one of the games the Camp liked to play, and he was counting his winnings.

In a very real sense, it was a game, the very subtle and entirely serious game of comparative rank which is played by all social animals. It is the method by which individuals arrange themselves – horses in a herd, wolves in a pack, people in a community – so that they can live together. The game pits two opposing forces against each other, both equally important to survival: individual autonomy and community welfare. The object is to achieve dynamic equilibrium.

At times and under certain conditions individuals can be nearly autonomous. An individual can live alone and have no worry about rank, but no species can survive without interaction between individuals. The ultimate price would be more final than death. It would be extinction. On the other hand, complete individual subordination to the group is just as devastating. Life is neither static nor unchanging. With no individuality, there can be no change, no adaptation and, in an inherently changing world, any species unable to adapt is also doomed.

Humans in a community, whether it is as small as two people or as large as the world, and no matter what form the society takes, will arrange themselves according to some hierarchy. Commonly understood courtesies and customs can help to smooth the friction and ease the stress of maintaining a workable balance within this constantly changing system. In some situations most individuals will not have to compromise much of their personal independence for the welfare of the community. In others, the needs of the community may demand the utmost personal sacrifice of the individual, even to life itself. Neither is more right than the other, it depends on the circumstances, but neither extreme can be maintained for long, nor can a society last if a few people exercise their individuality at the expense of the community.

Ayla often found herself comparing Clan society with that of the Mamutoi, and began to get a glimmer of this principle as she thought about the different styles of leadership of Brun and the Lion Camp's headman and headwoman. She saw Talut return the Speaking Staff to its customary place and recalled that when she first arrived at the Mamutoi Camp, she thought that Brun was a better leader than Talut.

Brun would have simply made a decision and the others would have followed his order, whether they liked it or not. Not many would even consider questioning whether they liked it or not. Brun never had to argue or shout. A sharp look or a curt command brought instant attention. It had seemed to her that Talut had no control over the noisy, contentious people, and that they had no respect for him.

Now she wasn't so sure. It seemed to her that it was more difficult to lead a group of people who believed everyone, woman and man, had the right to speak out and be listened to. She still thought Brun had been a good leader for his society, but she wondered if he could have led these people who aired their views so freely. It could become very loud and noisy when everyone had an opinion and did not hesitate to make it known, but Talut never allowed it to go beyond certain bounds. Though he was certainly strong enough to have forced his will on people, he chose to lead by consensus and accommodation instead. He had certain sanctions and beliefs to call upon, and techniques of his own to get attention, but it took a different kind of strength to persuade rather than coerce. Talut gained respect by giving respect.

As Ayla walked towards a knot of people standing near the firepit, she glanced around the hearth looking for the wolf puppy. It was a subliminal gesture, and when she didn't see him she assumed he had found some place to hide during the commotion.

". . . Frebec certainly got his way," Tornec was saying, "thanks to Tulie and Barzec."

"For Fralie's sake, I'm glad," Tronie said, relieved to know the Reindeer Hearth would not be pushed over or squeezed. "I just hope it will keep Frebec quiet for a while. He really started a big fight this time."

"I don't like big fights like that," Ayla said, remembering that the fight had started over Frebec's complaint that her animals had more room than he did.

"Don't let it bother you," Ranec said. "It's been a long winter. Something like that happens around this time every year. It's just a little diversion to create some excitement."

"But he wouldn't have had to make such a fuss to get more room," Deegie said. "I heard mother and Barzec talking about it long before he brought it up. They were going to give space to the Crane Hearth as a gift for Fralie's baby. All Frebec needed to do was ask."

"That's why Tulie is such a good headwoman," Tronie said. "She thinks of things like that."

"She is good, and so is Talut," Ayla said.

"Yes, he is." Deegie smiled. "That's why he is still headman. No one stays leader for long if he can't command the respect of his people. I think Branag will be as good. He had Talut to learn from." The warm feelings between Deegie and her mother's brother went deeper than the formal avuncular relationship that, along with the status and inheritance from her mother, assured the young woman of a high standing among the Mamutoi.

"But who would become leader instead, if Talut didn't have respect?" Ayla asked. "And how?"

"Well . . . ah . . ." Deegie began. Then the young people turned to Mamut to answer her question.

"If it is the old former leaders turning over active leadership to a younger brother and sister, who have been selected – usually relatives – there is a period of learning, then a ceremony, then the older leaders become advisers," the shaman and teacher said.

"Yes. That's what Brun did. When he was younger, he respected old Zoug and paid attention to his advice, and when he got older, he turned the leadership over to Broud, the son of his mate. But what happens if a Camp loses respect for a leader? A young leader?" Ayla asked, very interested.

"The change would not happen quickly," Mamut said, "but people just would not turn to him after a while. They would go to someone else, someone who could lead a more successful hunt, or handle problems better. Sometimes the leadership is relinquished, sometimes a Camp just breaks up, with some going with the new leader, and some staying with the old. But leaders don't usually give up their positions or authority easily, and that can cause problems, even fights. Then the decision would get turned over to the Councils. The headman or headwoman who has shared leadership with someone who causes trouble, or is held responsible for a problem, is seldom able to start up a new Camp, though it may not be her" – Mamut hesitated, and Ayla noticed that his eyes darted towards the old woman of the Crane Hearth, who was talking to Nezzie – "that person's fault. People want leaders they can depend on, and distrust those who have had problems . . . or tragedies."

Ayla nodded, and Mamut knew she understood, both what he had said and what he had implied. The conversation continued, but Ayla's mind had wandered back to the Clan. Brun had been a good leader, but what would his clan do if Broud was not? She wondered if they would turn to a new leader, and who it might be. It would be a long time before the son of Broud's mate was old enough. A persistent worry that had been nagging for her attention suddenly broke through.

"Where's Wolf?" she said.

She hadn't seen him since the argument, and no one else had either. Everyone started looking. Ayla searched her bed platform, and then every other corner of the hearth, even the curtained-off area with the basket of ashes and horse dung, which she had shown the pup. She was beginning to feel the same panic that a mother feels when her child is missing.

"Here he is, Ayla!" she heard Tornec say, with relief, but she felt her stomach churn when he added, "Frebec has him." Her surprise bordered on shock as she watched him approach. She was not the only one who stared in amazed disbelief.

Frebec, who never overlooked an opportunity to derogate Ayla's animals, or her, for her association with them, was cradling the wolf puppy gently in his arms. He handed the wolf over to her, but she noticed a moment of hesitation, as though he gave up the small creature reluctantly, and she saw a softer look in his eyes than she had ever seen there before.

"He must have got scared," Frebec explained. "Fralie said suddenly he was there, at the hearth, whining. She didn't know where he came from. Most of the children were there, too, and Crisavec picked him up and put him on a storage platform, near the head of his bed. But there's a deep niche in the wall there. It goes quite a way into the hillside. The wolf found it, and crawled all the way to the back, and then he wouldn't come out."

"It must have reminded him of his den," Ayla said.

"That's what Fralie said. It was too hard for her to go and get him, as big as she is, and I think she was afraid after hearing Deegie tell about you going into a wolf den. She didn't want Crisavec to go in after him, either. When I got there, I had to go in and get him out." Frebec paused then, and when he continued, Ayla heard a note of wonder in his voice. "When I reached him, he was so glad to see me, he licked me all over the face. I tried to get him to stop."

Frebec assumed a more detached and unconcerned manner to cover up the fact that he was obviously moved by the naturally winning ways of the frightened baby wolf. "But when I put him down, he cried and cried until I picked him up again." Several people had gathered around by then. "I don't know why he picked the Crane Hearth, or me, to run to when he was looking for a safe place."

"He thinks of the Camp as his pack now, and he knows you are a member of the Camp, especially after you brought him out of the den he found," Ayla replied, trying to reconstruct the circumstances.

Frebec had been feeling the flush of victory when he returned to his hearth, and something deeper that made him feel an unaccustomed warmth; a sense of belonging as an equal. They hadn't just ignored him or made fun of him. Talut always listened to him, just as though he had the status to warrant it, and Tulie, the headwoman herself, had offered to give him some of her space. Crozie had even sided with him.

A lump came in his throat when he saw Fralie, his very own, treasured, high-status woman who had made it all possible; his beautiful pregnant woman who would soon give birth to the first child of his own hearth, the hearth Crozie had given him, the Crane Hearth. He'd been annoyed when she told him the wolf was hiding in the niche, but the pup's eager acceptance of him, in spite of all his harsh words, surprised him. Even the new baby wolf welcomed him, and then would only be soothed by him. And Ayla said it was because the wolf knew he was a member of the Lion Camp. Even a wolf knew he belonged.

"Well, you better keep him here from now on," Frebec cautioned as he turned to go. "And watch out for him. If you don't, he could get stepped on."

After Frebec left, several of the people who had been standing around looked at each other in complete bewilderment.

"That was a change. I wonder what got into him?" Deegie said. "If I didn't know better, I'd say he actually likes Wolf!"

"I didn't think he had it in him," Ranec said, feeling more respect than he ever had for the man of the Crane Hearth.

24

The four-legged creatures of the Mother's domain had always been either food, fur, or the personification of spirits to the Lion Camp. They knew animals in their natural environment, knew their movements and migration patterns, knew where to look for them and how to hunt them. But the people of the Camp had never known individual animals before Ayla came with the mare and the young stallion.

The interaction of the horses with Ayla and, as time passed, with other people in varying degrees, was a constant source of surprise. It had never occurred to anyone before that such animals would respond to a human, or that they could be trained to come at a whistle or to carry a rider. But even the horses with all their interest and appeal did not hold the fascination to the Camp of the baby wolf. They respected wolves as hunters, and on occasion, adversaries. Sometimes a wolf was hunted for a winter pelt, and though it was rare, an occasional human fell to a pack of wolves. Most often wolves and humans tended to respect and avoid each other.

But the very young always exert a special appeal; it is the innate source of their survival. Babies, including baby animals, touch some inner chord that resonates in response, but Wolf – the name by which he came to be known – held a special charm. From the first day that the fuzzy little dark grey pup waddled on unsteady legs on the floor of the earthlodge, he entranced the human population. His eager puppy ways were hard to resist, and he quickly became a favourite of the Camp.

It helped, although the people of the Camp didn't realise it, that human ways and wolf ways were not so different. Both were intelligent, social animals who organised themselves within an overall pattern of complex and changing relationships, which benefited the group while accommodating individual differences. Because of the similarities of social structures and certain characteristics which had evolved independently in both canines and humans, a unique relationship was possible between them.

Wolf's life began under unusual and difficult circumstances. As the only surviving pup of a litter born to a lone wolf who had lost her mate, he never knew the security of a wolf pack. Rather than the comfort of litter mates or a solicitous aunt or uncle who would have stayed close by in the event that his mother left for a short time, he had experienced loneliness unusual for a wolf pup. The only other wolf he had known was his mother, and his memory of her was blurring as Ayla took her place.

But Ayla was something more. By deciding to keep and raise the wolf puppy, she became the human half of an extraordinary bond that developed between two entirely different species – canines and humans – a bond that would have profound and lasting effects.

Even if there had been other wolves around, Wolf was too young when he was found to have properly bonded with them. At his age of a month or so, he would have just begun coming out of the den to meet his relatives, the wolves that he would have identified with for the rest of his life. He imprinted instead on the people, and horses, of the Lion Camp.

It was the first, but it would not be the last time. By accident or design, as the idea spread, it would happen again, many times in many places. The ancestors of all the domestic canine breeds were wolves, and in the beginning they retained their essential wolf characteristics. But as time went on, the generations of wolves born and raised within a human environment began to differ from the original wild canines.

Animals born with normal genetic variations in colour, shape and size – a dark coat, a white spot, a curved-up tail, a smaller or larger size – which would have pushed them to the periphery or out of the pack, were often favoured by humans. Even genetic aberrations in the form of midgets or dwarfs or heavy-boned giants that would not have survived to reproduce in the wild were kept, and thrived. Eventually unusual or aberrant canines were bred to preserve and strengthen certain traits that were desirable to humans, until the outward similarity of many dogs to the ancestral wolf was remote indeed. Yet the wolf traits of intelligence, protectiveness, loyalty, and playfulness remained.

Wolf was quick to pick up cues of relative rank within the Camp, as he would have been within a wolf pack, though his interpretation of status might not have matched the notions of the humans. Though Tulie was headwoman of the Lion Camp, to Wolf, Ayla was the ranking female; in a wolf pack the mother of the litter was the female leader and she seldom allowed any other females to bear young.

No one in the Camp knew precisely what the animal thought or felt, or if he even had thoughts and feelings that could be understood by humans, but it didn't matter. The people of the Camp judged by behaviour, and from Wolf's actions no one doubted that he loved and worshipped Ayla beyond measure. Wherever she was, he was always aware of her, and at a whistle, a snap of the fingers, a beckoning gesture, even a nod, he was at her feet, looking up with adoration in his eyes, eagerly anticipating her least wish. He was totally unselfconscious in his responses, and entirely forgiving. He whined in abject despair when she scolded him, and wriggled with ecstasies of delight when she relented. He lived for her attention. His greatest joy was when she played or romped with him, but even a word or a pat was sufficient to elicit excited licking and other obvious signs of devotion.

With no one else was Wolf quite so effusive. With most he displayed varying degrees of friendliness or acceptance, which caused some surprise that the animal could show such a range of feelings. His reaction to Ayla strengthened the Camp's perception that she had a magical ability to control animals, and it increased her stature.

The young wolf had a little more difficulty determining who the male leader in his human pack was. The one who held that position in the wolf pack was the object of the most solicitous attention of all the other wolves. A greeting ceremony in which the male leader was mobbed by the rest of the pack eager to lick his face, sniff his fur, and crowd in close, often ending with a wonderful communal howling ceremony, commonly affirmed his leadership. But the human pack offered no such deference to any particular male.

Wolf did notice, however, that the two large four-legged members of his unconventional pack greeted the tall blond man with more enthusiasm than any other person, except Ayla. In addition, his scent lingered strongly around Ayla's bed and the nearby area, which included Wolf's basket. In the absence of other clues, Wolf leaned towards ascribing pack leadership to Jondalar. His inclination was strengthened when his friendly advances were rewarded with warm and playful attention.

The half-dozen children who played together were his litter mates and Wolf could often be found with them, frequently at the Mammoth Hearth. Once they developed a proper respect for sharp little teeth, and learned not to provoke a defensive snap, the children found the wolf liked to be handled, petted, and fondled. He was tolerant of unintentional excess, and seemed to know the difference between Nuvie squeezing him a bit too hard when she carried him, and Brinan pulling his tail just to hear him yelp. The former was suffered with forbearance, the latter rewarded with a nip of retribution. Wolf loved to play and always managed to get in the middle of wrestling, and the children quickly learned that he loved to retrieve things that were thrown. When they all crumpled in a tired heap, falling asleep wherever they happened to be, the wolf pup was often among them.

After the first night when she had promised never to let the wolf harm anyone, Ayla made a decision to train him with purpose and thought.

Her training of Whinney, in the beginning, had been accidental. She had acted on impulse the first time she climbed on the mare's back, and hadn't known she was intuitively learning to control the horse the more she rode. Though she was now aware of the signals she had developed and used them consciously, her means of control were still largely intuitive, and Ayla believed that Whinney obeyed her commands because she wanted to.

Training the cave lion had been somewhat more purposeful. By the time she found the injured cub, she knew an animal could be encouraged to follow her wishes. Her first efforts at training had been directed at controlling the lion kitten's rambunctious affection. She trained by love, the way children were raised by the Clan. She rewarded his gentle behaviour with her affection, and firmly pushed him aside, or got up and walked away when he forgot to sheath his claws or played too rough. When out of excitement, he bounded towards her with unchecked enthusiasm, he learned to stop when she put up her hand and said "Stop!" in a firm voice. The lesson was so well learned that even when he became a full-grown male cave lion nearly as tall but heavier than Whinney, he would stop at Ayla's command. She invariably responded with affectionate rubs and scratches, and occasionally a full-length hug, rolling with him on the ground. As he grew older, he learned many things, even to hunt with her.

Ayla soon realised that the children could benefit from some understanding of the ways of wolves. She began to tell them stories about the time she was learning to hunt and studying wolves along with other carnivorous animals. She explained that wolf packs had a female leader, and a male leader, like the Mamutoi, and told them that wolves communicated with certain postures and gestures along with vocal sounds. She showed them, on hands and knees, the stance of a leader – head up, ears perked up, tail straight out in back – and the posture of one approaching a leader – crouching down a little lower and licking the leader's muzzle – adding the sounds with perfect mimicry. She described stay-away warnings, and playful behaviour. The puppy often participated.

The children enjoyed it, and often the adults listened in with equal pleasure. Soon wolf signals were incorporated into the play of the youngsters, but none used them better, or with more understanding, than the child whose own language was spoken primarily with signs. An extraordinary relationship developed between the wolf and the boy that surprised the people of the Camp, and made Nezzie shake her head in wonder. Rydag not only used the wolf signals, including many of the sounds, but he seemed to take them a step further. To people watching, it often appeared that they were actually talking to each other, and the young animal seemed to know that the boy required particular care and attention.

From the beginning, Wolf was less rambunctious, gentler around him, and in his puppy way, protective of him. Except for Ayla, there was no one whose company Wolf preferred. If Ayla was busy, he looked for Rydag, and was often found sleeping near him or on his lap. Ayla wasn't entirely sure herself how Wolf and Rydag came to understand each other so well. Rydag's innate skill at reading subtle nuances in the wolf's signals might explain the boy's ability, but how could a young wolf puppy know the needs of a weak human child?

Ayla developed modified wolf signals along with other commands to train the puppy. The first lesson, after several accidents, was to use a basket of dung and ashes as the humans did, or to go outside. It was surprisingly easy; Wolf seemed embarrassed over his messes, and cringed when Ayla scolded him about them. The next lesson was more difficult.

Wolf loved to chew on leather, particularly boots and shoes, and breaking him of the habit proved vexatious and frustrating. Whenever she caught him at it and scolded him, he was contrite, and abjectly eager to please, but he was recalcitrant and would go right back to it again, sometimes the moment she turned her back. Anyone's footwear was in jeopardy, but most especially her favourite soft leather stockings. He couldn't seem to leave them alone. She had to hang them up high where he could not reach them or they would have been torn to shreds. But as much as she objected to his chewing on her things, she felt far worse when he ruined someone else's. She was responsible for bringing him to the lodge, and felt any damage he did was her fault.

Ayla was sewing the finishing beadwork on to the white leather tunic when she heard a commotion from the Fox Hearth.

"Hey! You! Give me that!" Ranec shouted.

Ayla knew from the sound that Wolf had got into something again. She ran to see what the problem was this time and saw Ranec and Wolf in a tug-of-war over a worn boot.

"Wolf! Drop it!" she said, dropping her hand in a quick gesture that came just short of his nose. The wolf pup let go immediately and hunched down with his ears slightly back and his tail down, and whined beseechingly. Ranec put his footwear on the platform.

"I hope he didn't ruin your boot," Ayla said.

"It doesn't matter anyway. It's an old one," Ranec said, smiling, and added admiringly, "You do know wolves, Ayla. He does exactly what you tell him."

"But only while I stand here and watch him," she said, looking down on the animal. Wolf was watching her, wriggling with expectation.

"The moment I turn my back, he'll be into something else he knows he's not supposed to touch. He'll drop it as soon as he sees me coming, but I don't know how to teach him not to get into people's things."

"Maybe he needs something of his own," Ranec volunteered, then he looked at her with his soft black glowing eyes, "or something of yours."

The puppy was scooching up to her, whining for her attention. Finally, impatient, he yipped a few times. "Stay there! Be still!" she commanded, upset with him. He backed down, lay on his paws, and looked up at her, utterly crushed.

Ranec watched, then said to Ayla, "He can't stand it when you're upset with him. He wants to know you love him. I think I know how he feels."

He moved closer and his dark eyes filled with the warmth and need that had touched her so deeply before. She felt a tingling response, and backed away, flustered. Then, to cover her agitation, she bent down and scooped up the wolf pup. Wolf excitedly licked her face, wriggling with happiness.

"See how happy he is now that he knows you care about him?" Ranec said. "It would make me happy to know you care about me. Do you?"

"Uh . . . of course, I care about you, Ranec," Ayla stammered, feeling uncomfortable.

He flashed a broad smile, and his eyes gleamed with a hint of mischief, and something deeper. "It would be a *pleasure* to show you how happy it makes me to know you care," he said, putting an arm around her waist, and moving in closer.

"I believe you," she said, ducking away. "You don't have to show me, Ranec."

It wasn't the first time he had made advances. Usually they were framed as jests that allowed him to let her know how he felt, while giving her the opportunity to avoid them without either of them losing face. She started walking back, sensing a more serious confrontation and wanting to avoid it. She had a feeling he would ask her to come to his bed, and she didn't know if she could refuse a man who commanded her to his bed, or even made a direct request. She understood it was her right, but the response to comply was so ingrained she wasn't sure that she could.

"Why not, Ayla?" he said, falling in step beside her. "Why won't you let me show you? You sleep alone now. You shouldn't sleep alone."

She felt a stab of remorse realising that she did sleep alone, but tried not to show it. "I don't sleep alone," she said, holding up the puppy. "Wolf sleeps with me, in a basket right here, near my head."

TMH-13

"That's not the same," Ranec said. His tone was serious and he seemed ready to push the issue. Then he stopped and smiled. He didn't want to rush her. He could tell she was upset. It hadn't been that long since the separation. He tried to turn the tension aside. "He's too small to keep you warm . . . but I must admit, he is appealing." He rubbed Wolf's head affectionately.

Ayla smiled and put the young wolf down in the basket. He immediately jumped out and then down to the floor, sat down and scratched himself, then scampered towards his feeding dish. Ayla began to fold up the white tunic to put it away. She rubbed the soft white leather and the white ermine fur, and straightened the little tails with the black tips, feeling her stomach tighten and a lump form in her throat. Her eyes stung from tears she fought to control. No, it wasn't the same, she thought. How could it be the same?

"Ayla, you know how much I want you, how much I care about you," Ranec said, standing behind her, "don't you?"

"I think so," she said, not turning, but closing her eyes.

"I love you, Ayla. I know you feel unsettled right now, but I want you to know. I loved you the first moment I saw you. I want to share my hearth with you, to make a joining with you. I want to make you happy. I know you need time to think about it. I'm not asking you to make a decision, but tell me you'll think about . . . letting me try to make you happy. Will you? Think about it?"

Ayla looked down at the white tunic in her hands, and her mind whirled. Why doesn't Jondalar want to sleep with me any more? Why did he stop touching me, stop sharing Pleasures with me, even when he was sleeping with me? Everything changed after I became Mamutoi. Didn't he want me to be adopted? If he didn't, why didn't he say so? Maybe he did want it; he said he did. I thought he loved me. Maybe he changed his mind. Maybe he doesn't love me any more. He never did ask me to join. What will I do if Jondalar leaves without me? The knot in her stomach felt as hard as a rock. Ranec cares for me, and he wants me to care about him. He is nice, and funny, he always makes me laugh . . . and he loves me. But I don't love him. I wish I could love him . . . maybe I should try.

"Yes, Ranec, I'll think about it," she said softly, but her throat tightened and ached as she spoke.

Jondalar watched Ranec leave the Mammoth Hearth. The tall man had become a watcher, though he felt embarrassed about it. It wasn't appropriate behaviour, either in this society or his own, for adults to stare or concern themselves unduly with the ordinary activities of another person, and Jondalar had always been especially sensitive to social conventions. It bothered him to appear so callow, but he couldn't help it. He tried to hide it, but he watched Ayla and the Mammoth Hearth constantly.

The carver's jaunty step and delighted smile as he returned to the Fox Hearth filled the tall visitor with dread. He knew it had to be something Ayla had said or done that caused the Mamutoi man such elation, and with his morbid imagination, he feared the worst.

Jondalar knew Ranec had become a constant visitor since he left the Mammoth Hearth, and he berated himself for creating the opportunity. He wished he could take back his words and the whole silly argument, but he was convinced it was too late to make amends. He felt helpless but, in a way, it was a relief to have some distance between them.

Though he didn't admit it to himself, his actions were motivated by more than a simple desire to allow her to choose the man she wanted. He had been hurt so deeply, part of him wanted to strike back; if she could reject him, he could reject her. But he also had a need to give himself a choice, to see if it was possible to get over his love for her. He sincerely wondered if it wouldn't be better for her to stay here, where she was accepted and loved, than to return with him to his people, and he feared what his own reaction would be if his people rejected her. Would he be willing to share an outcast life with her? Would he be willing to move away, leave his people again, especially after making such a long Journey to return? Or would he reject her, too?

If she chose someone else to love, then he'd be forced to leave her behind, and he would not be faced with such a decision. But the thought of her loving someone else filled him with such stomach-wrenching, breath-suffocating, throat-clenching, eye-burning, unbearable pain, he didn't know if he could survive . . . or if he wanted to. The more he fought with himself not to show his love, the more possessive and jealous he became, and the more he hated himself for it.

The turmoil of trying to sort out his powerful mixed emotions was taking its toll. He couldn't eat or sleep, and was looking gaunt and wasted. His clothes were beginning to hang on his tall frame. He couldn't concentrate, not even on a beautiful new piece of flint. Sometimes he wondered if he was losing his senses, or possessed by some baneful night spirit. He was so torn with love for Ayla, grief that he was losing her, and fear of what might happen if he didn't let her go, that he couldn't bear to stay too close to her. He was afraid he would lose control of himself, and do something he would regret. But he couldn't stop watching her.

The Lion Camp was forgiving of the minor indiscretion of their visitor. They were aware of his feelings for Ayla in spite of his attempts to hide them. Everyone in the Camp talked about the painful predicament the three young people were in. The solution to their problem seemed so simple to those looking from the outside. Ayla and Jondalar obviously cared for each other, so why didn't they just tell each other how they felt, and then invite Ranec to share their union? But Nezzie sensed it was not so simple. The wise, motherly woman felt that Jondalar's love for Ayla was too strong to be held off by the lack of a few words. Something much deeper was coming between them. And she, more than anyone, understood the depth of Ranec's love for the young woman. She did not believe that this was a situation that could be resolved with a shared union. Ayla would have to make a choice.

As though the idea held some compelling power, ever since Ranec had asked Ayla to think about sharing his hearth, and brought up the painfully obvious fact that she now slept alone, she hadn't been able to think about anything else. She had clung to the belief that Jondalar would forget their harsh words and return, especially since it seemed that every time she glanced towards the cooking hearth, she caught a glimpse, between the support posts and objects hanging from the ceiling in the intervening hearths, of him as he turned away. It made her think he was still interested enough to be looking in her direction. But each night that she spent alone diminished her hope.

"Think about it . . ." Ranec's words repeated themselves in Ayla's mind as she crushed dried burdock and sweet fern leaves for a tea for Mamut's arthritis, thinking about the dark smiling man and wondering if she could learn to love him. But the thought of her life without Jondalar made her stomach ache with a strange emptiness. She added fresh wintergreen and hot water to the bowl of crushed leaves, and brought it to the old man.

She smiled when he thanked her, but she seemed preoccupied, and sad. She had been abstracted all day. Mamut knew she had been upset since Jondalar moved away, and he wished he could help. He had seen Ranec talking to her earlier and he considered trying to talk to her about it, but he believed nothing happened in Ayla's life without purpose. He was convinced the Mother had created her present difficulties for a reason, and he hesitated to interfere. Whatever trials she and the two young men were undergoing were necessary. He watched her going out to the horse annexe, and was aware when she returned sometime later.

Ayla banked the fire, walked back to her bed platform, undressed and prepared for sleep. It was an ordeal facing the night knowing Jondalar would not be sleeping beside her. She busied herself with little tasks to delay settling herself into her furs, knowing she would lie awake half the night. Finally, she picked up the wolf puppy and sat on the edge of the bed, cuddling, stroking, and talking to the warm, loving, little animal, until he went to sleep in her arms. Then she put him in his basket, petting him until he settled down again. To make up for Jondalar's absence, Ayla lavished love on the wolf.

Mamut realised he was awake and opened his eyes. He could barely make out vague shapes in the darkness. The lodge was quiet, the night quiet that was filled only with the slight rustlings, heavy breathing and low rumbles of sleep. He slowly turned his head towards the faint red glow of the embers in the firepit, trying to discover what had brought him out of his deep sleep to full wakefulness. He heard a strained breath nearby, and a stifled sob, and pushed his covers aside.

"Ayla? Ayla, are you in pain?" Mamut said softly. She felt a warm hand on her arm.

"No," she said, her voice husky with strain. Her face was turned towards the wall.

"You are crying."

"I'm sorry I woke you. I should have been more quiet."

"You were quiet. It wasn't your noise that woke me, it was your need. The Mother called me to you. You are in pain. You are hurting inside, isn't that so?"

Ayla took a deep, painful breath, straining to repress the cry that wanted expression. "Yes," she said. She turned to face him, and he saw tears glistening in the muted light.

"Then cry, Ayla. You should not hold it in. You have reason to be in pain, and you have a right to cry," Mamut said.

"Oh, Mamut," she cried in a great heaving sob, then still restraining the sound, but with the relief of his permission, quietly wept her heartbreak and anguish.

"Do not hold back, Ayla. It is good for you to cry," he said, sitting on the edge of her bed and patting her gently. "It will all turn out as it should, as it is meant to be. It's all right, Ayla."

When she finally stopped, she found a piece of soft leather to wipe her face and nose, then sat up beside the old man. "I feel better, now," she said.

"It is always best to cry when you feel the need, but it is not over, Ayla."

Ayla bowed her head. "I know." Then she turned to him and said, "But why?"

"Someday you will know why. I believe your life is directed by powerful forces. You were picked for a special fate. It is not an easy burden you carry; look what you have already been through in your young life. But your life will not be all pain, you will have great joys. You are loved, Ayla. You draw love to you. That is given to you to help you bear the burden. You will always have love . . . perhaps too much . . ."

"I thought Jondalar loved me . . . ."

"Don't be too certain he doesn't, but many other people love you, including this old man," Mamut said, smiling. Ayla smiled, too. "Even a wolf, and horses love you. Haven't there been many who have loved you?"

"You're right. Iza loved me. She was my mother. It didn't matter that I wasn't born to her. When she died, she said she loved me best . . . Creb loved me . . . even though I disappointed him . . . hurt him." Ayla stopped for a moment, then continued. "Uba loved me . . . and Durc." She stopped again. "Do you think I'll ever see my son again, Mamut?"

The shaman paused before answering. "How long has it been since you've seen him?"

"Three . . . no, four years. He was born in early spring. He was three years when I left. He is close to Rydag in years . . ." Suddenly Ayla looked at the old shaman and spoke with earnest excitement. "Mamut, Rydag is a mixed child, just like my son. If Rydag can live here, why can't Durc? You went to the peninsula and came back, why couldn't I go and get Durc and bring him back here? It's not so very far."

Mamut frowned, considering his reply. "I can't answer that, Ayla. Only you can, but you must think about it very carefully before you decide what is best, not only for yourself, but for your son. You are Mamutoi. You have learned to speak our language, and you have learned many of our customs, but you have much to learn yet of our ways."

Ayla wasn't listening to the shaman's carefully chosen words. Her mind was already racing ahead. "If Nezzie could take in a child who can't even speak, why not one who could speak? Durc could, if he had a language to learn. Durc could be a friend to Rydag. Durc could help him, run and get things for him. Durc is a good runner."

Mamut let her continue her enthusiastic recitation of Durc's virtues until she stopped of her own accord, then he asked her, "When would you plan to go for him, Ayla?"

"As soon as I can. This spring . . . No, it's too hard to travel in spring, too much flooding. I'll have to wait until summer." Ayla paused. "Maybe not. This is the summer of the Clan Gathering. If I don't get there before they leave, I'll have to wait until they return. But, by then, Ura will be with them . . ."

"The girl who was Promised to your son?" Mamut asked.

"Yes. In a few years they will mate. Clan children grow up sooner than the Others . . . than I did. Iza didn't think I'd ever become a woman. I was so slow compared with Clan girls . . . Ura could be a woman, though, and ready to have a mate, and her own hearth." Ayla frowned. "She was a baby when I saw her, and Durc . . . The last time

I saw Durc, he was a little boy. Soon he'll be a man, providing for his mate, a mate who could have children. I don't even have a mate. My son's mate could have a child before I do."

"Do you know how old you are, Ayla?"

"Not exactly, but I always count my years in late winter, about now. I don't know why." She frowned again. "I guess it's time for me to add another year. That means I must be . . ." She closed her eyes to concentrate on the counting words. "I am eighteen years now, Mamut. I am getting old!"

"You were eleven when your son was born?" he asked, surprised. Ayla nodded. "I have known of some girls who became women at nine or ten, but that's very young. Latie is not yet a woman, and she is in her twelfth year."

"She will be soon. I can tell," Ayla said.

"I think you are right. But you are not so old, Ayla. Deegie is seventeen years, and she won't be joined until this summer at the Summer Meeting."

"That's right, and I promised I would be part of her Matrimonial. I can't go to a Summer Meeting and a Clan Gathering both." Mamut saw her pale. "I can't go to a Clan Gathering, anyway. I'm not even sure if I could go back to the Clan. I am cursed. I am dead. Even Durc might think I'm a spirit and be afraid of me. Oh, Mamut. What should I do?"

"You must think about it all very carefully before you decide what is best," he replied. She looked upset, and he decided to change the subject. "But you have time. It is not yet spring. The Spring Festival will be here before we know it, though. Have you thought about the root and the ceremony you spoke of? Are you willing to include that ceremony in the Spring Festival?"

Ayla felt a chill. The idea frightened her, but Mamut would be there to help. He would know what to do, and he did seem so interested in wanting to learn about it.

"All right, Mamut. Yes, I will do it."

Jondalar knew of the change in the relationship between Ayla and Ranec immediately, though he didn't want to accept it. He watched them for several days until he could no longer deny to himself that Ranec all but lived at the Mammoth Hearth, and that his presence was welcomed and enjoyed by Ayla. No matter how he tried to convince himself that it was for the best and that he had done the right thing in moving away, he could not ease the pain of losing her love or overcome the hurt of being excluded. In spite of the fact that he was the one who had withdrawn from her, and voluntarily left her bed and company, he now felt she was rejecting him.

It didn't take them long, Jondalar thought. He was there the next day, hanging around her, and she could hardly wait for me to leave before she welcomed him. They must have just been waiting for me to go. I should have known . . .

What are you blaming her for? You're the one who left, Jondalar, he said to himself. She didn't tell you to go. After the first time, she didn't go back to him. She was right there, ready for you, and you know it . . .

So now she's ready for him. And he's eager. Can you blame him? Maybe it's for the best. She's wanted here, they're more used to flatheads . . . Clan. And she's loved . . .

Yes, she's loved. Isn't that what you want for her? To be accepted, and to have someone love her . . .

But I love her, he thought with a welling up of pain and anguish. O Mother! How can I stand it? She's the only woman I've ever loved. I don't want her to be hurt, I don't want her to be turned out. Why her? O, Doni, why did it have to be her?

Maybe I should leave. That's it. I'll just leave, he thought, beyond the ability to think clearly at the moment.

Jondalar strode towards the Lion Hearth, and interrupted Talut and Mamut who were discussing the coming Spring Festival. "I'm leaving," he blurted out. "What can I do to trade for some supplies?" He had a manic look of desperation.

A knowing glance passed between the headman and the shaman. "Jondalar, my friend," Talut said, clapping him on the shoulder, "we'll be happy to give you any supplies you need, but you can't leave now. Spring is coming, but look outside, a blizzard is blowing, and late season blizzards are the worst."

Jondalar calmed down and realised his sudden impulse to leave was impossible. No one in his right mind would start out on a long journey now.

Talut felt a relaxation of tension in Jondalar's muscles, as he kept on talking. "In spring, it will flood, and there are many rivers to cross. Besides, you can't travel this far from your home, winter with the Mamutoi, and not hunt mammoth with the Mammoth Hunters, Jondalar. Once you return, you will never have the chance again. The first hunt will be in early summer, soon after we all get to the Summer Meeting. The best time to start travelling would be right after that. You would be doing me a great favour if you would consider staying with us at least until the first mammoth hunt. I'd like you to show that spear-thrower of yours."

"Yes, of course, I'll think about it," Jondalar said. Then he looked the big red-haired headman in the eyes. "And thanks, Talut. You're right. I can't leave yet."

Mamut was sitting cross-legged in his favourite place for meditating, the bed platform next to his that was used as storage for the extra reindeer-hide bedsheets, furs, and other bedding. He wasn't so much meditating as thinking. Since the night he had been awakened by her tears, he was much more aware of Ayla's despair over Jondalar's leaving. Her wretched unhappiness had left a deep impression on him. Though she managed to hide the extent of her feelings from most people, he was more conscious now of small details of her behaviour that he might have missed before. Though she genuinely seemed to enjoy Ranec's company, and laughed at his jokes, she was subdued, and the care and attention she lavished on Wolf and the horses had a quality of desolate longing.

Mamut paid closer attention to the tall visitor and noticed the same desolation in Jondalar's behaviour. He seemed filled with tormented anxiety, though he, too, tried to hide it. After his desperate impulse to leave in the middle of a storm, the old shaman feared that Jondalar's good judgment was becoming impaired at the thought of losing Ayla. To the old man who dealt so intimately with the spirit world of Mut and Her fates, that implied a deeper compulsion than simply young love. Perhaps the Mother had plans for him, too; plans that involved Ayla.

Though Mamut was reluctant to step in, he wondered why the Mother had shown him that She was the force behind their mutual feelings. Though he was convinced that ultimately She would arrange circumstances to suit Her, perhaps She wanted him to help in this case.

As he was pondering whether and how to make the Mother's wishes known, Ranec came into the Mammoth Hearth, obviously looking for Ayla. Mamut knew she had taken the wolf pup out for a ride on Whinney and would not be back for some time. Ranec looked around, then saw the old man and approached him.

"Do you know where Ayla is, Mamut?" he asked.

"Yes. She is out with the animals."

"I wondered why I hadn't seen her for a while."

"You are seeing a lot of her, lately."

Ranec grinned. "I hope to see a lot more of her."

"She did not arrive here alone, Ranec. Doesn't Jondalar have some prior interest?"

"He might have, when they first came, but he gave it up. He left the hearth." Ranec said. Mamut noted a defensiveness in his tone.

"I think there is still strong feeling between them. I don't think the separation would be permanent if their deep attachment were given the chance to grow back, Ranec."

"If you are telling me to back away, Mamut, I'm sorry. It's too late. I also have a strong feeling for Ayla." Ranec's voice cracked with the emotion he felt. "Mamut, I love her, I want to join with her, make a hearth with her. It's time I settled down with a woman, and I want her children at my hearth. I've never met anyone like her. She's everything I ever dreamed of. If I can convince her to agree, I want to announce our Promise at the Spring Festival, and join in the Matrimonial this summer."

"Are you sure that's what you want, Ranec?" Mamut asked. He was fond of Ranec, and he knew it would please Wymez if the dark boy he brought back from his travels would find a woman and settle down. "There are many Mamutoi women who would welcome a joining with you. What will you say to that pretty young red-haired woman you have almost Promised? What is her name? Tricie?" Mamut was certain that if a blush would have shown, Ranec's face would be red.

"I will say . . . I will say I am sorry. I can't help it. There is no one else I want but Ayla. She is Mamutoi now. She should join with a Mamutoi. I want it to be me."

"If it is meant to be, Ranec," Mamut said kindly, "it will be, but remember this. The choice is not yours. It is not even hers. Ayla was chosen by the Mother for a purpose, and given many gifts. No matter what you decide, or what she decides, Mut has first claim on her. Any man who joins with her, joins also with her purpose."

25

As that ancient earth tilted her icy northern face imperceptibly closer to the great shining star she circled, even the lands near the glaciers felt a kiss of gentle warmth and slowly awakened from the sleep of a deeper and colder winter. Spring stirred reluctantly at first, then, with the urgency of a season whose time was short, threw off the frozen cover in an exuberant rush that watered and quickened the soil.

The drops trickling from branches and archways in the first unfrozen noon warmth hardened into icicles as the nights cooled. In the gradually warming days that followed, the long tapered shafts grew, then slipped their icy grip and pierced drifts of snow, shrunk to mounds of slush drained off by muddy water. The rills, runnels, and rivulets of melting snow and ice joined together into streams to carry away the accumulated moisture that had been held in cold suspension. The surging streams raced down old channels and gullies, or cut new ones into the fine loess, sometimes aided and directed by an antler shovel or an ivory scoop.

The ice-bound river groaned and creaked in its struggle to loosen winter's hold as the melt poured into its hidden current. Then, with no warning, a sharp report, heard even in the lodge, followed by a second crack and then a booming rumble, announced that the ice no longer held back the flooding tide. The chunks and floes, bobbing, dipping, turning on end, caught up and swept along by the swift powerful stream, marked a turning point of the season.

As though the cold was washed out with the tide, the people of the Camp, as confined as the river by the frigid cold, spilled out of the earthlodge. Though it was warmer only by comparison, the restrained indoor life shifted to energetic activity outside. Any excuse to go outdoors was greeted with enthusiasm, even spring cleaning.

The people of the Lion Camp were clean, by their own standards. Though moisture in the form of ice and snow was plentiful, it took fire, and large supplies of fuel, to make water. Even so, some of the ice and snow they melted for cooking and drinking was used to wash, and they took sweatbaths periodically. Personal areas were generally well organised, tools and implements were cared for, the few clothes that were worn indoors were brushed, occasionally washed and well maintained. But by the end of winter, the stench inside the earthlodge was incredible.

Contributing to the stink was food in various stages of preservation or decay, cooked, uncooked, and rotten; burning oils, often rancid since fresh congealed lumps of fat were usually added to old oil in the lamps; baskets used for defecation, not always dumped immediately; containers of urine saved and left standing to become ammoniacal by the decomposition of urea through bacteria; and people. Though sweatbaths were healthful and cleansed the skin, they did little to eliminate normal body odours, but that was not their purpose. Personal odour was part of a person's identity.

The Mamutoi were accustomed to the rich and pungent natural odours of everyday living. Their sense of smell was well-developed and used, like sight or hearing, to maintain awareness of their environment. Not even the smells of the animals were thought to be unpleasant; they were natural, too. But as the season warmed, even noses accustomed to the ordinary odours of life began to notice the consequences of twenty people living together in close quarters for an extended period. Spring was the time when the drapes were pulled back to air the lodge, and the accumulated debris of the entire winter was cleaned up and thrown out.

In Ayla's case, that included shovelling out the horse dung from the annexe. The horses had weathered the winter well, which pleased Ayla, but it was not surprising. Steppes horses were hardy animals, adapted to the rigours of harsh winters. Though they had to forage for themselves, Whinney and Racer were free to come and go at will to a place of protection well beyond that usually available to their wild cousins. In addition, water, and even some food was provided for them. Horses matured quickly in the wild, necessary, under normal circumstances, for survival, and Racer, like other colts who had been born the same time, had reached his full growth. Though he would fill out a bit more in the next few years, he was a sturdy young stallion, slightly bigger than his dam.

Spring was also the time of shortages. The supply of certain foods, particularly favoured vegetable products, was exhausted, and other foods were running low. When they took stock, everyone was glad they had decided to go on the last bison hunt. If they hadn't, they might now be low on meat. But though the meat filled them, it left them unsatisfied. Ayla, recalling Iza's spring tonics for Brun's clan, decided to do the same for the Camp. Her tisanes of various dried herbs, including iron-rich yellow dock, and scurvy-preventing rose hips, relieved the underlying vitamin lack that caused the craving for fresh food, but it did not eliminate the desire. Everyone hungered for the first fresh greens. The need for her medical knowledge went beyond spring tonics, however.

Well-insulated and heated by several fires, lamps, and natural body heat, it was warm in the semi-subterranean longhouse. Even when it was bitterly cold out, few clothes were worn inside. During the winter they were careful to dress properly before going outdoors, but when the snow began to melt, such caution was abandoned. Though the temperature hovered barely above freezing, it felt so much warmer, people went outdoors wearing little more than their usual indoor clothing. With spring rains and melting snows, they often were wet and chilled before they went back in, which lowered their resistance.

Ayla was busier treating coughs, sniffles and sore throats in the warming days of spring than she ever was in the coldest depths of winter. The epidemic of spring colds and respiratory infections afflicted everyone. Even Ayla took to her bed for a few days to nurse a slight fever and heavy chest cough. Before they were hardly into the season, she had treated nearly everyone in the Lion Camp. Depending upon the need, she provided medicinal teas, steam treatments, hot plasters for throats and chests, and a sympathetic and convincing bedside manner. Everyone was praising the efficacy of her medicine. If nothing else, she made people feel better.

Nezzie told her they always got spring colds, but when Mamut came down with the illness shortly after she did, Ayla ignored her own residual symptoms to take care of him. He was a very old man, and she worried about him. A severe respiratory infection could be fatal. The shaman, however, for all his great age, still had remarkable stamina and recovered more quickly than some others in the lodge. Though he enjoyed her devoted attention, he urged her to see to others who needed her care more, and to rest herself.

She needed no urging when Fralie developed a fever, and a deep, body-racking cough, but her willingness to help made no difference. Frebec would not allow Ayla into the hearth to treat Fralie. Crozie argued furiously with him, and everyone in the Camp agreed with her, but he was adamant. Crozie even argued with Fralie, trying to convince her to ignore Frebec, to no avail. The sick woman merely shook her head and coughed.

"But why?" Ayla said to Mamut, sipping a hot drink with him and listening to Fralie's latest coughing spasm. Tronie had taken Tasher, who was between Nuvie and Hartal in age, to her hearth. Crisavec slept with Brinan at the Aurochs Hearth so the sick and pregnant woman could rest, but Ayla felt it every time Fralie coughed.

"Why won't he let me help her? He can see that other people feel better, and she needs it more than anyone. Coughing like that is too hard on her, especially now."

"That's not a difficult question, Ayla. If one believes the people of the

Clan are animals, it's impossible to believe they understand anything about healing medicine. And if you grew up with them, how could you know anything about it?"

"But they are not animals! A Clan medicine woman is very skilled."

"I know that, Ayla. I know better than anyone the skill of a Clan medicine woman. I think everyone here knows it now, even Frebec. At least they appreciate your ability, but Frebec doesn't want to back down after all the arguing. He's afraid he will lose face."

"What's more important? His face or Fralie's baby?"

"Fralie must think Frebec's face is more important."

"It's not Fralie's fault. Frebec and Crozie are trying to force her to choose between them, and she won't choose."

"That's Fralie's decision."

"That's just the trouble. She doesn't want to make a decision. She refuses to make a choice."

Mamut shook his head. "No, she is making a choice, whether she means to or not. But the choice is not between Frebec and Crozie. How close is she to giving birth?" he asked. "She looks ready to me."

"I'm not sure, but I don't think she is ready yet. She looks bigger because she's so thin, but the baby is not in position yet. That's what worries me. I think it's too soon."

"There is nothing you can do about it, Ayla."

"But if Frebec and Crozie wouldn't argue so much about everything . . ."

"That doesn't have anything to do with it. That's not Fralie's problem, that's between Frebec and Crozie. Fralie doesn't have to let herself be caught in the middle of their problem. She can make her own decisions, and in fact, she is. She is choosing to do nothing. Or rather, if your fears are founded – and I believe they are – she is choosing whether to give birth now or later. She may be choosing between life for her baby, and death . . . and may be endangering herself as well. But, it's her choice, and there may be more to it than any of us know."

Mamut's comments stayed on her mind long after the conversation was over, and she went to bed still thinking about them. He was right, of course. In spite of Fralie's feelings for her mother and Frebec, it wasn't her fight. Ayla tried to think of some way she could convince Fralie, but she had tried before, and now with Frebec keeping her away from his hearth, she had no opportunity to talk about it. When she went to sleep the worry was heavy on her mind.

She woke up in the middle of the night, and lay still, listening. She wasn't sure what woke her, but she thought it was the sound of Fralie's voice moaning in the darkness of the earthlodge. After a long silence, she decided it must have been a dream. Wolf whimpered, and she reached up to comfort him. Perhaps he was having a bad dream, too, and that's what woke her. Her hand stopped before it reached the pup as she strained to hear what she thought was a muffled moan.

Ayla pulled the covers back and got up. Quietly, she stepped around the drape and felt her way to the basket to relieve herself, then pulled a tunic over her head and went to the fireplace. She heard a muffled cough, then a spasm of coughs, that finally stopped in an equally muffled moan. Ayla stirred the coals, added a bit of kindling and bone shavings until she had a small fire, then dropped in a few cooking stones and reached for the waterbag.

"You can make some tea for me, too," Mamut said in a quiet voice from the dark of his sleeping platform, then pushed back his covers and sat up. "I think we'll all be up soon."

Ayla nodded, and poured extra water in the cooking basket. There was another coughing spell, then stirring around and subdued voices from the Crane Hearth.

"She needs something to quiet the cough, and something to calm the labour . . . if it's not too late. I think I'll check my medicines," Ayla said, putting her drinking bowl down, then hesitated, ". . . just in case someone asks."

She picked up a firebrand and Mamut watched her moving among the racks of dried plants she had brought back with her from the valley. It's a wonder to watch her practise her healing arts, Mamut thought. She's young to have such skill, though. If I were Frebec, I would have been more concerned about her youth, and possible inexperience, than her background. I know she was trained by the best, but how can she know so much already? She must have been born with it, and that medicine woman, Iza, must have seen her gift from the beginning. His musing was interrupted by another coughing spell from the Crane Hearth.

"Here, Fralie, have a drink of water," Frebec said anxiously.

Fralie shook her head, unable to talk, trying to control the cough. She was on her side, up on one elbow, holding a piece of soft leather to her mouth. Her eyes were glazed with fever, and her face red from the exertion. She glanced at her mother, who was sitting on the bed across the passageway, glaring at her.

Crozie's anger, and her distress, were both apparent. She had tried everything to convince her daughter to ask for help: persuasion, argument, diatribe; nothing worked. Even she had got some medicine from Ayla for her cold, and it was stupid of Fralie not to use the help that was available. It was all the fault of that stupid man, that stupid Frebec, but it did no good to talk about it. Crozie had decided she would not say another word.

Fralie's cough subsided, and she dropped back down on the bed, exhausted. Maybe the other pain, the one she didn't want to admit to, would not come this time. Fralie waited, holding her breath so as not to disturb anything, fearfully anticipating. An ache started in her lower back. She closed her eyes and took a deep breath, and tried to will it away. She put a hand on the side of her distended stomach and felt the muscles contract as the pain, and her anxiety, increased. It's too soon, she thought. The baby shouldn't be coming for at least another moon cycle.

"Fralie? Are you all right?" Frebec said, still standing there with the water.

She tried to smile at him, seeing his distress , his feeling of helplessness. "It's this cough," she said. "Everyone gets sick in spring."

No one understood him, she thought, least of all her mother. He was trying so hard to show everyone that he was worth something. That's why he wouldn't give in, that's why he argued so much, and was so quick to take offence. He embarrassed Crozie. He didn't understand that you showed your worth – the number and quality of your affiliations, and the strength of your influence – by how much you could claim from kin and kind to give away, so everyone could see it. Her mother had tried to show him by giving him the right to the Crane, not just the hearth Fralie brought to him when they joined, but the right to claim the Crane as his own birthright.

Crozie had expected gracious acquiescence to her wishes and requests, to show that he appreciated and understood that the Crane Hearth, which was still hers in name, though she had little else, was his to claim. But her demands could be excessive. She had lost so much, it was hard for her to give away any of her remaining claim to status, particularly to one who had so little. Crozie feared he would diminish it, and she needed constant reassurance that it was appreciated. Fralie wouldn't shame him by trying to explain. It was a subtle thing, something you grew up knowing . . . if you always had it. But Frebec never had anything.

Fralie began to feel an ache in her back again. If she lay there quietly, maybe it would go away . . . if she could keep from coughing. She was beginning to wish she could talk to Ayla, at least to get something for the cough, but she didn't want Frebec to think she was siding with her mother. And long explanations would just irritate her throat, and make Frebec defensive. She began coughing again, just as the contraction was reaching a peak. She muffled a cry of pain.

"Fralie? Is it . . . more than the cough?" Frebec asked, looking at her hard. He didn't think a cough should make her moan like that.

She hesitated. "What do you mean, more?" she asked.

"Well, the baby . . . but you've had two children, you know how to do these things, don't you?"

Fralie became lost in a racking cough, and when she regained control, she sidestepped the question.

Light was beginning to show around the edges of the smoke-hole cover when Ayla went back to her bed to finish dressing. Most of the Camp had been awake half the night. First it was Fralie's uncontrollable cough that woke them, but soon it became apparent that she was suffering from more than a cold. Tronie was having some difficulty with Tasher, who wanted to return to his mother. She picked him up and carried him to the Mammoth Hearth instead. He still wailed, so Ayla took him and carried him around the large hearth, offering him objects to distract him. The wolf puppy followed her. She carried Tasher through the Fox Hearth and the Lion Hearth, and then into the cooking hearth.

Jondalar watched her approaching, trying to quiet and comfort the child, and his heart beat faster. In his mind he willed her to come closer, but he felt nervous and anxious. They had hardly spoken since he moved away and he didn't know what to say. He looked around trying to think of something that might appease the baby, and noticed a small bone from a leftover roast.

"He might want to chew on this," Jondalar volunteered, when she stepped into the large communal hearth, holding the bone out to her.

She took the bone and put it in the child's hand. "Here, would you like this, Tasher?"

The meat was gone, but it still had some flavour. He put the knob end in his mouth, tasted, decided he liked it, and finally quieted.

"That was a good idea, Jondalar," Ayla said. She was holding the three-year-old, standing close and looking up at him.

"My mother used to do that when my little sister was cranky," he said.

They looked at each other, hungering for the sight of each other and filling their eyes, not saying anything, but noticing every feature, every shadow and line, every detail of change. He's lost weight, Ayla thought. He looks haggard. She's worried, upset about Fralie, she wants to help, Jondalar thought. O Doni, she's so beautiful.

Tasher dropped the bone, and Wolf snatched it.

"Drop it!" Ayla commanded. Reluctantly, he put it down, but stood guard over it.

"You might as well let him have it now. I don't think Frebec would like it too well if you gave the bone to Tasher after Wolf had it in his mouth."

"I don't want him to keep taking things that aren't his."

"He didn't really take it. Tasher dropped it. Wolf probably thought it was meant for him," Jondalar said reasonably.

"Maybe you're right. I guess it wouldn't hurt to let him keep it." She signalled, and the young wolf dropped his guard and picked up the bone again, then walked directly to the sleeping furs Jondalar had spread out on the floor, near the flint-working area. He made himself comfortable on top of them, then began gnawing on the bone.

"Wolf, get away from there," Ayla said, starting after him.

"It's all right, Ayla . . . if you don't mind. He comes often and makes himself at home. I . . . rather enjoy him."

"No, I don't mind," she said, then smiled. "You always were good with Racer, too. Animals like you, I think."

"But not like you. They love you. I do . . ." Suddenly he stopped. His forehead knotted in a frown and he closed his eyes. When he opened his eyes, he stood up straighter and stepped back a pace. "The Mother has granted you a rare gift," he said, his tone and demeanour much more formal.

Suddenly she felt hot tears in her eyes, and a pain in her throat. She looked down at the ground, then stepped back a pace, too.

"From the sound of things, I think Tasher will have a brother or sister before long," Jondalar said, changing the subject.

"I'm afraid so," Ayla said.

"Oh? You don't think she should have the baby?" Jondalar said, surprised.

"Of course, but not now. It's too soon."

"Are you sure?"

"No, I'm not sure. I haven't been allowed to see her," Ayla said.

"Frebec?"

Ayla nodded. "I don't know what to do."

"I can't understand why he still belittles your skill."

"Mamut says he doesn't think that 'flatheads' know anything about healing, so he doesn't believe I could have learned anything from them. I think Fralie really needs help, but Mamut says she must ask for it."

"Mamut is probably right, but if she really is going to have a baby, she might ask."

Ayla shifted Tasher, who had stuck a thumb in his mouth, and seemed content with that for the moment. She noticed Wolf on Jondalar's familiar furs that had been, until recently, next to hers. The furs, and his nearness, made her remember Jondalar's touch, the way he could make her feel. She wished his furs were still on her bed platform. When she looked at him again, her eyes held her desire, and Jondalar felt such an instant response, he ached to reach for her, but held back. His reaction confused Ayla. He had started to look at her the way that always brought a rush of tingling feeling deep inside. Why had he stopped? She was crushed, but she had felt a moment of . . . something . . . hope, perhaps. Maybe she could find a way to reach him, if she kept trying.

"I hope she does," Ayla said, "but it may be too late to stop the labour." She started to leave, and Wolf got up to follow her. She looked at the animal, and then at the man, paused, and then asked, "If she does ask for me, Jondalar, will you keep Wolf here? I can't have him following me and getting in the way at the Crane Hearth."

"Yes, of course I will," he said, "but will he come here?"

"Wolf, go back!" she said. He looked at her with a little whine in his throat, seeming to question. "Go back to Jondalar's bed!" she said, raising her arm and pointing. "Go to Jondalar's bed," she repeated. Wolf lowered his tail, crouched down, and went back. He sat down on top of the furs, and watched her. "Stay there!" she commanded. The young wolf lowered himself down, rested his head on his paws, and his eyes followed her as she turned and left the hearth.

Crozie, still sitting on her bed, watched as Fralie cried out and thrashed. Finally the pain passed, and Fralie took a deep breath, but that brought on a coughing spasm, and her mother thought she noticed a look of desperation. Crozie was feeling desperate, too. Somebody had to do something. Fralie was well into labour, and the cough was weakening her. There wasn't much hope for the baby any more, it was going to be born too early, and infants born too soon didn't survive. But Fralie needed something to ease her cough and her pain, and later, she would need something to ease her sorrow. It had done no good to talk to Fralie, not with that stupid man around. Couldn't he see that she was in trouble?

Crozie studied Frebec, who was hovering around Fralie's bed looking helpless and worried. Maybe he did, she thought. Maybe she should try again, but would it do any good talking to Fralie?

"Frebec!" Crozie said. "I want to talk to you."

The man looked surprised. Crozie seldom addressed him by name, or announced that she wanted to talk to him. She usually just screamed at him.

"What do you want?"

"Fralie is too stubborn to listen, but it must be obvious to you by now that she is having the baby . . ."

Fralie interrupted with a choking coughing spasm.

"Fralie, tell me the truth," Frebec said when her cough eased. "Are you having the baby?"

"I . . . I think so," she said.

He grinned. "Why didn't you tell me?"

"Because I hoped it wasn't true."

"But why?" he asked, suddenly upset. "Don't you want this baby?"

"It's too soon, Frebec. Babies that are born too soon don't live," Crozie answered for her.

"Don't live? Fralie, is something not right? Is it true this baby won't live?" Frebec said, shocked and stricken with fear. The feeling that something was terribly wrong had been growing in him all through the day, but he had not wanted to believe it, and he didn't think it could be this wrong.

"This is the first child of my hearth, Fralie. Your baby, born to my hearth." He kneeled beside the bed and held her hand. "This baby has to live. Tell me this baby will live," he pleaded. "Fralie, tell me this baby will live."

"I can't tell you. I don't know." Her voice was strained and hoarse.

"I thought you knew about these things, Fralie. You're a mother. You have two children already."

"Each one is different," she whispered. "This one has been difficult from the beginning. I was worried that I might lose it. There was so much trouble . . . finding a place to settle . . . I don't know. I just think it's too early for this baby to be born."

"Why didn't you tell me, Fralie?"

"What would you have done about it?" Crozie said, her tone restrained, almost hopeless. "What could you do? Do you know anything about pregnancy? Childbirth? Coughs? Pain? She didn't want to tell you because you've done nothing but insult the one who could help her. Now the child will die, and I don't know how weak Fralie is."

Frebec turned to Crozie. "Fralie? Nothing can happen to Fralie! Can it? Women have babies all the time."

"I don't know, Frebec. Look at her, judge for yourself."

Fralie was trying to control a cough that threatened, and the ache in her back was starting again. Her eyes were closed, and her brows drawn in. Her hair was tangled and stringy and her face shiny with sweat. Frebec jumped up and started to leave the hearth. "Where are you going, Frebec?" Fralie asked.

"I'm going to get Ayla."

"Ayla? But I thought . . ."

"She's been saying you were having trouble ever since she got here. She was right about that. If she knew that much, maybe she is a Healer. Everyone keeps saying she is. I don't know if it's true, but we've got to do something . . . unless you don't want me to."

"Get Ayla," Fralie whispered.

The excited tension communicated itself through the earthlodge as Frebec marched down the passageway towards the Mammoth Hearth.

"Ayla, Fralie is . . ." he barely began, too nervous and upset to worry about saving face.

"Yes, I know. Ask someone to get Nezzie to come and help me, and bring that container. Careful, it's hot. It's a decoction for her throat," Ayla said, hurrying towards the Crane Hearth.

When Fralie looked up and saw Ayla, she suddenly felt a great relief.

"The first thing we have to do is straighten this bed and make you comfortable," Ayla said, pulling at the bedding and covers, and bolstering her with furs and pillows for support.

Fralie smiled and suddenly noticed, for some reason, that Ayla still spoke with an accent. No, not really an accent, she thought. She just had difficulty with certain sounds. Strange how easy it was to get used to something like that. Crozie's head appeared next above her bed. She handed Ayla a piece of folded leather.

"Here's her birthing blanket, Ayla." They opened it out and while Fralie shifted, they spread it beneath the woman. "It's about time they got you, but it's too late to stop the birth now," Crozie said. "Too bad, I had an intuition that this one would be a girl. It's a shame she will die."

"Don't be too certain of that, Crozie," Ayla said.

"This baby is coming early. You know that."

"Yes, but don't give up this child to the next world, yet. There are things that can be done, if it's not too early . . . and if the birth goes well." Ayla looked down at Fralie. "Let's wait and see."

"Ayla," Fralie said, her eyes shining, "do you think there's hope?"

"There is always hope. Now, drink this. It will quiet your cough, and make you feel better. Then we'll see how far along you are."

"What's in it?" Crozie demanded.

Ayla studied the woman for a moment before replying. There had been command implicit in her tone, but Ayla sensed that concern and interest motivated the question. The tone of her request was more a style of speaking, Ayla decided, as though she was accustomed to giving orders. But it could be misunderstood as unreasonable or demanding when someone who was not in a position of leadership assumed a commanding tone.

"The inner bark of wild black cherry, to calm her, and to calm her cough and relieve the pain of labour," Ayla explained, "boiled with the dried root of blue cohosh, first ground to a powder, to help the pushing muscles work harder to hurry delivery. She's too far into labour to stop it."

"Hmm," Crozie vocalised, nodding approval. She had been as interested in verifying Ayla's expertise as she was in knowing the exact ingredients. Crozie was satisfied, from her reply, that Ayla was not just dispensing a remedy someone had told her about, but that she knew what she was doing. Not because she knew the properties of the plants, but because Ayla did.

*   *   *

Everyone stopped for a few moments to visit and offer moral support as the day progressed, but the encouraging smiles had a quality of sadness. They knew Fralie was facing an ordeal that had very little hope of a happy outcome. Time dragged for Frebec. He didn't know what to expect and felt lost, unsure. The times he had been around when women were giving birth, he didn't remember that it took so long, and it didn't seem to him that childbirth was this difficult for other women. Did they all thrash and strain, and cry out like that?

There wasn't room for him at his hearth with all the women there, and he wasn't needed, anyway. No one even noticed him sitting on Crisavec's bed, watching and waiting. Finally, he got up and walked away, not sure where to go. He decided he was hungry and headed for the cooking hearth hoping to find leftover roast or something. In the back of his mind, he thought about seeking out Talut. He felt a need to talk to someone, to share this experience with someone who might understand. When he reached the Mammoth Hearth, Ranec, Danug, and Tornec were standing near the firepit talking to Mamut, partially blocking the passageway. Frebec held back, not feeling like confronting them, to ask them to move. He hesitated, but he couldn't just stand there for ever, and started across the central space of the Mammoth Hearth towards them.

"How is she, Frebec?" Tornec asked.

He was vaguely startled by the friendly question. "I wish I knew," he replied.

"I know how you feel," Tornec said, with a wry smile. "I never feel more useless than when Tronie is giving birth. I hate seeing her in pain and keep wishing there was something I could do to help, but there never is. It's a woman's thing, she has to do it. It always surprises me afterwards how she forgets the trouble and the pain as soon as she sees the baby and knows it will be . . ." He stopped, realising he had said too much. "I'm sorry, Frebec. I didn't mean . . ."

Frebec frowned, then turned to Mamut. "Fralie said she thought this baby was coming too soon. Crozie said babies that come too soon don't live. Is that true? Will this baby die?"

"I can't answer that, Frebec. It is in the hands of Mut," the old man said, "but I do know that Ayla isn't giving up. It depends how soon. Babies born early are small and weak, that's why they usually die. But they don't always die, especially if it's not too early, and the longer they live, the better their chances are. I don't know what she can do, but if anyone can do anything, Ayla can. She was given a powerful gift, and I can assure you, no Healer could have had better training. I know from first-hand experience how skilled Clan medicine women are. One of them once healed me."

"You! You were healed by a flathead woman?" Frebec said. "I don't understand. How? When?"

"When I was a young man, on my Journey," Mamut said.

The young men waited for him to continue his story, but it soon became apparent that he was volunteering no further information.

"Old man," Ranec said, with a broad smile, "I wonder how many stories and secrets are hidden within the years of your long life."

"I have forgotten more than your full life's worth, young man, and I remember a great deal. I was old when you were born."

"How old are you?" Danug asked. "Do you know?"

"There was a time when I kept track by drawing a reminder on the spirit skin of a hide each spring of a significant event that happened during the year. I filled up several, the ceremonial screen is one of them. Now I am so old, I no longer count. But I will tell you, Danug, how old I am. My first woman had three children." Mamut looked at Frebec. "The firstborn, a son, died. The second child, a girl, had four children. The oldest was a girl, and she grew up to give birth to Tulie and Talut. You, of course, are the first child of Talut's woman. The woman of Tulie's firstborn may be expecting a child by now. If Mut grants me another season, I may see the fifth generation. That's how old I am, Danug."

Danug was shaking his head. That was older than he could even imagine.

"Aren't you and Manuv kin, Mamut?" Tornec asked.

"He is the third child of a younger cousin's woman, just as you are the third child of Manuv's woman."

Just then, there seemed to be some excitement at the Crane Hearth and they all turned to look.

"Now, take a deep breath," Ayla said, "and push once more. You're almost there."

Fralie gasped for breath and bore down hard, holding on to Nezzie's hands.

"Good! That's good!" Ayla encouraged. "Here it comes. Here it comes! Good! There we are!"

"It's a girl, Fralie!" Crozie said. "I told you this one would be a girl!"

"How is she?" Fralie asked. "Is she . . ."

"Nezzie, will you help her push out the afterbirth?" Ayla said, cleaning mucus from the infant's mouth as she struggled to take her first breath. There was an awful silence. Then a heart-stopping, miraculous, cry of life.

"She's alive! She's alive!" Fralie said, tears of relief and hope in her eyes.

Yes, she was alive, Ayla thought, but so small. She had never seen such a tiny baby. Yet, she was alive, struggling and kicking and breathing. Ayla put the baby face down across Fralie's stomach, and reminded herself that she had seen only Clan newborns. Babies of the Others were probably smaller to begin with. She helped Nezzie with the afterbirth, then turned the infant over and tied the umbilical cord in two places with the pieces of red-dyed sinew she had prepared. With a sharp flint knife, she cut the cord between the ties. For better or for worse, she was on her own; an independent, living, breathing human being. But the next few days would be critical.

Ayla examined the baby carefully while she was cleaning her. She seemed perfect, just exceptionally small and her cry was weak. Ayla wrapped her in a soft skin blanket, and handed her to Crozie. When Nezzie and Tulie had taken away the birthing blanket, and Ayla made sure Fralie was clean and comfortable, packed with an absorbent padding of mammoth wool, her new daughter was put in the crook of Fralie's arm. Then, she motioned to Frebec to come and see the first daughter of his hearth. Crozie hovered close.

Fralie unwrapped her, then looked up at Ayla with tears in her eyes. "She's so little," she said, cuddling the tiny infant. Then she untied the front of her tunic and put the baby to her breast. The newborn nuzzled, found the nipple, and from the smile on Fralie's face, Ayla knew she suckled. But in a few moments, she let go, and seemed exhausted from the effort.

"She's so small . . . will she live?" Frebec asked Ayla, but it was more a plea.

"She is breathing. If she can suckle, there is hope, but to live, she will need help. She must be kept warm, and she must not be allowed to use what little strength she has for anything but nursing. All the milk she drinks must be for growing," Ayla said. Then she gave both Frebec and Crozie a stern look. "There can be no more fighting at this hearth if you want her to live. It will make her upset, and you cannot let her become upset if she is to grow. She should not even be allowed to cry, she does not have the strength to cry. It will take her milk away from growing."

"How can I keep her from crying, Ayla? How will I know when to feed her if she doesn't cry?" Fralie said.

"Both Frebec and Crozie must help you because she must be with you every moment, just as though you were still pregnant, Fralie. I think the best way would be to make a carrier that will hold her to your breast. That way, you will keep her warm. She will be comforted by your closeness and the sound of your heart, because she is used to it. But most important, any time she needs to nurse, she need only turn her head to reach your nipple, Fralie. Then she won't use up strength she needs for growing with crying."

"What about changing her?" Crozie asked.

"Coat her skin with some of that soft tallow I gave you, Crozie, I'll make more. Use clean, dry dung packed around her to absorb her waste. Throw it out when she needs changing, but don't move her too much. And you must rest, Fralie, and not move around too much with her. It will do you good, too. We need to try to keep your cough calmed down. If she can survive the next few days, then every day she lives will make her stronger. With your help, Frebec, and Crozie, she has a chance."

A feeling of subdued hope pervaded the lodge as the drapes were closed on a red sun settling into a bank of clouds hovering on the horizon. Most people had finished their evening meal, and were stoking fires, cleaning things up, putting down children, and gathering together for the evening conversation and company. Several people were sitting around the fireplace of the Mammoth Hearth, but conversation was held down to a low murmur, as though loud voices were somehow inappropriate.

Ayla had given Fralie a mild relaxing drink, and left her to sleep. She would get little enough sleep in the days to come. Most infants settled into a routine of sleeping for a reasonable time before waking up to be fed, but Fralie's new baby couldn't nurse very long at one time, and therefore didn't sleep much before needing to nurse again. Fralie would have to get her sleep in a series of short naps, too, until the baby grew stronger.

It was almost strange to see Frebec and Crozie working together, helping each other to help Fralie, and being exceedingly courteous and restrained. It might not last, but they were trying, and some of their animosity seemed to be draining off.

Crozie had gone to bed early. It had been a difficult day and she wasn't so young any more. She was tired and she expected to be up to help Fralie later. Crisavec was still sleeping with Tulie's son, and Tronie was keeping Tasher. Frebec sat alone at the Crane Hearth, looking at the fire, feeling mixed emotions. He felt anxious and protective over the tiny infant, the first child of his hearth, and fearful. Ayla had put her in his arms to hold for a few moments while she and Crozie were making Fralie comfortable. He stared at her, awed that someone so small could be so perfect. Her diminutive hands even had fingernails. He was afraid to move, afraid he would break her, and was greatly relieved when Ayla took her back, yet he was reluctant to let her go.

Suddenly Frebec stood up and started down the passageway. He didn't want to be alone on this night. He stopped at the edge of the Mammoth Hearth and looked at the people sitting around the fire. They were the younger people of the Camp, and in the past, he would have walked by them on his way to the cooking hearth to visit with Talut and Nezzie or Tulie and Barzec or Manuv or Wymez or, lately, with Jondalar, and sometimes Danug. Even though Crozie was often at the cooking hearth, it was easier to ignore her than to face the possibility of being ignored by Deegie or disdained by Ranec. But Tornec had been friendly earlier, and his woman had given birth, and he knew how it felt. Frebec took a deep breath and walked towards the fireplace.

They broke into laughter just as he reached Tornec, and for a moment, he thought they were laughing at him. He was tempted to leave.

"Frebec! There you are!" Tornec said.

"I think there is still some tea left," Deegie said. "Let me pour you some."

"Everyone tells me she's a beautiful little girl," Ranec said. "And Ayla says she has a chance."

"We're lucky to have Ayla here," Tronie said.

"Yes, we are," Frebec replied. No one said anything for a moment. It was the first good word Frebec had ever said about Ayla.

"Maybe she can be named at the Spring Ceremony," Latie said. Frebec hadn't noticed her sitting next to Mamut in the shadow. "That would be good luck."

"Yes, it would," Frebec said, reaching for the cup Deegie gave him, and feeling a little more comfortable.

"I'm going to have a part in the Spring Ceremony, too," she announced, half shyly and half proudly.

"Latie is a woman," Deegie told him with the slightly condescending air of a big sister informing another adult who is knowledgeable.

"She will have her Rites of First Pleasures at the Summer Meeting this year," Tronie added.

Frebec nodded, and smiled at Latie, not quite sure what to say.

"Is Fralie still sleeping?" Ayla asked.

"She was when I left."

"I think I will go to bed, too," she said, getting up. "I'm tired." She put her hand on Frebec's arm. "Will you come and get me when Fralie wakes up?"

"Yes, I will, Ayla . . . and . . . uh . . . thank you," he said softly.

"Ayla, I think she's growing," Fralie said. "I'm sure she feels heavier, and she's starting to look around. She's nursing longer, too, I think."

"It's been five days. I think she may be getting stronger," Ayla agreed.

Fralie smiled, then tears came to her eyes. "Ayla, I don't know what I would have done without you. I've been blaming myself for not coming to you sooner. This pregnancy didn't feel right from the beginning, but when mother and Frebec started fighting, I couldn't take sides."

Ayla just nodded.

"I know mother can be difficult, but she has lost so much. She was a headwoman, you know."

"I guessed as much."

"I was the oldest of four children, I had two sisters and a brother . . . I was about Latie's age when it happened. Mother took me to the Deer Camp to meet the son of their headwoman. She wanted to arrange a union. I didn't want to go, and I didn't like him when I met him. He was older, and more concerned about my status than me, but before the visit was over, she managed to get me to agree. The arrangements were made for our joining at the Matrimonial the next summer. When we got back to our Camp . . . oh, Ayla, it was awful . . ." Fralie closed her eyes, trying to control herself.

"No one knows what happened . . . there was a fire. It was an old lodge, built by mother's uncle. People said the thatching, and wood, and bone must have been all dried out. They think it must have started at night . . . no one got out . . ."

"Fralie, I'm sorry," Ayla said.

"We had no place to go, so we turned around and went back to the Deer Camp. They were sorry for us, but not happy about it. They were afraid of bad luck, and we'd lost status. They wanted to break the agreement, but Crozie argued before the Council of Sisters and held them to it. The Deer Camp would have lost influence and status if they'd backed out. I was joined that summer. Mother said I had to. It was all we had left, but there was never much happiness in the union, except for Crisavec and Tasher. Mother was always fighting with them, particularly with my man. She was used to being headwoman, used to making decisions and having respect. It wasn't easy for her to lose it. She couldn't give it up. People started thinking of her as a bitter, nagging complainer, and didn't want to be around her." Fralie paused, then continued.

"When my man was gored by an aurochs, the Deer Camp said we were bad luck, and made us leave. Mother tried to arrange another union for me. There was some interest. I still had my birth status, they can't take away what you are born with, but no one wanted mother. They said she was bad luck, but I think they just didn't like her complaining all the time. I couldn't blame her, though. They just didn't understand.

"The only one who made an offer was Frebec. He didn't have much to offer" – Fralie smiled – "but he offered everything he had. I wasn't sure about him at first. He never had much status, and he doesn't always know how to act – he embarrasses mother. He wants to be worthwhile, so he tries to make himself important by saying nasty things about . . . other people. I decided to go away with him for a trial. Mother was surprised when we came back and I told her I wanted to accept his offer. She never has understood . . ."

Fralie looked at Ayla, and smiled gently. "Can you imagine what it was like being joined with someone who didn't want you, and never did care about you from the beginning? Then finding a man who wanted you so much he was willing to give everything he had, and promise everything he would ever get? That first night, after we went away together, he treated me like . . . a special treasure. He couldn't believe he had the right to touch me. He made me feel . . . I can't explain it . . . wanted. He's still like that when we're alone, but he and mother started fighting right away. When it became a matter of pride between them over whether I would see you, I couldn't take away his self-respect, Ayla."

"I think I understand, Fralie."

"I kept trying to tell myself that things weren't so bad, and your medicine did help me. I always believed he would change his mind when the time came, but I wanted it to be his idea, not something I forced him to do."

"I'm glad he did."

"But I don't know what I would have done if my baby had . . ."

"We can't be sure yet, but I think you are right. She does seem stronger," Ayla said.

Fralie smiled. "I've decided on a name for her, I hope it makes Frebec happy. I've decided to call her Bectie."

Ayla was standing by an empty storage platform sorting through a variety of dried vegetation. There were small piles of barks, roots, and seeds, little stacks of stems, bowls of dried leaves, flowers, fruits, and some whole plants. Ranec approached her, trying to be inconspicuous about hiding something behind his back.

"Ayla, are you busy?" he said.

"No, not really, Ranec. I've been going through my medicines, to see what I will be needing. I was out today with the horses. Spring is really coming – it's my favourite season. Green buds are starting, and pussy willows – I've always loved those fuzzy little flowers. Soon everything will be greening."

Ranec smiled at her enthusiasm. "Everyone is looking forward to the Spring Festival. That's when we celebrate new life, new beginnings, and with Fralie's new baby and Latie's new womanhood, we have much to celebrate."

Ayla frowned slightly. She wasn't sure if she was looking forward to her part in the Spring Ceremony. Mamut had been training her, and some very interesting things had been happening, but it was a little frightening. Not as much as she thought it would be, though. Everything would be fine. She smiled again.

Ranec had been watching her, wondering what was going through her mind, and trying to think of a way to approach the subject he had come for. "The ceremony could be especially exciting this year . . ." He paused, searching for the right words.

"I suppose you're right," Ayla said, still thinking about her part in the festival.

"You don't sound very excited," Ranec said, smiling.

"Don't I? I really am looking forward to Fralie naming the baby, and I'm so pleased for Latie. I remember how happy I was when I finally became a woman, and how relieved Iza was. It's just that Mamut is planning something and I'm not sure about it."

"I keep forgetting that you haven't been Mamutoi very long. You don't know what a Spring Festival is all about. No wonder you're not anticipating it like everyone else." He shifted his feet nervously and looked down, then back at her. "Ayla, you might anticipate it more, I would, too, if . . ." Ranec stopped, decided to change his approach, and held out the object he'd been hiding. "I made this for you."

Ayla saw what he held. She looked up at Ranec, her eyes wide with surprise and delight when she saw it. "You made this for me? But why?"

"Because I wanted to. It's for you, that's all. Think of it as a spring gift," he said, urging her to take it.

She took the ivory carving, holding it carefully, and examined it. "This is one of your bird-woman figures," Ayla said with awe and pleasure, "like the one you showed me before, but it's not the same one."

His eyes lit up. "I made it especially for you, but I should warn you," he said with mock seriousness, "I put magic in it, so you will . . . like it, and the one who made it."

"You didn't have to put magic in it for that, Ranec."

"You like it, then? Tell me, what do you think of it?" Ranec asked, though he usually didn't ask people what they thought of his work; it didn't matter to him what they thought. He worked for himself, and to please the Mother, but this time he wanted, more than anything, to please Ayla. He had put his heart, his yearning, and his dreams into every notch he cut, every line he etched, hoping this carving of the Mother would work magic on the woman he loved.

She looked closely at the figure and noticed the downward-pointing triangle. It was the symbol of woman she had learned, and one reason three was the number of generative power and sacred to Mut. The angle was repeated as chevrons, on what would be the front of the carving, if it were a woman, or the back, if it were a bird. The whole object was decorated with rows of chevrons and parallel lines in a fascinating geometric design, which was pleasing to look at by itself, but suggested more.

"It's beautifully made, Ranec. I especially like the way you did these lines. The pattern reminds me of feathers, in a way, but it also makes me think of water, like on the maps," Ayla said.

Ranec's smile turned into a delighted grin. "I knew it! I knew you would see it! The feathers of Her spirit when She becomes a bird and flies back in spring, and the birth waters of the Mother that filled the seas."

"It's wonderful, Ranec, but I can't keep it," she said, trying to give it back.

"Why not? I made it for you," he said, refusing to take it.

"But what can I give you back? I have nothing to equal the value of this."

"If that is what's worrying you, I have a suggestion. You have something I want that is worth much more than this chunk of ivory," Ranec said, smiling, his eyes flashing with humour . . . and love. He became more serious. "Join with me, Ayla. Be my woman. I want to share a hearth with you, I want your children to be the children of my hearth."

Ayla was reluctant to answer. Ranec could see her hesitation, and kept on talking, trying to persuade her. "Think how much we have in common. You're a Mamutoi woman, I'm a Mamutoi man, but both of us were adopted. And if we join, neither of us would have to move to another Camp. We could both stay in Lion Camp, and you could still take care of Mamut, and Rydag, and that would make Nezzie happy. But most important, I love you, Ayla, I want to share my life with you."

"I . . . don't know what to say."

"Say 'yes', Ayla. Let's announce it, include a Promise Ceremony in the Spring Festival. Then we can formalise the union at the Matrimonial this summer, when Deegie does."

"I'm not sure . . . I don't think . . ."

"You don't have to answer yet. Think about it if you want to." He had hoped she would agree immediately. Now he realised it might take time, but he didn't want her to say no. "Just tell me you'll give me the chance to show you how much I love you, how much I want you, how happy we can be together."

Ayla remembered what Fralie had said. It did make her feel special to know a man wanted her, that there was a man who cared about her and didn't keep avoiding her all the time. And she liked the thought of staying here where people loved her, people she loved. The Lion Camp were like her family, now. Jondalar would never stay. She had known that for a long time. He wanted to go back to his own home, and he had wanted to take her with him, once. Now he didn't seem to want her at all.

Ranec was nice, she did like him, and joining with him would mean staying here. And if she was going to have another baby, she should have it soon. She wasn't getting any younger. In spite of what Mamut had said, eighteen years seemed old to her. It would be so wonderful to have another baby, she thought. Like Fralie's baby. Only stronger. She could have a baby with Ranec. Would it have Ranec's features, his deep black eyes, his soft lips, his short wide nose, so different from the large, sharp, beaky noses of the men of the Clan? Jondalar's nose was between them in size and shape . . . why was she thinking about Jondalar?

Then an idea occurred to her that made her heart race with excitement. If I stay here and join with Ranec, she thought, maybe I could go and get Durc! Next summer, perhaps. There won't be a Clan Gathering then. What about Ura? Why not get her, too? If I go away with Jondalar, I know I'll never see Durc again. The Zelandonii live too far away, and Jondalar won't want to go back for Durc and take him with us. If only Jondalar would stay, and become Mamutoi . . . but he won't. She looked at the dark man, and saw the love in Ranec's eyes. Maybe I should think about joining with him.

"I said I would think about it, Ranec," she said.

"I know you did, but if you need more time to think about making a Promise, at least come to my bed, Ayla. Give me a chance to show you how much I care for you. Tell me you'll do that much. Come to my bed, Ayla" – taking her hand.

She looked down, trying to sort out her feelings. She felt a strong, though subtle, compulsion to obey him. Although she recognised it for what it was, it was difficult to overcome a feeling that she should go to his bed. But more than that, she wondered if she should give him a chance, perhaps have a trial with him, like Fralie did with Frebec.

Ayla nodded, still looking down. "I'll come to your bed."

"Tonight?" he said, shaking with joy and feeling like shouting.

"Yes, Ranec. If you want. I'll come to your bed, tonight."

26

Jondalar positioned himself so that he could see most of the Mammoth Hearth by looking down the passageway and through the open areas of the hearths that separated them. He had made such a habit of watching Ayla, he hardly thought about it any more. It didn't even embarrass him; it was a part of his existence. No matter what he was doing, she was always on his mind, often just at the edge of awareness. He knew when he slept and when she was awake, when she ate and when she worked on some project. He knew when she went out and knew who came to see her, and how long they stayed. He even had some idea what they talked about.

He knew Ranec had been spending most of his time there. Though he didn't like seeing them together, he also knew that Ayla had not been intimate with him, and seemed to avoid any close contact. Her actions had lulled him into a certain acceptance of the situation, and eased his anxieties, so he was unprepared for the sight of her walking with Ranec to the Fox Hearth as everyone was getting ready for bed. He couldn't believe it at first. He assumed she was just going to get something and would return to her own bed. The realisation that she was planning to spend the night with the carver did not come to him until he saw her command Wolf to go to the Mammoth Hearth.

But when it did, it was like a fire exploding in his head, that spread its burning pain and rage through his body. He was devastated. His first impulse was to rush to the Fox Hearth and tear her away. He had visions of Ranec mocking him, and he wanted to smash that dark smiling face, demolish that scornful derisive smile. He fought to control himself, and finally grabbed his parka and rushed outside.

Jondalar breathed in huge gulps of cold air, trying to cool his flaming jealousy, and almost seared his lungs with the cold. An early spring cold snap that dipped below freezing had hardened slush, turned rivulets into treacherous slides and trampled mud into uneven bumps and dips making it difficult to walk. He lost his footing in the dark and scrambled to keep his balance. When he reached the horse annexe, he went back in.

Whinney blew a greeting and Racer snorted and nudged him in the dark, looking for affection. He had spent a lot of time with the horses over the difficult winter, and even more during the uncertain spring. They welcomed his company and he relaxed in their warm, unquestioning presence. A movement of the inner drape caught his eye. Then he felt paws on his leg, and heard a pleading whine. He reached down and picked up the wolf pup.

"Wolf!" he said, smiling, but pulling back as the eager animal licked his face. "What are you doing here?" Then he lost his smile. "She made you leave, didn't she? You're used to her being there near you, and you miss her. I know how you feel. It's hard getting used to sleeping alone after she has slept beside you."

As he petted and stroked the little wolf, Jondalar felt an easing of tension, and he was reluctant to put him down. "What should I do with you, Wolf? I hate to make you go back. I suppose I could let you sleep with me."

Then he frowned, realising he was faced with a dilemma. How was he going to get back to his bed with the pup? It was cold out, and he wasn't sure if the little animal would want to go outside with him, but if he went in through the Mammoth Hearth opening, he would have to walk through the Fox Hearth to reach his bed. Nothing in the world could have induced him to walk through the Fox Hearth at that moment. Jondalar wished he had his sleeping furs with him. With no fire it was cool in the annexe, but sleeping in furs between the horses would have been warm enough. He had no choice. He would have to take the puppy out with him and back in through the front entrance.

He patted the horses, then cuddling the puppy close to his chest, pushed back the drape and stepped out into the cold night. The wind, more noticeable this time, stung his face with an icy slap, and parted the fur of his parka. Wolf tried to squirm closer and whimpered, but made no move to get away. Jondalar moved carefully over the rough frozen ground and was relieved to reach the front arch.

The lodge was quiet when he stepped into the cooking hearth. He walked to his sleeping furs, and put Wolf down, glad that he seemed content to stay. Quickly, he pulled off his parka and footwear, then crawled into the furs taking the small wolf with him. He had found it was not as warm on the floor in the open area of the hearth as it was on the enclosed sleeping platforms, and he slept in his indoor clothes, which left them rumpled. It took a few moments to find a comfortable position and settle down, but before long the warm bundle of fur curled up next to him was asleep.

Jondalar was not so fortunate. As soon as he closed his eyes, he heard the night sounds and stiffened in resistance. Normally the breathing, shuffling, coughing, whispering sounds of the Camp at night were background noise, easily ignored, but Jondalar's ears heard what he did not want to hear.

Ranec eased Ayla back on his furs, then looked down at her. "You are so beautiful, Ayla, so perfect. I want you so much, I want you to be with me always. Oh, Ayla . . ." he said, then bent down to breathe into her ear, and breathe in her woman scent. She felt his full soft mouth on hers, and felt herself respond. After a while, he put his hand on her stomach, then began slowly to move it in a circular motion, exerting gentle pressure.

Soon he reached up and cupped a breast, and then he lowered his head and took a hardened nipple in his mouth and sucked. She moaned as the tingling reached inside and moved her hips towards him. He pushed himself against her, and she felt a warm hardness next to her thigh, as he reached to take her other nipple in his mouth, and suckled hard, making little pleasure noises.

He ran his hand down her side and hip, then across her leg and up the inside of her thigh, found her moist folds and reached inside her. She felt him search her depths and pushed up against him. He eased himself around until he was pressed against her, while he suckled one breast, and then the other, and then nuzzled between them.

"Oh, Ayla. My beautiful woman, my perfect woman. How have you made me ready so soon? It is the Mother's way, Her secrets you command. My perfect woman . . ."

He was suckling again, she could feel the pressure as he pulled, and it sent shivers through her. Inside her, she felt a moving in and out, then his hand found her place of Pleasure. She cried out as he rubbed it, rhythmically, harder and faster. Suddenly, she was ready. She pushed against him moving her hips, crying out, and reaching for him.

He moved between her legs as she lifted them, helped guide him, then uttered a sigh of Pleasure as she felt him enter. His body moved back and forth, feeling the sensation building as he cried her name.

"Oh Ayla, Ayla, I want you so much. Be my woman, Ayla. Be my woman," Ranec said, as a great surge built. Her cries came in little rhythmic pants. He moved faster and faster until the warm wave of indescribable sensation broke free and washed over them.

Ayla breathed hard, catching her breath, as Ranec sprawled out on top of her. It had been a long time since she had shared Pleasures. The last time had been the night of her adoption, and she realised now that she had missed it. Ranec had been so delighted to have her and so eager to please, he almost tried too hard, but she had been more ready than she thought she would be, and though everything happened quickly, she did not feel unsatisfied.

"It was perfect for me," Ranec whispered. "Are you happy, Ayla?"

"Yes, Pleasures with you feel good, Ranec," she said. She heard him sigh.

They both lay still, enjoying the aftermath, but Ayla's thoughts went back to his question. Was she happy? She wasn't unhappy. Ranec was a good and considerate man, and she had felt Pleasure, but . . . something was missing. It was not the same as it had been with Jondalar, but she didn't know what the difference was.

Maybe it was just that she wasn't quite used to Ranec yet, she thought as she tried to shift to a more comfortable position. He was beginning to feel a bit heavy. Ranec, feeling her movement, pulled up, smiled at her, then rolled over and lay beside her on his side, nestling close to her.

He nuzzled her neck, then whispered in her ear, "I love you, Ayla. I want you so much. Say you will be my woman."

Ayla didn't answer. She couldn't answer yes, and she wouldn't answer no.

Jondalar gritted his teeth and clutched at his sleeping fur, wadding it up in his fist as he listened, against his will, to the murmuring, hard breathing, and heavy rhythmic movement from the Hearth of the Fox. He pulled the covers over his head, but could not block out the muffled sound of Ayla's voice crying out. He bit on a piece of leather to keep from making any sounds, but high in the back of his throat, his own voice cried out in pain and utter despair. Wolf, hearing, whimpered, scooted close to him, and licked the salty tears that the man tried to squeeze back.

He couldn't stand it. Jondalar could not bear the thought of Ayla with Ranec. But it was her choice, and his. What if she went back to the carver's bed again? He couldn't bear hearing that again. But what could he do? Leave. He could leave. He had to leave. Tomorrow. In the morning, at first light, he would leave.

Jondalar didn't sleep. He lay stiff with tension inside his furs when he realised they had only been resting, they were not through. Finally, when only the sounds of sleep could be heard in the lodge, he still didn't sleep. He heard Ayla and Ranec over and over again in his mind, and envisioned them together.

With the first hint of light outlining the covered smoke hole, before anyone was stirring, he was up stuffing his sleeping furs into a haversack. Then putting on his parka and footwear, and taking his spears and the spear-thrower, he quietly walked to the first archway and pushed back the drape. Wolf started to follow him, but Jondalar told him to "stay" in a hoarse whisper, and let the drape fall behind him.

Once outside, he pulled the hood up against the sharp wind and tied it tight around his face, leaving little more than an opening to see. He pulled on the mittens that dangled from his sleeves by cords, shifted the haversack, and started out walking up the slope. The ice crunched under his feet, and he stumbled in the dim light of the early grey morning, blinded by hot tears, now that he was alone.

The wind blew hard and cold when he reached the top, buffeting him with crosscurrents. He paused, trying to decide which way to go, then turned south, following the river. It was difficult walking. The freeze had been enough to form a crust of ice over some of the melting drifts, and he sunk through up to his knees, and had to pull his feet out with every step. Where there were no snowdrifts, the ground was hard and rough, and often slick. He slipped and slid, and fell once, bruising his hip.

As the morning progressed, no glowing sun penetrated the heavy overcast sky. The only evidence of its appearance was the diffused but growing light of the shadowless grey day. He plodded along, his thoughts turned inward, hardly paying attention to where he was going.

Why couldn't he bear the thought of Ayla and Ranec together? Why was it so hard for him to let her make her own choice? Did he want her just to himself? Did other men ever feel this way? Feel this pain? Was it that another man touched her? Was it fear that he was losing her?

Or was it more than that? Did he feel he deserved to lose her? She spoke easily about her life with the Clan, and he was as accepting as anyone else, until he thought about what his own people might think. Would she feel as free to talk about her childhood with the Zelandonii? She fitted in so well with the Lion Camp. They accepted her without reservation, but would they if they knew about her son? He hated to think that way. If he felt so ashamed of her, maybe he ought to give her up, but he couldn't bear the thought of losing her.

His thirst finally penetrated the murky niches of his introspection. He stopped and reached for his waterbag, then discovered he had forgotten to take it. At the next snowdrift, he broke through the crust of ice and put a handful of snow in his mouth, holding it there until it melted. It was second nature, he didn't even have to think about it. He had been trained from childhood not to eat snow for thirst without melting it first, preferably before it was put in the mouth. Swallowing snow chilled the body, and even melting it in the mouth was a last resort.

The missing waterbag made him consider his situation, for a moment. He had forgotten food, too, he realised, but it slipped out of his mind again. He was too caught up in remembering, over and over again, the sounds from the lodge, and the scenes and thoughts they created in his mind.

He came across an expanse of white, and hardly paused before plodding ahead into the drift. If he had observed his surroundings, he might have seen that it was more than a snowdrift, but he wasn't thinking. After the first few steps he broke through the crust, not into a drift of snow, but knee-deep into a pool of standing meltwater. His leather footwear, coated with fat, was waterproof enough to withstand a certain amount of snow, even wet, melting snow, but not water. The shock of cold finally snapped him out of his self-absorbed preoccupation. He waded out, breaking through more ice, and felt the added chill brought by the wind.

What a stupid thing to do, he thought. I don't even have a change of clothes with me. Or food. Or a waterbag. I have to go back. I'm not prepared for travelling at all, what can I have been thinking of? You know what you were thinking of, Jondalar, he said to himself, closing his eyes as the pain clutched him.

He was feeling the cold in his feet and lower legs, and the uncomfortable sloppy wetness. He wondered if he should try to dry out before he started back, then he realised he didn't have a firestone with him, or even a fire drill and tinder, and his footwear had liners of felted mammoth wool. Even wet, they would keep his feet from freezing, if he kept moving. He started back, berating himself for his stupidity, yet dreading every step.

As he retraced his own footsteps, he found himself thinking of his brother. He recalled the time Thonolan had been caught in quicksand at the mouth of the Great Mother River, and wanted to stay there and die. For the first time, Jondalar fully understood why Thonolan had lost his will to live after Jetamio died. His brother had chosen to stay with the people of the woman he loved, he remembered. But Jetamio had been born to the river people, he thought. Ayla was as much a stranger as he was to the Mamutoi. No, he corrected himself, that's not true. Ayla is a Mamutoi, now.

When he neared the lodge, Jondalar saw a large bulky figure coming towards him.

"Nezzie was worried about you and sent me to look for you. Where have you been?" Talut said as he fell in behind Jondalar.

"I went for a walk."

The big headman nodded. That Ayla had shared Pleasures with Ranec was no secret, but neither was Jondalar's anguish as private as he thought.

"Your feet are wet."

"I broke through the ice of a pool, thinking it was a snowdrift."

As they headed down the slope towards the Lion Camp, Talut said, "You should change your boots right away, Jondalar. I have an extra pair I will give you."

"Thank you," the younger man said, suddenly aware that he was very much an outsider. He had nothing of his own, and was entirely dependent on the goodwill of the Lion Camp, even for the necessary clothes and supplies to travel. He didn't like asking for more, but he had no choice if he was going to leave, and once he was gone, he would no longer be eating their food and making other demands on their resources.

"There you are," Nezzie said, as he walked in the earthlodge. "Jondalar! You're cold and wet! Take off those boots and let me get you something hot to drink."

Nezzie brought him a hot drink, and Talut gave him a pair of old boots and a dry pair of trousers. "You can keep these," he said.

"I'm grateful, Talut, for everything you've done for me, but I need to ask a favour. I have to leave. I must return to my home. I've been gone too long. It's time I started back, but I need some travelling gear, and some food. Once it warms up, it will be easier to find food along the way, but I need some to start out with."

"I'd be glad to give you what you need. Though my clothes are a little big on you, you can wear them," the big headman said, then grinning and smoothing his bushy red beard, he added, "but I have a better idea. Why not ask Tulie to outfit you?"

"Why Tulie?" Jondalar asked, puzzled.

"Her first man was about your size, and I'm sure she still has many of his clothes. They were of the finest quality, Tulie made sure of that."

"But why should she give them to me?"

"You still haven't collected on your future claim, and she's in debt to you. If you tell her you want it in a travelling outfit and supplies, she would make sure you have the best there is, to relieve her obligation," Talut said.

"That's right," Jondalar said with a smile. He'd forgotten the wager he'd won. It made him feel better to know he wasn't entirely without resources. "I will ask her."

"But you are not planning to leave yet, are you?"

"Yes, I am. As soon as I can," Jondalar said.

The headman sat down for some serious discussion. "It is not wise to travel yet. Everything is melting. Look what happened just going for a walk," Talut said, "and I was looking forward to you coming with us to the Summer Meeting and hunting mammoth with us."

"I don't know," Jondalar said. He noticed Mamut near one of the

422

firepits, eating, and was reminded of Ayla. He didn't think he could stand it another day. How could he possibly stay until the Summer Meeting?

"Early summer is a better time to start a long trek. It's safer. You should wait, Jondalar."

"I'll think about it," Jondalar said, though he had no intention of staying any longer than he absolutely had to.

"Good, do that," Talut said, getting up. "Nezzie told me to make sure you had some of her hot soup for breakfast. She put the last of the good roots in it."

Jondalar finished tying Talut's footwear, then got up and walked to the firepit where Mamut was finishing a bowl of soup. He greeted the old man, then reached for one of the bowls stacked nearby, and ladled some out for himself. He sat beside the shaman, pulled out his eating knife, and stabbed a piece of meat.

Mamut wiped out his bowl and put it down, then turned to Jondalar. "I could not help but overhear that you are planning to leave soon."

"Yes, tomorrow or the next day. As soon as I can get ready," Jondalar said.

"That's too soon!" Mamut said.

"I know. Talut said it was a bad time of year to travel, but I've travelled in bad seasons before."

"That's not what I mean. You must stay until the Spring Festival," he said, with absolute seriousness.

"I know it's a big occasion, everyone is talking about it, but I really need to go."

"You cannot go. It is not safe."

"Why? What difference will a few more days make? There will still be melting and flooding." The young visitor couldn't understand the old man's insistence that he stay for a festival that had no particular meaning for him.

"Jondalar, I have no doubt that you can travel in any weather. I wasn't thinking of you. I was thinking of Ayla."

"Ayla?" Jondalar said with a frown, as his stomach tightened into a knot. "I don't understand."

"I have been training Ayla in some practices of the Mammoth Hearth, and planning a special ceremony for this Spring Festival with her. We will be using a root she brought with her from the Clan. She used it once . . . with the guidance of her Mog-ur. I have experience with several magic plants that can lead one to the spirit world, but I have never used this root, and Ayla has never used it alone. We will both be trying something new. She seems to have . . . some concerns, and . . .

423

certain changes might be upsetting. If you leave, it could have an unforeseeable effect on Ayla."

"Are you saying there is some danger to Ayla in this root ceremony?" Jondalar asked, his eyes full of distress.

"There is always some element of danger in dealing with the spirit world," the shaman explained, "but she has travelled there alone, and if it happens again, without guidance or training, she could lose her way. That is why I am training her, but Ayla will need the help of those who have feelings for her, love for her. It is essential that you be here."

"Why me?" Jondalar said. "We are . . . not together any more. There are others here who have feelings . . . who love Ayla. Others she has feelings for."

The old man stood up. "I cannot explain it to you, Jondalar. It is a sense, an intuition. I can only say that when I heard you speak of leaving, a terrible, dark foreboding came over me. I'm not sure what it means, but I would . . . prefer . . . no, I will put it more strongly than that. Don't leave, Jondalar. If you love her, promise me you won't leave until after the Spring Festival," Mamut said.

Jondalar stood up and looked at the ancient, inscrutable face of the old shaman. It was not like him to make such a request without reason, but why was it so important for him to be here? What did Mamut know that he didn't? Whatever it was, Mamut's qualms filled him with apprehension. He could not leave if Ayla was in danger. "I will stay," he said. "I promise I will not leave until after the Spring Festival."

It was a few days before Ayla returned to Ranec's bed, though not because he hadn't been encouraging her. It was difficult for her to refuse him the first time he asked her outright. Her childhood training had been so strong, she felt that she had done something terribly wrong when she said no, and almost expected Ranec to be angry. But he took it with understanding, and said he knew she needed some time to think.

Ayla had learned of Jondalar's long walk the morning after her night with the dark carver, and she suspected it had something to do with her. Was it his way of showing that he still cared for her? But Jondalar was, if anything, even more distant. He avoided her whenever possible, and spoke only when it was necessary. She decided she must be wrong. He didn't love her. She was desolate when she finally began to accept it, but tried not to show it.

Ranec, on the other hand, made it abundantly clear that he loved her. He continued to press her for both her presence in his furs, and to join him at his hearth in a formally recognised union; to be his woman. She finally consented to share his furs again, largely because of his understanding, but held back her commitment to a more permanent relationship. She spent several nights with him, but then decided to refrain again for a time, this time finding it easier to refuse. She felt everything was moving too fast. He wanted to make the announcement of their Promise at the Spring Festival, which was only a few days away. She wanted time to think about it. She enjoyed Pleasures with Ranec, he was loving and knew how to please, and she cared for him. She liked him very much, in fact, but something was missing. She felt it as a vague sort of incompleteness. Though she wanted to, and wished she could, she did not love him.

Jondalar did not sleep when Ayla was with Ranec, and the strain was beginning to show. Nezzie thought he had lost more weight, but in Talut's old clothes, which hung on him, and an unkempt winter beard, it was hard to tell. Even Danug noticed that he seemed gaunt and worn, and he thought he knew the cause. He wished there was something he could do to help, he cared deeply for both Jondalar and Ayla, but no one could help. Not even Wolf, though the puppy brought more comfort than he knew. Whenever Ayla was absent from the hearth, the young wolf sought out Jondalar. It made the man feel he was not alone in his grief and rejection. He found himself spending more time with the horses as well, he even slept with them sometimes to get away from the painful scenes in the lodge, but he made a point of staying away when Ayla was around.

The weather turned warm the next few days, and it became more difficult for Jondalar to avoid her. In spite of the slush and high water, she rode the horses more often and though he tried to slip away when he saw her coming into the annexe, several times he found himself stammering excuses and leaving quickly after accidentally meeting her. Frequently she took Wolf, and occasionally Rydag, riding with her, but when she wanted to be free of responsibilities, she left the puppy behind in the boy's care, to his delight. Whinney and Racer were entirely familiar and comfortable with the young wolf, and Wolf seemed to enjoy the association of the horses whether he was on Whinney's back with Ayla, or running alongside trying to keep up. It was good exercise and a welcome excuse for her to get away from the earthlodge, which felt small and confining after the long winter, but she couldn't escape from the turmoil of strong feelings that whirled around and within her.

She had begun encouraging and directing Racer by voice, whistle, and signal while riding Whinney, but whenever she thought she should start getting him used to carrying a rider, it made her think of Jondalar and she held off. It wasn't so much a conscious decision as a delaying tactic, and a wild wish that everything would somehow work out as she had once hoped, and that Jondalar would train him and ride him.

Jondalar was thinking much the same thing. On one of their chance meetings, Ayla had encouraged him to take Whinney out for a ride, insisting that she was too busy, and that the horse needed the exercise after the long winter. He'd forgotten what sheer excitement it was to race into the wind on the back of a horse. And when he saw Racer pounding along beside him, and then pulling ahead of his dam, he dreamed of being on the young stallion's back riding beside Ayla and Whinney. Though he could generally direct the mare, he felt she was simply tolerating him, and always felt uneasy about it. Whinney was Ayla's horse, and though he eyed the brown stallion and felt a real affection for him, in his mind, Racer was Ayla's too.

As the weather warmed, Jondalar thought more about leaving. He decided to take Talut's advice and ask for his future claim from Tulie in the form of much-needed clothing and travelling equipment. As the headman had suggested, Tulie was delighted to relieve her obligation so easily.

Jondalar was tying a belt around his new deep brown tunic, when Talut strode into the cooking hearth. The Spring Festival would be the day after next. Everyone was trying on finery in preparation for the big day and relaxing after sweatbaths and a dunk in the cold river. For the first time since he left home, Jondalar had a surplus of well-made, beautifully decorated clothing as well as backpacks, tents, and other travelling gear. He had always enjoyed good quality, and his appreciation was not lost on Tulie. She had suspected all along, and now was convinced, that whoever the Zelandonii were, Jondalar came from people of high status.

"It looks like it was made for you, Jondalar," Talut said. "The beadwork across the shoulders falls just right."

"Yes, the clothes do fit well, and Tulie was more than generous. Thanks for the suggestion."

"I'm glad you decided not to leave right away. You'll enjoy the Summer Meeting."

"Well . . . ah . . . I'm not . . . Mamut . . . " Jondalar struggled for words to explain why he had not gone when he first planned to.

". . . and I'll make sure you are invited on the first hunt," Talut continued, assuming that Jondalar had stayed because of his counsel and invitation.

"Jondalar?" Deegie said, a little shocked. "From the back I thought you were Darnev!" She walked around him, with a smile on her face, looking him over. She liked what she saw. "You shaved," she said.

"It's spring. I decided it was time," he said, smiling back, his eyes telling her that she was attractive, too.

She was caught by his blue eyes, and his compelling attraction, then laughed, and decided it was time he was cleaned up and in decent clothes. He'd been looking so scruffy in his straggly, untrimmed beard and Talut's hand-me-downs, she'd forgotten how handsome he was.

"You wear that outfit well, Jondalar. It suits you. Wait until you get to the Summer Meeting. A stranger always gets a lot of attention, and I think the Mamutoi women will want to make you feel very welcome," Deegie said, with a teasing smile.

"But . . ." Jondalar gave up trying to explain that he wasn't planning to go to the Summer Meeting with them. He could tell them later, when he left.

He tried on another outfit after they left, one more suited to travelling or everyday wear, then went outside looking for the headwoman to thank her again, and show her how well the clothes fitted. In the entrance foyer, he met Danug, Rydag, and Wolf just coming in. The youth was holding Rydag with one arm and Wolf with the other. They had a fur wrapped around them and their hair was still damp. Danug had carried the boy up from the river after their sweatbath. He put them both down.

"Jondalar, you look good," Rydag signalled. "All ready for Spring Festival?"

"Yes. Are you?" he signed back.

"I have new clothes, too. Nezzie make for me, for Spring Festival," Rydag replied, smiling.

"For the Summer Meeting, too," Danug added. "She made new clothes for me, and for Latie and Rugie."

Jondalar noticed that Rydag's smile faded when Danug talked about the Summer Meeting. He didn't seem to look forward to the big summer gathering as much as the others.

When Jondalar pushed back the heavy drape and started out, Danug, not wanting the words to be heard, whispered to Rydag, "Should we have told him that Ayla is right outside? Every time he sees her, he runs away from her."

"No. He want see her. She want see him. Make right signals, wrong words," Rydag signed.

"You're right, but why can't they see it? How can they make each other understand?"

"Forget words. Make signals," Rydag replied, with his un–Clanlike smile, then picked up the wolf puppy and carried him into the lodge.

Jondalar discovered what the youngsters didn't tell him the moment he stepped out. Ayla was outside the front entrance with the two horses. She had just given Wolf to Rydag to take care of, and she was looking forward to a long, hard ride to work off the tension she was feeling.

Ranec wanted her agreement before the Spring Festival, and she couldn't make up her mind. She hoped the ride would help her think. When she saw Jondalar, her first reaction was to offer to let him ride Whinney, as she had done before, knowing that he loved it, and hoping that his love of the horses would bring him closer to her. But she wanted to ride. She had been anticipating it, and was just ready to leave.

When she looked at him again, she caught her breath. He had scraped off his beard with one of his sharp flint blades, and he looked so much the way he did when they were in her valley the previous summer, it made her heart pound and her face flush. He reacted to her physical signals with unconscious signals of his own, and the magnetic pull of his blue eyes drew her.

"You have removed your beard," Ayla said.

Without realising it, she had spoken in Zelandonii. It took him a moment before he realised what was different, then, he couldn't help but smile. He hadn't heard his own language in a long time. The smile encouraged her, and a thought came to her.

"I was just going out to ride on Whinney, and I have been thinking that someone needs to start getting Racer used to a rider. Why don't you come with me and try to ride him? It's a good day for it. The snow is almost gone, new grass is coming in, but the ground is not so hard yet, in case someone falls off," she said, rushing ahead before something happened that would make him change and become distant again.

"Uh . . . I don't know," Jondalar hesitated. "I thought you would want to ride him first."

"He's used to you, Jondalar, and no matter who rides him first, it would help to have two people. One to calm and settle him while the other gets on."

"I suppose you're right," he said, frowning. He didn't know if he should go out on the steppes with her, but he didn't know how to refuse, and he did want to ride the horse. "If you really want me to, I guess I could."

"I'll go and get a lead rope, and the guider you made for him," Ayla said, racing to the annexe before he could change his mind. "Why don't you start walking them up the slope?"

He began to have second thoughts, but she was gone before he could reconsider. He called the horses to him and started up to the broad flat plains above. Ayla caught up with them when they were near the top. She had a haversack and a waterbag as well as the halter and a rope. When they reached the steppes, Ayla led Whinney to a mound she had used before when she let some of the members of the Lion Camp, particularly the younger ones, ride the mare. With a practised leap, she was on the back of the hay-coloured horse.

"Get on, Jondalar. We can ride double."

"Ride double?" he said, almost in a panic. He hadn't considered riding double with Ayla, and was ready to bolt.

"Just until we find a nice open stretch of flat ground. We can't try it here. Racer might run into a gully or down the slope," she said.

He felt caught. How could he say he wouldn't ride double with her for a short distance? He walked to the mound, and carefully sat astride the mare, trying to sit back and avoid touching Ayla. The moment he was on, she signalled Whinney into a fast trot.

There was no preventing it. Try as he might, on the jouncing horse, he could not keep from sliding next to her. He could feel the warmth of her body through their clothing, smell the light pleasant odour of the dried cleansing flowers she used for washing, mixed with her familiar feminine scent. With each step the horse took, he felt her legs, her hips, her back pressed against him, and felt his manhood rise in response. His head was whirling, and he fought with himself to keep from kissing her neck, reaching around to hold a full, firm breast.

Why did he agree to this? Why didn't he put her off? What difference did it make if he ever rode Racer? They would never ride together. He had heard people talking, Ayla and Ranec were going to announce their Promise at the Spring Festival, and afterwards, he would leave and start on his long Journey home.

Ayla signalled Whinney to stop. "What do you think, Jondalar? There's a good flat stretch ahead."

"Yes, it looks fine," he said, quickly, and pulling his leg back around, jumped down.

Ayla lifted her leg over and slid off the other side. She was breathing fast, her face was flushed, her eyes glittering. She had breathed deeply of his man smell, melted into the warmth of his body, and shivered when she felt the hard, hot bump of his manhood. I could feel his need, she thought. Why was he in such a hurry to get away from me? Why doesn't he want me? Why doesn't he love me any more?

On opposite sides of the mare, they both tried to compose themselves. Ayla whistled for Racer, a whistle different from the one she used to call Whinney, and by the time she had patted him, and scratched him, and talked to him, she was ready to face Jondalar again.

"Do you want to put the guiding straps on his head?" she asked him, leading the young stallion towards a pile of large bones she noticed.

"I don't know. What would you do?" he said. He was also in control of himself again, and beginning to get excited about riding the young horse.

"I never did use anything to guide Whinney, except the way I moved, but Racer is used to being guided by the straps. I think I would use them," she said.

They both put the halter on Racer. Sensing something, he was friskier than usual, and they stroked and patted him to calm him down. They stacked up a couple of mammoth bones to give Jondalar something to stand on to mount the horse, then led the young horse beside them. At Ayla's suggestion, Jondalar rubbed his neck, and his back, and down his legs, and leaned across him, scratching him and stroking him, and getting him entirely familiar with the feel of the man.

"When you first get on him, hold him around the neck. He may rear to try to shake you off his back," Ayla said, trying to think of last-minute advice. "But he did get used to carrying the load on the way back from the valley, so he may not have much trouble getting used to you. Hold the lead rope, so it doesn't fall on the ground and trip him, but I would just let him run, wherever he wants to go, until he gets tired. I'll follow on Whinney. Are you ready?"

"I think so," he said, smiling nervously.

Jondalar stood on the big bones, leaned across the shaggy, sturdy animal, talking to him, while Ayla held his head. Then he eased a leg across his back, settled himself down, and clasped his arms around Racer's neck. When he felt the weight, the dark stallion laid his ears back. Ayla let go. He leaped up on his hind legs once, then he arched his back, trying to dislodge the load, but Jondalar held on. Then true to his name, the young horse broke out in a fast gallop and raced across the steppes.

Jondalar squinted into the cold wind, and felt a tremendous upsurge of sheer exhilaration. He watched the ground blur beneath him, and couldn't believe it. He was actually riding the young stallion, and it was every bit as exciting as he had imagined it would be. He closed his eyes and felt the tremendous power of the muscles bunching and straining beneath him, and a sense of magical wonder washed over him, as though for the first time in his life, he was sharing in the wonder and creation of the Great Earth Mother Herself.

He felt the young horse tiring, and, hearing other hoofbeats, opened his eyes to see Ayla and Whinney racing beside him. He smiled his wonder and delight at her, and the smile she returned made his heart pound faster. Everything else faded to insignificance for the moment. Jondalar's entire world was an unforgettable ride on the back of a racing stallion and the achingly beautiful smile on the face of the woman he loved.

Racer finally slowed, then drew to a halt. Jondalar jumped off. The young horse stood with his head hanging down almost to the ground, feet spread apart, sides heaving as he breathed hard. Whinney pulled up and Ayla jumped down. She took some pieces of soft leather out of the haversack, gave one to Jondalar, to rub down the sweaty animal, then she did the same for Whinney. The two exhausted horses crowded close together, leaning on each other for reassurance.

"Ayla, as long as I live, I'll never forget that ride," Jondalar said.

He hadn't been so relaxed for a long time, and she felt his excitement. They looked at each other, smiled, laughed, sharing the wonder of the moment. Without thinking, she reached up to kiss him, he started to respond, then suddenly, he remembered Ranec. He stiffened, withdrew her arms from around his neck.

"Don't play with me, Ayla," he said, his voice hoarse with control, as he pushed her away.

"Play with you?" she said, hurt filling her eyes.

Jondalar closed his eyes, clenched his teeth, shook with the strain of trying to maintain control. Then, suddenly, like an ice dam bursting, it was too much. He grabbed her, kissed her; a hard, mouth-bruising, desperate kiss. The next instant she was on the ground, his hands beneath her tunic, tearing at her drawstring.

She tried to help him, to untie it for him, but he couldn't wait. Impatiently, he grabbed at the waist of her soft leather leggings with both hands, and with the strength of denied passion that could be denied no more, she heard the ripping as he tore out the seams. He fumbled with the opening of his own trousers, then he was on top of her, wild in his frenzy, as his hard, throbbing shaft probed and searched.

She reached down to help guide him, feeling her own excitement mount as she realised what he so desperately wanted. But what was driving him to such ardent fury? What caused this craving need? Couldn't he see that she was ready for him? She had been ready for him the whole winter. There was never a time that she wasn't ready for him. As though her body itself had been trained from childhood to respond to his need, his signal, he had only to want her for her to want him. That was all she had been waiting for. Tears of need and love were in her eyes; she had waited so long for him to want her again.

With a passion as much denied as his, she opened to him, welcomed him, gave to him what he thought he was taking. She thrilled to the sensation of his long, hard member seeking her depths, filling her. He pulled back, and she hungered for him to return, to fill her again. She pushed to meet him when he did, pushed herself against his warm shaft, and felt the feeling deep inside tingle and grow. She arched her back to feel his movement, to press her place of Pleasure against him, to meet him again.

He cried out with the unbelievable joy of her. He had felt that way from the first time. They fitted together, matched each other, her depth for his size, as though she was made for him, and he for her. O, Mother. O, Doni, how he had missed her. How he had wanted her. How he loved her. He drove in, felt the warm, wet caress of her enfold him, take him in, reach for more, until his full shaft was buried within her.

Deep surges of Pleasure washed over him, coming in waves that matched his movements. He drove in again, and again, as she reached for him, hungered for him, ached for him. With wild abandon, with no restraint, he came back, and back to her, faster and faster, and she met him every time, felt her tension grow with his, until the peak, the crest, the last wave of Pleasure broke over them both.

He rested on top of her, in the middle of the open steppes just burgeoning with new life. Then suddenly he clutched her, buried his head in her neck, and cried her name. "Ayla, oh, my Ayla, my Ayla."

He kissed her neck, kissed her throat, kissed her mouth, then kissed a closed eye. Then he stopped, as abruptly as he began. He pulled up and looked down at her.

"You're crying! I've hurt you! O, Great Mother, what have I done?" he said. He jumped up and looked down at her, lying on the bare ground, her clothes torn. "Doni. O, Doni, what have I done? I forced her. How could I do such a thing? To her, who only knew this pain in the beginning. Now I have done it to her. O, Doni. O, Mother. How could you let me do it?"

"No, Jondalar!" Ayla said, sitting up. "It's all right. You didn't hurt me."

But he wouldn't hear her. He turned his back, not able to look at her, and covered himself. He could not turn back. He walked away, angry at himself, filled with shame, and remorse. If he couldn't trust himself not to hurt her, he would have to stay away from her, and make sure she stayed away from him. She is right to choose Ranec, he thought. I don't deserve her. He heard her get up and go to the horses. Then he heard her walking towards him, and felt her hand on his arm.

"Jondalar, you didn't . . ."

He spun around. "Stay away from me!" he snarled, full of guilty anger at himself.

She backed off. What had she done wrong now? "Jondalar . . . ?" she said again, taking a step towards him.

"Stay away from me! Didn't you hear me? If you don't stay away from me, I may lose control and force you again!" It came out sounding like a threat.

"You didn't force me, Jondalar," she said as he turned and strode off. "You cannot force me. There is no time I am not ready for you . . ."

But his thoughts were so full of remorse and self-loathing, he didn't hear her.

432

He kept walking, back towards the Lion Camp. She watched him go for some time, trying to sort out her confusion. Then she went back for the horses. She took Racer's lead rope in her hand, and holding on to Whinney's stand-up mane, mounted the mare, and quickly caught up to Jondalar.

"You're not going to walk all the way back, are you?" she said.

He didn't answer at first, didn't even turn around to look at her. If she thought he was going to ride double with her again . . . he thought, as she pulled up alongside. Out of the corner of his eye, he saw that she was leading the young stallion behind her, and he finally turned to face her.

He looked at her with tenderness and yearning. She seemed more appealing, more desirable, and he loved her more than ever, now that he was sure he'd spoiled it all. She ached to be near him, to tell him how wonderful it had been, how full and complete she felt, how she loved him. But he had been so angry, and she was so confused, she didn't know what to say.

They stared at each other, wanting each other, drawn to each other, but their silent shout of love went unheard in the roar of misunderstanding, and the clatter of culturally ingrained beliefs.

27

"I think you should ride back on Racer," Ayla said. "It's a long way to walk."

A long way, he thought. How long had he walked from his home? But he nodded, and followed her to a rock beside a small creek. Racer wasn't used to having riders. It was better to ease on him gently still. The stallion's ears went back, and he pranced a few skittish steps, but he settled down quickly and followed behind his dam as he had done many times before.

They didn't speak on the way back, and when they arrived, they were both glad that people were either inside the lodge, or at some distance from it. Neither of them was in a mood for casual conversation. As soon as they stopped, Jondalar dismounted and headed for the front entrance. He turned back just as Ayla was going into the annexe, feeling he should say something.

"Uh . . . Ayla?"

She stopped and looked up.

"I meant it, you know. I'll never forget this afternoon. The ride, I mean. Thank you."

"Don't thank me, Jondalar. Thank Racer."

"Yes, well, Racer didn't do it alone."

"No, you did it with him."

He started to say something else, then changed his mind, frowned, looked down, and went in through the front archway.

Ayla stared for a moment at the place he had been, closed her eyes, and struggled to swallow down a sob that threatened to start a flood. When she regained her composure, she went in. Though the horses had drunk from streams along the way, she poured water into their large drinking bowls, then pulled out the soft leather cloths, and started rubbing down Whinney again. Soon she just had her arms around the mare, leaning against her, her forehead pressed on the shaggy neck of her old friend, the only friend she'd had when she lived in the valley. Soon Racer was leaning on her, and she was caught in a vice between the two horses, but the familiar pressure was comforting.

Mamut had seen Jondalar come in the front, and heard Ayla and the horses in the annexe. He had the distinct feeling that something was very wrong. When he saw her come into the Mammoth Hearth, her dishevelled appearance made him wonder if she had fallen and hurt herself, but it was more than that. Something was troubling her. From the shadows of his platform he watched her. She changed, and he noticed her clothing was torn. Something must have happened. Wolf came racing in, followed by Rydag and Danug, who proudly held up a net bag with several fish in it. Ayla smiled and complimented the fishers, but as soon as they headed for the Lion Hearth to deposit their catch and collect more compliments, she picked up the young wolf and held him in her arms, and rocked back and forth. The old man was worried. He got up and walked over to Ayla's bed platform.

"I'd like to go over the Clan ritual with the root again," Mamut said. "Just to make sure we do everything right."

"What?" she said, her eyes focusing on him. "Oh . . . if you want, Mamut." She put Wolf into his basket, but he immediately jumped out and headed for the Lion Hearth and Rydag. He was in no mood to rest.

She had obviously been deep in some thought that was distressing her. She looked as though she had been crying, or was about to. "You said," he began, trying to get her to talk, and perhaps unburden herself, "Iza told you how to prepare the drink."

"Yes."

"And she told you how to prepare yourself. Do you have everything you need?"

"It's necessary to purify myself. I don't have exactly the same things, it's a different season, but I can use other things to cleanse myself."

"Your Mog-ur, your Creb, he controlled the experience for you?"

She hesitated. "Yes."

"He must have been very powerful."

"The Cave Bear was his totem. It chose him, gave him power."

"In the ritual with the root, were others involved?"

Ayla hung her head, then nodded.

There was something she hadn't told him, Mamut thought, wondering if it was important. "Did they assist him in controlling it?"

"No. Creb's power was greater than all of them. I know, I felt it."

"How did you feel it, Ayla? You never did tell me. I thought women of the Clan were barred from participating in the deepest rituals."

She looked down again. "They are," she mumbled.

He lifted her chin. "Perhaps you should tell me about it, Ayla."

She nodded. "Iza never did show me how to make it, she said it was too sacred to be wasted for practice, but she tried to tell me exactly how to do it. When we got to the Clan Gathering, the Mog-urs didn't want

435

me to make the drink for them. They said I was not Clan. Maybe they were right," Ayla added, putting her head down again. "But, there was no one else."

Was she pleading for understanding? Mamut wondered.

"I think I made it too strong, or too much. They didn't finish it all. Later, after the datura and the women's dance, I found it. I was dizzy, all I could think of was that Iza said it was too sacred to be wasted. So I drank it. I don't remember what happened after that, and yet I'll never forget it. Somehow, I found Creb and the Mog-urs, and he took me all the way back to the beginning of the memories. I remember breathing the warm water of the sea, burrowing in the loam . . . Clan and the Others, we both came from the same beginnings, did you know that?"

"I'm not surprised," Mamut said, thinking how much he would have given for that experience.

"But I was frightened, too, especially before Creb found me, and guided me. And . . . since then, I'm . . . not the same. Sometimes my dreams frighten me. I think he changed me."

Mamut was nodding. "That could explain it," he said. "I wondered how you could do so much without training."

"Creb changed, too. For a long time, it wasn't the same between us. With me, he saw something he hadn't seen before. I hurt him, I don't know how, but I hurt him," Ayla said, as tears welled up.

Mamut put his arms around her as she cried softly on his shoulder. Then her tears became the threatened flood, and she sobbed and shook with more recent grief. Her sadness for Creb brought up the tears she had been holding back, the tears of her sorrow, confusion, and thwarted love.

Jondalar had been watching from the cooking hearth. He had wanted to go to her, somehow make amends, and was trying to think of what to say when Mamut went over to talk to her. When he saw Ayla crying, he was sure she had told the old shaman. Jondalar's face burned with shame. He couldn't stop thinking about the incident on the steppes, and the more he thought about it, the worse it became.

And afterwards, he said to himself, all you did was walk away. You didn't even try to help her, didn't even try to tell her you were sorry, or how terrible you felt. Jondalar hated himself and wanted to leave, to pack up everything and leave, and not face Ayla or Mamut, or anyone, again, but he had promised Mamut he would stay until after the Spring Festival. Mamut already must think I am contemptible, he thought. Would breaking a promise be that much worse? But it was more than his promise that held him. Mamut had said Ayla might be in danger, and no matter how much he hated himself, how much he wanted to run away, Jondalar could not leave Ayla to face that danger alone.

"Do you feel better now?" Mamut said, when she sat up and wiped her eyes.

"Yes," she said.

"And you were not harmed?"

Ayla was surprised by his question. How did he know? "No, not at all, but he thinks so. I wish I could understand him," she said, as tears threatened again. Then she tried to smile. "I didn't cry so much when I lived with the Clan. It made them uneasy. Iza thought I had weak eyes, because they watered when I was sad, and she would always treat them with special medicine when I cried. I used to wonder if it was just me, or if all the Others had watery eyes."

"Now you know," Mamut smiled. "Tears were given to us to relieve pain. Life is not always easy."

"Creb used to say a powerful totem is not always easy to live with. He was right. The Cave Lion gives powerful protection, but difficult tests, too. I have always learned from them, and have always been grateful, but it is not easy."

"But necessary, I believe. You were chosen for a special purpose."

"Why me, Mamut?" Ayla cried out. "I don't want to be special. I just want to be a woman, and find a mate, and have children, like every other woman."

"You must be what you must be, Ayla. It is your fate, your destiny. If you were not able to do it, you would not have been chosen. Perhaps it is something only a woman can do. But don't be unhappy, child. Your life will not be all trials and tests. There will be much happiness, too. It just may not turn out as you want it to, or as you think it should."

"Mamut, Jondalar's totem is the Cave Lion, too, now. He was chosen and marked, too, like I was." Her hands unconsciously reached for the scars on her leg, but they were covered by her leggings. "I thought he was chosen for me, because a woman with a powerful totem must have a man with a powerful totem. Now, I don't know. Do you think he will be my mate?"

"It is for the Mother to decide, and no matter what you do, you cannot change that. But if he was chosen, there must be a reason for it."

Ranec knew Ayla had gone riding with Jondalar. He, too, had gone fishing with some of the others, but he worried the whole day that the tall, handsome man would win her back. In Darnev's clothes, Jondalar was a striking figure, and the carver, with his well-developed aesthetic sensibility, was quite aware of the visitor's undeniably compelling quality, particularly for women. He was relieved to see they were still separated, and seemed to be as distant as ever, but when he asked her to come to his bed, she said she was tired. He smiled and told her to get some rest, glad to see that she was, at least, sleeping alone, if she wasn't going to sleep with him.

Ayla was not so much tired as emotionally spent when she went to bed, and she lay awake for a long time, thinking. She was glad Ranec hadn't been at the lodge when she and Jondalar returned, and grateful that he wasn't angry when she refused him – she still kept expecting anger, and punishment for daring to be disobedient. But Ranec was not demanding, and his understanding almost changed her mind.

She tried to sort out what had happened, and even more, her feelings about it. Why did Jondalar take her if he didn't want her? And why had he been so rough with her? He was almost like Broud. Then why was she so ready for Jondalar? When Broud had forced her, it had been an ordeal. Was it love? Did she feel Pleasures because she loved him? But Ranec made her feel Pleasures, and she didn't love him, or did she?

Maybe she did, in a way, but that wasn't it. Jondalar's impatience made it seem like her experience with Broud, but it was not the same. He was rough, and excited, but he didn't force her. She knew the difference. Broud had wanted only to hurt her, and make her yield to him. Jondalar wanted her, and she had responded deeply, with every ounce of her being, and felt satisfied and completed. She would not have felt that way if he had hurt her. Would he have forced her if she hadn't wanted him? No, she thought, he wouldn't have. She was convinced that if she had objected, if she had pushed him away, he would have stopped. But she hadn't objected, she had welcomed him, wanted him, and he must have felt it.

He wanted her, but did he love her? Just because he wanted to share Pleasures with her didn't mean he still loved her. Maybe love could make Pleasures better, but it was possible to have one without the other. Ranec showed her that. Ranec loved her, she had no doubt about him. He wanted to join with her, wanted to settle with her, wanted her children. Jondalar had never asked her to join, never said he wanted her children.

He loved her once, though. Maybe she felt Pleasures because she loved him, even if he didn't love her any more. But he still wanted her, and he took her. Why was he so cold afterwards? Why had he rejected her again? Why had he stopped loving her? Once she thought she knew him. Now, she didn't understand him at all. She rolled over and curled into a tight ball, and wept quietly again, wept with wanting Jondalar to love her again.

★   ★   ★

"I'm glad I thought about inviting Jondalar along on the first mammoth hunt," Talut said to Nezzie as they retired to the Lion Hearth. "He's been so busy making that spear all night, I think he must really want to go."

Nezzie looked at him, raising an eyebrow and shaking her head. "Mammoth hunting is the farthest thing from his mind," she said, then tucked a fur around the sleeping blonde head of her youngest daughter, and smiled with gentle affection at the girl-woman form of her eldest, curled up next to her younger sister. "We're going to have to think about a separate place for Latie next winter, she'll be a woman, but Rugie will miss her."

Talut glanced back and saw the visitor brushing off chips of flint while he tried to see Ayla through the intervening hearths. When he didn't see her, he looked towards the Fox Hearth. Talut turned his head and saw Ranec getting into his bed alone, but he, too, kept glancing towards Ayla's bed. Nezzie is probably right, he thought.

Jondalar had stayed up until the last person left the cooking hearth, working on a long flint blade that he would haft to a sturdy shaft the same way Wymez did, learning how to make a Mamutoi mammoth hunting spear by first making an exact copy of one. The part of his mind that was always aware of the nuances of his craft had already thought of ideas for possible improvements, or at least interesting experiments, but the work was a familiar process that took little concentration, which was just as well. He couldn't think about anything but Ayla, and he was only using the work as a way to avoid company and conversation and be alone with his thoughts.

He felt a great relief when he saw her going to her bed alone earlier, he didn't think he could have borne it if she had gone to Ranec's bed. He carefully folded his new clothes, then got into new sleeping furs which were spread out on top of his old travelling roll. He folded his hands behind his head and stared up at the too-familiar ceiling of the cooking hearth. He had lain awake studying it too many nights. He still ached with remorse and shame, but not, on this night, with the burning ache of need, and as much as he hated himself for it, he remembered the Pleasure of the afternoon. He thought about it, carefully recalling every moment, turning over every detail in his mind, slowly savouring now what he had not taken time to think about then.

He was more relaxed than he had been since Ayla's adoption, and he slipped into a half-dozing, musing reverie. Had he imagined that she had been so willing? He must have; she could not have been that eager for him. Had she really responded with such feeling? Reaching for him as though she had wanted him as much as he wanted her? He felt the pull in his loins as he thought of her again, of filling her, of her deep warmth embracing him fully. But the need was easier, more like a warm afterglow, not the driving, hurting pain that was a combination of repressed desire, powerful love, and burning jealousy. He thought about Pleasuring her – he loved to Pleasure her – and he started to get up to go to her again.

It was only when he pushed back the cover and sat up, when he started to act on the urge brought on by his dreamy intimate ruminations, that the consequences of the afternoon struck him. He couldn't go to her bed. Not ever. He could never touch her again. He had lost her. It was no longer a matter of choice. He had destroyed any chance he had that she might choose him. He had taken her by force, against her will.

Sitting on his sleeping furs, with his feet on a floor mat and his elbows leaning on his bent-up knees, he held his bowed head and felt an agony of shame. His body shook with silent heaves of disgust. Of all the despicable things he had done in his life, this unnatural act was by far the worst.

There was no worse abomination, not even the child of mixed spirits, or the woman who gave birth to one, than a man who took a woman against her will. The Great Earth Mother Herself decried it, forbade it. One had only to observe the animals of Her creation to know how unnatural it was. No male animal ever took a female against her will.

In their season the stags might fight each other for the privilege of Pleasuring the does, but when the male deer tried to mount the female, she had only to walk away if she didn't want him. He could try and try, but she had to allow it, she had to stand for it. He could not force her. It was the same for every animal. The female wolf or the she-lion invited the male of her choice. She rubbed against him, passed her tempting odour before his nose, and moved her tail aside when he mounted, but she would turn angrily on any male who tried to mount against her will. He paid dearly for his audacity. A male could be as persistent as he liked, but the choice was always the female's. That was the way the Mother meant it to be. Only the human male ever forced a female, only an unnatural, abominable human male.

Jondalar had often been told, by Those Who Served the Mother, that he was favoured by the Great Earth Mother and all women knew it. No woman could refuse him, not even the Mother Herself. That was his gift. But even Doni would turn Her back on him now. He hadn't asked, not Doni, not Ayla, not anyone. He had forced her, taken her against her will.

Among Jondalar's people, any man who committed such a perversion was shunned – or worse. When he was growing up, young boys talked among themselves about being painfully unmanned. Though he never

440

knew anyone who was, he believed it was a fitting punishment. Now, he was the one who should be punished. What could he have been thinking of? How could he have done such a thing?

And you worried about her not being accepted, he said to himself. You were afraid she would be rejected, and you weren't sure if you could live with that. Who would be rejected now? What would they think of you if they knew? Especially after . . . what happened before. Not even Dalanar would take you in now. He would strike you from his hearth, turn you away, disclaim all ties. Zolena would be appalled. Marthona . . . he hated to think how his mother would feel.

Ayla had been talking to Mamut. She must have told him, that must have been why she was crying. He leaned his forehead against his knees and covered his head with his arms. Whatever they did to him, he deserved. He sat hunched over for some time, imagining the terrible punishments they would impose on him. He even wished they would do something terrible to him, to relieve the burden of guilt that weighed him down.

But eventually reason prevailed. He realised that no one had said a word to him about it all evening. Mamut even spoke to him about the Spring Festival and never brought it up. Then what had she been crying about? Maybe she was crying about it, but just never said anything. He lifted his head and looked across the darkened hearths in her direction. Could that be? Of all people, she had more right than anyone to claim redress. She had already had more than her share of unnatural acts forced on her by that brutal flathead . . . What right did he have to speak ill of that other man? Was he any better?

Yet, she had kept it to herself. She did not denounce him, did not demand his punishment. She was too good for him. He didn't deserve her. It was right that she and Ranec should Promise, Jondalar thought. Even as the thought entered his mind, he felt a tight knot of pain, as he understood that would be his punishment. Doni had given him what he had wanted most. She had found him the only woman he could ever love, but he couldn't accept her. And now he had lost her. It was his own fault, he would accept his punishment, but not without grieving.

As long as he could remember, Jondalar had fought for self-control. Other men showed emotion – laughed, or angered, or wept – far more easily than he, but above all, he resisted tears. Since the time he had been sent away and lost his tender credulous youth in a night of crying for the loss of home and family, he had wept only once: in Ayla's arms for the loss of his brother. But once again, on that night, he grieved. In the dark earthlodge of people who lived a year's Journey away from his home, he wept silent, unstoppable tears for the loss he felt most keenly of all. The loss of the woman he loved.

The long-awaited Spring Festival was both a new year's celebration and a festival of thanksgiving. Held not at the beginning, but at the height of the season when the first green buds and shoots were well established and could be harvested, it marked the start of the yearly cycle for the Mamutoi. With fervent joy and unspoken relief, that could only be fully appreciated by those who lived on the edge of survival, they welcomed the greening of the earth, which guaranteed life for themselves and the animals with whom they shared the land.

On the deepest, coldest nights of the harsh glacial winter, when it seemed the air itself would freeze, doubt that warmth and life would ever return again could arise in the most believing heart. Those times when spring seemed most remote, memories and stories of previous Spring Festivals relieved deep-seated fears and gave renewed hope that the Earth Mother's cycle of seasons would indeed continue. They made each Spring Festival as exciting and memorable as possible.

For the big Spring Feast, nothing left over from the previous year would be eaten. Individuals and small groups had been out for days fishing, hunting, trapping, and gathering. Jondalar had put his spear-thrower to good use and was pleased to contribute a pregnant bison entirely by himself, thin and gaunt though she was. Every edible vegetable product they could find was collected. Birch and willow catkins; the young unfolding stems of ferns as well as the old rootstocks which could be roasted, peeled, and pounded into flour; the juicy inner cambium bark of pines and birch, sweet with new rising sap; a few purplish-black curlewberries, filled with hard seeds, growing beside the small pink flowers on the ever-bearing low shrub; and from sheltered areas, where they had been covered with snow, bright red lingonberries, frozen and thawed to a soft sweetness, lingered with the dark leathery leaves on low tufted branches.

Buds, shoots, bulbs, roots, leaves, flowers of every description; the earth abounded with delicious fresh foods. Shoots and young pods of milkweed were used for sweetening. New green leaves of clover, pigweed, nettles, balsam-root, dandelion, wild lettuce and sorrel would be cooked or eaten raw; thistle stalks and, especially, sweet thistle roots were searched out. Lily bulbs were a favourite, and cattail shoots and bulrush stems. Sweet, flavourful liquorice roots could be eaten raw or roasted in ashes. Some plants were collected for sustenance, others mainly for the flavour they imparted, and many were used for teas. Ayla knew the medicinal qualities of most of them, and gathered some for her uses, as well.

On rocky slopes, the narrow tubular new shoots of wild onion were picked, and in dry, bare places, small leaves of lemony sorrel. Coltsfoot was collected from damp open ground near the river. Its slightly salty taste made it useful for seasoning, though Ayla gathered some for coughs and asthma. Garlicky-tasting ramson greens were picked for taste and flavour, as were tart juniper berries, peppery tiger lily bulbs, flavourful basil, sage, thyme, mint, linden, which grew as a prostrate shrub, and a variety of other herbs and greens. Some would be dried and stored, some used to season the recently caught fish and the various kinds of meats brought back for the feast.

The fish were plentiful, and favoured at this time of year, since most of the animals were still lean from the ravages of winter. But fresh meat, including at least one, symbolic, spring-born young animal – this year a tender bison calf – was always included in the feast. To make a feast of only the fresh products of the earth showed that the Earth Mother was offering her full bounty again, that She would continue to provide for and nurture Her children.

With the foraging and collecting of foods for the feast, the anticipation of the Spring Festival had been building up for days. Even the horses could sense it. Ayla noticed they were nervous. In the morning she took them outside, some distance from the earthlodge, to curry and brush them. It was an activity that relaxed Whinney and Racer and that relaxed her, and it gave her an excuse to get off by herself to think. She knew she should give Ranec an answer today. Tomorrow was the Spring Festival.

Wolf was curled up nearby, watching her. He sniffed the air, lifted his head and looked, and banged his tail against the ground, signalling the approach of someone friendly. Ayla turned, and felt her face flush and her heart pound.

"I was hoping I'd find you alone, Ayla. I'd like to talk to you, if you don't mind," Jondalar said, in a strangely subdued voice.

"No, I don't mind," she said.

He was shaved, his light hair pulled back neatly and tied at the nape of his neck, and he was wearing one of his new outfits from Tulie. He looked so good to her – handsome was the word Deegie used – he almost took her breath away, and her voice caught in her throat. But it was more than his appearance that moved Ayla. Even when he was wearing Talut's hand-me-downs, he looked good to her. His presence filled the space around him and touched her, as though he were a glowing ember that warmed her, even standing apart. It was a warmth that was not heat, but larger, more filling, and she wanted to touch that warmth, ached to feel it enfold her, and swayed towards him. But something in his eyes held her back, something ineffably sad that she had not seen there before. She stood quietly, waiting for him to speak.

He closed his eyes for a moment, gathering his thoughts, not sure how to begin. "Do you remember, when we were together in your valley, before you could speak very well, you wanted to tell me something once that was important, but you didn't know the words for it? You began to speak to me in signs – I remember thinking your movements were beautiful, almost like a dance."

She remembered only too well. She had been trying to tell him then what she wished she could tell him now: how she felt about him, how he filled her with a feeling that she still had no words for. Even to say she loved him was not enough.

"I'm not sure there are words to say what I need to say. 'Sorry' is just a sound that comes out of my mouth, but I don't know how else to say it. I'm sorry, Ayla, more than I can say. I had no right to force you, but I can't take back what has already been done. I can only say it won't ever happen again. I'll be leaving soon, as soon as Talut thinks it's safe to travel. This is your home. People here care about you . . . love you. You are Ayla of the Mamutoi. I am Jondalar of the Zelandonii. It's time for me to go home."

Ayla couldn't speak. She looked down, trying to hide the tears she couldn't hold back, then turned around and began to rub down Whinney, unable to look at Jondalar. He was leaving. He was going home and he hadn't asked her to go with him. He didn't want her. He didn't love her. She swallowed her sobs as she rubbed the brush over the horse. Not since she'd lived with the Clan had she fought so hard to hold back tears, struggled not to show them.

Jondalar stood there, staring at her back. She doesn't care, he thought. I should have left a long time ago. She had turned her back on him; he wanted to turn around and leave her to her horses, but the silent body language of her motions signalled a message that he couldn't put into words. It was only a sense, a feeling that something wasn't right, but it made him reluctant to go.

"Ayla . . . ?"

"Yes," she said, keeping her back turned and struggling to keep her voice from cracking.

"Is there . . . anything I can do before I leave?"

She didn't answer immediately. She wanted to say something that would change his mind, and tried frantically to think of a way to bring him closer to her, to keep him interested. The horses, he liked Racer. He liked riding him.

"Yes, there is," she finally said, fighting to sound normal.

He had turned to go when she didn't answer, but turned back quickly.

"You could help me train Racer . . . as long as you're here. I don't have as much time to take him out as I should." She allowed herself to turn around and face him again.

444

Did he imagine that she looked pale, that she was trembling? "I don't know how long I'll be here," he said, "but I'll do what I can." He started to say more, he wanted to tell her he loved her and that he was leaving because she deserved more. She deserved someone who would love her without reservation, someone like Ranec. He looked down while he searched for the right words.

Ayla was afraid she wouldn't be able to hold back the tears much longer. She turned to the mare and began to brush her again, then dropped the brush and was astride her and riding in one smooth action. Jondalar looked up and stepped back a few paces, surprised, and watched Ayla and the mare galloping up the slope, with Racer and the young wolf following behind. He stood there long after they were out of sight, then slowly walked back to the lodge.

The anticipation and tension were so intense on the night before the Spring Festival that no one could sleep. Both children and adults stayed up late. Latie was in a state of especially high excitement, feeling impatient one moment and nervous the next about the short puberty ceremony that would announce her readiness to begin preparations for the Celebration of Womanhood that would take place at the Summer Meeting.

Though she had reached physical maturity, her womanhood would not be complete until the ceremony that would culminate in the First Night of Pleasures when a man would open her so that she could receive the impregnating spirits joined by the Mother. Only when she was capable of motherhood was she considered a woman in all respects and, therefore, available for establishing a hearth and joining with a man to form a union. Until then, she would exist in the in-between state of no-longer-child but not-yet-woman, when she would learn about womanhood, motherhood, and men from older women and Those Who Served the Mother.

The men, except for Mamut, had been chased out of the Mammoth Hearth. All the women had gathered there while Latie was being instructed for the ceremony the next night, to offer moral support, advice, and helpful suggestions to the fledgling woman. Though she was there as an older woman, Ayla was learning as much as the young woman.

"You won't have much to do tomorrow night, Latie," Mamut was explaining. "Later you will have more to learn, but this is just to give notice. Talut will make the announcement, then I will give you the muta. Keep it in a safe place until you are ready to establish your own hearth."

Latie, sitting in front of the old man, nodded, feeling shy, but rather enjoying all the attention.

"You understand, after tomorrow, you must never be alone with a man, or even speak to any man alone, until you are fully a woman," Mamut said.

"Not even Danug or Druwez?" Latie asked.

"No, not even them," he said. The old shaman explained that during this transitional time, when she lacked the protection of both the guardian spirits of childhood and the full power of womanhood, she was considered very vulnerable to malignant influences. She would be required to stay within the watchful eye of some woman at all times, and must not even be alone with her brother or her cousin.

"What about Brinan? Or Rydag?" the young woman asked.

"They are still children," Mamut said. "Children are always safe. They have protective spirits hovering around all the time. That's why you must be protected now. Your guardian spirits are leaving you, making way for the life force, the Mother's power, to enter."

"But Talut or Wymez wouldn't harm me. Why can't I talk to them alone?"

"Male spirits are drawn to the life force, just as you will find that men are drawn to you now. Some male spirits are jealous of the Mother's power. They may try to take it from you, at this time, when you are vulnerable. They cannot use it to create life, but it is a powerful force. Without proper precaution, a male spirit may enter and even if he doesn't steal your life force, he may damage or overpower it. Then you may never have children, or your desires may become those of a male, and you will wish to share Pleasures with women."

Latie's eyes opened wide. She didn't know it was that dangerous. "I'll be careful, I won't let any male spirit come too close, but . . . Mamut . . ."

"What is it, Latie?"

"What about you, Mamut? You're a man."

Several women giggled, and Latie blushed. Maybe it was a stupid question.

"I would have asked the same question," Ayla remarked. Latie gave her a grateful look.

"It is a good question," Mamut said. "I am a man, but I also Serve Her. It would probably be safe to talk to me any time, and of course, for certain rituals when I am acting as One Who Serves, you will have to speak to me alone, Latie. But I think it would still be a good idea not to come just to visit me or to speak to me unless another woman is with you."

Latie nodded, frowning seriously, beginning to feel the responsibility of establishing a new relationship with people she had known and loved all her life.

"What happens when a male spirit steals the life force?" Ayla asked, very curious about these interesting beliefs of the Mamutoi that were somewhat similar to, yet very different from the traditions of the Clan.

"Then you have a powerful shaman," Tulie said.

"Or an evil one," Crozie added.

"Is that true, Mamut?" Ayla asked. Latie looked surprised and puzzled, and even Deegie, Tronie, and Fralie turned to Mamut with interest.

The old man gathered his thoughts, trying to choose his answer carefully. "We are only Her children," he began. "It is difficult for us to know why Mut, the Great Mother, selects some of us for special purposes. We only know that She has Her reasons. Perhaps there are times when She has need for someone of exceptional power. Some people may be born with certain gifts. Others may be chosen later, but no one is chosen without Her knowledge." Several eyes shifted towards Ayla, trying not to be conspicuous about it.

"She is the Mother of all," he continued. "No one can know Her completely, in all Her faces. That's why the face of the Mother is unknown on the figures that represent Her." Mamut turned to the oldest woman of the Camp. "What is evil, Crozie?"

"Evil is malicious harm. Evil is death," the old woman replied with conviction.

"The Mother is all, Crozie. The face of Mut is the birth of Spring, the bounty of Summer, but it is also the little death of Winter. Hers is the power of life, but the other face of life is death. What is death but return to Her to be reborn? Is death evil? Without death, there can be no life. Is evil malicious harm? Perhaps, but even those who seem to work evil, do so for Her reasons. Evil is a force She controls, a means to accomplish Her purposes; it is only an unknown face of the Mother."

"But what happens when a male force steals the life force of a woman?" Latie asked. She didn't want philosophies, she wanted to know.

Mamut looked at her speculatively. She was almost a woman, she had the right to be told. "She will die, Latie."

The girl shivered.

"Even if it is stolen. Some may remain, enough for her to start a new life. The life force that resides in a woman is so powerful, she may not know it was stolen until she is giving birth. When a woman dies in childbirth, it is always because a male spirit stole her life force before she was opened. That's why it is not healthy to wait too long for the Womanhood Ceremony. If the Mother had made you ready last fall, I would have talked to Nezzie about arranging a gathering of a few Camps to have a ceremony so you would not go through the winter unprotected, even though it means you would have missed the excitement of the celebration at the Summer Meeting."

447

"I'm glad I won't have to miss it, but . . ." Latie paused, still more concerned about life force than celebration, "does a woman always die?"

"No, sometimes she struggles to keep her life force, and if it is powerful, she may not only keep it, but the male force as well, or a part of it. Then she has the power of both in one body."

"Those are the ones who become powerful shamans," Tulie volunteered.

Mamut nodded. "Often, that is true. In order to learn how to use the power of both female and male, many people turn to the Mammoth Hearth for guidance, and many of those are called to Serve Her. They are often very good Healers, or Travellers in the Mother's underworld."

"What about the male spirit that does steal the life force?" Fralie asked, putting her new baby over her shoulder and patting gently. She knew it was a question her mother wanted to ask.

"That's the one who is evil," Crozie said.

"No," Mamut said, shaking his head. "That is not true. The male force is just attracted to a woman's life force. It cannot help itself, and men don't usually know that their male force has taken a young woman's life force until they discover they are not attracted to women, but prefer the company of other men. Young men are vulnerable then. They don't want to be different, they don't want anyone to know their male spirit may have harmed some woman. They often feel great shame, and rather than come to the Mammoth Hearth, they try to hide it."

"But there are evil ones among them with great power," Crozie said. "Power to destroy an entire Camp."

"The force of male and female in one body is very powerful. Without guidance, it can become perverted and malicious, and may want to cause illness and misfortune, even death. Even without such power, a person wishing misfortune on another can cause it to happen. With it, the results are almost inevitable, but with proper guidance, a man with both forces can become just as powerful a shaman as a woman with both forces, and is often more careful to use it only for good."

"What if a person like that doesn't want to be a shaman?" Ayla asked. She may have been born with her "Gifts" but she still had feelings of being pushed into something she wasn't sure she wanted.

"They don't have to," Mamut said. "But it's easier for them to find companionship, others like themselves, from among Those Who Serve the Mother."

"Do you remember those Sungaea travellers we met many years ago, Mamut?" Nezzie asked. "I was young then, but wasn't there some confusion about one of their hearths?"

"Yes, I remember, now that you mention it. We were just returning from the Summer Meeting, several Camps still travelling together when we met them. No one was quite sure what to expect, there had been some raiding, but finally we had a friendship fire with them. Some Mamutoi women got upset because one Sungaea man wanted to join them in their 'mother's place'. It took a lot of explaining to make it understood that the hearth which we thought consisted of one woman and her two co-mates was really one man and *his* two co-mates, except that one of them was a woman, and one of them was a man. The Sungaea referred to him as 'she'. He was bearded, but dressed in women's clothes, and though he had no breasts, he was 'mother' to one of the children. He certainly acted like the child's mother. I'm not sure if the child had been given to him by the woman of that hearth, or by another woman, but I was told that he experienced all the symptoms of pregnancy, and the pain of delivery."

"He must have wanted to be a woman very much," Nezzie commented. "Maybe he didn't steal some woman's life force. Maybe he was born in the wrong body. That can happen, too."

"But did he have stomach aches every moon time?" Deegie asked. "There's the test of a woman." Everyone laughed.

"Do you have moon-time stomach aches, Deegie? I can give you something to help, if you want," Ayla said.

"I may ask, next time."

"Once you have a child, it won't be so bad, Deegie," Tronie said.

"And when you're carrying, you don't have to worry about absorbent packing, and disposing of it properly," Fralie said. "But you do look forward to having them," she added, smiling at the sleeping face of her small but healthy daughter, and wiping away a dribble of milk from the corner of her mouth. She looked up at Ayla, suddenly curious. "What did you use when you were . . . younger?"

"Soft leather straps. They work well, especially if you need to travel, but sometimes I folded them over, or stuffed them with mouflon wool, or fur, or even bird down. Sometimes soft fluff from plants, crushed together. Never with dried mammoth dung, before, but it works, too."

Mamut had the ability to efface his presence and fade into the background when he chose, so that the women forgot he was there and spoke freely in a way they would never have done if another man had been there. Ayla was aware of him, however, and observed him quietly observing them. Finally, when the conversation slowed down, he spoke to Latie again.

"Some time soon, you will want to find a place for your personal communion with Mut. Pay attention to your dreams. They will help you find the right place. Before you visit your personal shrine, you will have to fast, and purify yourself, always acknowledge the four directions and the underworld and sky, and make offerings and sacrifices to Her,

449

particularly if you want Her help, or a blessing from Her. It's especially important when the time comes that you want to have a child, Latie, or when you learn you are going to have one. Then you must go to your personal shrine and burn a sacrifice to Her, a gift that will go up to Her in the smoke."

"How will I know what to give Her?" Latie asked.

"It could be something you find or something you make. You will know if it feels right. You will always know."

"When you want a special man, you can ask Her, too," Deegie said, with a conspiratorial smile. "I can't tell you how many times I asked for Branag."

Ayla glanced at Deegie, and resolved to find out more about personal shrines.

"There is so much to learn!" Latie said.

"Your mother can help you, and Tulie, too," Mamut said.

"Nezzie has asked me and I've agreed to be a Watching Woman this year, Latie," Tulie mentioned.

"Oh, Tulie! I'm so glad," Latie said. "Then I won't feel so alone."

"Well," the headwoman said, smiling at the girl's eager welcome, "it's not every year that the Lion Camp has a new woman."

Latie frowned with concentration, then asked in a soft voice, "Tulie what is it like? In the tent, I mean. That night."

Tulie looked at Nezzie, and smiled. "Are you a little worried about it?"

"Yes, a little."

"Don't worry. It will all be explained to you. You'll know what to expect."

"Is it anything like the way Druwez and I played when we were children? He would bounce on me so hard . . . I think he was trying to be Talut."

"Not really, Latie. Those were children's games, you were only playing, trying to be grown up. You were both very young then, too young."

"That's true, we were very young," Latie said, feeling very much older now. "Those are games for little children. We stopped playing like that a long time ago. In fact, we don't play anything any more. Lately, neither Danug or Druwez will even talk to me very much."

"They will want to talk to you," Tulie said. "I am sure of it, but remember, you must not talk to them very much, now, and not ever be alone with them."

Ayla reached for the large waterbag that was hanging by a leather strap from a peg pounded into one of the supporting posts. It was made from the stomach of a giant deer, a megaceros, which had been cured to maintain its naturally watertight character. It was filled through the lower opening, which was folded over and closed off. A short piece of a foreleg bone with a natural hollow in the middle had been grooved all the way around near one end. To form a pouring spout, the skin of the opening of the deer stomach was tied to the bone by wrapping a cord tightly around it at the groove.

Ayla pulled out the stopper – a thick strip of leather that had been passed up through the hollow and knotted in one place several times – poured water into the watertight basket she used for making her special morning tea, and pushed the leather knot back into the pouring spout to close it off. The red-hot cooking stone sputtered as she dropped it into the water. She stirred it around a few times to draw off as much heat from the stone as possible, then fished it out with two flat sticks, and put it back in the fire. With the damp sticks, she picked up another hot stone and dropped it into the water. When the water was simmering, she dropped in a measured amount of a mixture of dried leaves, roots, and particularly the fine vinelike stems of golden thread and left it to steep.

She had been especially careful to remember to take Iza's secret medicine. She hoped the powerful magic would work for her as well as it had worked for Iza for so many years. She did not want a baby now. She was too unsure.

After she dressed, she poured the tisane into her personal drinking cup, then sat down on a mat near the fire and tasted the strong-tasting, rather bitter drink. She had grown accustomed to the taste in the morning. This was her time for waking up, and it was part of her morning routine. As she sipped, she mused about the activities that would take place that day. This was it, the auspicious day everyone had been looking forward to, the day of the Spring Festival.

The happiest event, to her, would be the naming of Fralie's baby. The tiny infant had grown and thrived, and no longer had to be held next to her mother's breast every moment. She was strong enough to cry now, and could sleep alone during the day, though Fralie rather liked keeping her close and often used the carrier out of preference. The Hearth of the Crane was much happier these days, not only because they shared the joy of the baby, but because Frebec and Crozie were learning they could live without arguing every moment. Not that there weren't still problems, but they were coping better, and Fralie herself was taking a more active role in trying to mediate.

Ayla was thinking about Fralie's baby when she looked up and saw Ranec watching her. This was also the day he wanted to announce their Promise, and with a jolt, she remembered that Jondalar had told her he

451

was leaving. Suddenly she found herself recalling that terrible night when Iza died.

"You are not Clan, Ayla," Iza told her. *"You were born to the Others, you belong with them. Go north, Ayla. Find your own people. Find your own mate."*

Find your own mate . . . she thought. Once she thought Jondalar would be her mate, but he was leaving, going to his home without her. Jondalar didn't want her . . .

But Ranec did. She wasn't getting younger. If she was ever going to have a baby, she should be starting one soon. She took a sip of Iza's medicine, and swirled the last of the liquid and the dregs in the cup. If she stopped taking Iza's medicine, and shared Pleasures with Ranec, would that start a baby inside her? She could try it and find out. Maybe she should join with Ranec. Settle with him, have the children of his hearth. Would they be beautiful dark babies with dark eyes and tight curly hair? Or would they be light like her? Maybe both.

If she stayed here, joined with Ranec, she wouldn't be so far from the Clan. She would be able to go and get Durc and bring him back. Ranec was good with Rydag, he might not mind having a mixed child at his hearth. Maybe she could formally adopt Durc, make him a Mamutoi.

The thought that it might really be possible to get her son filled her with longing. Maybe it was just as well that Jondalar was leaving without her. If she left with him, she would never see her son again. But if he left without her, she would never see Jondalar again.

The choice had been made for her. She would stay. She would join with Ranec. She tried to think about all the positive elements, to convince herself that it would be better to stay. Ranec was a good man, and he loved her and wanted her. And she did like him. It wouldn't be so terrible to live with him. She could have babies. She could find Durc and bring him to live with them. A good man, her own people, and she would have her son again. That was more than she ever dreamed possible at one time. What more could she ask for? Yes, what more, if Jondalar was leaving?

I'll tell him, she thought. I'll tell Ranec he can announce our Promise today. But as she got up and walked towards the Hearth of the Fox, her mind was filled with only one thought. Jondalar was leaving without her. She would never see Jondalar again. Even as the realisation came to her, she felt the crushing weight, and closed her eyes to fight back her grief.

"Talut! Nezzie!" Ranec ran out of the lodge looking for the headman and his adoptive mother. When he saw them, he was so excited he could hardly speak. "She agreed! Ayla agreed! The Promise, we're going to do it! Ayla and me!"

He didn't even see Jondalar, and if he had, it wouldn't have mattered. Ranec couldn't think of anything except that the woman he loved, the woman he wanted more than any in the world, had agreed to be his. But Nezzie saw Jondalar, saw him blanch, saw him grab the curved mammoth tusk of the archway for support, and saw the pain on his face. Finally he let go and walked down towards the river, and a fleeting worry crossed her thoughts. The river was swollen and full. It would be easy to swim out and get swept away.

"Mother, I don't know what to wear today. I can't make up my mind," Latie wailed, nervous about the first ceremony that would acknowledge her elevated status.

"Let's take a look," Nezzie said, casting a last glance towards the river. Jondalar was not in sight.

28

Jondalar spent the entire morning walking along the river, his mind in a turmoil, hearing over and over again Ranec's joyful words: Ayla had agreed. They would announce their Promise at the ceremony that evening. He kept telling himself that he had expected it all along, but faced with it, he realised he hadn't. It had come as a much bigger shock than he ever imagined it would. Like Thonolan after he lost Jetamio, he wanted to die.

Nezzie had had some basis for her fears. Jondalar had not walked down towards the river for any particular purpose. It just happened to be the direction he took, but once he reached the turbulent watercourse, he found it strangely compelling. It seemed to offer peace, relief from pain and sorrow and confusion, but he only stared at it. Something equally compelling held him back. Unlike Jetamio, Ayla was not dead, and as long as she was alive, a small fire of hope could burn, but more than that, he feared for her safety.

He found a secluded area screened by brush and small trees overlooking the river, and tried to prepare for the ordeal of the evening's festivities, which would include the Promise Ceremony. He told himself it wasn't as though she was actually joining with Ranec this evening. She was only Promising to establish a hearth with him sometime in the future, and he had made a promise, too. Jondalar had told Mamut he would stay until after the Spring Festival, but it wasn't the promise that held him. Though he had no idea what it could be, or what he might be able to do, he could not leave knowing that Ayla faced some unknown danger even if it meant watching her Promise to Ranec. If Mamut, who knew the ways of the spirits, sensed some danger to her, Jondalar could only expect the worst.

Around noon, Ayla told Mamut that she was going to begin her preparations for the Root Ceremony. They had gone over the details several times until she felt reasonably sure that she hadn't forgotten anything important. She gathered up clean clothing, a soft, absorbent, buckskin deer hide, and several other things, but instead of leaving through the annexe, she headed towards the cooking hearth on her way out. She both wanted to see Jondalar, and hoped she wouldn't, and was disappointed and relieved to find only Wymez at the toolmaking area. He said he hadn't seen Jondalar since early that morning, but was happy to give her the small nodule of flint she wanted.

When she reached the river, she walked upstream along it for a distance, looking for a place that felt right. She stopped where a small creek joined the large river. The little waterway had washed around a rock outcrop which formed a high bank on the opposite side, blocking the wind. A screen of new-budding brush and trees made it a secluded, protected spot, and also provided dry wood from the previous year's deadfall.

Jondalar watched the river from his secluded vantage point, but he was so introspective, he didn't really see the wild, muddy, rushing water. He hadn't even been aware of the changing shadows as the sun climbed higher in the sky, and was startled when he heard someone approaching. He was in no mood for conversation, for trying to be pleasant and friendly on this day of celebration for the Mamutoi, and quickly slipped behind some brush to wait, unnoticed, until the person passed by. When he saw Ayla coming, and then obviously deciding to stay, he was at a loss. He thought about slipping away quietly, but Ayla was too good a hunter. She would hear him, he was sure. Then he thought about just coming out of the bushes, making some excuse about relieving himself, and going on his way, but he did neither.

Trying to remain as unobtrusive as possible, he stayed hidden and watched. He couldn't help himself, he couldn't even make himself look away, even though he soon realised she was preparing herself for the coming ritual, thinking she was alone. At first, he was just overwhelmed by her presence, then he became fascinated. It was as though he had to watch.

Ayla quickly started a fire with a firestone and a piece of flint, and put in cooking stones to heat. She wanted to make her purification ritual as close as possible to the way it was done in the Clan, but some changes could not be helped. She had considered making fire in the Clan way, by twirling a dry stick between her palms against a flat piece of wood until it created a hot ember. But in the Clan, women were not supposed to carry fire, or make it for ritual purposes in any case, and she decided if she was going to break with tradition enough to make her own fire, she might as well use her firestone.

Women were, however, allowed to make knives and other stone tools, so long as the tools weren't used for hunting weapons or to make them.

She had decided she needed a new amulet pouch. The decorated Mamutoi bag she now used would not be appropriate for a Clan ritual. To make a proper Clan amulet pouch, she felt she needed a Clan knife, which was why she had asked Wymez for an unbroken nodule of flint. She searched near the waters and found a river-rounded, fist-sized pebble to use as a hammerstone. With it, she knocked off the outer chalky-grey cortex of the small nodule of flint, in the process beginning to pre-shape it. She hadn't made her own tools for some time, but she hadn't forgotten the technique, and soon became involved in her task.

When she finished, the dark grey glossy stone had the shape of a roughly oval cylinder with a flattened top. She examined it, knocked off another sliver, then took careful aim and knocked a chip from the edge of the flat top at the narrow end of the oval to make a striking platform. Turning the stone to position it at just the right angle, she struck at the place she had nicked out. A rather thick flake fell away, having the same shape as the pre-formed oval top, and an edge that was razor sharp.

Though she used only the hammerstone, and did it with the ease and quickness of experience, she had made a perfectly serviceable, very sharp knife, which had required careful and precise control, but she had no intention of keeping it. It was a knife meant to be held in the hand, not hafted, and with all the fine blade-type tools she now had, most of them with handles, she had no need for a Clan knife, except for this special use. Without pausing to blunt the extremely sharp edge to make it easier and safer to hold, Ayla cut a long thin strip from the edge of the buckskin she brought with her, and slashed off an end, out of which she cut a small circle. Then she picked up the hammerstone again. After carefully knocking a couple of pieces of the flint away, the knife now was an awl with a sharp point. She used it to poke holes all the way around the circle of leather, and then threaded the leather lace through them.

She removed the decorated pouch from around her neck, undid the knot, and poured her sacred objects, the signs from her totem, into her hand. She studied them for a moment, then clutched them to her breast, before putting them into the new, simpler, Clan-style pouch and pulling the lace tight. She had made a decision to stay with the Mamutoi and join with Ranec, but somehow she didn't expect to find a sign from her Cave Lion confirming that it was the right decision.

With the amulet finished, she went to the creek and dipped water into the cooking basket, and added the hot stones from the fire. It was too early in the year to find lathering soaproot, and the countryside was too open for horsetail fern, which grew in shady damp places. She had to find alternatives to the traditional Clan cleansing agents.

After putting the sweet-smelling, lather-producing, dried coelanthus flowers into the hot water, she added fronds of wood fern and a few columbine flowers she had picked on her way, and then budding birch twigs for the smell of wintergreen, and put the container aside. It had taken long and hard thought to decide what to use to replace the flea and lice-killing insecticide made from the equisetic acid she would have extracted with an infusion from the fern. As it turned out, Nezzie inadvertently told her.

She undressed quickly, then picked up two tightly woven containers of liquid and headed for the river. One contained the pleasantly aromatic mixture she had just made, the other held stale urine.

Jondalar had asked her to show him Clan techniques for knapping flint once before, and he had been impressed, but he was fascinated to watch her working, in her imagined privacy, with such calm assurance and skill. She worked without bone hammers or punches, but she manufactured the tools she wanted quickly, making it seem effortless, but he wondered if he could do as well using only a hammerstone. He knew it took tremendous control, yet she had told him the Clan toolmaker she had learned from was far better than she. His estimation of flathead toolmaking skills suddenly increased.

She made the leather pouch quickly, too. The simple pouch was little more than serviceable, but the construction was ingenious, in its way. It wasn't until he watched her handle the objects in her pouch, and noticed the way she held them that he became aware of a melancholy air about her, an aura of sadness and grief. She should be full of joy, yet she seemed unhappy. He must be imagining it.

His breath caught in his throat when she began to undress, and the sight of her full, ripe beauty made him want her with a need that almost overpowered him. But the thought of his unspeakable actions the last time he wanted her, kept him away. She had taken to wearing braids again, during the winter, in a style similar to Deegie's, and as she unloosened her long hair, he remembered the first time he had seen her unclothed, in the heat of the summer in her valley, golden and beautiful and wet after a swim. He told himself not to look, and he had an opportunity to slip away when she entered the river, but if his life had depended upon it, he could not have moved.

Ayla started her cleansing process with stale urine. The ammoniacal fluid was harsh, and smelled strong, but it dissolved oils and grease on her skin and in her hair, and it killed any lice or fleas she might have picked up. It even tended to lighten the hair. The waters of the river, still full of glacial melt, were icy cold, but the shock was invigorating, and the churning of the silty, gritty river, even at the calmer edge, scoured away dirt and oils along with the sharp smell of ammonia.

Her body was pink from the cleansing and the cold water and she shivered when she got out, but the sweet-scented mixture was still warm and lathered into saponin-rich, slippery suds when she rubbed it all over her body and into her hair. This time, she headed for a pool near the mouth of the creek that held water less muddy than the river to rinse. When she emerged, she wrapped the soft buckskin around her to dry off, while she worked out the tangles in her hair with her stiff brush and an ivory hairpin. It felt good to be fresh and clean.

Though he ached to join her, and hungered to Pleasure her, Jondalar felt a certain satisfaction just filling his sight with her. It was more than seeing her lush body, rich with womanly curves, yet firm and shapely, with the flat, hard muscles that implied strength. He enjoyed watching her, seeing her naturally graceful movements, seeing her work with the ease of experience and practised skill. When making fire, or the tool she wanted, she knew exactly how to proceed and wasted no motions. Jondalar had always admired her ability and expertise, her intelligence. It was part of her appeal to him. Among all the other emotions, he had missed being with her, and just watching her fulfilled a need to be near her.

Ayla was nearly dressed when the "yip, yip" of the young wolf made her look up and smile.

"Wolf! What are you doing here? Did you run away from Rydag?" she said, as the puppy jumped up on her in greeting, pleased and excited to have found her. Then he began sniffing around the area while she gathered up her things.

"Well, now that you've found me, we can go back. Come on, Wolf. Let's go. What are you after in those bushes . . . Jondalar!"

Ayla was stunned beyond words when she discovered what the young wolf had been after, and Jondalar was too embarrassed to speak, yet their eyes held, and spoke more than words could say. But they would not believe what they saw. Finally Jondalar attempted to explain.

"I was . . . uh . . . walking by, and . . . uh . . ."

He gave up, not even trying to finish his lame attempt at an excuse, turned and walked quickly away. Ayla followed him back towards the Camp more slowly, trudging up the slope towards the earthlodge. Jondalar's behaviour confused her. She wasn't sure how long he had been there, but she knew he had been watching her, and wondered why he had been hiding from her. She didn't know what to think, but as she went into the lodge through the annexe to the Mammoth Hearth to find Mamut so he could complete her preparations, she remembered the way Jondalar had looked at her.

Jondalar did not return to the Camp immediately. He wasn't sure he could face her, or anyone, just then. When he neared the path from the river up to the lodge, he turned around and walked back, and soon found himself at the same secluded spot.

He walked to the remains of the little fire, kneeled down and felt the slight heat with his hand, and half closed his eyes remembering the scene he had secretly watched. When he opened his eyes, he spied the flint core she had left behind, and picked it up to examine it. Then he saw the chips and flakes she had struck off, and fitted some of them back on, to study the process more closely. Near scraps of leather, he saw the awl. He picked it up and looked it over. It wasn't made in the style he was accustomed to. It seemed too simple, almost crude, but it was a good, effective tool. And sharp, he thought, when it nicked his finger.

The tool she had made reminded him of Ayla, seemed, in its way, to represent the enigma of her, the apparent contradictions. Her innocent candour, shrouded in mystery; her simplicity, steeped in ancient knowledge; her honest naivety, surrounded by the depth and wealth of her experience. He decided to keep it, to remind himself of her always, and wrapped the sharp tool in the leather scraps to take it with him.

The feast was eaten in the warmth of the afternoon, inside at the cooking hearth, but with the archway drapes, even those of the new annexe, thrown back and tied open to allow fresh air and easy access. Many of the festivities were conducted outside, particularly games and competitions – wrestling seemed to be a favoured spring sport – and singing and dancing.

Gifts were exchanged to wish luck, happiness, and good will, in emulation of the Great Earth Mother, who was again bringing life and warmth to the land, to show their appreciation of the gifts of the earth She bestowed on them. The gifts were usually small items such as belts and knife sheaths, animal teeth with holes pierced through the root or grooved for cord to wrap around for suspension as pendants, and strings of beads which could be used as they were or sewn on to clothing. This year the new thread-puller was a favourite gift to give and receive, along with needle cases, little tubes of ivory or hollow bones of birds, in which to hold them. Nezzie had made the first one, which she kept with a square of mammoth skin used as a thimble in her decorated sewing pouch. Several others borrowed her idea.

The firestones owned by each hearth were considered magic and held sacred, and kept in the niche along with the figure of the Mother, but Barzec gave away several tinder kits which he devised, that were re-marked on with great enthusiasm. They were convenient for carrying and contained materials especially easy to light with the fire-starting spark – fluffy fibres, crushed dried dung, slivers of wood – and had a place for the firestone and flint striker when travelling.

With the chilling wind of evening, the Camp took their warm feelings inside and closed the heavy insulating drapes behind them. There was a time of settling down, of changing to their ceremonial clothes or adding the final decorative pieces, of refilling cups with a favourite beverage, a brisk herbal tea, or Talut's bouza. Then they all found their way to the Mammoth Hearth for the serious part of the Spring Festival.

Ayla and Deegie beckoned to Latie to invite her to sit with them; she was almost one of them now, almost a young woman. Danug and Druwez looked at her with unaccustomed shyness as she passed. She straightened her shoulders and held her head high, but refrained from speaking. Their eyes followed after her. Latie smiled as she sat between the two women, feeling very special, and very much that she belonged.

Latie had been playmate and friend to the boys when they were children, but she was not a child any more, nor a girl to be ignored or disdained by young males. She had passed into the magically attractive, slightly threatening, and altogether mysterious world of woman. Her body had changed its shape, and she could cause unexpected, uncontrollable feelings and responses in their bodies just by walking by. Even a direct look could be disconcerting.

But more daunting was something they had only heard about. She could make blood come out of her body with no wound and seemingly no pain, and somehow that made her able to draw the magic of the Mother into herself. They didn't know how, they only knew that one day she would bring forth new life from inside her body; one day Latie would make children. But first a man would have to make her a woman. That would be their role – not with Latie, of course, she was sibling and cousin, too closely related. But someday, when they were older and had more experience, they might be selected to perform that important function, because even though she could make blood, a female could not make children until a man made her a woman.

The coming Summer Meeting would prove enlightening for the two young men, also, particularly Danug, since he was older. They were never pushed, but when they were ready, there would be women who had dedicated themselves to honour the Mother for a season, who would make themselves available to young men, to give them experience, and to teach them the ways and the mysterious joys of women.

Tulie walked to the centre of the group, holding up and shaking the Speaking Staff, and waited for the people to quiet down. When she had everyone's attention, she gave the decorated ivory shaft to Talut, who was in full regalia, including his mammoth-tusk headpiece. Mamut appeared, dressed in an ornately decorated white leather cape. He held a cunningly fashioned shaft of wood that seemed to be a single piece, except that one end was a dry, bare, dead branch, and the other end bursting with green buds and small new leaves. He gave it to Tulie. As headwoman, the Spring Ceremony was hers to open. Spring was the women's time of the year; the time of birth and new life, the time of new beginnings. She held the double-ended shaft in both hands, over her head, pausing for full effect, then brought it down sharply across her knee, breaking it in two, symbolising the end of the old and the beginning of the new year, and the start of the ceremonial part of the evening.

"The Mother has smiled upon us with great favour this past cycle," Tulie began. "We have so much to celebrate, it will be difficult to know which significant event to use to mark the counting of the year. Ayla was adopted as a Mamutoi, so we have a new woman, and the Mother has chosen to make Latie ready for womanhood, so we soon will have another." Ayla was surprised to hear herself included. "We have a new baby girl to be named and numbered among us, and a new Union to be announced." Jondalar closed his eyes and swallowed hard. Tulie continued, "We have come through the winter well and healthy, and it is time for the cycle to begin again."

When Jondalar looked up, Talut had stepped forward and had the Speaking Staff. He saw Nezzie signal to Latie. She got up, smiled nervously at the two young women who had made her feel so secure, and approached the big, flaming-haired man of her hearth. Talut smiled at her with encouragement and loving affection. She saw Wymez standing beside her mother. His smile, though less infectious, was just as full of pride and love for his sister's daughter, and his heir, who would soon be a woman. It was an important moment for them all.

"I am very proud to give notice that Latie, the first daughter of the Lion Hearth, has been made ready to become a woman," Talut said, "and to announce that she will be included in the Ceremony of Womanhood at the Meeting this summer."

Mamut stepped towards her and handed her an object. "This is your muta, Latie," he said. "With this as a place for the Mother to reside, you can establish a hearth of your own someday. Keep it in a safe place."

Latie took the carved ivory object and went back to her place, and was delighted to show her muta to those nearby. Ayla was interested. She knew it had been made by Ranec because she had one like it, and recalling the words that had been spoken, she began to realise why he had given it to her. She needed a muta to establish a hearth with him.

"Ranec must be trying to work out something new," Deegie commented, seeing the bird-woman figure. "I haven't seen one like this before. It's very unusual. I'm not sure if I understand it. Mine looks more like a woman."

"He gave me one like Latie's," Ayla said. "I thought of it as both a woman and a bird, depending upon how you look at it." Ayla took Latie's muta and showed it from different angles and perspectives. "He said he wanted it to represent the Mother in Her spiritual form."

"Yes, I can see it, now that you showed me," Deegie said. She gave the little figure back to Latie, who cradled it carefully in her hands.

"I like it. It's not like everyone else's, and it means something special," Latie said, glad that Ranec gave her a muta that was so unique. Even though he had never lived at the Lion Hearth, Ranec was her brother, too, but he was so much older than Danug that he felt more like an uncle than a brother. She didn't always understand him, but she looked up to him, and knew that he was esteemed by all the Mamutoi as a carver. She would have been happy with any muta made by him, but she was pleased that he had chosen to give her one like Ayla's. He would only give a carving that he considered his best to Ayla.

The ceremony for the naming of Fralie's baby had already begun, and the three young women turned their attention to it. Ayla recognised the ivory plaque incised with cut marks that Talut was holding up, and felt a moment of concern, remembering her adoption. But the ceremony was obviously one that was quite common. Mamut must know what to do. As she watched Fralie present her infant to the shaman and the headman of the Lion Camp, Ayla suddenly remembered another naming ceremony. It had been spring then, she recalled, only she had been the mother, and she had presented her baby fearfully, expecting the worst.

She heard Mamut say, "What name have you chosen for this child?" And she heard Fralie reply, "She is to be called Bectie." But in her mind, Ayla heard Creb say, "Durc. The boy's name is Durc."

Tears were in her eyes as she felt again her gratitude, and her relief, when Brun accepted her son, and Creb named him. She looked up and noticed Rydag, who was sitting in the midst of several children with Wolf on his lap, watching her, with the same large, brown, ancient eyes that reminded her so much of Durc. She felt a sudden longing to see her son again, but then was struck with a realisation. Durc was mixed, like Rydag, but he had been born to the Clan, named and accepted by the Clan, raised by the Clan. Her son was Clan, and she was dead to the Clan. She shuddered, and tried to dispel the thoughts.

The sound of an infant's shocked howl snapped Ayla's attention back to the ceremony. The baby's arm had been nicked with a sharp knife, and a mark cut into the ivory plaque. Bectie had been named and numbered among the Mamutoi. Mamut was pouring the stinging solution on the small cut, making the tiny baby who had never known any pain voice her displeasure even louder, but the angry insistent squall of the infant brought a smile to Ayla's face. In spite of her early birth, Bectie had grown strong. She was healthy enough to cry. Fralie held Bectie out for all to see, then cuddling the infant, she sang a song of comfort and joy in a high, sweet voice, which quieted the baby. When she was through, she went back to her place near Frebec and Crozie. Within a few moments, Bectie began to cry again, but the baby's cries ceased with a suddenness that announced she had been offered the best of comforts.

Deegie nudged her, and Ayla realised the time had come. It was her turn. She was being beckoned forward. For a moment, she couldn't move. Then she wanted to run away, but there was no place to go. She didn't want to make this Promise to Ranec, she wanted Jondalar, wanted to beg him not to leave without her, but when she looked up and saw Ranec's eager, happy, smiling face, she took a deep breath, then stood up. Jondalar didn't want her, and she had told Ranec she would Promise. Reluctantly, Ayla walked towards the co-leaders of the Camp.

The dark man watched her coming towards him, out of the shadows and into the light of the central fire, and his breath caught in his throat. She was wearing the pale leather outfit Deegie had given her, the one that was so perfect for her, but her hair was not up in braids or buns, or one of the complex styles that incorporated beads or ornaments usually worn by the Mamutoi women. In deference to the Clan root ceremony, she had let her hair hang loose, and the thick, shining waves that fell below her shoulders gleamed in the firelight, and framed her unique, finely sculptured face with a golden halo. At that moment, Ranec was convinced she was the Mother incarnate, born into the body of the perfect Spirit Woman. He wanted her for his woman so much, it was almost a pain, an ache of yearning, and he could hardly believe this night was true.

Ranec was not alone in being awed by her beauty. As she stepped into the light of the fire, the whole Camp was caught by surprise. The Mamutoi clothing, richly elegant, and the glorious natural beauty of her hair, made a stunning combination, enhanced by the dramatic lighting. Talut thought of the value she would add to the Lion Camp, and Tulie was determined to set a very high Bride Price, even if she had to contribute half of it herself, for the status it would bestow on all of them. Mamut, already convinced that she was destined to Serve the Mother in some important way, took note of her instinctive sense of timing, and natural flair for the dramatic, and knew that someday she would be a force to be reckoned with.

But no one felt the impact of her presence more than Jondalar. He was as dazzled by her beauty as Ranec, but Jondalar's mother had been a leader, and then his brother after her, Dalanar had founded and was the leader of a new group, and Zolena had reached the highest rank of the Zelandonii. He had grown up among the natural leaders of his own people, and he sensed the qualities that were noticed by the Lion Camp's co-leaders and shaman. As though someone had kicked him in the stomach and knocked the wind out of him, he suddenly understood what he had lost.

As soon as Ayla reached Ranec's side, Tulie began.

"Ranec of the Mamutoi, son of the Fox Hearth of the Lion Camp, you have asked Ayla of the Mamutoi, daughter of the Mammoth Hearth of the Lion Camp, and protected by the Spirit of the Cave Lion, to join together to form a union and establish a hearth. Is this true, Ranec?"

"Yes, it is true," he answered, then turned to Ayla with a smile of absolute joy.

Talut then addressed Ayla. "Ayla of the Mamutoi, daughter of the Mammoth Hearth of the Lion Camp, and protected by the Spirit of the Cave Lion, do you agree to this union with Ranec of the Mamutoi, son of the Fox Hearth of the Lion Camp?"

Ayla closed her eyes and swallowed before she responded. "Yes," she finally said, in a barely audible voice, "I agree."

Jondalar, sitting at the back near the wall of the lodge, closed his eyes and clenched his jaw until his temples throbbed. It was his own fault. If he hadn't forced her, maybe she wouldn't be turning now to Ranec. But she had already turned to him, she had been sharing his bed. From the first day she was adopted by the Mamutoi, she had shared his bed. No, he had to admit, that wasn't quite true. After that first night, she didn't share the carver's bed at all until after they had that stupid argument, and he left the Mammoth Hearth. Why had they argued? He hadn't been angry with her, he was just worried about her. Then why had he left the Mammoth Hearth?

Tulie turned to Wymez, who was standing next to Ranec, beside Nezzie. Ayla hadn't even noticed him. "Do you accept this union between the son of the Fox Hearth and the daughter of the Mammoth Hearth?"

"I accept this union, and welcome it," Wymez replied.

"And you, Nezzie?" Tulie asked. "Will you accept a union between your son, Ranec, and Ayla, if a suitable Bride Price can be arranged?"

"I accept the union," the woman replied.

Talut spoke next, to the old man beside Ayla. "Mamutoi Spirit Seeker, he who has relinquished name and hearth, he who was called, he who is dedicated to the Mammoth Hearth, he who speaks to the Great Mother of all, the One Who Serves Mut," the headman said, carefully reciting all the shaman's names and appellations, "does the Mamut agree to a union between Ayla, daughter of the Mammoth Hearth, and Ranec, son of the Fox Hearth?"

Mamut did not answer immediately. He looked at Ayla, who was standing with her head bowed. She waited, and when he didn't speak, she looked at him. He studied her expression, noted her posture, the aura about her.

"The daughter of the Mammoth Hearth may join with the son of the Fox Hearth, if she wishes," he finally said. "There is nothing to ban such a joining. She does not need my approval or acceptance, or anyone's. The choice is hers. The choice will always be hers, no matter where she is. If ever she needs permission, I give it to her. But she will always remain the daughter of the Mammoth Hearth."

Tulie eyed the old man. She felt there was more to his words than there seemed. There was something ambiguous about his response and she wondered what he meant, but she decided she could think about it later.

"Ranec, son of the Fox Hearth and Ayla, daughter of the Mammoth Hearth, have declared their intention to join together. They wish to form a union to mingle their spirits, and to share one hearth. All those concerned have concurred," Tulie said, then turned to the carver. "Ranec, if you are joined, will you promise to give Ayla the protection of yourself and your male spirit, will you care for her when she is blessed by the Mother with new life, and will you accept her children as the children of your hearth?"

"Yes, I promise. It is what I want more than anything," Ranec said.

"Ayla, if you are joined, will you promise to care for Ranec and give him the protection of your mother's power, will you welcome the Mother's Gift of Life without reservation, and will you share your children with the man of your hearth?" Tulie said.

Ayla opened her mouth to speak, but no sound came out at first. She coughed and cleared her throat, then finally replied, but her answer was almost inaudible. "Yes, I promise."

"Do all hear and witness this Promise?" Tulie said to the people who were gathered.

"We hear and witness," the group responded. Then Deegie and Tornec began to beat a slow rhythmic pace on their bone instruments, subtly changing the tone to accompany the voices which started chanting.

"You will be joined at the Summer Matrimonial, so that all the Mamutoi may witness," Tulie said. "Circle the hearth three times to assure the Promise."

Ranec and Ayla, side by side, marched slowly around the hearth to the sound of the tonal music and chanting people. It was done. They were Promised. Ranec was ecstatic. He felt as though his feet barely touched the ground as he walked. His happiness was so all-consuming it was impossible to believe that Ayla didn't share it. He had noticed a certain reluctance, but he made excuses, assumed it was shyness, or that she was tired, or nervous. He loved her so much, it was beyond him to consider that she didn't love him the same way.

But Ayla felt heavy at heart as she circled the firepit, though she tried not to show it. Jondalar slumped down, unable to support himself, as though his very bones had collapsed, feeling like an empty, discarded pouch. More than anything, he wanted to leave, to run from the sight of the beautiful woman he loved walking beside the happily grinning dark-skinned man.

When they completed the third circuit, there was a pause in the ceremonies for well-wishing and gift-giving, to all of the celebrants. Gifts for Bectie included the space given to the Crane Hearth by the Aurochs Hearth, as well as an amber and seashell necklace, and a small knife in a decorated sheath, that were the beginning of the wealth she would accumulate in her lifetime. Latie was given personal gifts important for a woman, and a beautiful and richly decorated summer tunic from Nezzie, to be worn during the festivities at the Summer Meeting. She would receive many more gifts from relatives and close friends in other Camps.

Ayla and Ranec were given household items: a ladle carved from a horn, a two-handled scraper that was used to soften the inner sides of furs, with a slot for a replaceable blade, woven floor mats, cups, bowls, platters. Though Ayla felt they received many things, they were only a token. They would receive many more at the Summer Meeting, but they, and the Lion Camp, would also be expected to give gifts in return. Small or large, gifts were never without obligations, and the accounting of who owed what to whom was a complex but endlessly fascinating game.

"Oh, Ayla, I'm so glad we're going to be joined at the same time!" Deegie said. "It will be so much fun planning it with you, but you'll be coming back here, and I'll be going off to build a new lodge. I'm going to miss you next year. It would be such great fun to know who the Mother blesses first. You or me. Ayla, you must be so happy."

"I guess I am," Ayla said, and then smiled though her heart wasn't in it.

Deegie wondered about her lack of enthusiasm. Somehow, Ayla just didn't seem to be as excited about being Promised as she had been. Ayla wondered, too. She should be happy, she wanted to be happy, but all she felt was lost hope.

During the general socialising, Ayla and Mamut slipped off to the

Aurochs Hearth to make their final preparations. When they were ready, they returned along the passageway, but Mamut stopped in the shadows between the Reindeer Hearth and the Mammoth Hearth. People were in small groups, deeply involved in conversations, and the shaman waited until no one was looking in their direction. Then he motioned to Ayla and they moved quickly into the ceremonial area, staying in the shadows until the last moment.

Mamut, unnoticed at first, stood silently in front of the fireplace near the screen, his cape brought around in front of him with his arms across his chest, his eyes apparently closed. Ayla, sitting cross-legged on the ground at his feet with her head bowed, had a cape draped across her shoulders as well. When they were seen, it was with the eerie feeling that they had suddenly appeared in their midst. No one had seen them coming. They were just there. The people quickly found places to sit filled with a sense of anticipation and excitement, prepared now for the mystery and magic of the Mammoth Hearth, and curious about this new ceremony that had been prepared.

But first Mamut wanted to establish the presence of the spirit world, to show the heightened reality of the altered sense in which he functioned to those who knew of it only by word of mouth, or perhaps results. The group quieted. In the silence, the sound of breathing grew loud, and the crackling of the fire. Moving air was an invisible presence whiffling in through the fireplace vents, and moaning a muted howl across partially opened smokeholes. So gradually that no one noticed when it began, the moaning wind became a humming monotone, then a rhythmic chant. As the assembled people joined in, enlarging the wavering tone with natural harmonies, the old shaman began a weaving, rocking, dancing movement. Then the tonal drum accented the rhythm, and the clack of a rattle that appeared to be several armbands held together and shaken.

Suddenly Mamut threw off his cape, and stood in front of the assembly stark naked. He had no pockets, no sleeves, no secret folds to hide anything. Imperceptibly, he seemed to grow before their eyes, his transparent shimmering presence filling the space. Ayla blinked, knowing the old shaman had not changed. If she concentrated, she could see the familiar shape of the old man with sagging skin and long, thin, bony arms and legs, but it was difficult.

He shrank back to his normal size, but seemed to have swallowed or somehow incorporated the shimmering presence, so that it outlined him with a glow that made him seem larger than life. He held out his open hands in front of him. They were empty. He clapped his hands once, then held both hands together. His eyes closed, and at first he stood still, but soon he was trembling, as though straining against a great force.

Slowly, with great effort, he pulled his hands apart. A black amorphous shape appeared between them, and more than one watcher shuddered. It had the ineffable feel, the smell, of evil; of something loathsome, foul, and frightening. Ayla felt the hairs rise on the back of her neck, and she held her breath.

As Mamut stretched his hands apart, the shape grew. The acrid smell of fear rose from the seated group. Everyone was sitting up straight, straining forward, chanting with a wailing intensity, and the tension within the lodge was almost unbearable. The shape grew darker, ballooned, writhed with a life of its own, or rather, the antithesis of life. The old shaman strained, his body shaking with the effort. Ayla concentrated on him, fearful for him.

Without forewarning, Ayla felt herself pulled in, drawn, and suddenly found herself with Mamut, in his mind or in his vision. She saw clearly now, understood the danger, and was appalled. He was in control of a thing beyond words, beyond comprehension. Mamut had pulled her in, both to protect her and to help him. As he worked to control it, she was with him, knowing and learning at the same time. As he forced his hands back together, the shape grew smaller, and she could see that he was pushing it back where it came from. A loud crack, like a thunderclap, sounded in her mind as his hands came together.

It was gone. Mamut had forced the evil away, and Ayla became aware that he had called upon other spirits to help him wrestle with the thing. She sensed vague animal shapes, guardian spirits, the Mammoth and the Cave Lion, perhaps even the Cave Bear, Ursus himself. Then, she was back, seated on a mat, looking at the old man who was just Mamut again. Physically, he was tired, but mentally, his abilities were sharpened, honed by the contest of wills. Ayla, too, seemed to see with a clearer vision, and she sensed that the guardian spirits were still present. She had had enough training, now, to realise that his purpose had been to clear away any lingering malevolent influences that might jeopardise her ceremony. They would be drawn to the evil he had called up, and driven out with it.

Mamut signalled for silence. Chanting and drumming both stopped. It was time for Ayla to begin the Clan root ceremony, but the shaman wanted to stress the importance of the Camp's assistance when the time came for them to chant again. Wherever the root ritual took them, the sound of the chanting could lead them back.

In the expectant silence of the night, Ayla began to beat out an unusual set of rhythms on an instrument unlike any they had ever seen. It was exactly what it seemed to be, a large wooden bowl, carved out of one piece of wood, turned upside down. She had brought it back with her from the valley, and it was surprising as much for its size as for the fact that it was used as an instrument. Trees large enough to have made such a bowl did not grow on the open, dry, and windy steppes. Even the periodically flooded river valley seldom grew very large trees, but the small valley where she had lived was protected from the worst of the cutting winds and had more than sufficient water for a few large coniferous trees. One had been struck down by lightning, and she had made the bowl from a section of it.

Ayla used a smooth wooden stick to produce the sound. Though some variation in tone could be achieved by striking different places, it was not a musical percussion instrument, as the resonant skull drum and scapula were; it was made for rhythms. The people of the Lion Camp were intrigued, but this was not their music, and they weren't entirely comfortable with it. The rhythmic sounds that Ayla made were distinctly foreign, but as she had hoped, they created an atmosphere to match, one with the feeling of the Clan. Mamut was overwhelmed by memories of the time he spent with them. The beats she finished with did not give a sense of closure, but rather created a feeling that more was expected, and left a sense of anticipation hanging in the air.

The Camp didn't know what to expect, but when Ayla threw off the cape and stood up, they were surprised by the designs painted on her body, circles in red and black colour. Except for some facial tattoos of those who belonged to the Mammoth Hearth, the Mamutoi decorated their clothing, not their bodies. For the first time, the people of the Lion Camp had a sense of the world Ayla had come from, a culture so alien they could not fully comprehend it. It was not simply a different style of tunic, or choice of predominant colour tones, or spear-type preference, or even a different language. It was a different way of thinking, but they did recognise that it was a human way of thinking.

They watched with fascination as Ayla filled the wooden bowl she had given to Mamut with water. Then she picked up a dry root they hadn't noticed, and began to chew it. It was difficult at first. The root was old and dry, and the juices had to be spat into the bowl. She was not supposed to swallow any. When Mamut had wondered again if the root could still be effective after so long a time, Ayla had explained it was likely to be stronger.

After what seemed like a very long time – she remembered that it had seemed to take a long time the first time – she spat the masticated pulp and the rest of the juices into the bowl of water. She stirred it with her finger until it was a watery white fluid. When she felt that it looked right, she gave the bowl to Mamut.

With the beating of his own drum, and the shaking of the bracelet rattle, the shaman signalled the right pace for the drummers and chanters to maintain, and then, with a nod to Ayla, indicated he was ready.

469

She was nervous, her former experience with the root had unpleasant associations and she went over every detail of the preparation in her mind, and tried to remember everything Iza had told her. She had done everything she could think of to make the ceremony as close to the Clan ritual as she could. She nodded back, and Mamut held the bowl to his lips, and took the first drink. When he finished half the bowl, he gave the rest to Ayla. She drank the other half.

The very taste was ancient, reminiscent of rich loam in deep, shaded primeval forests, of strange giant trees and a canopy of green filtering out sun and light. She began to feel the effects almost immediately. A feeling of nausea overcame her, and a dizzying sense of vertigo. As the lodge whirled around and around, her vision clouded and her brain seemed to expand and grow tight in her head. Suddenly the lodge disappeared, and she was in another place, a dark place. She felt lost, and had a moment of panic. Then she had a sensation that someone was reaching for her, and realised Mamut was in the same place. Ayla was relieved to find him, but Mamut was not in her mind as Creb had been, and he did not direct her, or himself, as Creb had done. He exerted no control at all, he was just there, waiting to see what would happen.

Faintly, as though they were inside the earthlodge and she was outside, Ayla heard the chanting and the resonant voice of the drums. She focused on the sound. It had a steadying effect, gave her a point of reference and a sense that she was not alone. Mamut's nearness was also a calming influence, though she wished for the strong guiding mind that had shown her the way before.

The darkness shaded into grey that became luminous, then iridescent. She sensed motion, as though she and Mamut were flying over the landscape again, but there were no distinguishing features, only a sensation of passage through the surrounding opalescent cloud. Gradually, as her speed increased, the misty cloud coalesced into a thin film of shimmering rainbow colours. She was sliding down a long translucent tunnel, with walls like the inside of a bubble, moving faster and faster, heading straight towards a searing white light, like the sun, but icy cold. She screamed, but made no sound, then burst into the light, and through it.

She was in a deep, cold, black void that had a terrifyingly familiar feel. She had been here before, but that time, Creb had found her and brought her out. Only vaguely, she sensed Mamut was still with her, but she knew he could not help her. The chanting of the people was no more than a dim reverberation. She was sure that if it ever stopped, she would never find her way back, but she wasn't sure if she wanted to go back. In this place there was no sensation, no feeling, only an absence that made her see her confusion, her aching love, and her desperate unhappiness. The black void was frightening, but it seemed no worse than the desolation she felt inside.

She sensed motion again, and the blackness fading. She was in a misty cloud again, but it was different, thicker, heavier. The cloud parted and a vista opened before her, but it had no meaning for her. It was not the gentle, random, natural landscape she knew. It was filled with unfamiliar shapes and forms; even, regular, with hard flat surfaces and straight lines, and large masses of bright garish unnatural colour. Some things moved, rapidly, or perhaps it only seemed that way. She didn't know, but she didn't like this place, and struggled to push it away from her, to get away from it.

Jondalar had watched Ayla drink the mixture, and frowned with concern when he saw her stagger, and her face turn pale. She gagged a few times, and then slumped to the ground. Mamut, too, had fallen, but it was not unusual for the shaman to drop to the ground when he went far into the other world in search of spirits, whether or not he ate or drank something to help him. Mamut and Ayla were laid out on their backs, while the chanting and drumming continued. He saw Wolf try to reach her, but the young animal was held away. Jondalar understood how Wolf felt. He wanted to rush to Ayla, and even glanced at Ranec to see what his reaction was, but the Lion Camp did not seem alarmed, and he hesitated to interfere in a sacred ritual. He joined in the chanting instead. Mamut had made a point of telling them how important it was.

After a long time had passed, and neither one of them had moved, he became more fearful for Ayla, and he thought he saw expressions of concern on the faces of some of the people. He stood up, and tried to see her, but the fires had burned low and the lodge was darkened. He heard a whimper, and looked down at Wolf. The young animal whimpered again and looked at him with pleading eyes. He started towards Ayla several times, and then came back to him.

He heard Whinney neighing from the annexe. She sounded distressed, as though she sensed danger. The tall man went to see what the problem was. It was unlikely, but a predator could slip in to the horse annexe, and perhaps endanger the horses while everyone was busy. Whinney nickered when she saw him. Jondalar could find nothing to account for the mare's behaviour, but she was obviously spooked about something. Not even his pats and comforting words seemed to settle her down. She kept heading towards the entrance to the Mammoth Hearth, though she had never attempted to go inside before. Racer was uneasy, too, sensitive, perhaps, to his dam's nervousness.

Wolf was at his feet again, whining and whimpering, running towards the Mammoth Hearth entrance, and then towards him again.

"What is it, Wolf? What's bothering you?" And what's bothering Whinney? he thought. Then it occurred to him what might bother both animals. Ayla! They must sense some danger to Ayla!

Jondalar strode back in, and saw that several people were now around both Mamut and Ayla, trying to wake them up. Unable to hold back any more, he rushed to Ayla. She was stiff, rigid with tense muscles, and cold. She hardly breathed.

"Ayla!" Jondalar cried out. "O, Mother, she looks almost dead! Ayla! O, Doni, don't let her die! Ayla, come back! Don't die, Ayla! Please don't die!"

He held her in his arms, calling out her name, with great urgency, over and over again, pleading with her not to die.

Ayla felt herself slipping farther and farther away. She tried to hear the chanting and drumming, but they were like a dim memory. Then, she thought she heard her name. She strained to listen. Yes, there it was again, her name, spoken urgently, with great need. She felt Mamut move closer, and together they focused on the chanting. She heard a faint hum of voices, and felt herself drawn towards the sound. Then in the distance, she heard the deep, vibrant, staccato voice of the drums speak the word "h-h-o-ooo-m-m-m". More clearly now, she heard her name cried out with anguish and need and overpowering love. She felt a gentle probing reach for her and touch the combined essence of her and Mamut.

Suddenly, she was moving, being pulled and pushed along a single glowing strand. She had an impression of intense speed. The heavy cloud surrounded her, and was gone. She passed through the void in the flick of an eye. The shimmering rainbow became a grey mist, and the next instant, she was in the lodge. Below her, her own body, unnaturally still with a grey pallor, was sprawled out on the floor. She saw the back of a blond man who was huddling over her, holding her. Then, she felt Mamut push her.

Ayla's eyelids flickered, then she opened her eyes and saw Jondalar's face looking down at her. The intense fear in his blue eyes changed to immense relief. She tried to speak, but her tongue felt thick, and she was cold, freezing cold.

"They're back!" she heard Nezzie say. "I don't know where they've been, but they're back. And they're cold! Bring furs, and something hot to drink."

Deegie brought an armful of furs from her bed, and Jondalar got out of the way so she could tuck them around Ayla. Wolf came rushing over, jumping up and licking her face, then Ranec brought a cup of hot tea. Talut was helping her to sit up. Ranec held the hot drink to her lips, and she smiled, gratefully. Whinney neighed from the annexe and Ayla recognised the sound of distress and fear. The woman sat up, feeling concern, and nickered back to calm and reassure the mare. Then she asked for Mamut, and insisted on seeing him.

She was helped up, a fur was draped over her shoulders, and she was led to the old shaman. He was bundled in furs and holding a cup of hot tea, too. He smiled at her, but there was a hint of worry in his eyes. Not wanting to unduly upset the Camp, he had tried to make less of their perilous experiment, but he did not want Ayla to misunderstand how serious their danger had been. She, too, wanted to talk about it, but both of them avoided direct references to the experience. Nèzzie quickly sensed their need to talk, and unobtrusively cleared everyone away and left them alone.

"Where were we, Mamut?" Ayla asked.

"I don't know, Ayla. I have not been there before. It was another place, perhaps another time. Maybe it was not a real place," he said, thoughtfully.

"It must have been," she said. "Those things felt like real things, and some of it was familiar. That empty place, that darkness, I was there with Creb."

"I believe you when you say your Creb was powerful. Perhaps even more than you realise, if he could direct and control that place."

"Yes, he was, Mamut, but . . ." A thought occurred to Ayla, but she wasn't sure if she could express it. "Creb controlled that place, he showed me his memories and our beginnings, but I don't think Creb ever went where we went, Mamut. I don't think he could. Maybe that's what protected me. He had certain powers, and he could control them, but they were different. The place we went this time, that was a new place. He couldn't go to a new place, he could only go where he had been. But maybe he saw that I could. I wonder if that's what made him so sad?"

Mamut nodded. "Perhaps, but more important, that place was far more dangerous than I imagined it would be. I tried to make light of it for the sake of the Camp. If we had been gone much longer, we would not have been able to return at all. And we did not come back by ourselves. We were helped by . . . by someone who had such a strong . . . desire for us to return, it overcame all obstacles. When such single-minded strength of will is directed to achieve its purpose, no boundary can resist, except, perhaps, death itself."

Ayla frowned, obviously troubled, and Mamut wondered if she knew who had brought them back, or understood why such single-minded purpose could be required for her protection. She would in time, but it was not for him to tell her. She had to find out for herself.

"I will never go to that place again," he continued. "I am too old. I do not want my spirit lost in that void. Someday, when you have developed your powers, you may want to go again. I would not advise it, but if you go, make sure you have powerful protection. Make sure someone waits for you who can call you back."

When Ayla walked back towards her bed, she looked for Jondalar, but he had backed off when Ranec brought the tea, and now he was staying out of the way. Though he hadn't hesitated to go to her when he felt she was in danger, he was unsure now. She had just Promised to the Mamutoi carver. What right did he have to be holding her in his arms? And everyone seemed to know what to do, bringing her hot drinks and furs. He had felt that, because he wanted her so much, he might have helped in some strange way, but when he thought about it, he began to doubt it. She was probably coming back then, anyway, he told himself. It was coincidence. I just happened to be there. She won't even remember.

Ranec went to Ayla when she was through talking to Mamut, and begged her to come to his bed, not to couple, just so he could hold her and keep her warm. But she insisted she would feel more comfortable in her own bed. He finally agreed, but lay awake in his furs for a long time, thinking. Though it had been apparent to everyone, he had been able to ignore Jondalar's continued interest in Ayla, in spite of his leaving the Mammoth Hearth. After this night, however, Ranec could not deny the strong feelings that the tall man still had for her, not after watching him plead with the Mother for her life.

He had no doubt that Jondalar had been instrumental in bringing Ayla back, but he did not want to believe that she returned his feelings in kind. She had Promised herself to him that night. Ayla was going to be his woman and share his hearth. He had feared for her, too, and the thought of losing her, whether to some peril, or to another man, only made him want her more.

Jondalar saw Ranec go to her, and breathed easier when he saw the dark man return to his hearth alone, but then he rolled over and pulled the furs over his head. What difference did it make if she went with him this night or not? She would go to him eventually. She had Promised herself to him.

29

Ayla usually counted her years at the end of winter, beginning her new year with the season of new life, and the spring of her eighteenth year had been glorious with a profusion of meadow flowers and the fresh green of new growth. It was welcomed as only a place of frigid winter wastelands could, but after the Spring Festival the season ripened quickly. As the bright flowers of the steppes faded, they were replaced by the fast-growing, lush crop of new grass – and the roaming grazers it brought. The seasonal migrations had begun.

Animals in great numbers and many different varieties were on the move across the open plains. Some converged until their numbers became uncountable, others assembled in smaller herds or family groups, but all derived their sustenance, their life, from the great, windswept, incredibly rich grasslands, and the glacier-fed river systems that cut through it.

Huge hordes of big-boned bison covered hills and dips with a living, bawling, restless, undulating mass that left raw trampled earth behind. Wild cattle, aurochs, were strung out for miles in the open woodlands along the major river valleys as they travelled northward, sometimes commingled with herds of elk and massive-antlered giant deer. Shy roe deer travelled through riverine woodlands and boreal forests in small parties to spring and summer feeding grounds, along with unsociable moose who also frequented the bogs and melt lakes of the steppes. Wild goats and mouflon, usually mountain-dwelling, took to the open plains in the cold northern lands, and mingled at watering places with small family groups of saiga antelope, and larger herds of steppe horses.

The seasonal movement of woolly animals was more limited. With their thick layer of fat and heavy double coats of fur, they were adapted for life near the glacier and could not survive too much warmth. They lived year-round in the northern periglacial regions of the steppes, where the cold was deeper but dry, and snow was slight, feeding in winter on the coarse, dry standing hay. The sheeplike musk-oxen were permanent inhabitants of the frozen north, and moved in small herds within a limited territory. Woolly rhinoceroses, who usually gathered only in family groups, and the larger herds of woolly mammoths, ranged further, but in winter they stayed north. In the slightly warmer and wetter continental steppes to the south, deep snows buried feed and caused the heavy animals to flounder. They went south in spring to fatten on the tender new grass, but as soon as it warmed, they would move north again.

The Lion Camp rejoiced to see the plains teeming with life again, and remarked upon each species as it appeared, especially the animals who thrived in deep cold. Those were the ones who most helped them to survive. A sighting of the enormous, unpredictable rhinos, with two horns, the front one long and low-slung, and two coats of reddish fur, a soft downy underwool and an outer layer of long guard hair, always brought exclamations of wonder.

Nothing, however, created such sheer excitement among the Mamutoi as the sight of mammoths. When the usual time for them to pass by drew near, someone from the Lion Camp was always on the lookout. Except from a distance, Ayla hadn't seen a mammoth since she lived with the Clan, and she was as excited as anyone when Danug came running down the slope one afternoon shouting, "Mammoths! Mammoths!"

She was among the first to rush out of the lodge to see them. Talut, who often carried Rydag perched on his shoulders, had been on the steppes with Danug, and she noticed Nezzie, with the boy on her hip, was straggling behind. She started back to help, then saw Jondalar take him from the woman and hoist him up to his shoulders. He received warm smiles from both. Ayla smiled, too, though he didn't see her. The expression was still on her face when she turned to Ranec who had jogged to catch up with her. Her tender, beautiful smile evoked in him an intense feeling of warmth and a fierce wish that she was already his. She couldn't help but respond to the love in his dark, flashing eyes and the compelling grin. Her smile remained for him.

On the steppes, the Lion Camp watched the huge shaggy creatures with silent awe. They were the largest animals in their land – indeed, they would have been in almost any land. The herd, with several young in it, was passing close by, and the old matriarch eyed the people warily. She stood about ten feet high at the shoulders, and had a high domed head and a hump on the withers, used to store additional fat for winter. A short back that sloped down steeply to the pelvis completed the characteristic and immediately recognisable profile. Her skull was large in proportion to her size, more than half the length of her relatively short trunk, from the end of which two sensitive, mobile, finger projections extended, an upper and a lower one. Her tail was short, also, and her ears were small, to conserve heat.

476

Mammoths were eminently suited to their frigid domain. Their skin was very thick, insulated by three inches or more of subcutaneous fat, and closely covered with a soft, dense undercoat, about an inch long. The coarse long outer hair, up to twenty inches in length, was a dark reddish-brown, and hung in neat layers over the thick winter downy wool, as a warm, moisture-shedding cover and windbreak. With efficient rasplike grinders, they consumed a winter diet of coarse dry grass, plus twigs and bark of birches, willows, and larches with as much ease as they did their summer diet of green grasses, sedges, and herbs.

Most impressive of all, the mammoths' immense tusks inspired amazement and awe. Originating close together out of the lower jaw, they first pointed steeply downward, then curved strongly outward, upward, and finally inward. In old males, a tusk could reach sixteen feet in length, but by then, they were crossed over in front. In young animals the tusks were effective weapons and built-in tools for uprooting trees and clearing snow from pasture and feed, but when the two points curved up and overlapped, they got in the way, and were more hindrance than help.

The sight of the enormous animals brought a flood of memories to Ayla of the first time she had seen mammoths. She recalled wishing, then, that she could go hunting with the men of the Clan, and remembered that Talut had invited her to go on the first mammoth hunt with the Mamutoi. She did like to hunt, and the idea that she might actually join the hunters this time gave her a tingle of anticipation. She began to really look forward to the Summer Meeting.

The first hunt of the season had important symbolic meaning. As massive and majestic as woolly mammoths were, the Mamutoi feeling for them went beyond wonder at their size. They depended upon the animal for much more than food, and in their need and desire to assure the continuance of the great beasts, they conceived a special relationship with them. They held them in reverence because they based their own identity on them.

Mammoths had no real natural enemies; no carnivorous animal regularly depended on them for sustenance. The huge cave lions, twice the size of any large feline, which normally preyed on the large grazers – aurochs, bison, giant deer, elk, moose, or horse – and could kill a full-grown adult, occasionally brought down a young, sick, or very old mammoth, but no four-legged predator, singly or in groups, could kill an adult mammoth in its prime. Only the Mamutoi, the human children of the Great Earth Mother, had been given the ability to hunt the largest of Her creatures. They were the chosen ones. Among all Her creations, they were preeminent. They were the Mammoth Hunters.

After the mammoth herd passed, the people of the Lion Camp followed eagerly behind them. Not to hunt them, that would come later.

They were after the soft, downy wool of their winter undercoats, which was being shed in large handfuls through the coarser outer guard hairs. The naturally coloured dark red wool, which was gathered from the ground and spiny brush that caught and held it, was considered a special gift from the Spirit Mammoth.

As chance provided, the white wool of mouflon which was shed naturally by the wild sheep in spring, the unbelievably soft earthy-brown downy wool of musk-ox, and the lighter red rhinoceros underwool were also gathered with great enthusiasm. In their minds, they offered thanks and appreciation to the Great Earth Mother who gave Her children everything they needed from Her abundance, vegetable products and animals, and materials like flint and clay. They only had to know where and when to look.

Though fresh vegetables – carbohydrates – were enthusiastically added to their diet, for all the rich variety available to them, the Mamutoi hunted little in spring and early summer, unless stored supplies of meat were very low. The animals were too lean. The deep, hard winter sapped them of the required concentrated sources of energy in the form of fat. Their perambulations were driven by the need to replenish. A few male bison were picked off, if the fur at the nape of the neck was still black, indicating fat still present in some measure, and a few pregnant females of several species, for the tender foetus meat and skin which made soft baby clothes, or undergarments. The major exception was reindeer.

Vast herds of reindeer migrated north, the antlered females with the last year's young leading the way along remembered trails to their traditional calving grounds, followed by the males. As with other herding animals, their ranks were thinned by wolves that ranged along their flanks searching out the weak and the old, and by several species of felines: large lynxes, long-bodied leopards, and an occasional massive cave lion. The large carnivores played host with their leavings to a great variety of secondary carnivores and scavengers, both four-legged and flying: foxes, hyenas, brown bears, civets, small steppe cats, wolverines, weasels, ravens, kites, hawks, and many more.

The two-legged hunters preyed on them all. The fur and feathers of their hunting competitors were not disdained, though reindeer were the primary game of the Lion Camp – not for the meat, although it did not go to waste. The tongue was considered a treat and much of the meat was dried for use in travelling food, but it was the hides they wanted. Commonly greyish-fawn, but ranging in colour from creamy white to almost black, with a reddish-brown cast in the young, the coat of the most northern ranging deer was both lightweight and warm. Because their fur was naturally insulating, no finer cold-weather clothing could be found than that made from reindeer hide, and it was without equal for bedding and ground sheets. With surrounds and pit traps, the Lion Camp hunted them every year, to replenish their own supplies and for gifts to take with them when they set out on their own summer migrations.

As the Lion Camp prepared for the Summer Meeting, excitement ran high. At least once every day, someone told Ayla how much she would like meeting some relative or friend, or how much they would want to meet her. The only one who seemed to lack enthusiasm for the gathering of the Camps was Rydag. Ayla had never seen the boy in such low spirits, and she worried about his health.

She watched him carefully for several days, and one unusually warm afternoon when he was outside watching several people stretching reindeer hides, she sat down beside him.

"I have made new medicine for you, Rydag, to take to the Summer Meeting," Ayla said. "It is fresher, and may be stronger. You will have to tell me if you feel any differences, better or worse," she said, using both hand signs and words, as she usually did with him. "How are you feeling now? Any changes lately?"

Rydag liked it when Ayla talked to him. Though he was profoundly grateful for his new ability to communicate with his Camp, their understanding and use of sign language was essentially simple and direct. He had understood their verbal language for years, but when they spoke to him, they tended to simplify it to match the signs they used. Her signs were closer in nuance and feeling to verbal speech, and they enhanced her words.

"No, feel same," the boy signed.

"Not tired?"

"No . . . . Yes. Always little tired." He smiled. "Not as much."

Ayla nodded, studying him carefully, checking for any visible symptoms, trying to assure herself that there was no change in his condition, at least none for the worse. She did not see any signs of physical deterioration, but he seemed dejected.

"Rydag, is something bothering you? Are you unhappy?"

He shrugged, and looked away. Then he looked back at her. "Not want to go," he signed.

"Where don't you want to go? I don't understand."

"Not want to go Meeting," he said, looking away again.

Ayla frowned, but didn't press. Rydag didn't seem to want to talk about it, and soon went inside the lodge. She followed him in through the front foyer, trying not to seem conspicuous, and from the cooking hearth watched him lie down on his bed. She was worried about him. He seldom went to bed voluntarily during the day. She saw Nezzie come in and stop to tie the front drape back. Ayla hurried towards her, to help.

"Nezzie, do you know what's wrong with Rydag? He seems so . . . unhappy," Ayla said.

"I know. He gets that way this time of year. It's the Summer Meeting. He doesn't like it."

"That's what he said. Why?"

Nezzie paused and looked full at Ayla. "You really don't know, do you?" The young woman shook her head. Nezzie shrugged. "Don't worry about it, Ayla. There's nothing you can do."

Ayla walked through the lodge along the passageway, and glanced at the boy. His eyes were closed, but she knew he wasn't sleeping. She shook her head, wishing she could help. She guessed it was something about his difference, but he had been to Meetings before.

She hurried through the empty Fox Hearth, and into the Mammoth Hearth. Suddenly, Wolf came bounding in through the front entrance and was at her heels, playfully jumping up. She commanded him down with a signal. He obeyed, but looked so hurt she relented and threw him the well-chewed-up piece of soft leather that had once been one of her favourite stocking-shoes. She had finally given it to him when it seemed to be the only way to break him of chewing up everyone else's shoes and boots. He quickly tired of his old toy, and getting down on his forelegs, wagged his tail and yipped at her. Ayla couldn't help smiling, and decided it was just too nice a day to stay inside. On the spur of the moment, she picked up her sling and a pouch of round stones she had gathered, and signalled Wolf to follow her. Seeing Whinney in the annexe, she decided to include the mare as well.

Ayla went out through the arched entrance of the annexe, followed by the hay-coloured horse, and the young grey wolf, whose fur and markings were typical of his species, unlike his black mother. She noticed Racer partway down the slope towards the river. Jondalar was with him. His shirt was off in the warm sun, and he was leading the young stallion by a rope. As promised, he had been training Racer, spending most of his time at it, in fact, and both he and the horse seemed to enjoy it.

He saw her, and motioned for her to wait as he started up towards her. It was unusual for him to approach her, or indicate that he wanted to speak to her. Jondalar had changed since the incident on the steppes. He no longer avoided her, exactly, but he seldom made an effort to talk to her, and when he did, he was like a stranger, reserved and polite. She had hoped the young stallion would bring him closer to her, but if anything, he seemed more distant.

She waited, watching the tall, muscular, handsome man approach her, and unbidden, the thought of her warm response to his need on the steppes came to her mind. In an instant, she felt herself want him. It was a reaction of her body, beyond her control, but as Jondalar neared, she noticed the colour rise to his face and his rich blue eyes fill with that special look. She saw the bulge of his manhood, though she'd had no intention of looking there, and felt herself reddening.

"Excuse me, Ayla. I don't want to disturb you, but I felt I should show you this new restrainer I worked out for Racer. You might want to use one like it for Whinney," Jondalar said, keeping his voice normal and wishing he could control the rest of himself.

"You are not disturbing me," Ayla said, although he was. She looked at the device made of thin strips of leather, braided and looped around each other.

The mare had come into heat earlier in the season. Soon after Ayla noticed Whinney's condition, she heard the distinctive neigh of a stallion on the steppes. Though Ayla had found her after the mare had gone to live with a stallion and herd before, she couldn't face the thought of giving up Whinney to a stallion. She might not get her friend back this time. Ayla had used a halterlike contrivance and a rope around the neck to restrain the mare – and the young stallion who had exhibited great interest and excitement – and kept them inside the annexe if she couldn't be with them. Since then, she continued to use a halter occasionally, though she preferred to allow Whinney the freedom to come and go as she wished.

"How does it work?" Ayla asked.

He demonstrated on Whinney with an extra one he had made for her. Ayla asked several questions in a seemingly dispassionate tone, but she was hardly paying attention. She was far more aware of Jondalar's warmth when she stood beside him, and of his faint, pleasantly masculine smell. She seemed unable to keep from staring, at his hands, at the play of muscles across his chest, and at the bump of his manhood. She hoped her questions would lead to further conversation, but as soon as he finished explaining the device, he left abruptly. Ayla watched him grab up his shirt, mount Racer and, guiding him with leads to the new bridle, ride up the slope. She considered, for a moment, going after him on Whinney, then changed her mind. If he was so anxious to get away from her, it must mean he didn't want her around.

Ayla stared after Jondalar until he was out of sight. Wolf eagerly yipping at her finally brought her attention back. She wrapped her sling around her head, and checked the stones in the pouch, then picked up the pup and put him on Whinney's withers. Then she mounted, and started up the slope in a different direction from the one Jondalar had taken. She had planned to go hunting with Wolf, and she might as well

481

do it. Wolf had begun to stalk and try to catch mice and small game on his own, and she had discovered that he was very good at flushing game for her sling. Though it was accidental at first, the wolf was quick to learn, and was already becoming trained to flush them at her command.

Ayla was right in one respect. Jondalar left in such a hurry not because he didn't want to be around her just then – but only because he did want to be around her all the time. He needed to get away from his own reactions to Ayla's nearness. She was Promised to Ranec now, and he had lost any claim he might have had on her. Lately, he had started riding when he wanted to get away from a difficult situation, or from the strain of fighting conflicting emotions, or just to think. He began to understand why Ayla so often had ridden off on Whinney when something was troubling her. Riding across the open grasslands astride the stallion, feeling the wind in his face, had both an exhilarating and a calming effect.

Once up on the steppes, he signalled Racer to a gallop, and leaned closer to the strong neck stretching forward. It had been surprisingly easy to accustom the horse to accepting a rider, but in many ways both Ayla and Jondalar had been getting him used to it for some time. It was harder to decide how to make Racer understand and want to go where his rider wanted to go.

Jondalar understood that Ayla's control of Whinney had worked itself out in such a natural way, that her directions were still largely unconscious, but he started with the idea of training the horse. His directions were much more purposeful, but as he was training the horse, he was teaching himself as well. He learned how to sit on the horse, how to work with the stallion's powerful muscles, not just bounce on his back, and he discovered that the animal's sensitivity to thigh pressure and shifts in body position made guiding him easier.

As he gained more confidence and became more comfortable, he rode more, which was exactly the kind of practice that was needed, but the more he associated with Racer, the more affection he felt for him, also. He had been fond of him from the beginning, but he was still Ayla's horse. He kept telling himself he was training Racer for her, but he hated thinking about leaving the young stallion behind.

Jondalar had planned to leave immediately after the Spring Festival, yet he was still there and he wasn't sure why. He thought of reasons – it was still too early in the unpredictable season, he had promised Ayla he would train Racer – but he knew they were just excuses. Talut thought he was staying to go to the Summer Meeting with them, and Jondalar didn't try to correct his impression, though he kept telling himself he would be gone before they left. Every night when he went to bed, and particularly if Ayla went to the Fox Hearth, he told himself he was leaving the next day, and every day he put it off. He struggled with himself, but every time he seriously thought of packing up and going, he remembered her lying cold and still on the floor of the Mammoth Hearth, and he couldn't leave.

Mamut had spoken to him the day after the Festival, and told him the root had been too powerful for him to control. It was too dangerous, the shaman said, he would never use it again. He had advised Ayla not to use it either, and cautioned her that she would need strong protection if she ever did. Without actually saying so, the old man implied that somehow Jondalar had reached out to Ayla and was responsible for bringing her back.

The shaman's words disturbed Jondalar, but he derived a strange sort of comfort from them, too. When the man of the Mammoth Hearth had feared for Ayla's safety, why had he asked him to stay? And why did Mamut say it was he who brought her back? She was Promised to Ranec, and there was no doubt of the carver's feeling for her. If Ranec was there, why did Mamut want him? Why didn't Ranec bring her back? What did the old man know? Whatever it was, Jondalar could not bear the thought of not being there if she needed him again, or of letting her face some terrible danger without him, but neither could he bear the thought of her living with another man. He couldn't decide whether to go or stay.

"Wolf! Put that down!" Rugie cried, angry and upset. She and Rydag were playing at the Mammoth Hearth where Nezzie had told them to go so she could pack. "Ayla! Wolf has my doll and won't put her down."

Ayla was sitting on the middle of her bed surrounded by neat piles of her things. "Wolf! Drop it!" she commanded. "Come here," she signalled.

Wolf dropped the doll, which was made of scraps of leather, and slunk with his tail between his legs to Ayla. "Up here," she said, patting the place at the head of her bed where he usually slept. The wolf pup jumped up. "Now, lie down, and don't bother Rugie and Rydag, any more." He lay down with his head on his paws, staring up at her with woeful, penitent eyes.

Ayla went back to sorting through her things, but soon stopped and watched the two children playing together on the floor of the Mammoth Hearth, not meaning to stare, but intrigued. They were playing "hearths", making believe they were sharing a hearth the way grown-up women and men did. Their "child" was the leather doll, fashioned into a human shape with a round head, a body, arms and legs, wrapped in a soft skin blanket. It was the doll that fascinated Ayla. She never had a doll, people of the Clan did not make images of any kind, drawn, sculpted, or fashioned out of leather, but it reminded her of a wounded rabbit she once brought back to the cave for Iza to heal. She had cuddled and rocked the rabbit the same way Rugie held and played with the doll.

Ayla knew it was usually Rugie who initiated the games. Sometimes they played that they were joined, other times that they were "leaders", a brother and sister in charge of their own camp. Ayla watched the little blonde girl and the brown-haired boy, suddenly conscious of his Clan features. Rugie thinks of him as her brother, Ayla thought, but she doubted that they would ever be co-leaders of a Camp.

Rugie gave the doll to Rydag to tend, then got up and walked away on some imagined errand. Rydag watched her go, then put the doll down, and looked up at Ayla and smiled. The boy wasn't as interested in the imaginary baby after Rugie failed to return in a short time. He preferred real babies, though he didn't mind going along with Rugie's play when she was there. After a while, Rydag got up and left, too. Rugie had forgotten the game, and the doll for a while, and Rydag went to find her, or to find something else to do.

Ayla went back to making her decisions about what to take along to the Summer Meeting. In the last year, it seemed, she had sorted through her things too many times, making decisions about what to take and what to leave. This time she was packing to travel, and would only take what she could carry. Tulie had already spoken to her about using the horses and travois to bring gifts; it would increase both her status and that of the Lion Camp. She picked up the hide she had dyed red and shook it out, trying to decide if she would need it. She had never been able to make up her mind what to make out of the red hide. She didn't know what she could use it for now, but red was sacred to the Clan, and besides, she liked it. She folded it up and put it with the few other things she wanted to take besides essentials: the carved horse she loved so much, which Ranec had given to her at her adoption, and the new muta; the beautiful flint point from Wymez; some jewellery, beads and necklaces; her outfit from Deegie, the white tunic she had made, and Durc's cloak.

Her mind wandered while she went through a few more items, and she found herself thinking about Rydag. Would he ever really have a mate, like Durc? She didn't think there would be any girls like him at the Summer Meeting. She wasn't sure he would even reach adulthood, she realised. It made her grateful that her son had been strong and healthy, and that he would have a mate. Broud's clan would be getting ready to go to the Clan Gathering about now, if they hadn't already left.

Ura would be expecting to go back with them to mate with Durc eventually, and probably dreading the thought of leaving her own clan. Poor Ura, it would be hard for her to leave the people she knew to go to live in a strange place with a strange clan. A thought crossed Ayla's mind that had not occurred to her before. Would she like Durc? Would he like her? She hoped so, because it wasn't likely they would have any other choice.

Thinking about her own son, Ayla reached for a pouch she had brought back from the valley, opened it and dumped out its contents. Her heart skipped a beat when she saw the ivory carving. She picked it up. It was of a woman, but not like any of the female carvings she had seen, and she realised now how unusual it was. Most muta, except for Ranec's symbolic bird-women, were full, round motherly shapes with only a knob, sometimes decorated, for a head. They were all meant to symbolise the Mother, but this was a carving of a slender woman, with the hair done in many small braids, the way she used to wear hers. Most surprising, it had a carefully carved face, with a fine nose and chin, and a suggestion of eyes.

She held the carving in her hand, and it blurred in front of her eyes as all the memories came back. Without knowing it, tears were streaming down her face. Jondalar had carved it, in the valley. When he made it, he said he wanted to capture her spirit so they would never be apart. That was why he made it to resemble her, even though no one was supposed to make an image in the likeness of an actual person, for fear of trapping the spirit. He said he wanted her to have the carving, so no one could use it for malicious purposes against her. It was her first muta, she realised. He gave it to her after her First Rites, when he had made her a real woman.

She would never forget that summer in her valley, just the two of them, together. But Jondalar was going to leave without her. She clutched the ivory figure to her chest and wished she was going with him. Wolf was whimpering at her in sympathy, inching forward because he knew he was supposed to stay where he was. She reached for him, and buried her face in his fur, while he tried to lick away her salty tears.

She heard someone coming down the passageway, and sat up quickly, wiped her face, and struggled to contain herself. She turned around as though she was looking for something behind her when Barzec and Druwez walked past, involved in their own conversation. Then she put the carving back in the pouch and carefully put it on top of the bright red leather hide she had dyed, to take with her. She could never leave her first muta behind.

*   *   *

Later that evening, when the Lion Camp was getting ready to share a meal, Wolf suddenly growled menacingly, and raced towards the front entrance. Ayla jumped up and ran after him, wondering what could be wrong. Several others followed her. When she pushed open the drape, she was surprised to see a stranger, a very frightened stranger, backing away from a half-grown wolf who looked ready to attack.

"Wolf! Come!" Ayla ordered. The wolf pup retreated reluctantly, but he still faced the strange man with bared teeth and a growl low in his throat.

"Ludeg!" Talut said, stepping forward with a big smile and a great bear hug. "Come in. Come inside. It's cold."

"I . . . ah . . . don't know," the man said, eyeing the young wolf. "Are there any more inside like that?"

"No. No others," Ayla said. "Wolf will not hurt you. I will not let him."

Ludeg looked at Talut, not knowing whether to believe the unfamiliar woman. "Why do you have a wolf in your lodge?"

"It is a long story, but one better told by a warm fire. Come in, Ludeg. The young wolf will not harm you. I promise," Talut said, casting a meaningful glance at Ayla, as he guided the young man through the archway.

Ayla knew exactly what his look meant. Wolf had better not hurt this stranger. She followed them in, signalling the young animal to stay beside her, but she didn't know how to tell him to stop growling. This was a new situation. She knew that wolves, though very affectionate and attached to their own packs, were known to attack and kill strangers who invaded their territory. Wolf's behaviour was perfectly understandable, but that didn't make it acceptable. He would have to get used to strangers, whether he liked it or not.

Nezzie greeted the son of her cousin warmly, took his haversack and his parka, and gave them to Danug to take to a spare bed platform at the Mammoth Hearth, then filled a plate and found a place for him to sit. Ludeg kept glancing towards the wolf warily, filled with nervous apprehension, and every time Wolf saw his look, the menacing rumble in his throat intensified. When Ayla shushed him, he flattened his ears back and crouched down, but the next moment, he was growling at the stranger again. She thought about restraining Wolf with a rope around his neck, but she didn't think that would solve anything. It would only make the defensive animal more anxious, and in turn put the man more on edge.

Rydag had been hanging back, shy around the visitor, even though he knew him, but he was quick to see the problem. He sensed that the man's tense wariness was contributing to it. Maybe if he saw that the wolf was friendly, Ludeg would relax. Most people were crowded into the cooking hearth, and when Rydag heard Hartal wake up, he got an idea. He went to the Reindeer Hearth and comforted the toddler, then took his hand and walked him towards the cooking hearth, but not to his mother. Instead he headed towards Ayla and Wolf.

Hartal had lately developed a strong attraction for the frisky pup, and the moment he saw the furry grey creature, he chortled with glee. With delight, Hartal ran towards the wolf, but his baby steps were unsteady. He stumbled and fell on him. Wolf yelped, but his only reaction was to lick the baby's face, which caused Hartal to giggle. He pushed the warm, wet tongue away, putting his pudgy little hands into the long jaws full of sharp teeth, then grabbed fistfuls of furry coat and tried to pull Wolf towards him.

Forgetting his nervousness, Ludeg stared with round-eyed surprise at the toddler manhandling the wolf, but more, at the fierce carnivore's patient, gentle acceptance. Nor could Wolf keep up his defensive watchfulness of the stranger under the assault, and he was not full-grown and not quite capable of the sustained persistence of adult members of his species. Ayla smiled at Rydag, knowing immediately that he had brought Hartal for exactly the purpose that had been achieved. When Tronie came and got her son, Ayla picked up Wolf, deciding the time was right to introduce him to the stranger.

"I think Wolf will get used to you faster if you let him learn your scent," she said to the young man.

Ayla spoke the language perfectly, but Ludeg noticed a difference in the way she said some of her words. He looked at her carefully for the first time, wondering who she was. He knew she had not been with the Lion Camp when they left last year. In fact, he didn't recall ever seeing her before, and he was certain he would have remembered such a beautiful woman. Where had she come from? He looked up and noticed a tall, blond stranger watching him.

"What do I need to do?" he asked.

"I think if you just let him smell your hand, it would help. He likes to be petted, too, but I would not try to rush it. He needs a little time to get to know you," Ayla said.

Rather tentatively, Ludeg reached out his hand. Ayla put Wolf down to let him sniff at it, but stayed protectively close. She didn't think Wolf would attack, but she wasn't sure. After a time, the man reached out to touch the thick, shedding fur. He had never touched a living wolf before, and it was rather exciting. He smiled at Ayla, and thought again how beautiful she was when she smiled back.

"Talut, I think I'd better tell my news quickly," Ludeg said. "I think the Lion Camp has stories I'd like to hear."

The big headman smiled. This was the kind of interest he welcomed. Runners usually came with news to tell, and were chosen as much because they liked to tell a good story as for their ability to run fast.

"Tell us, then. What news do you bring?" Talut asked.

"Most important is the change of gathering place for the Summer Meeting. The Wolf Camp is hosting. The Meeting place that was chosen last year was washed out. I have other news, sad news. I stopped off at a Sungaea Camp for a night. There is sickness, killing sickness. Some have died, and when I left, the son and daughter of the headwoman were very sick. There was some doubt if they would live."

"Oh, that's terrible!" Nezzie said.

"What kind of sickness do they have?" Ayla asked.

"It seems to be in the chest. High fever, deep cough, and hard to breathe."

"How far is this place?" Ayla asked.

"Don't you know?"

"Ayla was a visitor, but she has been adopted," Tulie said. Then she turned to Ayla. "It is not too far."

"Can we go there, Tulie? Or can someone take me there? If those children are sick, maybe I can help."

"I don't know. What do you think, Talut?"

"It's out of the way if the Summer Meeting is going to be held at Wolf Camp, and they are not even related, Tulie."

"I think Darnev had distant kin at that Camp," Tulie said. "And it is a shame for a young brother and sister to be so sick."

"Perhaps we should go, but we should leave then, as soon as we can," Talut said.

Ludeg had been listening with great interest. "Well, now that I've told you my news, I'd like to know about the Lion Camp's new member, Talut. Is she really a Healer? And where did the wolf come from? I never heard of having a wolf in a lodge."

"And that's not all," Frebec said. "Ayla has two horses, a mare and a young stallion, too."

The visitor looked at Frebec in disbelief, then settled back and prepared to listen to the stories the Lion Camp had to tell.

In the morning, after a long night of storytelling, Ludeg was given an example of Ayla's and Jondalar's horse-riding skills, and was suitably impressed. He left for the next Camp ready to spread the word of the new Mamutoi woman, along with his news of the changed location of the Summer Meeting. The Lion Camp decided to leave the next morning, and the balance of the day was spent in last-minute preparations.

Ayla decided to take more medicines than she usually carried in her medicine bag, and was going through her supply of herbs, talking with Mamut while he packed. The Clan Gathering was much on her mind, and watching the old shaman favour his stiff joints, she recalled that the old people of the Clan, unable to make the long trek, had been left behind. How was Mamut going to manage a long trip? It bothered her enough to go outside and look for Talut, to ask.

"I carry him most of the way, on my back," Talut explained.

She noticed Nezzie adding a bundle to the pile of things that would be hauled on the travois by the horses. Rydag was sitting on the ground nearby looking disconsolate. Suddenly Ayla went looking for Jondalar. She found him arranging the travelling pack Tulie had given him.

"Jondalar! There you are," she said.

He looked up, startled. She was the last person he expected to see at that moment. He had just been thinking about her, and how to say goodbye to her. He had decided this was the time, when everyone was leaving the lodge, for him to leave, too. But instead of going with the Lion Camp to the Summer Meeting, he would go the other way and begin his long trek home.

"Do you know how Mamut gets to the Summer Meeting?" Ayla asked.

The question took him entirely by surprise. It was not the most pressing thing on his mind. He wasn't even sure what she was talking about. "Uh . . . no," he said.

"Talut has to carry him, on his back. And then there's Rydag. He has to be carried, too. I was thinking, Jondalar, you've been training Racer, he's used to carrying someone on his back now, isn't he?"

"Yes."

"And you can control him, he will go where you want him to, won't he?"

"Yes, I think so."

"Good! Then there's no reason Mamut and Rydag can't ride to the Meeting on the horses. They can't guide them, but you and I can lead them. It would be so much easier on everyone, and Rydag has been so unhappy lately, it might raise his spirits. Remember how excited he was the first time he rode on Whinney? You don't mind, do you, Jondalar? We don't need to ride, everyone else is walking," Ayla said.

She was so pleased and excited about the idea, it was obvious she hadn't even considered that he might not be going with them. How could he refuse her? he thought. It was a good idea, and the Lion Camp had done so much for him, it seemed the least he could do.

"No. I don't mind walking," Jondalar said. He felt a strange sense of lightness as he watched Ayla go to tell Talut, as though a terrible weight had been lifted. He hurried to finish packing, then picking up his gear, went to join the rest of the Camp. Ayla was supervising the loading of the two travois. They were nearly ready to go.

Nezzie saw him coming and smiled at him. "I'm glad you decided to come with us and help Ayla with the horses. Mamut is going to be much more comfortable, I think, and look at Rydag! I haven't seen him this excited about going to a Summer Meeting ever."

Why did he have the feeling, Jondalar wondered, that Nezzie knew he had been thinking of going home?

"And think what an impression it will make when we arrive not only with horses, but with people riding on them," Barzec said.

"Jondalar, we were waiting for you. Ayla wasn't sure who should ride on which horse," Talut said.

"I don't think it makes any difference," Jondalar said. "Whinney is a little easier to ride. She doesn't bounce you as hard."

He noticed that Ranec was helping Ayla balance the loads. He cringed inwardly when he saw them laughing together, and realised how temporary his reprieve was. He had only put off the inevitable, but he was committed now. After Mamut made mysterious gestures and spoke esoteric words, he stuck a muta in the ground at the front entrance to guard the lodge, and then with help from Ayla and Talut, mounted Whinney. He seemed nervous, but it was hard to tell. Jondalar thought he was hiding it well.

Rydag was not nervous, though, he had been on the back of a horse before. He was just excited when the tall man picked him up and put him on Racer's back. He had never ridden the stallion. He grinned at Latie, who was watching him, with a mixture of concern for his safety, delight at his new experience, and just a bit of envy. She had observed Jondalar training the horse, as much as she could from a distance, since it was hard to convince another woman to go with her just to stand around and watch – there were drawbacks to adulthood. She decided training a young horse wasn't necessarily magical. It just took patience, and of course, a horse to train.

A last check was made of the Camp, and then they started up the slope. Halfway up, Ayla stopped. Wolf did too, watching her expectantly. She looked back at the earthlodge where she had found a home and acceptance among her own kind. She missed its snug security already, but it would be there when they returned, ready to shelter them again through a long cold winter. Wind riffled the drape across the archway of mammoth tusks at the entrance, and she could see the skull of the cave lion above it. The Lion Camp seemed lonely without people. Ayla of the Mamutoi shivered with a sudden uneasy pang of sadness.

30

The great grasslands, bountiful source of life in that cold land, displayed yet another face of the renewing cycle as the Lion Camp travelled. The bluish-violet and yellow flowers of the last dwarf iris were fading but still colourful, and fernleaf peonies were in full bloom. A broad bed of the dark red blossoms filling the entire depression between two hills caused exclamations of wonder and appreciation from the travellers. But it was the young blue grass and ripening fescue and feather grasses that predominated, turning the steppes into waves of softly billowing silver accented by shadows of blue sage. Not until later, after the young grass grew ripe and the feather grass lost its plumes, would the rich plains change from silver to golden.

The young wolf took delight in discovering the multitude of small animals that lived and thrived on the vast prairie. He dashed after polecats and stoats – ermine in summer-brown coats – and backed off when the dauntless predators held their ground. When mice, voles, and velvety-furred shrews, who were used to evading foxes, scurried into holes burrowed just below the surface, Wolf chased gerbils, hamsters and long-eared, prickly hedgehogs. Ayla laughed at his look of startled surprise when a thick-tailed jerboa, with short forelegs, and three toes on its long hind legs, bounded away in jumps and dived into the burrow in which it had hibernated all winter. Hares, giant hamsters, and great jerboas were large enough for a meal, and tasty when skinned and skewered over an evening fire. Ayla's sling brought down several that Wolf flushed.

The digging steppe rodents were beneficial, loosening and turning over the topsoil, but some changed the character of the land with their extensive burrowing. As the Lion Camp hiked overland, the ubiquitous holes of spotted susliks were too numerous to count, and in some areas they had to wend their way around hundreds of grass-covered mounds, two to three feet high, each a community of steppe marmots.

Susliks were the preferred prey of black kites, though the long-winged hawks also fed on other rodents, and carrion and insects as well. The graceful birds usually detected the unsuspecting susliks while soaring in the air, but the kite could also hover like a kestrel, the native falcon, or fly very low to take its prey by surprise. Besides hawks and falcons, the tawny eagle favoured the prolific little rodent. On one occasion, when Ayla noticed Wolf striking a pose that caused her to look closer, she saw one of the large dark brown predatory birds land near its nest on the ground, bringing a suslik to its young. She watched with interest, but neither she nor the wolf disturbed them.

A host of other birds lived off the bounty of the open land. Larks and pipits were everywhere on the steppes, willow grouse, ptarmigan, and partridges, sand grouse and great bustards, and beautiful demoiselle cranes, bluish-grey with black heads and white tufts of feathers behind the eyes. They arrived to nest in spring, flourished on a diet of insects, lizards and snakes, and left in fall in great V-shaped formations, trumpeting across the sky.

Talut had started out by setting a pace that he was accustomed to using when travelling with the whole Camp, one that would not push the slower members of the band too hard. But he found they were moving much faster than usual. The horses were making a difference. By carrying gifts, trade goods and hides for tents on the travois, and the people who had to be helped, on their backs, they had lightened everyone's load. The headman was pleased at their increased pace, especially since they were going out of their way, but it also presented a problem. He had planned the route they would take, and the stops, to take advantage of certain known watering places. Now, he was having to reconsider as he went.

They had stopped near a small river, though it was still early in the day. The steppes sometimes gave way to woods near water, and they set up camp in a large field partially surrounded by trees. After Ayla removed the travois from Whinney, she decided to take Latie for a ride. The girl enjoyed helping with the horses, and the animals showed a strong attachment in return. As they rode double through a small grove of trees, a mixture of spruce, birch, hornbeam, and larch, they came to a flowering glade, a small luxuriant meadow that was a verdant piece of the steppes, enclosed by trees. Ayla stopped, and whispered quietly into the ear of the young woman sitting astride the horse in front of her.

"Be very still, Latie, but look over there, near the water."

Latie looked where Ayla indicated, frowned at first when she couldn't see anything, then smiled when she saw a saiga antelope hind with two small young ones raise her head, wary, but uncertain. Then Latie saw several others. The spiral horns grew straight out of the head of the small antelope, tipping back slightly at the end, and its large nose overhung, giving it a distinctive long face.

Sitting quietly on the back of the horse, watching, the sound of birds became noticeable: the cooing of doves, the merry lilt of a warbler, the call of a woodpecker. Ayla heard the beautiful flutelike note of a golden oriole, and gave it back, mimicking so exactly it confused the bird. Latie wished she could whistle like that.

Ayla gave Whinney a slight signal that edged her slowly towards the park-like opening in the woods. Latie almost shook with excitement when they drew near the antelope, and she saw another hind with two young ones. Suddenly there was a shift in wind, and all the saigas lifted their heads, and in an instant were bounding through the woods towards the open steppes. A streak of grey followed them, and Ayla knew who had caused them to run.

By the time Wolf returned, panting, and plopped down, Whinney was grazing peacefully, and the two young women were sitting in the sunny meadow picking wild strawberries. A handful of the colourful flowers was on the ground beside Ayla, bright red blooms with long thin petals that appeared to have been dipped in a bright red dye, and bunches of large golden-yellow flowerheads, mixed in with white, downy spheres.

"I wish there was enough to bring some back," Ayla said, putting another tiny, but exceptionally sweet and flavourful berry in her mouth.

"There would have to be a lot more. I wish there was more for me," Latie said, with a big smile. "Besides, I want to think of this as a special place, just for us, Ayla." She put a strawberry in her mouth and closed her eyes, savouring the taste. Her expression turned thoughtful. "Those baby antelope, they really were young, weren't they? I never was that close to such young ones before."

"It's Whinney, that's why we can get so close. Antelopes aren't afraid of horses. But Wolf here," Ayla said, looking towards the animal. He looked up at the sound of his name. "He's the one who chased them away."

"Ayla, can I ask you something?"

"Of course. You can always ask something."

"Do you think I could find a horse someday? I mean a little one, that I could take care of the way you took care of Whinney, so it would get used to me."

"I don't know. I didn't plan to find Whinney. It just happened. It would be hard to find a little one. All mothers protect their young."

"If you wanted to get another horse, a little horse, how would you do it?"

"I never thought about it . . . I suppose if I wanted a young horse . . . let me think . . . you'd have to catch its mother. Remember the bison hunt last fall? If you were hunting horses, and drove a herd into a surround like that, you wouldn't have to kill them all. You could keep

493

a young one, or two. Maybe you could even separate a young one from the rest, and then let the others go, if you didn't need them." Ayla smiled. "I find it harder to hunt horses, now."

When they returned, most people were sitting around a large fire, eating. The two young women helped themselves and sat down.

"We saw some saigas," Latie said. "Even little ones."

"I think you saw some strawberries, too," Nezzie commented drily, seeing her daughter's red-stained hands. Latie blushed, remembering that she had wanted to keep them all for herself.

"There weren't enough to bring any back," Ayla said.

"It wouldn't have mattered. I know Latie and strawberries. She would eat a whole field of them, without sharing any, if she had the chance."

Ayla noticed Latie's embarrassment, and changed the subject. "I also picked some coltsfoot for coughs, for the sick Camp, and a red-flowered plant – I don't know the name – whose root is very good for deep coughs and bringing up phlegm from the chest," she said.

"I didn't know that was why you were picking those flowers," Latie said. "How do you know they have that kind of sickness?"

"I don't know, but since I saw the plants, I thought I might as well get some, especially since we were so sick with that kind of sickness. How long before we get there, Talut?"

"It's hard to tell," the headman said. "We're travelling faster than usual. We should reach the Sungaea Camp in another day or so, I think. The map Ludeg made for me was very good, but I hope we're not too late. Their sickness is worse than I thought."

Ayla frowned. "How do you know?"

"I found signs that were left by someone."

"Signs?" Ayla said.

"Come with me. I'll show you," Talut said, putting his cup down and getting up. He led her to a pile of bones near the water. Bones, particularly big ones such as skulls, could be found all over the plains, but as they drew near, it was obvious to Ayla that it was not a natural arrangement. Someone had purposefully stacked them up. A mammoth skull with broken tusks had been placed on top of the heap, upside-down.

"That is a sign of bad news," Talut said, pointing to the skull. "Very bad. Do you see this lower jaw, with the two spine bones leaning against it? The point of the jaw shows which way to go, and the Camp is two days away."

"They must need help, Talut! Is that why they put this sign here?"

Talut pointed to a piece of charred birchbark, held down by the broken end of the left tusk. "See this?" he said.

"Yes. It's burned black, like it was in a fire."

"It means sickness, killing sickness. Someone has died. People are afraid of that kind of sickness, and this is a place people often stop. That sign was not put here to ask for help, but to warn people away."

"Oh, Talut! I must go. The rest of you don't have to, but I must go. I can leave now, on Whinney."

"And what will you tell them when you get there?" Talut said. "No, Ayla. They won't let you help. No one knows you. They are not even Mamutoi, they are Sungaea. We have talked about it. We knew you would want to go. We started out this way, and we will go with you. I think, because of the horses, we can make it in one day instead of two."

The sun was skimming the edge of the earth when the band of travellers from the Lion Camp approached a large settlement situated on a broad natural terrace some thirty feet above a wide, swift river. They stopped when they were noticed by some people, who stared in amazement before running towards one of the shelters. A man and a woman emerged. Their faces were reddened with a salve of ochre, and their hair was covered with ashes.

It's too late, Talut thought, as he and Tulie approached the Sungaea Camp, followed by Nezzie and Ayla, who was leading Whinney with Mamut on her back. It was obvious they had interrupted something important. When the visitors were about ten feet away, the man with the red-coloured face raised his arm and held up his hand, palm facing front. It was an obvious signal to stop. He spoke to Talut in a language that was different, yet there was something familiar about it to Ayla. She felt she should be able to understand it; a similarity to Mamutoi, perhaps. Talut answered, in his own language. Then the man spoke again.

"Why has the Lion Camp of the Mamutoi come here at this time?" he said, speaking now in Mamutoi. "There is sickness, and great sadness at this Camp. Did you not see the signs?"

"Yes, we saw the signs," Talut said. "We have with us one who is a daughter of the Mammoth Hearth, a skilled Healer. The runner, Ludeg, who passed by here some days ago, told us of your troubles. We were preparing to travel to our Summer Meeting, but first, Ayla, our Healer, wished to come here to offer her skills. One of us was related to one of you; we are kin. We came."

The man looked at the woman standing beside him. It was obvious that she was grieving, and she gathered herself together with some effort.

"It is too late," she said. "They are dead." Her voice trailed off in a wail, and she cried out in anguish, "They are dead. My children, my babies, my life, they are dead." Two people stepped up on either side of the woman and led her away.

"My sister has suffered a great sorrow," the man said. "She has lost both a daughter and a son. The girl was nearly a woman, the boy a few years younger. We all grieve."

Talut shook his head in sympathy. "It is indeed a great sorrow. We share your grief, and offer whatever solace we may. If it is within your custom, we would like to stay to add our tears to yours as they are returned to the breast of the Mother."

"Your kindness is appreciated, and will always be remembered, but there are still those among us who are sick. It may be dangerous for you to stay. It may be dangerous for you to have come."

"Talut, ask him if I can look at the ones who are still sick. I may be able to help them," Ayla said quietly.

"Yes, Talut. Ask if Ayla may look at the sick ones," Mamut added. "I think she will be able to say if it's safe for us to stay."

The man with the red face looked hard at the old man sitting on the horse. He had been amazed when he first saw the horses, but he did not want to seem overwhelmed, and he was so numbed with grief he had put his curiosity aside for the moment, while he acted as spokesman for his sister, and his Camp. But when Mamut spoke, the strange sight of a man sitting on the back of a horse was suddenly brought to his awareness with new impact.

"How does that man come to be sitting on a horse?" he finally blurted out. "Why does the horse stand still for it? And that other one, back there?"

"It is a long story," Talut said. "The man is our Mamut, and the horses answer to our Healer. When there is time, we will be happy to tell you about it, but first, Ayla would like to look at your sick ones. She may be able to help them. She will be able to tell us if the evil spirits still linger, and if she can contain them and make them harmless; whether it is safe for us to stay."

"You say she is skilled. I must believe you. If she can command the horse spirit, she must have powerful magic. Let me speak to those within."

"There is one other animal you should know about," Talut said, then turned to the woman. "Call him, Ayla."

She whistled, and even before Rydag could let him go, Wolf had wriggled free. The Sungaea man and other bystanders were startled as the young wolf came racing towards them, but even more surprised when he stopped at Ayla's feet, and looked up at her with expectation. At her signal, he dropped down to his stomach, but his alert attention focused on the strangers made them uneasy.

Tulie had been carefully observing the reactions of the Sungaea Camp and quickly realised what a powerful impression the tractable animals had made. They had enhanced the stature of the people they were associated with, and the Lion Camp as a whole. Mamut, by the simple act of sitting on the back of the horse, had garnered prestige. They watched him with wary glances, and his words had carried great authority, but the response to Ayla was even more revealing. They looked at her with awe, and a kind of fearful reverence.

The headwoman realised that she had grown accustomed to the horses, but she recalled her own apprehension the first time she had seen Ayla with her horses, and it wasn't hard to put herself in their place. She had been there when Ayla brought the tiny wolf pup to the lodge, and she had watched him grow up, but looking at Wolf as a stranger might see him, she realised he would not be seen as a puppyish young animal. He might be young, but, to all appearances, he was nearly a full-grown wolf, and the horse was a mature mare. If Ayla could bend the will of high-strung horses and the spirit of independent wolves to her command, what other forces could she control? Especially when told she was the daughter of the Mammoth Hearth, and a Healer.

Tulie wondered what kind of reception they would receive when they arrived at the Summer Meeting, but she wasn't at all surprised when Ayla was invited in to examine the ailing members of the Camp. The Mamutoi settled down to wait. When Ayla came out, she went to Mamut, Talut and Tulie.

"I think they have what Nezzie calls spring sickness, fever, and tightness in the chest, and trouble breathing, except they got it later in the season, and harder," Ayla explained. "Two older people died earlier, but it is most sad when children die. I'm not sure why they did. Young people are usually strong enough to recover from this kind of sickness. Everyone else seems to be over the worst of it. Some of them are coughing a lot, and I can help make them a little more comfortable, but no one seems seriously ill any more. I would like to fix something to help the mother. She is taking it very hard. I can't blame her. I am not absolutely certain, but I don't think it will endanger us to stay for the burial. I don't think we should stay inside their lodges, though."

"I would have suggested we set up our own tents, if we decided to stay," Tulie said. "It's hard enough for them without having strangers in their midst all the time, and they aren't even Mamutoi. Sungaea are . . . different."

Ayla was awakened in the morning by the sound of voices not too far from the tent. She quickly got up, dressed, and looked out. Several people were digging a long, narrow trench. Tronie and Fralie were outside, sitting near a fire nursing their babies. Ayla smiled and joined them. The smell of sage tea rose from a steaming cooking basket. She scooped out a cup and sat with the two women, sipping the hot liquid.

"Are they going to bury them today?" Fralie asked.

"I think so," Ayla said. "I don't think Talut wanted to ask outright, but I got that impression. I can't understand their language, though I can catch a few words now and then."

"They must be digging the grave. I wonder why they are making it so long?" Tronie said.

"I don't know, but I'm glad we'll be leaving soon. I know it's right for us to stay, but I don't like burials," Fralie said.

"No one does," Ayla said. "I wish we could have got here a few days earlier."

"You don't know if you could have done anything for those children anyway," Fralie said.

"I feel so sorry for the mother," Tronie commented. "It would be hard enough to lose one child, but to lose two at the same time . . . I don't know if I could stand it." She cuddled Hartal to her, but it only made the toddler squirm to get away.

"Yes. It is hard to lose a child," Ayla said. Her voice was so grim, it made Fralie look, and wonder. Ayla put her cup down and got up. "I saw some wormwood growing nearby. The root makes a very strong medicine. I don't often use it, but I want to make something to calm and relax the mother, and it needs to be strong."

The Lion Camp observed or peripherally participated in various activities and ceremonies during the day, but towards evening the atmosphere changed, became charged with an intensity that caught up even the visitors. The heightened emotions evoked genuine cries of sorrow and grief from the Mamutoi when the two children were solemnly carried out of a lodge on hammock-like biers, and brought around to each person for a final farewell.

As the people who were carrying the stretchers slowly walked by the mourning visitors, Ayla noticed that the children had been clothed in beautifully made and elegantly decorated finery, as though dressed for an important festival. She could not help but be impressed and intrigued. Pieces of variously dyed and naturally coloured leathers and furs had been carefully stitched together into intricate geometric patterns in making the tunics and long trousers, outlined and highlighted by solid areas that were filled in with thousands of small ivory beads. A stray thought passed through her mind. Had all the work been done using only a sharp awl? Maybe someone would appreciate the small, sharp-pointed, ivory shaft with the hole in the end.

She also noticed headbands and belts, and across the shoulders of the girl, a cape with fascinating designs that were worked into a material which appeared to have been constructed out of strands of the underwool shed by the passing woolly beasts. She wanted to touch it, examine it closely, and learn how it had been made, but it would not have been appropriate. Ranec, standing beside her, noticed it, too, and commented on the intricate pattern of right-angled spirals. Ayla hoped that before they left, she could find out more about how it was made, perhaps in exchange for one of her ivory points with a hole.

Both children were also adorned with jewellery made of shells, animal canines, bone; the boy even had a large, unusual stone which had been pierced to wear as a pendant. Unlike the adults whose hair was in disarray and covered with ashes, their hair was neatly combed and arranged in elaborate styles – the boy in braids, the girl with large buns on either side of her head.

Ayla could not dispel the feeling that the children were only sleeping and would wake up any moment. They looked too young, too healthy, with their round-cheeked, unlined faces to be gone, to have passed into the realm of the spirits. She felt a shudder pass through her, and involuntarily glanced towards Rydag. She caught Nezzie's eye and looked away.

Finally the bodies of the children were brought to the long, narrow trench. They were lowered into it and placed head to head. A woman with a peculiar headdress and a long beaded tunic stood up and began a keening, high-pitched chant that sent shivers through everyone. She wore many necklaces and pendants around her neck that jangled and clicked when she moved, and several loose ivory bracelets around her arms, consisting of several separate half-inch-wide bands. Ayla realised they were similar to ones some of the Mamutoi used.

A deep reverberating drumbeat sounded with the familiar tone of a mammoth skull drum. Keening and chanting, the woman began to weave and sway, rising up on her toes and lifting her feet, sometimes facing different directions, but staying in one place. As she danced, she waved her arms about sharply and rhythmically, causing her bracelets to rattle. Ayla had met her, and though they had not been able to converse, she felt drawn to her. Mamut had explained that she was not a medicine woman as Ayla was, but one who could communicate with the spirit world. She was the Sungaea counterpart of Mamut – or Creb, Ayla realised with a jolt. It was still difficult for her to conceive of a woman Mog-ur.

The man and woman with the red faces sprinkled powdered red ochre over the children, making Ayla think of the red ochre salve that Creb had rubbed on Iza's body. Several other things were ceremoniously added to the grave: shafts of mammoth tusk that had been straightened, spears, flint knives and daggers, carvings of a mammoth, a bison, and a horse – not as well made as Ranec's, Ayla thought. She was surprised to see a long ivory staff, decorated with a circular, spoked, wheel-like carving to which feathers and other objects were attached, laid beside each child. When the people of the settlement joined in the wailing, keening song of the woman, Ayla quietly leaned forward and whispered to Mamut. "Those staffs look like Talut's. Are they Speaking Staffs?"

"Yes, they are. The Sungaea are related to the Mamutoi, more closely than some people want to admit," Mamut said. "There are some differences, but this burial ceremony is very much like ours."

"Why would they put Speaking Staffs in a grave with children?"

"They are given those things which they will need when they wake up in the spirit world. As the daughter and son of the headwoman, they are a sister and brother who were destined to become co-leaders, if not in this lifetime, then the next," Mamut explained. "It is necessary to show their rank so they do not lose status there."

Ayla watched for a while, then, when they started to put the dirt back in, she spoke to Mamut again.

"Why are they buried like that, head to head?"

"They are brother and sister," he said, as though the rest was self-explanatory. Then he saw her puzzled expression and continued, "It can be a long, difficult, and confusing Journey to the spirit world, especially for those who are so young. They need to be able to communicate, to help and comfort each other, but it is an abomination to the Mother for a brother and sister to share Pleasures. If they wake up side by side, they may forget they are brother and sister, and couple by mistake, thinking they were sleeping together because they were meant to be joined. Head to head, they can encourage each other on the journey, and still not be confused about their relationship when they reach the other place."

Ayla nodded. It seemed logical, but as she watched the grave being filled in, she fervently wished they had got there a few days sooner. Maybe she couldn't have helped, but she could have tried.

Talut stopped at the edge of a small waterway, looked upstream and then downstream, then consulted the marked piece of ivory he held in his hand. He checked the position of the sun, studied some cloud formations in the north, and sniffed the wind. Finally he examined the area nearby.

"We camp here for the night," he said, shrugging off his haversack and packframe. He walked towards his sister as she was deciding where the primary tent would be placed, so the adjoining ones that utilised part of the same structural supports would have plenty of level ground. "Tulie, what would you say to stopping to do a little trading? I was looking at these maps Ludeg made. It didn't occur to me at first, but seeing where we are, look," he said, showing her two different pieces of ivory with marks scratched on them, "here's the map showing the way to Wolf Camp, the new location of the Summer Meeting, and here's the quick one he made showing the way to Sungaea Camp. From here, it wouldn't be much out of our way to visit Mammoth Camp."

"You mean Musk-Ox Camp," Tulie said, with annoyed disdain. "It was presumptuous of them to rename their Camp. Everyone has a Mammoth Hearth, but no one should name a Camp for the mammoth. Aren't we all Mammoth Hunters?"

"But Camps are always named after the headman's hearth, and their new headman is their Mamut. Besides, that doesn't mean we can't trade with them – if they are not gone for the summer. You know they are related to Amber Camp, and they always have some amber to trade," Talut said, knowing his sister's weakness for the warm, gold-hued stones of petrified resin. "Wymez says they have access to good flint, too. We have plenty of reindeer hides, not to mention some nice furs."

"I don't know how a man can establish a hearth when he doesn't even have a woman, but I just said they were presumptuous. We can still trade with them. Of course we should stop, Talut." The headwoman's expression changed to an enigmatic smile. "Yes, by all means. I think it would be interesting for the 'Mammoth' Camp to meet *our* Mammoth Hearth."

"Good. We'd better leave early, then," Talut said, but he regarded her with puzzlement, and shook his head, wondering what his clever and astute sister was thinking.

When the Lion Camp reached a large sinuous river gouging a channel between steep banks of loess soil, similar to the setting near their lodge, Talut headed out to a promontory between ravines and carefully scanned the surrounding terrain. He saw deer and aurochs near the water on the floodplain below, grazing in a green meadow dotted with small trees. Some distance farther, he noticed a large pile of jumbled bones that had been carried by flooding waters and slammed against a high bank where the river turned sharply. Tiny figures scuttled over the accumulation of dried bones, and he saw several of them carrying away pieces.

"They are still here," he announced. "They must be building."

The travellers trooped down a slope towards the Camp, situated on a broad terrace no more than fifteen feet above the level of the river, and if Ayla had been surprised at the lodge of the Lion Camp, she was astounded by the Mammoth Camp. Rather than a single large, sod-covered, semi-subterranean longhouse that Ayla had likened to a cave or even a human-size burrow, in this Camp, several individual round lodges were clustered together on the terrace. They, too, were solid and sturdy under a thick layering of sod covered with clay, and patches of grass grew around the edges, but not on the top. They reminded Ayla of nothing so much as huge, bald, marmot mounds.

As they approached, she could understand why the tops were bare. Just as they did, the Mammoth Camp also used the roofs of their dwellings as viewing platforms. Two of the lodges each supported a crowd of onlookers, and though the watchers had turned their attention to the visitors, that was not the reason they were up on the rounded roofs. When the Lion Camp passed around a lodge that blocked their view, Ayla saw the object of their interest, and was astonished.

Talut had been right. They were building. Ayla had overheard Tulie's remarks about the name these people had chosen for themselves, but after seeing the lodge they were making, it seemed most appropriate. Though it might end up looking like all the others when it was completed, the way they used mammoth bones as structural supports seemed to capture a special quality of the animal. It was true that the Lion Camp had used mammoth bones in the supporting framework of their lodge, and had selected certain pieces and trimmed them to fit, but the bones used in this dwelling did more than support. They were selected and arranged so that the structure managed to convey the essence of the mammoth in a way that expressed the beliefs of the Mamutoi.

To create the design, they first brought up large numbers of the same skeletal parts of many mammoths from the bone pile below. They began with a circle, about sixteen feet across at the base, of mammoth skulls placed so that the solid surface of the foreheads faced inward. The opening was the familiar archway, constructed of two large curved tusks, anchored on each side in the socket of a mammoth skull, and joined at the top. Around the outside and half-way up was a circular wall made of, perhaps, a hundred mammoth mandibles, the V-shaped lower jaws, stacked with the pointed chins down one on top of another four deep.

The overall effect of these stacks of V's placed side by side was the most impressive concept of the construction, and the most meaningful. Together they created a zigzag pattern, similar to the pattern used to symbolise water on the maps. And beyond that, as Ayla had learned from Mamut, the zigzag symbol for water was also the most profound symbol for the Great Mother, Creator of all Life. They represented the downward-pointing triangle of Her mound, the external expression of Her womb. Multiplied many times over, the symbol represented all life; not only water, but the birth waters of the Mother which had flooded the land and filled the seas and rivers when She gave birth to all life on earth. There could be no doubt that this would be the lodge of the Mammoth Hearth.

The circular wall was not completed, but they were working on the rest of the lodge, wedging in shoulder blades and pelvic bones and pieces of spine in a rhythmically symmetrical yet tightly fitted way. An open framework of wood inside provided additional support for the structure and it appeared that the roof would be constructed of mammoth tusks.

"This is the work of a true artist!" Ranec said, stepping closer and openly admiring their handiwork.

Ayla knew he would approve. She noticed Jondalar standing a little distance away holding Racer's lead rope. She realised that he was no less impressed or appreciative of the inspired mind that had conceived of the idea. In fact the entire Lion Camp was at a loss for words. But as Tulie had suspected, the Mammoth Camp was just as astounded by their visitors – or rather, by the tame animals that travelled with them.

There was a period of mutual staring in wonder and amazement, and then a woman and man, both somewhat younger than the leaders of the Lion Camp, came forward to greet Tulie and Talut. The man had been hauling heavy mammoth bones up the slope – these were by no means temporary dwellings that would be carried from place to place, but a permanent settlement – and he was stripped to the waist and sweaty. His face was heavily tattooed, and Ayla had to remind herself not to stare. He not only had a chevron pattern on his left cheek, like the Mamut of the Lion Camp, but a symmetrical arrangement of zigzags, triangles and diamond shapes, and right-angle spirals in two colours, blue and red.

The woman had obviously been working, too, and was also bare from the waist up, but rather than pants, she wore a wrapped skirt that fell to just below her knees. She had no tattoos, but the side of her nose was pierced and she wore a labret made of a small piece of carved and polished amber through the hole.

"Tulie, Talut, what a surprise! We were not expecting you, but in the name of the Mother, we welcome the Lion Camp," the woman said.

"In the name of Mut, we thank you for your welcome, Avarie," Tulie said. "We did not mean to come at an inconvenient time."

"We were nearby, Vincavec," Talut added, "and could not pass without stopping."

"It is never inconvenient for the Lion Camp to visit," the man said, "but how do you happen to be nearby? This is not on the way to Wolf Camp for you."

"The runner that came to tell us that the Meeting place had been changed stopped off at the Sungaea Camp as he was making his stops and told us they were very sick. We have a new member, a Healer, Ayla of the Mammoth Hearth," Talut said, beckoning her forward, "and she wanted to go and see if she could help. We have just come from there."

"Yes, I know that Sungaea Camp," Vincavec said, then turned to Ayla. For a moment she felt his eyes bore into her. She hesitated for a moment, still not entirely used to returning the direct look of a stranger, but she sensed this was not a moment for shyness, or the modesty of a Clan woman, and returned his intense gaze. Suddenly he laughed, and his pale grey eyes gleamed with approval, and a look that appreciated her womanliness. She noticed then that he was a striking, attractive man, not because he was handsome or for any particular feature, although the tattoos did make him stand out, but because of a quality of strength of will and intelligence. He looked up at Mamut sitting on Whinney.

"So you're still with us, old man," he said, obviously pleased, then added with a knowing smile, "and still coming up with surprises. Since when have you become a Caller? Or do we need another name? Two horses and a wolf travelling with the Lion Camp? This is more than a Gift of Calling."

"Another name might be appropriate, Vincavec, but it is not my Gift. The animals answer to Ayla."

"Ayla? It seems the old Mamut has found himself a worthy daughter." Vincavec looked her over again, with obvious interest. He didn't notice Ranec glower, but Jondalar did. He understood the feeling, and for the first time, felt a strange sort of kinship with the carver.

"Enough standing here talking," Avarie said. "We have plenty of time for that. The travellers must be tired, and hungry. You must let me arrange a meal for you, and a place to rest."

"We can see that you are making a new lodge, Avarie. You don't need to go to trouble for us. A place to set up tents will be enough," Tulie said. "Later, we would be pleased to share a meal with you, and perhaps show you some fine reindeer skins and furs we happen to have with us."

"I have a better idea!" Talut boomed, shrugging off his packframe where he stood. "Why don't we help you? You may have to tell me where to put it, but I have back enough to carry a mammoth bone or two."

"Yes, I'd like to help," Jondalar volunteered, leading Racer forward and helping Rydag off. "That's an unusual lodge. I have never seen anything quite like it."

"By all means. We welcome your help. Some of us are in a hurry to get to the Summer Meeting, but a lodge needs a summer to set up properly, so we needed to build it before we left. The Lion Camp is most generous," Vincavec said, wondering how many pieces of amber their generosity was going to cost when the trading started. Then he decided it would be worth it to get his lodge finished, and quiet some of the complainers.

Vincavec hadn't noticed the tall blond man in the crowd of people at first, but he looked twice, then glanced back at Ayla who was unharnessing Whinney from the travois. He was a stranger, as Ayla was, and he seemed as comfortable with the horses as she did. But then the little flathead seemed familiar with the wolf, and he was no stranger any more. It must have something to do with the woman. The Mamut-headman of the Mammoth Camp turned his attention back to Ayla. He noticed the brown-skinned carver was hovering around her; Ranec always did have an eye for the beautiful and the exceptional, he thought. In fact, he was acting possessive, but then who was the stranger? Wasn't he associated with the woman? Vincavec glanced at Jondalar, and noted that he was watching Ayla and Ranec.

Something was going on here, Vincavec decided, then smiled. Whatever the relationships, if they were both so interested, it was likely the woman was not formally joined, yet. He looked her over once again. She was a striking woman, and a daughter of the Mammoth Hearth, a Healer, or so they claimed, and she certainly had some unique talent with animals. A woman of high status, no doubt, but where had she come from? And why was it always the Lion Camp that turned up with someone unusual?

The two headwomen were standing inside an almost complete, but empty new earthlodge. Although the outside was covered, the zigzag pattern of the walls was subtly apparent on the inside.

"Are you sure you won't travel with us, Avarie?" Tulie said. A new string of large amber beads graced her neck. "We'd be happy to wait a few more days, until you are ready."

"No, you go ahead. I know everyone is anxious to get to the Meeting, and you have already done too much. The lodge is nearly finished, and without you, we would never have been so far along."

"It was our pleasure to work with you. I must admit, the new lodge is quite impressive. It is an honour to the Mother. Your brother is truly remarkable. One can almost feel the Mother's presence inside." She was sincere, and Avarie knew it.

"Thank you, Tulie, and we will not forget your help. That's why we don't want to keep you any longer. You are already late because you stayed to help us. All the best places will be taken."

"It won't take us long to get there now. Our load is considerably lighter. Mammoth Camp strikes a hard bargain."

Avarie's eyes glanced at the big headwoman's new necklace. "Not nearly as hard a bargain as Lion Camp," she said.

Tulie agreed. She believed the Lion Camp had got the better of the bargaining, but it was unseemly to admit to it. She changed the subject. "Well, we'll look forward to seeing you there. If we can, we'll try to mark a place for you."

"We would appreciate that, but I suspect we'll be the last ones. We will have to take what we can get. We will look for you, though," Avarie said, as they walked out.

"We'll leave in the morning, then," Tulie said. The two women embraced, and touched cheeks, then the headwoman of the Lion Camp started towards the tents.

"Oh, Tulie, in case I don't see Ayla to tell her before you go, please thank her again for the firestone," Avarie said, then added in an apparently offhand way, "Have you set a Bride Price for her yet?"

"We have been thinking about it, but she has so much to offer, it's difficult," Tulie said, then turned to go. After a few steps, she turned back and smiled. "She and Deegie have become so close, Ayla is almost like a daughter to me."

Tulie could hardly suppress a smile as she walked away. She thought she had noticed Vincavec paying particular attention to Ayla, and she knew Avarie's comment was no casual remark. He had put his sister up to it. It would not be a bad match, Tulie thought, and having ties with the Mammoth Camp could prove beneficial. Of course, Ranec has first claim. They are, after all, Promised, but if someone like Vincavec made an offer, it wouldn't hurt to consider it. At the very least, it would raise her value. Yes, Talut had a good idea when he suggested they stop and do some trading.

Avarie watched her go. So Tulie is going to negotiate the Bride Price, herself. I thought as much. Perhaps we should stop off at Amber Camp on the way, I know where mother keeps the raw stone, and if Vincavec is going to try for Ayla, he's going to need everything he can get. I never saw a woman drive a harder bargain than Tulie, Avarie thought with begrudging admiration. She hadn't particularly cared for the big headwoman of the Lion Camp before, but these past few days when they had a chance to get better acquainted, she had come to respect her, and even like her. Tulie had worked hard with them and was generous with her praise when it was deserved, and if she was a formidable trader, well, that was the headwoman's role. In fact, if she were young and ready to make a joining, Avarie thought, she wouldn't mind having someone like Tulie negotiating her Bride Price.

★   ★   ★

From the Mammoth Camp, the Lion Camp travelled in a generally northerly direction, for the most part following the river. Near the great waterways that coursed down the continent, the northern landscape changed continually and displayed a rich diversity of plant life. Their trek took them from tundra fells and loess plains to reedy forest lakes, from lush bogs to windy knolls and grassy meadows bright with summer blooms. Though the northern plants were stunted, the flowers were often larger and more brilliant than southern varieties. Ayla could identify most of them, though she didn't always know what to call them. When they passed them, or if she was out riding or walking alone, she often picked some to bring to Mamut, or Nezzie, or Deegie, or someone to tell her the names.

The closer they came to the place of the Summer Meeting, the more Ayla found reasons to make side trips. Summer had always been the time when she wanted solitude. It had been her pattern for as long as she could remember. In the winter, she accepted the confinement imposed by severe weather, whether it was to the cave of Brun's clan, or the one in her valley, or the Mamutoi earthlodge. But in summer, though she did not like to be alone at night, she had often enjoyed getting off by herself during the day. It was her time to think her own thoughts, and follow her own impulses, free from the restriction of being watched too much, either because of suspicion, or love.

When they stopped for the evening, it was easy enough to say she wanted to identify plants or to hunt, and she did both, using the spear-thrower as well as her sling to bring back fresh meat, but she really wanted to get away alone. She needed time to think. She was dreading their arrival, and couldn't quite understand why. She had met enough people now, and had been easily enough accepted, so she knew that wasn't the problem. But the closer they got, the more excited Ranec became, and the more morose Jondalar seemed. And the more she wished she could avoid this gathering of the Camps.

On their last night of travelling, Ayla returned from a long walk with a handful of flowers. She noticed that a patch of ground near the fire had been smoothed out, and that Jondalar was making marks in it with the drawing knife. Tornec had a broken piece of ivory in his hand and a sharp knife out, and was studying marks.

"Here she is," Jondalar said. "Ayla can tell you better than I can. I'm not sure I could find my way back to the valley from Lion Camp, and I know I couldn't do it from here. We've taken too many turns and detours."

"Jondalar was trying to make a map showing the way to the valley where you found the firestones," Talut said.

"I've been looking ever since we left, and I haven't seen one firestone,"

507

Tornec added. "I'd like to make a trip there sometime and get some more. The ones we have won't last forever. Mine already has a big groove in it."

"I'm having trouble judging distance," Jondalar said. "We travelled on horseback, so it's hard to say how many days it would take on foot. And we explored a lot, stopped when we felt like it, didn't follow any logical trail. I'm almost certain we went back across the river that runs through your valley, farther north. Maybe more than once. When we went back, it was almost winter, and many landmarks had changed."

Ayla put down the flowers, and picked up the drawing knife, and tried to think about how to make a map to the valley. She started to make a line, and then hesitated.

"Don't worry about trying to do it from here," Talut encouraged. "Just think about how to get there from Lion Camp."

Ayla crinkled her brow in concentration. "I know I could show you the way from Lion Camp," she said, "but I still don't understand maps very well. I don't think I know how to draw one."

"Well, don't worry about it," Talut said. "We don't need a map, if you can show us the way. Maybe after we return from the Summer Meeting, we can make a trip there." Then he motioned with his red-bearded chin towards the flowers. "What did you bring back this time, Ayla?"

"That's what I want you to tell me. I know what they are, but I don't know what you call them."

"I know that red one is a geranium," Talut said. "And this is poppy."

"More flowers?" Deegie said, just joining them.

"Yes. Talut told me these two," Ayla said.

"Let's see, that's heather, and that's cushion pink," Deegie said, then sat down beside Ayla. "We're almost there. Talut says some time tomorrow. I can hardly wait. Tomorrow I'll see Branag, and then it won't be long until we are finally joined. I don't even know if I'll be able to sleep tonight."

Ayla smiled at her. Deegie was so excited, it was hard not to share her enthusiasm, but it only served to remind her that she, too, would soon be joined. Jondalar's talk about the valley and going back there had renewed her ache of longing for him. She had been watching him, trying not to make it obvious, and she had a distinct feeling that he had been observing her. She kept meeting his eyes briefly before both looked away.

"Oh, Ayla, there are so many people I want you to meet, and I'm so glad we are going to be joined at the same Matrimonial. That's something we'll always have together."

Jondalar got up. "I need to go . . . and . . . uh . . . set up my sleeping roll," he said, then hurried away.

Deegie watched Ayla's eyes follow after him, and was almost certain she saw tears being held back. She shook her head. Ayla just didn't seem like a woman who was about to join and establish a new hearth with a man she loved. There was no joy, no excitement. Something was missing. Something called Jondalar.

31

In the morning the Lion Camp continued upstream, staying on the plateau of the plains, but catching glimpses of the swift waterway below on their left, cloudy with glacial runoff and churning with silt. When they reached a fork, a place where two major rivers joined, they took the left branch. After fording two large tributaries, putting most of their possessions in a bowl boat they had brought along for that purpose, they descended to the floodplain and travelled through the woods and grassy meadows of the river valley.

Talut kept watching the system of hollows and ravines on the high right bank across the river, comparing the actual landscape to the ivory scratched with symbols, whose meaning was still unclear to Ayla. Ahead, near a sharp bend, was the highest point of the opposite shoreline, rising some two hundred feet above the water. On their side, a broad grassy field and patches of woods extended inland for some miles. As they drew closer, Ayla noticed a bone cairn, with a wolf skull on top. A peculiar arrangement of rocks extended across the river in the direction Talut was heading.

The river there was wide and shallow, and would have been fordable in any case, but someone had made the crossing even easier. Piles of rock and gravel, and some bone, had been placed and spread out in the manner of stepping-stones to make a pathway for people to cross the river, while diverting the flow of water to the spaces in between.

Jondalar paused to look more closely. "What a clever idea!" he remarked. "You could cross the river here without even getting your feet wet."

"The best places to put lodges are on that side – those deep hollows give good protection from the wind – but the best hunting is on this side," Barzec explained. "This walkway washes out with the floods, but Wolf Camp builds a new one every year. They seem to have gone to extra trouble this year, probably to make it easier for visitors."

Talut started across. Ayla noticed Whinney was extremely agitated, and thought the horse was nervous about the stepping-stone path with the watery spaces in between, but the mare followed her without incident.

The headman paused more than halfway over. "Right here, it's good fishing," he said. "The current runs fast, so it's deep. Salmon come up this far. Sturgeon, too. And other fish, pike, trout, catfish." He directed his comments at Ayla and Jondalar in particular, though he included any of the youngsters who had not been there before. It had been some years since Lion Camp had visited Wolf Camp as a group.

On the other side, as Talut led them towards a wide ravine, perhaps a half-mile across at the top, Ayla heard a strange sound, like a loud hum or a muted roar. They gradually climbed uphill. Sixty feet or so above the level of the river and one hundred and fifty yards back, they came to the bottom of the large ravine. Ayla looked ahead, and gasped. Protected by steep walls, a half-dozen separate round lodges, clustered in a row, were comfortably settled within the nearly mile-long hollow. But it wasn't the round earthlodges that made Ayla gasp.

It was the people. In all her life, Ayla had never seen so many people. Well over a thousand human souls, more than thirty Camps, had gathered together for the Mamutoi Summer Meeting. The length and breadth of the entire area was filled with tents. There were at least four or five times as many people as had come together for the Clan Gathering – and everyone was staring at her.

Or rather, at her horses and Wolf. The young canine cowered against her leg, just as thunderstruck as she. She sensed panic in Whinney and was sure Racer felt the same. Fear for them helped her overcome her own feelings of sheer terror at the sight of so many human beings. She looked up and saw Jondalar hanging on the lead rope, struggling to keep Racer from rearing, while the frightened boy hung on tight.

"Nezzie, get Rydag!" she called out. The woman had already seen the problem and hardly needed Ayla's words to impel her to move. Ayla helped Mamut down, and put her arm around the mare's neck, leading her towards the young stallion to help calm him. The wolf followed after her.

"I'm sorry, Ayla. I should have thought about how the horses would react to so many people," Jondalar said.

"You knew there would be this many?"

"I . . . didn't know, but I guessed there might be about as many as would come to a Zelandonii Summer Meeting."

"I think we should try to set up Cattail Camp some place out of the way," Tulie said, speaking up to get everyone's attention. "Maybe here, near the edge of the encampment. We'll be farther away from every-thing" – she was looking around as she spoke – "but Wolf Camp has a creek running through their hollow this year, and it turns this way."

Tulie had been anticipating the reaction of the people, and she hadn't been disappointed. They had been seen crossing the river, and everyone there had crowded close to watch the arrival of the Lion Camp. But she had not anticipated that the animals might be overwhelmed by their initial introduction to a herd of humanity.

"How about over there, near the wall?" Barzec suggested. "It's not too level, but we can even it out."

"It looks fine to me. Are there any objections?" Talut said, looking pointedly at Ayla. She and Jondalar just led the animals that way, wanting to get them settled. The Lion Camp began clearing out rocks and brush and levelling a place to set up their large, double-skinned, communal tent.

Living in a tent was made much more comfortable by using two layers of hides. The insulating layer of air between them helped to keep the warmth in, and moisture condensing in the cool of the evening ran down the inner side of the outer hides to the ground. The inner hides, which were tucked under the interior ground cloths, kept draughts out as well. Though not nearly as permanent as the earthlodge at Lion Camp, it was a more substantial structure than the single-wall overnight shelter that was only a part of the full summer tent, which they used when travelling. They referred to their summer home as Cattail Camp to differentiate the summer location, wherever it happened to be, from the winter site, when they spoke of it, though they still thought of themselves as belonging to a group called Lion Camp.

The tent was divided into four interdependent conical sections, each with a separate fireplace, supported by sturdy, flexible young trees, although mammoth rib bones, or other long bones, could have and had been used. The central section, which was largest, would house the Lion Hearth, the Fox Hearth, and the Mammoth Hearth. While the tent lodge was not as roomy as the earthlodge, it would be used primarily for sleeping, and it was seldom that everyone would be in the tent sleeping at the same time. Other activities, private, social, and public, would take place outdoors, so setting up also meant defining territory beyond the walls of the tent. The placement of Cattail Hearth, the main exterior cooking hearth, was a matter of some importance.

While they worked to set up their tent and stake out their territory, the rest of the people at the Meeting began to recover from their initial stunned silence, and began to talk excitedly among themselves. Ayla finally discovered the source of the peculiar muted roar. She recalled, when she first arrived at Lion Camp, how noisy she thought it was when everybody spoke at once. This was that noise many times over; it was the combined voices of the entire throng.

No wonder Whinney and Racer were so skittish, Ayla thought. The constant hum of humanity made her skittish, too. She wasn't used to it. The Clan Gathering had not been as big, but even if it had, it would never have been as noisy. They used few words to communicate; a gathering of the people of the Clan was quiet. But with people who used verbal speech, except for rare occasions, it was always noisy within an encampment. Like the wind on the steppes, the voices never ceased, they only varied in intensity.

Many people hurried to greet the Lion Camp, offering to help set up and arrange their place, and were greeted warmly, but Talut and Tulie passed several meaningful glances between themselves. They didn't remember having so many friends who were so willing to help before. With the help of Latie, Jondalar, and Ranec, and for a while, Talut, Ayla set up a place for the horses. The two young men worked together easily, but spoke little. She turned down offers of help from the curious, explaining that the horses were shy and strangers would make them nervous. But that only made it obvious that she was the one in control of the animals, and engendered more curiosity. Word of her spread quickly.

At the farthest edge of the encampment, slightly around a curve of the wall of the ravine that opened on to the river valley, they constructed an awninglike lean-to, utilising the hide tent she and Jondalar had used when they travelled together, supported by small trees and sturdy branches. It was somewhat hidden from the sight of the people camped in the hollow, but the view of the river and the beautiful wooded meadows across was expansive.

They were moving in and setting up places to sleep in the somewhat more crowded quarters when a delegation from Wolf Camp, along with several others, came to welcome them officially. They were in the host Camp's territory, and though it was expected, it was more than courtesy to extend to all visitors the use of the Wolf Camp's hereditary fishing weirs, berry, nut, seed, and root beds and hunting grounds. Even though the Summer Meeting would not last the entire season, hosting such a large group would take its toll, and it was necessary to find out if some particular area should be avoided so as not to overtax the resources of the region.

Talut had been quite surprised when told of the change in the location of the Summer Meeting. The Mamutoi didn't, as a rule, meet at a home Camp. Usually they chose some location that was out on the steppes or in some large river valley that could accommodate such concentrations of people more easily.

"In the name of the Great Mother of all, the Lion Camp is welcome," a thin, grey-haired woman said.

Tulie was shocked to see her. She had been a woman of uncommon grace and robust health, who had shouldered the responsibility of her co-leadership with ease, but she seemed to have aged ten years in the last season. "Marlie, we appreciate your hospitality. In the name of Mut, we thank you."

"I see you have done it again," a man said, grasping both of Talut's hands in greeting.

Valez was younger than his sister, but for the first time, Tulie noticed that he also showed signs of age. It made her suddenly aware of her own mortality. She had always thought Marlie and Valez were close to her in age.

"But I think this is your biggest surprise," Valez continued. "When Toran came running in, shouting something about horses walking across the river with you, everyone had to go and look. And then someone spied the wolf . . ."

"We won't ask you to tell us about them now," Marlie said, "though I must admit I am curious. You'll just have to repeat it again too many times. We might as well wait until this evening so you can tell everyone at once."

"Marlie is right, of course," Valez said, though he had been ready to hear the story right then. He also noticed that his sister seemed especially tired. He feared this would be her last Summer Meeting. That was why he had agreed to host it when the place that had originally been selected was washed out by a change in the course of the river. They would be handing over their co-leadership this season.

"Please make use of whatever you need. Are you settled in comfortably? I'm sorry you have to be so far away, but you are late. I wasn't even sure that you were coming," Marlie said.

"We took a roundabout way," Talut agreed. "But this is the best place. It's better for the animals. They aren't used to so many people."

"I'd like to know how they got used to one!" a voice called out. Tulie's eyes lit up as a tall young man approached, but Deegie got to him first.

"Tarneg! Tarneg!" she cried out as she rushed to embrace him. The rest of the Aurochs Hearth were not far behind her. He hugged his mother, and then Barzec, and all had tears in their eyes. Then Druwez, Brinan, and Tusie clamoured for his attention. He put his arms around the shoulders of both boys, hugged them and told them how much they had grown, and then picked up Tusie. After a mutual hug and a tickle which produced delighted giggles, Tarneg put her down.

"Tarneg!" Talut boomed.

"Talut, you old bear!" Tarneg returned in a voice as powerful as the two men hugged. There was a strong family resemblance – he was nearly as much a bear as his uncle – but Tarneg had his mother's darker colouring. He bent down to rub Nezzie's cheek with his, then with a mischievous grin, he put his arms around the rotund woman and picked her up.

"Tarneg! What are you doing? Put me down," she scolded.

He set her lightly down on her feet, then winked at her. "Now I know I'm as good a man as you, Talut," Tarneg said, and laughed out loud. "Do you know how long I've wanted to do that? Just to prove I could?"

"It is not necessary to . . . :" Nezzie began.

Talut threw back his head and roared with laughter. "It takes more than that, young man. When you can match me in the furs, you'll be as good a man as I am."

Nezzie gave up trying to scold her dignity back, and just looked at her great bear of a man, shaking her head with exasperated fondness. "What is it about Summer Meetings that makes old men want to prove they are young again?" she said. "Well, at least it gives me a rest." She caught Ayla's interested look.

"I wouldn't put a wager on that!" Talut said. "I'm not so old that I can't still clear the way to the lioness of my hearth just because I'm shovelling other drifts."

"Hmmmf," Nezzie shrugged, turning away, disdaining to reply.

Ayla was standing near both horses, and keeping the wolf close by so he wouldn't growl and frighten people, but she had been watching the entire scene with intense interest, including the reactions of the people around. Danug and Druwez looked slightly embarrassed. Though they'd had no experience, yet, they did know what subject was being discussed, and it had been very much on their minds. Tarneg and Barzec were grinning from ear to ear. Latie was blushing and trying to hide behind Tulie, who looked on as though all this foolishness was beneath her. Most people were smiling benignly, even Jondalar, Ayla noticed, which surprised her. She had wondered if the reasons for his actions towards her had something to do with customs that were very different. Perhaps, unlike the Mamutoi, the Zelandonii did not believe people had the right to choose their own partners, but he did not seem disapproving.

As Nezzie passed her on the way into the tent, Ayla noticed a knowing little smile playing across her mouth, too. "Happens every year," she said in a half-whisper. "He's got to make a big scene, tell everyone what a man he is, and the first few days, even find another 'drift' or two – although she always looks like me, blonde and plump. Then, when he thinks no one is noticing any more, he's happy enough to spend most of his nights at Cattail Camp – and not so happy if I'm not there."

"Where do you go?"

"Who can tell? With a Meeting this size, even though you know everyone, or at least every Camp, you don't know everyone well. Each year there is someone to get to know better. Though I admit, often enough it's another woman with growing children and a new way to season mammoth. Sometimes a man catches my eye, or I catch his, but I don't need to make a big scene about it. It's all right for Talut to brag, but if the truth were known, I don't think he would like it if I bragged."

"So you don't," Ayla said.

"It's a small enough thing to do to preserve harmony and good will at the hearth . . . and, well, to please him."

"You really love him, don't you?"

"That old bear!" Nezzie started to object, then smiled and the softness crept into her eyes. "We had our times, in the beginning – you know how loud he can be – but I never did let him get the best of me, or shout me down. I think that's what he likes about me. Talut could break a man in half, if he wanted to, but that's not his way. He can get angry sometimes, but there is no cruelty in him. He would never hurt someone weaker than he is – and that's almost everyone! Yes, I love him, and when you love a man, you want to do things to please him."

"Would you . . . not go with another man who caught your eye, even if you wanted to, if it would please him?"

"At my age, that wouldn't be hard, Ayla. In fact, if the truth were known, I don't have a lot to brag about. When I was younger, I still looked forward to Summer Meetings for some new faces and some playful games, and even a turn in the furs once in a while, but I think Talut is right about one thing. There aren't many men who can match him. Not because of all the 'drifts' he can shovel, but because he cares how he does it."

Ayla nodded with understanding. Then she frowned, thinking, What do you do if there are two men, and each of them cares?

"Jondalar!"

Ayla looked up when she heard the strange voice call his name. She saw him smile and stride towards a woman and greet her warmly.

"So you are still with the Mamutoi! Where's your brother?" the woman said. She was a powerful-looking woman, not tall, but muscular.

Jondalar's forehead knotted in pain. Ayla could see from the woman's expression that she knew.

"How did it happen?"

"A lioness stole his kill, and he chased her back to her den. Her mate got him, wounded me, too," Jondalar said in as few words as possible.

The woman nodded sympathetically. "You say you were wounded? How did you get away?"

Jondalar looked towards Ayla, and saw that she had been watching them. He led the woman towards her. "Ayla, this is Brecie of the Mamutoi, headwoman of Willow Camp . . . or rather Elk Camp. Talut said that's the name of your winter Camp. This is Ayla of the Mamutoi, daughter of the Mammoth Hearth of Lion Camp."

Brecie was taken aback. Daughter of the Mammoth Hearth! Where did she come from? She wasn't with Lion Camp last year. Ayla was not even a Mamutoi name.

"Brecie," Ayla said. "Jondalar told me about you. You are the one who saved him and his brother from the sinking sands of Great Mother River, and you are Tulie's friend. I am pleased to meet you."

That is certainly not a Mamutoi accent, and it's not Sungaea, Brecie thought. It's not Jondalar's accent, either. I'm not sure it's an accent at all. She really speaks Mamutoi very well, but she has a peculiar way of swallowing some words. "I am pleased to meet you . . . Ayla, did you say?" Brecie asked.

"Yes, Ayla."

"That's an unusual name." When no explanation was forthcoming, Brecie continued, "You seem to be the one who is, uh . . . watching these . . . animals." It occurred to her that she had never been quite so close to a living animal, at least one who was standing still and not trying to run away.

"That's because they answer to her," Jondalar volunteered with a smile.

"But didn't I see you with one of them? I will admit, you caught me by surprise, Jondalar. In those clothes, for a moment, I thought you were Darnev, and when you were leading a horse, I thought either I was imagining things, or that Darnev had returned from the spirit world."

"I am learning about these animals from Ayla," Jondalar said. "She's the one who saved me from the cave lion, too. Believe me, she has a way with animals."

"That seems obvious," Brecie said, this time looking down at Wolf, who was not as nervous, though his alert attention seemed more menacing. "Is that why she was adopted by the Mammoth Hearth?"

"That's one reason," Jondalar said.

It had been a stab in the dark on Brecie's part, the guess that Ayla had recently been adopted by the Mamut of the Lion Camp. Jondalar's answer confirmed her speculations. It didn't, however, answer where she came from. Most people assumed she came with the tall blond man, perhaps a hearth mate or a sister, but she knew Jondalar had arrived in their territory with only his brother. Where had he found this woman?

"Ayla! How nice to see you again."

She looked up to see Branag arm in arm with Deegie. They embraced with warmth, and rubbed cheeks. Though she had only met him once, he felt like an old friend, and it was nice to know *someone* at this Meeting.

"Mother wants you to come and meet the headwoman and headman of Wolf Camp," Deegie said.

"Of course," Ayla said, rather glad for an excuse to get away from the sharp-eyed Brecie. Ayla had noticed the quick mind at work in the woman's shrewd guesses, and felt a little uncomfortable around her. "Jondalar, will you stay here with the horses?" She had noticed a few other people had walked over with Branag and Deegie, and were edging closer to the animals. "This is still all new to them, and they are happier when someone they know is around. Where's Rydag? He can watch Wolf."

"He's inside," Deegie said.

Ayla turned to look, and noticed him standing shyly in the entrance. "Tulie wants me to meet headwoman. Will you watch Wolf?" Ayla signalled and spoke.

"I watch," he signalled, glancing at the crowd of people around, a bit apprehensively. Rydag came out slowly, then sat down beside Wolf and put his arm around him.

"Look at that! She even talks to flatheads. She must be good with animals!" a sneering voice shouted from the crowd. Several people laughed.

Ayla spun around and glared, looking for the one who spoke.

"Anyone can talk to them – you can talk to a rock, too – it's getting them to talk back," another voice said, which caused more laughter.

Ayla turned in that direction, almost sputtering, so angry she could hardly speak.

"Is someone here trying to say that boy is an animal?" A more familiar voice spoke out. Ayla frowned as a member of the Lion Camp came forward.

"I am, Frebec. Why not? He doesn't know what I'm saying. Flatheads are animals, you've said it often enough."

"Now I'm saying I was wrong, Chaleg. Rydag knows exactly what you're saying, and it's not hard to get him to talk back to you. You just have to learn his language."

"What language? Flatheads can't talk. Who's telling you these stories?"

"Sign language. He speaks with his hands," Frebec said. There was general derisive laughter. Ayla was watching him, curious now. Frebec did not like being laughed at.

"Don't believe me, then," he said, shrugging and starting to walk away, as though it didn't matter, then he turned to face the man who had been ridiculing Rydag. "But I'll tell you something else. He can talk to that wolf, too, and if he tells that wolf to get you, I wouldn't wager on your chances."

Unknown to Chaleg, Frebec had been signalling to the boy; the hand motions meant nothing to the stranger. Rydag in turn had questioned Ayla. The whole Lion Camp was watching, taking delight in knowing what was coming by means of this secret language, which they could speak in front of all these people without their knowing it.

Without turning around, Frebec continued, "Why don't you show him, Rydag?"

Suddenly Wolf was no longer sitting peacefully with the arm of a child around him. In one smooth leap, Wolf was at the man, hackles raised, teeth bared, and a growl that raised the hair on the back of every onlooker's neck. The man's eyes opened round as he jumped back in sheer terror. Most of the people near him jumped back as well, but Chaleg kept on going. At Rydag's signal, Wolf calmly walked back to his place beside the boy, looking rather pleased with himself, turned around a few times, then settled down with his head on his paws, and watched Ayla.

It was taking a chance, Ayla conceded to herself. However, the signal that was given was not exactly one to attack. It was a game the children played with Wolf, a pouncing, mock-attack game that young wolves often played with each other, except Wolf had been taught to curb his bite. Ayla had been using a similar signal on their hunting forays when she wanted him to flush game for her. Though sometimes he ended up pouncing and killing the animals for himself, it was nothing like a signal to actually hurt someone, and Wolf hadn't touched the man. He had only leaped towards him. But the danger was that he might have.

Ayla knew how protective wolves were about their own territory, or their own pack. They would kill to defend it. Yet, as she watched him walk back, she thought, if wolves could laugh, he'd be laughing. She could not help but feel that he knew what was going on; that the idea was only to bluff, and he knew just how to do it. It wasn't just a mock attack, there was nothing playful about the way he moved. He gave every signal of attack. He had just stopped short. The sudden exposure to masses of people had been difficult for the young wolf, but he had acquitted himself well. And seeing the look on that man's face made it worth taking the chance. Rydag was not an animal!

Branag looked a little shocked, but Deegie was grinning as they joined Tulie and Talut, and another couple. Ayla was formally introduced to the co-leaders of the host Camp, and immediately knew what everyone else knew. Marlie was very ill. She shouldn't even be standing here, Ayla thought, mentally prescribing medicines and preparations for her. As she noticed her colour, the look of her eye, the texture of her skin and hair, Ayla wondered if anything could help her, but she sensed the strength of the woman; she would not give in easily. That could be more important than medicines.

"That was quite a demonstration, Ayla," Marlie said, noticing the interesting peculiarity of her speech. "Was it the boy or you controlling the wolf?"

"I don't know," she said, smiling. "Wolf responds to signals, but we both gave them."

"Wolf? You say it like a name," Valez said.

"It is his name."

"Do the horses have names, too?" Marlie asked.

"The mare is *whinny*." Ayla said it like the sound a horse would make, and Whinney nickered back, causing smiles, but nervous ones. "Most people just say her name, Whinney. The stallion is her son. Jondalar named him Racer. It is a word from his language that means one who likes to run fast and beat the others."

Marlie nodded. Ayla looked hard at the woman for a moment, then turned to Talut. "I am very tired from working to make that place for the horses. Do you see that big log? Would you bring it here so I can sit?"

For a moment the big headman was totally startled. It was so out of character. Ayla simply would not ask such a thing, especially in the middle of a conversation with the headwoman of the host Camp. If anyone needed a place to sit, Marlie did. Then it hit him. Of course! Why hadn't he thought of it before? He hurried to get the log and manhandled it back himself.

Ayla sat down. "I hope you don't mind. I really am tired. Won't you join me, Marlie?"

Marlie sat, shaking a little. After a while, she smiled. "Thank you, Ayla. I hadn't planned to stay here so long. How did you know I was feeling dizzy?"

"She's a Healer," Deegie said.

"A Caller and a Healer? That's an unusual combination. No wonder the Mammoth Hearth claimed her."

"There is something I'd like to prepare for you, if you would take it," Ayla said.

"Healers have seen me, but you are welcome to try, Ayla. Now, before the subject is lost forever, there is a question I want to ask. Were you certain the wolf would not harm that man?"

Ayla paused only a moment. "No. I was not certain. He is still very young, and not always completely reliable. But I thought I was close enough to block his attack if he didn't stop it short himself."

Marlie nodded. "People are not always completely reliable; I would not expect animals to be. If you had said otherwise, I would not have believed you. Chaleg will complain, you know, as soon as he recovers, to save face. He will bring it to the Council of Brothers, and they will bring it to us."

"Us?"

"The Council of Sisters," Tulie said. "The Sisters are the final authority. They are closer to the Mother."

"I am glad I was here to see it. Now I don't have to worry about sorting through conflicting stories that are unbelievable to begin with," Marlie said. She shifted her gaze and studied the horses and then Wolf. "They seem to be perfectly normal animals, not spirits or other magic things. Tell me, what do the animals eat when they are with you, Ayla? They do eat?"

"The same things they always eat. Wolf eats mostly meat, either raw or cooked. He's like another person in the lodge, and usually eats what I eat, even vegetables. Sometimes I hunt for him, but he's getting good at catching mice and small animals for himself. The horses eat grass and grains. I was thinking of taking them down to that meadow across the river soon and leaving them there for a while."

Valez looked down across the water, and then at Talut. Ayla could see he was thinking. "I don't like to say this, Ayla, but it could be dangerous to leave them there alone."

"Why?" she asked, with an edge of panic to her voice.

"Hunters. They look like any other horses, particularly the mare. The dark colour of the young one is unusual enough. We should be able to pass the word not to kill any brown horses, especially if they seem very friendly. But the other one . . . every other horse on the steppes is that colour, and I don't think we can ask people not to kill horses. It is the favourite meat of some people," Valez explained.

"Then I'll have to go with her," Ayla said.

"You can't do that!" Deegie cried. "You'll miss out on everything."

"I can't let anything hurt her," Ayla said. "I'll just have to miss things."

"That would be too bad," Tulie said.

"Can't you think of something?" Deegie said.

"No . . . if only she was brown, too," Ayla said.

"Well, why not make her brown?"

"Make her brown? How?"

"What if we mix some colour, like I do for leather, and rub it on her?"

Ayla thought for a while. "I don't think it will work. It's a good idea, Deegie, but the trouble is, making her brown really won't make much difference. Even Racer is still in danger. A brown horse still looks like a horse, and if someone is hunting horses, it won't be easy to remember not to kill brown ones."

"That's true," Talut said. "Hunters think about hunting, and two brown horses that aren't afraid of people would make very tempting targets."

"How about a different colour like . . . red? Why not make Whinney a red horse? A bright red horse. Then she'd really stand out."

Ayla made a face. "I don't like the thought of making her a red horse, Deegie. She would look so strange. It is a good idea, though. Everyone would know she is not an ordinary horse. I think we should do it, but a bright red horse . . . Wait! I have another idea." Ayla rushed into the tent. She dumped her travelling pack out on top of her sleeping furs, and found what she was looking for near the bottom. She ran out with it.

"Look, Deegie! Remember this?" Ayla said, opening out the bright red hide she had dyed herself. "I never could think of anything to make with it. I just liked it for the colour. I can tie this on Whinney when she's out in the meadow alone."

"That is a bright red!" Valez said, smiling and nodding his head. "I think it will work. With that on, anyone who saw her would know she is a special horse, and would probably hesitate to hunt her, even without being told. We can announce it tonight that the horse with the red cover and the brown one with her are not to be hunted."

"It might not hurt to tie something on Racer, too," Talut said. "It wouldn't have to be as bright, but something made by a person so anyone who gets close enough to throw a spear will know he is not ordinary."

"I would suggest," Marlie added, "that since all people are not entirely reliable, sometimes telling is not enough. It might be wise for you and your Mamut to contrive some prohibition against killing the horses. A good curse could scare off anyone who might be tempted to see how mortal those animals are."

"You can always say that Rydag will send Wolf to get anyone who hurts them," Branag said, with a smile. "That story is probably all over the Meeting by now, and grown bigger with each telling."

"That may not be such a bad idea," Marlie said, standing up to go. "At least it could be spread around as a rumour."

They watched the co-leaders of the Wolf Camp go, then shaking her head sadly, Tulie went to finish getting settled in. Talut decided to go find out who was organising competitions to set up a spear-thrower competition, and stopped to talk to Brecie and Jondalar. The three left together. Deegie and Branag walked with Ayla towards the horses.

"I know just the person to tell to start the rumour going," Branag said. "With the stories going around already, even if they aren't entirely believed, I think they will avoid the horses. I don't think anyone will want to take a chance that Rydag might send the wolf after him. I've been meaning to ask, how did Rydag know to signal the wolf?"

Deegie looked at the man to whom she was Promised with surprise. "I guess you don't know, do you? I don't know why I should think that just because I know something, you know it, too. Frebec wasn't just making something up to defend Lion Camp. He was telling the truth. Rydag understands everything that everyone says. He always has. We just didn't know it until Ayla taught us all his sign language so we could understand him. When Frebec was pretending to walk away, he told Rydag, and Rydag asked Ayla. We all knew what they were saying, so we knew what was going to happen."

"Is that true?" Branag asked. "You were talking to each other and no one knew it!" He laughed. "Well, if I'm going to be in on the Lion Camp's surprises, maybe I should learn this secret language, too."

"Ayla!" Crozie called, coming out of the tent. They stopped and let her catch up. "Tulie just told me what you decided to do to mark the horses," she said, coming towards them. "Smart idea, and red will stand out on a light-coloured horse, but you don't have two bright red hides. When I was unpacking, I found something I'd like you to have." She unwrapped a bundle that had recently been untied, took out a folded hide and shook it open.

"Oh, Crozie!" Ayla exclaimed. "This is beautiful!" She breathed in wonder at a chalk-white leather cape decorated with ivory beads in subtle repetitive triangles, and hedgehog quills, dyed ochre red and sewn on in patterns of right-angled spirals and zigzags.

Crozie's eyes lit up at her admiration. Having made a tunic, Ayla understood the difficulty of making leather white. "It's for Racer. I think white against his dark brown coat will stand out."

"Crozie, it's too beautiful for that. It will get dirty and dusty, and especially if he tries to roll with it on, it will lose the decorations. I can't let Racer wear this out in the field," Ayla said.

Crozie looked at her sternly. "If someone is out hunting horses and sees a brown horse with a white decorated cover on his back, do you think that hunter is likely to aim a spear at him?"

"No, but you have put too much work into that to let it get ruined."

"The work was put in many years ago," Crozie said, then with a softening expression and a misting of her eyes, she added, "It was made for my son, Fralie's brother. I have never been able to give it to anyone else. I could not bear to see someone else wear it, and I could not throw it away. I have just dragged it around from place to place, a useless piece of hide, the work wasted. If this hide will help protect that animal, it will no longer be useless, the work will have some value. I want you to have it, for what you have given me."

Ayla took the proffered package, but looked puzzled. "What have I given you, Crozie?"

"It's not important," she said abruptly. "Just take it."

Frebec, hurrying into the tent, looked up and saw them, and smiled, full of self-satisfaction, before going in. They smiled back.

"I was very surprised when Frebec came forward to defend Rydag," Branag commented. "I would have thought he would be the last one."

"He's changed a lot," Deegie said. "He still likes to argue, but he's not so hard to get along with. He's willing to listen sometimes."

"Well, he never was afraid to step up and say what he thought," Branag said.

"Maybe that's what it was," Crozie said. "I never did understand what Fralie saw in him. I tried my best to talk her out of joining with him. He didn't have a thing to offer. His mother had no status, he had no particular talents, I thought she was throwing herself away. Maybe just having the nerve to ask says something for him, and he really did want her. I suppose I should have trusted her judgment all along, after all, she is my daughter. Just because someone comes from poor beginnings doesn't mean he may not want to better himself."

Branag looked at Deegie, and then Ayla, over Crozie's head. In his opinion, she had changed even more than Frebec.

32

Ayla was alone in the tent. She glanced over the area which would be her place for the duration of their stay, trying to find one more article to fold, one more object to arrange, one more reason to delay leaving the confines of Cattail Camp. As soon as she was ready, Mamut had told her, he wanted to take her to meet the people with whom she was associated with in a unique way, the Mamuti, those who belonged to the Mammoth Hearth.

She looked upon the meeting as an ordeal, certain they would want to question her, evaluate her, and judge whether she had a right to be included within their ranks. In her heart, she didn't believe she did. She didn't feel possessed of unique talents and special gifts. She was a Healer because she had learned the skills and knowledge of a medicine woman from Iza. There was no great magic in having the animals, either. The mare answered to her because, when she was alone, and lonely, in her valley, she had taken in a motherless foal for company, and Racer was born there. She saved Wolf because she owed it to his mother, and she knew by then that animals raised around people would be friendly. It wasn't a big mystery.

Rydag had stayed inside the tent with her for a while, after she examined him, asked him some specific questions about how he felt, and made a mental note to adjust his medicine. Then he went out and sat with Wolf to watch the people. Nezzie had agreed with her that he seemed in a much better mood. The woman was full of self-righteous delight, and praise for Frebec, who had heard and overheard so many words of praise, he was almost embarrassed. Ayla had never seen him smile so much, and knew that part of his happiness was the sense of acceptance and belonging. She understood the feeling.

Ayla looked around one last time, picked up a rawhide container and attached it to her belt, then sighed and walked outside. Everyone seemed to be gone except Mamut, who was talking to Rydag. Wolf saw her and raised his head as she approached, which caused Rydag and Mamut to look also.

"Is everyone gone? Maybe I should stay here and watch Rydag until someone comes back," she said, quick to volunteer.

"Wolf watch me," Rydag signed, with a grin. "No one stay long when see Wolf. I tell Nezzie go. You go, Ayla."

"He's right. Wolf seems content to stay here with Rydag, and I can't think of a better guardian," Mamut said.

"What if he gets sick?" Ayla said.

"I get sick, I tell Wolf, 'get Ayla'." Rydag made the signal they had worked out before in practice and play. Wolf jumped up, put his paws on Ayla's chest and reached up to lick her jaw, eager to get her attention.

She smiled, ruffed up his neck, then signalled him down.

"I want stay here, Ayla. I like watching. River. Horses in meadow. People walk by." Rydag grinned. "Not always see me, stare at tent, stare at horse place. Then see Wolf. Funny people."

Mamut and Ayla both smiled at his simple delight in seeing the surprised reactions of people.

"Well, I suppose it will be all right. Nezzie wouldn't have left him if she didn't think he would be safe," Ayla said, conceding her last internal argument against leaving. "I'm ready to go, Mamut."

As they walked together towards the permanent lodges of Wolf Camp, Ayla noticed a denser concentration of tents and Camps, and many more people milling around between them. She was glad they were on the outside edge, where she could look out and see trees and grass, and the river and meadow. Several people nodded or spoke to them as they passed. Ayla watched Mamut, noting how he acknowledged their greetings, and responded the same way.

One lodge at the end of the somewhat uneven row of six seemed to be the focal point of activities. Ayla noticed a cleared area with no household Camps near the dwelling, and realised it must be the place where people gathered. The Camps that were immediately adjacent to the clearing did not have the look of usual household areas. One of them had a fence made of openly spaced mammoth bones, branches and dried brush marking the territorial boundaries. As they passed it, Ayla heard her name called. She stopped, surprised at who had called her from the other side of the fence.

"Latie!" she said, then recalled what Deegie had told her. As long as Latie was still at the lodge of the Lion Camp, the restriction on her association with males did not limit her movements or activities too much. However, once they reached the Meeting place, it was necessary that she be kept in seclusion. Several other young women were with her, all smiling and giggling. She was introduced to Latie's age mates, who seemed to be somewhat in awe of her.

"Where are you going, Ayla?"

"To the Mammoth Hearth," Mamut answered for her.

Latie nodded as though she should have known. Ayla noticed Tulie in the enclosed yard area around a tent which was decorated with painted designs in red ochre, talking to several other women. She waved and smiled.

"Latie, look! A red-foot!" one of her friends said, in hushed tones of excitement. Everyone stopped to stare, and the young women giggled. Ayla found herself looking with great interest at the woman who sauntered past, noticing as she walked that the bottoms of her bare feet were a rich bright red. She had been told about them, but this was the first one she had seen. She seemed to be a perfectly ordinary woman, Ayla thought. Yet, there was a quality to her that made one look twice.

The woman approached a knot of young men, whom Ayla hadn't seen before, loitering near a stand of small trees across the clearing. Ayla thought her walk became more exaggerated as she neared them, her smile more languorous, and she suddenly noticed her red feet more. The woman stopped to talk to the young men, and her liquid laugh floated across the empty space. As she and the old man walked away, Ayla remembered the conversation the women, and Mamut, had had the evening before the Spring Festival.

All the young females who were in the transitional state of not-yet-women were under constant surveillance – but not only by the chaperones. Ayla noticed, now, several groups of young men standing around the fringes of the prohibited area where Latie and her age mates were staying, hoping to catch a glimpse of the forbidden, and therefore all the more desirable, young women. At no time in her life was a woman the object of greater interest by the male population. The young women enjoyed their unique status and the special attention it brought, and were just as interested in the other gender, though they disdained to show it openly. They spent most of their time peeking out of the tent or around the fence, speculating about the various males, who paraded and lounged around the periphery with exaggerated casualness.

Though the young men who watched, and were watched in return, might eventually form a hearth with those just now becoming women, they were not the ones likely to be chosen for the first, important initiation. The young women and the older female advisers who shared their tent discussed several possibilities from among the older and more experienced men. Those being considered were usually approached privately before the eventual selection was made.

The day before the ceremony, the young women who were staying together in one tent – occasionally there were too many for one tent and two Camps of young women would be established – would go out as a group. When they found a man with whom they wanted to spend the night, they would surround and "capture" him. The men thus captured were required to go along with the initiates – few men objected to the requirement. That night, after some preliminary rituals, they would all go together into the darkened tent, grope to find each other, and spend the night exploring the differences and learning the Pleasures of each other. Neither the young women nor the men were supposed to know with whom they eventually coupled, though in actual practice, they usually did. The watching older women made sure there was no undue roughness, and were available on the rare occasion that advice was necessary. If, for some reason, any of the young women were not opened, it could be accommodated in a quiet second night's ritual without overtly placing blame on anyone in particular.

Neither Danug nor Druwez would be invited to Latie's tent, primarily because they were too closely related, but also because they were too young. Other women who had celebrated their First Rites in previous years, particularly those who had no children yet, could choose to stand in for the Great Mother and teach Her way to young men. After a special ceremony, which honoured them and set them apart for the season, the soles of the feet of these women would be stained with a deep red dye that would not wash off, though eventually it would wear off, to signify that they were available to help young men gain experience. Many also wore red leather bands tied around their upper arms, ankles, or waists.

Though some teasing was inevitable, the women appreciated the underlying seriousness of their task. Understanding his natural shyness, and the driving urge behind his eagerness, they treated each young man with consideration, teaching him to know a woman tenderly, so that someday he might be chosen to make a woman, so that someday she might make a child. And to show them how pleased She was with this offering of themselves, Mut blessed many of these women. Even those who had been joined for some time, and had never borne life in their wombs, were often pregnant by the end of the season.

Next to the not-yet-women, the red-footed women were the most sought after by all ages of men. For the rest of his years, nothing could so quickly stimulate a man of the Mamutoi as the flash of a red foot when a woman walked by, and knowing it, some women tinged their feet reddish to make themselves more attractive. Though a woman who had made such a dedication of herself was free to choose any man, her service was for the younger ones and any older man who managed to convince her to share his company felt himself favoured.

Mamut directed Ayla towards a Camp that was not far from the Rites of Womanhood Camp. At first glance it seemed to be an ordinary tent within a household Camp. The difference, she noticed, was that everyone was tattooed. Some, like old Mamut, just had a simple dark blue chevron pattern high on the right cheekbone: three or four broken lines, like the lower parts of downward-pointing triangles, stacked up, one nestled within the other. They reminded her of the lower jawbones of mammoths that had been used to construct Vincavec's lodge. The tattoos of others, particularly the men, Ayla noticed, were much more elaborate. The patterns incorporated not only chevrons, but triangles, zigzags, rhomboids, and right-angled spirals, in both blue and red.

Ayla was glad they had stopped off at Mammoth Camp before coming to the Meeting. She knew she would have been startled by their decorated faces, if she had not already met Vincavec. As fascinating and complex as the tattoos on the faces of these people were, none were as intricate as his.

The next difference she noticed was that although there seemed to be a preponderance of women at this Camp, there were no children. They had obviously been left in someone's care at the household Camps. Ayla quickly understood that this was not considered to be a place for children. This was a place for adults to gather, for serious meetings, discussions, and rituals – and gaming. Several people were playing games with marked bones, sticks, and pieces of ivory in the outdoor area of the Camp.

Mamut walked up to the entrance of the tent, which was open, and scratched on the leather. Ayla looked into the dim interior over his shoulder, trying not to appear conspicuous to those lounging around outside, but they, too, were trying, without seeming too eager, to get a closer look at her. They were curious about the young woman, whom old Mamut had not just accepted into training but adopted as a daughter. She was a stranger, it was said, not even Mamutoi. No one even knew where she came from.

Many of them had made a point of walking past Cattail Camp to see the horses and the wolf, and they were surprised and impressed to see the animals, though they did not want to show it. How could anyone control a stallion? Or make a mare stand quietly with so many people – and a wolf – around? Why was the wolf so docile with the people of Lion Camp? He behaved like a normal wolf around everyone else. No one else could get near him, or even within the boundaries of their Camp without an invitation and, it was said, he had attacked Chaleg.

The old man motioned Ayla inside, and they both sat down near a large fireplace, though only a small flame burned within it, off to one side, near the woman who sat across. She was a heavy woman. Ayla had never seen anyone quite so fat and wondered how she could have walked any distance to get there.

"I have brought my daughter to meet you, Lomie," the old Mamut said.

"I wondered when you were coming," she replied.

Then, before she said anything else, she moved a red-hot stone from the fire with sticks. She opened up a packet of leaves and dropped a few on the stone and leaned closer to breathe in the smoke that curled up. Ayla smelled sage, and less pronounced, mullein and lobelia. She watched the woman closely, noted a heaviness of breathing, which was soon relieved, and realised she suffered a chronic cough, probably asthma.

"Do you make a cough syrup from the root of mullein, too?" Ayla asked her. "It can help." She had been reluctant to speak up at first, and wasn't sure why she did without having been introduced, but she wanted to help, and somehow it felt like the right thing to do.

Lomie's head jerked up, startled, and she looked at the young blonde woman with new interest. The hint of a smile glanced across Mamut's face.

"She is a Healer, too?" Lomie said to Mamut.

"I believe there is none better, not even you, Lomie."

Lomie knew it was not said lightly. Old Mamut had great respect for her skill. "And here I thought you had only adopted a pretty young woman to ease your last years, Mamut."

"Ah, but I did, Lomie. She has eased my winter arthritis, and other assorted aches and pains," he said.

"I'm glad to know there is more to her than can be seen. She is young for it, though."

"There is more to her than you know, Lomie, in spite of her youth."

Lomie turned then. "You are Ayla."

"Yes, I am Ayla of the Lion Camp of the Mamutoi, daughter of the Mammoth Hearth . . . and protected by the Cave Lion," Ayla finished, as Mamut had instructed her.

"Ayla of the Mamutoi. Hmmm . . . It has an unusual sound, but then so does your voice. Not unpleasant, though. Stands out. Makes people notice you. I am Lomie, Mamut of the Wolf Camp and Healer of the Mamutoi."

"First Healer," Mamut corrected.

"How can I be First Healer, old Mamut, if she is my equal?"

"I did not say Ayla was your equal, Lomie. I said there is none better. Her background is . . . unusual. She was trained by . . . someone with a great depth of knowledge in certain Healing ways. Could you have identified the subtle smell of mullein, masked by the heavy aroma of sage, so quickly if you hadn't known it was there? And then known what you were treating yourself for?"

Lomie started to speak, then hesitated, and did not respond. Mamut continued, "I think she would have known just by looking at you. She has a rare gift for knowing, and an amazing knowledge of remedies and treatments, but she lacks skill in just those ways that you are most proficient, finding and relieving the problem that creates the illness, and helping someone want to get well. She could learn much from you, and I hope you will consent to train her, but I think there is much you could learn from her as well."

Lomie turned to Ayla. "And is that what you want?"

"It is what I want."

"If you know so much already, what do you think you can learn from me?"

"I am a medicine woman. It is . . . who I am . . . my life. I could not be otherwise. I was trained by one who was . . . First, but from the beginning she taught me there is always more to learn. I would be grateful to learn from you," Ayla said. Her sincerity was not feigned. She was hungry to talk to someone with whom she could share ideas and discuss treatments, and learn.

Lomie paused. Medicine woman? Where had she heard that name for Healer before? She put the thought aside for the moment. It would come to her.

"Ayla has a gift for you," Mamut said. "Call in anyone you want, but then, if you will, close the flap."

Everyone who was outside had either come in while they were talking, or was standing at the entrance. They all crowded in. No one wanted to miss anything. When everyone was settled and the entrance flap closed and tied, Mamut picked up a handful of dirt from a drawing circle and put out the small flame, but the bright daylight could not be kept out entirely. It beamed in through the smoke hole, and dimly, through the hide walls. It would not be quite as dramatic a demonstration in the dimly lit tent as it had been within the dark earthlodge, but every one of the Mamuti would recognise its possibilities.

Ayla untied the small carrying container from her waistband, one she and Mamut had asked Barzec to make, and withdrew tinder, firestone, and flint. After everything was ready, Ayla paused, and for the first time in many moon cycles, sent a silent thought to her totem. It wasn't a specific request, but she thought about a big, impressive, fast lighting spark, so the effect would be what Mamut wanted. Then she picked up the flint and struck it sharply against the iron pyrite. It flashed brightly, even in the tent, then went out. She struck again, and this time it took, and soon the small fire in the fireplace was burning again.

The Mamuti were wise in the ways of artifice and accustomed to creating effects. They prided themselves on being able to recognise how they were accomplished. Little surprised them, but Ayla's fire trick left them without words.

"The magic is in the firestone itself," old Mamut said, as Ayla put the materials back in the rawhide container, and gave it to Lomie. Then the tone and quality of his voice changed. "But the way to draw the fire out of it was shown to Ayla. I did not need to adopt her, Lomie. She was born to the Mammoth Hearth, chosen by the Mother. She can only follow her destiny, but now I know that I was chosen to be part of it, and why I was given so many years."

His words sent a thrill of shivers and raised hairs through everyone in the tent of the Mammoth Hearth. He had touched upon the real mystery, the deeper calling that each one of them felt in some measure beyond the superficial trappings and casual cynicism. Old Mamut was a phenomenon. His very existence was magical. No one had ever lived so long. His name was even lost in the passage of years. They were each a Mamut, shaman of their Camps, but he was simply Mamut, his name and calling had become one. No one there doubted that there was some purpose for his many years. If he said Ayla was the reason, then she was touched by the deep and unexplainable mysteries of life and the world around them, which each one of them felt called upon to struggle with.

Ayla was preoccupied when she and Mamut left the tent. She, too, had felt tension, a stirring of gooseflesh when old Mamut spoke of her destiny, but she didn't want to be the object of such intense interest by powers beyond her control. It was frightening, all this talk of destiny. She wasn't any different from anyone else, and she didn't want to be. She didn't like it when her speech was commented upon, either. At Lion Camp no one noticed any more. She had forgotten that there were some words she just couldn't get right, no matter how hard she tried.

"Ayla! There you are. I was looking for you."

She looked up at the sparkling dark eyes and wide flashing smile of the dark-skinned man to whom she was Promised. She smiled back. He was just the one she needed to take her mind off her troubling thoughts. She turned to Mamut to see if he still wanted her. He smiled and told her to go and have a look around the encampment with Ranec.

"I want you to meet some carvers. Some of them are doing fine work," Ranec said, leading her with an arm around her waist. "We always have a Camp near the Mammoth Hearth. Not just carvers, other artists, too."

He was excited, and Ayla sensed the same exhilaration she felt when she realised Lomie was a Healer. Even though there might be some competition in relation to ability and the status each was accorded, no one understood the nuances of a craft or skill like another person who practised it. Only with another Healer could she discuss the relative merits of mullein versus wintergreen in the treatment of coughs, for example, and she had missed those kinds of discussions. She had seen how Jondalar, Wymez, and Danug could spend unbelievable amounts of time talking about flint and toolmaking, and she realised that Ranec also enjoyed the contact of others who worked with ivory.

As they walked across part of the cleared area, Ayla noticed Danug and Druwez with several other young men, smiling and shuffling nervously while talking to a red-footed woman. Danug looked up and saw her and smiled, then made a quick excuse and loped across a few yards of trampled and dried grass to join them. They waited for him to catch up.

"I saw you talking to Latie, and was going to bring some friends to meet you, Ayla, but we can't go too close to Giggle-Girl Camp . . . uh, I mean, uh –" Danug blushed, realising he had given away the nickname the young men had for the place where they were not allowed.

"It's all right, Danug. They do giggle a lot."

The tall young man relaxed. "Not that there's anything wrong with that. Are you in a hurry? Can you come over and meet them now?"

Ayla gave Ranec a questioning glance.

"I was just going to take her to meet some people, too," Ranec said. "But there is no hurry. We can come over and meet your friends first."

As they started back towards the group of young men, Ayla noticed the red-footed woman was still there.

"I wanted to meet you, Ayla," the woman said after Danug made the introductions. "Everyone is talking about you, wondering where you came from, and why those animals answer to you. You have given us all a mystery that I'm sure we'll be talking about for years." She smiled, and gave Ayla a sly wink. "Take my advice. Don't tell anyone where you come from. Keep them guessing. It's more fun."

Ranec laughed. "She may be right, Ayla," he said. "Tell me, Mygie, why are you wearing red feet this year?"

"After Zacanen and I scattered the hearth, I didn't want to stay with his Camp, but I wasn't sure if I wanted to go back to my mother's Camp, either. This just seemed like the right thing to do. It gives me a place to stay for a while, and if the Mother chooses to give me a child for it, I wouldn't be sorry. Oh, that reminds me, did you know the Mother gave another woman a baby of your spirit, Ranec? You remember Tricie? Marlie's daughter? The one who lives here, at Wolf Camp? She chose red feet last year. This year she has a boy. Toralie's little girl was dark, like you, but not this one. I saw him. He's very light, with red hair even brighter than hers, but he looks just like you. Same nose and everything. She calls him Ralev."

Ayla looked at Ranec with a peculiar smile on her face, and noticed his colour deepen. He's blushing, she thought, but you have to know him well to notice. I'm sure he remembers Tricie.

"I think we'd better go, Ayla," Ranec said, putting his arm around her waist as though to urge her back across the clearing. But she resisted a moment.

"It's been very interesting to talk to you, Mygie. I hope we talk again," Ayla said, then turned to Nezzie's son. "I'm pleased you asked me to come and meet your friends, Danug." She smiled, one of her beautiful, breathtaking smiles at him and Druwez. "And I am happy to have met all of you," she added, looking at each one of the young men in turn. Then she left with Ranec.

Danug watched her walking away, then heaved a big sigh. "I wish Ayla was wearing red feet," he said. He heard several comments of agreement.

When Ranec and Ayla passed the large lodge, which was surrounded by the clearing on three sides, she heard the sound of drums coming from it, and some other interesting sounds which she had not heard before. She glanced towards the entrance, but it was closed. Just as they were turning into another Camp on the edge of the clearing, someone stepped in their path.

"Ranec," a woman said. She was shorter than average, with creamy white skin spattered with freckles. Her eyes, brown flecked with gold and green, sparked with anger. "So you did arrive with the Lion Camp. When you didn't stop by our lodge to say hello, I thought maybe you had fallen in the river, or got caught in a stampede." Her tone was venomous.

"Tricie! I . . . uh . . . I was going to . . . um . . . we had to set up Camp," Ranec said. Ayla had never seen the glib, smooth-talking man so tongue-tied, and his face would have been as red as Mygie's feet, if his brown skin hadn't hidden it.

"Aren't you going to introduce me to your friend, Ranec?" Tricie said sarcastically. It was obvious she was upset.

"Yes," Ranec said, "I'd like you to meet her. Ayla, this is Tricie, a . . . a . . . friend of mine."

"I had something to show you, Ranec," Tricie said, rudely ignoring the introduction, "but I don't suppose it matters now. Hinted Promises don't mean much. I suppose this is the woman you will be joined with in the Matrimonial this season." There was hurt as well as anger in her voice.

Ayla guessed what the problem was, and sympathised, but was not quite sure how to handle this difficult situation. Then, she stepped forward, and held out both her hands.

"Tricie, I am Ayla, of the Mamutoi, daughter of the Mammoth Hearth of the Lion Camp, protected by the Cave Lion."

The formality of the greeting reminded Tricie that she was the daughter of a headwoman, and Wolf Camp was hosting the Summer

Meeting. She did have a responsibility. "In the name of Mut, the Great Mother, Wolf Camp welcomes you, Ayla of the Mamutoi," she said.

"I was told your mother is Marlie."

"Yes, I am Marlie's daughter."

"I met her earlier. She is a remarkable woman. I am pleased to meet you."

Ayla heard Ranec breathe a sigh of relief. She glanced at him, and over his shoulder, noticed Deegie heading towards the lodge from which she had heard the drumming. On impulse, she decided Ranec should work out his relationship with Tricie alone.

"Ranec, I see Deegie over there, and there are some things I want to talk to her about. I will come and meet the carvers later," Ayla said, and quickly left.

Ranec was stunned by her hurried departure, and suddenly realised he was going to have to face Tricie and make some explanations, whether he wanted to or not. He looked at the pretty young woman standing there waiting, angry and vulnerable. Her red hair, a particularly vibrant shade like none he had ever seen, along with her red feet, had made her doubly appealing last season, and she was an artist, too. He was impressed with the quality of her work. Her baskets were exquisite, and the exceptional mat on his floor came from her hands. But she took her offering to the Mother so seriously, she would not even consider an experienced man at first. Her resistance only inflamed his desire for her.

He hadn't actually Promised, though. True, he had seriously considered it, and would have if she hadn't been dedicated. She was the one who had refused a formal Promise, fearing it would anger Mut and cause Her to withdraw Her blessing. Well, Ranec thought, the Mother could not have been too angry if She had drawn from his essence to make Tricie's baby. He guessed that was what she wanted to show him, that she already had a child to bring to his hearth, and one of his spirit, besides. It would have made her irresistible under other circumstances, but he loved Ayla. If he'd had enough to offer, he might have considered asking for them both, but since a choice had to be made, there was no question. Just the thought of living without Ayla put a knot of panic in the pit of his stomach. He wanted her more than any woman he'd ever wanted in his life.

Ayla called out to Deegie, and when she caught up with her, they walked together.

"I see you've met Tricie," Deegie said.

"Yes, but she seemed to need to talk to Ranec, so I was glad I saw you. It gave me the chance to get away and let them be alone," Ayla said.

"I don't doubt she wanted to talk to him. It was all over the Camp last season that they were planning to Promise."

"She has a child, you know. A son."

"No, I didn't! I've hardly had the chance to say more than hello to people, and no one told me. That's going to make her worth more and raise her Bride Price. Who told you?"

"Mygie did, one of the red-foots. She says the boy is of Ranec's spirit."

"That spirit moves around! There are a couple of young ones with his essence. You can't always tell for sure with the other men whose spirit it is, but you can with him. His colouring comes through," Deegie said.

"Mygie said this boy is very light, and red-haired, but looks like Ranec, in the face."

"That would be interesting! I think I may have to go to see Tricie later," Deegie said with a smile. "The daughter of one headwoman ought to pay a visit to the daughter of another headwoman, especially of the host Camp. Do you want to come with me when I go?"

"I'm not sure . . . yes, I think I would," Ayla said.

They had reached the curved arch entrance of the lodge from which the unusual sounds were coming. "I was going to stop here, at the Music Lodge. I think you might enjoy it," Deegie said, then scratched on the leather door covering. While they waited for someone to untie it from inside, Ayla glanced around.

Southeast of the entrance was a fence made of seven skulls of mammoths plus other bones, filled in with hard-packed clay to make it solid. Probably a windbreak, Ayla thought. In the hollow where the settlement was located, the only wind would come from the river valley. On the northeast she counted four huge outdoor hearths and two distinct work areas. One appeared to be for making tools and implements out of ivory and bone, the others must have been primarily concerned with working the flint which was found nearby. Ayla saw Jondalar and Wymez, and several other men and women who were also flint workers, she guessed. She should have known that would be where to find him.

The drape was pulled back, and Deegie beckoned Ayla to follow her in, but someone at the entrance stopped her.

"Deegie, you know we don't let visitors in here," she said. "We're practising."

"But, Kylie, she is a daughter of the Mammoth Hearth," Deegie said, surprised.

"I don't see any tattoo. How can she be Mamut without a tattoo?"

"This is Ayla, daughter of old Mamut. He adopted her to the Mammoth Hearth."

"Oh. Just a moment, let me ask."

Deegie was impatient while they waited again, but Ayla looked more closely at the lodge, and got the impression that it had slumped, or fallen in somewhat.

"Why didn't you tell me she's the one with the animals?" Kylie said when she came back. "Come in."

"You should know I wouldn't bring anyone here who wasn't acceptable," Deegie said.

It was not dark in the lodge, the smoke hole was somewhat bigger than usual, and allowed light inside, but it did take a while for eyes to adjust after the bright sunshine outside. At first, Ayla thought the person Deegie was talking to was a child. But when she saw her, Ayla realised she was probably somewhat older, not younger than her tall, stocky friend. The misimpression was caused by the difference in size between the two women. Kylie was small with a slender build, almost dainty, and next to Deegie, it was easy to mistake her for a child, but her lithe, supple movements bespoke the confidence and experience of maturity.

Though the shelter had seemed large from the outside, there was less room inside than Ayla had imagined. The ceiling was lower than usual, and half the usable space in the room was taken up by four mammoth skulls, which were partially buried in the floor with the tusk sockets upright. The trunks of small trees had been placed in the sockets, and were used as supports to brace the ceiling, which had slumped or fallen in. It struck Ayla, as she looked around, that this lodge was far from new. The wood and the thatching had the greyness of age. There were none of the usual household goods or large cooking hearths to be seen, only one small fireplace. The floor had been swept clean, leaving only dark traces of the former major hearths.

Ropes had been strung between the supporting uprights, and drapes, which could be used to divide the space, hung from them, bunched up at one end. Thrown over the ropes, or hanging from pegs on the posts, was the most unusual array of objects Ayla had ever seen. Colourful outfits, fantastic and ornate headgear, strings of ivory beads and seashells, pendants of bone and amber, and some things she couldn't begin to understand.

There were several people in the lodge. Some were sitting around a small fireplace, sipping from cups; a couple more were in the light streaming in through the smoke hole, sewing garments. To the left of the entrance, several people were sitting or kneeling on mats on the floor near large mammoth bones, decorated with red lines and zigzags. Ayla identified a leg bone, a shoulder blade, two lower jawbones, a pelvis bone, and a skull. They were greeted warmly, but Ayla felt they were interrupting something. Everyone seemed to be looking at them, as though waiting to find out why they had come.

"Don't stop practising for us," Deegie said. "I brought Ayla to meet you, but we don't want to interrupt. We'll wait until you are ready to stop." The people turned back to their task, while Deegie and Ayla sat down on mats nearby.

A woman who was kneeling in front of the large femur began tapping out a steady beat with a hammer-shaped section of reindeer antler, but the sounds she was producing were more than rhythmic. As she hit the leg bone in different places, a resonant, melodic sound emerged, which changed in pitch and tone. Ayla looked more closely, wondering what caused the unusual timbre.

The leg bone was about thirty inches long and rested horizontally on two props that kept it off the ground. The epiphysis at the upper end had been removed, and some of the spongy inner material had been taken out, enlarging the natural canal. The bone was painted across the top with evenly spaced zigzag stripes in dark ochre red, similar to the patterns found so frequently on everything from footwear to house construction, but these seemed to serve more than a decorative or symbolic function. After watching for a while, Ayla felt sure the woman who was playing the leg-bone instrument was using the pattern of stripes as a guide to where she should strike to produce the tone she wanted.

Ayla had heard skull drums and Tornec's scapula played. All had some tonal variation, but she had never heard such a range of musical tones before. These people seemed to think she had some magical gifts, but this seemed more magical than anything she had ever done. A man began to tap on the mammoth shoulder blade like Tornec's with an antler hammer. The timbre and tone had a different resonance, a sharper quality, yet the sound complemented and added interest to the music that the woman played on the leg bone.

The large triangular-shaped scapula was about twenty-five inches long, with a narrow neck at the top, broadening out to about twenty inches along the bottom edge. He held the instrument by the neck, upright, in a vertical position, with the wide bottom resting on the ground. It was also painted with parallel, zigzag stripes in bright red. Each stripe, about the width of a small finger, was divided by spaces of equal width, and each one had a perfectly straight and even edge. In the centre of the broad lower area most frequently struck, the red pattern of stripes was worn away and the bone was shiny from long, repeated use.

When the rest of the mammoth bone instruments joined in, Ayla held her breath. At first she could only listen, overwhelmed by the complex sound of the music, but after a while, she concentrated on each one individually.

An older man played the larger of the lower jawbones, but rather than an antler hammer, he used an end piece of mammoth tusk, about twelve inches long, grooved around to make a knob at the thicker end. The mandible itself was painted, like the other instruments, but only on the right half. It was turned and rested steady, supported by the left undecorated side, which kept the right playing half off the ground for a clear, undamped sound. While he was playing, he tapped along the parallel zigzag red bands that were painted within the hollow as well as along the outer edge of the cheek, and the piece of ivory was rubbed over the ridged surface of the tooth, to create a rasping accent.

A woman played the other jawbone, which was from a younger animal. It was twenty inches long, and fifteen inches across at its widest part, and was also painted with red zigzag stripes on the right side. A deep hole, about two inches wide by five inches long, where a tooth had been removed, altered the resonance and emphasised the higher-pitched tone.

The woman who played the pelvic-bone instrument also held it upright, resting one edge on the ground. She tapped, with an antler hammer, mostly in the centre of the bone where a small natural inward curvature was found. The sounds were intensified and the changes in tone distinct at that place, and the red stripes painted there were almost entirely worn away.

Ayla was familiar with the strong, resonant, lower tones of the mammoth skull drum played by a young man. It was like the drums played by Deegie and Mamut with such skill. The drum was also painted where it was struck, on the forehead and roof of the skull, but in this case it did not have zigzag lines, but a distinctly different pattern of branched lines and disconnected marks and dots.

After the people stopped playing, on a satisfactorily conclusive note, they became involved in a discussion. Deegie joined in, but Ayla just listened, trying to understand the unfamiliar terms, but not wanting to intrude.

"The piece needs balance as well as harmony," the woman who played the leg-bone instrument was saying. "I think we could introduce a wind reed before Kylie dances."

"I'm sure you could convince Barzec to sing that part, Tharie," Deegie said.

"It would be better to work him in later. Kylie and Barzec both would be too much. One would detract from the other. No, I think a five-tone crane wind reed would be best. Let's try it, Manen," she said to a man with a neatly trimmed beard, who had joined them from the other group.

Tharie started playing again, and this time, the sounds were becoming familiar to the newcomer. Ayla felt pleased to be allowed to watch, and wanted nothing more than to sit quietly and enjoy this new experience. With the introduction of the haunting tones of the wind reed, a flutelike instrument made of the hollow leg bone of a crane, Ayla was suddenly reminded of the eerie spiritual voice of Ursus, the Great Cave Bear, from the Clan Gathering. Only one Mog-ur could make that sound. It was a secret passed down through his line, but he had held something to his mouth. It must have been the same kind of thing, she thought.

Nothing, however, moved Ayla so much as when Kylie started dancing. Ayla noticed first that she wore loose bracelets on each arm, similar to the Sungaea dancer's. Each bracelet was made of a set of five thin strips of mammoth ivory, perhaps a half-inch wide, incised with diagonal cut marks radiating out from a central diamond shape in a way that created an overall zigzag pattern when all five were held together. A small hole had been bored through at each end to tie them together, and they rattled together when she moved in a certain way.

Kylie stayed in one place, more or less, sometimes slowly assuming impossible positions which she held, and other times making acrobatic movements, which caused the loose bracelets she wore on each arm to rattle as emphasis. The motions of the supple, strong woman were so graceful and smooth, she made it look easy, but Ayla knew she could never have made them. She was enthralled with the performance, and found herself making spontaneous comments after she was through, the way the Mamutoi so often did.

"How do you do that? It was wonderful! Everything. The sounds, the movements. I have never seen anything like it," Ayla said. The smiles of appreciation showed her comments were well received.

Deegie sensed that the musicians felt satisfied and their need for intense concentration had passed. They were more relaxed now, ready for a rest, and ready to satisfy their curiosity about the mysterious woman who had apparently come out of nowhere and was now a Mamutoi. The coals in the fireplace were stirred, wood added, and cooking rocks, and water for tea poured into a wooden cooking bowl.

"Certainly you've seen *something* like it, Ayla," Kylie said.

"No, not at all," Ayla protested.

"What about the rhythms you were showing me?" Deegie said.

"That's not the same at all. Those are just simple Clan rhythms."

"Clan rhythms?" Tharie asked. "What are Clan rhythms?"

"The Clan are the people I grew up with," Ayla started to explain.

"They are deceptively simple," Deegie interrupted, "but they evoke strong feelings."

"Can you show us?" the young man who played the skull drum asked.

Deegie looked at Ayla. "Shall we, Ayla?" she asked, then went on to explain to the others. "We've been playing around with them a little."

"I guess we could," Ayla said.

"Let's do it," Deegie said. "We need something to make a deep steady beat, muffled, no resonance, like something striking the ground, if Ayla can use your drum, Marut."

"I think wrapping a piece of leather around this striker might work," Tharie said, volunteering her leg-bone instrument.

The musicians were intrigued. The promise of something new was always interesting. Deegie kneeled on the mat in Tharie's place, and Ayla sat cross-legged close to the drum and tapped it to get the feel. Then Deegie hit the leg-bone instrument in a few places until Ayla indicated the sound was right.

When they were ready, Deegie began beating a slow steady pace, changing the tempo slightly until she saw Ayla nod, but not changing the tone at all. Ayla closed her eyes, and when she felt herself moving to Deegie's steady beat, she joined in. The timbre of the skull drum was too resonant to replicate exactly the sounds Ayla remembered. It was difficult to create the sense of a sharp crack of thunder, for example; the sharp staccato of beats came out more like a sustained rumbling, but she had been practising with a drum like it. Soon she was weaving an unusual contrapuntal rhythm around the strong steady beat, a seemingly random pattern of staccato sounds that varied in tempo. The two sets of rhythms were so distinct they bore no relationship to each other, yet a stressed beat of Ayla's rhythms coincided with every fifth beat of Deegie's steady sound, almost as if by accident.

The two rhythms had the effect of producing an increasing sense of expectation, and after a while, a slight feeling of anxiety until the two beats, though it seemed impossible that they ever would, came together. With each release, another surge of tension mounted. At the moment when it seemed no one could stand it any more, Ayla and Deegie stopped before a concluding beat, and left a heightened expectation hanging in the air. Then, to Deegie's surprise as much as anyone's, a windy, reedy, flute-like whistle was heard, with a haunting, eerie not-quite melody, that sent a shiver through the listeners. It ended on a note of closure, but a sense of otherworldliness still lingered.

No one said a word for some moments. Finally Tharie said, "What strange, asymmetrical, compelling music." Then several people wanted Ayla to show them the rhythms, eager to try them out.

"Who played the wind reed?" Tharie asked, knowing it wasn't Manen, who had been standing beside her.

"No one did," Deegie said. "It wasn't an instrument. Ayla was whistling."

"Whistling? How does anyone whistle like that?"

"Ayla can imitate any whistling sound," Deegie said. "You ought to hear her bird calls. Even they think she's a bird. She can get them to come and eat out of her hand. It's part of her way with animals."

"Would you show us a bird whistle, Ayla?" Tharie said, in a tone that sounded unbelieving.

She didn't think it was really the place, but went through a quick repertoire of bird whistles, which brought the astonished looks Deegie had expected.

Ayla was grateful when Kylie offered to show her around. She was shown some of the costumes and other paraphernalia, and discovered that some of the head pieces were actually face masks. Most things were coloured garishly bright, but worn at night, by firelight, the colours of the costumes would stand out, yet appear normal. Someone was grinding red ochre from a small pouch, and mixing it into fat. With a chill, she remembered Creb rubbing a paste of red ochre on Iza's body before her burial, but she was told it would be used to decorate and add colour to the faces and bodies of the players and dancers. She noticed ground charcoal and white chalk, too.

Ayla watched a man sewing beads on a tunic, using an awl, and it occurred to her how much easier it would be with a thread-puller, but she decided to have Deegie bring one over. She was getting too much attention as it was, and it made her uncomfortable. They looked at strings of beads and other jewellery, and Kylie held up two conical spiral seashells to her ears.

"Too bad your ears are not pierced," she said. "These would look nice on you."

"They are nice," Ayla said. She noticed the holes in Kylie's ears then, and in her nose as well. She liked Kylie, and admired her, and felt a rapport that could lead to friendship.

"Why don't you take them anyway? You can talk to Deegie or Tulie and have them do it. And you really should have a tattoo, Ayla. Then you can go wherever you want, and won't have to keep explaining that you belong to the Mammoth Hearth."

"But I'm really not Mamut," Ayla said.

"I think you are, Ayla. I'm not sure what the rites are, but I know Lomie would not hesitate if you told her you were ready to dedicate yourself to the Mother."

"I'm not sure if I am ready."

"Maybe not, but you will be. I feel it in you."

When she and Deegie left, Ayla realised she had been given something very special, a private look behind the scenes that few people were allowed to see. It was a place of mystery, even uncloaked and explained, but how much more magical and supernatural it must seem, she thought, when seen from outside. Ayla glanced towards the flint-working area as they were leaving, but Jondalar was not there.

She followed as Deegie walked through the encampment, heading towards the back of the hollow, looking for friends and relations, and finding out where all the various Camps were located. They passed an area where three Camps, tucked in among brush, faced a clearing. There was a noticeable feeling about the area that was different, but Ayla couldn't put her finger on it at first. Then she began to notice specific details. The tents were ragged, and not well hung, and holes were poorly patched, if at all. A strong unpleasant smell and the buzz of flies called her attention to a rotting piece of meat left on the ground between two tents, and then she noticed more garbage strewn haphazardly around. She knew that children often got dirty, but the ones that were staring at them looked like they hadn't been clean for some time. Their clothes were grimy, their hair unkempt, their faces dirty. There was an unsavoury squalor about the place.

Ayla noticed Chaleg lounging in front of one tent. Her appearance there took him by surprise, and his first expression was one of malicious hatred. It shocked her. Only Broud had ever looked at her that way before. Then Chaleg covered it, but the insincere, malevolent smile was almost worse than the blatant hatred.

"Let's leave this area," Deegie said, with a sniff of disdain. "It's always a good idea to know where they are, so you know what to avoid."

Suddenly there was a loud eruption of screaming and shouting as two children, a boy in his early teens and a girl about eleven years, came running out of one of the tents.

"You give that back to me! Do you hear? You give that back to me!" the girl screamed as she chased after the boy.

"You've got to catch me first," the boy taunted, holding something in her face and shaking it.

"You . . . oh, you . . . Give that back!" the girl screamed again and ran after him with a new burst of speed.

The boy's smile made it clear that he was taking great delight in the girl's anger and frustration, but when he turned back to look at her, he failed to notice an exposed root. He tripped and fell heavily, and the girl was on top of him, hitting and pounding with all her might. He hit her in the face then, with great force, and brought a spurt of blood from her nose. She cried out, and struck him back in the mouth, tearing his lip.

"Help me, Ayla!" Deegie said, as she descended on the two children rolling on the ground. She wasn't quite as strong as her mother, but she was a tall and strong young woman, and when she grabbed the boy, who happened to be on top of his sister at that moment, there was no resisting her. Ayla held on to the girl, who was struggling to get back at the boy again.

"What do you think you're doing?" Deegie said sternly. "How can you bring this shame upon yourselves? Hitting, striking each other, and brother and sister besides. Well, you two are coming with me. We'll get this taken care of right now!" she said, as she dragged the reluctant boy by the arm. Ayla followed behind with the girl, who was now struggling to get away.

People stared as they walked past, firmly leading the blood-spattered children, and then followed behind. By the time Deegie and Ayla had brought the children to the lodges in the centre of the Camp, word had gone on ahead, and a group of women were waiting. Tulie was among them, Ayla noticed, and Marlie, and Brecie, headwomen, she realised, who made up the Council of Sisters.

"She started it . . ." the boy shouted.

"He took my . . ." the girl started to yell back.

"Quiet!" Tulie said, firmly and loudly, her eyes blazing fury.

"There are no excuses for hitting, for striking another person," Marlie said, as hard and angry as Tulie. "You are both old enough to know that, and if you don't, you will now. Bring the leather thongs," she commanded.

A young man ran into one of the lodges, and soon Valez emerged, holding several straps of leather. The girl looked horror-stricken, and the boy's eyes widened. He struggled to get away, broke free, and started to run, but Talut, who was just coming from Cattail Camp, caught him in a quick dash, and brought him back.

Ayla was concerned. Both children needed their hurts attended to, but more than that, what were they going to do to them? After all, they were just children.

While Talut held the boy, another man took one of the long leather thongs and began to wrap it around him, tying his right arm down to his side. It was not tight enough to cut off circulation, but it held the arm immobile. Then someone brought the girl up, who began to cry when her right arm was tied down to her side.

"But . . . but he took my . . ."

"It doesn't matter what he took," Tulie said.

"There are other ways of getting it back," Brecie said. "You could have come to the Council of Sisters. That's why we have Councils."

"What do you think would happen if everyone was allowed to strike each other just because someone disagreed, or teased, or took something?" another woman said.

"You both must learn," Marlie said, as the boy's left ankle was tied to the girl's right ankle, "there is no bond as strong as the bond between brother and sister. It is the bond of birth. So that you will remember, you will be bound to each other for two days, and the hands that hit each other held down so they cannot rise in anger. You must help each other now. One cannot go where the other cannot go. One cannot sleep unless the other lies down. One cannot eat, or drink, or wash, or do any personal act without the other. You will learn to depend on each other, as you must do all your lives."

"And all who see you will know the abomination you have committed upon each other," Talut announced loudly, so that all heard.

"Deegie," Ayla said in a quiet voice, "they do need help, the girl's nose is still bleeding, and the boy's mouth is swollen."

Deegie went to Tulie and whispered in her ear. The woman nodded, then stepped forward. "Before you return to your Camp, go with Ayla to the Mammoth Hearth, where she will look to the hurts you inflicted upon each other."

The first lesson in cooperation they had to learn was how to match their steps, so they could walk with their ankles tied together. Deegie went with Ayla and the youngsters to the Mammoth Hearth, and after they were cleaned up and treated, both young women watched them hobble away together.

"They were really fighting," Ayla said as they walked back to Cattail Camp, "but the boy did take something from the girl."

"It doesn't matter," Deegie said. "Hitting is not the way to get it back. They must learn fighting is unacceptable. It's obvious they didn't learn that at their own Camp, so they must learn it here. It makes you understand why Crozie was so reluctant to have Fralie join with Frebec."

"No, why?"

"Didn't you know? Frebec came from one of those Camps. All three are closely related. Chaleg is Frebec's cousin."

"Well, Frebec has certainly changed a lot."

"That's true, but I'll be honest with you. I'm still not sure about him. I think I'll hold judgment until he's really put to the test."

Ayla couldn't keep her mind off the children, or the thought that there was something for her to learn from this experience. Judgment had been swift and absolutely without recourse. They hadn't even been given a chance to explain, and no one considered looking at their injuries first – she still didn't even know their names. But they weren't seriously hurt, and there was no doubt they had been fighting. While the punishment was swift, and they were not likely to forget it, it was not painful, though they might feel the hurt of humiliation and ridicule for many years.

"Deegie," Ayla said, "about those children, their left arms are free. What will keep them from untying those bonds?"

"Everyone will know it. As humiliating as it may be to have to walk around the encampment tied together with their arms held down, it would be far worse if they took the bindings off. It would be said that they were controlled by the evil spirits of anger, that they couldn't even control themselves enough to learn the value of each other's help. They'd be shunned, and shamed even worse."

"I don't think they will ever forget this," Ayla said.

"And neither will a lot of other youngsters. Even the arguing will be less for a while, though it doesn't hurt them to yell at each other a little," Deegie said.

Ayla was eager to get back to the familiarity of Cattail Camp. She had met so many people and seen so many things, her mind was in a whirl. It would take a while to absorb it all, but she couldn't help but look when they passed by the flint-working area again. This time, she saw Jondalar, but she also saw someone else whom she had not expected to see. Mygie was there, looking adoringly up into his startling blue eyes, and Ayla thought the way she was standing was particularly exaggerated. Jondalar was smiling at Mygie, an easy, comfortable smile that she hadn't seen for a long time, and he had that look in his eyes that she hadn't seen for a long time, either.

"I thought those red-footed women were supposed to be concerned with teaching young men," Ayla said, thinking nobody needed to teach Jondalar anything.

Deegie noticed Ayla's expression, and quickly saw the reason for her frown. She could understand it, but on the other hand, it had been a long and difficult winter for him, too.

"He does have physical needs, Ayla, just like you do."

Suddenly Ayla blushed. She was the one, after all, who had been sharing Ranec's bed, while Jondalar slept alone. Why should she be upset if he found a woman to make Pleasures with here at the Summer Meeting? She should have expected it, but she knew why. She wanted him to make Pleasures with her. It wasn't so much the idea of his choosing Mygie; it was that he hadn't chosen her.

"If he's going to look for a woman, it's best if he can find an agreeable red-foot," Deegie continued. "They can't make commitments. By the time the season is over, unless the feeling is very strong, it won't last through a long winter. I don't think his feeling for Mygie will be very strong, Ayla, and she might help him to relax and think more clearly."

"You're right, Deegie. What difference does it make? He's leaving after the mammoth hunt, he says . . . and I have Promised to join with Ranec," Ayla said.

Then, she thought, as they walked through the crowds of people, I will go back to the Clan, and find Durc, and bring him here. He can become a Mamutoi, and share our hearth, and be a friend to Rydag. And he can bring Ura, too, so he will have a mate . . . and I will live here with all my new friends, and Ranec, who loves me, and Durc, my son . . . my only child . . . and Rydag, and the horses, and Wolf . . . And I'll never see Jondalar again, Ayla thought, as a cold bleakness filled her.

33

Rugie and Tusie came running into the main section of the tent, giggling and smiling.

"There's another one outside," Rugie announced.

Ayla quickly looked down, Nezzie and Tulie gave each other a knowing glance, Fralie smiled, and Frebec grinned.

"Another what?" Nezzie asked, to make sure, though she knew.

"Another 'legation," Tusie said, with the self-important tone of being tired of all this nonsense.

"Between the delegations and your duties as a guardian, you're having a busy summer, Tulie," Fralie said, cutting up some meat for Tasher, but she knew the headwoman was in her glory to be the focal point of all the interest shown in the Lion Camp and its members.

Tulie and Ayla went out, then Nezzie did, too, to lend support, since almost everyone else seemed to be gone already. Fralie and Frebec walked to the tent opening to see who had come. Frebec followed the three women out, but Fralie stayed back to keep the children out of the way. A group of people was standing outside of the territory which Wolf had determined belonged to the Lion Camp. He had marked the invisible boundaries with his scent, and patrolled them regularly. Anyone could come up to them, but no one could step one foot within them without clear indication of welcome from someone he knew.

The animal was between the people and the tent, in a defensive pose, which included bared teeth and a low growl, and none of the visitors was willing to test his intentions. Ayla signalled him to her side, and gave him the "friend" sign, which she had spent all of one morning teaching him to accept, from her and everyone else in Lion Camp. Against his better instincts, it meant that he must allow outsiders within the boundaries of the territory of his pack. Though repeat visitors were more easily tolerated than complete strangers, he made it known that he didn't like company, and was always relieved when they left.

Occasionally, just to get him used to large numbers of people, Ayla took him through the encampment, keeping him close to her. It always brought stares and gapes to see the woman walking confidently with a wolf at her heel, and that made Ayla uncomfortable, but she felt it was necessary. As similar as wolf ways and people ways were, if people were going to be his pack, there were some things about them Wolf was going to have to get used to. People liked each other's company, even that of strangers, and they liked to gather in large groups.

But Wolf did not spend all his time within Cattail Camp. He often went down to the meadow with the horses, and off on forays by himself, or with individual people. Ayla mostly, but sometimes with Jondalar, or Danug, or, strangely enough to many people, with Frebec.

Frebec called the animal to him, and walked him towards the horse lean-to, to keep him out of the way. Wolf did make people nervous, and that could have a less than positive effect upon the delegations that came to court Ayla on behalf of some man. The men were not interested in joining with Ayla to form a union, they knew she was Promised to Ranec. They weren't looking for a mate, they were looking for a sister. The delegations were coming with offers to adopt her.

As astute and knowledgeable as she was about the nature and customs of her people, not even Tulie had considered the scope of that possibility. But the first time she was approached by a woman of her acquaintance, who had only sons, asking if she would entertain an offer from her hearth and Camp for Ayla's adoption, Tulie immediately understood the implications.

"I should have realised from the beginning," Tulie explained to the Camp later, "that a single woman of high status, beauty, and talents would make an extremely desirable sister, particularly since she was adopted by the Mammoth Hearth. That is not usually considered a family hearth. We, or rather, Ayla, does not have to accept any of them, unless, of course, she wants to, but the offers alone increase her value."

Tulie's eyes had been full of glee when she considered how much Ayla was contributing to the status and worth of the Lion Camp. In her heart, she almost wished Ayla had not Promised to Ranec. Her Bride Price could be astounding if she were available. On the other hand, that would mean the Lion Camp would lose her, and keeping the treasure was perhaps better than losing it even for a good price. As long as no set value was placed, speculation would always make it greater. But the offers they were getting for her adoption opened up a whole new realm of possibilities. She could be adopted in name, without leaving the Lion Camp. She could even become a headwoman, if her potential brother had the right connections, and ambition. And if Ayla and Deegie were both headwomen, with direct ties back to Lion Camp, it could bring tremendous influence. All these thoughts were going through Tulie's mind as they approached this new delegation.

Ayla had begun to understand that variations in the pattern of designs used to decorate clothing and footwear were a means of defining group identity. Though they all used the same basic geometric shapes, a preponderance of one over the other – chevrons over diamond shapes, for example – and the way they were combined, were significant indicators of Camp affiliation and ties to other Camps. Unlike Tulie, however, she did not yet recognise instantly from those patterns, and from personal acquaintance of the people, exactly where to place them within the overall fabric of hierarchy and relationships within the group.

The status of some Camps was so high Tulie would have accepted less in material goods because of the affiliations and value they brought. Others might be good possibilities if they were willing to pay enough. Based on the offers already received, Tulie dismissed this group at one glance. They were hardly worth talking to. They simply didn't have enough to bring to the relationship to make the association worthwhile. As a result, Tulie was extremely pleasant to them, but did not invite them in, and they understood they had come with too little, too late. Simply making the offer had its compensations, however. It was a way of allying themselves with Lion Camp, which increased its influence, and that would be remembered favourably.

While they were standing outside the tent, making pleasantries, Frebec noticed Wolf striking a defensive posture, and growling towards the river. Suddenly he was off.

"Ayla!" Frebec called out. "Wolf is after something!"

She whistled, loud, piercing, and urgent, then hurried to look down on the path leading to the river. She watched Wolf return, followed by a new group of people. But these were not strangers.

"It's Mammoth Camp," Ayla said. "I see Vincavec."

Tulie turned to Frebec. "Will you see if you can find Talut? We should greet them properly, and you might tell Marlie or Valez they have finally arrived."

Frebec nodded and left.

The delegation that had come to make an offer were too curious to leave now. Vincavec was the first to reach them, saw the delegation, Ayla, and Tulie, and quickly understood the gist of the circumstances. He let his backframe drop, and came forward with a smile.

"Tulie, it must be auspicious that you are the first person we see, since you are the first person I wanted to see," Vincavec said, reaching for both her hands and rubbing her cheek with his cheek like a dear old friend.

"Why should I be the first person you want to see?" Tulie said, smiling in spite of herself. He was a charmer.

He ignored the question. "Tell me, why are your guests dressed in their finest? A delegation, perhaps?"

A woman spoke up. "We have made an offer to adopt Ayla," she said with dignity, as though the offer had not been effectively turned down. "My son has no sister."

Even Ayla could almost see Vincavec's mind working, but it took only a moment for him to understand the entire situation, and a moment more to make a decision and act on it.

"Well, I am going to make an offer, too, more formally later, but to give you something to think about, Tulie, I want to propose a joining." He turned to Ayla and took both of her hands. "I want to join with you, Ayla. I want you to come and make my Mammoth Hearth something more than a name. Only you can give me that, Ayla. It is your hearth to bring, but in return, I can give you Mammoth Camp."

Ayla was startled, and overwhelmed. Vincavec knew she had already made a commitment. Why would he ask for her? Even if she wanted to, could she suddenly change her mind and join with him? Was it so easy to break a Promise?

"She is already Promised to Ranec," Tulie said.

Vincavec looked directly at the big headwoman, and smiled knowingly, then reached into a pouch and pulled out his closed hand. He opened it and held in his palm two beautiful, polished, matched pieces of amber. "I hope he has a good Bride Price, Tulie."

Tulie's eyes opened wide. His offer was enough to take her breath away. He had effectively told her to name her price, and name it in amber if she wanted to, though of course, she wouldn't, not entirely. Her eyes narrowed then. "It is not for me to decide, Vincavec. Ayla makes her own choices."

"I know, but take these as my gift to you, Tulie, for all your help in building my lodge," he said, and pressed them on her.

Tulie was torn. She should refuse. To accept them would give him an advantage over her, but it was Ayla's decision, and Promised or not, she was free to make that choice. Why should she object? As she closed her hand over the amber, she saw Vincavec's expression of triumph, and Tulie felt as though she had been bought for two pieces of amber. He knew she would consider no other offer. If he could convince Ayla, she was his. But Vincavec doesn't know Ayla, Tulie thought. No one does. She might call herself Mamutoi, but she was a stranger still, and who could tell what would move her? She watched as the man with the startling tattooed face turned his full attention on the young woman, and she saw Ayla's reaction. Without question, there was interest.

"Tulie! How nice to see you again!" Avarie was approaching, holding out her hands. "We're so late, all the best places are taken. Do you know a good place to set up Camp? Where are you set up?"

"Right here," Nezzie said, coming up to greet the Mammoth Camp's headwoman next. She had been very interested in the exchange between Tulie and Vincavec, and had noted his expression, too. It was not going to make Ranec happy to know Vincavec was going to make an offer for Ayla, but Nezzie wasn't at all sure that the Mamut-headman of the Mammoth Camp was going to find Ayla all that easy to convince, no matter what he offered.

"You're here? So far away from everything?" Avarie said.

"With the animals, it's the best place for us. They get nervous around crowds," Tulie said, as though it had been chosen on purpose.

"Vincavec, if Lion Camp is here, why don't we camp nearby?" Avarie said.

"It is not a bad place. There are advantages, more room to spread out," Nezzie said. If both Lion Camp and Mammoth Camp are here, she thought, some of the interest from the centre will move here, too.

Vincavec smiled at Ayla. "I can think of nothing I'd rather do than set up near Lion Camp," he said.

Talut came striding into Camp then, and greeted the co-leaders of Mammoth Camp in his booming voice. "Vincavec! Avarie! You finally made it! What held you up?"

"We made some stops along the way," Vincavec said.

"Ask Tulie to show you what he brought her," Nezzie said.

Tulie still felt a little embarrassed, and wished Nezzie hadn't said anything, but she opened her hand and held out the amber for her brother to see.

"Those are beautiful pieces," Talut said. "You decided to do some trading, I see. Did you know Willow Camp has white spiral seashells?"

"Vincavec wants more than seashells," Nezzie said. "He wants to make an offer for Ayla . . . for his hearth."

"But she's Promised to Ranec," Talut said.

"A Promise is only a Promise," Vincavec said.

Talut looked at Ayla, then Vincavec, then Tulie. Then he laughed. "Well, this is one Summer Meeting that won't be forgotten for a long time."

"It wasn't only the stop at Amber Camp," Avarie said. "Seeing you, Talut, with your big red mane reminds me. We kept trying to go around a cave lion with a reddish mane, but he seemed to be heading in the same direction we were. I didn't see a pride, but I think we'd better warn people there are lions around."

"There are always lions around," Talut said.

"Yes, but this one was acting strange. Lions don't usually bother with people that much, but for a while, I thought he was stalking us. He came so close I had trouble sleeping one night. He was the biggest cave lion I ever saw. I still shake when I think about it," Avarie said.

Ayla listened carefully, frowning, then shook her head. No. Just coincidence, she thought. There are a lot of big cave lions.

"When you get set up, come up to the clearing. We're talking about the mammoth hunt and the Mammoth Hearth is planning the Hunting Ceremony. It won't hurt to have another good Caller. I'm sure you will want mammoth meat for the Matrimonial Feast, since you plan to be a part of it, Vincavec!" Talut said. He started to leave, then he turned around to Ayla. "Since you are going to hunt mammoth with us, why don't you come back with me, and bring your spear-thrower? I was going to come and get you, anyway."

"I'll walk with you," Tulie said. "I have to go to the Womanhood Camp and see Latie."

"This is good quality. Especially for blade tools, like chisels, scrapers, drills," Jondalar said, hunkering down on one knee, examining the smooth grey interior face of fine-structured flint. He had used a specially shaped piece of fresh antler, strong and resilient enough to resist breaking, as a digger and a lever to pry out the exposed lump of hard silica from its chalky matrix. Then he broke it open with a hammerstone.

"Wymez says some of the best flint comes from here," Danug said.

Jondalar motioned up at the perpendicular cliff face of a river gorge that had been worn down over time by the churning water. More lumps of the hard flint encased in a white opaque crust jutted out from the somewhat less hard chalky stone. "Flint is always best if you can get it from the source. This is similar to Dalanar's flint mine and his is the best stone in our region."

"The Wolf Camp certainly thinks this is the best flint," Tarneg said. "The first time I came here, I was with Valez. You should have heard him rave. With this place so close to their Camp, they count these workings as theirs. You did the right thing in asking their permission to come, Jondalar."

"It's only courtesy. I know how Dalanar feels about his mine."

"What's so special about this stone? I've often seen flint on river floodplains," Tarneg said.

"Sometimes you can find good nodules that were recently washed out, on floodplains, and they are a lot easier to get. It's work digging them out of the rock. But flint tends to dry out if it lies in the open very long," Jondalar said. "Then the flakes come off shorter, more abruptly."

"If it's been on the surface too long, Wymez sometimes buries flint in damp soil for a while to make it easier to work," Danug said.

"I've done that. It can help, but it depends on the size of the nodule, and how dry it is. If it's a big piece, it can't be too old. It works best for small ones, even down to egg-size, but those are hardly worthwhile to work, unless they are really fine quality."

"We do something similar with mammoth tusk," Tarneg said. "As a first step we wrap the tusk in damp skins and bury it with hot ashes. The ivory changes, becomes denser but easier to work, and easier to bend. It's the best way to straighten a whole tusk."

"I wondered how you did that," Jondalar said, then he paused, obviously thinking. "My brother would have wanted to learn about it. He was a spear-maker. He could make a good straight shaft, but he understood the properties of wood, how to bend and shape it. I think he would have understood your process, too. Perhaps knowledge of your methods is one reason Wymez was so quick to grasp the idea of heating flint to make it more workable. He is one of the best workers of flint I've ever known."

"You're a good flint man, too, Jondalar," Tarneg said. "Even Wymez speaks highly of you, and he doesn't praise easily. You know, I've been thinking. I'm going to need a good flint worker for Aurochs Camp. I know you've been saying you are going back to your home, but it sounds like a long trip. Would you consider staying if you had a place to stay? What I mean is, how would you like to join my Camp?"

Jondalar's forehead furrowed as he tried to think of a way to refuse Tarneg's offer without offending. "I'm not sure, I'd have to think about it."

"I know Deegie likes you, I'm sure she'd agree. And you wouldn't have any trouble finding someone to make a hearth with," Tarneg encouraged. "I've been noticing the women around you, even the red-foots. First it was Mygie, now all the rest of them find reasons to visit the flintworkers' area. It must be because you are new around here. Women are always curious about men they don't know." He smiled. "I've heard more than one man wishing he was a tall, blond stranger. They'd all like to get a red-foot interested again, but it's Danug's turn, this time." Tarneg smirked knowingly at his young cousin.

Jondalar and Danug both looked uncomfortable. Jondalar stood up, and looked away to shift attention elsewhere, and in an incidental way, he noticed that around these two men, he was not exceptionally tall. The three of them were near the same size, and Danug still had some growing in him. He was going to be a second Talut. But there were all sizes of men at the Meeting, just as there were at Zelandonii Summer Meetings.

"Well, I wish you would think about Aurochs Camp, Jondalar. Now that Deegie and Branag are finally going to be joined, we'll be building this autumn, though I haven't decided yet whether to make a single lodge, like Lion Camp, or the smaller individual ones for each family.

I tend to be old-fashioned. I like the big ones best, but a lot of the younger people want a place with just their own relations, and I admit, when people start arguing, it could be nice to have your own place to go."

"I appreciate the offer, Tarneg," Jondalar said. "I mean that, but I don't want to give you a false impression. I am going home. I have to go back. I could give you a lot of reasons, that I need to bring back word of my brother's death, for example. But the truth is, I don't know why I have to go. I just do."

"Is it because of Ayla?" Danug asked with a worried frown.

"That's part of it. I admit, I don't look forward to seeing her sharing a hearth with Ranec, but I was trying to convince her to come back with me when we met you. Now it looks like I'll be going back alone anyway . . . I'm not looking forward to that either, but that doesn't change anything. I still have to go."

"I'm not sure I understand, but I wish you good fortune, and may the Mother smile on your Journey. When do you think you'll leave?" Tarneg said.

"Soon after the mammoth hunt."

"Speaking of the mammoth hunt, we should be getting back. They are planning it this afternoon," Tarneg said.

They started walking along the river that was a tributary to the major waterway near the settlement, and began clambering over rocks at a place where the walls narrowed in. Working their way out of the gorge around a precipitous ledge, they came upon a group of young men shouting words of insult or encouragement to two of them who were fighting. Druwez was among the spectators.

"What's going on here?" Tarneg said, wading into their midst and pulling the fighters apart. One was bleeding from the mouth, the other had an eye that was swelling shut.

"They're just having a . . . competition," someone said.

"Yes, they're . . . uh . . . practising . . . for the wrestling games."

"This is no competition," Tarneg said. "This is a fight."

"No, honest, we weren't fighting," the boy with the puffy eye said, "just playing around a little."

"You call black eyes and broken teeth playing around? If you were just practising, you wouldn't have to come here to this out-of-the-way place where no one would see you. No, this was planned. I think you'd better tell me what's going on."

No one volunteered an answer, but there was a lot of shuffling of feet.

"What about the rest of you?" Tarneg said, eyeing the other youths, "What are all of you doing here? Including you, Druwez. What do you think mother and Barzec are going to do when they find out you were here, encouraging a fight? I think you'd better tell me what's going on here."

Still no one would say.

"I think we'd better take you back and let the Councils decide what to do with you. The Sisters will find some way to let you work off your urge to fight, and make a good example of you, besides. Maybe they'll even ban all of you from mammoth hunts."

"Don't tell on them, Tarneg," Druwez pleaded. "Dalen was only trying to stop them."

"Stop them? Maybe you should tell me what this fight is about," Tarneg said.

"I think I know," Danug said. Everyone turned to look at the tall young man. "It's because of the raid."

"What raid?" Tarneg said. This was sounding serious.

"Some people were talking about making a raid on a Sungaea Camp," Danug explained.

"You know raiding has been banned. The Councils have been trying to negotiate a friendship fire and establish trading with the Sungaea. I hate to think of the trouble a raid would cause," Tarneg said. "Whose idea was this raid?"

"I don't know," Danug said. "One day everyone was talking about it. Someone discovered a Sungaea Camp a few days away. The plan was to say they were going hunting, and instead go and wreck their Camp, steal their food, and chase them away. I told them I wasn't interested, and I thought they were stupid to do it. They would just make trouble for themselves and everyone else. Besides, we stopped at a Sungaea Camp on our way here. A brother and sister had just died. Maybe it isn't the same Camp, but they probably all are feeling bad about it. I didn't think it was right to raid them."

"Danug can do that," Druwez said. "No one's going to call him a coward, because no one wants to fight him. But when Dalen said he wasn't going on any raid, either, then a whole bunch of them started saying he was afraid of a fight. That's when he said he'd show them he wasn't afraid to fight anyone. We said we'd come with him so they wouldn't gang up on him."

"Which one of you is Dalen?" Tarneg said. The boy with the broken tooth and bleeding mouth stepped forward. "Who are you?" he said to the other one, whose eye was already turning black and blue. He refused to answer.

"They call him Cluve. He's Chaleg's nephew," Druwez volunteered.

"I know what you're trying to do," Cluve said sullenly. "You're going to put all the blame on me just because Druwez is your brother."

"No, I wasn't going to put blame on anyone. I'm going to let the Council of Brothers decide. You can all expect to get a summons from them, including my brother. Now, I think you'd better clean yourselves up. If you go back to the Meeting looking like that, everyone will know you were fighting, and no one would be able to keep it from the Sisters. I don't have to tell you what will happen to you if they find out you were fighting about a raid."

The young men hurried to leave before Tarneg changed his mind, but they left in two groups, one with Cluve, the other with Dalen. Tarneg made a point of noticing who went with whom. Then the three of them continued back to the Meeting.

"There's something I'd be interested in knowing, if you don't mind," Jondalar said. "Why would you let the Council of Brothers decide what to do with these young men? Would they really keep it from the Council of Sisters?"

"The Sisters have no tolerance for fighting, and won't listen to any excuses, but many of the Brothers went on raids when they were young men, or were in a fight or two, just to make a little excitement. Didn't you ever fight someone when you weren't supposed to, Jondalar?'

"Well, yes, I guess I did. And got caught, too."

"The Brothers are more lenient, especially towards the one who was fighting in a good cause, even though Dalen should have told someone about the raid rather than fighting to show them he wasn't afraid. It seems easier for a man to condone that sort of thing. The Sisters say fighting always leads to more fighting, and that may be true, but Cluve was right about one thing," Tarneg said. "Druwez is my brother. He wasn't really encouraging the fight, he was trying to help out his friend. I hate to see him get into trouble for that."

"Did you ever fight anyone, Tarneg?" Danug asked.

The future headman looked at his younger cousin for a moment, then nodded. "Once or twice, but not too many men want to challenge me. Like you, I'm bigger than most. Sometimes those competitions are more fight than anyone admits to, though."

"I know," Danug said, with a thoughtful expression.

"But at least they are under watchful eyes that won't let anyone get badly hurt, and they don't get carried any farther and start a revenge fight." Tarneg glanced at the sky. "It's close to noon, later than I thought. We'd better hurry if we want to hear about the mammoth hunt."

When Ayla and Talut reached the clearing, he led her towards a slight rise off to one side that lent itself naturally as a gathering place for smaller

557

groups and was used for both casual and special meetings. One was in progress and Ayla scanned the crowd of people looking for a glimpse of Jondalar. That was all she ever saw of him lately. From the moment they arrived, he seemed to lose himself in the throng, leaving Cattail Camp early in the morning, and coming back late, if at all. When she did see him, he was often with some woman, usually a different one each time. She found herself making disparaging remarks to Deegie and some others about his many partners. She was not the only one. She'd heard Talut remark that he wondered if Jondalar was trying to make up for the whole winter in one short season. His exploits were talked about by many around the Camps, often with humour and a backhanded sort of admiration, both for his apparent stamina, and his obvious appeal. It wasn't the first time that his attractiveness to women was the subject of talk, but it was the first time he didn't really care.

Ayla laughed at the comments, too, but in the darkness of night, she held back tears and wondered what was wrong with her. Why didn't he ever choose her? Yet there was a strange comfort in seeing him with many different women. At least she knew he hadn't found any particular one to replace her.

She didn't know that Jondalar was trying to stay away from Cattail Camp as much as possible. In the closer quarters of the tent, he was much more conscious of her and Ranec sleeping together – not in the same bed every night, since she felt she needed the privacy of her own bed sometimes – but next to each other. It was easy enough to stay around the flint-working area during the day, and that led to invitations to meet people and share meals. For the first time since he was a young man, he was making friends of his own, not with the help of his brother, and he discovered it wasn't so difficult.

The women gave him an excuse to stay away at night, too, if not all night, at least until late. He had little real feeling for any of them, but he felt guilty about using them for a place to stay, and made up for it in the way he knew best, which made him all the more irresistible. It had been the experience of many women that a man as handsome as Jondalar was more concerned with satisfying himself than her, but he was skilled enough to make any woman feel well cared for. It was a release for him, he wasn't having to fight his own powerful urges as well as trying to cope with his confused feelings, and he enjoyed the women, but in the same way he had always enjoyed women, on a superficial level. He hungered for the deeper feelings he'd always searched for and that no woman aroused in him, except Ayla.

Ayla saw him coming back from the Wolf Camp's flint mine, along with Tarneg and Danug, and as she often did when she saw him, she felt her heart pound and her throat ache. She noticed Tulie approach the three men, and then saw her walking away with Jondalar while Tarneg and Danug continued towards them. Talut waved the two over.

"I want to ask you about the customs of your people, Jondalar," Tulie said when they had found a private place to talk. "I know you honour the Mother, and that speaks well for you and your Zela . . . Zelandonii, but do you also have a ceremonial initiation into womanhood with understanding and gentleness?"

"First Rites? Yes, of course. How could anyone not care about how a young woman is opened the first time? Our rituals are not quite the same as yours, but I think the purpose is the same," Jondalar said.

"Good. I have been talking with some women. They speak highly of you, you've been recommended several times, and that's important, but more important is that Latie has asked for you. Would you be willing to be a part of her initiation?"

Jondalar realised he should have known what was coming. It wasn't as though he hadn't been asked before, but for some reason he thought she just wanted to know about the customs of his people. In the past, he had always been more than willing to participate, and he was tempted, but this time he hesitated. He had also felt a terrible guilt afterwards, for using the deeply sacred ceremony to satisfy his own needs for the deeper feelings it evoked. He wasn't sure he could handle those mixed feelings right now, particularly with someone he liked as much as Latie.

"Tulie, I have participated in similar rituals, and I understand the honour you and Latie have offered me, but I think I must refuse. I realise we have no real relationship, but I have lived with Lion Camp all winter, and in that time I have come to regard Latie as a sister," Jondalar said, "a special younger sister."

Tulie nodded. "That's too bad, Jondalar. In many ways, you would be the perfect one. You come from so far away, there is no possible relationship between you. But I can understand how she could come to feel like a sister. You haven't exactly shared the same hearth, but Nezzie has treated you with the affection of a son, and Latie is a person with much promise. There is no worse abomination in the eyes of the Mother than for a man to initiate a woman born of his own mother. If you feel like a brother, I'm afraid it would taint the ceremony. I'm glad you told me this."

They walked back together towards the people sitting and standing on the slope and where it levelled out into the clearing. Jondalar noticed that Talut was talking, and even more interesting, Ayla was standing beside him with her spear-thrower.

"You've seen how far Ayla can throw a spear with this spear-throwing weapon," Talut was saying, "but I'd like to have them both show it to you under better circumstances, where you can really see what it can do. I know most of us like to use a larger spear with the shaped points Wymez developed for hunting mammoths, but this throwing weapon has some real advantages. Some of us at Lion Camp have experimented with it. This will throw a good-size spear, but it takes practice, just like throwing a spear by hand does. Most grow up throwing spears, in games and hunting. They are used to throwing, but if they could see how well it works, I'm sure many people would give it a try. Ayla says she plans to use it on the mammoth hunt, and I'm sure Jondalar will, too, so some people will see what it can do. We've talked about a contest, but it hasn't quite worked out yet. When we return from the hunt, I think we should plan to have a big contest, with all kinds of competitions."

There were general expressions of agreement to his suggestion, then Brecie said, "I think a big contest is a good idea, Talut. I wouldn't mind seeing two or three days of it. We've been working on a throwing stick. Some of us have got several birds from a flock with one throw. In the meantime, I think we should let the Mamuti work out the best day to leave, and do some Calling for mammoths. And if we have nothing more to talk about, I have to get back to my Camp."

The meeting started to break up, then there was a sudden flurry of interest as Vincavec strode into the clearing, followed by his Camp, the delegation that had been talking about adopting Ayla, and the last of Lion Camp, Nezzie and Rydag. The people from the delegation began to spread the news that the Mamut-headman of the Mammoth Camp was willing to pay any Bride Price Tulie wanted to Ayla, in spite of the fact that she was already Promised.

"You know he claims the right to name his Camp after the Mammoth Hearth, just because he's Mamut," Jondalar heard a woman saying to another woman nearby, "but he can't claim any hearth until he's joined. The woman brings the hearth. He just wants her because she's a daughter of the Mammoth Hearth, to make his so-called Mammoth Camp acceptable."

Jondalar happened to be standing near Ranec when he overheard someone tell him. He was surprised to feel a sense of compassion when he saw the dark man's expression. It occurred to him that if anyone knew how Ranec was feeling at that moment, he did. But at least he knew that the man who had convinced Ayla to live with him loved her. It seemed obvious that Vincavec wanted Ayla just to serve his own purposes, not because he cared about her.

Ayla, too, was overhearing pieces of conversation in which her name was mentioned. She didn't like overhearing. In the Clan, she could have averted her eyes so as not to eavesdrop, but when communication was entirely verbal, she could not close her ears.

And then, suddenly, she wasn't hearing anyone, except the tone of taunting voices from several older children, and the word "flathead"

"Look at that animal, all dressed up like people," an older boy said, pointing his finger at Rydag, and laughing.

"They dress the horses, why not the flathead?" someone else added, with more laughter.

"She claims he's a person, you know. They say he understands everything you say, and can even talk," another of the youngsters said.

"Sure, and if she could get the wolf to walk on his hind legs, she'd probably call him a person, too."

"Maybe you'd better be careful what you say. Chaleg says the flathead can make the wolf go after you. He says the flathead made the wolf attack him, and he's taking it to the Council of Brothers."

"Well, doesn't that prove he's an animal? If he can make another animal attack?"

"My mother says she doesn't think it's right for them to bring animals to a Summer Meeting."

"My uncle said he doesn't mind the horses, so much, or even the wolf, so long as they keep them away, but he thinks they ought to be banned from bringing that flathead to meetings and ceremonies that are meant for people."

"Hey, flathead! Go on, get out of here. Go back to your pack, with the other animals, where you belong."

At first Ayla was too stunned to react to the openly derogatory comments. Then she saw Rydag close his eyes and look down, and start to head back towards Cattail Camp. With blazing anger, she stormed up to the youngsters.

"What is wrong with you? How can you call Rydag an animal? Are you blind?" Ayla said with barely restrained fury. Several people stopped to see what was going on. "Can't you see he understands every word you say? How can you be so cruel? Do you feel no shame?"

"Why should my son feel shame?" a woman said, coming to her youngster's defence. "That flathead is an animal, and shouldn't be allowed at ceremonies that are sacred to the Mother."

Several more people were crowding around now, including most of the Lion Camp. "Ayla, don't pay attention to them," Nezzie said, trying to cool her rage.

"Animal! How dare you say he's an animal! Rydag is just as much a person as you are," Ayla cried, turning on the woman.

"I don't have to be insulted like that," the woman said. "I'm no flathead woman."

"No, you aren't! She would be more human than you are. She would have more compassion, more understanding."

"How do you know so much?"

"No one knows better than I. They took me in, raised me when I lost my people and had no one else. I would have died if it hadn't been for the compassion of a woman of the Clan," Ayla said. "I was proud to be a woman of the Clan, and a mother."

"No! Ayla, don't!" she heard Jondalar saying, but she was past all caring.

"They are human, and so is Rydag. I know, because I have a son like him."

"Oh, no." Jondalar cringed, as he pushed his way forward to stand beside her.

"Did she say she had a son like him?" a man said. "A son of mixed spirits?"

"I'm afraid you've done it now, Ayla," Jondalar said quietly.

"She mothered an abomination? You better get away from her." A man came forward to the woman who had been arguing with Ayla. "If she draws that kind of spirit to her, it might get inside some other woman, too."

"That's right! You better get away from her, too," another man said to the obviously pregnant woman standing beside him, as he led her away. Other people were drawing back, their expressions full of repugnance and fear.

"Clan?" one of the musicians said. "Those rhythms she played, didn't she say they were Clan rhythms? Is that who she meant? Flatheads?"

As Ayla looked around, she felt a moment of panic, and an urge to run from all these people who were looking at her with such disgust. Then she closed her eyes and took a deep breath, lifted her chin and stood her ground defiantly. What right did they have to say her son was less than human? From the corner of her eye she saw Jondalar standing beside and just behind her, and was more grateful than she could say.

Then, on her other side, another man stepped forward. She turned and smiled at Mamut, and Ranec as well. Then Nezzie was standing with her, and Talut, and then, of all people, Frebec. Almost as one, the rest of the Lion Camp stood beside her.

"You are wrong," Mamut said to the throng, in the voice that seemed too powerful to come from one so old. "Flatheads are not animals. They are people, and children of the Mother as much as you are. I, too, lived with them for a time, and hunted with them. Their medicine woman healed my arm, and I learned my way to the Mother through them. The Mother does not mix spirits, there are no horse-wolves, or lion-deer. The people of the Clan are different, but the difference is insignificant.

No children like Rydag, or Ayla's son, could be born if they were not human, too. They are not abominations. They are simply children."

"I don't care what you say, old Mamut," the pregnant woman said. "I don't want a flathead child or a mixed one. If she already had one, that spirit may linger around her."

"Woman, Ayla is no threat to you," the old shaman replied. "The spirit that was chosen for your child is already there. It cannot be changed now. It was not Ayla's doing that gave her baby the spirit of a flathead man, she did not draw that spirit to her. It was the Mother's choice. You must remember, a man's spirit never lingers far from the man himself. Ayla grew up with the Clan. She became a woman while she lived with them. When Mut decided to give her a child, She could only choose from the men who were nearby, and they were all men of the Clan. Of course the spirit of one of them was chosen to enter her, but you don't see any men of the Clan around here now, do you?"

"Old Mamut, what if there were some flathead men nearby?" a woman shouted out from the crowd.

"I believe they would have to be very close, even share the same hearth, before that spirit would be chosen. The people of the Clan are human, but there are some differences. While life is better than no life to the Mother, which is why Ayla was given a child when she wanted one, it is not easy to blend the two. With so many Mamutoi men around, one of them would be chosen first."

"That's what you say, old man," another voice called out. "I'm not so sure it's true. I'm keeping my woman away from her."

"No wonder she's so good with animals, she grew up with them." Ayla turned and saw that it was Chaleg who was talking.

"Does that mean their magic is stronger than ours?" Frebec replied. There was some uneasy shuffling in the crowd.

"I've heard her say it's not magic. She says anyone can do it." Frebec recognised the voice of the Mamut of Chaleg's Camp.

"Then why hasn't anyone done it before?" Frebec said. "You are Mamut. If anyone can do it, let me see you go out and ride back on a horse. Why don't you bring a wolf under your control? I've seen Ayla whistle birds down out of the sky."

"Why are you standing up for her, Frebec, against your own family, your own Camp?" Chaleg asked.

"What Camp is my Camp? The one that turned me out, or the one that took me in? My hearth is the Hearth of the Crane, my Camp is Lion Camp. Ayla lived near us all winter. Ayla was there when Bectie was born, and she is not mixed. The daughter of my hearth would not even be here now, if it hadn't been for Ayla."

Jondalar listened to Frebec with a lump in his throat. In spite of what he said, it took real courage to face down his own cousin, his own relatives, the Camp of his birth. Jondalar could hardly believe this was the same man who had been such a big troublemaker. He had been so quick to condemn Frebec in the beginning, yet who was the one who had felt embarrassed for Ayla? Who was the one who feared what people would say if she said anything about her background? Who was the one that was afraid he would be rejected by his family and his people if he stood up for her? Jondalar felt shamed. Frebec had shown him what a coward he was. Frebec, and Ayla.

When he'd seen her swallow down her fear, and lift her chin to face them all, he had never felt more proud of anyone in his life. Then the Lion Camp stood up with her, and he could hardly believe it. The ones that counted were the ones that cared. Jondalar forgot as he thought about Ayla and the Lion Camp with praise and pride, that he had been the first one to rush to her side.

34

The Lion Camp returned to Cattail Camp to discuss the unexpected crisis. An initial suggestion to leave immediately was quickly abandoned. They were, after all, Mamutoi, and this was the Summer Meeting. Tulie had stopped by for Latie so that she could be included in the discussions, and prepared for the possibility of unkind comments directed at her, Ayla, or the Lion Camp. She was asked if she wanted to delay her womanhood rites. Latie defended Ayla vehemently, and decided she would return to the special Camp for the ceremony and ritual, and just let anyone try to say anything bad about Ayla, or the Lion Camp.

Then Tulie asked Ayla why she hadn't mentioned her son before. Ayla explained she didn't like to talk about him because it still hurt too much, and Nezzie quickly made it clear that she had been told in the very beginning. Mamut also admitted to knowing about him. Though the headwoman wished she had known and wondered why she was not told, she did not blame Ayla. She considered whether she would have thought about the young woman any differently, had she known, and admitted she might not have credited her with as much potential value or status. Then she began to question her position. Why should it make a difference? Was Ayla any different?

Rydag was very upset and depressed, and nothing Nezzie said or did seemed to help. He wouldn't eat, wouldn't go out of the tent, wouldn't communicate except to respond to a direct question. He would only sit and hug the wolf. Nezzie was grateful for the animal's patience. Ayla decided to see if there was anything she could do. She found him sitting with the wolf on his sleeping roll in a dark corner. Wolf lifted his head, and banged his tail on the ground at her approach.

"Is it all right if I sit down here with you, Rydag?" she asked.

He shrugged an assent. She sat beside him and asked how he felt, speaking aloud to him, but automatically signing the words, too, until she realised it was probably too dark to see. It struck her then, the real advantage to being able to speak with words. It wasn't that you couldn't speak as well with signals and hand signs, it was that you weren't limited by only what you could see.

It was like the difference between thrusting with a spear when hunting, like the Clan did, or throwing it. Both were effective weapons for bringing meat home, but one had greater range and possibilities. She had seen how useful motions and signs, which were not understood by everyone, could be, particularly for secret or private communication, but overall, there was a greater advantage in speaking with words that could be heard and understood. With a full verbal language, you could speak to someone who was behind a barrier, or in a different room, or even shout across a distance, or to a large group. You could speak when someone's back was turned, or when you were holding something, which freed the hands for other purposes, and you could speak softly in the dark.

Ayla sat quietly with the boy for some time, not asking questions, just offering closeness and company. After a while, she started talking to him, telling Rydag about the time she lived with the Clan.

"In some ways, this Meeting reminds me of the Clan Gathering," Ayla said. "Here, even if I look the same as everyone, I feel different. There, I was different . . . taller than any of the men by then . . . just a big ugly woman. It was awful when we first got there. They almost weren't going to let Brun's clan stay because they brought me. They said I wasn't Clan, but Creb insisted that I was. He was the Mog-ur, and they didn't dare dispute him. It's a good thing Durc was only a baby. When they saw him, they thought he was deformed, and they all stared. You know how it feels. But he wasn't deformed. He was just a mixture, like you are. Or maybe you are more like Ura. Her mother was Clan."

"You say before, Ura will join with Durc?" Rydag asked, turning towards the light from the fire to make his motions seen. He was intrigued in spite of himself.

"Yes. Her mother came to me, and it was arranged. She was so relieved to know there was another child, a boy, like her daughter. She was so afraid Ura would never find a mate. To be honest, I didn't think about it much. I was just grateful that Durc was accepted into the Clan."

"Durc is Clan? He is mixed, but Clan?" the boy signed.

"Yes, Brun accepted him, Creb named him. Not even Broud can take that away from him. And everyone loves him – except Broud – even Oga, Broud's mate. She nursed him, when I lost my milk, right along with her son, Grev. They grew up together like brothers, and they are good friends. Old Grod made Durc a little spear, just his size." Ayla smiled at the memory. "Uba loves him best, though. Uba is my sister, like you and Rugie. She is Durc's mother now. I gave him to Uba when Broud made me leave. He may look a little different, but yes, Durc is Clan."

"I hate it here," Rydag motioned with vehement anger. "I wish I am Durc and live with Clan."

Rydag's comment startled Ayla. Even after they talked more, and she finally convinced him to eat something, and then tucked him into his bed, it stayed on her mind.

Ranec watched Ayla all evening. He noticed how she would stop in the middle of some activity, like lifting a bite of food to her mouth, for example, while her eyes glazed over with a faraway look, or a frown of concentration creased her forehead. He knew her thoughts were weighing heavily on her mind, and he wanted so much to comfort her, share them with her.

Everyone stayed at Cattail Camp that night, and the tent was crowded. Ranec waited until Ayla finally started to slide into her fur bedroll, then he quickly went to his.

"Will you share my furs tonight, Ayla?" Ranec watched her close her eyes and frown. "I don't mean for Pleasures," he added quickly, "unless you want to. I know this has been a hard day for you . . ."

"I think it's been harder for Lion Camp," Ayla said.

"I don't think it's been any harder, but that doesn't matter. I just want to give you something, Ayla. My furs to keep you warm, my love to comfort you. I want to be close to you tonight."

She nodded acquiescence, and slid into Ranec's bedroll with him, but she could not sleep, could not even rest comfortably, and he was aware of it.

"Ayla, what's troubling you? Would you like to talk about it?" Ranec said.

"I've been thinking about Rydag, and my son, but I don't know if I can talk about it. I just need to think about it."

"You'd rather be in your own bed, wouldn't you?" he finally said.

"I know you want to help, Ranec, and that in itself helps more than I can say. I can't tell you how much it meant to me when I saw you there, standing beside me. I am so grateful to the Lion Camp, too. Everyone has been so good, so wonderful to me, almost too wonderful. I learned so much from them, and I was so proud to be Mamutoi, to say they were my people. I thought all the Others – the ones I used to call the Others – were like the Lion Camp, but now I know that isn't true. Like the Clan, most people are good people, but not everyone, and even good people are not good about everything. I had some ideas and . . . I was making some plans . . . but, I need to think, now."

"And you can think better in your own bed, not cramped in here with me. Go ahead, Ayla, you'll still be next to me," Ranec said.

Ranec wasn't the only one who had been watching Ayla, and when Jondalar saw her get out of Ranec's bedroll and into her own, he had a strange set of mixed feelings. He was relieved that he wouldn't have to grit his teeth against the sounds of them sharing Pleasures, but he felt a pang of regret for Ranec. If he had been in the dark carver's place, he would have wanted to hold Ayla, and comfort her, try to take on some of her pain. It would have hurt him if she had left his bed to sleep alone.

After Ranec fell asleep and a deep stillness settled on the Camp, Ayla quietly got up, slipped on a light parka against the night-time chill, and went outside into the dark starlit night. In a moment, Wolf was beside her. They walked towards the horse lean-to, and were welcomed by a nicker from Racer, and a soft blow of recognition from Whinney. After patting and scratching, and quiet words, Ayla put her arms around Whinney's neck, and leaned on her.

How many times had the hay-coloured mare been her friend when she needed one? Ayla smiled. What would the Clan think of her friends? Two horses and a wolf! She was grateful for their presence, their company, but there was still an emptiness inside her. Someone was missing, the one she wanted most. Yet he had been there. Even before the Lion Camp stood up for her. She didn't even know where he came from. Suddenly Jondalar was just there, beside her, standing against them all. Against their repugnance, their disgust. It had been terrible, worse than the Clan Gathering. It wasn't just that she was different. They feared her, hated her. That's what he'd been trying to tell her all along. But even if she'd known, it wouldn't have made any difference. She couldn't let them pick on Rydag, or malign her son.

From the opening of the tent, another pair of eyes watched her. Jondalar could not sleep either. He had seen her get up, and quietly followed her. How many times had he seen her like that with Whinney? He was happy that she had the animals to turn to, but he ached to be in the mare's place. But it was too late. She didn't want him, and he couldn't blame her. With a sudden realisation, he saw through his emotional confusion, saw his actions with a new clarity, and realised that he had done it himself. In the very beginning, he wasn't just being "fair" and letting her make her own choice. He had turned away from her, out of petty jealousy. He was hurt, and wanted to hurt back.

There was more to it than that, admit it, Jondalar, he said to himself. You were hurt, but you knew how she was raised. She didn't even understand your jealousy. When she went to Ranec's bed that night, she was only being a "good Clan woman". That was the real problem, her Clan background. You were ashamed of it. You were ashamed to love her, afraid you would have to face what she faced today. You didn't know if you could stand up for her. No matter how much you said you loved her, you were afraid you'd turn against her, too. Well, there is no shame in loving her, the shame is in your own cowardice. And now it's too late. She didn't need you. She stood up for herself, and then the whole Lion Camp stood up for her. She doesn't need you at all, and you don't deserve her.

Finally the chill drove Ayla back in. She glanced towards Jondalar's sleeping place when she entered the tent. He was rolled over on his side, facing the other way. She slipped into her bed, and felt a heavy, sleeping hand reach for her. Ranec did love her, she knew that. And she loved him, too, in her own way. She lay still, and listened to Ranec's steady breathing. After a while he rolled the other way and the hand was gone.

Ayla tried to sleep, but she couldn't stop thinking. She had wanted to go for Durc and bring him back to Lion Camp to live with her. Now she questioned if that would be best for him. Would he be happier here with her than he would be living with the Clan? Could he be happy living with people who would hate him? Who would call him flathead and worse, a half-animal abomination? With the Clan, he was known, and loved; he was one of them. Maybe Broud hated him, but even at the Clan Gathering, he would have friends. He was accepted, he would be allowed to join in the competitions, and the ceremonies – did Durc have the Clan memories? she wondered.

If she couldn't take him away, could she go back to the Clan and live? Now that she had found people like herself, could she ever accept Clan ways, again? They would never allow her to keep her animals. Would she be willing to give up Whinney and Racer, and Wolf, and be only Durc's mother? Does Durc need a mother? He was a baby when I left, but he's not a baby any more. By now, Brun is teaching him to hunt.

He has probably made his first small kills, and brought them back to show Uba. Ayla smiled to herself at the picture that evoked. Uba would praise him so highly, and tell him what a brave, strong hunter he is.

Durc has a mother! she realised. Uba is his mother. Uba has raised him, taken care of him, nursed his little cuts and scrapes. How can I take him away from her? Who would take care of her when she gets old? Even when he was a baby, the other women in the Clan were more mother to him than I was after I lost my milk.

How can I go back and get him, anyway? I am cursed. To the Clan, I am dead! If Durc saw me, I would only frighten him, and everyone else. Even if there was no death curse on me, would he be happy to see me? Would he even remember me?

He was hardly more than a baby when I left. By now, he is at the Clan Gathering and has met Ura. He's young yet, but he must be thinking about the time when they will mate. He is planning to make a hearth – just as I am, she thought. Even if I could convince him I wasn't a spirit, Durc would have to bring Ura with him, and Ura would be miserable here. It will be difficult enough for her to leave her own clan and live with Durc and his clan, but to move into a world in which nothing was familiar would be so much worse. Especially a world where she would be hated and misunderstood.

What if I went back to the valley? And then brought Durc and Ura to live there? But Durc needs people . . . and so do I. I don't want to live alone, why should Durc want to live alone in a valley with me?

I've been thinking of myself, not Durc. It would not be better for him to come here. It would not make him happy. It would only make me happy. But I am not Durc's mother any more. Uba is his mother. I am nothing to him but a memory of a mother who died, and maybe it's better that way. The Clan is his world, and like it or not, this is my world. I cannot go back to the Clan; Durc cannot come here. There is no place in this world where my son and I can live together, and be happy.

Ayla woke early the next morning. Even after she did finally go to sleep, she did not sleep well. She woke often from dreams of shaking earth and crumbling caves, and felt uneasy and depressed. She helped Nezzie heat water for soup and grind grains for a morning meal, and was glad for the opportunity to talk with her.

"I feel terrible about all the trouble I've caused, Nezzie. The whole Lion Camp is being shunned because of me," Ayla said.

"Don't even say that. It's not your fault, Ayla. We had a choice, and we made it. You were only defending Rydag, and he is a member of Lion Camp, too, at least to us."

"All this trouble has made me realise something," Ayla continued. "Ever since I left the Clan, I've always thought about going back to get my son someday. Now I know I never can. I can't bring him here, and I can't go back there. But knowing that I'll never see him makes me feel that I just lost him all over again. I wish I could cry, grieve for him, mourn for him, but I just feel dry and empty."

Nezzie was sorting through yesterday's fresh-picked berries and pulling off the stems. She stopped and gave Ayla a level gaze. "Everyone suffers disappointments in life. Everyone loses loved ones. Some are real tragedies. You lost your people when you were young. That was a tragedy, but there was nothing you could do about it. It's worse if you blame yourself. Wymez lives every day of his life blaming himself for the death of the woman he loved. I think Jondalar blames himself for his brother's death. You've lost a son. It is hard for a mother to lose a child, but you do have something. You know he is probably still alive. Rydag lost his mother . . . someday I will lose him."

After breakfast, Ayla went out. Most people were staying around Cattail Camp. She looked towards the centre of the Meeting, then at

Larch Camp, the newly set up summer home of the Mammoth Camp. She was surprised to see Avarie looking across at her. She wondered how they felt today about setting up the Camp so close to Lion Camp.

Avarie went to the tent her brother had designated as the Mammoth Hearth, scratched on the leather, then without waiting for a response, went in. Vincavec had spread his fur bedroll out so that it took up almost half the floor space. In the middle was a backrest, an ornately decorated hide stretched across a mammoth bone frame that had been lashed together with rawhide. He was sitting up on his furs, lounging against the backrest.

"The feelings are mixed," she said without preamble.

"I can imagine," Vincavec replied. "Lion Camp worked hard with us putting up the lodge. By the time they left, everyone was feeling more than friendly towards them. And Ayla with her horses and wolf was fascinating – and a little awe-inspiring. But now, if old stories and customs are to be believed, Lion Camp is sheltering an abomination, a woman of unbridled evil, who draws animal flathead spirits to her like a fire draws moths at night, and spreads them around to the other women. What do you think, Avarie?"

"I don't know, Vincavec. I like Ayla, and she doesn't seem like an evil person to me. The boy doesn't seem like an animal, either. He's just weak and can't talk, but I do believe he understands. Maybe he is human, and maybe the other flatheads are, too. Maybe the old Mamut is right. The Mother just chose a spirit from the only men near Ayla when She gave her a baby. I didn't know she lived with a pack of flatheads once, though, or that the old man did."

"That old man has lived so many years, he's forgotten more things than a double handful of younger men have ever learned, and he's often right. I have a feeling about this, Avarie. I don't think it will have lasting bad effects. There is something about Ayla that makes me think the Mother watches out for her. I think she may come out of this more powerful than she was before. Let's find out how Mammoth Camp feels about siding with Lion Camp."

"Where's Tulie?" Fralie asked, looking around the tent.

"She went with Latie back to the Womanhood Camp," Nezzie said. "Why?"

"Do you remember that Camp that came offering to adopt Ayla, just before Mammoth Camp arrived?"

Ayla looked at Fralie questioningly.

"Yes," Nezzie said. "The one Tulie didn't think had enough to offer."

"They are outside asking for Tulie, again."

"I'll go see what they want," Nezzie said.

Ayla waited inside, not really wanting to face them, if she didn't have to. After a few moments, Nezzie returned.

"They still want to adopt you, Ayla," she said. "The headwoman of that Camp has four sons. They want you for a sister. She says if you have already had one son, it proves you are capable of having children. They have increased their offer. Maybe you should go out and welcome them, in the name of the Mother."

Tulie and Latie walked with purposeful strides through the encampment, side by side, looking straight ahead, ignoring the curious stares of the people they passed.

"Tulie! Latie! Wait a moment," Brecie called out, hurrying to catch up with them. "We were just getting ready to send a runner to you, Tulie. We'd like to invite you to share a meal with us at Willow Camp this evening."

"Thank you, Brecie. I appreciate your invitation. Of course we'll come. I should have known we could count on you."

"We've been friends a long time, Tulie. Sometimes old tales are believed just because they are old. Fralie's baby looks fine to me."

"And she was born early, too. Bectie wouldn't even be alive, if it wasn't for Ayla," Latie said, quick to defend her friend.

"I did wonder where she came from, though. Everyone thought she came with Jondalar. They are both tall and blond, but I knew better. I remember when we pulled him and his brother out of the muck near Beran Sea. She wasn't with them, then, and I knew that wasn't a Mamutoi accent, or a Sungaea accent either. But I still don't know how she controls those horses and that wolf."

Tulie was feeling much better as they continued towards the centre of the hollow, and the earthlodges of Wolf Camp.

"How many does that make?" Tarneg asked Barzec as another delegation was leaving.

"Almost half the Camps have made some gesture of reconciliation," Barzec said. "I can think of one or two more who might still decide to join with us."

"But that still leaves about half the Camps," Talut said. "And some of them are arguing pretty hard against us. Some are even saying we should leave."

"Yes, but look who they are, and Chaleg is the only one I've heard who is saying we should leave," Tarneg said.

"But they're Mamutoi, too, and even seeds blown by ill winds can take root," Nezzie said.

"I don't like this split," Talut said. "There are too many good people on both sides. I wish I could think of some way to make it right again."

"Ayla feels terrible, too. She says that she's causing problems for Lion Camp. Did you see the look on her face when those youngers that were fighting started calling her 'animal woman'?"

"Do you mean the ones that we caught by the ri –?" Danug started to ask, but Tarneg quickly interrupted.

"She means the brother and sister that Ayla and Deegie caught hitting each other." Danug would have to be careful. He had almost slipped and mentioned something about the boys that were fighting, Tarneg thought.

"I've never seen Rydag so upset," Nezzie continued. "Every year the Meetings have been harder on him. He doesn't like the way people treat him, but this year is worse . . . maybe because it's so much better for him at Lion Camp now. I'm afraid all this is not good for him, but I don't know what to do. Even Ayla's worried, and that worries me more."

"Where is Ayla now?" Danug asked.

"Out with the horses," Nezzie said.

"I think she should take it as a compliment when they call her 'animal woman'. You must admit, she is good with animals," Barzec said. "Some people even think she can speak with their spirits from the other world."

"Some of the others say it just proves that she lived with animals," Tarneg reminded him. "And accuse her of drawing different kinds of spirits that are not so welcome."

"Ayla still says anyone can make animals friendly," Talut said.

"She tries to make less of it," Barzec said. "That may be why some of the others don't put as much importance on it. People are more used to someone like Vincavec, someone who lets you know how great he thinks he is."

Nezzie looked at Tulie's man, and wondered why he didn't seem to care much for Vincavec. The Mammoth Camp had been one of the first to take their side.

"You may be right, Barzec," Tarneg said. "It's strange how quickly you can get used to having animals around, when they behave so well. They don't seem unnatural. They're just like any other animal, except you can get close to them, and touch them. But when you think about it, it is beyond reason. Why should that wolf obey a signal from a weak child that he could easily tear apart? Why should those horses let someone sit on their backs and ride them? And what would make a person even think to try it?"

"I wouldn't be surprised if Latie tried it, some day," Talut said.

"If anyone will, she will," Danug said. "Did you see her when she was here? First place she went was the horse lean-to. She missed them more than anyone. I think she's in love with those horses."

Jondalar had been listening without making any comment. The situation Ayla had caused for herself by admitting her background was painful and debasing, but in many ways it hadn't been as bad as he had imagined it would be. He was surprised that she hadn't been more thoroughly denounced. He had expected her to be vilified, driven out, completely ostracised. Was the taboo worse among his people, or did he just think it was?

When the Lion Camp stood up for her, he thought they must be a rare exception, who might be more forgiving because of Rydag. Then, when Vincavec and Avarie of Mammoth Camp came to offer support, Jondalar began to reconsider, and when more and more of the Camps voluntarily came to offer support to the Lion Camp, he was forced to inspect his own beliefs.

Jondalar was a physical man. He understood concepts such as love, compassion, anger, with an empathy that was based on his own feelings, even though he could not express them well. He could discuss intangible philosophies and matters of the spirit with intelligence, but they were not his passion, and he accepted his society's positions without deep misgivings. But Ayla had faced the crowd with such dignity and quiet strength, respect for her soared. It gave him a rare insight.

He began to understand that just because some people thought certain behaviour was wrong, that didn't make it so. A person could resist popular belief and stand up for personal principles, and though there might be consequences, not everything would necessarily be lost. In fact, something important might be gained, if only within oneself. Ayla was not expelled from the people who had so recently adopted her. Half of them were willing to accept her, and believed her to be a woman of rare talents and courage.

The other half were of a different mind, but not all for the same reasons. Some saw it as an opportunity to gain influence and status by opposing the powerful Lion Camp at a time when their position was threatened. Others were genuinely incensed that a woman who was so depraved could be allowed to live among them. In their opinion, she personified evil, even more so because she did not appear to be evil. She looked like any other woman, more attractive than most, but she had duped them by a trick of controlling animals that she must have learned when she lived with the bestial flathead abominations, who had even fooled some people into thinking they were human.

Many feared her. By her own admission, she had spawned one of those misbegotten half-animals, and now threatened every other woman at the Summer Meeting. No matter what old Mamut said, everyone knew certain male spirits were consistently drawn to the same woman. The Lion Camp had allowed Nezzie to keep that animal child, and now look what they had! More animals, and an abomination of a woman who had probably been drawn to him. The entire Lion Camp ought to be banned.

The Mamutoi were a close-knit people. Almost everyone could count at least one relative or friend in every Camp. But now the fabric of their lives threatened to be torn apart, and many people, including Talut, were very distressed. The Councils convened, but ended up wrangling over the dispute. This was an unprecedented situation, and they didn't have the means or the strategies to resolve it.

The bright afternoon sun did little to dispel the sombre mood of the encampment. Walking Whinney up the path towards Cattail Camp, Ayla noticed the place where red-ochred earth had been dug out of the ground, and it reminded her of her visit to the Music Lodge. Though they were still practising, and still planning a big celebration after the mammoth hunt, there wasn't the same sense of expectation and excitement about it. Even the happiness Deegie had felt about her Matrimonial, and Latie about her elevation to the status of woman, were dampened by the differences that threatened to disrupt the entire Summer Meeting.

Ayla talked about leaving, but Nezzie told her it would not solve anything. She had not caused the problem. Her presence had only brought into the open a deep and basic difference between the two factions. Nezzie said the problem had been brewing ever since she took in Rydag. Many people still disapproved of him being allowed to live with them.

Ayla worried about Rydag. He seldom smiled and she noticed an absence of his gentle humour. He had no appetite, and she didn't think he was sleeping well. He seemed to enjoy listening to her talk about her life with the Clan, but he seldom joined in on conversations.

She settled Whinney into the lean-to, and saw Jondalar on the broad, grassy meadow below riding towards the river crossing on Racer. He seemed different lately. Not quite so distant, but saddened.

On the spur of the moment, Ayla decided to go to the clearing at the centre of the encampment and see what activities were going on. The Wolf Camp insisted that since they were hosting the Meeting, they could not take sides, but she believed they favoured the Lion Camp's position. She was not going to hide. She was not an "abomination", the Clan were people, and so were Rydag and her son. She wanted to do something, show herself. Maybe visit the Mammoth Hearth, or the Music Lodge, or talk to Latie.

She set out with determined steps, nodding to those who acknowledged her, ignoring those who did not, and when she neared the Music Lodge, she saw Deegie coming out.

"Ayla! You are just the person I want to see. Are you going any place special?"

"I just decided to get away from Lion Camp."

"Good! I was going to visit Tricie, and see her baby. I've been wanting to visit, but she's been gone every time I've tried. Kylie just told me she's there now. Do you want to come with me?"

"Yes."

They walked towards the headwoman's lodge. "We came to pay a visit, Tricie," Deegie explained at the entrance, "and to see your baby."

"Come in," Tricie said. "I just put him down, but I don't think he's asleep yet."

Ayla stayed back while Deegie picked him up and held him, cooing and talking to him. "Don't you want to see him, Ayla?" Tricie finally said. It was almost a challenge.

"I do want to see him."

She took the baby from Deegie's arms and studied him carefully. His skin was so white it was nearly translucent, and his eyes such a pale blue they had almost no colour at all. His hair was a bright orangey-red, but it had all the texture and tight, springy curl of Ranec's. Most distinctive, his face was an infant version of Ranec's face. Ayla knew without doubt that Ralev was Ranec's baby. Ranec had started him as surely as Broud had started Durc growing inside her. She couldn't help but wonder, when she joined with him, would she have a baby like this some day?

Ayla talked to the infant in her arms. He looked up at her with interest, as though he was fascinated, then he smiled and cooed a soft little delighted laugh. Ayla hugged him to her, closed her eyes and felt the softness of his cheek against hers, and felt her heart melt.

"Isn't he beautiful, Ayla?" Deegie said.

"Yes, isn't he beautiful?" Tricie asked, her tone sharper.

Ayla looked at the young mother. "No, he's not beautiful." Deegie gaped at her with surprise. "No one could ever say he is beautiful, but he is the most . . . lovable baby I have ever seen. Not a woman in the world could resist him. He doesn't have to be beautiful. There is something special about him, Tricie. I think you are very lucky to have him."

The mother's smile softened. "I think I am, too, Ayla. And I agree, he is not beautiful, but he is good, and so lovable."

Suddenly there was a commotion outside, shouting and wailing. The three young women hurried to the entranceway.

"O Great Mother! My daughter! Someone help her!" a woman wailed.

"What's wrong? Where is she?" Deegie asked.

"A lion! A lion has her! Down in the meadow. Someone help her, please!" Several men with spears were already running towards the path.

"A lion? No, it can't be!" Ayla said, as she started running after the men.

"Ayla! Where are you going?" Deegie called after her, trying to catch up.

"To get the girl," Ayla called back.

She raced towards the path. A crowd of people was standing near the top of it watching the men with spears running down the path. Beyond them, in plain sight on the grassy floodplain across the river, was a massive cave lion, with a shaggy reddish mane, circling a tall young girl, who was too petrified to move. Ayla looked down, studied the animal closely to make sure, then ran into Lion Camp. Wolf jumped up on her.

"Rydag!" she called. "Come and get Wolf! I've got to get that girl." When Rydag came out of the tent, she commanded the wolf, "Stay!" in her firmest tone, then told the boy not to let him go. Only then did she whistle for Whinney.

She jumped on the mare's back, and raced down the path. The men with spears were already crossing the river when she guided Whinney around them. As soon as she reached firm ground on the other side, she urged Whinney into a gallop, and headed straight for the lion and the girl. The people watching from the top of the path looked on with wonder and amazement.

"What does she think she can do?" someone said, angrily. "She doesn't even have a spear. The girl seems unharmed so far, but rushing at the lion with a horse might incite him. If that child is harmed, it will be her fault."

Jondalar overheard the comment, as well as several other people from the Lion Camp, who turned to him questioningly. He just watched Ayla, swallowing the misgivings that rose in his throat. He couldn't be sure, but she must have been, or she would never have gone down there with Whinney.

As Ayla and Whinney neared, the huge cave lion stopped and faced her. There was a scar on his nose, a familiar scar. She remembered when he got it.

"Whinney, it's Baby! It really is Baby!" she cried, as she brought the horse to a stop and slid off.

577

She ran towards the lion, not even considering that he might not remember her. This was her Baby. She was his mother. She had raised him from a small cub, taken care of him, hunted with him.

It was just that fearlessness that he remembered. He started towards her, as the girl watched with fear. The next thing Ayla knew, the lion had tripped her, to knock her down, and she had her arms around his big shaggy neck, hugging him full-length, while he wrapped his forelegs around her in the closest thing to an embrace he could accomplish.

"Oh, Baby, you came back. How did you ever find me?" she cried, wiping her tears of joy in his rough mane.

Finally she sat up, and felt a raspy tongue lick her face. "Stop that!" she said, smiling. "I won't have any skin left." She scratched him in his favourite places, and a low, rumbling growl let her know his pleasure. He rolled over on his back so she could scratch his stomach. Ayla noticed the girl, tall, with long blonde hair, standing wide-eyed, watching them.

"He was looking for me," Ayla said to her. "I think he mistook you for me. You can go now, but walk, don't run."

Ayla scratched Baby on his stomach and behind his ears, until the girl walked into the waiting arms of a man, who clasped her to him with obvious relief, then led her up the path. The rest were standing back, holding their spears in readiness. Among them she saw Jondalar, with his spear-thrower poised in readiness, and beside him a shorter, dark-skinned man. Talut was on the other side of Ranec, and Tulie beside him.

"You have to go, Baby. I don't want you to get hurt. Even if you are the biggest cave lion on the earth, a spear can stop you," Ayla said, talking in the special language that grew out of Clan words and signs and animal sounds. Baby was familiar with the sounds, and certain of the signals. He rolled over and got up. Ayla hugged him around the neck, and then she couldn't resist. She slid her leg over and eased on to his back, and hung on to his reddish mane. It was not the first time.

She felt hard, powerful muscles bunch beneath her, then with a leap, he was off, and in an instant, reached the full speed of a lion on the chase. Though she had ridden the lion before, she had never been able to develop any signals to direct him. He went where he wanted to go, but he allowed her to go with him. It was always an exciting wild ride, and she loved it for just that reason. Ayla clung to his mane, as the wind whipped her face, and breathed in his strong, rangy odour.

Ayla felt him turn and slow – the lion was a sprinter, unlike the wolf, he had no endurance for the long distance – and she looked ahead to see Whinney waiting, patiently grazing. The horse nickered as they approached, and tossed her head. Baby's lion smell was strong and disturbing, but the mare had helped to raise this animal from a cub, and in her own way had mothered him. Though he was nearly as tall at the withers as she was, and longer and heavier, the horse had no fear of this particular lion, especially when Ayla was with him.

When the lion stopped, Ayla slid off his back. She hugged him and scratched him again, then with a signal that was suggestive of casting a stone with a sling, she told him to go. Tears fell, as she watched him walk away, his tail weaving from side to side. When she heard the distinctive tone of his *"hnk, hnk, hnk"* grunting voice, that she would recognise anywhere, she sobbed in answer. The tears flooded and her vision blurred as the big tawny cat with the reddish mane disappeared into the tall grass. She knew, somehow, that she would never ride him again; that she would never see her wild, unlikely, lion son again.

The *"hnk, hnk"* grunts continued until finally the huge cave lion, gigantic compared with his later counterparts, sounded a deep, full-bellied, shattering roar that could be heard for miles. He shook the very earth with his farewell.

Ayla signalled to Whinney, and started walking back. As much as she loved riding her mare, she wanted to remember the feel of that last wild ride as long as she could.

Jondalar finally tore his eyes away from the mesmerising scene and noticed the expressions on the faces of the others. He could see what they were thinking. Horses were one thing, even a wolf maybe, but a cave lion? He beamed a wide, smug grin of pride and relief. Let someone question his stories now!

The men started up the path after Ayla, feeling almost foolish carrying spears no one had had any use for. The people who had been watching stood back as she neared, making way for the woman and the horse, and stared after her with stunned disbelief and awe. Even the Lion Camp, who had heard Jondalar's stories, and knew about her life in the valley, could not believe what they had seen.

35

Ayla had been selecting the clothing to take along on the hunt – it could be very cold at night, she was told. They would be in sight of the gigantic wall of ice that was the leading edge of the glacier. To her surprise, Wymez had brought her several expertly made spears, and was explaining to her the merits of the spear point he had devised for hunting mammoth. It was an unexpected gift, and after all the adulation and other strange behaviour from the Mamutoi, she wasn't sure how to respond. But he put her at ease with his special warm smile, and told her he had been planning this gift ever since she Promised to join with the son of his hearth. She had asked him about adapting it to work with a spear-thrower when Mamut came into the tent.

"The Mamutoi would like to talk to you. They want you to help with the Call to bring the mammoths, Ayla," he said. "They think if you spoke to the Spirit Mammoth, she would be willing to give us many."

"But I already told you. I don't have any special powers," Ayla pleaded. "I don't want to talk to them."

"I know, Ayla. I explained that you may have a Calling talent, but you are untrained. They insist that I ask you. After they saw you ride the lion and tell him to go, they are convinced that you would have a strong influence on the Spirit Mammoth, trained or not."

"That was Baby, Mamut. The lion I raised. I couldn't do that with just any lion."

"Why do you speak of that lion as though you are his mother?" a voice said from the entrance. A large figure was standing there. "Are you his mother?" Lomie said, coming into the tent at Mamut's beckoning gesture.

"In a way, I guess. I raised him from a cub. He was hurt, he'd been caught in a stampede and kicked in the head. I call him Baby because he was just a baby when I found him. I never named him anything else. He was always just Baby, even when he got big," Ayla explained. "I don't know how to Call animals, Lomie."

"Then why did that lion appear, at a most providential moment, if you didn't Call him?" Lomie asked.

"It was just by chance. There's nothing mysterious about it. He probably picked up my scent, or Whinney's scent, and came looking for me. He used to come back for a visit sometimes, even after he found a mate and his own pride. Ask Jondalar."

"If he wasn't under special influence, why didn't he hurt that girl? She didn't have any 'mother' relationship with him. She said he knocked her down, and she thought he was going to eat her, but he only licked her face."

"I think the only reason he stopped that girl was because she looks a little like me. She's tall, and has blonde hair. He grew up with a person, not with other lions, so he thinks of people as his family. And he always used to trip me or knock me down when he hadn't seen me for a while, if I didn't stop him. It's his way of being playful. He wanted to be hugged, and scratched," Ayla explained. She noticed that the tent had filled up with Mamutoi, while she was talking.

Wymez stepped back out of the way with a sly smile on his face. She wouldn't go to them, so they came to her, he thought. He frowned when he noticed Vincavec edging in closer. It would be hard on Ranec if Ayla decided to choose him instead. He had never seen the son of his hearth so upset as when he learned of Vincavec's offer. Wymez had to admit it, it had upset him, too.

Vincavec watched Ayla as she answered the questions. He was not easily overwhelmed. He was, after all, headman and Mamut, and privy to the schemes of temporal influence as well as the guises of supernatural power. But like the other Mamutoi, he was called to the Mammoth Hearth because he felt an urge to explore deeper dimensions, to discover and explain the reasons beyond appearances, and he could be moved by a truly inexplicable mystery, or demonstration of manifest power.

From their first meeting, he had sensed a mystery about Ayla that intrigued him, and a quality of quiet strength, as though her mettle had already been tested. His interpretation was that the Mother watched out for her, and that was why her problem would be resolved. But he'd had no inkling of the means, and he was genuinely surprised at the result. He knew no one would dream of opposing her now, or those who sheltered her. Nor would anyone object to her background, or the son she once bore. Her power was too great. Whether she would use it for beneficial or malicious purposes was incidental – like summer and winter, or day and night, they were two faces of the same substance – except that no one wanted to incur her personal enmity. If she could control a cave lion, who knew what she could do?

Vincavec, along with old Mamut and the other Mamutoi, had been raised in the same environment, reared in the same culture, and the patterns of belief that evolved to accommodate their existence were ingrained, were a part of their mental and moral fibre.

Their lives were largely conceived to be preordained, since they had little control over them. Illness struck without reason, and though it could be treated, some might die while others survived. Accidents were equally unpredictable, and if they happened when one was alone, were often fatal. Harsh climates and rapidly shifting weather patterns, brought on by the proximity of massive land glaciers, could cause drought or floods that had an immediate effect on the natural environment upon which they were dependent. A summer too cold, or with too much rain, could stunt plant growth, decrease animal populations, and change their migration patterns, and could result in hardship for the mammoth-hunting people.

The structure of their metaphysical universe paralleled their physical world, and was useful in providing answers to unresolvable questions – questions that could cause great anxiety without some acceptable and, based on their precepts, reasonable explanation. But any structure, no matter how useful, is also limiting. The animals of their world roamed freely, the plants grew at random, and the people were intimately familiar with these patterns. They knew where certain plants grew, and understood the behaviour of animals, but it never occurred to them that the patterns could be changed; that animals and plants, and people, were born with an innate capacity for change and adaptation. That, indeed, without it, they would not survive.

Ayla's control over the animals she had raised was not perceived as natural; no one had ever tried to tame or domesticate an animal before. The Mamuti, anticipating the need for explanations to relieve the anxieties caused by this startling innovation, had mentally searched the theoretical construct of their metaphysical world for answers that would satisfy. It was not a simple act of taming animals that she had done. Instead, Ayla had demonstrated a supernatural power far beyond anyone's imagination. Her control over animals, it seemed obvious, could only be explained by her access to the original Spirit form and therefore to the Mother Herself.

Vincavec, like old Mamut and the rest of the Mamuti, was now convinced that Ayla was not just Mamut – One Who Served the Mother – she had to be something more. Perhaps she embodied some supernatural presence; she might even be Mut Herself, incarnate. It was all the more believable because she did not flaunt it. But whatever her power, he was sure some important destiny awaited her. There was a reason for her existence, and he fervently wanted to be a part of it. She was the chosen of the Great Earth Mother.

"All your explanations have merit," Lomie said, persuasively, after she heard all of Ayla's objections, "but would you be willing to participate in the Calling ceremony, even if you don't think you have any Talent for it? Many people here are convinced that you will bring good luck to the mammoth hunt if you join in the Call, and offering good luck won't hurt you. It would make the Mamutoi very happy."

Ayla saw no way that she could refuse, but she was not comfortable with the adulation she had been getting. She almost hated to walk through the encampment now, and was looking forward to the mammoth hunt the next day with great excitement, and relief at the chance to get away for a while.

Ayla woke up and looked out the open triangular end of the lean-to travelling tent. Daylight was beginning to illuminate the eastern edge of the sky. She got up quietly, trying not to wake Ranec or anyone else, and slipped outside. The damp chill of early morning hung in the air, but no swarms of flying insects yet, for which she was grateful. Last night the air had been thick with them.

She walked to the edge of a black pool of stagnant water covered with slime and pollen; breeding grounds for the swarms of midges, gnats, blackflies, and mostly mosquitoes, that had risen to meet them like a high-pitched humming swirl of dark smoke. The insects had worked themselves under clothing, leaving a trail of red swollen bites, and swarmed around the eyes and choked the mouths of hunters and horses.

The fifty men and women selected for the first mammoth hunt of the season had reached the disagreeable but inevitable bogs. The permanently frozen ground beneath the surface layer, softened now by spring and summer melt, allowed no drainage to percolate through. Where the accumulation of melt was greater than could be dissipated by evaporation, the result was standing water. On any extended trek in the warmer season, it was likely that tracts of accumulated ground moisture would be found, ranging from large shallow melt lakes to still ponds that reflected the moving sky to swampy mires.

It had been too late in the afternoon to decide whether to attempt to cross the bog or find a way around it. Camp was quickly set up and fires lit to deter the flying hordes. The first night on the trek, those who had not seen Ayla's firestone used before made the usual exclamations of surprise and awe, but by now it was taken for granted that she would light the fire. The tents they used were simple shelters made of several hides that had been sewn together to make one large covering. Its shape depended upon structural materials that were found or brought with them. A mammoth skull with large tusks still intact might be used to hold up the hide cover, or the supple strength of a living dwarf willow could be bent to the task, even mammoth spears served double duty as tent poles on occasion. Sometimes it was just used as an extra ground cloth. This time the cover hide, which was shared by the hunters from Lion Camp with a few others, was draped across a slanting ridgepole with one end jammed into the ground and the other braced up by the crotch of a tree.

After they had made camp, Ayla searched around the dense vegetation near the bog and was pleased to find certain small plants with hand-shaped, dark green leaves. Digging down to the underground system of roots and rhizomes, she collected several, and boiled the greenish-yellow goldenseal root to make a healing and insect-repelling wash for the sore eyes and throats of the horses. When she used it on her own mosquito-bitten skin, several others asked to use it and she ended up treating the insect bites of the entire hunting party. She added more of the pounded root to fat to make a salve for the next day. Then she found a patch of fleabane and pulled up several plants to throw on the fire, as an additional deterrent along with ordinary smoke to help keep a small area close to the fire relatively insect free.

But in the cool damp of morning the flying scourges were quiescent. Ayla shivered and rubbed her arms, but made no move to return for a warmer covering. She stared at the dark water, hardly noticing the gradual encroachment of light from the east filling the entire vault of the sky, and bringing into sharp focus the tangled vegetation. She felt a warm fur drape her shoulders. Gratefully she pulled it around her, and felt arms encircle her waist from behind.

"You're cold, Ayla. You've been out here a long time," Ranec said.

"I couldn't sleep," she replied.

"What's wrong?"

"I don't know. Just an uneasy feeling. I can't explain it."

"You've been troubled ever since the Calling ceremony, haven't you?" Ranec said.

"I hadn't thought about it. You may be right."

"But you didn't participate. You only watched."

"I didn't want to participate, but I'm not sure. Something may have happened," Ayla said.

Immediately after breakfast, the hunters packed up and started travelling again. At first they attempted to skirt the bog, but there appeared to be no way around without making a long detour. Talut and several other hunt leaders peered into the dense, swampy thicket overhung by a cold misty fog, conferred with some of the others, and finally decided on a route that seemed to offer the easiest passage through.

The waterlogged ground near the edge soon gave way to a quivering fen. Many of the hunters removed their footwear and plunged into the cold, muddy water barefoot. Ayla and Jondalar led the nervous horses in more carefully. Cold-loving vines and long beards of greenish-grey lichen hung from dwarf birch, willow, and alder growing so closely together they formed a miniature arctic jungle. Footing was treacherous. With no solid ground to bind the roots and give stability, the trees grew at unlikely angles and sprawled along the ground, and the hunters struggled to make their way across fallen trunks, twisted brush, and partially submerged roots and branches that snared unsuspecting feet. Tufts of reeds and sedge grass looked deceitfully more substantial than they were, and mosses and ferns camouflaged stinking stagnant pools.

Progress was slow and exhausting. By midmorning, when they stopped to rest, everyone was sweating and warm, even in the shade. Starting out again, Talut ran into a particularly tenacious branch of an alder, and exploding in a rare outburst of anger, chopped at the tree furiously with his massive axe. The bright orange liquid seeping out of gashes in the offending tree resembled blood, and gave Ayla an unpleasant feeling of foreboding.

Nothing was so welcome as firm ground. Tall ferns and even taller grasses, more than the height of a man, grew on the rich clearing near the bog. They turned east to avoid wetlands that extended towards the west, then climbed a rise out of the depression in the plains filled by the bogs, and sighted the joining of a large river and a tributary. Talut, Vincavec, and the leaders of some of the other Camps stopped to consult maps marked on ivory, and scratched more marks on the ground with knives.

As they approached the river, they passed through the middle of a birch forest. Not a forest of the tall sturdy trees of warmer climates, these birches were stunted and dwarfed by the harsh periglacial conditions, yet they were not without beauty. As though pruned and shaped on purpose into endlessly fascinating individual shapes, each tree had a distinctive, pale, delicate grace. But the thin, frail, pendulous branches were misleading. When Ayla tried to break one, it was tough as sinew, and in the wind, they flailed the competing vegetation into submission.

"They're called the 'Old Mothers'."

Ayla spun around and saw Vincavec.

"An appropriate name, I think. They remind one never to misjudge the strength of an old woman. This is a sacred grove, and they are guardians of somuti," he said, pointing towards the ground.

The small quivering light green birch leaves did not entirely block out the sun, and dappled patterns of shade danced lightly on the forest floor thick with leaf mould. Then Ayla noticed, sprouting from the moss under certain trees, the large, white-spotted, bright red mushrooms.

"Those mushrooms, is that what you call somuti? They are poisonous. They can kill you," Ayla said.

"Yes, of course, unless you know the secrets of preparing them. That is so they will not be used inappropriately. Only those who are chosen may explore the world of somuti."

"Do they have medicinal qualities? I know of none," she asked.

"I don't know. I'm not a Healer. You'd have to ask Lomie," Vincavec said. Then, before she knew it, he had taken both her hands, and was looking at her, or rather, looking into her, she felt. "Why did you fight me at the Calling ceremony, Ayla? I had prepared the way to the underland for you, but you resisted me."

Ayla felt a strange sense of internal conflict, pulled two ways. Vincavec's voice was warm and compelling, and she felt a great desire to lose herself in the black depths of his eyes, to float in the cool dark pools, to give in to anything he wished. But she also felt an overpowering need to break away, to hold herself apart and maintain her own identity. With a wrenching effort of will, she tore her eyes away, and caught a glimpse of Ranec watching them. He quickly turned aside.

"You may have prepared a way, but I wasn't prepared," Ayla said, avoiding Vincavec's gaze. She looked up when he laughed. His eyes were grey, not black.

"You're good! You're strong, Ayla. I've never met anyone like you. You are so right for the Mammoth Hearth, for the Mammoth Camp. Tell me you'll share my hearth," Vincavec said, with every bit of persuasion and feeling he could bring to bear.

"I have Promised Ranec," she said.

"That doesn't matter, Ayla. Bring him along, if you wish. I would not mind sharing the Mammoth Hearth with so gifted a carver. Take us both! Or I'll take you both." He laughed again. "It would not be the first time. A man has a certain appeal, too!"

"I . . . I don't know," she said, then looked up at the muffled pounding of hooves.

"Ayla, I'm going to take Racer into the river and brush down his legs. Mud is caked up and drying on them. Do you want me to take Whinney, too?" Jondalar said.

"I'll take her myself," Ayla said, glad for the excuse to get away. Vincavec was fascinating, but a little frightening.

"She's over there, near Ranec," Jondalar said, turning towards the river.

Vincavec's eyes followed after the tall blond man. I wonder what part he plays in all this, the Mamut-headman thought. They arrived together, and he understands her animals, perhaps as well as she does, but they don't seem to be lovers, and it's not because he has trouble with women.

Avarie tells me they love him, but he never touches Ayla, never sleeps with her. It's said he turned down the Womanhood ritual because his feelings were too brotherly. Is that how he feels towards Ayla? Brotherly? Is that why he interrupted us and directed her back to the carver? Vincavec frowned, then carefully pulled up several of the large mushrooms and, with a cord, tied them upside down to the branches of the "Old Mothers" to dry. He planned to get them on the way back.

After they crossed the tributary, they reached a drier area, with open treeless bogs, farther apart. The honking, clacking, and squealing of waterfowl warned them of the large melt lake ahead. They set up camp not far from it and several people headed for the water to bring back supper. No fish were to be found in the temporary bodies of water, unless they happened to become part of a year-round river or stream, but amid the roots of tall phragmite reeds, bulrushes, sedges, and cattails swam the tadpoles of edible frogs and fire-bellied toads.

By some mysterious seasonal signal a vast array of birds, mostly waterfowl, came north to join the ptarmigan, the golden eagle, and the snowy owl. The spring thaw, that brought renewed plant growth and the great reedy marshes, invited the uncountable numbers of migrating fowl to stop, build nests, and proliferate. Many birds fed on the immature amphibians, and some on the adults, as well as newts and snakes, seeds and bulbs, on the inevitable insects, even on small mammals.

"Wolf would love this place," Ayla said to Brecie as she watched a couple of circling birds, with sling in hand, hoping they would come in closer to the edge so she wouldn't have to wade out too far to retrieve them. "He's getting very good at going in after them for me."

Brecie had promised to show Ayla her throwing stick, and wanted to see the young woman's much-touted expertise with the sling. Both had been mutually impressed. Brecie's weapon was an elongated, roughly diamond-shaped, crosswise section of leg bone, with the knobby epiphysis at the end removed and the edge sharpened. Its flight was circular, and thrown into a flock, several birds could be killed at one time. Ayla thought the throwing stick was much better for hunting birds than her sling, but the sling had more general application. She could also hunt animals with it.

"You brought the horses, why did you leave the wolf behind?" Brecie asked.

"Wolf is still so young I wasn't sure how he'd behave on a mammoth hunt, and I didn't want to take the chance that anything would go wrong on this one. The horses, though, can help bring meat back. Besides, I think Rydag would have been lonely without Wolf," Ayla said. "I miss them both."

Brecie was tempted to ask Ayla if she really did have a son like Rydag, then changed her mind. The subject was just too sensitive.

As they continued to head north over the next few days, a distinctive change came over the landscape. The bogs disappeared and, once they left the noisy birds behind, the sound of wind filled the treeless open plains with an eerie, wailing silence and a sense of desolation. The skies became overcast with a dull grey, featureless cloud cover that obscured the sun and hid the stars at night, but it seldom rained. Instead, the air felt drier, and colder, with a sharp wind that seemed to sap even the moisture from exhaled breath. But an occasional break in the clouds at evening vanquished the dull monotony of the heavens with a sunset so glowing, and so brilliant as it reflected off the moisture-laden upper skies, it left the travellers without words to describe it, daunted by its sheer beauty.

It was a land of far horizons. Low rolling hill followed low rolling hill, with no jagged peaks to lend distance and perspective, and no reed-green marshes to relieve the endless greys, browns, and dusty golds. The plains seemed to go on forever in all directions, except towards the north. There the vast sweep was swallowed by a dense misty fog that hid all signs of the world beyond, and deceived the eye about the distance to it.

The character of the land was neither grassy steppes nor frozen tundra, but a blend of both. Frost and drought-resistant tufted grasses, herbs with dense root systems, miniature woody shrubs of sagebrush and wormwood mingled with white arctic bell heather, miniature rhododendron, and pink crowberry flowers dominated the dainty purple blooms of alpine heath. Blueberry bushes no more than four inches high promised, nonetheless, a profusion of full-sized berries, and prostrate birch crawled along the ground like woody vines.

But even dwarfed trees were scarce with two sets of growing conditions opposing them. On true northern tundra, summer temperature is too low for germination and growth of tree seeds. On steppes, howling winds, that absorb moisture before it can accumulate, sweep across the landscape, and are as much a prohibiting factor as the cold. The combination left the land both frozen and dry.

Landscape even more bleak greeted the band of hunters as they pushed towards the thick white fog ahead. Bare rock and rubble was exposed, but it was covered with lichens; clinging scaly crusts of yellow, grey, brown, even bright orange that seemed more rock than plant. A few flowering herbs and miniature shrubs persisted, and the tough grasses and sedges covered sizeable patches. Even in this wild dreary place of cold dry winds that seemed incapable of supporting life, life went on.

Clues began to appear that hinted at the secret hidden within the mists. Scratches etched into large slabs of rock; long ridges of sand, stones and gravel; large stones out of place, as though dropped from the sky by an invisible giant hand. Water washed across the stony ground, in thin streams and gushing cloudy torrents, with no discernible pattern, and as they drew closer cold moisture in the air could at last be felt. Dirty snow lingered in shaded nooks, and in a depression beside a large boulder, old snow surrounded a small pool. Deep within it were shelves of ice of a rich and vivid shade of blue.

The wind shifted in the afternoon, and by the time the travellers set up camp, it was snowing, a dry, blowing snow. Talut and the others were conferring, disturbed. Vincavec had Called to the Mammoth Spirit several times to no avail. They had expected to find the great beasts before this.

At night, lying quietly in her bed, Ayla became aware of mysterious sounds that seemed to be coming from deep within the earth: grindings, poppings, chortlings, gurglings. She couldn't identify them, had no idea where they came from, and it made her nervous. She tried to sleep, but she kept waking up. Finally towards morning, exhaustion overcame her, and she gave in to slumber.

Ayla knew it was late when she woke up. It seemed unusually bright and everyone else was out of the tent. She grabbed her parka, but got only as far as the opening. When she looked out, she stopped and stared with her mouth hanging open. The shift in the wind had cleared away the summer mist of steaming ice temporarily. She bent her head back to look up at the wall of a glacier towering over her that was so incredibly massive the top was lost in clouds.

Its sheer size made it seem closer than it was, but some gigantic chunks that had once tumbled down the steep jagged wall were strewn together in a jumbled heap perhaps a quarter of a mile away. Several people were standing around them. She realised they were the scale that had given her a proper sense of the true size of the immense barrier of ice. The glacier was an incredible spectacle, and incredibly beautiful. In the sunlight – Ayla suddenly noticed the sun was out – it sparkled with millions of shattered crystals of ice that glinted with tints of prismatic hues, but the deep underlying colour had tones of the same startling blue that she had seen in the pool. There were no words adequate to describe it; overwhelming had no meaning beside its magnificence, its grandeur, its power.

Ayla finished dressing hurriedly, feeling she had missed out on something. She poured herself a cup of what seemed to be leftover tea with a slight film of ice already forming on top, and discovered it was meat broth instead. She paused only a moment before deciding it was fine, and drank it down. Then she scooped out a ladleful of congealed cooked grains, wrapped them in a thick slice of cold roast meat, and headed towards the rest of the hunters at a fast pace.

"I wondered if you were ever going to wake up," Talut said, when he saw her coming.

"Why didn't you wake me?" Ayla asked, then took her last bite.

"It's not wise to wake someone who is sleeping so soundly, unless it's an emergency," Talut answered.

"The spirit needs time for its night travels, so it can come back refreshed," Vincavec added, coming around to greet her. He made a motion to take both her hands, but she evaded them, quickly brushed his cheek with hers, and was off to examine the ice.

The huge chunks had obviously fallen with some force. They were deeply imbedded, and the ground was churned up around them. That they had also been there for several years was soon apparent, as well. An accumulation of wind-blown grit, picked up from the rock that was ground to flour at the margins of the ice, coated the top surfaces with a thick layer of dark grey dirt, striated in some places with intervening white layers of compact snow. The surfaces themselves were pitted and rough from melting and refreezing unevenly over the years, and a few small tenacious plants had actually taken root on the ice.

"Come up here, Ayla," Ranec called. She looked up and saw him standing on top of a high block, tilted slightly askew. She was surprised to see Jondalar beside him. "It's easy if you come around the side."

Ayla went around the jumbled pile of ice blocks and clambered up a series of broken shards and slabs. The gritty rock dust ground into the ice made the usually slick surface rough and footing reasonably secure. With a little care, it was easy to climb and move around. When she reached the highest place, Ayla stood up, then closed her eyes. The buffeting wind pushed against her, as though testing her resolve to withstand its force, and the voice of the great wall rumbled, moaned, and cracked nearby. She turned her head towards the intense light above, seen even through closed eyelids, and sensed with the skin of her face the cosmic struggle between the heat from the heavenly fire-ball, and the cold of the massive ice wall. The air itself tingled with indecision.

Then she opened her eyes. Ice commanded the view, filled her vision. The enormous, majestic, formidable expanse of ice that reached the sky marched across the entire breadth of the land as far as she could see. Mountains were insignificant beside it. The sight filled her with a humbling exultation, an awe-inspiring excitement. Her smile brought acknowledging smiles from Jondalar and Ranec.

"I've seen it before," Ranec said, "but I could see it as many times as there are stars in the sky and never get tired of it." Both Ayla and Jondalar nodded in agreement.

"It can be dangerous, though," Jondalar added.

"How did this ice get here?" Ayla asked.

"The ice moves," Ranec said. "Sometimes it grows, sometimes it shrinks back. This split off when the wall was here. This pile was much bigger then. It has been shrinking, like the wall." Ranec studied the glacier. "I think it was farther away last time. The ice may be growing again."

Ayla swept her gaze across the open landscape then, noticing how much farther she could see from her higher vantage point. "Oh, look!" she cried, pointing towards the southeast. "Mammoths! I see a herd of mammoths!"

"Where?" Ranec said, suddenly excited.

The excitement spread through the hunters like fire. Talut, who had started around the side at the sound of the word "mammoths", was already halfway up the ice pile. He reached the top in a few strides, put his hand across his forehead as a sunshade, and looked where Ayla had pointed.

"She's right! There they are! Mammoths!" he boomed, unable to restrain his emotion, or the volume of his voice.

Several others were climbing up the ice, each looking for a place to view the great tusked creatures. Ayla stepped down out of the way so Brecie could stand in her place.

There was a certain relief in sighting the mammoths, as well as excitement. At least they were finally showing themselves. Whatever it was that the Spirit Mammoth had been waiting for, she had finally allowed her creatures of this world to present themselves to those who were chosen by Mut to hunt mammoths.

One of the women of Brecie's Camp mentioned to one of the men that she had seen Ayla standing on the very top of the ice pile with her eyes closed, turning her head as though Seeking something, or perhaps Calling it, and when she opened her eyes, there were the mammoths. The man nodded in understanding.

Ayla was staring down at the shape of the pile of ice below, about ready to descend. Talut appeared beside her, smiling as big a grin as she had ever seen.

"Ayla, you have made this headman a very happy man," the red-bearded giant said.

"I didn't do anything," Ayla said. "I just happened to see them."

"That's enough. Whoever happened to see them first would have made me a very happy man. But I'm glad it was you," Talut said.

Ayla smiled at him. She really did love the big headman. She thought of him as an uncle, or a brother, or a friend, and she felt he cared about her the same way.

"What were you looking at down there, Ayla?" Talut said, starting to follow her down.

"Nothing in particular. I was just noticing that you can see the shape of this pile from here. See how it comes in on the side where we climb up and then curves back around?"

Talut gave it a cursory look, then found himself looking closer. "Ayla! You've done it again!"

"Done what?"

"You have made this headman a very happy man!"

His smile was contagious. She smiled back. "What makes you happy this time, Talut?" she said.

"You made me notice the shape of this ice pile. It's like a blind canyon. Not quite complete, but we can fix that. Now I know how we're going to hunt those mammoths!"

No time was lost. The mammoths could decide to move away, or the weather could change again. The hunters had to take advantage of the opportunity immediately. The hunt leaders conferred, then quickly sent out several scouts to investigate the lay of the land and the size of the herd. While they were gone, a wall of rock and ice was built to block the open space in one side of the cold canyon, making the tumbled pile of ice into an enclosure with only one opening. When the scouts returned, the hunters gathered to devise a plan to drive the huge woolly animals into the trap.

Talut told how Ayla and Whinney had helped to drive bison into a trap. Many people were quite interested, but they all reached the conclusion that with the huge behemoths, a single rider on horseback would not be able to start a concerted drive, though she might be of some help. To get them started towards the trap, some other means would have to be found.

Fire was the answer. Late summer lightning storms had set enough dry fields on fire that even massive mammoths, who feared little, had a healthy respect for it. At this season of the year, however, it might be difficult to get a grass fire going. The fire would have to be in the form of torches, held in the hands of the drivers.

"What'll we use for torches?" someone asked.

"Dry grass and mammoth dung, bound together and dipped in fat," Brecie said, "so they'll catch fast and burn hot."

"And we can use Ayla's firestone to start them quickly," Talut added. There were nods of agreement.

"We're going to need fire in more than one place," Brecie said, "and in the right sequence."

"Ayla has given each of the hearths of Lion Camp a firestone. We have several with us. I have one, and so does Ranec. Jondalar has one, too," Talut said, aware of the added prestige his announcement gave them. Too bad Tulie isn't here, he thought. She would have appreciated the moment. Ayla's firestones were priceless, particularly since they were apparently not too abundant.

"Once we get the mammoths moving, how do we make sure they head for the trap?" the woman from Brecie's Camp asked. "This is open country."

The plan they worked out was simple and direct. They constructed two rows of cairns out of broken chunks of ice and rock, fanning out from the opening of the ice canyon. Talut, with his massive axe, made short work of breaking the large glacier shards into pieces small enough to carry. Several torches were deposited behind each cairn in readiness. Of the fifty hunters, a few chose places within the canyon itself, behind protective blocks of ice, for the first frontal assault. Others ranged out behind the stone cairns. The rest, primarily the fastest, strongest runners – for all their great bulk, mammoths were capable of great bursts of speed for short distances – would split into two groups, to circle around both sides of the herd.

Brecie began explaining some traits and vulnerabilities of mammoths and how to hunt them to the younger hunters, who had not hunted the great shaggy beasts before. Ayla listened carefully, and walked into the ice canyon with them. The headwoman of Elk Camp would lead the frontal assault from inside and wanted to inspect the trap and select her place.

As soon as they were within the icy walls, Ayla noticed the drop in temperature. With the fire they had made to melt the fat for the torches, and the exertion of cutting grass and carrying hunks of ice, she hadn't noticed the cold. Yet, they were so near the great glacier that water left out overnight usually had a film of ice in the morning even in summer, and parkas were necessary during the day. Inside the frozen enclosure the cold was intense, but as Ayla looked around the spacious chamber in the midst of the jagged tumble of ice, she felt she had entered another place, a white and blue world of stark and chilling beauty.

Like the rocky canyons near her valley, large blocks, newly sheared from the walls, lay scattered and broken on the ground. Above them sharp-edged pinnacles and soaring spires of sparkling white shaded in the cracks and corners to a deep, rich, vivid blue. She was reminded, suddenly, of Jondalar's eyes. The softer, rounded edges of older blocks and slabs scattered in fallen heaps, worn down with time and covered with a fine wind-blown grit, invited climbing and exploring.

Ayla did, just out of curiosity, while the others were looking for hunting places. She would not be waiting here for the mammoths. She and Whinney would help chase the woolly tuskers, as would Jondalar and Racer. The speed of the horses would be helpful, and she and Jondalar would each provide a firestone for one of the groups of drivers. Ayla noticed more people gathering around the entrance and hurried out. Whinney was following Jondalar and Racer from the campsite. Ayla whistled and the mare cantered ahead of them.

The two groups of drivers started towards the mammoth herd, swinging wide to circle around behind without causing too much disturbance. Ranec and Talut were each behind one of the rows of cairns that converged towards the ice canyon, ready to supply quick fire when it was needed. Ayla waved at Talut and smiled at Ranec as she passed them waiting near a pile of ice and stone. Vincavec was on the same side as Ranec, she noticed. She returned his smile, too.

Ayla walked ahead of Whinney, her spears and spear-thrower secured in the holders of the pack baskets, along with the group's torches. Several other hunters were nearby, but no one spoke much. Everyone was concentrating on the mammoths, fervently hoping that the hunt would be successful. Ayla glanced back at Whinney, then at the herd ahead. They were still grazing in the same field of grass where she had first seen them not so very long ago, she realised. Everything had happened so fast she'd hardly had time to think. They had accomplished a great deal in a very short time.

She had always wanted to hunt mammoth, and a chill of anticipation shot through her when she realised that she was actually about to participate in the first mammoth hunt of her life. Though there was something utterly ridiculous about it, when she stopped to consider it. How could creatures as small and weak as humans challenge the huge, shaggy, tusked beast, and hope to succeed? Yet here she was, ready to take on the largest animal that walked the land, with nothing more than a few mammoth spears. No, that wasn't entirely true. She also had the intelligence, experience, and cooperation of the other hunters. And Jondalar's spear-thrower.

Would the new spear-thrower he developed to be used with the bigger spears work? They had tried them out, but she still wasn't totally comfortable with hers.

Ayla caught sight of Racer and the other group coming towards them through the dry grass, and the mammoth herd seemed to be moving more. Were they becoming nervous about the people trying to edge around them? The pace of her group was quickening; others were worried, too. A signal was passed to get the torches. Ayla quickly pulled them out of Whinney's packbaskets and handed them out. They waited anxiously, watching the other group get its torches. Then, the hunt leader signalled.

Ayla slipped off her mittens and squatted down over a small pile of fireweed lint and crushed dung. The others hovered close, waiting. She struck her fire-starting flint against the yellowish-grey chunk of iron pyrite. The spark died. She struck again. It seemed to take. She struck again, adding more sparks to the smouldering tinder, and tried to blow it into flame. Then a sudden gust of wind came to her aid, and the fire suddenly enveloped the tinder and crushed dung. She added a few lumps of tallow to help it burn hotter, and sat back while the first of the hunters held their torches to the flames. They lit each other's torches, then began to fan out.

There was no absolute signal to begin the drive. It began slowly, as the disorganised hunters made dashes towards the giant beasts, shouting and waving their smoky, movable flames. But most of the Mamutoi were experienced mammoth hunters, and used to hunting together. Soon the efforts became more concerted as both groups of drivers combined and the shaggy elephants began moving towards the cairns.

A big she-mammoth, the matriarch of the herd, seeming to notice a purpose in the confusion, turned aside. Ayla started running towards her, screaming and waving her torch. She had a sudden recollection of trying to chase a herd of horses once, alone, with only smoky torches to assist. All but one of the horses got away – no, two, she thought. The nursing mare fell into her pit trap, but not the little yellow foal. She glanced back at Whinney.

The screaming trumpet of the she-mammoth caught her by surprise. She turned back in time to see the old matriarch eyeing the weak, insignificant creatures who were carrying the smell of danger, then start a run, in Ayla's direction. But this time, the young woman was not alone. She looked up to see Jondalar at her side, then several others, more than the huge tusked woolly wanted to face. Lifting her trunk to trumpet a warning of fire, she rose up and screamed again, then dodged back.

The patch of dry standing hay was on higher ground, not subject to the summer runoff of the glacier, and though there were mists, no rain had fallen for many days. The fires that had been used to start the torches were left untended and soon they spread through the grass, encouraged by the sharp wind. The mammoths noticed the fire first, not only the smell of burning grass, but of scorched earth and smouldering brush; the familiar smell of a prairie fire and even more threatening. The old matriarch trumpeted again, joined now by a chorus of blaring screams as the shaggy reddish-brown beasts, young and old, picked up speed and stampeded towards an unknown but far greater danger.

A crosswind sent a billow of smoke towards the hunters racing to keep up with the herd. Ayla, ready to mount Whinney, glanced back at the blaze, and understood what had impelled the great behemoths in their panic. She watched for a moment as the crackling red flames hungrily devoured their way across the field, spitting sparks and belching smoke. But she knew the fire was no real threat. Even if it managed to cross the areas of rocky bare ground, the ice canyon itself would stop it. She noticed Jondalar was already on Racer, following close behind the retreating mammoths, and hurried after him.

Ayla could hear her hard breathing when she passed the young woman from Brecie's Camp, who had run all the way, staying close behind the great beasts. It would be harder for them to turn aside once they were committed to the route that would take them inevitably into the cold canyon, and the two women smiled at each other when the herd entered the lane between the cairns. Ayla rode ahead; it was her turn to harry them now.

She noticed fires starting up along the way behind the cairns, at the sides and a little ahead of the ponderous giants. They did not want to light the torches too far ahead of them and risk turning the herd aside now that they were so close. Suddenly she was approaching the opening in the ice. She pulled Whinney aside, grabbed her spears and jumped off, and felt the vibrations of the earth as the last mammoth pounded into the trap. She dashed in and joined the chase, following close on the heels of an old bull with tusks crossed over in front. More burnable materials, which had been piled into mounds at the opening, were lit in an attempt to keep the frightened animals inside. Jogging around a fire, Ayla again entered the cold enclosure.

No longer was it a place of stark, serene beauty. Instead blaring screams of mammoths echoed off hard, icy walls, grating on the ears, and racking on the nerves. Ayla was filled with almost unbearable tension, part fear, part excitement. She swallowed her fear, and fitted her first spear into the groove in the middle of the spear-thrower.

The she-mammoth had moved towards the far end, looking for a way to lead the herd out, but Brecie was waiting there, up high on a block of ice. The old matriarch raised her trunk and trumpeted her frustration, and the headwoman of Elk Camp hurled a spear down her open throat. The scream was cut short in a gurgle of liquid that spouted from her mouth and sprayed the cold white ice with warm red blood.

The young man from Brecie's Camp threw a second spear. The long, sharp flint point pierced the tough hide and lodged deep in the abdomen. Another spear followed, and also found the soft underbelly, tearing a

596

long gash from the weight of the shaft. The mammoth uttered a hoarse rattle of pain as blood and shiny grey-white ropes of intestines gushed from the wound. Her hind legs became tangled in her own viscera. Yet another spear was cast at the doomed beast, but hit a rib bone and bounced off. The one that followed found a space between two ribs for the long, flat, thin blade to pierce.

The old she-mammoth sunk to her knees, tried once to rise up, then fell over on her side. Her trunk rose once more in an effort to cry a warning, then slowly, almost gracefully, dropped to the ground. Brecie touched a spear to the head of the valiant old cow, praised her brave struggle, and thanked the Great Mother for the sacrifice which allowed Earth's children to survive.

Brecie was not the only one who stood over a brave mammoth and thanked the Mother. Teams of hunters had informally grouped together for a multiple attack on each animal. Spears that were thrown allowed them to stay out of range of the tusks and trunks and heavy feet of the mammoths they singled out, but they also had to watch out for the animals that were the prey of other hunters in the close quarters. Blood pouring out of the wounded and dying beasts softened the ice of the partially frozen ground, then froze in bright red slicks, making footing hazardous. The icy canyon was a mêlée of hunters' shouts and mammoths' screams, and the glimmering walls amplified and reverberated every sound.

After watching a few moments, Ayla went after a young bull, whose heavy tusks were long and curved, but still useful as weapons. She settled the heavy spear on the new thrower, trying to get the right feel. She recalled Brecie saying that the stomach was one of the more vulnerable places on a mammoth, and Ayla had been quite impressed by the disembowelling of the herd matriarch. She took aim and with a hard throw, cast the lethal weapon across the icy canyon.

It flew fast and true, and struck the abdominal cavity. But with the power of the weapon and the strength of her throw, and without others ready to assist, she should have aimed for a more vital spot. A spear in the stomach was not immediately fatal. He was bleeding profusely, mortally wounded, but the pain enraged him, giving him the strength to turn on his attacker. The bull mammoth blared a challenge, lowered his head and thundered towards the young woman.

The long-distance cast of the spear-thrower gave Ayla her only advantage. She dropped her spears and raced towards a block of ice. But her foot slipped as she tried to climb up. She scrambled behind it just as the huge mammoth slammed into it with all his force. His massive tusks cracked the gigantic block of frozen water in two and jammed it back, knocking the wind out of Ayla. Then screaming his frustration, and his dying, he jabbed and tore at the slab of ice, trying to get at the creature behind it. Suddenly two spears flew in quick succession, and found the maddened bull. One landed in his neck, the other cracked a rib with such tremendous force, it reached his heart.

The mammoth crumpled in a heap beside the broken ice. His blood spilled from his wounds into deep red pools that steamed, then chilled, then hardened on the cold glacial ice. Still shaking, Ayla crawled out from behind the block.

"Are you all right?" Talut said, reaching her in time to help her stand up.

"Yes, I think so," she said, somewhat breathless.

Talut reached for the spear that was sticking out of the mammoth's chest, gave a mighty heave and yanked it out. A new spate of blood poured forth as Jondalar reached them.

"Ayla, I was certain he had you!" Jondalar said. The look on his face was more than worried. "You should have waited until I came . . . or someone came to help you. Are you sure you're all right?"

"Yes, I am, but I'm very glad you two were around," she said, then smiled. "Hunting mammoth can be exciting."

Talut studied her carefully for a moment. She'd had a close call. That mammoth almost had her, but she did not seem unusually upset. A little breathless and excited, but that was normal. He grinned and nodded, then examined the point and shaft of his spear. "Hah! It's still good!" he said. "I can get another one with this sticker!" He waded back into the fray.

Ayla's eyes followed the big headman, but Jondalar was looking at her; his heart was still pounding with fear for her. He'd almost lost her! That mammoth nearly killed her! Her hood was thrown back and her hair was in disarray. Her eyes were sparkling with excitement. Her face was flushed and she was breathing hard. She was beautiful in her excitement, and the effect was immediate and overwhelming.

His beautiful woman, he thought. His wonderful, exciting Ayla. What would he have done if he'd lost her? He felt the blood rush to his loins. His fear at the thought of losing her, and his love, awakened his need, and filled him with a strong desire to hold her. He wanted her. He wanted her more than he'd ever wanted her in his life. He could have taken her that instant, right there on the cold, bloody floor of the ice canyon.

She glanced up at him and saw his look, felt the irresistible charisma of eyes as vividly blue as a deep glacial pool, but warm. He wanted her. She knew he wanted her, and she wanted him with a fire that seared her and would not be quenched. She loved him, more than she dreamed it

598

was possible to love anyone. She stretched up to him, reaching for him, hungering for his kiss, for his touch, for his love.

"Talut just told me about it!" Ranec said, running towards them, panic in his voice. "Is that the bull?" He looked stunned. "Are you sure you are not hurt, Ayla?"

Ayla stared at Ranec for a moment, uncomprehending, and saw a veil drop over Jondalar's eyes as he stepped back. Then the sense of Ranec's question reached her.

"No, I'm not hurt, Ranec. I'm fine," Ayla said, but she wasn't sure if it was true. Her mind was in a turmoil as she watched Jondalar yank his spear out of the mammoth's neck and walk away. She watched him go.

She's not my Ayla any more, and it's my own fault! he thought. Suddenly he remembered the incident on the steppes the first time he rode Racer, and was filled with remorse, and shame. He knew what a terrible crime that was, and yet he could have done it again. Ranec was a better man for her. He had turned his back on her, and then defiled her. He didn't deserve her. He had hoped he was beginning to accept the inevitable, hoped that some day, after he returned to his home, he might forget Ayla. He was even able to enjoy a level of friendship with Ranec. But now he knew that the pain of losing her would never go away, he would never get over Ayla.

He saw a mammoth, the last one standing, a young one that had somehow escaped the carnage. Jondalar heaved his spear at the animal with such violent force, it was brought to its knees. Then he stalked out of the icy canyon. He had to get away, to be alone. He walked until he knew he was out of sight of the rest of the hunters. Then he put his hands up to his head, and gritted his teeth, and tried to get himself under control. He dropped to the ground and pounded his fists on the earth.

"O Doni," he cried out, trying to rid himself of his pain and misery, "I know it's my fault. I was the one who turned my back on her and pushed her away. It wasn't just jealousy, I was ashamed to love her. I was afraid she wouldn't be good enough for my people, afraid she wouldn't be accepted, and I would be turned out because of her. But I don't care about that any more. I'm the one who's not good enough for her, but I love her. O Great Mother, I love her, and I want her. Doni, how I want her! No other woman means anything. I come away from them empty. Doni, I want her back. I know it's too late, now, but I want my Ayla back."

36

Talut was never more in his element than when they butchered mammoths. Bare-chested, sweating profusely, swinging his massive axe as though it were a child's toy, he cracked bones and ivory, split tendons, and ripped through tough skin. He enjoyed the work and knowing it helped his people, took delight in using his powerful body and making the effort less for someone else, grinned with pleasure as he used his massive muscles in a way that no one else could, and everyone who watched him had to smile, too.

Skinning the thick hides from the huge animals, however, took many people, just as curing and tanning the skins would when they returned. Even bringing them back required cooperative effort, which was why they selected only the best. The same held true for every other part of the huge animals, from tusks to tails. They were especially discriminating in their selection of meat, picking only the choicest cuts, preferring those rich with fat, and leaving the rest.

But the wastage was not as great as it seemed. The Mamutoi had to carry everything on their backs, and the transport of poor quality lean meat could cost them more calories than they gained. With careful selection, the food they brought back would feed many people for a long time, and they would not have to hunt again soon. Those who hunted, and depended on hunting for food, did not overkill. They simply utilised wisely. They lived close to the Great Earth Mother, knew and understood their dependence on Her. They did not squander Her resources.

The weather stayed remarkably clear while the hunters butchered, causing dramatic swings in temperature between midday and midnight. Even so, near the great glacier, the days could get quite warm in the bright summer sun – warm enough, with the desiccating wind, to dry some of the leaner meat, and make it reasonable to carry back. But nights always belonged to the ice. On the day of their departure, a shift in the wind brought scattered clouds in the west, and a noticeable cooling.

Ayla's horses were never so appreciated as when she loaded them for the trip back. Every hunter was preparing a full load, and immediately understood the benefits of the pack animals. The travois provoked particular interest. Several people had wondered why Ayla insisted on dragging the long poles with her; they were obviously not spears. Now they were nodding approval. One of the men, jokingly, even picked up a partially loaded travois and dragged it himself.

Though they woke early, eager to get back, it was mid-morning before they got underway. Sometime after noon, the hunters climbed a long, narrow hill of sand, gravel, and boulders, deposited long before by the leading edge of the glacier broaching farther south. When they reached the rounded ridge of the esker, they stopped for a rest, and looking back, Ayla saw the glacier unshrouded by mists from the perspective of distance for the first time. She could not stop looking at it.

Gleaming in the sun, a few clouds in the west obscuring its upper reaches, a continuous barrier of ice the height of a mountain stretched across the land as far as she could see, marking a boundary beyond which none could go. It was truly the end of the earth.

The front edge was uneven, accommodating minor local differences in terrain, and a climb to the top would have revealed dips and ridges, seracs, and crevices quite extensive on a human scale, but in relation to its own size, the surface was uniformly level. Sweeping beyond imagination, the vast inexorable glacier sheathed a quarter of the earth's surface with a glittering carapace of ice. Ayla kept looking back when they started out again, and watched the western clouds move in and the mists rise, veiling the ice in mystery.

In spite of their heavy packs, they travelled faster on the trek back than they had on the way there. Each year the terrain changed enough over the winter that the route, even to well-known places, had to be re-explored. But the way to the northern glacier, and back, was now known. Everyone was jubilant and in good spirits about the successful hunt, and eager to return to the Meeting. No one seemed weighted down by their load, except Ayla. As they travelled, the feeling of foreboding she had experienced on their way north became even stronger on the way back, but she avoided any mention of her misgivings.

The carver was so full of anxious anticipation he found it hard to contain himself. The anxiety stemmed largely from Vincavec's continuing interest in Ayla, though he felt a vague sense of deeper conflicts as well. But Ayla was still Promised to him, and they were carrying the meat for the Matrimonial Feast. Even Jondalar seemed to have accepted the joining, and although nothing was explicitly stated, Ranec sensed that the tall man was siding with him against Vincavec. The Zelandonii man had many admirable qualities, and a tentative relationship was developing. Nonetheless, Ranec felt Jondalar's presence was a tacit threat to his joining with Ayla, and could be an obstacle that stood between him and complete happiness. Ranec would be happy when he finally left.

Ayla was not looking forward to the Matrimonial Ceremony at all, though she knew she should have been. She knew how much Ranec loved her, and she believed she could be happy with him. The idea of having a baby like Tricie's filled her with delight. In her own mind, Ayla knew beyond doubt that Ralev was Ranec's child. Not the result of any mixing of spirits, she was sure that he had started the child with his own essence when he shared Pleasures with Tricie. Ayla liked the red-haired woman, and felt sorry for her. She decided she would not mind sharing Ranec and the hearth with her and Ralev, if Tricie wanted to.

It was only in the darkest depths of night that Ayla admitted to herself that she might be just as happy not living at Ranec's hearth at all. She had generally avoided sleeping with him during the trip out, except for a few occasions when he seemed to be in special need of her, not physically, but because he wanted reassurances and closeness. On the way back, she had not been able to share Pleasures with Ranec. Instead, in her bed at night, she could think only of Jondalar. The same questions went through her mind over and over again, but she could come to no conclusion.

When she thought of the day of the hunt, of her close call with the bull mammoth, and of the look of aching need in Jondalar's eyes, she wondered if it was possible that he still loved her. Then why had he been so distant all winter? Why had he stopped finding Pleasure in her? Why had he left the Mammoth Hearth? She remembered that day on the steppes the first time he rode Racer. When she thought of his desire, his need, and her willing and eager acceptance, she could not sleep for wanting him, but the memory was clouded by his rejection, and her feelings of pain and confusion.

After one particularly long day, and a late meal, Ayla was among the first to leave the fire and head for the tent. She had turned down Ranec's hopeful implied request to share his furs with a smile and a comment about being tired after the day's trek, and then, seeing his disappointment, felt bad. But she was tired, and very uncertain about her feelings. She caught sight of Jondalar near the horses before she entered the tent. He was turned away from her, and she watched him, unintentionally fascinated by the shape of his body, the way he moved, the way he stood. She knew him so well, she thought she could recognise him by the shadow he cast. Then she noticed her body had responded to him unintentionally, too. She was breathing faster and her face was flushed, and she felt so drawn to him, she started in his direction.

But it's no use, she thought. If I went over to talk to him, he would just back away, make some excuses, and then go find someone else to talk to. Ayla went into the tent, still full of the feelings he had caused in her, and crawled into her furs.

She had been tired, but now she couldn't sleep, and tossed and turned, trying to deny her yearning for him. What was wrong with her? He didn't seem to want her, why should she want him? But then why did he look at her that way sometimes? Why did he want her so much that time on the steppes? It was as though he was so drawn to her, he couldn't help it. A thought struck her then, and she frowned. Maybe he was drawn to her, the way she was drawn to him, but maybe he didn't want to be. Had that been the problem all along?

She felt herself redden again, but this time with chagrin. Thinking about it that way, it suddenly seemed to make sense, all his avoiding her and running away from her. Was it because he didn't *want* to want her? When she thought of all the times she had tried to approach him, tried to talk to him, tried to understand him, when all he wanted was to avoid her, she felt humiliated. He doesn't want me, she thought. Not like Ranec does. Jondalar said he loved me, and talked about taking me with him, when we were in the valley, but he never asked me to join with him. He never said he wanted to share a hearth, or that he wanted my children.

Ayla felt hot tears at the corners of her eyes. Why should I care about him, when he doesn't really care about me? She sniffed, and wiped her eyes with the backs of her hands. All this time when I've been thinking about him, and wanting him, he just wanted to forget me.

Well, Ranec wants me, and he makes good Pleasures, too. And he is so good to me. He wants to share a hearth with me, and I haven't even been very nice to him. And he makes nice babies, too, at least Tricie's baby is nice. I think I should start being nicer to Ranec, and forget about Jondalar, she thought. But even as the words formed in her mind, her tears broke forth again, and try as she would she could not stop the thought that rose up from deep within. Yes, Ranec is good to me but Ranec is not Jondalar, and I love Jondalar.

Ayla was still awake when people started to come into the tent. She watched Jondalar come through the opening, and saw him look in her direction, hesitating. She looked back at him for a moment, then she raised her chin and looked away. Ranec came in just then. She sat up and smiled at him.

"I thought you were tired. That's why you went to bed early," the carver said.

"I thought I was, but I couldn't go to sleep. I think maybe I'd like to share your furs, after all," she said.

The brightness of Ranec's smile could have rivalled the sun, if it had been shining.

"It's a good thing nothing can keep me awake when I'm tired," Talut said with a good-natured grin, as he sat down on his sleeping roll to untie his boots. But Ayla noticed that Jondalar did not smile. He had closed his eyes, but it didn't hide his grimace of pain, or the slump of defeat as he walked towards his sleeping place. Suddenly, he turned around and hurried back out of the tent. Ranec and Talut exchanged a glance, but then the dark man looked at Ayla.

When they reached the bog, they decided to look for a way around. They were carrying too much to fight their way through it again. The ivory route map of the previous year was consulted, and a decision was made to change direction the following morning. Talut was sure it would not take any more time to go the long way around, though he had some trouble convincing Ranec, who could not abide any delays.

The evening before they decided to take the new route, Ayla felt unusually edgy. The horses had been skittish all day, too, and even the attention of brushing and currying them hadn't settled them down. Something felt wrong. She didn't know what it was, just a strange unease. She started walking across the open steppes, trying to relax, and wandered away from camp.

She spied a covey of ptarmigan, and looked for her sling, but she had forgotten it. Suddenly, for no apparent reason, they took flight in a panic. Then a golden eagle appeared above the horizon. With deceptively slow wing motions, it rode the currents of air, and seemed in no great hurry. Yet, more quickly than she realised, the eagle was gaining on the low-flying grouse. Suddenly, in a flurry of speed, the eagle snatched its victim in strong talons, and squeezed the ptarmigan to death.

Ayla shuddered and hurried back to camp. She stayed up late, talking to people, trying to distract herself. But when she went to bed, sleep came slowly, and then was filled with unsettling dreams. She woke often, and sometime around daybreak, found herself awake again, and unable to go back to sleep. Slipping out of her bedroll, she went out of the tent, and started up the fire to boil water.

She sipped her morning tea as the sky grew lighter, staring absently at a thin stalk with a dried flower umbel growing near the fireplace. A half-eaten haunch of cold roast mammoth had been raised up high, on top of a tripod of mammoth spears, directly over the fire, to protect it from marauding animals. Recognition of the wild carrot plant dawned on her, and noticing a fractured branch with a pointed end in the woodpile, she used it as a digging stick to uncover the root a few inches below the surface. Then she noticed several more dried flower umbels, and while she was digging them, she saw some thistle stalks, crisp and juicy after the spines were scraped off. Not far from the thistles, she found a big puffball mushroom, still white and fresh, and day lilies with crisp new buds. By the time people were stirring, Ayla had a large basket pot of soup, thickened with cracked grains, simmering.

"This is wonderful!" Talut said, scooping up a second serving with an ivory ladle. "What made you decide to cook such a delicious breakfast this morning?"

"I couldn't sleep, and then I noticed all the vegetables growing nearby. It took my mind off . . . things," she said.

"I slept like a bear in winter," Talut said, then studied her closely, wishing Nezzie was there. "Is something troubling you, Ayla?"

She shook her head. "No . . . well, yes. But I don't know what it is."

"Are you sick?"

"No, it's not that. I just feel . . . strange. The horses notice something, too. Racer is hard to manage, and Whinney is nervous . . ."

Suddenly Ayla dropped her cup, and clutching her arms as though to protect herself, stared in horror at the southeastern sky. "Talut! Look!" A column of dark grey was rising upwards in the distance, and a massive, billowing dark cloud was filling up the sky. "What is it?"

"I don't know," the big headman said, looking as frightened as she felt. "I'll get Vincavec."

"I am not sure, either." They turned towards the voice of the tattooed shaman. "It's coming from the mountains in the southeast." Vincavec was struggling to keep his composure, he was not supposed to show his fears, but it was not easy. "It must be a sign from the Mother."

Ayla was sure some terrible catastrophe was happening for the earth to spew forth like that with such force. The dark grey column must have been unbelievably huge to look so large from so far away, and the cloud, roiling and surging angrily, was growing larger. High winds were beginning to push it westward.

"It's the milk of Doni's Breast," Jondalar said, more matter-of-factly than he felt, using a word from his own language. Everyone was out of the tents now, staring at the terrifying eruption and the huge bloated cloud of seething volcanic ash.

"What is . . . that word you said?" Talut asked.

"It's a mountain, a special kind of mountain that spouts. I saw one when I was very young," Jondalar said. "We call them the 'Breasts of the Mother'. Old Zelandoni told us the legend about them. The one I saw was far away on the high midlands. Later a man who was travelling, and was closer to it, told us what he saw. It was a very exciting story, but he was scared. There were some small earthquakes, then the top of the mountain blew right off. It sent up a big spout like that, and made a black cloud that filled the sky. It's not like a regular cloud, though. It's full of a light dust, like ash. That one" – he motioned towards the huge black cloud that was streaming towards the west – "looks like it's blowing away from us. I hope the wind doesn't shift. When that ash settles, it covers everything. Sometimes very deep."

"It must be far away," Brecie said. "We can't even see the mountains from here, and there are no sounds, no roars and rumbles and shaking of the ground. Just that huge spout and the great dark cloud."

"That's why, even if the ash falls around here, it may not be too bad. We're far enough away."

"You said there were earthquakes? Earthquakes are always a sign from the Mother. This must be, too. The Mamuti will have to meditate on this, find its meaning," Vincavec said, not wanting to appear less knowledgeable than the stranger.

Ayla did not hear much beyond "earthquake". There was nothing in the world she feared so much as earthquakes. She had lost her family when she was five to a violent rending of the solid earth, and another earthquake had killed Creb when Broud had expelled her from the Clan. Earthquakes had always presaged devastating loss, wrenching change. She kept control of herself only by the thinnest edge.

Then, out of the corner of her eye, she caught a familiar movement. The next instant, a streak of grey fur raced towards her, jumped up, and put wet, muddy paws on her chest. She felt the lick of a raspy tongue on her jaw.

"Wolf! Wolf! What are you doing here?" she said, as she ruffed up his neck. Then she stopped, horror-stricken, and cried out. "Oh, no! It's Rydag! Wolf has come for me, to take me to Rydag! I must go. I must go immediately!"

"You'll have to leave the travois and the horses' back loads here, and ride back," Talut said. The pain in his eyes was evident. Rydag was the son of his hearth just as much as any of Nezzie's children, and the headman loved him. If he could have, if he wasn't so big, Ayla would have offered to let him ride Racer and come back with her.

She ran into the tent to dress and saw Ranec. "It's Rydag," she said.

"I know. I just heard you. Let me help. I'll put some food and water in your pack. Will you need your bedroll? I'll pack it, too," he said, while she was wrapping ties around her boots.

"Oh, Ranec," Ayla said. He was so good to her. "How can I thank you!"

"He's my brother, Ayla."

Of course! she thought. Ranec loves him, too. "I'm sorry. I'm not thinking right. Do you want to come back with me? I was thinking of asking Talut, but he's too big to ride Racer. You could, though."

"Me? Get up on a horse? Never!" Ranec said, looking startled and pulling back a little.

Ayla frowned. She hadn't realised he felt so strongly about the horses, but now that she thought about it, he was one of the few who had never asked for a ride. She wondered why.

"I wouldn't have the first idea how to guide him, and . . . I'm afraid I'd fall off, Ayla. It's all right for you, that's one of the things I love about you, but I'll never ride a horse," Ranec said. "I prefer my own two feet. I don't even like boats."

"But someone must go with her. She should not go back alone," Talut said from just beyond the entrance.

"She won't," Jondalar said. He was dressed in travelling clothes, standing beside Whinney, holding Racer's bridle.

Ayla breathed a great sigh of relief, and then frowned. Why was he going with her? He never wanted to go anywhere with her, alone. He didn't really care about her. She was glad he would be with her, but she wasn't going to tell him. She had already humiliated herself too many times.

Whilst she put the carrying bags on Whinney, Ayla noticed Wolf slurping water from Ranec's dish. He had gobbled down half a plate of meat as well.

"Thank you for feeding him, Ranec," she said.

"Just because I won't ride a horse doesn't mean I don't like the animals, Ayla," the carver said, feeling diminished. He hadn't wanted to tell her he was afraid to ride a horse.

She nodded, and smiled. "I'll see you when you get to Wolf Camp," Ayla said. They embraced, and kissed, and Ayla thought he held her to him almost too fervently. She hugged Talut as well, and Brecie, and brushed Vincavec's cheek, then mounted. The wolf was immediately at Whinney's heels.

"I hope Wolf's not too tired to run back after running all the way here," Ayla said.

"If he gets tired, he can ride double with you on Whinney," Jondalar said, sitting on Racer, trying to keep the nervous stallion calm.

"That's right. I'm not thinking," Ayla said.

"Take care of her, Jondalar," Ranec said. "When she's worried about someone else, she forgets to take care of herself. I want her to be well for our Matrimonial.''

"I'll take care of her, Ranec. Don't worry, you will have a well and healthy woman to bring to your hearth,'' Jondalar replied.

Ayla looked from one to the other. More was being said than the words.

They travelled steadily until midday, then stopped to rest and lunch on travelling food. Ayla was so deeply worried about Rydag, she would have preferred to keep on going, but the horses needed the rest. She wondered if he had sent Wolf for her himself. It seemed likely. Anyone else would send a person. Only Rydag would reason that Wolf was smart enough to understand the message and follow her trail to find her. But he wouldn't do it, unless . . . it was very important.

The disturbance to the southeast frightened her. The great column spewing into the sky had stopped, but the cloud was still there, spreading out. The fear of strange earth convulsions was so basic to her, and so deep, that she was in a mild state of shock. Only her overriding fear for Rydag forced her to stay in control of herself.

But with all her fears, Ayla was strongly conscious of Jondalar. She had almost forgotten how happy it made her feel to be with him. She had dreamed of riding with him on Whinney and Racer, just the two of them together, with Wolf loping alongside. While they rested, she watched him, but surreptitiously, with a Clan woman's ability to efface herself, to see without being seen. Just looking at him gave her a feeling of warmth and a desire to be closer, but her recent insight into his unexplainable behaviour, and her embarrassment over pushing herself on him when she wasn't wanted, made her reluctant to show her interest. If he didn't want her, she didn't want him, or at least, she wasn't going to let him know that she did.

Jondalar was watching her, too, wanting to find a way to talk to her, to tell her how much he loved her, to try to win her back. But she seemed to be avoiding him, he couldn't catch her eye. He knew how upset she was about Rydag – he feared the worst himself – and didn't want to intrude on her. He wasn't sure it was the right time to bring up his personal feelings, and after all this time, he didn't quite know how to begin. Riding back, he had wild visions of not even stopping at Wolf Camp, of continuing on with her, maybe all the way back to his home. But he knew that was impossible. Rydag needed her, and she was Promised to Ranec. They were going to join. Why should she want to go with him?

They didn't rest long. As soon as Ayla thought the horses were rested enough, they started riding again. But they had travelled only a short distance when they saw someone coming. He hailed them from a distance, and when they got closer, they saw it was Ludeg, the messenger who had brought them the new location of the Summer Meeting.

"Ayla! You're the one I am looking for. Nezzie sent me to get you. I'm afraid I have bad news for you. Rydag is very sick," Ludeg said. Then he looked around. "Where is everyone else?"

"They are coming. We came on ahead as soon as we found out," Ayla said.

"But how could you find out? I'm the only runner that was sent," Ludeg asked.

"No," Jondalar said. "You're the only human runner that was sent, but wolves can run faster."

Suddenly Ludeg noticed the young wolf. "He didn't go hunting with you, how did Wolf get here?"

"I think Rydag sent him," Ayla said. "He found us on the other side of the bog."

"It's a good thing, too," Jondalar added. "You might have missed the hunters. They've decided to go around the bog on the way back. It's easier when you're heavily loaded to stay on dry ground."

"So they found mammoth. Good, that will make everyone happy," Ludeg said, then he looked at Ayla. "I think you'd better hurry. It's lucky you're this close."

Ayla felt the blood drain from her face.

"Would you like a ride back, Ludeg?" Jondalar asked, before they hurried away. "We can ride double."

"No. You need to go ahead. You've already saved me a long trip. I don't mind the walk back."

Ayla raced Whinney all the way back to the Summer Meeting. She was off the horse and in the tent before anyone knew she was back.

"Ayla! You're here! You made it in time. I was afraid he would be gone before you got here," Nezzie said. "Ludeg must have travelled fast."

"It wasn't Ludeg who found us. It was Wolf," Ayla said, throwing off her outerwear and rushing to Rydag's bed.

She had to close her eyes to overcome the shock for a moment. The set of his jaw and the lines of strain told her more than any words that he was in pain, terrible pain. He was pale, but dark hollows circled his eyes, and his cheekbones and brow ridges protruded in sharp angles. Every breath was an effort and caused more pain. She looked up at Nezzie, who was standing beside the bed.

"What happened, Nezzie?" She fought to hold back tears, for his sake.

"I wish I knew. He was fine, then all of a sudden he got this pain. I

609

tried to do everything you told me, gave him the medicine. Nothing helped," Nezzie said.

Ayla felt a faint touch on her arm. "I glad you come," the boy signed.

Where had she seen that before? That struggle to make signs with a body too weak to move? Iza. That's how she was when she died. Ayla had just returned from a long trek then, and a long stay at the Clan Gathering. But she just went to hunt mammoth this time. They weren't gone very long. What happened to Rydag? How did he get so sick so fast? Had it been coming up on him slowly all along?

"You sent Wolf, didn't you?" Ayla asked.

"I know he find," the boy motioned. "Wolf smart."

Rydag closed his eyes then, and Ayla had to turn her head aside, and close her eyes. It hurt to see the way he laboured to breathe, to see his pain.

"When did you last have your medicine?" Ayla asked, when he opened his eyes and she could look at him.

Rydag shook his head slightly. "Not help. Nothing help."

"What do you mean, nothing will help? You're not a medicine woman. How do you know? I'm the one who knows that," Ayla said, trying to sound firm and positive.

He shook his head slightly again. "I know."

"Well, I'm going to examine you, but first, I'm going to get you some medicine," Ayla said, but it was more that she was afraid she would break down right there. He touched her hand as she started to leave.

"Not go." He closed his eyes again, and she watched him struggle for one more tortured breath, and then another, powerless to do anything. "Wolf here?" he finally signed.

Ayla whistled, and whoever it was outside that had been trying to keep Wolf from going in the tent, suddenly found it impossible. He was there, jumping up on the boy's bed, trying to lick his face. Rydag smiled. It was almost more than Ayla could stand, that smile on a Clan face that was so uniquely Rydag. The rambunctious young animal could be too much. Ayla motioned him down.

"I send Wolf. Want Ayla," Rydag motioned again. "I want . . ." He didn't seem to know the word in signs.

"What is it you want, Rydag?" Ayla encouraged.

"He tried to tell me," Nezzie said. "But I couldn't understand him. I hope you can. It seems so important to him."

Rydag closed his eyes and wrinkled his brow, and Ayla had the feeling he was trying to remember something.

"Durc lucky. He . . . belongs. Ayla, I want . . . Mog-ur."

He was trying so hard, and it was taking so much out of him, but all

Ayla could do was try to understand. "Mog-ur?" The sign was silent. "You mean a man of the spirit world?" Ayla said, aloud.

Rydag nodded, encouraged. But the expression on Nezzie's face was unfathomable. "Is that what he's been trying to say?" the woman asked.

"Yes, I think so," Ayla said. "Does that help?"

Nezzie nodded, a short, clipped nod of anger. "I know what he wants. He doesn't want to be an animal, he wants to go to the spirit world. He wants to be buried . . . like a person."

Rydag was nodding now, agreeing.

"Of course," Ayla said. "He is a person." She looked perplexed.

"No. He's not. He was never numbered among the Mamutoi. They wouldn't accept him. They said he was an animal," Nezzie said.

"You mean he cannot have a burial? He cannot walk the spirit world? Who says he can't?" Ayla's eyes blazed with fury.

"The Mammoth Hearth," Nezzie said. "They won't allow it."

"Well, am I not the daughter of the Mammoth Hearth? I will allow it!" Ayla stated.

"It won't do any good. Mamut would, too. The Mammoth Hearth has to agree, and they won't agree," Nezzie said.

Rydag had been listening, hopeful, but now his hope was dimming. Ayla saw his expression, his disappointment, and was more angry than she had ever been.

"The Mammoth Hearth doesn't have to agree. They are not the ones who decide if someone is human or not. Rydag is a person. He is no more an animal than my son is. The Mammoth Hearth can keep their burial. He doesn't need it. When the time comes, I will do it, the Clan way, the way I did it for Creb, the Mog-ur. Rydag will walk the world of the Spirits, Mammoth Hearth or no!"

Nezzie glanced at the boy. He seemed more relaxed now. No, she decided. At peace. The strain, the tension, he had been showing was gone. He touched Ayla's arm.

"I am not animal," he signed.

He seemed about to say something else. Ayla waited. Then suddenly she realised there was no sound, no struggle to take one more tortured breath. He was not in pain any more.

But Ayla was. She looked up and saw Jondalar. He had been there all along, and his face was as racked with grief as hers, or Nezzie's. Suddenly all three of them were clinging together, trying to find solace in each other.

Then another showed his grief. From the floor beneath Rydag's bed, a low whine rose in a furry throat, then yips that extended and deepened and soared into Wolf's first full, ringing howl. When his breath ran out, he began again, crying out his loss in the sonorous, eerie, spine-tingling, unmistakable tones of wolfsong. People gathered at the entrance of the tent to look, but were hesitant to enter. Even the three who were awash in their own sorrow paused to listen and wonder. Jondalar thought to himself that animal or human, no one could ask for a more poignant or awesome elegy.

After the first racking tears of grief were spent, Ayla sat beside the small thin body, unmoving, but her tears had not stopped. She stared into space, silently remembering her life with the Clan, and her son, and the first time she saw Rydag. She loved Rydag. He had come to mean as much to her as Durc and, in a certain way, stood in for him. Even though her son had been taken from her, Rydag had given her an opportunity to know more about him, to learn how he might be growing and maturing, how he might look, how he might think. When she smiled at Rydag's gentle humour, or was pleased at his perceptiveness and intelligence, she could imagine that Durc had the same kind of understanding. Now Rydag was gone, and her tenuous link to Durc was gone. Her grief was for both.

Nezzie's grief was not less, but the needs of the living were important, too. Rugie climbed up on her lap, hurt and confused that her playmate, and friend, and brother, couldn't play any more, couldn't even make words with his hands. Danug was stretched out full-length on his bed, his head buried under a cover, sobbing, and someone had to go and tell Latie.

"Ayla? Ayla," Nezzie finally said. "What do we have to do to bury him in the Clan way? We need to start getting him ready."

It took Ayla a moment to comprehend that someone was talking to her. She frowned, and focused on Nezzie. "What?"

"We have to get him ready for burial. What do we have to do? I don't know anything about Clan burials."

No, none of the Mamutoi did, she thought. Especially the Mammoth Hearth. But she did. She thought about the Clan burials she had seen and considered what should be done for Rydag. Before he can be buried in the Clan way, he has to be Clan. That means he has to be named, and he needs an amulet with a piece of red ochre in it. Suddenly, Ayla got up and rushed out.

Jondalar went after her. "Where are you going?"

"If Rydag is going to be Clan, I have to make him an amulet," she said.

Ayla stalked through the encampment, obviously angry, marching past the Camp of the Mammoth Hearth without even a glance, and straight to the flint-workers' area. Jondalar followed behind. He had some idea what she was up to. She asked for a flint nodule, which no one was ready to refuse her. Then she looked around and found a hammerstone, and cleared herself a place to work.

As she began to preshape the flint in the Clan way, and the Mamutoi flint-knappers realised what she was doing, they were eager to watch, and crowded as close as they dared. No one wanted to raise her ire even more, but this was a rare opportunity. Jondalar had tried to explain the Clan techniques once, after Ayla's background became generally known, but his training was different. He didn't have the necessary control using their methods. Even when he succeeded, they thought it was his own skill, not the unusual process.

Ayla decided to make two separate tools, a sharp knife and a pointed awl, and bring them both back to Cattail Camp to make the amulet. She managed to make a serviceable knife, but she was so full of grief and anger, her hands shook. The first time she tried to make the more difficult narrow, sharp point, she shattered it, and then noticed that many people were watching her, which made her nervous. She felt that the Mamutoi flint-workers were judging the Clan way of making tools, and she was not representing them well, and then was angry that she should even care. The second time she tried, she broke it, too. Her frustration brought angry tears, which she kept trying to wipe away. Suddenly, Jondalar was kneeling in front of her.

"Is this what you want, Ayla?" he asked, holding up the piercing tool she had made for the special Spring Festival Ceremony.

"That's a Clan tool! Where did you get . . . that's the one I made!" she said.

"I know. I went back and got it that day. I hope you don't mind."

She was surprised, puzzled, and strangely pleased. "No, I don't mind. I'm glad you did, but why?"

"I wanted . . . to study it," he replied. He couldn't quite bring himself to say he wanted it to remember her by, to tell her he thought he would be leaving without her. He didn't want to leave without her.

She took her tools back to Cattail Camp, and asked Nezzie for a piece of soft leather. After she got it, the woman watched her make the simple, gathered pouch.

"They look a little more crude, but those tools really work very well," Nezzie remarked. "What is the pouch for?"

"It's Rydag's amulet, like the one I made for the Spring Festival. I have to put a piece of red ochre in it, and name him the way the Clan does. He should have a totem, too, to protect him on his way to the world of the Spirits." She paused, and wrinkled her brow. "I don't know what Creb did to discover a person's totem, but it was always right . . . maybe I can share my totem with Rydag. The Cave Lion is a powerful totem, difficult to live with sometimes, but he was tested many times. Rydag deserves a strong, protective totem."

"Is there anything I can do? Does he need to be prepared? Dressed?" Nezzie asked.

"Yes, I'd like to help, too," Latie said. She was standing at the entrance with Tulie.

"And so would I," Mamut added.

Ayla looked up and saw almost the entire Lion Camp wanting to help and looking to her for direction. Only the hunters were missing. She was filled with a great warmth for these people who had taken in a strange orphaned child and accepted him as their own, and a righteous anger at the members of the Mammoth Hearth who would not even give him a burial.

"Well, first, someone can get some red ochre, crush it up, like Deegie does to colour leather, and mix it in some rendered fat to make a salve. That has to be rubbed all over him. It should be Cave Bear fat, for a proper Clan burial. The Cave Bear is sacred to the Clan."

"We don't have Cave Bear fat," Tornec said.

"There are not many Cave Bears around here," Manuv added.

"Why not mammoth fat, Ayla?" Mamut suggested. "Rydag wasn't just Clan. He was mixed. He was part Mamutoi, too, and the mammoth is sacred to us."

"Yes, I think we could use that. He was Mamutoi, too. We shouldn't forget that."

"How about dressing him, Ayla?" Nezzie asked. "He's never even worn the new clothes I made for him this year."

Ayla frowned, then nodded agreement. "Why not? After he's coloured with red ochre, the way the Clan does, he could be dressed in his best clothes, like the Mamutoi do for burials. Yes, I think that's a good idea, Nezzie."

"I never would have guessed red ochre was a sacred colour at their burials, too," Frebec commented.

"I didn't even think they buried their dead," Crozie said.

"Obviously, the Mammoth Hearth didn't either," Tulie said. "They are going to be in for a surprise."

Ayla asked Deegie for one of the wooden bowls she had given her as an adoption gift, made in the Clan style, and used it to mix the red ochre and mammoth fat into a coloured salve. But it was Nezzie, Crozie, and Tulie, the three oldest women of Lion Camp, who rubbed it on him, and then dressed him. Ayla put aside a small dab of the oily red paste for later, and put a lump of the red iron ore into the pouch she had made.

614

"What about wrapping him?" Nezzie said. "Shouldn't he be wrapped, Ayla?"

"I don't know what that means," Ayla said.

"We use a hide or a fur, or something, to carry him out, and then it's wrapped around him before he is laid in the grave," Nezzie explained.

It was another Mamutoi custom, Ayla realised, but it seemed that with dressing him so richly and putting all his jewellery on him, there was already more Mamutoi than Clan to this burial. The three women were watching her expectantly. She looked back at Tulie, then Nezzie. Yes, maybe Nezzie was right. Something should be used to carry him, some kind of bedding or cover. Then she looked at Crozie.

Suddenly, though she hadn't thought of it for some time, she remembered something: Durc's cloak. The cloak she had used to carry her son close to her breast when he was an infant, and to support him on her hip when he was a toddler. It was the one thing she had taken with her from the Clan that had no necessary purpose. Yet, how many nights when she was alone had Durc's carrying cloak given her a sense of connection with the only place of security she had known, and to those she had loved? How many nights had she slept with that cloak? Cried into it? Rocked it? It was the one thing she owned that had belonged to her son, and she wasn't sure if she could give it up, but did she really need it? Was she going to carry it around with her for the rest of her life?

Ayla noticed Crozie looking at her again, and remembered the white cape, the one that Crozie had made for her son. She had carried it around with her for many years, because it meant so much to her. But she had given it up for a good purpose, to Racer, to protect him. Wasn't it more important for Rydag to be wrapped in something that had come from the Clan, when he was sent on his way to walk in the spirit world, than for her to carry Durc's cloak around? Crozie had finally let the memory of her son go. Maybe it was time for her to let Durc go, too, and just be grateful that he was more than a memory.

"I have something to wrap him in," Ayla said. She rushed to her sleeping place and from the bottom of a pile, she pulled out a folded hide and shook it out. She held the soft, supple, old leather of her son's cloak to her cheek once more, and closed her eyes, remembering. Then she walked back and gave it to Rydag's mother.

"Here's a wrapping," she told Nezzie, "a Clan wrapping. It once belonged to my son. Now it will help Rydag in the spirit world. And thank you, Crozie," she added.

"Why are you thanking me?"

"For everything you've done for me, and for showing me that all mothers must let go sometime."

"Hmmmf!" the old woman said, trying to look stern, but her eyes glistened with feeling. Nezzie took the cloak from Ayla and covered Rydag.

By then it was dark. Ayla had planned to do a simple ceremony inside the tent, but Nezzie asked her to wait until morning and conduct the ceremony outside, to show everyone at the Meeting Rydag's humanity. It would also give the hunters a little more time to return. No one wanted Talut and Ranec to miss Rydag's funeral, but they could not wait too long.

Late the next morning they carried the body outside and laid it out on the cloak. Many people from the Meeting had gathered around, and more were coming. Word had spread that Ayla was going to give Rydag a flathead burial, and everyone was curious. She had the small bowl of red ochre paste and the amulet, and had begun calling the Spirits to attend, as Creb had always done, when another commotion arose. Much to Nezzie's relief, the hunters returned, and with all of the mammoth meat. They had taken turns dragging back the two travois, and were already planning variations of it to make a sledge that people could drag more easily.

The ceremony was postponed until the mammoth meat was stored, and Talut and Ranec were told what had happened, but no one objected when it was resumed quickly. The death of the mixed Clan child at the Summer Meeting of the Mamutoi had created a real dilemma. He had been called an abomination, an animal, but animals were not buried; their meat was stored. Only people were buried, and they did not like to leave the dead unburied for long. Though the Mamutoi weren't quite willing to grant Rydag human status, they knew he wasn't really an animal, either. No one revered the Spirit of flatheads as they did deer, or bison, or mammoths, and no one was ready to store Rydag's body beside the mammoth carcasses. He was an abomination precisely because they saw his humanity, but degraded it and would not recognise it. They were glad to let Ayla and the Lion Camp dispose of Rydag's body in a way that seemed to resolve the problem.

Ayla stood up on a mound to begin the ceremony again, trying to remember the signs Creb had made for this part. She didn't know exactly what all the signs meant, they were taught only to Mog-urs, but she did know the general purpose and content, and explained as she went along for the benefit of the Lion Camp, and the rest of the Mamutoi who were watching.

"I am Calling the Spirits now," she said. "The Spirit of the Great Cave Bear, the Cave Lion, the Mammoth, all the others, and the Ancient Spirits, too, of Wind and Mist and Rain." Then she reached down for the small bowl. "Now I'm going to name him and make him part of the Clan," she said, and dipping her finger in the red paste, Ayla drew a line from his forehead to his nose. Then she stood up and said with signs and words, "The boy's name is Rydag."

There was a quality about her, the tone of her voice, the intensity of her expressions as she tried to remember exactly the correct signs and movements, even her strange speech mannerism, that held people fascinated. The story of her standing on the ice Calling the mammoths was spreading fast. No one doubted that this daughter of the Mammoth Hearth had every right to conduct this ceremony, or any ceremony, whether she had a Mamut tattoo or not.

"Now he is named in the Clan way," Ayla explained, "but he also needs a totem to help him find the world of the Spirits. I do not know his totem, so I will share my totem, the Spirit of the Cave Lion, with him. It is a very powerful, protective totem, but he is worthy."

Next, she exposed Rydag's small, thin, right leg, and with the red ochre paste, drew four parallel lines on his thigh. Then she stood and announced in words and signs, "Spirit of Cave Lion, the boy, Rydag, is delivered into your protection." Then she slipped the amulet, tied to a cord, around his neck. "Rydag is now named and accepted by the Clan," she said, and fervently hoped it was true.

Ayla had chosen a place, somewhat away from the settlement, and Lion Camp had requested and received permission from Wolf Camp to bury him there. Nezzie wrapped the small stiff body in Durc's cloak, then Talut picked up the boy and carried him to the place of burial. He was not ashamed of the tears that fell as he laid Rydag in the shallow grave.

The people of the Lion Camp stood around the dip in the ground that had been deepened only slightly, and watched as several things were put into the grave with him. Nezzie brought food and placed it beside him. Latie added his favourite little whistle. Tronie brought a string of bones, the deer vertebrae that he had used when he tended the babies and young children of Lion Camp during the past winter. It was what he loved doing most, because it was something useful he could do. Then, unexpectedly, Rugie ran to the grave and dropped in her favourite doll.

At Ayla's signal, everyone from the Lion Camp picked up a stone and carefully laid it on the cloak-wrapped figure: the beginning of his grave cairn. It was then that Ayla began the burial ceremony. She didn't try to explain, the purpose seemed clear enough. Using the same signs that Creb had used at Iza's funeral, and that she, in turn, had used to honour Creb when she found him in the rubble-strewn cave, Ayla's movements gave meaning to a burial rite that was far more ancient than any there could know, and more beautiful than anyone had imagined.

She was not using the simplified sign language that she had taught to the Lion Camp. This was the full, complex, rich Clan language in which movements and postures of the entire body had shades and nuances of meaning. Though many of the signs were esoteric – even Ayla didn't know the full meaning – many ordinary signs were also included, some of which the Lion Camp did know. They were able to understand the essence, know that it was a ritual for sending someone to a world beyond. To the rest of the Mamutoi, Ayla's movement had the appearance of a subtle, yet expressive dance, full of hand movements, and arm movements, stances and gestures. She evoked in them with her silent grace, the love and the loss, the sorrow and the mythic hope of death.

Jondalar was overwhelmed. His tears flowed as freely as any member of the Lion Camp's. As he watched her beautiful silent dance, he was reminded of a time in her valley – it seemed so long ago now – when she once had tried to tell him something with the same kind of graceful movements. Even then, though he didn't understand it was a language, he had sensed some deeper meaning in her expressive gestures. Now that he knew more, he was surprised at how much he didn't know, yet how beautiful he thought it was when Ayla moved that way.

He remembered the posture she used when they first met, sitting cross-legged on the ground and bowing her head, waiting for him to tap her shoulder. Even after she could speak, she would use it sometimes. It always embarrassed him, particularly after he knew it was a Clan gesture, but she had told him it was her way of trying to say something that she didn't have the words for. He smiled to himself. It was hard to believe she couldn't talk when he first met her. Now, she was fluent in two languages: Zelandonii and Mamutoi, three, if he counted Clan. She had even picked up a little Sungaea in the short time she spent with them.

As he watched her move through the Clan ritual, filled with memories of the valley, and memories of their love, he wanted her more than he'd ever wanted anything in his life. But Ranec was standing close to her, as enraptured as he. Every time Jondalar looked at Ayla, he could not avoid seeing the dark-skinned man. The moment he arrived, Ranec had sought her out, and he made a point of letting Jondalar know that she was still Promised to him. And Ayla seemed distant, elusive. He had made some attempts to talk to her, to express his sorrow, but after their first moments of shared grief, she seemed unwilling to accept his efforts to console her. He wondered if he was imagining it. As upset as she was, what else could he expect?

Suddenly, all heads turned at the sound of a steady beat. Marut, the drummer, had gone to the Music Lodge, and brought his mammoth-skull drum back. Music was usually played at Mamutoi funerals, but the sounds he was making were not the usual Mamutoi rhythms. They were the unfamiliar, strangely fascinating rhythms of the Clan that Ayla had shown him. Then the bearded musician, Manen, began to play the simple flute tones she had whistled. The music matched, in an unexplainable way, the movements of the woman who was dancing a ritual as evanescent as the sound of music itself.

Ayla had almost completed the ritual, but she decided to repeat it, since they were playing Clan sounds. The second time they went through it, the musicians began to improvise. With their expertise and skill, they made the simple Clan sounds into something else, which was neither Clan nor Mamutoi, but a mixture of both. A perfect accompaniment, Ayla thought, for the funeral of a boy who was a mixture of both.

Ayla went through one last repetition with the musicians, and she wasn't sure when her tears started, but she could see she was not alone. There were many wet eyes, and not only from among the Lion Camp.

As she finished for the third time, a heavy dark cloud that had been approaching from the southeast began to blot out the sun. It was the season for thunderstorms, and some people looked for shelter. Instead of water, a light dust began to fall, very light at first. Then the volcanic ash from the eruption in the faraway mountains fell heavier.

Ayla stood by Rydag's grave cairn feeling the feathery soft volcanic ash sifting down on her, coating her hair, her shoulders, clinging to her arms, her eyebrows, even her eyelashes, turning her into a monochrome figure in pale beige-grey. The fine light dust covered everything, the stones of the cairn, the grass, even the brown dust of the path. Logs and bush alike took on the same hue. It covered the people standing by the grave as well, and to Ayla, they all began to look the same. Differences were lost in the face of such awesome powers as movements of the earth, and death.

37

"This stuff is terrible!" Tronie complained, shaking out a bed covering at the edge of a gully, and causing more ash to billow up. "We've been cleaning it up for days, but it's in the food, in the water, clothes, beds. It gets into everything, and you can't get rid of it."

"What we need is another good rain," Deegie said, throwing out some dirty water that had been used to wash down the hide covering of the tent. "Or a good snowstorm. That would settle it. This is one year I'm going to look forward to winter."

"I'm sure you are," Tronie said, then looked at her sideways and grinned, "but I think it's because you'll be joined by then and living with Branag."

A beatific smile transformed Deegie's face as she thought of her upcoming nuptials. "I won't deny that, Tronie," she said.

"Is it true that the Mammoth Hearth was talking about postponing the Matrimonial because of this ash?" Tronie asked.

"Yes, and the Womanhood Rites, too, but everyone objected. I know Latie doesn't want to wait, and I don't either. They finally agreed. They don't want any more bad feelings. A lot of people thought they were wrong about Rydag's funeral," Deegie said.

"But some people agreed with them," Fralie said, approaching with a basketful of ash. She dumped it into the gully. "No matter what they had decided, someone would have thought they were wrong."

"I guess you had to live with Rydag to know," Tronie said.

"I'm not so sure," Deegie said. "He lived with us a long time, but I never thought of him as quite human until Ayla came."

"I don't think she's as anxious for the Matrimonial as you, Deegie," Tronie said. "I wonder if something is wrong with her. Is she sick?"

"I don't think so," Deegie said. "Why?"

"She's not acting right. She's preparing to be joined, but she doesn't seem to be looking forward to it. She's getting a lot of gifts, and everything, but she doesn't seem happy. She should be like you. Every time someone says 'join', you smile, and get a dreamy look on your face."

"Not everyone looks forward to their joining the same way," Fralie said.

"She did feel very close to Rydag," Deegie commented. "And she is grieving, as much as Nezzie. If he had been Mamutoi, the Matrimonial probably would be delayed."

"I feel bad about Rydag, too, and I miss him – he was so good with Hartal," Tronie said. "We all feel bad, though he was in so much pain I was relieved. I think something else is bothering Ayla."

She did not add that she had wondered about Ayla joining with Ranec from the beginning. There was no reason to make an issue of it, but in spite of Ranec's feeling for her, Deegie still thought Ayla felt more for Jondalar, though she seemed to be ignoring him lately. She saw the tall Zelandonii man come out of the tent, and walk towards the centre of the Meeting area. He seemed preoccupied.

Jondalar nodded in response to people who acknowledged him as he passed, but his thoughts were turned inward. Was he imagining it? Or was Ayla really avoiding him? After all the time that he had spent trying to stay out of her way, he still couldn't quite believe, now that he wanted to talk to her alone, that she was avoiding him. In spite of her Promise to Ranec, some part of him always believed that all he had to do was to stop avoiding her and she would be available to him again. It wasn't that she had seemed so eager, exactly, but that she seemed open to him. Now, she seemed closed. He had decided the only way to find out was to face her directly, but he was having trouble finding her at a time and place where they could talk.

He saw Latie coming towards him. He smiled and stopped to watch her. She walked with an independent stride now, smiled confidently at people who nodded greetings. There is a difference, he thought. It always amazed him to see the change that First Rites brought. Latie was no longer a child, or a giggling, nervous girl. Though she was still young, she moved with the assurance of a woman.

"Hello, Jondalar," she said, smiling.

"Hello, Latie. You're looking happy." A lovely young woman, he thought to himself as he smiled. His eyes conveyed his feelings. She responded with an indrawn breath and widened eyes, and then a look that answered his unconscious invitation.

"I am. I was getting so tired of staying in one place all the time. This is the first chance I've had to walk around by myself . . . or with anyone I want." She swayed a little closer as she looked up at him. "Where are you going?"

"I'm looking for Ayla. Have you seen her?"

Latie sighed, then smiled in a friendly way.

"Yes, she was watching Tricie's baby for a while. Mamut is looking for her, too."

"Don't blame them all, Ayla," Mamut said. They were sitting outside in the warm sunshine, in the shade of a big alder bush. "There were several who disagreed. I was one."

"I don't blame you, Mamut. I don't know if I blame anyone, but why can't they see? What makes people hate them so much?"

"Maybe because they can see how much we are alike, so they look for differences." He paused, then continued, "You should go to the Mammoth Hearth before tomorrow, Ayla. You can't be joined until you do. You're the last one, you know."

"Yes, I suppose I should," Ayla said.

"Your reluctance is giving Vincavec hope. He asked me again today if I thought you were considering his offer. He said, if you didn't want to break your Promise, he was going to talk to Ranec about accepting him as a co-mate. His offer could increase your Bride Price substantially, and give very high status to all of you. How would you feel about it, Ayla? Would you be willing to accept Vincavec as a co-mate with Ranec?"

"Vincavec said something about that on the hunt. I'd have to talk to Ranec and see how he feels about it," Ayla said.

Mamut thought she showed remarkably little enthusiasm, either way. This was a bad time for their joining, with her grief still so strong, but with all the offers and attention, it was hard to counsel waiting. He noticed that she was suddenly distracted, and turned to see what she was watching. Jondalar was coming towards them. She seemed nervous and took a step as though she was in a hurry to go, but she couldn't just break off her conversation with Mamut so abruptly.

"There you are, Ayla. I've been looking for you. I'd like to talk to you."

"I'm busy with Mamut now," she said.

"I think we're through, if you want to talk to Jondalar," Mamut said.

Ayla looked down, and then at the old man, avoiding Jondalar's troubled gaze, then said softly, "I don't think we have anything to say to each other, Mamut."

Jondalar felt his face drain, then a shock of blushing heat. She had been avoiding him! She didn't even want to talk to him. "Uh . . . well, uh . . . I'm . . . I'm sorry I bothered you," he said, backing away. Then, wishing he could find a place to hide, he rushed off.

Mamut observed her closely. After he left, she watched him go, her eyes even more troubled than his. He shook his head, but refrained from speaking as they walked together back to Lion Camp.

As they neared, Ayla noticed Nezzie and Tulie coming towards them. Rydag's death had been hard on Nezzie. Just the day before she had brought what was left of his medicine back, and they had both wept. Nezzie didn't want it around as a sad reminder, but wasn't sure if she should throw it away. It made Ayla realise that with Rydag gone, the need to help Nezzie treat him was gone, too.

"We were looking for you, Ayla," Tulie said. She seemed delighted with herself the way someone would who had been planning a big surprise, and that was rare for the big headwoman. The two women opened out something that was carefully folded. Ayla's eyes opened wide, and the two women looked at each other and grinned. "Every bride needs a new tunic. Usually it is the man's mother who makes it, but I wanted to help Nezzie."

It was a stunning garment of golden yellow leather, exquisitely and ornately decorated; certain sections of it were solidly filled in with designs in ivory beads, highlighted by many small amber beads.

"It's so beautiful, and there's so much work in it. The beadwork alone must have taken days and days. When did you make it?" Ayla asked.

"We started it after you announced your Promise, and finished it here," Nezzie said. "Come in the tent and try it on."

Ayla looked at Mamut. He smiled and nodded. He had been aware of the project, and even conspired with them in the surprise. The three women went into the tent, and towards Tulie's sleeping section. Ayla undressed, but she wasn't quite sure how to wear the garment. The women put it on her. It was a specially made tunic that opened down the front, and was tied closed with a finger-woven sash of red mammoth wool.

"You can wear it closed like this if you just want to wear it to show someone," Nezzie said, "but for the ceremony, you should open it like this." She pulled back the top of the front opening and retied the sash. "A woman proudly shows her breasts when she is joined, when she brings her hearth to form a union with a man."

The two women stepped back to admire the bride-to-be. She has breasts to be proud of, Nezzie thought. Mother's breasts, that she can nurse with. Too bad she has no mother here to be with her. She would make any woman proud.

"Can we come in now?" Deegie said, peeking in the tent. All the women of the Camp came in then to admire Ayla in her finery. It seemed they all were in on the surprise.

"Close it now, so you can go outside and show the men," Nezzie said, closing and retying the mating tunic again. "You shouldn't wear it open in public until the ceremony."

Ayla stepped outside the tent to the smiling approval and pleasure of the men of the Lion Camp. Others, who were not of the Lion Camp, were watching her as well. Vincavec had known of the surprise, and made a point of being close by. When he saw her, he resolved that in some way he was going to join with her, if he had to co-mate with ten men.

Another man who was not of the Lion Camp, though most people thought of him in that way, was watching, too. Jondalar had followed them back, not quite willing to accept her rebuff, or even believe it. Danug told him, and he waited with the others. When she first stepped out, he filled his eyes with the sight of her, then he closed them and his forehead knotted with pain. He had lost her. She was showing her intention to join with Ranec the next day. He took a deep breath and clamped his teeth together. He could not stay to see her joined with the dark-skinned carver of the Lion Camp. It was time for him to leave.

After Ayla changed back into her regular clothing and left again with Mamut, Jondalar hurried into the tent. He was glad to find it empty. He packed his travelling gear, thanking Tulie again in his mind, laid out everything he would take, and then covered it with a sleeping fur. He planned to wait until morning, say goodbye to everyone, and leave immediately after breakfast. He wouldn't tell anyone until then.

During the day Jondalar visited with special friends he had made at the Meeting, not saying goodbye, but thinking it. In the evening he spent time with each member of the Lion Camp. They were like family. It was going to be hard leaving, knowing he would never see them again. It was even harder finding a way to talk to Ayla, at least once more. He watched her, and when she and Latie went out to the horse lean-to, he quickly followed them.

The words of their conversation were superficial and uncomfortable, but there was an intensity about him that filled Ayla with an uneasy tension. When she went back in, he stayed and brushed the young stallion until it got dark. The first time he saw Ayla, she was helping Whinney give birth, he remembered. He'd never seen anything like that before. It was going to be hard leaving him, too. Jondalar felt more for Racer than he ever thought it was possible to feel for an animal.

Finally he went in the tent, and crawled into his bed. He closed his eyes, but sleep would not come. He lay awake and thought of Ayla, of their time in the valley and their love that grew slowly. No, not so slowly. He loved her from the beginning, he had just been slow to recognise it, slow to appreciate it, so slow he lost it. He threw away her love, and he would pay for the rest of his life. How could he have been so stupid? He would never forget her, or the pain of losing her, and he would never forgive himself.

It was a long, difficult night, and when the first light of dawn barely glimmered through the tent opening, he could stand it no longer. He couldn't say goodbye, to her or anyone, he just had to leave. Quietly, he gathered up his travel clothing, packs, and sleeping roll, and slipped outside.

"You decided not to wait. I thought as much," Mamut said.

Jondalar spun around. "I . . . ah . . . I have to go. I can't stay any more. It's time I . . . ah," he stammered.

"I know, Jondalar. I wish you good Journey. You have a long way to go. You must decide for yourself what is best, but remember this, a choice cannot be made if there is none to make." The old man ducked into the tent.

Jondalar frowned, and he walked towards the horse lean-to. What did Mamut mean? Why did Those Who Served the Mother always speak words that could not be understood?

When he saw Racer, Jondalar had a fleeting impulse to ride away on him, at least take away that much, but Racer was Ayla's horse. He patted both of them, gave the brown stallion a hug around the neck, and then noticed Wolf, and gave him an affectionate rub. Then he quickly got up and started walking down the path.

When Ayla woke up the sun was streaming in. It looked like a perfect day. Then she remembered this was the day of the Matrimonial celebration. The day didn't seem so perfect any more. She sat up and looked around. Something was wrong. It had always been her habit to glance over in Jondalar's direction when she first woke up. He wasn't there. Jondalar is up early this morning, she thought. She couldn't get over the feeling that something was very wrong.

She got up, dressed, and went outside to wash and find a twig for her teeth. Nezzie was beside the fire, looking at her, strangely. The feeling that something wasn't right grew distinctly stronger. She glanced towards the horse lean-to. Whinney and Racer seemed fine, and there was Wolf. She went back in the tent and looked around again. Many people were up and gone for the day. Then she noticed that Jondalar's place was empty. He wasn't just gone for the day. His sleeping roll and travelling packs, everything was missing. Jondalar was gone!

Ayla ran out in a panic. "Nezzie! Jondalar is gone! He's not just at Wolf Camp someplace, he's gone. And he left me behind!"

"I know, Ayla. I've been expecting it, haven't you?"

"But he didn't even say goodbye! I thought he was going to stay until the Matrimonial."

"That's the last thing he ever wanted to do, Ayla. He never wanted to see you join with someone else."

"But . . . but . . . Nezzie, he didn't want me. What else could I do?"

"What do you want to do?"

"I want to go with him! But he's gone. How could he leave me? He was going to take me with him. That's what we planned. What happened to everything we had planned, Nezzie?" she said, in a sudden burst of tears. Nezzie held out her arms, and comforted the sobbing young woman.

"Plans change, Ayla. Lives change. What about Ranec?"

"I'm not the right one for him. He should join with Tricie. She's the one who loves him," Ayla said.

"Don't you love him? He loves you."

"I wanted to love him, Nezzie. I tried to love him, but I love Jondalar. Now Jondalar is gone." Ayla sobbed anew. "He doesn't love me."

"Are you so sure?" Nezzie asked.

"He left me, and he didn't even say goodbye. Nezzie, why did he leave without me? What did I do wrong?" Ayla pleaded.

"Do you think you did something wrong?"

Ayla stopped and frowned. "He wanted to talk to me yesterday, and I wouldn't talk to him."

"Why wouldn't you talk to him?"

"Because . . . because he didn't want me. All last winter, when I loved him so much, and wanted to be with him, he didn't want me. He wouldn't even talk to me."

"So when he did want to talk to you, you wouldn't talk to him. It happens that way sometimes," Nezzie said.

"But I do want to talk to him, Nezzie. I want to be with him. Even if he doesn't love me, I want to be with him. But now he's gone. He just got up and walked away. He can't be gone! He can't be gone . . . far . . ."

Nezzie looked at her and almost smiled.

"How far could he be, Nezzie? Walking? I can walk fast, maybe I can catch up with him. Maybe I should go after him and see what he wanted to talk to me about. Oh, Nezzie, I should be with him. I love him."

"Then, go after him, child. If you want him, if you love him, go after him. Tell him how you feel. At least give him the chance to tell you what he wanted to say."

"You're right!" Ayla wiped away tears with the back of her hand and tried to think. "That's what I should do. I'm going to do it. Right now!" she said, and started running down the path, even before Nezzie could say another word. She raced across the stepping-stones of the river, and into the field. Then she stopped. She didn't know which way to go, she'd have to track him, and it would take forever to catch up with him this way.

Suddenly, Nezzie heard two piercing whistles. She smiled as the wolf zipped past her, and Whinney perked her ears and followed him. Racer trailed after. She watched down the slope as the wolf loped towards the young woman.

When he got closer, Ayla signalled, and spoke. "Find Jondalar, Wolf. Find Jondalar!"

The wolf started sniffing the ground and the air currents, and when he started off, Ayla noticed the slight traces of trampled grass and broken twigs. She leaped on Whinney's back, and followed.

It was only after she started riding that the questions came to her. What am I going to say to him? How can I tell him that he promised to take me with him? What if he won't listen? What if he doesn't want me?

Rain had washed the coating of volcanic ash from trees and leaves, but Jondalar strode through the meadows and woodlands of the floodplain oblivious to the beauty of a rare summer day. He didn't quite know where he was going, he just followed the river, but with each step that took him farther away, his thoughts weighed heavier.

Why am I leaving without her? Why am I travelling alone? Maybe I should go back, ask her to come with me? But she doesn't want to come with you. She's a Mamutoi. These are her people. She chose Ranec, not you, Jondalar, he said to himself. Yes, she chose Ranec, but did you give her any choice? Then he stopped. What was it Mamut said? Something about choice? "A choice cannot be made if there is none to make." What did he mean?

Jondalar shook his head in exasperation, and then, he realised, he knew. I never gave her a choice. Ayla didn't choose Ranec, at least not at first. Maybe the night of the adoption she had a choice . . . or did she? She was raised by the Clan. No one ever told her she had a choice. And then I pushed her away. Why didn't I give her a choice before I left? Because she wouldn't talk to you.

No, because you were afraid she wouldn't choose you. Stop lying to yourself. After all that time, she finally decided not to talk to you, and you were afraid she wouldn't choose you, that's why, Jondalar. So you didn't give her the chance. Are you any better off now?

Why don't you go back and give her a choice? At least make the offer? But what will you say to her? She's getting ready for the big ceremony. What will you offer? What can you offer?

You could offer to stay. You could even offer to co-mate with Ranec. Could you stand that? Could you share her with Ranec? If the only other choice is not having her at all, could you stay here and share her?

Jondalar stood still, closed his eyes, and frowned. Only if he had no other choice. What he wanted most was to take her home, and make it her home. The Mamutoi had accepted her, were the Zelandonii less accepting? Some of them, maybe not all of them, but he couldn't promise.

Ranec has the Lion Camp, and many other affiliations. You can't even offer her your people, your affiliations. You don't know if they will accept her, or you. You don't have anything to offer, except yourself.

If he could offer her no more than that, what would they do if his people wouldn't accept them? We could go somewhere else. We could even come back here. He frowned. That's a lot of travelling. Maybe he should just offer to stay, establish himself here. Tarneg said he wanted a flint-knapper for his new Camp. What about Ranec? More important, what about Ayla? What if she didn't want him at all?

Jondalar was so engrossed in his thoughts, he didn't hear the dull thud of hoofbeats until Wolf suddenly jumped up on him.

"Wolf? What are you doing . . ." He looked up and stared in disbelief as Ayla slid off Whinney's back.

She walked towards him, shy now, so afraid he would turn his back on her again. How could she tell him? How could she make him listen? What could she do if he wouldn't listen to her? Then she recalled those first wordless days, and the way she had learned to ask someone to listen a lifetime ago. She dropped to the ground, gracefully, from long practice, and bowed her head, and waited.

Jondalar gaped at her, didn't understand for a moment, then remembered. It was her signal. When she wanted to tell him something important, but didn't have the words, she used that Clan signal. But why was she speaking to him in the language of the Clan now? What did she want to tell him that was so important?

"Get up," he said. "You don't have to do that." Then he remembered the proper response. He tapped her shoulder. When Ayla looked up, she had tears in her eyes. He hunkered down on one knee to wipe them away. "Ayla, why are you doing this? Why are you here?"

"Jondalar, yesterday you tried to tell me something, and I wouldn't listen to you. Now I want to tell you something. It is difficult to say, but I want you to listen. That's why I'm asking you this way. Will you listen, and not turn away?"

Hope blazed so hot Jondalar couldn't speak. He only nodded, and held her hands.

"Once you wanted me to go away with you," she began, "and I didn't want to leave the valley." She stopped to take a deep breath. "Now, I want to go with you, anywhere with you. Once you told me that you loved me, that you wanted me. Now, I think you don't want to love me, but I still want to go with you."

"Get up, Ayla, please," he said, helping her up. "What about Ranec? I thought you wanted him." His arms were still around her.

"I don't love Ranec. I love you, Jondalar. I never stopped loving you. I don't know what I did to make you stop loving me."

"You love me? You still love me? Oh, Ayla, my Ayla," Jondalar said, crushing her to him. Then he looked at her as though he was seeing her for the first time, and his eyes filled with his love. She reached up and his mouth found hers. They came together, holding each other, with a hard and tender passion, full of love, full of longing.

Ayla couldn't believe she was in his arms, that he was holding her, wanting her, loving her, after all this time. Tears filled her eyes, then she tried to stop them, afraid he would misunderstand them again, then she didn't care and let the tears fall.

He looked down at her beautiful face. "You're crying, Ayla."

"It's only because I love you. I have to cry. It's been so long, and I love you so much," she said.

He kissed her eyes, her tears, her mouth, and felt it open to him, gently, firmly.

"Ayla, are you really here?" he said. "I thought I'd lost you, and I knew it was my own fault. I love you, Ayla, I never stopped loving you. You must believe that. I never stopped loving you, even though I know why you thought so."

"But you didn't want to love me, did you?"

He closed his eyes and his forehead knotted with the pain of the truth. He nodded. "I was ashamed that I loved someone who came from the Clan, and I hated myself for feeling ashamed of the woman I loved. I've never been so happy with anyone as I have with you. I love you, and when it was just the two of us, everything was perfect. But when we were with other people . . . every time you did something that you learned from the Clan, I was embarrassed. And I was always afraid you'd say something, and then everyone would know that I loved a woman who was . . . abomination." He could hardly say the word.

"Everyone used to tell me I could have any woman I wanted. No woman could refuse me, they said, not even the Mother Herself. It seemed to be true. What they didn't know was that I never knew a woman I really wanted, until I met you. But what would they say if I brought you home? If Jondalar could have anyone, why would he bring home . . . the mother of a flathead . . . an abomination? I was afraid they wouldn't accept you, and turn me away, too, unless . . . I turned against you. I was afraid I might, if I had to choose between my people and you."

Ayla was frowning. She looked down. "I didn't understand. That would be a hard decision for you to make."

"Ayla," Jondalar said, turning her face up to look at him. "I love you. Maybe only now do I realise how important that is to me. Not just that

629

you love me, but that I love you. Now I know, for me there is only one choice. You are more important to me than my people, or anyone. I want to be wherever you are." Her eyes overflowed again, try as she might to stop them. "If you want to stay here and live with the Mamutoi, I will stay and become Mamutoi. If you want me to share you with Ranec . . . I will do that, too."

"Is that what you want to do?"

"If it's what you want . . ." Jondalar started to say, then remembered Mamut's words. Maybe he ought to give her a choice, tell her his preference. "I want to be with you, that's most important, believe me. I would be willing to stay here, if that's what you want, but if you ask me what I want, I want to go home, and take you with me."

"Take me with you? You aren't ashamed of me any more? You're not ashamed of the Clan, and Durc?"

"No. I'm not ashamed of you. I'm proud of you. And I'm not ashamed of the Clan either. You, and Rydag, have taught me something very important, and maybe it's time to try and teach some others. I've learned so many things that I want to take back to my people. I want to show them the spear-thrower, and Wymez's methods of working flint, and your firestones, and the thread-puller, and the horses and Wolf. With all that, they may even be willing to listen to someone trying to tell them that the people of the Clan are children of the Earth Mother, too."

"The Cave Lion is your totem, Jondalar," Ayla said with the finality of absolute knowledge.

"You've said that before. What makes you so sure?"

"Remember when I told you powerful totems are hard to live with? Their tests are very hard, but their gifts, what you learn from them, make it all worth it. You have been through a hard test, but are you sorry now? This year has been hard for both of us, but I have learned so much, about myself, and about the Others. I am not afraid of them any more. You have learned very much, too, about yourself and about the Clan. I think you feared them, in a different way. Now you have overcome it. The Cave Lion is a Clan totem, and you don't hate them any more."

"I think you must be right, and I'm glad a Clan Cave Lion totem has chosen me, if that means I am acceptable to you. I have nothing to offer you, Ayla, except myself. I can't promise any affiliations, not even my people. I cannot make promises, because I don't know if the Zelandonii will accept you. If they don't, we'll have to find some other place to go. I will become a Mamutoi if you want, but I would rather take you home and have Zelandoni tie the knot for us."

"Is that like joining?" Ayla asked. "You never asked me to join with you before. You asked me to come with you, but you never asked me to make a hearth with you."

"Ayla, Ayla, what's wrong with me? Why do I take it for granted that you know everything, already? Maybe it's because you know so much that I don't know, and you've learned so much, so fast, that I forget you've just learned it. Maybe I ought to learn a sign for saying things that I don't have words for."

Then, with an amused smile of delight, he hunkered down in front of her with one knee to the ground. He wasn't quite sitting cross-legged, with his head bowed, the way she always did, but he was looking up at her. Ayla was obviously disconcerted, and uncomfortable, which pleased him, because that was always how he felt.

"What are you doing, Jondalar? Men aren't supposed to do that. They don't have to ask permission to speak."

"But I have to ask, Ayla. Will you come back with me, and join with me, and have Zelandoni tie the knot, and make a hearth with me, and make some children for me?"

Ayla started crying again, and felt silly for all the tears she had been shedding. "Jondalar, I never wanted anything else. Yes, to all those things. Now, please, get up."

He stood up, and took her in his arms, feeling happier than he ever had in his life. He kissed her, then held her to him as though he was afraid to let her go, afraid he might lose her, as he very nearly did before.

He kissed her again, and need for her grew with the wonder of her being there. She felt it, and her body responded and was ready for him. But he wanted no taking of her this time. He wanted her fully, completely. He backed away, and shrugged off the travelling pack he still wore. Then he took out a ground cloth and spread it out. Wolf suddenly came bounding up to him.

"You're going to have to stay away for a while," he said, then smiled at Ayla.

She commanded Wolf away, and smiled back at Jondalar. He sat down on the ground cloth and reached his hand up to her. She joined him, already tingling, anticipating, and wanting him so much.

He kissed her then, lightly, and reached for her breast, and savoured even the small familiarity of its full, round shape through her light tunic. She remembered, too, and more. Quickly, she pulled the tunic off. He reached for her with both hands, and the next instant, she was on her back, with his mouth firmly on hers. His hand caressed a breast, and found the nipple, and then a warm wet mouth was on her other nipple. She moaned as the drawing sensation sent waves of feeling deep inside to the place that hungered for him. She rubbed his arms, and his broad back, then the back of his neck, and his hair. For just an instant, she was

631

surprised that it wasn't tightly curled. The thought left as quickly as it came.

He was kissing her again, his tongue gently probing. She took his in, then probed back, remembering that his touch was never too much, or too frenzied, but sensitive and knowing. She delighted in the memory, and in the renewal of it. It was almost like the first time, learning him again, and remembering how well he knew her. How many nights had she longed for him?

He tasted the warmth of her mouth, then the salt of her throat. She felt warm shivers tracing her jaw, then the side of her neck. He kissed her shoulder, nibbled lightly, and suckled, playing with the sensitive places he knew were there. Unexpectedly, he took her nipple again. She gasped at the sudden increase in feeling. Then she sighed, and moaned with pleasure as he played them both.

He sat up then, and looked at her, then closed his eyes as though he wanted to memorise her. She was smiling when he opened them again.

"I love you, Jondalar, and I have wanted you so much."

"Oh, Ayla, I ached with wanting you, and yet I almost gave you up. How could I, when I love you so much?" He was kissing her again, holding her tight, as though he feared he might lose her yet. She clung to him with the same fervour. And suddenly, there was no waiting. He held both her breasts, and then untied her waistband. She lifted her hips and pushed off her half-length summer pants, while he unfastened his own, pulled off his shirt, yanked off his footwear.

He hugged her around the waist with his head on her stomach, then moved down between her legs, kissed her mound of hair. Then he stopped for a moment, pushed her legs apart, and with both hands, held her open, and looked at the deep pink folds, like soft moist flower petals. Then like a bee he dipped and tasted. She cried out, and arched to him, while he explored each petal, each fold, each crease, nibbling, suckling, teasing, revelling in giving her Pleasure, as he had wanted to for days without number.

This was Ayla. This was his Ayla. This was her taste, her honey, and his own member was so full, so eager. He wanted to wait, wanted this to last, but suddenly she could not. She was breathing hard, and fast, panting, gasping, calling out to him. She reached for him, pulled him up, then reached down to guide him to her warm deep well.

As he slid in, he breathed a deep sigh, and let his full shaft glide in and in, until she enfolded him fully. This was his Ayla. This was the woman he fitted, the one who fitted him, who held him all. He stayed for a moment, luxuriating in her full embrace. It had been like this with her from the first time, and every time. How could he have dreamed of giving her up? The Mother must have made Ayla just for him, so they could honour Her in full measure, so they could please Her with their Pleasures, as She meant them to.

He pulled back, and felt her thrust to him as he thrust to her. He pulled back again, and pushed, and back and in again. Then suddenly, he was ready, and she was crying out, and they pulled back and in once more, and the wave rolled up and reached the peak, and broke over them in a release of shuddering spent delight.

The resting was part of the Pleasure. She loved the feel of his weight on her then. He was never heavy. Usually he got up first, before she was ready for him to. She could smell herself on him, and it made her smile, reminding her of the Pleasures they had just shared. She never felt quite so complete as then, when they were through, and he was still there, inside her.

He loved the feel of her full body under his, and it had been so long, so stupidly long. But she loved him. How could she still love him after all that? How could he be so lucky? Never, ever again would he let her go.

Finally, he pulled out, rolled over, and smiled at her.

"Jondalar?" Ayla said, after a while.

"Yes."

"Let's go swimming. The river isn't far. Let's go swimming like we used to in the valley, before we go back to Wolf Camp."

He sat up beside her, and smiled. "Let's go!" he said, was up in an instant, then helped her up. Wolf stood up, too, and wagged his tail.

"Yes, you can come with us," Ayla said, as they picked up their things and headed for the river. Wolf leaped after them eagerly.

After they swam and bathed and played with Wolf in the river, and the horses had rolled, and grazed, and relaxed, away from the crowd, Ayla and Jondalar dressed, feeling refreshed, and hungry.

"Jondalar?" Ayla said, standing by the horses.

"Yes."

"Let's ride double on Whinney. I want to feel you close to me."

All the way back, Ayla thought about how she was going to tell Ranec. She was not looking forward to it. When they arrived, he was waiting for her, and was obviously not happy. He had been looking for her. Everyone else had been getting ready for the Matrimonial that evening, either to attend or to participate. Nor did it please him to see them riding double on Whinney, with Racer tagging behind.

"Where have you been? You should be dressed by now."

"I have to talk to you, Ranec."

"We don't have time to talk," he said, with a frantic look in his eye.

633

"I'm sorry, Ranec. We have to talk. Some place where we can be alone."

He could only acquiesce. Ayla went into the tent first, and took something from her pack. They walked down the slope towards the river, and then along its bank. Finally, Ayla stopped, reached inside her tunic, and pulled out the carving of a woman transcending into her spiritual bird form, the muta Ranec had carved for her.

"I have to give this back to you, Ranec," Ayla said, holding it out to him.

Ranec jumped back, as though he had been burned. "What do you mean? You can't give that back! You need it to make a hearth. You need it for our Matrimonial," he said, an edge of panic creeping into his voice.

"That's why I have to give it back. I can't make a hearth with you. I'm leaving."

"Leaving? You can't leave, Ayla. You Promised. Everything's arranged. The Matrimonial is tonight. You said you would join with me. I love you, Ayla. Don't you understand, I love you." The panic rose in Ranec's voice with each statement.

"I know," Ayla said softly. The shock and pain in his eyes hurt her. "I Promised, and everything is arranged. But I have to leave."

"But why? Why now, all of a sudden?" Ranec asked, his voice high-pitched, almost strangled.

"Because I have to leave now. It's the best time to travel, and we have a long way to go. I'm going with Jondalar. I love him. I never stopped loving him. I thought he didn't love me . . ."

"When you thought he didn't love you, then I was good enough? Is that how it was?" Ranec said. "All the time we spent together, you were wishing it was him. You never loved me at all."

"I wanted to love you, Ranec. I care about you. I wasn't always wishing for Jondalar, when I was with you. You made me happy many times."

"But not always. I wasn't good enough. You were perfect, but I wasn't always perfect for you."

"I never looked for perfect. I love him, Ranec. How long could you love me knowing that I love someone else?"

"I could love you until I die, Ayla, and into the world beyond. Don't you understand? I will never love anyone again the way I love you. You can't leave me." The dark, magnetic artist was pleading with her, with tears in his eyes; he had never pleaded for anything before in his life.

Ayla was feeling his pain, and she wished there was something she could do to make it less. But she could not give him the one thing he wanted. She could not love him the way she loved Jondalar.

"I'm sorry, Ranec. Please. Take the muta." She held it out again.

"Keep it!" he said, with as much venom as he could. "Maybe I'm not good enough for you, but I don't need you. I can have my pick of this place. Go ahead, run off with your flint-knapper. I don't care."

"I can't keep it," Ayla said, putting the muta down on the ground at his feet. She bowed her head and turned to go.

She walked back along the river, with pain in her heart for the pain she had caused. She hadn't meant to hurt him so badly. If there had been any other way, she would have chosen it. She hoped that never again would someone love her that she couldn't love back.

"Ayla?" Ranec called out. She turned back and waited for him to catch up with her. "When are you leaving?"

"As soon as I can get packed."

"It's not true, you know. I do care." His face was etched with grief and pain. She wanted to run to him, comfort him, but she didn't dare encourage him. "I always knew you loved him, from the beginning," he said. "But I loved you so much, and I wanted you so much, I didn't want to see it. I tried to convince myself that you loved me, and I hoped, in time, you really would."

"Ranec, I'm so sorry," she said. "If I hadn't loved Jondalar first, I would have loved you. I could have been happy with you. You were so good to me, and you always made me laugh. I do love you, you know. Not the way you want, but I will always love you."

His black eyes were full of anguish. "I'll never stop loving you, Ayla. I'll never forget you. I'll take this love to my grave," Ranec said.

"Don't say that! You deserve more happiness than that."

He laughed, a bitter, hard laugh. "Don't worry, Ayla. I'm not ready for that grave, yet. At least not enough to make it happen. And some day, I may join with a woman, make a hearth, and she will have children. I may even love her. But no other woman will ever be you, and I will never feel about another woman the way I feel about you. You can only happen once in any man's lifetime." They started walking back.

"Will it be Tricie?" Ayla asked. "She loves you."

Ranec nodded. "Perhaps. If she'll have me. Now that she has a son, she will be in even greater demand, and she had plenty of offers before."

Ayla stopped, and looked at Ranec. "I think Tricie will have you. She's hurt now, but that's because she loves you so much. But there is something else you should know. Her son, Ralev, he's your son, Ranec."

"You mean he's the son of my spirit?" Ranec frowned. "You are probably right."

"No, I don't mean he's the son of your spirit. I mean Ralev is your son, Ranec. He is the son of your body, your essence. Ralev is your son just as much as he is Tricie's son. You started him growing inside her, when you shared Pleasures with her."

"How do you know I shared Pleasures with her?" Ranec said, looking a little uncomfortable. "She was a red-foot last year, and very dedicated."

"I know because Ralev was born, and he is your son. That's how all life is started. That's why Pleasures honour the Mother. It is the beginning of life. I know this, Ranec. I promise you, it is true, and this promise cannot be broken," Ayla said.

Ranec frowned with concentration. It was a strange new idea. Women were mothers. They gave birth to children, daughters and sons. But could a man have a son? Could Ralev be his son? Yet Ayla said it. It had to be. She carried the essence of Mut. She was the Spirit Woman. She might even be the Great Earth Mother incarnate.

Jondalar checked the packs again, then led Racer to the head of the path, where Ayla was saying goodbye. Whinney was packed, and waiting patiently, but Wolf was running excitedly between them, knowing something was happening.

It had been difficult for Ayla to leave behind the people she loved when she was expelled from the Clan, but she'd had no choice. Saying goodbye, voluntarily, to the people she loved in the Lion Camp, knowing she would never see them again, was even harder. She had cried so many tears already this day, she wondered how she had any more to shed, yet her eyes watered anew each time she hugged another friend.

"Talut," she sobbed, hugging the big, red-haired headman. "Did I ever tell you it was your laughter that made me decide to visit? I was so scared of the Others, I was ready to ride back to the valley, until I saw you laughing."

"You are going to have me crying in a moment, Ayla. I don't want you to go."

"I already am crying," Latie said. "I don't want you to go, either. Remember the first time you let me touch Racer?"

"I remember when she let Rydag ride Whinney," Nezzie said. "I think that was the happiest day of his life."

"I'm going to miss the horses, too," Latie wailed, as she clung to Ayla.

"Maybe you can get a little horse of your own some day, Latie," Ayla said.

"I will miss the horses, too," Rugie said.

Ayla picked her up and gave her a squeeze. "Then maybe you'll have to get a little horse, too."

"Oh, Nezzie," Ayla cried. "How can I thank you? For everything? You know, I lost my mother when I was little, but I'm very lucky. I've had two mothers to replace her. Iza took care of me when I was a little girl, but you are the mother I needed to become a woman."

636

"Here," Nezzie said, handing her a package, and trying not to give way to tears entirely. "It's your Matrimonial tunic. I want you to have it for your joining with Jondalar. He is like a son to me, too. And you are like my daughter."

Ayla hugged Nezzie again, then looked up at her big, strapping son. When she hugged Danug, he hugged her back with no reservations. She felt the maleness of his strength, and the warmth of his body, and a momentary spark of his attraction to her as he whispered in her ear, "I wish you had been my red-foot."

She backed off, and smiled. "Danug! You are going to be such a man! I wish I were staying to see you grow into another Talut."

"Maybe, when I'm older, I'll make a long Journey and come to visit you!"

She hugged Wymez next, and she looked for Ranec, but he was not around. "I'm sorry, Wymez," she said.

"I am sorry, too. I wanted you to stay with us. I would have liked to have seen the children you would have brought to his hearth. But Jondalar is a good man. May the Mother smile on your Journey."

Ayla took Hartal from Tronie's arms, and was delighted at his giggle. Then Manuv picked up Nuvie, for Ayla to kiss.

"She is here only because of you. I will not forget it, and neither will she," Manuv said. Ayla embraced him, then Tronie and Tornec, too.

Frebec held Bectie, while Ayla made her last farewells to Fralie and the two boys. Then she embraced Crozie. She held back stiffly at first, though Ayla felt her shaking. Then the old woman clutched her, tight, and there was a tear glistening in her eye.

"Don't forget how to make white leather," she commanded.

"I won't, and I have the tunic with me," Ayla said, then with a sly smile, she added, "But, Crozie, from now on you should remember. Never play Knucklebones with a member of the Mammoth Hearth."

Crozie looked at her in surprise, and then cackled a laugh, as Ayla turned to Frebec. Wolf had joined them, and Frebec rubbed behind his ears.

"I'm going to miss this animal," he said.

"And this animal," Ayla said as she gave him a hug, "is going to miss you!"

"I will miss you, too, Ayla," he said.

Ayla found herself in the middle of a crush of people from the Aurochs Hearth, as all the children and Barzec crowded around her. Tarneg was there, too, with his woman. Deegie waited with Branag, and then the two young women collapsed in each other's arms in a new freshet of wet eyes.

"In some ways, it's harder to say goodbye to you than anyone,

Deegie," Ayla said. "I never had a friend like you, who was my age, and could understand me."

"I know, Ayla. I can't believe you're leaving. Now, how are we going to know who has a baby first?"

Ayla backed away and looked at Deegie, critically, then smiled. "You will. You already have one started."

"I wondered about it! Do you really think so?"

"Yes. I'm sure of it."

Ayla noticed Vincavec was standing beside Tulie. She brushed his tattooed cheek lightly before she turned to the headwoman of Lion Camp.

"You surprised me," he said. "I didn't know he would be the one. But then, everyone has weaknesses." He gave Tulie a knowing glance.

Vincavec was displeased that his reading of the situation was so far off. He had totally discounted the tall blond man, and he was somewhat miffed at Tulie because she had accepted his matched pieces of amber knowing that it was not likely he would be getting what he was bargaining for, in spite of the fact that he had pushed them on her. He had been making pointed comments implying that she had accepted his amber because of her weakness for it, and that she didn't give full value. Since they were ostensibly a gift, she couldn't return them, and he was taking full value in his cutting remarks.

Tulie glanced at Vincavec before she approached Ayla, making sure he was watching, then she gave the young woman a warm and sincere embrace.

"I have something for you. I'm sure everyone will agree, these are perfect for you," she said, then dropped two, beautiful, matched pieces of amber in Ayla's hand. "They will match your matrimonial tunic. You might consider wearing them on your ears."

"Oh, Tulie," Ayla said. "This is too much. They are beautiful!"

"They are not too much, Ayla. They were meant for you," Tulie said, looking back triumphantly at Vincavec.

Ayla noticed Barzec was smiling, too, and Nezzie was nodding her head in agreement.

It was hard for Jondalar to leave the Lion Camp, too. They had made him welcome, and he had grown to love them. Many of his goodbyes were tearful. The last person he spoke to was Mamut. They embraced and rubbed cheeks, then Ayla joined them. "I want to thank you," Jondalar said. "I think you knew from the beginning that I had a hard lesson to learn." The old shaman nodded. "But I have learned a great deal from you and the Mamutoi. I have learned what has meaning and what is superficial, and I know the depths of my love for Ayla. I have no more reservations. I will stand beside her against my worst enemies or best friends."

"I will tell you now something else you must know, Jondalar," Mamut said. "I knew her destiny was with you from the beginning, and when the volcano erupted, I knew she would be leaving with you soon. But remember this. Ayla's destiny is much greater than anyone knows. The Mother has chosen her, and her life will have many challenges, and so will yours. She will have need of your protection, and the strength your love has gained. That is why you had to learn that lesson. It is never easy to be chosen, but there are always great benefits, too. Take care of her, Jondalar. You know, when she worries about others, she forgets to take care of herself."

Jondalar nodded. Then Ayla hugged the old man, smiling through dewy eyes.

"I wish Rydag were here. I miss him so much. I learned lessons, too. I wanted to go back for my son, but Rydag taught me that I must let Durc live his own life. How can I thank you for everything, Mamut?"

"No thanks are necessary, Ayla. Our paths were meant to cross. I have been waiting for you without knowing it, and you have given me much joy, my daughter. You were never meant to go back for Durc. He was your gift to the Clan. Children are always a joy, but pain, too. And they all must lead their own lives. Even Mut will let Her children go their own way, some day, but I fear for us if we ever neglect Her. If we forget to respect our Great Earth Mother, She will withhold Her blessings, and no longer provide for us."

Ayla and Jondalar mounted the horses, waved, and said last goodbyes. Most of the encampment had come to wish them a good Journey. As they started out, Ayla kept looking for one last person. But Ranec had already said his goodbyes and he could not face a more public farewell.

Ayla finally saw him when they started down the path, standing alone, off by himself. With a great heaviness of spirit, she stopped and waved to him.

Ranec waved back, but in his other hand he held clutched to his breast a piece of ivory, carved into the shape of a transcendent bird-woman figure. Into every notch that was carved, every line that was etched, he had lovingly carved every hope of his aesthetic and sensitive soul. He had made it for Ayla, hoping it would charm her to his hearth, as he hoped his laughing eyes and sparkling wit would charm her to his heart. But as the artist of great talent and charm and laughter watched the woman he loved ride away, no smile graced his face, and his laughing black eyes were filled with tears.